CW00957596

MURIEL SPARK

OMNIBUS 1

MURIEL SPARK

OMNIBUS 1

·

THE PRIME OF MISS JEAN BRODIE

·

THE COMFORTERS

·

THE ONLY PROBLEM

·

THE DRIVER'S SEAT

·

MEMENTO MORI

CONSTABLE · LONDON

The Prime of Miss Jean Brodie
first published in Great Britain 1961
by Macmillan & Co
Copyright © Muriel Spark 1961

The Comforters
first published in Great Britain 1957
by Macmillan & Co
Copyright © Muriel Spark 1957

The Only Problem
first published in Great Britain 1984
by The Bodley Head Ltd
Copyright © Copyright Administration Ltd 1984

The Driver's Seat
first published in Great Britain 1970
by Macmillan & Co
Copyright © Copyright Administration Ltd 1970

Memento Mori
first published in Great Britain 1959
by Macmillan & Co
Copyright © Copyright Administration Ltd 1959

This edition first published in Great Britain 1993
by Constable and Company Ltd
3 The Lanchesters
162 Fulham Palace Road
London W6 9ER
ISBN 0 09 472580 2
Set in Monophoto Imprint 11pt by
Servis Filmsetting Ltd, Manchester
Printed in Great Britain by
St Edmundsbury Press Ltd
Bury St Edmunds, Suffolk

A CIP catalogue record for this book
is available from the British Library

Contents

THE PRIME OF
MISS JEAN BRODIE

ONE

The boys, as they talked to the girls from Marcia Blaine School, stood on the far side of their bicycles holding the handlebars, which established a protective fence of bicycle between the sexes, and the impression that at any moment the boys were likely to be away.

The girls could not take off their panama hats because this was not far from the school gates and hatlessness was an offence. Certain departures from the proper set of the hat on the head were overlooked in the case of fourth-form girls and upwards so long as nobody wore their hat at an angle. But there were other subtle variants from the ordinary rule of wearing the brim turned up at the back and down at the front. The five girls, standing very close to each other because of the boys, wore their hats each with a definite difference.

These girls formed the Brodie set. That was what they had been called even before the headmistress had given them the name, in scorn, when they had moved from the Junior to the Senior school at the age of twelve. At that time they had been immediately recognizable as Miss Brodie's pupils, being vastly informed on a lot of subjects irrelevant to the authorized curriculum, as the headmistress said, and useless to the school as a school. These girls were discovered to have heard of the Buchmanites and Mussolini, the Italian Renaissance painters, the advantages to the skin of cleansing cream and witch-hazel over honest soap and water, and the word 'menarche'; the interior decoration of the London house of the author of *Winnie the Pooh* had been described to them, as had the love lives of Charlotte Brontë and of Miss Brodie herself. They were aware of the existence of Einstein and the arguments of those who considered the Bible to be untrue. They knew the rudiments of astrology but not the date of the Battle of Flodden or the capital of Finland. All of the Brodie set, save one, counted on its fingers, as had Miss Brodie, with accurate results more or less.

By the time they were sixteen, and had reached the fourth form, and loitered beyond the gates after school, and had adapted themselves to the orthodox régime, they remained unmistakably Brodie, and were all famous in the school, which is to say they were held in suspicion and not much liking. They had no team spirit and very little in common with each other outside their continuing friendship with Jean Brodie. She still taught in the Junior department. She was held in great suspicion.

Marcia Blaine School for Girls was a day school which had been partially endowed in the middle of the nineteenth century by the wealthy widow of an Edinburgh bookbinder. She had been an admirer of Garibaldi before she died. Her manly portrait hung in the great hall, and was honoured every Founder's Day by a bunch of hard-wearing flowers such as chrysanthemums or dahlias. These were placed in a vase beneath the portrait, upon a lectern which also held an open Bible with the text underlined in red ink, 'O where shall I find a virtuous woman, for her price is above rubies.'

The girls who loitered beneath the tree, shoulder to shoulder, very close to each other because of the boys, were all famous for something. Now, at sixteen, Monica Douglas was a prefect, famous mostly for mathematics which she could do in her brain, and for her anger which, when it was lively enough, drove her to slap out to right and left. She had a very red nose, winter and summer, long dark plaits, and fat, peg-like legs. Since she had turned sixteen, Monica wore her panama hat rather higher on her head than normal, perched as if it were too small and as if she knew she looked grotesque in any case.

Rose Stanley was famous for sex. Her hat was placed quite unobtrusively on her blonde short hair, but she dented in the crown on either side.

Eunice Gardiner, small, neat, and famous for her spritely gymnastics and glamorous swimming, had the brim of her hat turned up at the front and down at the back.

Sandy Stranger wore it turned up all round and as far back on her head as it could possibly go; to assist this, she had attached to her hat a strip of elastic which went under the chin. Sometimes Sandy chewed this elastic and when it was chewed down she sewed on a new piece. She was merely notorious for her small, almost non-existent, eyes, but she was famous for her vowel sounds which, long ago in the long past, in the Junior school, had enraptured Miss Brodie. 'Well, come and recite for us please, because it has been a tiring day.'

> 'She left the web, she left the loom,
> She made three paces thro' the room,
> She saw the water-lily bloom,
> She saw the helmet and the plume,
>   She look'd down to Camelot.'

'It lifts one up,' Miss Brodie usually said, passing her hand outwards from her breast towards the class of ten-year-old girls who were listening for the bell which would release them. 'Where there is no vision,' Miss Brodie had assured them, 'the people perish. Eunice, come and do a somersault in order that we may have comic relief.'

But now, the boys with their bicycles were cheerfully insulting Jenny Gray about her way of speech which she had got from her elocution classes. She was going to be an actress. She was Sandy's best friend. She wore her hat with the front brim bent sharply downwards; she was the prettiest and most graceful girl of the set, and this was her fame. 'Don't be a lout, Andrew,' she said with her uppish tone. There were three Andrews among the five boys, and these three Andrews now started mimicking Jenny: 'Don't be a lout, Andrew,' while the girls laughed beneath their bobbing panamas.

Along came Mary Macgregor, the last member of the set, whose fame rested on her being a silent lump, a nobody whom everybody could blame. With her was an outsider, Joyce Emily Hammond, the very rich girl, their delinquent, who had been recently sent to Blaine as a last hope, because no other school, no governess, could manage her. She still wore the green uniform of her old school. The others wore deep violet. The most she had done, so far, was to throw paper pellets sometimes at the singing master. She insisted on the use of her two names, Joyce Emily. This Joyce Emily was trying very hard to get into the famous set, and thought the two names might establish her as a something, but there was no chance of it and she could not see why.

Joyce Emily said, 'There's a teacher coming out,' and nodded towards the gates.

Two of the Andrews wheeled their bicycles out on to the road and departed. The other three boys remained defiantly, but looking the

other way as if they might have stopped to admire the clouds on the
Pentland Hills. The girls crowded round each other as if in discussion. 'Good afternoon,' said Miss Brodie when she approached the
group. 'I haven't seen you for some days. I think we won't detain
these young men and their bicycles. Good afternoon, boys.' The
famous set moved off with her, and Joyce, the new delinquent,
followed. 'I think I haven't met this new girl,' said Miss Brodie,
looking closely at Joyce. And when they were introduced she said:
'Well, we must be on our way, my dear.'

Sandy looked back as Joyce Emily walked, and then skipped, leggy
and uncontrolled for her age, in the opposite direction, and the Brodie
set was left to their secret life as it had been six years ago in their
childhood.

'I am putting old heads on your young shoulders,' Miss Brodie had
told them at that time, 'and all my pupils are the crème de la crème.'

Sandy looked with her little screwed-up eyes at Monica's very red
nose and remembered this saying as she followed the set in the wake of
Miss Brodie.

'I should like you girls to come to supper tomorrow night,' Miss
Brodie said. 'Make sure you are free.'

'The Dramatic Society . . .' murmured Jenny.

'Send an excuse,' said Miss Brodie. 'I have to consult you about a
new plot which is afoot to force me to resign. Needless to say, I shall
not resign.' She spoke calmly as she always did in spite of her forceful
words.

Miss Brodie never discussed her affairs with the other members of
the staff, but only with those former pupils whom she had trained up
in her confidence. There had been previous plots to remove her from
Blaine, which had been foiled.

'It has been suggested again that I should apply for a post at one of
the progressive schools, where my methods would be more suited to
the system than they are at Blaine. But I shall not apply for a post at a
crank school. I shall remain at this education factory. There needs
must be a leaven in the lump. Give me a girl at an impressionable age,
and she is mine for life.'

The Brodie set smiled in understanding of various kinds.

Miss Brodie forced her brown eyes to flash as a meaningful
accompaniment to her quiet voice. She looked a mighty woman with

her dark Roman profile in the sun. The Brodie set did not for a moment doubt that she would prevail. As soon expect Julius Caesar to apply for a job at a crank school as Miss Brodie. She would never resign. If the authorities wanted to get rid of her she would have to be assassinated.

'Who are the gang, this time?' said Rose, who was famous for sex-appeal.

'We shall discuss tomorrow night the persons who oppose me,' said Miss Brodie. 'But rest assured they shall not succeed.'

'No,' said everyone. 'No, of course they won't.'

'Not while I am in my prime,' she said. 'These years are still the years of my prime. It is important to recognize the years of one's prime, always remember that. Here is my tram-car. I dare say I'll not get a seat. This is nineteen-thirty-six. The age of chivalry is past.'

Six years previously, Miss Brodie had led her new class into the garden for a history lesson underneath the big elm. On the way through the school corridors they passed the headmistress's study. The door was wide open, the room was empty.

'Little girls,' said Miss Brodie, 'come and observe this.'

They clustered round the open door while she pointed to a large poster pinned with drawing-pins on the opposite wall within the room. It depicted a man's big face. Underneath were the words 'Safety First'.

'This is Stanley Baldwin who got in as Prime Minister and got out again ere long,' said Miss Brodie. 'Miss Mackay retains him on the wall because she believes in the slogan "Safety First". But Safety does not come first. Goodness, Truth and Beauty come first. Follow me.'

This was the first intimation, to the girls, of an odds between Miss Brodie and the rest of the teaching staff. Indeed, to some of them, it was the first time they had realized it was possible for people glued together in grown-up authority to differ at all. Taking inward note of this, and with the exhilarating feeling of being in on the faint smell of row, without being endangered by it, they followed dangerous Miss Brodie into the secure shade of the elm.

Often, that sunny autumn, when the weather permitted, the small girls took their lessons seated on three benches arranged about the elm.

'Hold up your books,' said Miss Brodie quite often that autumn, 'prop them up in your hands, in case of intruders. If there are any intruders, we are doing our history lesson . . . our poetry . . . English grammar.'

The small girls held up their books with their eyes not on them, but on Miss Brodie.

'Meantime I will tell you about my last summer holiday in Egypt . . . I will tell you about care of the skin, and of the hands . . . about the Frenchman I met in the train to Biarritz . . . and I must tell you about the Italian paintings I saw. Who is the greatest Italian painter?'

'Leonardo da Vinci, Miss Brodie.'

'That is incorrect. The answer is Giotto, he is my favourite.'

Some days it seemed to Sandy that Miss Brodie's chest was flat, no bulges at all, but straight as her back. On other days her chest was breast-shaped and large, very noticeable, something for Sandy to sit and peer at through her tiny eyes while Miss Brodie on a day of lessons indoors stood erect, with her brown head held high, staring out of the window like Joan of Arc as she spoke.

'I have frequently told you, and the holidays just past have convinced me, that my prime has truly begun. One's prime is elusive. You little girls, when you grow up, must be on the alert to recognize your prime at whatever time of your life it may occur. You must then live it to the full. Mary, what have you got under your desk, what are you looking at?'

Mary sat lump-like and too stupid to invent something. She was too stupid ever to tell a lie; she didn't know how to cover up.

'A comic, Miss Brodie,' she said.

'Do you mean a comedian, a droll?'

Everyone tittered.

'A comic paper,' said Mary.

'A comic paper, forsooth. How old are you?'

'Ten, ma'am.'

'You are too old for comic papers at ten. Give it to me.'

Miss Brodie looked at the coloured sheets. '*Tiger Tim's* forsooth,' she said, and threw it into the waste-paper basket. Perceiving all eyes upon it she lifted it out of the basket, tore it up beyond redemption and put it back again.

'Attend to me, girls. One's prime is the moment one was born for.

Now that my prime has begun – Sandy, your attention is wandering. What have I been talking about?'

'Your prime, Miss Brodie.'

'If anyone comes along,' said Miss Brodie, 'in the course of the following lesson, remember that it is the hour for English grammar. Meantime I will tell you a little of my life when I was younger than I am now, though six years older than the man himself.'

She leaned against the elm. It was one of the last autumn days when the leaves were falling in little gusts. They fell on the children who were thankful for this excuse to wriggle and for the allowable movements in brushing the leaves from their hair and laps.

'Season of mists and mellow fruitfulness. I was engaged to a young man at the beginning of the War but he fell on Flanders' Field,' said Miss Brodie. 'Are you thinking, Sandy, of doing a day's washing?'

'No, Miss Brodie.'

'Because you have got your sleeves rolled up. I won't have to do with girls who roll up the sleeves of their blouses, however fine the weather. Roll them down at once, we are civilized beings. He fell the week before Armistice was declared. He fell like an autumn leaf, although he was only twenty-two years of age. When we go indoors we shall look on the map at Flanders, and the spot where my lover was laid before you were born. He was poor. He came from Ayrshire, a countryman, but a hard-working and clever scholar. He said, when he asked me to marry him, "We shall have to drink water and walk slow." That was Hugh's country way of expressing that we would live quietly. We shall drink water and walk slow. What does the saying signify, Rose?'

'That you would live quietly, Miss Brodie,' said Rose Stanley who six years later had a great reputation for sex.

The story of Miss Brodie's felled fiancé was well on its way when the headmistress, Miss Mackay, was seen to approach across the lawn. Tears had already started to drop from Sandy's little pig-like eyes and Sandy's tears now affected her friend Jenny, later famous in the school for her beauty, who gave a sob and groped up the leg of her knickers for her handkerchief. 'Hugh was killed,' said Miss Brodie, 'a week before the Armistice. After that there was a general election and people were saying "Hang the Kaiser!" Hugh was one of the Flowers of the Forest, lying in his grave.' Rose Stanley had now begun to weep. Sandy slid her wet eyes sideways, watching the advance of Miss Mackay, head and shoulders forward, across the lawn.

'I am come to see you and I have to be off,' she said. 'What are you little girls crying for?'

'They are moved by a story I have been telling them. We are having a history lesson,' said Miss Brodie, catching a falling leaf neatly in her hand as she spoke.

'Crying over a story at ten years of age!' said Miss Mackay to the girls who had stragglingly risen from the benches, still dazed with Hugh the warrior. 'I am only come to see you and I must be off. Well, girls, the new term has begun. I hope you all had a splendid summer holiday and I look forward to seeing your splendid essays on how you spent them. You shouldn't be crying over history at the age of ten. My word!'

'You did well,' said Miss Brodie to the class, when Miss Mackay had gone, 'not to answer the question put to you. It is well, when in difficulties, to say never a word, neither black nor white. Speech is silver but silence is golden. Mary, are you listening? What was I saying?'

Mary Macgregor, lumpy, with merely two eyes, a nose and a mouth like a snowman, who was later famous for being stupid and always to blame and who, at the age of twenty-three, lost her life in a hotel fire, ventured, 'Golden.'

'What did I say was golden?'

Mary cast her eyes around her and up above. Sandy whispered, 'The falling leaves.'

'The falling leaves,' said Mary.

'Plainly,' said Miss Brodie, 'you were not listening to me. If only you small girls would listen to me I would make of you the crème de la crème.'

TWO

Mary Macgregor, although she lived into her twenty-fourth year, never quite realized that Jean Brodie's confidences were not shared with the rest of the staff and that her love-story was given out only to her pupils. She had not thought much about Jean Brodie, certainly never disliked her, when, a year after the outbreak of the Second World War, she joined the Wrens, and was clumsy and incompetent, and was much blamed. On one occasion of real misery – when her first and last boy-friend, a corporal whom she had known for two weeks, deserted her by failing to turn up at an appointed place and failing to come near her again – she thought back to see if she had ever really been happy in her life; it occurred to her then that the first years with Miss Brodie, sitting listening to all those stories and opinions which had nothing to do with the ordinary world, had been the happiest time of her life. She thought this briefly, and never again referred her mind to Miss Brodie, but had got over her misery, and had relapsed into her habitual slow bewilderment, before she died while on leave in Cumberland in a fire in the hotel. Back and forth along the corridors ran Mary Macgregor, through the thickening smoke. She ran one way; then, turning, the other way; and at either end the blast furnace of the fire met her. She heard no screams, for the roar of the fire drowned the screams; she gave no scream, for the smoke was choking her. She ran into somebody on her third turn, stumbled and died. But at the beginning of the nineteen-thirties, when Mary Macgregor was ten, there she was sitting blankly among Miss Brodie's pupils. 'Who has spilled ink on the floor – was it you, Mary?'

'I don't know, Miss Brodie.'

'I dare say it was you. I've never come across such a clumsy girl. And if you can't take an interest in what I am saying, please try to look as if you do.'

These were the days that Mary Macgregor, on looking back,

found to be the happiest days of her life.

Sandy Stranger had a feeling at the time that they were supposed to be the happiest days of her life, and on her tenth birthday she said so to her best friend Jenny Gray who had been asked to tea at Sandy's house. The speciality of the feast was pineapple cubes with cream, and the speciality of the day was that they were left to themselves. To Sandy the unfamiliar pineapple had the authentic taste and appearance of happiness and she focused her small eyes closely on the pale gold cubes before she scooped them up in her spoon, and she thought the sharp taste on her tongue was that of a special happiness, which was nothing to do with eating, and was different from the happiness of play that one enjoyed unawares. Both girls saved the cream to the last, then ate it in spoonfuls.

'Little girls, you are going to be the crème de la crème,' said Sandy, and Jenny spluttered her cream into her handkerchief.

'You know,' Sandy said, 'these are supposed to be the happiest days of our lives.'

'Yes, they are always saying that,' Jenny said. 'They say, make the most of your schooldays because you never know what lies ahead of you.'

'Miss Brodie says prime is best,' Sandy said.

'Yes, but she never got married like our mothers and fathers.'

'They don't have primes,' said Sandy.

'They have sexual intercourse,' Jenny said.

The little girls paused, because this was still a stupendous thought, and one which they had only lately lit upon; the very phrase and its meaning were new. It was quite unbelievable. Sandy said, then, 'Mr Lloyd had a baby last week. He must have committed sex with his wife.' This idea was easier to cope with and they laughed screamingly into their pink paper napkins. Mr Lloyd was the Art master to the Senior girls.

'Can you *see* it happening?' Jenny whispered.

Sandy screwed her eyes even smaller in the effort of seeing with her mind. 'He would be wearing his pyjamas,' she whispered back.

The girls rocked with mirth, thinking of one-armed Mr Lloyd, in his solemnity, striding into school.

Then Jenny said, 'You do it on the spur of the moment. That's how it happens.'

Jenny was a reliable source of information, because a girl employed by her father in his grocer shop had recently been found to be pregnant, and Jenny had picked up some fragments of the ensuing fuss. Having confided her finds to Sandy, they had embarked on a course of research which they called 'research', piecing together clues from remembered conversations illicitly overheard, and passages from the big dictionaries.

'It all happens in a flash,' Jenny said. 'It happened to Teenie when she was out walking at Puddocky with her boy friend. Then they had to get married.'

'You would think the urge would have passed by the time she got her *clothes* off,' Sandy said. By 'clothes' she definitely meant to imply knickers, but 'knickers' was rude in this scientific context.

'Yes, that's what I can't understand,' said Jenny.

Sandy's mother looked round the door and said, 'Enjoying yourselves, darlings?' Over her shoulder appeared the head of Jenny's mother. 'My word,' said Jenny's mother, looking at the tea-table, 'they've been tucking in!'

Sandy felt offended and belittled by this; it was as if the main idea of the party had been the food.

'What would you like to do now?' Sandy's mother said.

Sandy gave her mother a look of secret ferocity which meant: you promised to leave us all on our own, and a promise is a promise, you know it's very bad to break a promise to a child, you might ruin all my life by breaking your promise, it's my birthday.

Sandy's mother backed away bearing Jenny's mother with her. 'Let's leave them to themselves,' she said. 'Just enjoy yourselves, darlings.'

Sandy was sometimes embarrassed by her mother being English and calling her 'darling', not like the mothers of Edinburgh who said 'dear'. Sandy's mother had a flashy winter coat trimmed with fluffy fox fur like the Duchess of York's, while the other mothers wore tweed or, at the most, musquash that would do them all their days.

It had been raining and the ground was too wet for them to go and finish digging the hole to Australia, so the girls lifted the tea-table with all its festal relics over to the corner of the room. Sandy opened the lid of the piano stool and extracted a notebook from between two sheaves of music. On the first page of the notebook was written,

The Mountain Eyrie
by
Sandy Stranger and Jenny Gray

This was a story, still in the process of composition, about Miss Brodie's lover, Hugh Carruthers. He had not been killed in the war, that was a mistake in the telegram. He had come back from the war and called to inquire for Miss Brodie at school, where the first person whom he encountered was Miss Mackay, the headmistress. She had informed him that Miss Brodie did not desire to see him, she loved another. With a bitter, harsh laugh, Hugh went and made his abode in a mountain eyrie, where, wrapped in a leather jacket, he had been discovered one day by Sandy and Jenny. At the present stage in the story Hugh was holding Sandy captive but Jenny had escaped by night and was attempting to find her way down the mountainside in the dark. Hugh was preparing to pursue her.

Sandy took a pencil from a drawer in the sideboard and continued:

'Hugh!' Sandy beseeched him, 'I swear to you before all I hold sacred that Miss Brodie has never loved another, and she awaits you below, praying and hoping in her prime. If you will let Jenny go, she will bring back your lover Jean Brodie to you and you will see her with your own eyes and hold her in your arms after these twelve long years and a day.'

His black eye flashed in the lamplight of the hut. 'Back, girl!' he cried, 'and do not bar my way. Well do I know that yon girl Jenny will report my whereabouts to my mocking erstwhile fiancée. Well do I know that you are both spies sent by her that she might mock. Stand back from the door, I say!'

'Never!' said Sandy, placing her young lithe body squarely in front of the latch and her arm through the bolt. Her large eyes flashed with an azure light of appeal.

Sandy handed the pencil to Jenny. 'It's your turn,' she said.

Jenny wrote: With one movement he flung her to the farthest end of the hut and strode out into the moonlight and his strides made light of the drifting snow.

'Put in about his boots,' said Sandy.

Jenny wrote: His high boots flashed in the moonlight.

'There are too many moonlights,' Sandy said, 'but we can sort that later when it comes to publication.'

'Oh, but it's a secret, Sandy!' said Jenny.

'I know that,' Sandy said. 'Don't worry, we won't publish it till our prime.'

'Do you think Miss Brodie ever had sexual intercourse with Hugh?' said Jenny.

'She would have had a baby, wouldn't she?'

'I don't know.'

'I don't think they did anything like that,' said Sandy. 'Their love was above all that.'

'Miss Brodie said they clung to each other with passionate abandon on his last leave.'

'I don't think they took their clothes off, though,' Sandy said, 'do you?'

'No. I can't see it,' said Jenny.

'I wouldn't like to have sexual intercourse,' Sandy said.

'Neither would I. I'm going to marry a pure person.'

'Have a toffee.'

They ate their sweets, sitting on the carpet. Sandy put some coal on the fire and the light spurted up, reflecting on Jenny's ringlets. 'Let's be witches by the fire, like we were at Hallowe'en.'

They sat in the twilight eating toffees and incanting witches' spells. Jenny said, 'There's a Greek god at the museum standing up with nothing on. I saw it last Sunday afternoon but I was with Auntie Kate and I didn't have a chance to *look* properly.'

'Let's go to the museum next Sunday,' Sandy said. 'It's research.'

'Would you be allowed to go alone with me?'

Sandy, who was notorious for not being allowed to go out and about without a grown-up person, said, 'I don't think so. Perhaps we could get someone to take us.'

'We could ask Miss Brodie.'

Miss Brodie frequently took the little girls to the art galleries and museums, so this seemed feasible.

'But suppose,' said Sandy, 'she won't let us look at the statue if it's naked.'

'I don't think she would notice that it was naked,' Jenny said.

'She just wouldn't see its thingummyjig.'

'I know,' said Sandy. 'Miss Brodie's above all that.'

It was time for Jenny to go home with her mother, all the way in the tram car through the haunted November twilight of Edinburgh across the Dean Bridge. Sandy waved from the window, and wondered if Jenny, too, had the feeling of leading a double life, fraught with problems that even a millionaire did not have to face. It was well known that millionaires led double lives. The evening paper rattlesnaked its way through the letter box and there was suddenly a six-o'clock feeling in the house.

Miss Brodie was reciting poetry to the class at a quarter to four, to raise their minds before they went home. Miss Brodie's eyes were half shut and her head was thrown back:

> 'In the stormy east wind straining,
> The pale yellow woods were waning,
> The broad stream in his banks complaining,
> Heavily the low sky raining
>   Over tower'd Camelot.'

Sandy watched Miss Brodie through her little pale eyes, screwed them smaller and shut her lips tight.

Rose Stanley was pulling threads from the girdle of her gym tunic. Jenny was enthralled by the poem, her lips were parted, she was never bored. Sandy was never bored, but she had to lead a double life of her own in order never to be bored.

> Down she came and found a boat
> Beneath a willow left afloat,
> And round about the prow she wrote
>   *The Lady of Shalott.*

'By what means did your Ladyship write these words?' Sandy inquired in her mind with her lips shut tight.

'There was a pot of white paint and a brush which happened to be standing upon the grassy verge,' replied the Lady of Shalott graciously. 'It was left there no doubt by some heedless member of the Unemployed.'

'Alas, and in all that rain!' said Sandy for want of something better to say, while Miss Brodie's voice soared up to the ceiling, and curled round the feet of the Senior girls upstairs.

The Lady of Shalott placed a white hand on Sandy's shoulder and gazed at her for a space. 'That one so young and beautiful should be so ill-fated in love!' she said in low sad tones.

'What can be the meaning of these words?' cried Sandy in alarm, with her little eyes screwed on Miss Brodie and her lips shut tight.

Miss Brodie said: 'Sandy, are you in pain?'

Sandy looked astonished.

'You girls,' said Miss Brodie, 'must learn to cultivate an expression of composure. It is one of the best assets of a woman, an expression of composure, come foul, come fair. Regard the Mona Lisa over yonder!'

All heads turned to look at the reproduction which Miss Brodie had brought back from her travels and pinned on the wall. Mona Lisa in her prime smiled in steady composure even though she had just come from the dentist and her lower jaw was swollen.

'She is older than the rocks on which she sits. Would that I had been given charge of you girls when you were seven. I sometimes fear it's too late, now. If you had been mine when you were seven you would have been the crème de la crème. Sandy, come and read some stanzas and let us hear your vowel sounds.'

Sandy, being half-English, made the most of her vowels, it was her only fame. Rose Stanley was not yet famous for sex, and it was not she but Eunice Gardiner who had approached Sandy and Jenny with a Bible, pointing out the words, 'The babe leapt in her womb'. Sandy and Jenny said she was dirty and threatened to tell on her. Jenny was already famous for her prettiness, and she had a sweet voice, so that Mr Lowther, who came to teach singing, would watch her admiringly as she sang 'Come see where golden-hearted spring ...'; and he twitched her ringlets, the more daringly since Miss Brodie always stayed with her pupils during the singing lesson. He twitched her ringlets and looked at Miss Brodie like a child showing off its tricks and almost as if testing Miss Brodie to see if she were at all willing to conspire in his un-Edinburgh conduct.

Mr Lowther was small, with a long body and short legs. His hair and moustache were red-gold. He curled his hand round the back of his ear and inclined his head towards each girl to test her voice. 'Sing ah!'

'Ah!' sang Jenny, high and pure as the sea maiden of the Hebrides whom Sandy had been talking about. But her eyes swivelled over to catch Sandy's.

Miss Brodie ushered the girls from the music room and, gathering them about her, said, 'You girls are my vocation. If I were to receive a proposal of marriage tomorrow from the Lord Lyon King-of-Arms I would decline it. I am dedicated to you in my prime. Form a single file, now, please, and walk with your heads up, *up*, like Sybil Thorndike, a woman of noble mien.'

Sandy craned back her head, pointed her freckled nose in the air and fixed her little pig-like eyes on the ceiling as she walked along in the file.

'What are you doing, Sandy?'

'Walking like Sybil Thorndike, ma'am.'

'One day, Sandy, you will go too far.'

Sandy looked hurt and puzzled.

'Yes,' said Miss Brodie, 'I have my eye upon you, Sandy. I observe a frivolous nature. I fear you will never belong to life's élite or, as one might say, the crème de la crème.'

When they had returned to the classroom Rose Stanley said, 'I've got ink on my blouse.'

'Go to the science room and have the stain removed; but remember it is very bad for the tussore.'

Sometimes the girls would put a little spot of ink on a sleeve of their tussore silk blouses so that they might be sent to the science room in the Senior school. There a thrilling teacher, a Miss Lockhart, wearing a white overall, with her grey short hair set back in waves from a tanned and weathered golfer's face, would pour a small drop of white liquid from a large jar on to a piece of cotton wool. With this she would dab the ink-spot on the sleeve, silently holding the girl's arm, intently absorbed in the task. Rose Stanley went to the science room with her inky blouse only because she was bored, but Sandy and Jenny got ink on their blouses at discreet intervals of four weeks, so that they could go and have their arms held by Miss Lockhart who seemed to carry six inches of pure air around her person wherever she moved in that strange-smelling room. This long room was her natural setting and she had lost something of her quality when Sandy saw her walking from the school in her box-pleat tweeds over to her sports car like an ordinary teacher. Miss Lockhart in the science room was to Sandy something apart, surrounded by three lanes of long benches set out with jars half-full of coloured crystals and powders and liquids, ochre and bronze and metal grey and cobalt blue, glass vessels of curious shapes, bulbous, or with pipe-like stems. Only once when Sandy went to the science room was there a lesson in progress. The older girls, big girls, some with bulging chests, were standing in couples at the benches, with gas jets burning before them. They held a glass tube full of green stuff in their hands and were dancing the tube in the flame, dozens of dancing green tubes and flames, all along the benches. The bare winter top branches of the trees brushed the windows of this long room, and beyond that was the cold winter sky with a huge red sun. Sandy, on that occasion, had the presence of mind to remember that her schooldays were supposed to be the happiest days of her life and she took the compelling news back to Jenny that the Senior school was going to be marvellous and Miss Lockhart was beautiful.

'All the girls in the science room were doing just as they liked,' said Sandy, 'and that's what they were supposed to be doing.'

'We do a lot of what we like in Miss Brodie's class,' Jenny said. 'My mummy says Miss Brodie gives us too much freedom.'

'She's not supposed to give us freedom, she's supposed to give us lessons,' said Sandy. 'But the science class is supposed to be free, it's allowed.'

'Well, I like being in Miss Brodie's,' Jenny said.

'So do I,' Sandy said. 'She takes an interest in our general knowledge, my mother says.'

All the same, the visits to the science room were Sandy's most secret joy, and she calculated very carefully the intervals between one ink-spot and another, so that there should be no suspicion on Miss Brodie's part that the spots were not an accident. Miss Lockhart would hold her arm and carefully dab the ink-stain on her sleeve while Sandy stood enthralled by the long room which was this science teacher's rightful place, and by the lawful glamour of everything there. It was on the occasion when Rose Stanley, after the singing lesson, was sent to the science room to get ink off her blouse that Miss Brodie told her class,

'You must be more careful with your ink. I can't have my girls going up and down to the science room like this. We must keep our good name.'

She added, 'Art is greater than science. Art comes first, and then science.'

The large map had been rolled down over the blackboard because they had started the geography lesson. Miss Brodie turned with her pointer to show where Alaska lay. But she turned again to the class and said: 'Art and religion first; then philosophy; lastly science. That is the order of the great subjects of life, that's their order of importance.'

This was the first winter of the two years that this class spent with Miss Brodie. It had turned nineteen-thirty-one. Miss Brodie had already selected her favourites, or rather those whom she could trust; or rather those whose parents she could trust not to lodge complaints about the more advanced and seditious aspects of her educational policy, these parents being either too enlightened to complain or too unenlightened, or too awed by their good fortune in getting their girls' education at endowed rates, or too trusting to question the value of what their daughters were learning at this school of sound reputation. Miss Brodie's special girls were taken home to tea and bidden not to tell the others, they were taken into her confidence, they understood her private life and her feud with the headmistress and the allies of the headmistress. They learned what troubles in her career Miss Brodie had encountered on their behalf. 'It is for the sake of you girls – my influence, now, in the years of my prime.' This was the beginning of the Brodie set. Eunice Gardiner was so quiet at first, it was difficult to see why she had been drawn in by Miss Brodie. But eventually she cut capers for the relief and amusement of the tea-parties, doing cartwheels on the carpet. 'You are an Ariel,' said Miss Brodie. Then Eunice began to chatter. She was not allowed to do cartwheels on Sundays, for in many ways Miss Brodie was an Edinburgh spinster of the deepest dye. Eunice Gardiner did somersaults on the mat only at Saturday gatherings before high teas, or afterwards on Miss Brodie's kitchen linoleum, while the other girls were washing up and licking honey from the depleted comb off their fingers as they passed it over to be put away in the food cupboard. It was twenty-eight years after Eunice did the splits in Miss Brodie's flat that she, who had become a nurse and married a doctor, said to her husband one evening:

'Next year when we go for the Festival –'

'Yes?'

She was making a wool rug, pulling at a different stitch. 'Yes?' he said.

'When we go to Edinburgh,' she said, 'remind me while we're there to go and visit Miss Brodie's grave.'

'Who was Miss Brodie?'

'A teacher of mine, she was full of culture. She was an Edinburgh Festival all on her own. She used to give us teas at her flat and tell us about her prime.'

'Prime what?'

'Her prime of life. She fell for an Egyptian courier once, on her travels, and came back and told us all about it. She had a few favourites. I was one of them. I did the splits and made her laugh, you know.'

'I always knew your upbringing was a bit peculiar.'

'But she wasn't mad. She was as sane as anything. She knew exactly what she was doing. She told us all about her love life, too.'

'Let's have it then.'

'Oh, it's a long story. She was just a spinster. I must take flowers to her grave – I wonder if I could find it?'

'When did she die?'

'Just after the war. She was retired by then. Her retirement was rather a tragedy, she was forced to retire before time. The head never liked her. There's a long story attached to Miss Brodie's retirement. She was betrayed by one of her own girls, we were called the Brodie set. I never found out which one betrayed her.'

It is time now to speak of the long walk through the old parts of Edinburgh where Miss Brodie took her set, dressed in their deep violet coats and black velour hats with the green and white crest, one Friday in March when the school's central heating system had broken down and everyone else had been muffled up and sent home. The wind blew from the icy Forth and the sky was loaded with forthcoming snow. Mary Macgregor walked with Sandy because Jenny had gone home. Monica Douglas, later famous for being able to do real mathematics in her head, and for her anger, walked behind them with her dark red face, broad nose and dark pigtails falling from her black hat and her legs already shaped like pegs in their black wool stockings. By her side walked Rose Stanley, tall and blonde with a yellow-pale skin, who had not yet won her reputation for sex, and whose conversation was all about trains, cranes, motor cars, Meccanos, and other boys' affairs. She was not interested in the works of engines or the constructive powers of the Meccanos, but she knew their names, the variety of colours in which they came, the makes of motor cars and their horse-power, the various prices of the Meccano sets. She was also an energetic climber of walls and trees. And although these concerns at Rose Stanley's eleventh year marked her as a tomboy, they did not go deep into her femininity and it was her superficial knowledge of these topics alone, as if they had been a conscious preparation, which stood her in good stead a few years later with the boys.

With Rose walked Miss Brodie, head up, like Sybil Thorndike, her nose arched and proud. She wore her loose brown tweed coat with the beaver collar tightly buttoned, her brown felt hat with the brim up at one side and down at the other. Behind Miss Brodie, last in the group, little Eunice Gardiner who, twenty-eight years later, said of Miss Brodie, 'I must visit her grave', gave a skip between each of her walking steps as if she might even break into pirouettes on the pavement, so that Miss Brodie, turning round, said from time to time, 'Now, Eunice!' And, from time to time again, Miss Brodie would fall behind to keep Eunice company.

Sandy, who had been reading *Kidnapped*, was having a conversation with the hero, Alan Breck, and was glad to be with Mary Macgregor because it was not necessary to talk to Mary.

'Mary, you may speak quietly to Sandy.'

'Sandy won't talk to me,' said Mary who later, in that hotel fire, ran hither and thither till she died.

'Sandy cannot talk to you if you are so stupid and disagreeable. Try to wear an agreeable expression at least, Mary.'

'Sandy, you must take this message o'er the heather to the Macphersons,' said Alan Breck. 'My life depends upon it, and the Cause no less.'

'I shall never fail you, Alan Breck,' said Sandy. 'Never.'

'Mary,' said Miss Brodie, from behind, 'please try not to lag behind Sandy.'

Sandy kept pacing ahead, fired on by Alan Breck whose ardour and thankfulness, as Sandy prepared to set off across the heather, had reached touching proportions.

Mary tried to keep up with her. They were crossing the Meadows, a gusty expanse of common land, glaring green under the snowy sky. Their destination was the Old Town, for Miss Brodie had said they should see where history had been lived; and their route had brought them to the Middle Meadow Walk.

Eunice, unaccompanied at the back, began to hop to a rhyme which she repeated to herself:

> Edinburgh, Leith,
> Portobello, Musselburgh
> *And* Dalkeith.

Then she changed to the other foot.

> Edinburgh, Leith . . .

Miss Brodie turned round and hushed her, then called forward to Mary Macgregor who was staring at an Indian student who was approaching,

'Mary, don't you *want* to walk tidily?'

'Mary,' said Sandy, 'stop staring at the brown man.'

The nagged child looked numbly at Sandy and tried to quicken her pace. But Sandy was walking unevenly, in little spurts forward and little halts, as Alan Breck began to sing to her his ditty before she took to the heather to deliver the message that was going to save Alan's life. He sang:

> This is the song of the sword of Alan:
> The smith made it,
> The fire set it;
> Now it shines in the hands of Alan Breck.

Then Alan Breck clapped her shoulder and said, 'Sandy, you are a brave lass and want nothing in courage that any King's man might possess.'

'Don't walk so fast,' mumbled Mary.

'You aren't walking with your head up,' said Sandy. 'Keep it up, up.'

Then suddenly Sandy wanted to be kind to Mary Macgregor, and thought of the possibilities of feeling nice from being nice to Mary instead of blaming her. Miss Brodie's voice from behind was saying to Rose Stanley, 'You are all heroines in the making. Britain must be a fit country for heroines to live in. The League of Nations . . .' The sound of Miss Brodie's presence, just when it was on the tip of Sandy's tongue to be nice to Mary Macgregor, arrested the urge. Sandy looked back at her companions, and understood them as a body with Miss Brodie for the head. She perceived herself, the absent Jenny, the ever-blamed Mary, Rose, Eunice, and Monica, all in a frightening little moment, in unified compliance to the destiny of Miss Brodie, as if God had willed them to birth for that purpose.

She was even more frightened then, by her temptation to be nice to Mary Macgregor, since by this action she would separate herself, and be lonely, and blameable in a more dreadful way than Mary who, although officially the faulty one, was at least inside Miss Brodie's category of heroines in the making. So, for good fellowship's sake, Sandy said to Mary, 'I wouldn't be walking with *you* if Jenny was here.' And Mary said, 'I know.' Then Sandy started to hate herself again and to nag on and on at Mary, with the feeling that if you did a thing a lot of times, you made it into a right thing. Mary started to cry, but quietly, so that Miss Brodie could not see. Sandy was unable to cope and decided to stride on and be a married lady having an argument with her husband:

'Well, Colin, it's rather hard on a woman when the lights have fused and there isn't a man in the house.'

'Dearest Sandy, *how* was I to know . . .'

As they came to the end of the Meadows a group of Girl Guides came by. Miss Brodie's brood, all but Mary, walked past with eyes ahead. Mary stared at the dark blue big girls with their regimented vigorous look and broader accents of speech than the Brodie girls used when in Miss Brodie's presence. They passed, and Sandy said to

Mary, 'It's rude to stare.' And Mary said, 'I wasn't staring.' Meanwhile Miss Brodie was being questioned by the girls behind on the question of the Brownies and the Girl Guides, for quite a lot of the other girls in the Junior School were Brownies.

'For those who like that sort of thing,' said Miss Brodie in her best Edinburgh voice, 'that is the sort of thing they like.'

So Brownies and Guides were ruled out. Sandy recalled Miss Brodie's admiration for Mussolini's marching troops, and the picture she had brought back from Italy showing the triumphant march of ·the black uniforms in Rome.

'These are the fascisti,' said Miss Brodie, and spelt it out. 'What are these men, Rose?'

'The fascisti, Miss Brodie.'

They were dark as anything and all marching in the straightest of files, with their hands raised at the same angle, while Mussolini stood on a platform like a gym teacher or a Guides mistress and watched them. Mussolini had put an end to unemployment with his fascisti and there was no litter in the streets. It occurred to Sandy, there at the end of the Middle Meadow Walk, that the Brodie set was Miss Brodie's fascisti, not to the naked eye, marching along, but all knit together for her need and in another way, marching along. That was all right, but it seemed, too, that Miss Brodie's disapproval of the Girl Guides had jealousy in it, there was an inconsistency, a fault. Perhaps the Guides were too much of a rival fascisti, and Miss Brodie could not bear it. Sandy thought she might see about joining the Brownies. Then the group-fright seized her again, and it was necessary to put the idea aside, because she loved Miss Brodie.

'We make good company for each other, Sandy,' said Alan Breck, crunching beneath his feet the broken glass among the blood on the floor of the ship's roundhouse. And taking a knife from the table, he cut off one of the silver buttons from his coat. 'Wherever you show that button,' he said, 'the friends of Alan Breck will come around you.'

'We turn to the right,' said Miss Brodie.

They approached the Old Town which none of the girls had properly seen before, because none of their parents was so historically minded as to be moved to conduct their young into the reeking network of slums which the Old Town constituted in those years.

The Canongate, The Grassmarket, The Lawnmarket, were names which betokened a misty region of crime and desperation: 'Lawnmarket Man Jailed.' Only Eunice Gardiner and Monica Douglas had already traversed the High Street on foot on the Royal Mile from the Castle or Holyrood. Sandy had been taken to Holyrood in an uncle's car and had seen the bed, too short and too broad, where Mary Queen of Scots had slept, and the tiny room, smaller than their own scullery at home, where the Queen had played cards with Rizzio.

Now they were in a great square, the Grassmarket, with the Castle, which was in any case everywhere, rearing between a big gap in the houses where the aristocracy used to live. It was Sandy's first experience of a foreign country, which intimates itself by its new smells and shapes and its new poor. A man sat on the icy-cold pavement; he just sat. A crowd of children, some without shoes, were playing some fight game, and some boys shouted after Miss Brodie's violet-clad company, with words that the girls had not heard before, but rightly understood to be obscene. Children and women with shawls came in and out of the dark closes. Sandy found she was holding Mary's hand in her bewilderment, all the girls were holding hands, while Miss Brodie talked of history. Into the High Street, and 'John Knox,' said Miss Brodie, 'was an embittered man. He could never be at ease with the gay French Queen. We of Edinburgh owe a lot to the French. We are Europeans.' The smell was amazingly terrible. In the middle of the road farther up the High Street a crowd was gathered. 'Walk past quietly,' said Miss Brodie.

A man and a woman stood in the midst of the crowd which had formed a ring round them. They were shouting at each other and the man hit the woman twice across the head. Another woman, very little, with cropped black hair, a red face and a big mouth, came forward and took the man by the arm. She said:

'I'll be your man.'

From time to time throughout her life Sandy pondered this, for she was certain that the little woman's words were 'I'll be your man', not 'I'll be your woman', and it was never explained.

And many times throughout her life Sandy knew with a shock, when speaking to people whose childhood had been in Edinburgh, that there were other people's Edinburghs quite different from hers, and with which she held only the names of districts and streets and monuments in common. Similarly, there were other people's nine-teen-thirties. So that, in her middle age, when she was at last allowed all those visitors to the convent – so many visitors being against the Rule, but a special dispensation was enforced on Sandy because of her Treatise – when a man said, 'I must have been at school in Edinburgh at the same time as you, Sister Helena,' Sandy, who was now some years Sister Helena of the Transfiguration, clutched the bars of the grille as was her way, and peered at him through her little faint eyes and asked him to describe his schooldays and his school, and the Edinburgh he had known. And it turned out, once more, that his was a different Edinburgh from Sandy's. His school, where he was a boarder, had been cold and grey. His teachers had been supercilious Englishmen, 'or near-Englishmen', said the visitor 'with third-rate degrees'. Sandy could not remember ever having questioned the quality of her teachers' degrees, and the school had always been lit with the sun or, in winter, with a pearly north light. 'But Edinburgh,' said the man, 'was a beautiful city, more beautiful then than it is now. Of course, the slums have been cleared. The Old Town was always my favourite. We used to love to explore the Grassmarket and so on. Architecturally speaking, there is no finer sight in Europe.'

'I was once taken for a walk through the Canongate,' Sandy said, 'but I was frightened by the squalor.'

'Well, it was the 'thirties,' said the man. 'Tell me, Sister Helena, what would you say was your greatest influence during the 'thirties? I mean, during your teens. Did you read Auden and Eliot?'

'No,' said Sandy.

'We boys were very keen on Auden and that group of course. We wanted to go and fight in the Spanish Civil War. On the Republican side, of course. Did you take sides in the Spanish Civil War at your school?'

'Well, not exactly,' said Sandy. 'It was all different for us.'

'You weren't a Catholic then, of course?'

'No,' said Sandy.

'The influences of one's teens are very important,' said the man.

'Oh yes,' said Sandy, 'even if they provide something to react against.'

'What was your biggest influence, then, Sister Helena? Was it political, personal? Was it Calvinism?'

'Oh no,' said Sandy. 'But there was a Miss Jean Brodie in her prime.' She clutched the bars of the grille as if she wanted to escape from the dim parlour beyond, for she was not composed like the other nuns who sat, when they received their rare visitors, well back in the darkness with folded hands. But Sandy always leaned forward and peered, clutching the bars with both hands, and the other sisters remarked it and said that Sister Helena had too much to bear from the world since she had published her psychological book which was so unexpectedly famed. But the dispensation was forced upon Sandy, and she clutched the bars and received the choice visitors, the psychologists and the Catholic seekers, and the higher journalist ladies and the academics who wanted to question her about her odd psychological treatise on the nature of moral perception, called 'The Transfiguration of the Commonplace'.

'We will not go into St Giles',' said Miss Brodie, 'because the day draws late. But I presume you have all been to St Giles's Cathedral?'

They had nearly all been in St Giles' with its tattered blood-stained banners of the past. Sandy had not been there, and did not want to go. The outsides of old Edinburgh churches frightened her, they were of such dark stone, like presences almost the colour of the Castle rock, and were built so warningly with their upraised fingers.

Miss Brodie had shown them a picture of Cologne Cathedral, like a wedding cake, which looked as if it had been built for pleasure and festivities, and parties given by the Prodigal Son in his early career. But the insides of Scottish churches were more reassuring because during the services they contained people, and no ghosts at all. Sandy, Rose Stanley and Monica Douglas were of believing though not church-going families. Jenny Gray and Mary Macgregor were Presbyterians and went to Sunday School. Eunice Gardiner was Episcopalian and claimed that she did not believe in Jesus, but in the Father, Son and Holy Ghost. Sandy, who believed in ghosts, felt that the Holy Ghost was a feasible proposition. The whole question was, during this winter term, being laid open by Miss Brodie who, at the same time as adhering to the strict Church of Scotland habits of her youth, and keeping the Sabbath, was now, in her prime, attending evening classes in comparative religion at the University. So her pupils heard all about it, and learned for the first time that some honest people did not believe in God, nor even Allah. But the girls were set to study the Gospels with diligence for their truth and goodness, and to read them aloud for their beauty.

Their walk had brought them into broad Chambers Street. The group had changed its order, and was now walking three abreast, with Miss Brodie in front between Sandy and Rose. 'I am summoned to see the headmistress at morning break on Monday,' said Miss Brodie. 'I have no doubt Miss Mackay wishes to question my methods of instruction. It has happened before. It will happen again. Meanwhile, I follow my principles of education and give of my best in my prime. The word "education" comes from the root e from ex, out, and duco, I lead. It means a leading out. To me education is a leading out of what is already there in the pupil's soul. To Miss Mackay it is a putting in of something that is not there, and that is not what I call education, I call it intrusion, from the Latin root prefix in meaning in and the stem trudo, I thrust. Miss Mackay's method is to thrust a lot of information into the pupil's head; mine is a leading out of knowledge, and that is true education as is proved by the root meaning. Now Miss Mackay has accused me of putting ideas into my girls' heads, but in fact that is her practice and mine is quite the opposite. Never let it be said that I put ideas into your heads. What is the meaning of education, Sandy?'

'To lead out,' said Sandy who was composing a formal invitation to Alan Breck, a year and a day after their breath-taking flight through the heather.

Miss Sandy Stranger requests the pleasure of Mr Alan Breck's company at dinner on Tuesday the 6th of January at 8 o'clock.

That would surprise the hero of *Kidnapped* coming unexpectedly from Sandy's new address in the lonely harbour house on the coast of Fife – described in a novel by the daughter of John Buchan – of which Sandy had now by devious means become the mistress. Alan Breck would arrive in full Highland dress. Supposing that passion struck upon them in the course of the evening and they were swept away into sexual intercourse? She saw the picture of it happening in her mind, and Sandy could not stand for this spoiling. She argued with herself, surely people have time to *think*, they have to stop to think while they are taking their clothes off, and if they stop to think, how can they be swept away?

'That is a Citroen,' said Rose Stanley about a motor car that had passed by. 'They are French.'

'Sandy, dear, don't rush. Take my hand,' said Miss Brodie. 'Rose, your mind is full of motor cars. There is nothing wrong with motor cars, of course, but there are higher things. I'm sure Sandy's mind is not on motor cars, she is paying attention to my conversation like a well-mannered girl.'

And if people take their clothes off in front of each other, thought Sandy, it is so rude, they are bound to be put off their passion for a moment. And if they are put off just for a single moment, *how* can they be swept away in the urge? If it all happens in a flash . . .

Miss Brodie said, 'So I intend simply to point out to Miss Mackay that there is a radical difference in our principles of education. Radical is a word pertaining to roots – Latin *radix*, a root. We differ at root, the headmistress and I, upon the question whether we are employed to educate the minds of girls or to intrude upon them. We have had this argument before, but Miss Mackay is not, I may say, an outstanding logician. A logician is one skilled in logic. Logic is the art of reasoning. What is logic, Rose?'

'To do with reasoning, ma'am,' said Rose, who later, while still in her teens, was to provoke Miss Brodie's amazement and then her awe and finally her abounding enthusiasm for the role which Rose then appeared to be enacting: that of a great lover, magnificently elevated above the ordinary run of lovers, above the moral laws, Venus incarnate, something set apart. In fact, Rose was not at the time in question engaged in the love affair which Miss Brodie thought she was, but it seemed so, and Rose was famous for sex. But in her mere eleventh year, on the winter's walk, Rose was taking note of the motor cars and Miss Brodie had not yet advanced far enough into her prime to speak of sex except by veiled allusion, as when she said of her warrior lover, 'He was a pure man', or when she read from James Hogg's poem 'Bonnie Kilmeny',

'Kilmeny was pure as pure could be'

and added, 'Which is to say, she did not go to the glen in order to mix with men.'

'When I see Miss Mackay on Monday morning,' said Miss Brodie,

'I shall point out that by the terms of my employment my methods cannot be condemned unless they can be proved to be in any part improper or subversive, and so long as the girls are in the least equipped for the end-of-term examination. I trust you girls to work hard and try and scrape through, even if you learn up the stuff and forget it next day. As for impropriety, it could never be imputed to me except by some gross distortion on the part of a traitor. I do not think ever to be betrayed. Miss Mackay is younger than I am and higher salaried. That is by accident. The best qualifications available at the University in my time were inferior to those open to Miss Mackay. That is why she holds the senior position. But her reasoning power is deficient, and so I have no fears for Monday.'

'Miss Mackay has an awfully red face, with the veins all showing,' said Rose.

'I can't permit that type of remark to pass in my presence, Rose,' said Miss Brodie, 'for it would be disloyal.'

They had come to the end of Lauriston Place, past the fire station, where they were to get on a tram-car to go to tea with Miss Brodie in her flat at Churchhill. A very long queue of men lined this part of the street. They were without collars, in shabby suits. They were talking and spitting and smoking little bits of cigarette held between middle finger and thumb.

'We shall cross here,' said Miss Brodie and herded the set across the road.

Monica Douglas whispered, 'They are the Idle.'

'In England they are called the Unemployed. They are waiting to get their dole from the labour bureau,' said Miss Brodie. 'You must all pray for the Unemployed, I will write you out the special prayer for them. You all know what the dole is?'

Eunice Gardiner had not heard of it.

'It is the weekly payment made by the State for the relief of the Unemployed and their families. Sometimes they go and spend their dole on drink before they go home, and their children starve. They are our brothers. Sandy, stop staring at once. In Italy the unemployment problem has been solved.'

Sandy felt that she was not staring across the road at the endless queue of brothers, but that it was pulling her eyes towards it. She felt once more very frightened. Some of the men looked over at the girls, but without seeing them. The girls had reached the tram stop. The men were talking and spitting a great deal. Some were laughing with hacking laughs merging into coughs and ending up with spits.

As they waited for the tram-car Miss Brodie said, 'I had lodgings in this street when first I came to Edinburgh as a student. I must tell you a story about the landlady, who was very frugal. It was her habit to come to me every morning to ask what I would have for breakfast, and she spoke like this: "Wud ye have a red herrin? – no ye wouldn't. Could ye eat a boilt egg? – no ye couldn't." The result was, I never had but bread and butter to my breakfast all the time I was in those lodgings, and very little of that.'

The laughter of the girls met that of the men opposite, who had now begun to file slowly by fits and starts into the labour bureau. Sandy's fear returned as soon as she had stopped laughing. She saw the slow jerkily moving file tremble with life, she saw it all of a piece like one dragon's body which had no right to be in the city and yet would not go away and was unslayable. She thought of the starving children. This was a relief to her fear. She wanted to cry as she always did when she saw a street singer or a beggar. She wanted Jenny to be there, because Jenny cried easily about poor children. But the snaky creature opposite started to shiver in the cold and made Sandy tremble again. She turned and said to Mary Macgregor who had brushed against her sleeve, 'Stop pushing.'

'Mary, dear, you mustn't push,' said Miss Brodie.

'I wasn't pushing,' said Mary.

In the tram-car Sandy excused herself from tea with Miss Brodie on the plea that she thought she had a cold coming on. Indeed she shivered. She wanted at that moment to be warmly at home, outside which even the corporate Brodie set lived in a colder sort of way.

But later, when Sandy thought of Eunice doing somersaults and splits on Miss Brodie's kitchen linoleum while the other girls washed up, she rather wished she had gone to tea at Miss Brodie's after all. She took out her secret notebook from between the sheets of music and added a chapter to 'The Mountain Eyrie', the true love story of Miss Jean Brodie.

THREE

The days passed and the wind blew from the Forth.

.　It is not to be supposed that Miss Brodie was unique at this point of her prime; or that (since such things are relative) she was in any way off her head. She was alone, merely, in that she taught in a school like Marcia Blaine's. There were legions of her kind during the nineteen-thirties, women from the age of thirty and upward, who crowded their war-bereaved spinsterhood with voyages of discovery into new ideas and energetic practices in art or social welfare, education or religion. The progressive spinsters of Edinburgh did not teach in schools, especially in schools of traditional character like Marcia Blaine's School for Girls. It was in this that Miss Brodie was, as the rest of the staff spinsterhood put it, a trifle out of place. But she was not out of place amongst her own kind, the vigorous daughters of dead or enfeebled merchants, of ministers of religion, University professors, doctors, big warehouse owners of the past, or the owners of fisheries who had endowed these daughters with shrewd wits, high-coloured cheeks, constitutions like horses, logical educations, hearty spirits and private means. They could be seen leaning over the democratic counters of Edinburgh grocers' shops arguing with the Manager at three in the afternoon on every subject from the authenticity of the Scriptures to the question what the word 'guaranteed' on a jam-jar really meant. They went to lectures, tried living on honey and nuts, took lessons in German and then went walking in Germany; they bought caravans and went off with them into the hills among the lochs; they played the guitar, they supported all the new little theatre companies; they took lodgings in the slums and, distributing pots of paint, taught their neighbours the arts of simple interior decoration; they preached the inventions of Marie Stopes; they attended the meetings of the Oxford Group and put Spiritualism to their hawk-eyed test. Some assisted in the Scottish Nationalist Movement;

others, like Miss Brodie, called themselves Europeans and Edinburgh a European capital, the city of Hume and Boswell.

They were not, however, committee women. They were not school teachers. The committee spinsters were less enterprising and not at all rebellious, they were sober churchgoers and quiet workers. The school-mistresses were of a still more orderly type, earning their keep, living with aged parents and taking walks on the hills and holidays at North Berwick.

But those of Miss Brodie's kind were great talkers and feminists and, like most feminists, talked to men as man-to-man.

'I tell you this, Mr Geddes, birth control is the only answer to the problem of the working class. A free issue to every household ...'

And often in the thriving grocers' shops at three in the afternoon:

'Mr Logan, Elder though you are, I am a woman in my prime of life, so you can take it from me that you get a sight more religion out of Professor Tovey's Sunday concerts than you do out of your kirk services.'

And so, seen in this light, there was nothing outwardly odd about Miss Brodie. Inwardly was a different matter, and it remained to be seen, towards what extremities her nature worked her. Outwardly she differed from the rest of the teaching staff in that she was still in a state of fluctuating development, whereas they had only too understandably not trusted themselves to change their minds, particularly on ethical questions, after the age of twenty. There was nothing Miss Brodie could not yet learn, she boasted of it. And it was not a static Miss Brodie who told her girls, 'These are the years of my prime. You are benefiting by my prime', but one whose nature was growing under their eyes, as the girls themselves were under formation. It extended, this prime of Miss Brodie's, still in the making when the girls were well on in their teens. And the principles governing the end of her prime would have astonished herself at the beginning of it.

The summer holidays of nineteen-thirty-one marked the first anniversary of the launching of Miss Brodie's prime. The year to come was in many ways the sexual year of the Brodie set, who were now turned eleven and twelve: it was a crowded year of stirring revelations. In later years, sex was only one of the things in life. That year it was everything.

The term opened vigorously as usual. Miss Brodie stood bronzed before her class and said, 'I have spent most of my summer holidays in Italy once more, and a week in London, and I have brought back a great many pictures which we can pin on the wall. Here is a Cimabue. Here is a larger formation of Mussolini's fascisti, it is a better view of them than that of last year's picture. They are doing splendid things as I shall tell you later. I went with my friends for an audience with the Pope. My friends kissed his ring but I thought it proper only to bend over it. I wore a long black gown with a lace mantilla, and looked magnificent. In London my friends who are well-to-do – their small girl has two nurses, or nannies as they say in England – took me to visit A. A. Milne. In the hall was hung a reproduction of Botticelli's *Primavera* which means the Birth of Spring. I wore my silk dress with the large red poppies which is just right for my colouring. Mussolini is one of the greatest men in the world, far more so than Ramsay MacDonald, and his fascisti –'

'Good morning, Miss Brodie. Good morning, sit down, girls,' said the headmistress who had entered in a hurry, leaving the door wide open.

Miss Brodie passed behind her with her head up, up, and shut the door with the utmost meaning.

'I have only just looked in,' said Miss Mackay, 'and I have to be off. Well, girls, this is the first day of the new session. Are we downhearted? No. You girls must work hard this year at every subject and pass your qualifying examination with flying colours. Next year you will be in the Senior school, remember. I hope you've all had a nice summer holiday, you all look nice and brown. I hope in due course of time to read your essays on how you spent them.'

When she had gone Miss Brodie looked hard at the door for a long time. A girl, not of her set, called Judith, giggled. Miss Brodie said to Judith, 'That will do.' She turned to the blackboard and rubbed out with her duster the long division sum she always kept on the blackboard in case of intrusions from outside during any arithmetic periods when Miss Brodie should happen not to be teaching arithmetic. When she had done this she turned back to the class and said, 'Are we downhearted no, are we downhearted no. As I was saying, Mussolini has performed feats of magnitude and unemployment is even farther abolished under him than it was last year. I shall be able to tell you a great deal this term. As you know, I don't believe in talking down to children, you are capable of grasping more than is generally appreciated by your elders. Education means a leading out, from *e*, out and *duco*, I lead. Qualifying examination or no qualifying examination, you will have the benefit of my experiences in Italy. In Rome I saw the Forum and I saw the Colosseum where the gladiators died and the slaves were thrown to the lions. A vulgar American remarked to me, "It looks like a mighty fine quarry." They talk nasally. Mary, what does to talk nasally mean?'

Mary did not know.

'Stupid as ever,' said Miss Brodie. 'Eunice?'

'Through your nose,' said Eunice.

'Answer in a complete sentence, please,' said Miss Brodie. 'This year I think you should all start answering in complete sentences, I must try to remember this rule. Your correct answer is "To talk nasally means to talk through one's nose". The American said, "It looks like a mighty fine quarry." Ah, it was there the gladiators fought. "Hail Caesar!" they cried. "These about to die salute thee!"'

Miss Brodie stood in her brown dress like a gladiator with raised arm and eyes flashing like a sword. 'Hail Caesar!' she cried again, turning radiantly to the window light, as if Caesar sat there. 'Who opened the window?' said Miss Brodie dropping her arm.

Nobody answered.

'Whoever has opened the window has opened it too wide,' said Miss Brodie. 'Six inches is perfectly adequate. More is vulgar. One should have an innate sense of these things. We ought to be doing history at the moment according to the time-table. Get out your history books and prop them up in your hands. I shall tell you a little more about Italy. I met a young poet by a fountain. Here is a picture of Dante meeting Beatrice – it is pronounced Beatri*chay* in Italian which makes the name very beautiful – on the Ponte Vecchio. He fell in love with her at that moment. Mary, sit up and don't slouch. It was a sublime moment in a sublime love. By whom was the picture painted?'

Nobody knew.

'It was painted by Rossetti. Who was Rossetti, Jenny?'

'A painter,' said Jenny.

Miss Brodie looked suspicious.

'And a genius,' said Sandy, to come to Jenny's rescue.

'A friend of – ?' said Miss Brodie.

'Swinburne,' said a girl.

Miss Brodie smiled. 'You have not forgotten,' she said, looking round the class. 'Holidays or no holidays. Keep your history books propped up in case we have any further intruders.' She looked disapprovingly towards the door and lifted her fine dark Roman head with dignity. She had often told the girls that her dead Hugh had admired her head for its Roman appearance.

'Next year,' she said, 'you will have the specialists to teach you history and mathematics and languages, a teacher for this and a teacher for that, a period of forty-five minutes for this and another for that. But in this your last year with me you will receive the fruits of my prime. They will remain with you all your days. First, however, I must mark the register for today before we forget. There are two new girls. Stand up the two new girls.'

They stood up with wide eyes while Miss Brodie sat down at her desk.

'You will get used to our ways. What religions are you?' said Miss Brodie with her pen poised on the page while, outside in the sky, the gulls from the Firth of Forth wheeled over the school and the green and golden tree-tops swayed towards the windows.

> 'Come autumn sae pensive, in yellow and gray,
> And soothe me wi' tidings o' nature's decay

– Robert Burns,' said Miss Brodie when she had closed the register. 'We are now well into the nineteen-thirties. I have four pounds of rosy apples in my desk, a gift from Mr Lowther's orchard, let us eat them now while the coast is clear – not but what the apples do not come under my own jurisdiction, but discretion is . . . discretion is . . . Sandy?'

'The better part of valour, Miss Brodie.' Her little eyes looked at Miss Brodie in a slightly smaller way.

Even before the official opening of her prime Miss Brodie's colleagues in the Junior school had been gradually turning against her. The teaching staff of the Senior school was indifferent or mildly amused, for they had not yet felt the impact of the Brodie set; that was to come the following year, and even then these senior mistresses were not unduly irritated by the effects of what they called Miss Brodie's experimental methods. It was in the Junior school, among the lesser paid and lesser qualified women, with whom Miss Brodie had daily dealings, that indignation seethed. There were two exceptions on the staff, who felt neither resentment nor indifference towards Miss Brodie, but were, on the contrary, her supporters on every count. One of these was Mr Gordon Lowther, the singing master for the whole school, Junior and Senior. The other was Mr Teddy Lloyd, the Senior girls' art master. They were the only men on the staff. Both were already a little in love with Miss Brodie, for they found in her the only sex-bestirred object in their daily environment, and although they did not realize it, both were already beginning to act as rivals for her attention. But so far, they had not engaged her attention as men, she knew them only as supporters, and was proudly grateful. It was the Brodie set who discerned, before she did, and certainly these men did, that Mr Lowther and Mr Lloyd were at pains to appear well, each in his exclusive right before Miss Brodie.

To the Brodie set Gordon Lowther and Teddy Lloyd looked rather like each other until habitual acquaintance proved that they looked very different. Both were red-gold in colouring. Teddy Lloyd, the art master, was by far the better-shaped, the better-featured and the more sophisticated. He was said to be half Welsh, half English. He spoke with a hoarse voice as if he had bronchitis all the time. A golden forelock of his hair fell over his forehead into his eyes. Most wonderful of all, he had only one arm, the right, with which he painted. The other was a sleeve tucked into his pocket. He had lost the contents of the sleeve in the Great War.

Miss Brodie's class had only once had an opportunity to size him up closely, and then it was in a dimmed light, for the blinds of the art room had been drawn to allow Mr Lloyd to show his lantern slides. They had been marched into the art room by Miss Brodie, who was going to sit with the girls on the end of a bench, when the art master came forward with a chair for her held in his one hand and presented in a special way with a tiny inflection of the knees, like a flunkey. Miss Brodie seated herself nobly like Britannia with her legs apart under her loose brown skirt which came well over her knees. Mr Lloyd showed his pictures from an exhibition of Italian art in London. He had a pointer with which he indicated the design of the picture in accompaniment to his hoarse voice. He said nothing of what the pictures represented, only followed each curve and line as the artist had left it off – perhaps at the point of an elbow – and picked it up – perhaps at the edge of a cloud or the back of a chair. The ladies of the *Primavera*, in their netball-playing postures, provided Mr Lloyd with much pointer work. He kept on passing the pointer along the lines of their bottoms which showed through the drapery. The third time he did this a collective quiver of mirth ran along the front row of girls, then spread to the back rows. They kept their mouths shut tight against these convulsions, but the tighter their lips, the more did the little gusts of humour escape through their noses. Mr Lloyd looked round with offended exasperation.

'It is obvious,' said Miss Brodie, 'that these girls are not of cultured homes and heritage. The Philistines are upon us, Mr Lloyd.'

The girls, anxious to be of cultured and sexless antecedents, were instantly composed by the shock of this remark. But immediately Mr Lloyd resumed his demonstration of artistic form, and again dragged his pointer all round the draped private parts of one of Botticelli's female subjects, Sandy affected to have a fit of spluttering coughs, as did several girls behind her. Others groped under their seat as if looking for something they had dropped. One or two frankly leant against each other and giggled with hands to their helpless mouths.

'I am surprised at *you*, Sandy,' said Miss Brodie. 'I thought you were the leaven in the lump.'

Sandy looked up from her coughs with a hypocritical blinking of her eyes. Miss Brodie, however, had already fastened on Mary Macgregor who was nearest to her. Mary's giggles had been caused by contagion, for she was too stupid to have any sex-wits of her own, and Mr Lloyd's lesson would never have affected her unless it had first affected the rest of the class. But now she was giggling openly like a dirty-minded child of an uncultured home. Miss Brodie grasped Mary's arm, jerked her to her feet and propelled her to the door where she thrust her outside and shut her out, returning as one who had solved the whole problem. As indeed she had, for the violent action sobered the girls and made them feel that, in the official sense, an unwanted ring-leader had been apprehended and they were no longer in the wrong.

As Mr Lloyd had now switched his equipment to a depiction of the Madonna and Child, Miss Brodie's action was the more appreciated, for no one in the class would have felt comfortable at being seized with giggles while Mr Lloyd's pointer was tracing the outlines of this sacred subject. In fact, they were rather shocked that Mr Lloyd's hoarse voice did not change its tone in the slightest for this occasion, but went on stating what the painter had done with his brush; he was almost defiant in his methodical tracing of lines all over the Mother and the Son. Sandy caught his glance towards Miss Brodie as if seeking her approval for his very artistic attitude and Sandy saw her smile back as would a goddess with superior understanding smile to a god away on the mountain tops.

It was not long after this that Monica Douglas, later famous for mathematics and anger, claimed that she had seen Mr Lloyd in the act of kissing Miss Brodie. She was very definite about it in her report to the five other members of the Brodie set. There was a general excited difficulty in believing her.

'When?'

'Where?'

'In the art room after school yesterday.'

'What were you doing in the art room?' said Sandy who took up the role of cross-examiner.

'I went to get a new sketch pad.'

'Why? You haven't finished your old sketch pad yet.'

'I have,' said Monica.

'When did you use up your old sketch pad?'

'Last Saturday afternoon when you were playing golf with Miss Brodie.'

It was true that Jenny and Sandy had done nine holes on the Braid Hills course with Miss Brodie on the previous Saturday, while the rest of the Brodie set wandered afield to sketch.

'Monica used up all her book. She did the Tee Woods from five angles,' said Rose Stanley in verification.

'What part of the art room were they standing in?' Sandy said.

'The far side,' Monica said. 'I know he had his arm round her and was kissing her. They jumped apart when I opened the door.'

'Which arm?' Sandy snapped.

'The right of course, he hasn't got a left.'

'Were you inside or outside the room when you saw them?' Sandy said.

'Well, in and out. I *saw* them, I tell you.'

'What did they say?' Jenny said.

'They didn't see me,' said Monica. 'I just turned and ran away.'

'Was it a long and lingering kiss?' Sandy demanded, while Jenny came closer to hear the answer.

Monica cast the corner of her eye up to the ceiling as if doing mental arithmetic. Then when her calculation was finished she said, 'Yes it was.'

'How do you know if you didn't stop to see how long it was?'

'I know,' said Monica, getting angry, 'by the bit that I did see. It was a small bit of a good long kiss that I saw, I could tell it by his arm being round her, and –'

'I don't believe all this,' Sandy said squeakily, because she was excited and desperately trying to prove the report true by eliminating the doubts. 'You must have been dreaming,' she said.

Monica pecked with the fingers of her right hand at Sandy's arm, and pinched the skin of it with a nasty half turn. Sandy screamed. Monica, whose face was becoming very red, swung the attaché case which held her books, so that it hit the girls who stood in its path and made them stand back from her.

'She's losing her temper,' said Eunice Gardiner, skipping.

'I don't believe what she says,' said Sandy, desperately trying to visualize the scene in the art room and to goad factual Monica into describing it with due feeling.

'I believe it,' said Rose. 'Mr Lloyd is an artist and Miss Brodie is artistic too.'

Jenny said, 'Didn't they see the door opening?'

'Yes,' said Monica, 'they jumped apart as I opened the door.'

'How did you know they didn't see you?' Sandy said.

'I got away before they turned round. They were standing at the far end of the room beside the still-life curtain.' She went to the classroom door and demonstrated her quick get-away. This was not dramatically satisfying to Sandy who went out of the classroom, opened the door, looked, opened her eyes in a startled way, gasped and retreated in a flash. She seemed satisfied by her experimental re-enactment but it so delighted her friends that she repeated it. Miss Brodie came up from behind her on her fourth performance which had reached a state of extreme flourish.

'What are you doing, Sandy?' said Miss Brodie.

'Only playing,' said Sandy, photographing this new Miss Brodie with her little eyes.

The question of whether Miss Brodie was actually capable of being kissed and of kissing occupied the Brodie set till Christmas. For the war-time romance of her life had presented to their minds a Miss Brodie of hardly flesh and blood, since that younger Miss Brodie belonged to the prehistory of before their birth. Sitting under the elm last autumn, Miss Brodie's story of 'when I was a girl' had seemed much less real, and yet more believable than this report by Monica Douglas. The Brodie set decided to keep the incident to themselves lest, if it should spread to the rest of the class, it should spread wider still and eventually to someone's ears who would get Monica Douglas into trouble.

There was, indeed, a change in Miss Brodie. It was not merely that Sandy and Jenny, recasting her in their minds, now began to try to imagine her as someone called 'Jean'. There was a change in herself. She wore newer clothes and with them a glowing amber necklace which was of such real amber that, as she once showed them, it had magnetic properties when rubbed and then applied to a piece of paper.

The change in Miss Brodie was best discerned by comparison with the other teachers in the Junior school. If you looked at them and then looked at Miss Brodie it was more possible to imagine her giving herself up to kissing.

Jenny and Sandy wondered if Mr Lloyd and Miss Brodie had gone further that day in the art room, and had been swept away by passion. They kept an eye on Miss Brodie's stomach to see if it showed signs of swelling. Some days, if they were bored, they decided it had begun to swell. But on Miss Brodie's entertaining days they found her stomach as flat as ever and at these times even agreed together that Monica Douglas had been telling a lie.

The other Junior school teachers said good morning to Miss

Brodie, these days, in a more than Edinburgh manner, that is to say it was gracious enough, and not one of them omitted to say good morning at all; but Sandy, who had turned eleven, perceived that the tone of 'morning' in good morning made the word seem purposely to rhyme with 'scorning', so that these colleagues of Miss Brodie's might just as well have said 'I scorn you' instead of good morning. Miss Brodie's reply was more than ever anglicized in its accent than was its usual proud wont. 'Good mawning,' she replied, in the corridors, flattening their scorn beneath the chariot wheels of her superiority, and deviating her head towards them no more than an insulting half-inch. She held her head up, up, as she walked, and often, when she reached and entered her own classroom, permitted herself to sag gratefully against the door for an instant. She did not frequent the staff common rooms in the free periods when her class was taking its singing or sewing lessons, but accompanied them.

Now the two sewing teachers were somewhat apart from the rest of the teaching staff and were not taken seriously. They were the two younger sisters of a third, dead, eldest sister whose guidance of their lives had never been replaced. Their names were Miss Ellen and Miss Alison Kerr; they were incapable of imparting any information whatsoever, so flustered were they, with their fluffed-out hair, dry blue-grey skins and birds' eyes; instead of teaching sewing they took each girl's work in hand, one by one, and did most of it for her. In the worst cases they unstitched what had been done and did it again, saying 'This'll not do', or 'That's never a run and fell seam'. The sewing sisters had not as yet been induced to judge Miss Brodie since they were by nature of the belief that their scholastic colleagues were above criticism. Therefore the sewing lessons were a great relaxation to all, and Miss Brodie in the time before Christmas used the sewing period each week to read *Jane Eyre* to her class who, while they listened, pricked their thumbs as much as was bearable so that interesting little spots of blood might appear on the stuff they were sewing, and it was even possible to make blood-spot designs.

The singing lessons were far different. Some weeks after the report of her kissing in the art room it gradually became plain that Miss Brodie was agitated before, during, and after the singing lessons. She wore her newest clothes on singing days.

Sandy said to Monica Douglas, 'Are you sure it was Mr Lloyd

who kissed her? Are you sure it wasn't Mr Lowther?'

'It was Mr Lloyd,' said Monica, 'and it was in the art room, not the music room. What would Mr Lowther have been doing in the art room?'

'They look alike, Mr Lloyd and Mr Lowther,' Sandy said.

Monica's anger was rising in her face. 'It was Mr Lloyd with his one arm round her,' she said. 'I saw them. I'm sorry I ever told you. Rose is the only one that believes me.'

Rose Stanley believed her, but this was because she was indifferent. She was the least of all the Brodie set to be excited by Miss Brodie's love affairs, or by anyone else's sex. And it was always to be the same. Later, when she was famous for sex, her magnificently appealing qualities lay in the fact that she had no curiosity about sex at all, she never reflected upon it. As Miss Brodie was to say, she had instinct.

'Rose is the only one who believes me,' said Monica Douglas.

When she visited Sandy at the nunnery in the late nineteen-fifties, Monica said, 'I really did see Teddy Lloyd kiss Miss Brodie in the art room one day.'

'I know you did,' said Sandy.

She knew it even before Miss Brodie had told her so one day after the end of the war, when they sat in the Braid Hills Hotel eating sandwiches and drinking tea which Miss Brodie's rations at home would not run to. Miss Brodie sat shrivelled and betrayed in her long-preserved dark musquash coat. She had been retired before time. She said, 'I am past my prime.'

'It was a good prime,' said Sandy.

They looked out of the wide windows at the little Braid Burn trickling through the fields and at the hills beyond, so austere from everlasting that they had never been capable of losing anything by the war.

'Teddy Lloyd was greatly in love with me, as you know,' said Miss Brodie, 'and I with him. It was a great love. One day in the art room he kissed me. We never became lovers, not even after you left Edinburgh, when the temptation was strongest.'

Sandy stared through her little eyes at the hills.

'But I renounced him,' said Miss Brodie. 'He was a married man. I renounced the great love of my prime. We had everything in common, the artistic nature.'

She had reckoned on her prime lasting till she was sixty. But this, the year after the war, was in fact Miss Brodie's last and fifty-sixth year. She looked older than that, she was suffering from an internal growth. This was her last year in the world and in another sense it was Sandy's.

Miss Brodie sat in her defeat and said, 'In the late autumn of nineteen-thirty-one – are you listening, Sandy?'

Sandy took her eyes from the hills.

In the late autumn of nineteen-thirty-one Miss Brodie was away from school for two weeks. It was understood she had an ailment. The Brodie set called at her flat after school with flowers and found no one at home. On inquiring at school next day they were told she had gone to the country to stay with a friend until she was better.

In the meantime Miss Brodie's class was dispersed, and squashed in among the classes of her colleagues. The Brodie set stuck together and were placed with a gaunt woman who was, in fact, a Miss Gaunt from the Western Isles who wore a knee-length skirt made from what looked like grey blanket stuff; this had never been smart even in the knee-length days; Rose Stanley said it was cut short for economy. Her head was very large and bony. Her chest was a slight bulge flattened by a bust bodice, and her jersey was a dark forbidding green. She did not care at all for the Brodie set who were stunned by a sudden plunge into industrious learning and very put out by Miss Gaunt's horrible sharpness and strict insistence on silence throughout the day.

'Oh dear,' said Rose out loud one day when they were settled to essay writing, 'I can't remember how you spell "possession". Are there two 's's or –?'

'A hundred lines of *Marmion*,' Miss Gaunt flung at her.

The black-marks book which eventually reflected itself on the end-of-term reports, was heavily scored with the names of the Brodie set by the end of the first week. Apart from inquiring their names for this purpose Miss Gaunt did not trouble to remember them. 'You, girl,' she would say to every Brodie face. So dazed were the Brodie girls that they did not notice the omission during that week of their singing lesson which should have been on Wednesday.

On Thursday they were herded into the sewing room in the early afternoon. The two sewing teachers, Miss Alison and Miss Ellen Kerr, seemed rather cowed by gaunt Miss Gaunt, and applied themselves briskly to the sewing machines which they were teaching the girls to use. The shuttle of the sewing machines went up and down, which usually caused Sandy and Jenny to giggle, since at that time everything that could conceivably bear a sexual interpretation immediately did so to them. But the absence of Miss Brodie and the presence of Miss Gaunt had a definite subtracting effect from the sexual significance of everything, and the trepidation of the two sewing sisters contributed to the effect of grim realism.

Miss Gaunt evidently went to the same parish church as the Kerr sisters, to whom she addressed remarks from time to time while she embroidered a tray cloth.

'My brothurr . . .' she kept saying, 'my brothurr says . . .'

Miss Gaunt's brother was apparently the minister of the parish, which accounted for the extra precautions Miss Alison and Miss Ellen were taking about their work today, with the result that they got a lot of the sewing mixed up.

'My brothurr is up in the morning at five-thirty . . . My brothurr organized a . . .'

Sandy was thinking of the next instalment of *Jane Eyre* which Miss Brodie usually enlivened this hour by reading. Sandy had done with Alan Breck and had taken up with Mr Rochester, with whom she now sat in the garden.

'You are afraid of me, Miss Sandy.'

'You talk like the Sphinx, sir, but I am not afraid.'

'You have such a grave, quiet manner, Miss Sandy – you are going?'

'It has struck nine, sir.'

A phrase of Miss Gaunt's broke upon the garden scene: 'Mr Lowther is not at school this week.'

'So I hear,' Miss Alison said.

'It seems he will be away for another week at least.'

'Is he ill?'

'I understand so, unfortunately,' said Miss Gaunt.

'Miss Brodie is ailing, too,' said Miss Ellen.

'Yes,' said Miss Gaunt. 'She too is expected to be absent for another week.'

'What is the trouble?'

'That I couldn't say,' said Miss Gaunt. She stuck her needle in and out of her embroidery. Then she looked up at the sisters. 'It may be Miss Brodie has the same complaint as Mr Lowther,' she said.

Sandy saw her face as that of the housekeeper in *Jane Eyre*, watching her carefully and knowingly as she entered the house, late, from the garden where she had been sitting with Mr Rochester.

'Perhaps Miss Brodie is having a love affair with Mr Lowther,' Sandy said to Jenny, merely in order to break up the sexless gloom that surrounded them.

'But it was Mr Lloyd who kissed her. She must be in love with Mr Lloyd or she wouldn't have let him kiss her.'

'Perhaps she's working it off on Mr Lowther. Mr Lowther isn't married.'

It was a fantasy worked up between them, in defiance of Miss Gaunt and her forbidding brother, and it was understood in that way. But Sandy, remembering Miss Gaunt's expression as she remarked 'It may be Miss Brodie has the same complaint as Mr Lowther', was suddenly not sure that the suggestion was not true. For this reason she was more reticent than Jenny about the details of the imagined love affair. Jenny whispered, 'They go to bed. Then he puts out the light. Then their toes touch. And then Miss Brodie . . . Miss Brodie . . .' She broke into giggles.

'Miss Brodie yawns,' said Sandy in order to restore decency, now that she suspected it was all true.

'No, Miss Brodie says "Darling". She says –'

'Quiet,' whispered Sandy, 'Eunice is coming.'

Eunice Gardiner approached the table where Jenny and Sandy sat, grabbed the scissors and went away. Eunice had lately taken a religious turn and there was no talking about sex in front of her. She had stopped hopping and skipping. The phase did not last long, but while it did she was nasty and not to be trusted. When she was well out of the way Jenny resumed:

'Mr Lowther's legs are shorter than Miss Brodie's, so I suppose she winds hers round his, and –'

'Where does Mr Lowther live, do you know?' Sandy said.

'At Cramond. He's got a big house with a housekeeper.'

In that year after the war when Sandy sat with Miss Brodie in the window of the Braid Hills Hotel and brought her eyes back from the hills to show she was listening, Miss Brodie said:

'I renounced Teddy Lloyd. But I decided to enter into a love affair, it was the only cure. My love for Teddy was an obsession, he was the love of my prime. But in the autumn of nineteen-thirty-one I entered an affair with Gordon Lowther, he was a bachelor and it was more becoming. That is the truth and there is no more to say. Are you listening, Sandy?'

'Yes, I'm listening.'

'You look as if you were thinking of something else, my dear. Well, as I say, that is the whole story.'

Sandy was thinking of something else. She was thinking that it was not the whole story.

'Of course the liaison was suspected. Perhaps you girls knew about it. You, Sandy, had a faint idea . . . but nobody could prove what was between Gordon Lowther and myself. It was never proved. It was not on those grounds that I was betrayed. I should like to know who betrayed me. It is incredible that it should have been one of my own girls. I often wonder if it was poor Mary. Perhaps I should have been nicer to Mary. Well, it was tragic about Mary, I picture that fire, that poor girl. I can't see how Mary could have betrayed me, though.'

'She had no contact with the school after she left,' Sandy said.

'I wonder, was it Rose who betrayed me?'

The whine in her voice – '. . . betrayed me, betrayed me' – bored and afflicted Sandy. It is seven years, thought Sandy, since I betrayed this tiresome woman. What does she mean by 'betray'? She was looking at the hills as if to see there the first and unbetrayable Miss Brodie, indifferent to criticism as a crag.

After her two weeks' absence Miss Brodie returned to tell her class that she had enjoyed an exciting rest and a well-earned one. Mr Lowther's singing class went on as usual and he beamed at Miss Brodie as she brought them proudly into the music room with their heads up, up. Miss Brodie now played the accompaniment, sitting very well at the piano and sometimes, with a certain sadness of countenance, richly taking the second soprano in 'How sweet is the shepherd's sweet lot', and other melodious preparations for the annual concert. Mr Lowther, short-legged, shy and golden-haired, no longer played with Jenny's curls. The bare branches brushed the windows and Sandy was almost as sure as could be that the singing master was in love with Miss Brodie and that Miss Brodie was in love with the art master. Rose Stanley had not yet revealed her potentialities in the working-out of Miss Brodie's passion for one-armed Teddy Lloyd, and Miss Brodie's prime still flourished unbetrayed.

It was impossible to imagine Miss Brodie sleeping with Mr Lowther, it was impossible to imagine her in a sexual context at all, and yet it was impossible not to suspect that such things were so.

During the Easter term Miss Mackay, the headmistress, had the girls in to tea in her study in small groups and, later, one by one. This was a routine of inquiry as to their intentions for the Senior School, whether they would go on the Modern side or whether they would apply for admission to the Classical.

Miss Brodie had already prompted them as follows: 'I am not saying anything against the Modern side. Modern and Classical, they are equal, and each provides for a function in life. You must make your free choice. Not everyone is capable of a Classical education. You must make your choice quite freely.' So that the girls were left in no doubt as to Miss Brodie's contempt for the Modern side.

From among her special set only Eunice Gardiner stood out to be a Modern, and that was because her parents wanted her to take a course in domestic science and she herself wanted the extra scope for gymnastics and games which the Modern side offered. Eunice, preparing arduously for Confirmation, was still a bit too pious for Miss Brodie's liking. She now refused to do somersaults outside of the gymnasium, she wore lavender water on her handkerchief, declined a try of Rose Stanley's aunt's lipstick, was taking a suspiciously healthy interest in international sport and, when Miss Brodie herded her set to the Empire Theatre for their first and last opportunity to witness the dancing of Pavlova, Eunice was absent, she had pleaded off because of something else she had to attend which she described as 'a social'.

'Social what?' said Miss Brodie, who always made difficulties about words when she scented heresy.

'It's in the Church Hall, Miss Brodie.'

'Yes, yes, but social what? Social is an adjective and you are using it as a noun. If you mean a social gathering, by all means attend your social gathering and we shall have our own social gathering in the presence of the great Anna Pavlova, a dedicated woman who, when she appears on the stage, makes the other dancers look like elephants. By all means attend your social gathering. We shall see Pavlova doing the death of the Swan, it is a great moment in eternity.'

All that term she tried to inspire Eunice to become at least a pioneer missionary in some deadly and dangerous zone of the earth, for it was intolerable to Miss Brodie that any of her girls should grow up not largely dedicated to some vocation. 'You will end up as a Girl Guide leader in a suburb like Corstorphine,' she said warningly to Eunice, who was in fact secretly attracted to this idea and who lived in Corstorphine. The term was filled with legends of Pavlova and her dedicated habits, her wild fits of temperament and her intolerance of the second-rate. 'She screams at the chorus,' said Miss Brodie, 'which is permissible in a great artist. She speaks English fluently, her accent is charming. Afterwards she goes home to meditate upon the swans which she keeps on a lake in the grounds.'

'Sandy,' said Anna Pavlova, 'you are the only truly dedicated dancer, next to me. Your dying Swan is perfect, such a sensitive, final tap of the claw upon the floor of the stage . . .'

'I know it,' said Sandy (in considered preference to 'Oh, I do my best'), as she relaxed in the wings.

Pavlova nodded sagely and gazed into the middle distance with the eyes of tragic exile and of art. 'Every artist knows,' said Pavlova, 'is it not so?' Then, with a voice desperate with the menace of hysteria, and a charming accent, she declared, 'I have never been understood. Never. Never.'

Sandy removed one of her ballet shoes and cast it casually to the other end of the wings where it was respectfully retrieved by a member of the common chorus. Pausing before she removed the other shoe, Sandy said to Pavlova, 'I am sure I understand you.'

'It is true,' exclaimed Pavlova, clasping Sandy's hand, 'because you are an artist and will carry on the torch.'

Miss Brodie said: 'Pavlova contemplates her swans in order to perfect her swan dance, she studies them. That is true dedication. You must all grow up to be dedicated women as I have dedicated myself to you.'

A few weeks before she died, when, sitting up in bed in the nursing home, she learnt from Monica Douglas that Sandy had gone to a convent, she said: 'What a waste. That is not the sort of dedication I meant. Do you think she has done this to annoy me? I begin to wonder if it was not Sandy who betrayed me.'

The headmistress invited Sandy, Jenny and Mary to tea just before the Easter holidays and asked them the usual questions about what they wanted to do in the Senior school and whether they wanted to do it on the Modern or the Classical side. Mary Macgregor was ruled out of the Classical side because her marks did not reach the required standard. She seemed despondent on hearing this.

'Why do you want so much to go on the Classical side, Mary? You aren't cut out for it. Don't your parents realize that?'

'Miss Brodie prefers it.'

'It has nothing to do with Miss Brodie,' said Miss Mackay, settling her great behind more firmly in her chair. 'It is a question of your marks or what you and your parents think. In your case, your marks don't come up to the standard.'

When Jenny and Sandy opted for Classical, she said: 'Because Miss Brodie prefers it, I suppose. What good will Latin and Greek be to you when you get married or take a job? German would be more useful.'

But they stuck out for Classical, and when Miss Mackay had accepted their choice she transparently started to win over the girls by praising Miss Brodie. 'What we would do without Miss Brodie, I don't know. There is always a difference about Miss Brodie's girls, and the last two years I may say a *marked* difference.'

Then she began to pump them. Miss Brodie took them to the theatre, the art galleries, for walks, to Miss Brodie's flat for tea? How kind of Miss Brodie. 'Does Miss Brodie pay for all your theatre tickets?'

'Sometimes,' said Mary.

'Not for all of us every time,' said Jenny.

'We go up to the gallery,' Sandy said.

'Well, it is most kind of Miss Brodie. I hope you are appreciative.'

'Oh, yes,' they said, united and alert against anything unfavourable to the Brodie idea which the conversation might be leading up to. This was not lost on the headmistress.

'That's splendid,' she said. 'And do you go to concerts with Miss Brodie? Miss Brodie is very musical, I believe?'

'Yes,' said Mary, looking at her friends for a lead.

'We went to the opera with Miss Brodie last term to see *La Traviata*,' said Jenny.

'Miss Brodie is musical?' said Miss Mackay again, addressing Sandy and Jenny.

'We saw Pavlova,' said Sandy.

'Miss Brodie is musical?' said Miss Mackay.

'I think Miss Brodie is more interested in art, ma'am,' said Sandy.

'But music is a form of art.'

'Pictures and drawings, I mean,' said Sandy.

'Very enlightening,' said Miss Mackay. 'Do you girls take piano lessons?'

They all said yes.

'From whom? From Mr Lowther?'

They answered variously, for Mr Lowther's piano lessons were not part of the curriculum and these three girls had private arrangements for the piano at home. But now, at the mention of Mr Lowther, even slow-minded Mary suspected what Miss Mackay was driving at.

'I understand Miss Brodie plays the piano for your singing lessons. So what makes you think she prefers art to music, Sandy?'

'Miss Brodie told us so. Music is an interest to her but art is a passion, Miss Brodie said.'

'And what are *your* cultural interests? I'm sure you are too young to have passions.'

'Stories, ma'am,' Mary said.

'Does Miss Brodie tell you stories?'

'Yes,' said Mary.

'What about?'

'History,' said Jenny and Sandy together, because it was a question they had foreseen might arise one day and they had prepared the answer with a brainracking care for literal truth.

Miss Mackay paused and looked at them in the process of moving the cake from the table to the tray; their reply had plainly struck her as being on the ready side.

She asked no further questions, but made the following noteworthy speech:

'You are very fortunate in Miss Brodie. I could wish your arithmetic papers had been better. I am always impressed by Miss Brodie's girls in one way or another. You will have to work hard at ordinary humble subjects for the qualifying examination. Miss Brodie is giving you an excellent preparation for the Senior school. Culture cannot compensate for lack of hard knowledge. I am happy to see you are devoted to Miss Brodie. Your loyalty is due to the school rather than to any one individual.'

Not all of this conversation was reported back to Miss Brodie.

'We told Miss Mackay how much you liked art,' said Sandy, however.

'I do indeed,' said Miss Brodie, 'but "like" is hardly the word; pictorial art is my passion.'

'That's what I said,' said Sandy.

Miss Brodie looked at her as if to say, as in fact she had said twice before, 'One day, Sandy, you will go too far for my liking.'

'Compared to music,' said Sandy, blinking up at her with her little pig-like eyes.

Towards the end of the Easter holidays, to crown the sex-laden year, Jenny, out walking alone, was accosted by a man joyfully exposing himself beside the Water of Leith. He said, 'Come and look at this.'

'At what?' said Jenny, moving closer, thinking to herself he had picked up a fallen nestling from the ground or had discovered a strange plant. Having perceived the truth, she escaped unharmed and unpursued though breathless, and was presently surrounded by solicitous, horrified relations and was coaxed to sip tea well sugared against the shock. Later in the day, since the incident had been reported to the police, came a wonderful policewoman to question Jenny.

These events contained enough exciting possibilities to set the rest of the Easter holidays spinning like a top and to last out the whole of the summer term. The first effect on Sandy was an adverse one, for she had been on the point of obtaining permission to go for walks alone in just such isolated spots as that in which Jenny's encounter had taken place. Sandy was now still forbidden lone walks, but this was a mere by-effect of the affair. The rest brought nothing but good.

The subject fell under two headings: first, the man himself and the nature of what he had exposed to view, and secondly the policewoman.

The first was fairly quickly exhausted.

'He was a horrible creature,' said Jenny.

'A terrible beast,' said Sandy.

The question of the policewoman was inexhaustible, and although Sandy never saw her, nor at that time any policewoman (for these were in the early days of the women police), she quite deserted Alan Breck and Mr Rochester and all the heroes of fiction for the summer term, and fell in love with the unseen policewoman who had questioned Jenny; and in this way she managed to keep alive Jenny's enthusiasm too.

'What did she look like? Did she wear a helmet?'

'No, a cap. She had short, fair, curly hair curling under the cap. And a dark blue uniform. She said, "Now tell me all about it."'

'And what did you say?' said Sandy for the fourth time.

For the fourth time Jenny replied: 'Well, I said, "The man was walking along under the trees by the bank, and he was holding something in his hand. And then when he saw me he laughed out loud and said, come and look at this. I said, at what? And I went a bit closer and I saw . . ." – but I couldn't tell the policewoman what I saw, could I? So the policewoman said to me, "You saw something nasty?" And I said "yes". Then she asked me what the man was like, and . . .'

But this was the same story all over again. Sandy wanted new details about the policewoman, she looked for clues. Jenny had pronounced the word 'nasty' as 'nesty', which was unusual for Jenny.

'Did she say "nasty" or "nesty"?' said Sandy on this fourth telling.

'Nesty.'

This gave rise to an extremely nasty feeling in Sandy and it put her off the idea of sex for months. All the more as she disapproved of the pronunciation of the word, it made her flesh creep, and she plagued Jenny to change her mind and agree that the policewoman had pronounced it properly.

'A lot of people say nesty,' said Jenny.

'I know, but I don't like them. They're neither one thing nor another.'

It bothered Sandy a great deal, and she had to invent a new

speaking-image for the policewoman. Another thing that troubled her was that Jenny did not know the policewoman's name, or even whether she was addressed as 'constable', 'sergeant', or merely 'miss'. Sandy decided to call her Sergeant Anne Grey. Sandy was Anne Grey's righthand woman in the Force, and they were dedicated to eliminate sex from Edinburgh and environs. In the Sunday newspapers, to which Sandy had free access, the correct technical phrases were to be found, such as 'intimacy took place' and 'plaintiff was in a certain condition'. Females who were up for sex were not called 'Miss' or 'Mrs', they were referred to by their surnames: 'Willis was remanded in custody...' 'Roebuck', saidCounsel,'was discovered to be in a certain condition.'

So Sandy pushed her dark blue police force cap to the back of her head and sitting on a stile beside Sergeant Anne Grey watched the spot between the trees by the Water of Leith where the terrible beast had appeared who had said 'Look at this' to Jenny, but where, in fact, Sandy never was.

'And another thing,' said Sandy, 'we've got to find out more about the case of Brodie and whether she is yet in a certain condition as a consequence of her liaison with Gordon Lowther, described as singing master, Marcia Blaine School for Girls.'

'Intimacy has undoubtedly taken place,' said Sergeant Anne, looking very nice in her dark uniform and short-cropped curls blondely fringing her cap. She said, 'All we need are a few incriminating documents.'

'Leave all that to me, Sergeant Anne,' said Sandy, because she was at that very time engaged with Jenny in composing the love correspondence between Miss Brodie and the singing master. Sergeant Anne pressed Sandy's hand in gratitude; and they looked into each other's eyes, their mutual understanding too deep for words.

At school after the holidays the Water of Leith affair was kept a secret between Jenny and Sandy, for Jenny's mother had said the story must not be spread about. But it seemed natural that Miss Brodie should be told in a spirit of sensational confiding.

But something made Sandy say to Jenny on the first afternoon of the term: 'Don't tell Miss Brodie.'

'Why?' said Jenny.

Sandy tried to work out the reason. It was connected with the undecided state of Miss Brodie's relationship to cheerful Mr Lowther, and with the fact that she had told her class, first thing: 'I have spent Easter at the little Roman village of Cramond.' That was where Mr Lowther lived all alone in a big house with a housekeeper.

'Don't tell Miss Brodie,' said Sandy.

'Why?' said Jenny.

Sandy made an effort to work out her reasons. They were also connected with something that had happened in the course of the morning, when Miss Brodie, wanting a supply of drawing books and charcoal to start the new term, sent Monica Douglas to fetch them from the art room, then called her back, and sent Rose Stanley instead. When Rose returned, laden with drawing books and boxes of chalks, she was followed by Teddy Lloyd, similarly laden. He dumped his books and asked Miss Brodie if she had enjoyed her holiday. She gave him her hand, and said she had been exploring Cramond, one should not neglect these little nearby seaports.

'I shouldn't have thought there was much to *explore* at Cramond,' said Mr Lloyd, smiling at her with his golden forelock falling into his eye.

'It has quite a lot of charm,' she said. 'And did you go away at all?'

'I've been painting,' he said in his hoarse voice. 'Family portraits.'

Rose had been stacking the drawing books into their cupboard and now she had finished. As she turned, Miss Brodie put her arm round Rose's shoulder and thanked Mr Lloyd for his help, as if she and Rose were one.

'N'tall,' said Mr Lloyd, meaning 'Not at all', and went away. It was then Jenny whispered, 'Rose has changed in the holidays, hasn't she?'

This was true. Her fair hair was cut shorter and was very shiny. Her cheeks were paler and thinner, her eyes less wide open, set with the lids half-shut as if she were posing for a special photograph.

'Perhaps she has got the Change,' said Sandy. Miss Brodie called it the Menarche but so far when they tried to use this word amongst themselves it made them giggle and feel shy.

Later in the afternoon after school, Jenny said: 'I'd better tell Miss Brodie about the man I met.'

Sandy replied, 'Don't tell Miss Brodie.'

'Why not?' said Jenny.

Sandy tried, but could not think why not, except to feel an

unfinished quality about Miss Brodie and her holiday at Cramond, and her sending Rose to Mr Lloyd. So she said, 'The policewoman said to try to forget what happened. Perhaps Miss Brodie would make you remember it.'

Jenny said, 'That's what I think, too.'

And so they forgot the man by the Water of Leith and remembered the policewoman more and more as the term wore on.

During the last few months of Miss Brodie's teaching she made herself adorable. She did not exhort or bicker and even when hard pressed was irritable only with Mary Macgregor. That spring she monopolized with her class the benches under the elm from which could be seen an endless avenue of dark pink May trees, and heard the trotting of horses in time to the turning wheels of light carts returning home empty by a hidden lane from their early morning rounds. Not far off, like a promise of next year, a group of girls from the Senior school were doing first-form Latin. Once, the Latin mistress was moved by the spring of the year to sing a folk-song to fit the clip-clop of the ponies and carts, and Miss Brodie held up her index finger with delight so that her own girls should listen too.

> Nundinarum adest dies,
> Mulus ille nos vehet.
> Eie, curre, mule, mule,
> I tolutari gradu.

That spring Jenny's mother was expecting a baby, there was no rain worth remembering, the grass, the sun and the birds lost their self-centred winter mood and began to think of others. Miss Brodie's old love story was newly embroidered, under the elm, with curious threads: it appeared that while on leave from the war, her late fiancé had frequently taken her out sailing in a fishing boat and that they had spent some of their merriest times among the rocks and pebbles of a small seaport. 'Sometimes Hugh would sing, he had a rich tenor voice. At other times he fell silent and would set up his easel and paint. He was very talented at both arts, but I think the painter was the real Hugh.'

This was the first time the girls had heard of Hugh's artistic leanings. Sandy puzzled over this and took counsel with Jenny, and it came to them both that Miss Brodie was making her new love story fit the old. Thereafter the two girls listened with double ears, and the rest of the class with single.

Sandy was fascinated by this method of making patterns with facts, and was divided between her admiration for the technique and the pressing need to prove Miss Brodie guilty of misconduct.

'What about those incriminating documents?' said Sergeant Anne Grey in her jolly friendly manner. She really was very thrilling.

Sandy and Jenny completed the love correspondence between Miss Brodie and the singing master at half-term. They were staying in the small town of Crail on the coast of Fife with Jenny's aunt who showed herself suspicious of their notebook: and so they took it off to a neighbouring village along the coast by bus, and sat at the mouth of a cave to finish the work. It had been a delicate question how to present Miss Brodie in both a favourable and an unfavourable light, for now, as their last term with Miss Brodie drew to a close, nothing less than this was demanded.

That intimacy had taken place was to be established. But not on an ordinary bed. That had been a thought suitable only for the enlivening of a sewing period, but Miss Brodie was entitled to something like a status. They placed Miss Brodie on the lofty lion's back of Arthur's Seat, with only the sky for roof and bracken for a bed. The broad parkland rolled away beneath her gaze to the accompanying flash and crash of a thunderstorm. It was here that Gordon Lowther, shy and smiling, small with a long body and short legs, his red-gold hair and moustache, found her.

'Took her,' Jenny had said when they had first talked it over.

'Took her – well, no. She gave herself to him.'

'She gave herself to him,' Jenny said, 'although she would fain have given herself to another.'

The last letter in the series, completed at mid-term, went as follows:

My Own Delightful Gordon,

Your letter has moved me deeply as you may imagine. But alas, I must ever decline to be Mrs Lowther. My reasons are twofold. I am dedicated to my Girls as is Madame Pavlova, and there is another in my life whose mutual love reaches out to me beyond the bounds of Time and Space. He is Teddy Lloyd! Intimacy has never taken place with him. He is married to another. One day in the art room we melted into each other's arms and knew the truth. But I was proud of giving myself to you when you came and took me in the bracken on Arthur's Seat while the storm raged about us. If I am in a certain condition I shall place the infant in the care of a worthy shepherd and his wife, and we can discuss it calmly as platonic acquaintances. I may permit misconduct to occur again from time to time as an outlet because I am in my Prime. We can also have many a breezy day in the fishing boat at sea.

I wish to inform you that your housekeeper fills me with anxiety like John Knox. I fear she is rather narrow, which arises from an ignorance of culture and the Italian scene. Pray ask her not to say 'You know your way up' when I call at your house at Cramond. She should take me up and show me in. Her knees are not stiff. She is only pretending that they are.

I love to hear you singing 'Hey Johnnie Cope'. But were I to receive a proposal of marriage tomorrow from the Lord Lyon King-of-Arms I would decline it.

Allow me, in conclusion, to congratulate you warmly upon your sexual intercourse, as well as your singing.

With fondest joy,
Jean Brodie

When they had finished writing this letter they read the whole correspondence from beginning to end. They were undecided then whether to cast this incriminating document out to sea or to bury it. The act of casting things out to sea from the shore was, as they knew, more difficult than it sounded. But Sandy found a damp hole half-hidden by a stone at the back of the cave and they pressed into it the notebook containing the love correspondence of Miss Jean Brodie, and never saw it again. They walked back to Crail over the very springy turf full of fresh plans and fondest joy.

FOUR

'I have enough gunpowder in this jar to blow up this school,' said Miss Lockhart in even tones.

She stood behind her bench in her white linen coat, with both hands on a glass jar three-quarters full of a dark grey powder. The extreme hush that fell was only what she expected, for she always opened the first science lesson with these words and with the gunpowder before her, and the first science lesson was no lesson at all, but a naming of the most impressive objects in the science room. Every eye was upon the jar. Miss Lockhart lifted it and placed it carefully in a cupboard which was filled with similar jars full of different coloured crystals and powders.

'These are bunsen burners, this is a test-tube, this is a pipette, that's a burette, that is a retort, a crucible . . .'

Thus she established her mysterious priesthood. She was quite the nicest teacher in the Senior School. But they were all the nicest teachers in the school. It was a new life altogether, almost a new school. Here were no gaunt mistresses like Miss Gaunt, those many who had stalked past Miss Brodie in the corridors saying 'good morning' with predestination in their smiles. The teachers here seemed to have no thoughts of anyone's personalities apart from their speciality in life, whether it was mathematics, Latin or science. They treated the new first-formers as if they were not real, but only to be dealt with, like symbols of algebra, and Miss Brodie's pupils found this refreshing at first. Wonderful, too, during the first week was the curriculum of dazzling new subjects, and the rushing to and from room to room to keep to the time-table. Their days were now filled with unfamiliar shapes and sounds which were magically dissociated from ordinary life, the great circles and triangles of geometry, the hieroglyphics of Greek on the page and the curious hisses and spits some of the Greek sounds made from the teacher's lips – 'psst ... psooch ...'

A few weeks later, when meanings appeared from among these sighs and sounds, it was difficult to remember the party-game effect of that first week, and that Greek had ever made hisses and spits or that 'mensarum' had sounded like something out of nonsense verse. The Modern side, up to the third form, was distinguished from the Classical only by modern or ancient languages. The girls on the Modern side were doing German and Spanish, which, when rehearsed between periods, made the astonishing noises of foreign stations got in passing on the wireless. A mademoiselle with black frizzy hair, who wore a striped shirt with real cufflinks, was pronouncing French in a foreign way which never really caught on. The science room smelt unevenly of the Canongate on that day of the winter's walk with Miss Brodie, the bunsen burners, and the sweet autumnal smoke that drifted in from the first burning leaves. Here in the science room – strictly not to be referred to as a laboratory – lessons were called experiments, which gave everyone the feeling that not even Miss Lockhart knew what the result might be, and anything might occur between their going in and coming out and the school might blow up.

Here, during that first week, an experiment was conducted which involved magnesium in a test-tube which was made to tickle a bunsen flame. Eventually, from different parts of the room, great white magnesium flares shot out of the test-tubes and were caught in larger glass vessels which waited for the purpose. Mary Macgregor took fright and ran along a single lane between two benches, met with a white flame, and ran back to meet another brilliant tongue of fire. Hither and thither she ran in panic between the benches until she was caught and induced to calm down, and she was told not to be so stupid by Miss Lockhart, who already had learnt the exasperation of looking at Mary's face, its two eyes, nose and mouth, with nothing more to say about it.

Once, in later years, when Sandy was visited by Rose Stanley, and they fell to speaking of dead Mary Macgregor, Sandy said,

'When any ill befalls me I wish I had been nicer to Mary.'

'How were we to know?' said Rose.

And Miss Brodie, sitting in the window of the Braid Hills Hotel with Sandy, had said: 'I wonder if it was Mary Macgregor betrayed me? Perhaps I should have been kinder to Mary.'

The Brodie set might easily have lost its identity at this time, not only because Miss Brodie had ceased to preside over their days which were now so brisk with the getting of knowledge from unsoulful experts, but also because the headmistress intended them to be dispersed.

She laid a scheme and it failed. It was too ambitious, it aimed at ridding the school of Miss Brodie and breaking up the Brodie set in the one stroke.

She befriended Mary Macgregor, thinking her to be gullible and bribable, and underrating her stupidity. She remembered that Mary had, in common with all Miss Brodie's girls, applied to go on the Classical side, but had been refused. Now Miss Mackay changed her mind and allowed her to take at least Latin. In return she expected to be informed concerning Miss Brodie. But as the only reason that Mary had wanted to learn Latin was to please Miss Brodie, the headmistress got no further. Give the girl tea as she might, Mary simply did not understand what was required of her and thought all the teachers were in league together, Miss Brodie and all.

'You won't be seeing much of Miss Brodie,' said Miss Mackay, 'now that you are in the Senior school.'

'I see,' said Mary, taking the remark as an edict rather than a probing question.

Miss Mackay laid another scheme and the scheme undid her. There was a highly competitive house system in the Senior school, whose four houses were named Holyrood, Melrose, Argyll and Biggar. Miss Mackay saw to it that the Brodie girls were as far as possible placed in different houses. Jenny was put in Holyrood, Sandy with Mary Macgregor in Melrose, Monica and Eunice went into Argyll and Rose Stanley into Biggar. They were therefore obliged to compete with each other in every walk of life within the school and on the wind-swept hockey fields which lay like the graves of the martyrs exposed to the weather in an outer suburb. It was the team spirit, they were told, that counted now, every house must go all out for the Shield and turn up on Saturday mornings to yell encouragement to the house. Inter-house friendships must not suffer, of course, but the team spirit . . .

This phrase was enough for the Brodie set who, after two years at Miss Brodie's, had been well directed as to its meaning.

'Phrases like "the team spirit" are always employed to cut across individualism, love and personal loyalties,' she had said. 'Ideas like "the team spirit"', she said, 'ought not to be enjoined on the female sex, especially if they are of that dedicated nature whose virtues from time immemorial have been utterly opposed to the concept. Florence Nightingale knew nothing of the team spirit, her mission was to save life regardless of the team to which it belonged. Cleopatra knew nothing of the team spirit if you read your Shakespeare. Take Helen of Troy. And the Queen of England, it is true she attends international sport, but she has to, it is all empty show, she is concerned only with the King's health and antiques. Where would the team spirit have got Sybil Thorndike? *She* is the great actress and the rest of the cast have got the team spirit. Pavlova . . .'

Perhaps Miss Brodie had foreseen this moment of the future when her team of six should be exposed to the appeal of four different competing spirits, Argyll, Melrose, Biggar and Holyrood. It was impossible to know how much Miss Brodie planned by deliberation, or how much she worked by instinct alone. However, in this, the first test of her strength, she had the victory. Not one of the senior house-prefects personified an argument to touch Sybil Thorndike and Cleopatra. The Brodie set would as soon have entered the Girl Guides as the team spirit. Not only they, but at least ten other girls who had passed through Brodie hands kept away from the playing grounds except under compulsion. No one, save Eunice Gardiner, got near to being put in any team to try her spirit upon. Everyone agreed that Eunice was so good on the field, she could not help it.

On most Saturday afternoons Miss Brodie entertained her old set to tea and listened to their new experiences. Herself, she told them, she did not think much of her new pupils' potentialities, and she described some of her new little girls and made the old ones laugh, which bound her set together more than ever and made them feel chosen. Sooner or later she inquired what they were doing in the art class, for now the girls were taught by golden-locked, one-armed Teddy Lloyd.

There was always a great deal to tell about the art lesson. Their first day, Mr Lloyd found difficulty in keeping order. After so many unfamiliar packed hours and periods of different exact subjects, the girls immediately felt the relaxing nature of the art room, and brimmed over with relaxation. Mr Lloyd shouted at them in his hoarse voice to shut up. This was most bracing.

He was attempting to explain the nature and appearance of an ellipse by holding up a saucer in his one right hand, high above his head, then lower. But his romantic air and his hoarse 'Shut up' had produced a reaction of giggles varying in tone and pitch.

'If you girls don't shut up I'll smash this saucer to the floor,' he said.

They tried but failed to shut up.

He smashed the saucer to the floor.

Amid the dead silence which followed he picked on Rose Stanley and indicating the fragments of saucer on the floor, he said, 'You with the profile – pick this up.'

He turned away and went and did something else at the other end of the long room for the rest of the period, while the girls looked anew at Rose Stanley's profile, marvelled at Mr Lloyd's style, and settled down to drawing a bottle set up in front of a curtain. Jenny remarked to Sandy that Miss Brodie really had good taste.

'He has an artistic temperament, of course,' said Miss Brodie when she was told about the saucer. And when she heard that he had called Rose 'you with the profile', she looked at Rose in a special way, while Sandy looked at Miss Brodie.

The interest of Sandy and Jenny in Miss Brodie's lovers had entered a new phase since they had buried their last composition and moved up to the Senior school. They no longer saw everything in a sexual context, it was now rather a question of plumbing the deep heart's core. The world of pure sex seemed years away. Jenny had turned twelve. Her mother had recently given birth to a baby boy, and the event had not moved them even to speculate upon its origin.

'There's not much time for sex research in the Senior school,' Sandy said.

'I feel I'm past it,' said Jenny. This was strangely true, and she did not again experience her early sense of erotic wonder in life until suddenly one day when she was nearly forty, an actress of moderate reputation married to a theatrical manager. It happened she was standing with a man whom she did not know very well outside a famous building in Rome, waiting for the rain to stop. She was surprised by a reawakening of that same buoyant and airy discovery of sex, a total sensation which it was impossible to say was physical or mental, only that it contained the lost and guileless delight of her eleventh year. She supposed herself to have fallen in love with the man, who might, she thought, have been moved towards her in his own way out of a world of his own, the associations of which were largely unknown to her. There was nothing whatever to be done about it, for Jenny had been contentedly married for sixteen years past; but the concise happening filled her with astonishment whenever it came to mind in later days, and with a sense of the hidden possibilities in all things.

'Mr Lowther's housekeeper,' said Miss Brodie one Saturday afternoon, 'has left him. It is most ungrateful, that house at Cramond is easily run. I never cared for her as you know. I think she resented my position as Mr Lowther's friend and confidante, and seemed dissatisfied by my visits. Mr Lowther is composing some music for song at the moment. He ought to be encouraged.'

The next Saturday she told the girls that the sewing sisters, Miss Ellen and Miss Alison Kerr, had taken on the temporary task of housekeepers to Mr Lowther, since they lived near Cramond.

'I think those sisters are inquisitive,' Miss Brodie remarked. 'They are too much in with Miss Gaunt and the Church of Scotland.'

On Saturday afternoons an hour was spent on her Greek lessons, for she had insisted that Jenny and Sandy should teach her Greek at the same time as they learned it. 'There is an old tradition for this practice,' said Miss Brodie. 'Many families in the olden days could afford to send but one child to school, whereupon that one scholar of the family imparted to the others in the evening what he had learned in the morning. I have long wanted to know the Greek language, and this scheme will also serve to impress your knowledge on your own minds. John Stuart Mill used to rise at dawn to learn Greek at the age of five, and what John Stuart Mill could do as an infant at dawn, I too can do on a Saturday afternoon in my prime.'

She progressed in Greek, although she was somewhat muddled about the accents, being differently informed by Jenny and Sandy who took turns to impart to her their weekly intake of the language. But she was determined to enter and share the new life of her special girls, and what she did not regard as humane of their new concerns, or what was not within the scope of her influence, she scorned.

She said: 'It is witty to say that a straight line is the shortest distance between two points, or that a circle is a plane figure bounded by one line, every point of which is equidistant from a fixed centre. It is plain witty. Everyone knows what a straight line and a circle are.'

When, after the examinations at the end of the first term, she looked at the papers they had been set, she read some of the more vulnerable of the questions aloud with the greatest contempt: 'A window cleaner carries a uniform 60-lb. ladder 15 ft long, at one end of which a bucket of water weighing 40 lb. is hung. At what point must he support the ladder to carry it horizontally? Where is the c.g. of his load?' Miss Brodie looked at the paper, after reading out this question as if to indicate that she could not believe her eyes. Many a time she gave the girls to understand that the solution to such problems would be quite useless to Sybil Thorndike, Anna Pavlova and the late Helen of Troy.

But the Brodie set were on the whole still dazzled by their new subjects. It was never the same in later years when the languages of physics and chemistry, algebra and geometry had lost their elemental strangeness and formed each an individual department of life with its own accustomed boredom, and become hard work. Even Monica Douglas, who later developed such a good brain for mathematics, was plainly never so thrilled with herself as when she first subtracted x from y and the result from a; she never afterwards looked so happy.

Rose Stanley sliced a worm down the middle with the greatest absorption during her first term's biology, although in two terms' time she shuddered at the thought and had dropped the subject. Eunice Gardiner discovered the Industrial Revolution, its rights and wrongs, to such an extent that the history teacher, a vegetarian communist, had high hopes of her which were dashed within a few months when Eunice reverted to reading novels based on the life of Mary Queen of Scots. Sandy, whose handwriting was bad, spent hours forming the Greek characters in neat rows in her notebooks while Jenny took the same pride in drawing scientific apparatus for her chemistry notes. Even stupid Mary Macgregor amazed herself by understanding Caesar's Gallic Wars which as yet made no demands on her defective imagination and the words of which were easier to her than English to spell and pronounce, until suddenly one day it appeared, from an essay she had been obliged to write, that she believed the document to date from the time of Samuel Pepys; and then Mary was established in the wrong again, being tortured with probing questions, and generally led on to confess to the mirth-shaken world her notion that Latin and shorthand were one.

Miss Brodie had a hard fight of it during those first few months when the Senior school had captivated her set, displaying as did the set that capacity for enthusiasm which she herself had implanted. But, having won the battle over the team spirit, she did not despair. It was evident even then that her main concern was lest the girls should become personally attached to any one of the senior teachers, but she carefully refrained from direct attack because the teachers themselves seemed so perfectly indifferent to her brood.

By the summer term, the girls' favourite hours were those spent unbrainfully in the gymnasium, swinging about on parallel bars, hanging upside down on wall bars or climbing ropes up to the ceiling, all competing with agile Eunice to heave themselves up by hands, knees, and feet like monkeys climbing a tropical creeper, while the gym teacher, a thin grey-haired little wire, showed them what to do and shouted each order in a broad Scots accent interspersed by her short cough, on account of which she was later sent to a sanatorium in Switzerland.

By the summer term, to stave off the onslaughts of boredom, and to reconcile the necessities of the working day with their love for Miss Brodie, Sandy and Jenny had begun to apply their new-found knowledge to Miss Brodie in a merry fashion. 'If Miss Brodie was weighed in air and then in water . . .' And, when Mr Lowther seemed not quite himself at the singing lesson, they would remind each other that an immersed Jean Brodie displaces its own weight of Gordon Lowther.

Presently, in the late spring of nineteen-thirty-three, Miss Brodie's Greek lessons on a Saturday afternoon came to an end, because of the needs of Mr Lowther who, in his house at Cramond which the girls had not yet seen, was being catered for quite willingly by those sewing mistresses, Miss Ellen and Miss Alison Kerr. Living on the coast nearby, it was simple for them to go over turn by turn and see to Mr Lowther after school hours, and prepare his supper and lay out provision for his breakfast; it was not only simple, it was enjoyable to be doing good, and it was also profitable in a genteel way. On

Saturdays either Miss Ellen or Miss Alison would count his laundry and keep house for him. On some Saturday mornings both were busy for him; Miss Ellen supervised the woman who came to clean while Miss Alison did the week's shopping. They never had been so perky or useful in their lives before, and especially not since the eldest sister had died, who had always told them what to do with their spare time as it cropped up, so that Miss Alison could never get used to being called Miss Kerr and Miss Ellen could never find it in her to go and get a book from the library, wanting the order from the late Miss Kerr.

But the minister's sister, gaunt Miss Gaunt, was secretly taking over the dead sister's office. As it became known later, Miss Gaunt approved of their arrangement with Gordon Lowther and encouraged them to make it a permanent one for their own good and also for private reasons connected with Miss Brodie.

Up to now, Miss Brodie's visits to Mr. Lowther had taken place on Sundays. She always went to church on Sunday mornings, she had a rota of different denominations and sects which included the Free Churches of Scotland, the Established Church of Scotland, the Methodist and the Episcopalian churches and any other church outside the Roman Catholic pale which she might discover. Her disapproval of the Church of Rome was based on her assertions that it was a church of superstition, and that only people who did not want to think for themselves were Roman Catholics. In some ways, her attitude was a strange one, because she was by temperament suited only to the Roman Catholic Church; possibly it could have embraced, even while it disciplined, her soaring and diving spirit, it might even have normalized her. But perhaps this was the reason that she shunned it, lover of Italy though she was, bringing to her support a rigid Edinburgh-born side of herself when the Catholic Church was in question, although this side was not otherwise greatly in evidence. So she went round the various non-Roman churches instead, hardly ever missing a Sunday morning. She was not in any doubt, she let everyone know she was in no doubt, that God was on her side whatever her course, and so she experienced no difficulty or sense of hypocrisy in worship while at the same time she went to bed with the singing master. Just as an excessive sense of guilt can drive people to excessive action, so was Miss Brodie driven to it by an excessive lack of guilt.

The side-effects of this condition were exhilarating to her special girls in that they in some way partook of the general absolution she had assumed to herself, and it was only in retrospect that they could see Miss Brodie's affair with Mr Lowther for what it was, that is to say, in a factual light. All the time they were under her influence she and her actions were outside the context of right and wrong. It was twenty-five years before Sandy had so far recovered from a creeping vision of disorder that she could look back and recognize that Miss Brodie's defective sense of self-criticism had not been without its beneficent and enlarging effects; by which time Sandy had already betrayed Miss Brodie and Miss Brodie was laid in her grave.

It was after morning church on Sundays that Miss Brodie would go to Cramond, there to lunch and spend the afternoon with Mr Lowther. She spent Sunday evenings with him also, and more often than not the night, in a spirit of definite duty, if not exactly martyrdom, since her heart was with the renounced teacher of art.

Mr Lowther, with his long body and short legs, was a shy fellow who smiled upon nearly everyone from beneath his red-gold moustache, and who won his own gentle way with nearly everybody, and who said little and sang much.

When it became certain that the Kerr sisters had taken over permanently the housekeeping for this bashful, smiling bachelor, Miss Brodie fancied he was getting thin. She announced this discovery just at a time when Jenny and Sandy had noticed a slimmer appearance in Miss Brodie and had begun to wonder, since they were nearly thirteen and their eyes were more focused on such points, if she might be physically beautiful or desirable to men. They saw her in a new way, and decided she had a certain deep romantic beauty, and that she had lost weight through her sad passion for Mr Lloyd, and this noble undertaking of Mr Lowther in his place, and that it suited her.

Now Miss Brodie was saying: 'Mr Lowther is looking thin these days. I have no faith in those Kerr sisters, they are skimping him, they have got skimpy minds. The supplies of food they leave behind on Saturdays are barely sufficient to see him through Sunday, let alone the remainder of the week. If only Mr Lowther could be persuaded to move from that big house and take a flat in Edinburgh, he would be so much easier to look after. He needs looking after. But he will not be persuaded. It is impossible to persuade a man who does not disagree, but smiles.'

She decided to supervise the Kerr sisters on their Saturdays at Cramond when they prepared for Mr Lowther's domestic week ahead. 'They get well paid for it,' said Miss Brodie. 'I shall go over and see that they order the right stuff, and sufficient.' It might have seemed an audacious proposition, but the girls did not think of it this way. They heartily urged Miss Brodie to descend upon the Kerrs and to interfere, partly in anticipation of some eventful consequence, and partly because Mr Lowther would somehow smile away any fuss; and the Kerr sisters were fairly craven; and, above all, Miss Brodie was easily the equal of both sisters together, she was the square on the hypotenuse of a right-angled triangle and they were only the squares on the other two sides.

The Kerr sisters took Miss Brodie's intrusion quite meekly, and that they were so unquestioning about any authority which imposed itself upon them was the very reason why they also did not hesitate later on to answer the subsequent questions of Miss Gaunt. Meantime Miss Brodie set about feeding Mr Lowther up, and, since this meant her passing Saturday afternoons at Cramond, the Brodie set was invited to go, two by two, one pair every week, to visit her in Mr Lowther's residence, where he smiled and patted their hair or pulled pretty Jenny's ringlets, looking meanwhile for reproof or approval, or some such thing, at brown-eyed Jean Brodie. She gave them tea while he smiled; and he frequently laid down his cup and saucer, went and sat at the piano and burst into song. He sang:

'March, march, Ettrick and Teviotdale,
Why the de'il dinna ye march *forward* in order?
March, march, Eskdale and Liddesdale,
All the Blue Bonnets are bound for the Border.'

At the end of the song he would smile his overcome and bashful smile and take his teacup again, looking up under his ginger eyebrows at Jean Brodie to see what she felt about him at the current moment. She was Jean to him, a fact that none of the Brodie set thought proper to mention to anyone.

She reported to Sandy and Jenny: 'I made short work of those Kerr sisters. They were starving him. Now it is I who see to the provisions. I am a descendant, do not forget, of Willie Brodie, a man of substance, a cabinet maker and designer of gibbets, a member of the Town Council of Edinburgh and a keeper of two mistresses who bore him five children between them. Blood tells. He played much dice and fighting cocks. Eventually he was a wanted man for having robbed the Excise Office – not that he needed the money, he was a night burglar only for the sake of the danger in it. Of course, he was arrested abroad and was brought back to the Tolbooth prison, but that was mere chance. He died cheerfully on a gibbet of his own devising in seventeen-eighty-eight. However all this may be, it is the stuff I am made of, and I have brooked and shall brook no nonsense from Miss Ellen and Miss Alison Kerr.'

Mr Lowther sang:

> 'O mother, mother, make my bed,
> O make it soft and narrow,
> For my true love died for me today.
> I'll die for him tomorrow.'

Then he looked at Miss Brodie. She was, however, looking at a chipped rim of a teacup. 'Mary Macgregor must have chipped it,' she said. 'Mary was here last Sunday with Eunice and they washed up together. Mary must have chipped it.'

Outside on the summer lawn the daisies sparkled. The lawn spread wide and long, one could barely see the little wood at the end of it and even the wood belonged to Mr Lowther, and the fields beyond. Shy, musical and gentle as he was, Mr Lowther was a man of substance.

Now Sandy considered Miss Brodie not only to see if she was desirable, but also to find out if there was any element of surrender about her, since this was the most difficult part of the affair to realize. She had been a dominant presence rather than a physical woman like Norma Shearer or Elizabeth Bergner. Miss Brodie was now forty-three and this year when she looked so much thinner than when she had stood in the classroom or sat under the elm, her shape was pleasanter, but it was still fairly large compared with Mr Lowther's. He was slight and he was shorter than Miss Brodie. He looked at her with love and she looked at him severely and possessively.

By the end of the summer term, when the Brodie set were all turned, or nearly turned, thirteen, Miss Brodie questioned them in their visiting pairs each week about their art lesson. The girls always took a close interest in Teddy Lloyd's art classes and in all he did, making much of details, so as to provide happy conversation with Miss Brodie when their turn came to visit her at Gordon Lowther's house at Cramond.

It was a large gabled house with a folly-turret. There were so many twists and turns in the wooded path leading up from the road, and the front lawn was so narrow, that the house could never be seen from the little distance that its size demanded and it was necessary to crane one's neck upward to see the turret at all. The back of the house was quite plain. The rooms were large and gloomy with Venetian blinds. The banisters began with a pair of carved lions' heads and carried up and up, round and round, as far as the eye could reach. All the furniture was large and carved, dotted with ornaments of silver and rose-coloured glass. The library on the ground floor where Miss Brodie entertained them held a number of glass bookcases so dim in their interiors that it was impossible to see the titles of the books without peering close. A grand piano was placed across one corner of the room, and on it, in summer, stood a bowl of roses.

This was a great house to explore and on days when Miss Brodie was curiously occupied in the kitchen with some enormous preparation for the next day's eating – in those months when her obsession with Mr Lowther's food had just begun – the girls were free to roam up the big stairs, hand-in-hand with awe, and to open the doors and look into the dust-sheeted bedrooms and especially into two rooms that people had forgotten to furnish properly, one of which had nothing in it but a large desk, not even a carpet, the other of which was empty except for an electric light bulb and a large blue jug. These rooms were icy cold, whatever the time of year. On their descending the stairs after these expeditions, Mr Lowther would often be standing waiting for them, shyly smiling in the hall with his hands clasped together as if he hoped that everything was to their satisfaction. He took roses from the bowl and presented one each to the girls before they went home.

Mr Lowther never seemed quite at home in his home, although he had been born there. He always looked at Miss Brodie for approval before he touched anything or opened a cupboard as if, really, he was not allowed to touch without permission. The girls decided that perhaps his mother, now four years dead, had kept him under all his life, and he was consequently unable to see himself as master of the house.

He sat silently and gratefully watching Miss Brodie entertain the two girls whose turn it was to be there, when she had already started on her project of fattening him up which was to grow to such huge proportions that her food-supplying mania was the talk of Miss Ellen and Miss Alison Kerr, and so of the Junior school. One day, when Sandy and Jenny were on the visiting rota, she gave Mr Lowther, for tea alone, an admirable lobster salad, some sandwiches of liver paste, cake and tea, followed by a bowl of porridge and cream. These were served to him on a tray for himself alone, you could see he was on a special diet. Sandy was anxious to see if Mr Lowther would manage the porridge as well as everything else. But he worked his way through everything with impassive obedience while she questioned the girls: 'What are you doing in the art class just now?'

'We're at work on the poster competition.'

'Mr Lloyd – is he well?'

'Oh yes, he's great fun. He showed us his studio two weeks ago.'

'Which studio, where? At his house?' – although Miss Brodie knew perfectly well.

'Yes, it's a great long attic, it –'

'Did you meet his wife, what was she like? What did she say, did she give you tea? What are the children like, what did you do when you got there? . . .'

She did not attempt to conceal from her munching host her keen interest in the art master. Mr Lowther's eyes looked mournful as he ate on. Sandy and Jenny knew that similar questions had been pressed upon Mary Macgregor and Eunice Gardiner the previous week, and upon Rose Stanley and Monica Douglas the week before. But Miss Brodie could not hear enough versions of the same story if it involved Teddy Lloyd, and now that the girls had been to his house – a large and shabby, a warm and unconventional establishment in the north of

Edinburgh – Miss Brodie was in a state of high excitement by very contact with these girls who had lately breathed Lloyd air.

'How many children?' said Miss Brodie, her teapot poised.

'Five, I think,' said Sandy.

'Six, I think,' said Jenny, 'counting the baby.'

'There are lots of babies,' said Sandy.

'Roman Catholics, of course,' said Miss Brodie, addressing this to Mr Lowther.

'But the littlest baby,' said Jenny, 'you've forgotten to count the wee baby. That makes six.'

Miss Brodie poured tea and cast a glance at Gordon Lowther's plate.

'Gordon,' she said, 'a cake.'

He shook his head and said softly, as if soothing her, 'Oh, no, no.'

'Yes, Gordon. It is full of goodness.' And she made him eat a Chester cake, and spoke to him in a slightly more Edinburgh way than usual, so as to make up to him by both means for the love she was giving to Teddy Lloyd instead of to him.

'You must be fattened up, Gordon,' she said. 'You must be two stone the better before I go on my holidays.'

He smiled as best he could at everyone in turn, with his drooped head and slowly moving jaws. Meanwhile Miss Brodie said:

'And Mrs Lloyd – is she a woman, would you say, in her prime?'

'Perhaps not yet,' said Sandy.

'Well, Mrs Lloyd may be past it,' Jenny said. 'It's difficult to say with her hair being long on her shoulders. It makes her look young although she may not be.'

'She looks really like as if she won't have any prime,' Sandy said.

'The word "like" is redundant in that sentence. What is Mrs Lloyd's Christian name?'

'Deirdre,' said Jenny, and Miss Brodie considered the name as if it were new to her although she had heard it last week from Mary and Eunice, and the week before that from Rose and Monica and so had Mr Lowther. Outside, light rain began to fall on Mr Lowther's leaves.

'Celtic,' said Miss Brodie.

Sandy loitered at the kitchen door waiting for Miss Brodie to come for a walk by the sea. Miss Brodie was doing something to an enormous ham prior to putting it into a huge pot. Miss Brodie's new ventures into cookery in no way diminished her previous grandeur, for everything she prepared for Gordon Lowther seemed to be large, whether it was family-sized puddings to last him out the week, or joints of beef or lamb, or great angry-eyed whole salmon.

'I must get this on for Mr Lowther's supper,' she said to Sandy, 'and see that he gets his supper before I go home tonight.'

She always so far kept up the idea that she went home on these week-end nights and left Mr Lowther alone in the big house. So far the girls had found no evidence to the contrary, nor were they ever to do so; a little later Miss Ellen Kerr was brought to the headmistress by Miss Gaunt to testify to having found Miss Brodie's nightdress under a pillow of the double bed on which Mr Lowther took his sleep. She had found it while changing the linen; it was the pillow on the far side of the bed, nearest the wall, under which the nightdress had been discovered folded neatly.

'How do you know the nightdress was Miss Brodie's?' demanded Miss Mackay, the sharp-minded woman, who smelt her prey very near and yet saw it very far. She stood with a hand on the back of her chair, bending forward full of ears.

'One must draw one's own conclusions,' said Miss Gaunt.

'I am addressing Miss Ellen.'

'Yes, one must draw one's own conclusions,' said Miss Ellen, with her tight-drawn red-veined cheeks looking shiny and flustered. 'It was crêpe de Chine.'

'It is non-proven,' said Miss Mackay, sitting down to her desk. 'Come back to me,' she said, 'if you have proof positive. What did you do with the garment? Did you confront Miss Brodie with it?'

'Oh, no, Miss Mackay,' said Miss Ellen.

'You should have confronted her with it. You should have said, "Miss Brodie, come here a minute, can you explain this?" That's what you should have said. Is the nightdress still there?'

'Oh, no, it's gone.'

'She's that brazen,' said Miss Gaunt.

All this was conveyed to Sandy by the headmistress herself at that subsequent time when Sandy looked at her distastefully through her little eyes and, evading the quite crude question which the coarse-faced woman asked her, was moved by various other considerations to betray Miss Brodie.

'But I must organize the dear fellow's food before I go home tonight,' Miss Brodie said in the summer of nineteen-thirty-three while Sandy leaned against the kitchen door with her legs longing to be running along the sea shore. Jenny came and joined her, and together they waited upon Miss Brodie, and saw on the vast old kitchen table the piled-up provisions of the morning's shopping. Outside on the dining-room table stood large bowls of fruit with boxes of dates piled on top of them, as if this were Christmas and the kitchen that of a holiday hotel.

'Won't all this give Mr Lowther a stoppage?' Sandy said to Jenny.

'Not if he eats his greens,' said Jenny.

While they waited for Miss Brodie to dress the great ham like the heroine she was, there came the sound of Mr Lowther at the piano in the library singing rather slowly and mournfully:

> 'All people that on earth do dwell,
> Sing to the Lord with cheerful voice.
> Him serve with mirth, his praise forth tell,
> Come ye before him and rejoice.'

Mr Lowther was the choir-master and an Elder of the church, and had not yet been quietly advised to withdraw from these offices by Mr Gaunt the minister, brother of Miss Gaunt, following the finding of the nightdress under the pillow next to his.

Presently, as she put the ham on a low gas and settled the lid on the pot Miss Brodie joined in the psalm richly, contralto-wise, giving the notes more body:

> 'O enter then his gates with praise,
> Approach with joy His courts unto.'

The rain had stopped and was only now hanging damply within the salt air. All along the sea front Miss Brodie questioned the girls, against the rhythm of the waves, about the appointments of Teddy Lloyd's house, the kind of tea they got, how vast and light was the studio, and what was said.

'He looked very romantic in his own studio,' Sandy said.

'How was that?'

'I think it was his having only one arm,' said Jenny.

'But he always has only one arm.'

'He did more than usual with it,' said Sandy.

'He was waving it about,' Jenny said. 'There was a lovely view from the studio window. He's proud of it.'

'The studio is in the attic, I presume?'

'Yes, all along the top of the house. There is a new portrait he has done of his family, it's a little bit amusing, it starts with himself, very tall, then his wife. Then all the little children graded downwards to the baby on the floor, it makes a diagonal line across the canvas.'

'What makes it amusing?' said Miss Brodie.

'They are all facing square and they all look serious,' Sandy said. 'You are supposed to laugh at it.'

Miss Brodie laughed a little at this. There was a wonderful sunset across the distant sky, reflected in the sea, streaked with blood and puffed with avenging purple and gold as if the end of the world had come without intruding on every-day life.

'There's another portrait,' Jenny said, 'not finished yet, of Rose.'

'He has been painting Rose?'

'Yes.'

'Rose has been sitting for him?'

'Yes, for about a month.'

Miss Brodie was very excited. 'Rose didn't mention this,' she said.

Sandy halted. 'Oh, I forgot. It was supposed to be a surprise. You aren't supposed to know.'

'What, the portrait, I am to see it?'

Sandy looked confused, for she was not sure how Rose had meant her portrait to be a surprise to Miss Brodie.

Jenny said, 'Oh, Miss Brodie, it is the fact that she's sitting for Mr Lloyd that she wanted to keep for a surprise.' Sandy realized, then, that this was right.

'Ah' said Miss Brodie, well pleased. 'That is thoughtful of Rose.'

Sandy was jealous, because Rose was not supposed to be thoughtful.

'What is she wearing for her portrait?' said Miss Brodie.

'Her gym tunic,' Sandy said.

'Sitting sideways,' Jenny said.

'In profile,' said Miss Brodie.

Miss Brodie stopped a man to buy a lobster for Mr Lowther. When this was done she said:

'Rose is bound to be painted many times. She may well sit for Mr Lloyd on future occasions, she is one of the crème de la crème.'

It was said in an inquiring tone. The girls understood she was trying quite hard to piece together a whole picture from their random remarks.

Jenny accordingly let fall, 'Oh, yes, Mr Lloyd wants to paint Rose in red velvet.'

And Sandy added, 'Mrs Lloyd has a bit of red velvet to put around her, they were trying it round her.'

'Are you to return?' said Miss Brodie.

'Yes, all of us,' Sandy said. 'Mr Lloyd thinks we're a jolly nice set.'

'Have you not thought it remarkable,' said Miss Brodie, 'that it is you six girls that Mr Lloyd has chosen to invite to his studio?'

'Well, we're a set,' said Jenny.

'Has he invited any other girls from the school?' – but Miss Brodie knew the answer.

'Oh, no, only us.'

'It is because you are mine,' said Miss Brodie. 'I mean of my stamp and cut, and I am in my prime.'

Sandy and Jenny had not given much thought to the fact of the art master's inviting them as a group. Indeed, there was something special in his acceptance of the Brodie set. There was a mystery here to be worked out, and it was clear that when he thought of them he thought of Miss Brodie.

'He always asks about you,' Sandy said to Miss Brodie, 'as soon as he sees us.'

'Yes, Rose did tell me that,' said Miss Brodie.

Suddenly, like migrating birds, Sandy and Jenny were of one mind for a run and without warning they ran along the pebbly beach into the air which was full of sunset, returning to Miss Brodie to hear of her forthcoming summer holiday when she was going to leave the fattened-up Mr Lowther, she was afraid, to fend for himself with the aid of the Misses Kerr, and was going abroad, not to Italy this year but to Germany, where Hitler was become Chancellor, a prophet-figure like Thomas Carlyle, and more reliable than Mussolini; the German brownshirts, she said, were exactly the same as the Italian black, only more reliable.

Jenny and Sandy were going to a farm for the summer holidays, where in fact the name of Miss Brodie would not very much be on their lips or in their minds after the first two weeks, and instead they would make hay and follow the sheep about. It was always difficult to realize during term times that the world of Miss Brodie might be half forgotten, as were the worlds of the school houses, Holyrood, Melrose, Argyll and Biggar.

'I wonder if Mr Lowther would care for sweetbreads done with rice,' Miss Brodie said.

FIVE

'Why, it's like Miss Brodie!' said Sandy. 'It's terribly like Miss Brodie.' Then, perceiving that what she had said had accumulated a meaning between its passing her lips and reaching the ears of Mr and Mrs Lloyd, she said, 'Though of course it's Rose, it's more like Rose, it's terribly like Rose.'

Teddy Lloyd shifted the new portrait so that it stood in a different light. It still looked like Miss Brodie.

Deirdre Lloyd said, 'I haven't met Miss Brodie, I think. Is she fair?'

'No,' said Teddy Lloyd in his hoarse way, 'she's dark.'

Sandy saw that the head on the portrait was fair, it was Rose's portrait all right. Rose was seated in profile by a window in her gym dress, her hands palm-downwards, one on each knee. Where was the resemblance to Miss Brodie? It was the profile perhaps; it was the forehead, perhaps; it was the type of stare from Rose's blue eyes, perhaps, which was like the dominating stare from Miss Brodie's brown. The portrait was very like Miss Brodie.

'It's Rose, all right,' Sandy said, and Deirdre Lloyd looked at her.

'Do you like it?' said Teddy Lloyd.

'Yes, it's lovely.'

'Well, that's all that matters.'

Sandy continued looking at it through her very small eyes, and while she was doing so Teddy Lloyd drew the piece of sheeting over the portrait with a casual flip of his only arm.

Deirdre Lloyd had been the first woman to dress up as a peasant whom Sandy had ever met, and peasant women were to be fashionable for the next thirty years or more. She wore a fairly long full-gathered dark skirt, a bright green blouse with the sleeves rolled up, a necklace of large painted wooden beads, and gipsy-looking ear-rings. Round her waist was a bright red wide belt. She wore dark brown stockings and sandals of dark green suede. In this, and various other costumes of similar kind, Deirdre was depicted on canvas in different parts of the studio. She had an attractive near-laughing voice. She said:

'We've got a new one of Rose. Teddy, show Sandy the new one of Rose.'

'It isn't quite at a stage for looking at.'

'Well, what about Red Velvet? Show Sandy that – Teddy did a splendid portrait of Rose last summer, we swathed her in red velvet, and we've called it Red Velvet.'

Teddy Lloyd had brought out a canvas from behind a few others. He stood it in the light on an easel. Sandy looked at it with her tiny eyes which it was astonishing that anyone could trust.

The portrait was like Miss Brodie. Sandy said, 'I like the colours.'

'Does it resemble Miss Brodie?' said Deirdre Lloyd with her near-laughter.

'Miss Brodie is a woman in her prime,' said Sandy, 'but there is a resemblance now you mention it.'

Deirdre Lloyd said: 'Rose was only fourteen at the time; it makes her look very mature, but indeed she is very mature.'

The swathing of crimson velvet was so arranged that it did two things at once, it made Rose look one-armed like the artist himself, and it showed the curves of her breast to be more developed than they were, even now, when Rose was fifteen. Also, the picture was like Miss Brodie, and this was the main thing about it and the main mystery. Rose had a large-boned pale face. Miss Brodie's bones were small, although her eyes, nose and mouth were large. It was difficult to see how Teddy Lloyd had imposed the dark and Roman face of Miss Brodie on that of pale Rose, but he had done so.

Sandy looked again at the other recent portraits in the studio, Teddy Lloyd's wife, his children, some unknown sitters. They were none of them like Miss Brodie.

Then she saw a drawing lying on top of a pile on the work-table. It was Miss Brodie leaning against a lamp post in the Lawnmarket with a working-woman's shawl around her; on looking closer it proved to be Monica Douglas with the high cheekbones and long nose. Sandy said:

'I didn't know Monica sat for you.'

'I've done one or two preliminary sketches. Don't you think that setting's rather good for Monica? Here's one of Eunice in her harlequin outfit, I thought she looked rather well in it.'

Sandy was vexed. These girls, Monica and Eunice, had not said anything to the others about their being painted by the art master. But now they were all fifteen there was a lot they did not tell each other. She looked more closely at this picture of Eunice.

Eunice had worn the harlequin dress for a school performance. Small and neat and sharp-featured as she was, in the portrait she looked like Miss Brodie. In amongst her various bewilderments Sandy was fascinated by the economy of Teddy Lloyd's method, as she had been four years earlier by Miss Brodie's variations on her love story, when she had attached to her first, war-time lover the attributes of the art master and the singing master who had then newly entered her orbit. Teddy Lloyd's method of presentation was similar, it was economical, and it always seemed afterwards to Sandy that where there was a choice of various courses, the most economical was the best, and that the course to be taken was the most expedient and most suitable at the time for all the objects in hand. She acted on this principle when the time came for her to betray Miss Brodie.

Jenny had done badly in her last term's examinations and was mostly, these days, at home working up her subjects. Sandy had the definite feeling that the Brodie set, not to mention Miss Brodie herself, was getting out of hand. She thought it perhaps a good thing that the set might split up.

From somewhere below one of the Lloyd children started to yell, and then another, and then a chorus. Deirdre Lloyd disappeared with a swing of her peasant skirt to see to all her children. The Lloyds were Catholics and so were made to have a lot of children by force.

'One day,' said Teddy Lloyd as he stacked up his sketches before taking Sandy down to tea, 'I would like to do all you Brodie girls, one by one and then all together.' He tossed his head to move back the golden lock of his hair from his eye. 'It would be nice to do you all together,' he said, 'and see what sort of a group portrait I could make of you.'

Sandy thought this might be an attempt to keep the Brodie set together at the expense of the newly glimpsed individuality of its members. She turned on him in her new manner of sudden irritability and said, 'We'd look like one big Miss Brodie, I suppose.'

He laughed in a delighted way and looked at her more closely, as if for the first time. She looked back just as closely through her little eyes, with the near-blackmailing insolence of her knowledge. Where-upon he kissed her long and wetly. He said in his hoarse voice, 'That'll teach you to look at an artist like that.'

She started to run to the door, wiping her mouth dry with the back of her hand, but he caught her with his one arm and said: 'There's no need to run away. You're just about the ugliest little thing I've ever seen in my life.' He walked out and left her standing in the studio, and there was nothing for her to do but to follow him downstairs. Deirdre Lloyd's voice called from the sitting-room. 'In here, Sandy.'

She spent most of the tea time trying to sort out her preliminary feelings in the matter, which was difficult because of the children who were present and making demands on the guest. The eldest boy, who was eight, turned on the wireless and began to sing in mincing English tones, 'Oh play to me, Gipsy' to the accompaniment of Henry Hall's band. The other three children were making various kinds of din. Above this noise Deirdre Lloyd requested Sandy to call her Deirdre rather than Mrs Lloyd. And so Sandy did not have much opportunity to discover how she was feeling inside herself about Teddy Lloyd's kiss and his words, and to decide whether she was insulted or not. He now said, brazenly, 'And you can call me Teddy outside of school.' Amongst themselves, in any case, the girls called him Teddy the Paint. Sandy looked from one to the other of the Lloyds.

'I've heard such a lot about Miss Brodie from the girls,' Deirdre was saying. 'I really must ask her to tea. D'you think she'd like to come?'

'No,' said Teddy.

'Why?' said Deirdre, not that it seemed to matter, she was so languid and long-armed, lifting the plate of biscuits from the table and passing them round without moving from the low stool on which she sat.

'You kids stop that row or you leave the room,' Teddy declared.

'Bring Miss Brodie to tea,' Deirdre said to Sandy.

'She won't come,' Teddy said, '– will she, Sandy?'

'She's awfully busy,' Sandy said.

'Pass me a fag,' said Deirdre.

'Is she still looking after Lowther?' said Teddy.

'Well, yes, a bit —'

'Lowther,' said Teddy, waving his only arm, 'must have a way with women. He's got half the female staff of the school looking after him. Why doesn't he employ a housekeeper? He's got plenty of money, no wife, no kids, no rent to pay, it's his own house. Why doesn't he get a proper housekeeper?'

'I think he likes Miss Brodie,' Sandy said.

'But what does she see in him?'

'He sings to her,' Sandy said, suddenly sharp.

Deirdre laughed. 'Miss Brodie sounds a bit queer, I must say. What age is she?'

'Jean Brodie,' said Teddy, 'is a magnificent woman in her prime.' He got up, tossing back his lock of hair, and left the room.

Deirdre blew a cloud of reflective smoke and stubbed out her cigarette, and Sandy said she would have to go now.

Mr Lowther had caused Miss Brodie a good deal of worry in the past two years. There had been a time when it seemed he might be thinking of marrying Miss Alison Kerr, and another time when he seemed to favour Miss Ellen, all the while being in love with Miss Brodie herself, who refused him all but her bed-fellowship and her catering.

He tired of food, for it was making him fat and weary and putting him out of voice. He wanted a wife to play golf with and to sing to. He wanted a honeymoon on the Hebridean island of Eigg, near Rum, and then to return to Cramond with the bride.

In the midst of this dissatisfaction had occurred Ellen Kerr's finding of a nightdress of quality folded under the pillow next to Mr Lowther's in that double bed on which, to make matters worse, he had been born.

Still Miss Brodie refused him. He fell into a melancholy mood upon his retirement from the offices of choir-master and Elder, and the girls thought he brooded often upon the possibility that Miss Brodie could not take to his short legs, and was all the time pining for Teddy Lloyd's long ones.

Most of this Miss Brodie obliquely confided in the girls as they grew from thirteen to fourteen and from fourteen to fifteen. She did not say, even obliquely, that she slept with the singing master, for she was still testing them out to see whom she could trust, as it would be her way to put it. She did not want any alarming suspicions to arise in the minds of their parents. Miss Brodie was always very careful to impress the parents of her set and to win their approval and gratitude. So she confided according to what seemed expedient at the time, and was in fact now on the look-out for a girl amongst her set in whom she could confide entirely, whose curiosity was greater than her desire to make a sensation outside, and who, in the need to gain further confidences from Miss Brodie, would never betray what had been gained. Of necessity there had to be but one girl; two would be dangerous. Almost shrewdly, Miss Brodie fixed on Sandy, and even then it was not of her own affairs that she spoke.

In the summer of nineteen-thirty-five the whole school was forced to wear rosettes of red, white and blue ribbons in the lapels of its blazers, because of the Silver Jubilee. Rose Stanley lost hers and said it was probably in Teddy Lloyd's studio. This was not long after Sandy's visit to the art master's residence.

'What are you doing for the summer holidays, Rose?' said Miss Brodie.

'My father's taking me to the Highlands for a fortnight. After that, I don't know. I suppose I'll be sitting for Mr Lloyd off and on.'

'Good,' said Miss Brodie.

Miss Brodie started to confide in Sandy after the next summer holidays. They played rounds of golf in the sunny early autumn after school.

'All my ambitions,' said Miss Brodie, 'are fixed on yourself and Rose. You will not speak of this to the other girls, it would cause envy. I had hopes of Jenny, she is so pretty; but Jenny has become insipid, don't you think?'

This was a clever question, because it articulated what was already growing in Sandy's mind. Jenny had bored her this last year, and it left her lonely.

'Don't you think?' said Miss Brodie, towering above her, for Sandy was playing out of a bunker. Sandy gave a hack with her niblick and said, 'Yes, a bit,' sending the ball in a little backward half-circle.

'And I had hopes of Eunice,' Miss Brodie said presently, 'but she seems to be interested in some boy she goes swimming with.'

Sandy was not yet out of the bunker. It was sometimes difficult to follow Miss Brodie's drift when she was in her prophetic moods. One had to wait and see what emerged. In the meantime she glanced up at Miss Brodie who was standing on the crest of the bunker which was itself on a crest of the hilly course. Miss Brodie looked admirable in her heather-blue tweed with the brown of a recent holiday in Egypt still warming her skin. Miss Brodie was gazing out over Edinburgh as she spoke.

Sandy got out of the bunker. 'Eunice,' said Miss Brodie, 'will settle down and marry some professional man. Perhaps I have done her some good. Mary, well Mary. I never had any hopes of Mary. I thought, when you were young children, that Mary might be something. She was a little pathetic. But she's really a most irritating girl, I'd rather deal with a rogue than a fool. Monica will get her B.Sc. with honours I've no doubt, but she has no spiritual insight, and of course that's why she's – '

Miss Brodie was to drive off now and she had decided to stop talking until she had measured her distance and swiped her ball. Which she did. '– that's why she has a bad temper, she understands nothing but signs and symbols and calculations. Nothing infuriates people more than their own lack of spiritual insight, Sandy, that is why the Moslems are so placid, they are full of spiritual insight. My dragoman in Egypt would not have it that Friday was their Lord's Day. "Every day is the Lord's day," he said to me. I thought that very profound, I felt humbled. We had already said our farewells on the day before my departure, Sandy, but lo and behold when I was already seated in the train, along the platform came my dragoman with a beautiful bunch of flowers for me. He had true dignity. Sandy, you will never get anywhere by hunching over your putter, hold your shoulders back and bend from the waist. He was a very splendid person with a great sense of his bearing.'

They picked up their balls and walked to the next tee. 'Have you ever played with Miss Lockhart?' Sandy said.

'Does she play golf?'

'Yes, rather well.' Sandy had met the science mistress surprisingly on the golf course one Saturday morning playing with Gordon Lowther.

'Good shot, Sandy. I know very little of Miss Lockhart,' said Miss Brodie. 'I leave her to her jars and gases. They are all gross materialists, these women in the Senior school, they all belong to the Fabian Society and are pacifists. That's the sort of thing Mr Lowther, Mr Lloyd and myself are up against when we are not up against the narrow-minded, half-educated crowd in the junior departments. Sandy, I'll swear you are short-sighted, the way you peer at people. You must get spectacles.'

'I'm not,' said Sandy irritably, 'it only seems so.'

'It's unnerving,' said Miss Brodie. 'Do you know, Sandy dear, all my ambitions are for you and Rose. You have got insight, perhaps not quite spiritual, but you're a deep one, and Rose has got instinct, Rose has got instinct.'

'Perhaps not quite spiritual,' said Sandy.

'Yes,' said Miss Brodie, 'you're right. Rose has got a future by virtue of her instinct.'

'She has an instinct how to sit for her portrait,' said Sandy.

'That's what I mean by your insight,' said Miss Brodie. 'I ought to know, because my prime has brought me instinct and insight, both.'

Fully to savour her position, Sandy would go and stand outside St Giles Cathedral or the Tolbooth, and contemplate these emblems of a dark and terrible salvation which made the fires of the damned seem very merry to the imagination by contrast, and much preferable. Nobody in her life, at home or at school, had ever spoken of Calvinism except as a joke that had once been taken seriously. She did not at the time understand that her environment had not been on the surface peculiar to the place, as was the environment of the Edinburgh social classes just above or, even more, just below her own. She had no experience of social class at all. In its outward forms her fifteen years might have been spent in any suburb of any city in the British Isles; her school, with its alien house system, might have been in Ealing. All she was conscious of now was that some quality of life peculiar to Edinburgh and nowhere else had been going on unbeknown to her all the time, and however undesirable it might be, she felt deprived of it; however undesirable, she desired to know what it was, and to cease to be protected from it by enlightened people.

In fact, it was the religion of Calvin of which Sandy felt deprived, or rather a specified recognition of it. She desired this birthright; something definite to reject. It pervaded the place in proportion as it was unacknowledged. In some ways the most real and rooted people whom Sandy knew were Miss Gaunt and the Kerr sisters who made no evasions about their belief that God had planned for practically everybody before they were born a nasty surprise when they died. Later, when Sandy read John Calvin, she found that although popular conceptions of Calvinism were sometimes mistaken, in this particular there was no mistake, indeed it was but a mild understanding of the case, he having made it God's pleasure to implant in certain people an erroneous sense of joy and salvation, so that their surprise at the end might be the nastier.

Sandy was unable to formulate these exciting propositions; nevertheless she experienced them in the air she breathed, she sensed them in the curiously defiant way in which the people she knew broke the Sabbath, and she smelt them in the excesses of Miss Brodie in her prime. Now that she was allowed to go about alone, she walked round the certainly forbidden quarters of Edinburgh to look at the blackened monuments and hear the unbelievable curses of drunken men and women, and comparing their faces with the faces from Morningside and Merchiston with which she was familiar, she saw, with stabs of new and exciting Calvinistic guilt, that there was not much difference.

In this oblique way, she began to sense what went to the makings of Miss Brodie who had elected herself to grace in so particular a way and with more exotic suicidal enchantment than if she had simply taken to drink like other spinsters who couldn't stand it any more.

It was plain that Miss Brodie wanted Rose with her instinct to start preparing to be Teddy Lloyd's lover, and Sandy with her insight to act as informant on the affair. It was to this end that Rose and Sandy had been chosen as the crème de la crème. There was a whiff of sulphur about the idea which fascinated Sandy in her present mind. After all, it was only an idea. And there was no pressing hurry in the matter, for Miss Brodie liked to take her leisure over the unfolding of her plans, most of her joy deriving from the preparation, and moreover, even if these plans were as clear to her own mind as they were to Sandy's, the girls were too young. All the same, by the time the girls were sixteen Miss Brodie was saying to her set at large: 'Sandy will make an excellent Secret Service agent, a great spy'; and to Sandy alone she had started saying 'Rose will be a great lover. She is above the common moral code, it does not apply to her. This is a fact which it is not expedient for anyone to hear about who is not endowed with insight.'

For over a year Sandy entered into the spirit of this plan, for she visited the Lloyds' frequently, and was able to report to Miss Brodie how things were going with the portraits of Rose which so resembled Miss Brodie.

'Rose,' said Miss Brodie, 'is like a heroine from a novel by D. H. Lawrence. She has got instinct.'

But in fact the art master's interest in Rose was simply a professional one, she was a good model; Rose had an instinct to be satisfied with this role, and in the event it was Sandy who slept with Teddy Lloyd and Rose who carried back the information.

It was some time before these things came to pass, and meanwhile Miss Brodie was neglecting Mr Lowther at Cramond and spending as much time as possible with Rose and Sandy discussing art, and then the question of sitting for an artist, and Rose's future as a model, and the necessity for Rose to realize the power she had within her, it was a gift and she an exception to all the rules, she was the exception that proved the rule. Miss Brodie was too cautious to be more precise and Rose only half-guessed at Miss Brodie's meaning, for she was at this time, as Sandy knew, following her instinct and becoming famous for sex among the schoolboys who stood awkwardly with their bicycles at a safe distance from the school gates. Rose was greatly popular with these boys, which was the only reason why she was famed for sex, although she did not really talk about sex, far less indulge it. She did everything by instinct, she even listened to Miss Brodie as if she agreed with every word.

'When you are seventeen or eighteen, Rose, you will come to the moment of your great fulfilment.'

'Yes, honestly I think so, Miss Brodie.'

Teddy Lloyd's passion for Jean Brodie was greatly in evidence in all the portraits he did of the various members of the Brodie set. He did them in a group during one summer term, wearing their panama hats each in a different way, each hat adorning, in a magical trans-figuration, a different Jean Brodie under the forms of Rose, Sandy, Jenny, Mary, Monica and Eunice. But mostly it was Rose, because she was instinctively a good model and Teddy Lloyd paid her five shillings a sitting, which Rose found useful, being addicted to the cinema.

Sandy felt warmly towards Miss Brodie at those times when she saw how she was misled in her idea of Rose. It was then that Miss Brodie looked beautiful and fragile, just as dark heavy Edinburgh itself could suddenly be changed into a floating city when the light was a special pearly white and fell upon one of the gracefully fashioned streets. In the same way Miss Brodie's masterful features became clear and sweet to Sandy when viewed in the curious light of the woman's folly, and she never felt more affection for her in her later years than when she thought upon Miss Brodie as silly.

But Miss Brodie as the leader of the set, Miss Brodie as a Roman matron, Miss Brodie as an educational reformer were still prominent. It was not always comfortable, from the school point of view, to be associated with her. The lack of team spirit alone, the fact that the Brodie set preferred golf to hockey or netball if they preferred anything at all, were enough to set them apart, even if they had not dented in the crowns of their hats and tilted them backwards or forwards. It was impossible for them to escape from the Brodie set because they were the Brodie set in the eyes of the school. Nominally, they were members of Holyrood, Melrose, Argyll and Biggar, but it had been well known that the Brodie set had no team spirit and did not care which house won the shield. They were not allowed to care. Their disregard had now become an institution, to be respected like the house system itself. For their own part, and without this repu-tation, the six girls would have gone each her own way by the time she was in the fourth form and had reached the age of sixteen.

But it was irrevocable, and they made the most of it, and saw that their position was really quite enviable. Everyone thought the Brodie set had more fun than anyone else, what with visits to Cramond, to

Teddy Lloyd's studio, to the theatre and teas with Miss Brodie. And indeed it was so. And Miss Brodie was always a figure of glamorous activity even in the eyes of the non-Brodie girls.

Miss Brodie's struggles with the authorities on account of her educational system were increasing throughout the years, and she made it a moral duty for her set to rally round her each time her battle reached a crisis. Then she would find them, perhaps, loitering with the bicycle boys after school, and the bicycles would rapidly bear the boys away, and they would be bidden to supper the following evening.

They went to the tram-car stop with her. 'It has been suggested again that I should apply for a post at one of the progressive, that is to say, crank schools. I shall not apply for a post at a crank school. I shall remain at this education factory where my duty lies. There needs must be a leaven in the lump. Give me a girl at an impressionable age and she is mine for life. The gang who oppose me shall not succeed.'

'No,' said everyone. 'No, of course they won't.'

The headmistress had not quite given up testing the girls of the Brodie set to see what they knew. In her frustration she sometimes took reprisals against them when she could do so under the guise of fair play, which was not often.

'If they do not try to unseat me on the grounds of my educational policy, they attempt personal calumny,' said Miss Brodie one day. 'It is unfortunate, but true, that there have been implications against my character in regard to my relations with poor Mr Lowther. As you girls well know, I have given much of my energy to Mr Lowther's health. I am fond of Mr Lowther. Why not? Are we not bidden to love one another? I am Gordon Lowther's closest friend, his confidante. I have neglected him of late I am afraid, but still I have been all things to Gordon Lowther, and I need only lift my little finger and he would be at my side. This relationship has been distorted . . . .'

It was some months, now, that Miss Brodie had neglected the singing master, and the girls no longer spent Saturday afternoons at Cramond. Sandy assumed that the reason why Miss Brodie had stopped sleeping with Gordon Lowther was that her sexual feelings were satisfied by proxy; and Rose was predestined to be the lover of Teddy Lloyd. 'I have had much calumny to put up with on account of my good offices at Cramond,' said Miss Brodie. 'However, I shall survive it. If I wished I could marry him tomorrow.'

The morning after this saying, the engagement of Gordon Lowther to Miss Lockhart, the science teacher, was announced in *The Scotsman*. Nobody had expected it. Miss Brodie was greatly taken aback and suffered untimely, for a space, from a sense of having been betrayed. But she seemed to recall herself to the fact that the true love of her life was Teddy Lloyd whom she had renounced; and Gordon Lowther had merely been useful. She subscribed with the rest of the school to the china tea-set which was presented to the couple at the last assembly of the term. Mr Lowther made a speech in which he called them 'you girlies', glancing shyly from time to time at Miss Brodie who was watching the clouds through the window. Sometimes he looked towards his bride to be, who stood quietly by the side of the headmistress half-way up the hall waiting till he should be finished and they could join him on the platform. He had confidence in Miss Lockhart, as everyone did, she not only played golf well and drove a car, she could also blow up the school with her jar of gunpowder and would never dream of doing so.

Miss Brodie's brown eyes were fixed on the clouds, she looked quite beautiful and frail, and it occurred to Sandy that she had possibly renounced Teddy Lloyd only because she was aware that she could not keep up this beauty; it was a quality in her that came and went.

Next term, when Mr Lowther returned from his honeymoon on the island of Eigg, Miss Brodie put her spare energy into her plan for Sandy and Rose, with their insight and instinct; and what energy she had to spare from that she now put into political ideas.

SIX

Miss Mackay, the headmistress, never gave up pumping the Brodie set. She knew it was useless to do so directly, her approach was indirect, in the hope that they would be tricked into letting fall some piece of evidence which could be used to enforce Miss Brodie's retirement. Once a term, the girls went to tea with Miss Mackay.

But in any case there was now very little they could say without implicating themselves. By the time their friendship with Miss Brodie was of seven years' standing, it had worked itself into their bones, so that they could not break away without, as it were, splitting their bones to do so.

'You still keep up with Miss Brodie?' said Miss Mackay, with a gleaming smile. She had new teeth.

'Oh, yes, rather . . .'

'Yes, oh yes, from time to time . . .'

Miss Mackay said to Sandy confidentially when her turn came round – because she treated the older girls as equals, which is to say, as equals definitely wearing school uniform – 'Dear Miss Brodie, she sits on under the elm, telling her remarkable life story to the junior children. I mind when Miss Brodie first came to the school, she was a vigorous young teacher, but now –' She sighed and shook her head. She had a habit of putting the universal wise saws into Scots dialect to make them wiser. Now she said, 'What canna be cured maun be endured. But I fear Miss Brodie is past her best. I doubt her class will get through its qualifying examination this year. But don't think I'm criticizing Miss Brodie. She likes her wee drink, I'm sure. After all, it's nobody's business, so long as it doesn't affect her work and you girls.'

'She doesn't drink,' said Sandy, 'except for sherry on her birthday, half a bottle between the seven of us.'

Miss Mackay could be observed mentally scoring drink off her list of things against Miss Brodie. 'Oh, that's all I meant,' said Miss Mackay.

The Brodie girls, now that they were seventeen, were able to detach Miss Brodie from her aspect of teacher. When they conferred amongst themselves on the subject they had to admit, at last, and without doubt, that she was really an exciting woman as a woman. Her eyes flashed, her nose arched proudly, her hair was still brown, and coiled matriarchally at the nape of her neck. The singing master, well satisfied as he was with Miss Lockhart, now Mrs Lowther and lost to the school, would glance at Miss Brodie from under his ginger eyebrows with shy admiration and memories whenever he saw her.

One of her greatest admirers was the new girl called Joyce Emily Hammond who had been sent to Blaine School as a last hope, having been obliged to withdraw from a range of expensive schools north and south of the border, because of her alleged delinquency which so far had not been revealed, except once or twice when she had thrown paper pellets at Mr Lowther and succeeded only in hurting his feelings. She insisted on calling herself Joyce Emily, was brought to school in the morning by a chauffeur in a large black car, though she was obliged to make her own way home; she lived in a huge house with a stables in the near environs of Edinburgh. Joyce Emily's parents, wealthy as they were, had begged for a trial period to elapse before investing in yet another set of school uniform clothing for their daughter. So Joyce Emily still went about in dark green, while the rest wore deep violet, and she boasted five sets of discarded colours hanging in her wardrobe at home besides such relics of governesses as a substantial switch of hair cut off by Joyce Emily's own hand, a post office savings book belonging to a governess called Miss Michie, and the charred remains of a pillow-case upon which the head of yet another governess called Miss Chambers had been resting when Joyce Emily had set fire to it.

The rest of the girls listened to her chatter, but in general she was disapproved of not only because of her green stockings and skirt, her shiny car and chauffeur, but because life was already exceedingly full of working for examinations and playing for the shield. It was the Brodie set to which Joyce Emily mostly desired to attach herself, perceiving their individualism; but they, less than anybody, wanted her. With the exception of Mary Macgregor, they were, in fact,

among the brightest girls in the school, which was somewhat a
stumbling-block to Miss Mackay in her efforts to discredit Miss
Brodie.

The Brodie set, moreover, had outside interests. Eunice had a boy
friend with whom she practised swimming and diving. Monica
Douglas and Mary Macgregor went slum-visiting together with
bundles of groceries, although Mary was reported to be always
making remarks like, 'Why don't they eat cake?' (What she actually
said was, 'Well, why don't they send their clothes to the laundry?'
when she heard complaints of the prohibitive price of soap.) Jenny
was already showing her dramatic talent and was all the time
rehearsing for something in the school dramatic society. Rose
modelled for Teddy Lloyd and Sandy occasionally joined her, and
was watchful, and sometimes toyed with the idea of inducing Teddy
Lloyd to kiss her again just to see if it could be done by sheer looking
at him insolently with her little eyes. In addition to these activities the
Brodie set were meeting Miss Brodie by twos and threes, and
sometimes all together after school. It was at this time, in nineteen-
thirty-seven, that she was especially cultivating Rose, and questioning Sandy, and being answered as to the progress of the great love
affair presently to take place between Rose and the art master.

So that they had no time to do much about a delinquent whose
parents had dumped her on the school by their influence, even if she
was apparently a delinquent in name only. Miss Brodie, however,
found time to take her up. The Brodie girls slightly resented this but
were relieved that they were not obliged to share the girl's company,
and that Miss Brodie took her to tea and the theatre on her own.

One of Joyce Emily's boasts was that her brother at Oxford had
gone to fight in the Spanish Civil War. This dark, rather mad girl
wanted to go too, and to wear a white blouse and black skirt and march
with a gun. Nobody had taken this seriously. The Spanish Civil War
was something going on outside in the newspapers and only once a
month in the school debating society. Everyone, including Joyce
Emily, was anti-Franco if they were anything at all.

One day it was realized that Joyce Emily had not been at school for
some days, and soon someone else was occupying her desk. No one
knew why she had left until, six weeks later, it was reported that she
had run away to Spain and had been killed in an accident when the

train she was travelling in had been attacked. The school held an abbreviated form of remembrance service for her.

Mary had gone to be a shorthand typist and Jenny had gone to a school of dramatic art. Only four remained of the Brodie set for the last year. It was hardly like being at school at all, there was so much free time, so many lectures and so much library research outside the school building for the sixth-form girls that it was just a matter of walking in and out. They were deferred to and consulted, and had the feeling that they could, if they wished, run the place.

Eunice was to do modern languages, although she changed her mind a year later and became a nurse. Monica was destined for science, Sandy for psychology. Rose had hung on, not for any functional reason, but because her father thought she should get the best out of her education, even if she was only going to the art school later on, or at the worst, become a model for artists or dress designers. Rose's father played a big part in her life, he was a huge widower, as handsome in his masculine way as was Rose in her feminine, proudly professing himself a cobbler; that was to say, he now owned an extensive shoe-making business. Some years ago, on meeting Miss Brodie he had immediately taken a hearty male interest in her, as so many men did, not thinking her to be ridiculous as might have been expected; but she would have none of Mr Stanley, for he was hardly what she would call a man of culture. She thought him rather carnal. The girls, however, had always guiltily liked Rose's father. And Rose, instinctive as she undoubtedly was, followed her instinct so far as to take on his hard-headed and merry carnality, and made a good marriage soon after she left school. She shook off Miss Brodie's influence as a dog shakes pond-water from its coat.

Miss Brodie was not to know that this would be, and meantime Rose was inescapably famous for sex and was much sought after by sixth-form schoolboys and first-year university students. And Miss Brodie said to Sandy: 'From what you tell me I should think that Rose and Teddy Lloyd will soon be lovers.' All at once Sandy realized that this was not all theory and a kind of Brodie game, in the way that so much of life was unreal talk and game-planning, like the prospects of a war and other theories that people were putting about in the air like pigeons, and one said, 'Yes, of course, it's inevitable.' But this was not theory; Miss Brodie meant it. Sandy looked at her, and perceived that the woman was obsessed by the need for Rose to sleep with the man she herself was in love with; there was nothing new in the idea, it was the reality that was new. She thought of Miss Brodie eight years ago sitting under the elm tree telling her first simple love story and wondered to what extent it was Miss Brodie who had developed complications throughout the years, and to what extent it was her own conception of Miss Brodie that had changed.

During the year past Sandy had continued seeing the Lloyds. She went shopping with Deirdre Lloyd and got herself a folkweave shirt like Deirdre's. She listened to their conversation, at the same time calculating their souls by signs and symbols, as was the habit in those days of young persons who had read books of psychology when listening to older persons who had not. Sometimes, on days when Rose was required to pose naked, Sandy sat with the painter and his model in the studio, silently watching the strange mutations of the flesh on the canvas as they represented an anonymous nude figure, and at the same time resembled Rose, and more than this, resembled Miss Brodie. Sandy had become highly interested in the painter's mind, so involved with Miss Brodie as it was, and not accounting her ridiculous.

'From what you tell me I should think that Rose and Teddy Lloyd will soon be lovers.' Sandy realized that Miss Brodie meant it. She had told Miss Brodie how peculiarly all his portraits reflected her. She had said so again and again, for Miss Brodie loved to hear it. She had said that Teddy Lloyd wanted to give up teaching and was preparing an exhibition, and was encouraged in this course by art critics and discouraged by the thought of his large family.

'I am his Muse,' said Miss Brodie. 'But I have renounced his love in order to dedicate my prime to the young girls in my care. I am his Muse but Rose shall take my place.'

She thinks she is Providence, thought Sandy, she thinks she is the God of Calvin, she sees the beginning and the end. And Sandy thought, too, the woman is an unconscious Lesbian. And many theories from the books of psychology categorized Miss Brodie, but failed to obliterate her image from the canvases of one-armed Teddy Lloyd.

When she was a nun, sooner or later one and the other of the Brodie set came to visit Sandy, because it was something to do, and she had written her book of psychology, and everyone likes to visit a nun, it provides a spiritual sensation, a catharsis to go home with, especially if the nun clutches the bars of the grille. Rose came, now long since married to a successful business man who varied in his line of business from canned goods to merchant banking. They fell to talking about Miss Brodie.

'She talked a lot about dedication,' said Rose, 'but she didn't mean your sort of dedication. But don't you think she was dedicated to her girls in a way?'

'Oh yes, I think she was,' said Sandy.

'Why did she get the push?' said Rose. 'Was it sex?'

'No, politics.'

'I didn't know she bothered about politics.'

'It was only a side line,' Sandy said, 'but it served as an excuse.'

Monica Douglas came to visit Sandy because there was a crisis in her life. She had married a scientist and in one of her fits of anger had thrown a live coal at his sister. Whereupon the scientist demanded a separation, once and for all.

'I'm not much good at that sort of problem,' said Sandy. But Monica had not thought she would be able to help much, for she knew Sandy of old, and persons known of old can never be of much help. So they fell to talking of Miss Brodie.

'Did she ever get Rose to sleep with Teddy Lloyd?' said Monica.

'No,' said Sandy.

'Was she in love with Teddy Lloyd herself?'

'Yes,' said Sandy, 'and he was in love with her.'

'Then it was a real renunciation in a way,' said Monica.

'Yes, it was,' said Sandy. 'After all, she was a woman in her prime.'

'You used to think her talk about renunciation was a joke,' said Monica.

'So did you,' said Sandy.

In the summer of nineteen-thirty-eight, after the last of the Brodie set had left Blaine, Miss Brodie went to Germany and Austria, while Sandy read psychology and went to the Lloyds' to sit for her own portrait. Rose came and kept them company occasionally.

When Deirdre Lloyd took the children into the country Teddy had to stay on in Edinburgh because he was giving a summer course at the art school. Sandy continued to sit for her portrait twice a week, and sometimes Rose came and sometimes not.

One day when they were alone, Sandy told Teddy Lloyd that all his portraits, even that of the littlest Lloyd baby, were now turning out to be likenesses of Miss Brodie, and she gave him her insolent black-mailing stare. He kissed her as he had done three years before when she was fifteen, and for the best part of five weeks of the summer they had a love affair in the empty house, only sometimes answering the door to Rose, but at other times letting the bell scream on.

During that time he painted a little, and she said: 'You are still making me look like Jean Brodie.' So he started a new canvas, but it was the same again.

She said: 'Why are you obsessed with that woman? Can't you see she's ridiculous?'

He said, yes, he could see Jean Brodie was ridiculous. He said, would she kindly stop analysing his mind, it was unnatural in a girl of eighteen.

Miss Brodie telephoned for Sandy to come to see her early in September. She had returned from Germany and Austria which were now magnificently organized. After the war Miss Brodie admitted to Sandy, as they sat in the Braid Hills Hotel, 'Hitler *was* rather naughty,' but at this time she was full of her travels and quite sure the new régime would save the world. Sandy was bored, it did not seem necessary that the world should be saved, only that the poor people in the streets and slums of Edinburgh should be relieved. Miss Brodie said there would be no war. Sandy never had thought so, anyway. Miss Brodie came to the point: 'Rose tells me you have become his lover.'

'Yes, does it matter which one of us it is?'

'Whatever possessed you?' said Miss Brodie in a very Scottish way, as if Sandy had given away a pound of marmalade to an English duke.

'He interests me,' said Sandy.

'Interests you, forsooth,' said Miss Brodie. 'A girl with a mind, a girl with insight. He is a Roman Catholic and I don't see how you can have to do with a man who can't think for himself. Rose was suitable. Rose has instinct but no insight.'

Teddy Lloyd continued reproducing Jean Brodie in his paintings.

'You have instinct,' Sandy told him, 'but no insight, or you would see that the woman isn't to be taken seriously.'

'I know she isn't,' he said. 'You are too analytical and irritable for your age.'

The family had returned and their meetings were dangerous and exciting. The more she discovered him to be still in love with Jean Brodie, the more she was curious about the mind that loved the woman. By the end of the year it happened that she had quite lost interest in the man himself, but was deeply absorbed in his mind, from which she extracted, among other things, his religion as a pith from a husk. Her mind was as full of his religion as a night sky is full of things visible and invisible. She left the man and took his religion and became a nun in the course of time.

But that autumn, while she was still probing the mind that invented Miss Brodie on canvas after canvas, Sandy met Miss Brodie several times. She was at first merely resigned to Sandy's liaison with the art master. Presently she was exultant, and presently again inquired for details, which she did not get.

'His portraits still resemble me?' said Miss Brodie.

'Yes, very much,' said Sandy.

'Then all is well,' said Miss Brodie. 'And after all, Sandy,' she said, 'you are destined to be the great lover, although I would not have thought it. Truth is stranger than fiction. I wanted Rose for him, I admit, and sometimes I regretted urging young Joyce Emily to go to Spain to fight for Franco, she would have done admirably for him, a girl of instinct, a —'

'Did she go to fight for Franco?' said Sandy.

'That was the intention. I made her see sense. However, she didn't have the chance to fight at all, poor girl.'

When Sandy returned, as was expected of her, to see Miss Mackay that autumn, the headmistress said to this rather difficult old girl with the abnormally small eyes, 'You'll have been seeing something of Miss Brodie, I hope. You aren't forgetting your old friends, I hope.'

'I've seen her once or twice,' said Sandy.

'I'm afraid she put ideas into your young heads,' said Miss Mackay with a knowing twinkle, which meant that now Sandy had left school it would be all right to talk openly about Miss Brodie's goings-on.

'Yes, lots of ideas,' Sandy said.

'I wish I knew what some of them were,' said Miss Mackay, slumping a little and genuinely worried. 'Because it is still going on, I mean class after class, and now she has formed a new set, and they are so out of key with the rest of the school, Miss Brodie's set. They are precocious. Do you know what I mean?'

'Yes,' said Sandy. 'But you won't be able to pin her down on sex. Have you thought of politics?'

Miss Mackay turned her chair so that it was nearly square with Sandy's. This was business.

'My dear,' she said, 'what do you mean? I didn't know she was attracted by politics.'

'Neither she is,' said Sandy, 'except as a side interest. She's a born Fascist, have you thought of that?'

'I shall question her pupils on those lines and see what emerges, if that is what you advise, Sandy. I had no idea you felt so seriously about the state of world affairs, Sandy, and I'm more than delighted –'

'I'm not really interested in world affairs,' said Sandy, 'only in putting a stop to Miss Brodie.'

It was clear the headmistress thought this rather unpleasant of Sandy. But she did not fail to say to Miss Brodie, when the time came, 'It was one of your own girls who gave me the tip, one of your set, Miss Brodie.'

Sandy was to leave Edinburgh at the end of the year and when she said goodbye to the Lloyds she looked round the studio at the canvases on which she had failed to put a stop to Miss Brodie. She congratulated Teddy Lloyd on the economy of his method. He congratulated her on the economy of hers, and Deirdre looked to see whatever did he mean? Sandy thought, if he knew about my stopping of Miss Brodie, he would think me more economical still. She was more fuming, now, with Christian morals, than John Knox.

Miss Brodie was forced to retire at the end of the summer term of nineteen-thirty-nine, on the grounds that she had been teaching Fascism. Sandy, when she heard of it, thought of the marching troops of black shirts in the pictures on the wall. By now she had entered the Catholic Church, in whose ranks she had found quite a number of Fascists much less agreeable than Miss Brodie.

'Of course,' said Miss Brodie when she wrote to tell Sandy the news of her retirement, 'this political question was only an excuse. They tried to prove personal immorality against me on many occasions and failed. My girls were always reticent on these matters. It was my educational policy they were up against which had reached its perfection in my prime. I was dedicated to my girls, as you know. But they used this political excuse as a weapon. What hurts and amazes me most of all is the fact, if Miss Mackay is to be believed, that it was one of my own set who betrayed me and put the inquiry in motion.

'You will be astonished. I can write to you of this, because you of all my set are exempt from suspicion, you had no *reason* to betray me. I think first of Mary Macgregor. Perhaps Mary has nursed a grievance, in her stupidity of mind, against me – she is such an exasperating young woman. I think of Rose. It may be that Rose resented my coming first with Mr L. Eunice – I cannot think it could be Eunice, but I did frequently have to come down firmly on her commonplace ideas. She wanted to be a Girl Guide, you remember. She was attracted to the Team Spirit – could it be that Eunice bore a grudge? Then there is Jenny. Now you know Jenny, how she went *off* and was never the same after she wanted to be an actress. She became so dull. Do you think she minded my telling her that she would never be a Fay Compton, far less a Sybil Thorndike? Finally, there is Monica. I half incline to suspect Monica. There is very little Soul behind the mathematical brain, and it may be that, in a fit of rage against that Beauty, Truth and Goodness which was beyond her grasp, she turned and betrayed me.

'You, Sandy, as you see, I exempt from suspicion, since you had no reason whatsoever to betray me, indeed you have had the best part of me in my confidences and in the man I love. Think, if you can, who it could have been. I must know which one of you betrayed me . . .'

Sandy replied like an enigmatic Pope: 'If you did not betray us it is impossible that you could have been betrayed by us. The word betrayed does not apply . . .'

She heard again from Miss Brodie at the time of Mary Macgregor's death, when the girl ran hither and thither in the hotel fire and was trapped by it. 'If this is a judgement on poor Mary for betraying me, I am sure I would not have wished . . .'

'I'm afraid', Jenny wrote, 'Miss Brodie is past her prime. She keeps wanting to know who betrayed her. It isn't at all like the old Miss Brodie; she was always so full of fight.'

Her name and memory, after her death, flitted from mouth to mouth like swallows in summer, and in winter they were gone. It was always in summer time that the Brodie set came to visit Sandy, for the nunnery was deep in the country.

When Jenny came to see Sandy, who now bore the name Sister Helena of the Transfiguration, she told Sandy about her sudden falling in love with a man in Rome and there being nothing to be done about it. 'Miss Brodie would have liked to know about it,' she said, 'sinner as she was.'

'Oh, she was quite an innocent in her way,' said Sandy, clutching the bars of the grille.

Eunice, when she came, told Sandy, 'We were at the Edinburgh Festival last year. I found Miss Brodie's grave, I put some flowers on it. I've told my husband all the stories about her, sitting under the elm and all that; he thinks she was marvellous fun.'

'So she was, really, when you think of it.'

'Yes, she was,' said Eunice, 'when she was in her prime.'

Monica came again. 'Before she died,' she said, 'Miss Brodie thought it was you who betrayed her.'

'It's only possible to betray where loyalty is due,' said Sandy.

'Well, wasn't it due to Miss Brodie?'

'Only up to a point,' said Sandy.

And there was that day when the inquiring young man came to see Sandy because of her strange book of psychology, 'The Transfiguration of the Commonplace', which had brought so many visitors that Sandy clutched the bars of her grille more desperately than ever.

'What were the main influences of your school days, Sister Helena? Were they literary or political or personal? Was it Calvinism?'

Sandy said: 'There was a Miss Jean Brodie in her prime.'

THE
COMFORTERS

PART ONE

ONE

On the first day of his holiday Laurence Manders woke to hear his grandmother's voice below.

'I'll have a large wholemeal. I've got my grandson stopping for a week, who's on the B.B.C. That's my daughter's boy, Lady Manders. He won't eat white bread, one of his fads.'

Laurence shouted from the window, 'Grandmother, I adore white bread and I have no fads.'

She puckered and beamed up at him.

'Shouting from the window,' she said to the baker.

'You woke me up,' Laurence said.

'My grandson,' she told the baker. 'A large wholemeal, and don't forget to call on Wednesday.'

Laurence looked at himself in the glass. 'I must get up,' he said, getting back into bed. He gave himself seven minutes.

He followed his grandmother's movements from the sounds which came clearly through the worn cottage floorboards. At seventy-eight Louisa Jepp did everything very slowly but with extreme attention, as some do when they know they are slightly drunk. Laurence heard a clink and a pause, a tinkle and a pause, breakfast being laid. Her footsteps clicked like a clock that is running down as she moved between the scullery and the little hot kitchen; she refused to shuffle.

When he was half dressed Laurence opened a tiny drawer on the top of the tall old-fashioned chest. It contained some of his grandmother's things, for she had given him her room. He counted three hairpins, eight mothballs; he found a small piece of black velvet embroidered with jet beads now loose on their thread. He reckoned the bit of stuff would be about two and a half inches by one and a half. In another drawer he found a comb with some of his grandmother's hair on it and noted that the object was none too neat. He got some pleasure from having met with these facts, three hairpins, eight mothballs, a comb none too neat, the property of his grandmother, here in her home in Sussex, now in the present tense. That is what Laurence was like.

'It is unhealthy,' his mother had lately told him. 'It's the only unhealthy thing about your mind, the way you notice absurd details, it's absurd of you.'

'That's what I'm like,' Laurence said.

As usual, she knew this meant deadlock, but carried on,

'Well, it's unnatural. Because sometimes you see things that you shouldn't.'

'Such as?'

She did not say, but she knew he had been in her room prying into her messy make-up drawer, patting the little bottles like a cat and naming them. She could never persuade him that this was wrong. After all, it was a violation of privacy.

Very often Laurence said, 'It would be wrong for you but it isn't for me.'

And always Helena Manders, his mother, would reply 'I don't see that', or 'I don't agree', although really she did in a way.

In his childhood he had terrorized the household with his sheer literal truths.

'Uncle Ernest uses ladies' skin food, he rubs it on his elbows every night to keep them soft' ... 'Eileen has got her pain' ... 'Georgina Hogg has three hairs on her chin when she doesn't pull them out. Georgina has had a letter from her cousin which I read.'

These were memorable utterances. Other items which he aired in the same breath, such as, 'There's been a cobweb on the third landing for two weeks, four days and fifteen hours, not including the time for the making' – these were received with delight or indifference according to mood, and forgotten.

His mother told him repeatedly, 'I've told you repeatedly, you are not to enter the maids' rooms. After all, they are entitled to their privacy.'

As he grew older he learned to conceal the sensational portions of his knowledge, imparting only what was necessary to promote his reputation for being remarkably observant. In those days his father was capable of saying, on the strength of a school report,

'I always knew Laurence would outgrow that morbid phase.'

'Let's hope he has,' Helena Manders had said. Parents change. In those days, Laurence was aware that she half-suspected him of practising some vague sexual perversion which she could not name, would not envisage, and which in any case he did not practise. Then, it was almost to put her at ease, to assure her that he was the same Laurence as of old, that he said, during the holidays of his last term,

'Eileen is going to have a baby.'

'She's a good Catholic girl,' Helena protested; she was herself a Catholic since her marriage. None the less, on challenging Eileen in the kitchen, the case turned out to be so. Eileen, moreover, defiantly refused to name the man. Laurence was able to provide this information.

'I've always kept up with Eileen's correspondence,' he explained. 'It enlivens the school holidays.'

'You've been in that poor girl's room, reading her letters behind her back, the poor thing!'

'Shall I tell you what her boy friend wrote?' Laurence said tyrannously.

'I'm shocked as you know,' she said, accepting that this made no impression. 'How you, a good Catholic – but apart from that, it's illegal, I believe, to read letters addressed to others,' she said, defeated.

Merely to give her the last word he pointed out, 'Well, you've got them married, my dear. A good Catholic marriage. That's the happy result of my shocking perusal of Eileen's letters.'

'The end doesn't justify the means.'

Pat it came out just as he had expected. An answer for everything. All the same, incidents like this helped to deaden the blow when she realized that Laurence was abandoning, and finally had abandoned religion.

Louisa Jepp sat at the table writing out her football pools as she waited for Laurence.

'Come down!' she said to the ceiling, 'and leave off your snooping, dear.'

As soon as he appeared she told him, 'If Manchester City had won last week I should have got thirty thousand.'

Louisa folded her football coupon and placed it under the clock. She gave all her attention to Laurence and his breakfast.

She was half-gipsy, the dark one and the youngest of a large red-haired family, which at the time of her birth owed its prosperity to the father's success as a corn dealer. The success was owing to good fortune in the first place, his having broken jail while waiting to come before the Bench, never afterwards returning to his gipsy tribe. It was a hundred and thirty years after this event that Louisa was sitting down to breakfast with Laurence.

Louisa's hair remains black, though there is not much of it. She is short, and seen from the side especially, her form resembles a neat double potato just turned up from the soil with its small round head, its body from which hang the roots, her two thin legs below her full brown skirt and corpulence. Her face, from the front, is square, receding in planes like a prism. The main lines on her face are deep, they must have been in gradual evidence since she was thirty, they seemed carved to the bone. But the little wrinkles are superficial, brushing the surface of her skin, coming and going like innumerable stars when she puckers a smile or unfolds a look of surprise. Her eyes are deep-set and black. Her hands and feet very small. She wears rimless spectacles. She is still alive, not much changed from that day when Laurence came down to breakfast. She was wearing a brown dress, a brown woollen jacket with gilt buttons, and a pair of diamond earrings embedded in her ears.

When Laurence had sized her up, as he always did with everyone, he dipped his fork into a jar and drew out something long, white and pickled.

'What can this be?'

'Chid'lings,' she said. 'They are beautiful.'

He was accustomed to Louisa's food: whelks, periwinkles, milts and roes, chitterlings and sweetbreads, giblets, brains and the tripes of ruminating animals. Louisa prepared them at long ease, by many processes of affusion, diffusion and immersion, requiring many pans of brine, many purifications and simmerings, much sousing and sweetening by slow degrees. She seldom bought an ordinary cut or joint, and held that people who went through life ignoring the inward vitals of shells and beasts didn't know what was good for them.

'If you won thirty thousand in the pool, what would you do?' Laurence said.

'Buy a boat,' she replied.

'I would paddle you up and down the river,' Laurence said. 'A houseboat would be nice. Do you remember that fortnight on the houseboat, my first year at prep school?'

'I mean a boat for crossing the sea. Yes, it was lovely on the houseboat.'

'A yacht? Oh, how grand.'

'Well, a good-sized boat,' said Louisa, 'that's what I'd buy. Suitable for crossing the Channel.'

'A motor cruiser,' Laurence suggested.

'That's about it,' she said.

'Oh, how grand.'

She did not reply, for he had gone too far with his 'Oh, how grand!'

'We could do the Mediterranean,' he said.

'Oh, how grand,' she said.

'Wouldn't it be more fun to buy a house?' Laurence had just remembered his mother's plea, 'If you get an opportunity do try to persuade her to take a little money from us and live comfortably in her own house.'

She answered, 'No. But if I won a smaller sum I'd buy this cottage. I'm sure Mr Webster would sell.'

'Oh, I'd love to think of you having the cottage for your very own. Smugglers Retreat is such a dear little house.' Even as he spoke Laurence knew that phrases like 'your very own' and 'dear little house' betrayed what he was leading up to, they were not his grandmother's style.

'I know what you're leading up to,' said Louisa. 'Help yourself to the cigarettes.'

'I have my own. Why won't you let father buy the cottage for you? He can afford it.'

'I manage very nicely,' said Louisa. 'Smoke one of these – they come from Bulgaria.'

'Oh, how grand!' But he added, 'How extremely smart and where did you get them from?'

'Bulgaria. I think through Tangiers.'

Laurence examined the cigarette. His grandmother, a perpetual surprise. She rented the cottage, lived as an old-age pensioner.

Her daughter Helena said frequently, 'God knows how she manages. But she always seems to have plenty of everything.'

Helena would tell her friends, 'My mother won't accept a penny. Most independent; the Protestant virtues, you know. God knows how she manages. Of course, she's half gipsy, she has the instinct for contriving ways and means.'

'Really! Then you have gipsy blood, Helena? Really, and you so fair, how romantic. One would never have thought –'

'Oh, it comes out in me sometimes,' Helena would say.

It was during the past four years, since the death of her husband, penniless, that Louisa had revealed, by small tokens and bit by bit, an aptitude for acquiring alien impenetrable luxuries.

Manders' Figs in Syrup, with its seventy-year-old trademark – an oriental female yearning her draped form towards, and apparently worshipping a fig tree – was the only commodity that Louisa was willing to accept from her daughter's direction. Louisa distributed the brown sealed jars of this confection among her acquaintance; it kept them in mind of the living reality underlying their verbal tradition, 'Mrs Jepp's daughter was a great beauty, she married into Manders' Figs in Syrup.'

'Tell your father,' said Louisa, 'that I have not written to thank him because he is too busy to read letters. He will like the Bulgarian cigarettes. They smell very high. Did he like *my* figs?'

'Oh yes, he was much amused.'

'So your mother told me when she wrote last. Did he *like* them?'

'Loved them, I'm sure. But we were awfully tickled.'

Louisa, in her passion for pickling and preserving, keeps up with the newest methods. Some foods go into jars, others into tins sealed by her domestic canning machine. When Louisa's own figs in syrup, two cans of them with neatly pencilled labels, had arrived for Sir Edwin Manders, Helena had felt uneasy at first.

'Is she having a lark with us, Edwin?'

'Of course she is.'

Helena was not sure what sort of a lark. She wrote to Louisa that they were all very amused.

'Did they enjoy the figs?' Louisa pressed Laurence.

'Yes, they were lovely.'

'They are as good as Manders', dear, but don't tell your father I said so.'

'Better than Manders',' Laurence said.

'Did you taste some, then?'

'Not actually. But I know they were most enjoyable, Mother said' (which Helena had not said).

'Well, that's what I sent them for. To be enjoyed. You shall have some later. I don't know what they are talking about – "much amused". Tell your father that I'm giving him the cigarettes for enjoyment, tell him that, my dear.'

Laurence was smoking his Bulgarian. 'Most heady,' he said. 'But Mother takes a fit when you send expensive presents. She knows you have to deny yourself and –'

He was about to say 'pinch and scrape', using his mother's lamenting words; but this would have roused the old lady. Besides, the phrase was obviously inaccurate; his grandmother was sur-rounded by her sufficiency, always behind which hovered a suspicion of restrained luxury. Even her curious dishes seemed chosen from an expansive economy of spirit rather than any consideration of their cost in money.

'Helena is a sweet girl, but she does deceive herself. I'm not in need of anything, as she could very well see, if she took the trouble. There is no need for Helena to grieve on my account.'

Laurence was away all day, with his long legs in his small swift car, gone to look round and about the familiar countryside and coastline, gone to meet friends of his own stamp and education, whom he sometimes brought back to show off to them his funny delicious grandmother. Louisa Jepp did many things during that day. She fed the pigeons and rested. Rather earnestly, she brought from its place a loaf of white bread, cut the crust off one end, examined the loaf, cut another slice, and looked again. After the third slice she began at the other end, cutting the crust, peering at the loaf until, at the fourth slice, she smiled at what she saw, and patting the slices into place again put back the loaf in the tin marked 'bread'.

At nine o'clock Laurence returned. The sitting-room which looked out on the village was very oblong in shape. Here he found his grandmother with visitors, three men. They had been playing rummy, but now they were taking Louisa's refreshments, seated along each side of the room. One was in an invalid chair; this was a young man, not more than twenty-four.

'Mr Hogarth, my grandson; my grandson, Mr Webster; and this is *young* Mr Hogarth. My grandson is on the B.B.C., my daughter's son, Lady Manders. You've heard him give the commentaries on the football and the races, Laurence Manders.'

'Heard you last Saturday.' This was Mr Webster, the oldest guest, almost as old as Louisa.

'Saw you this morning,' Laurence said.

Mr Webster looked surprised.

'With the baker's van,' Laurence added.

Louisa said, 'Laurence is very observant, he has to be for his job.'

Laurence, who was aglow from several drinks, spoke the obliging banality, 'I never forget a face', and turning to the elder Hogarth he said, 'For instance, I'm sure I've seen your face somewhere before.' But here, Laurence began to lose certainty. 'At least – you resemble someone I know but I don't know who.'

The elder Hogarth looked hopelessly at Louisa, while his son, the boy in the invalid chair, said, 'He looks like me. Have you seen me before?'

Laurence looked at him.

'No,' he said, 'I haven't. Nobody at all like you.'

Then, in case he should have said the wrong thing, considering the young man was a cripple, Laurence rattled on.

'I may take up detective work one of these days. It would be quite my sort of thing.'

'Oh no, you could never be a detective, Laurence,' Louisa said, very seriously.

'Now, why not?'

'You have to be cunning to be a detective. The C.I.D. are terribly sly and private detectives will stoop to anything. You aren't a bit sly, dear.'

'I notice extraordinary things,' Laurence boasted casually, lolling his brown head along the back of the sofa. 'Things which people think are concealed. Awful to be like that, isn't it?'

Laurence had the feeling that they didn't like him, they suspected him. He got nervous, and couldn't seem to say anything right. They more and more seemed not to like him as he went on and on compulsively about the wonderful sleuth he would make. And all the time he was talking he actually was taking them in, sleuth-like.

Their presence in his grandmother's house was strange and surprising, and for that reason alone did not really surprise him. Louisa is pouring out tea. She calls the young Hogarth 'Andrew'. His father is 'Mervyn' to her. Webster is 'Mr Webster'.

Mr Webster with his white hair, white moustache and dark nautical jacket is not easy to identify with his early-morning appearance – the tradesman in a sandy-brown overall who calls with the bread: Laurence felt pleased with himself for recognizing Mr Webster, who wore brown suede shoes, size ten by Laurence's discernment, whose age might be going on seventy-five, and who, by his voice, is a Sussex man.

Mervyn Hogarth was thin and small. He had a washed-out sandy colouring. Louisa had prepared for him a thin slice of brown bread and butter.

'Mervyn has to eat often, in small snacks, for his gastric trouble,' Louisa explained. By his speech, the elder Hogarth is a knowing metropolitan product. God knows what he is doing at Louisa's, why he is on sufficiently familiar visiting terms for first names and gastric confidences. But Laurence was not a wonderer. He observed that the elder Hogarth wore unpressed flannels and an old ginger tweed jacket with the air of one who can afford to go careless. The son Andrew, with full red lips, was square and large-faced with glasses. He was paralysed in the legs.

As Louisa asked Laurence, 'Did you have a nice outing, dear?' Andrew winked at him.

Laurence resented this, an injustice to his grandmother. He felt averse to entering a patronizing conspiracy with Andrew against the old lady; he was on holiday for a special reason connected with a love affair, he wanted a change from the complications of belonging to a sophisticated social group. The grandmother refreshed him, she was not to be winked about. And so Laurence smiled at Andrew, as if to say, 'I acknowledge your wink. I cannot make it out at all. I take it you mean something pleasant.'

Andrew started looking round the room; he seemed to have missed something that should be there. At last he fixed on the box of Bulgarian cigarettes on Louisa's sideboard; reaching out he opened the box and helped himself to one. Mr Webster tried to exchange a glance with Louisa disapproving of her guest's manners, but she would not be drawn in to it. She rose and passed the open box to Laurence.

Andrew told him, 'They are Bulgarian.'

'Yes, I know. Rather odd, aren't they?'

'They grow on one,' Andrew remarked.

'Bulgarian!' his father exclaimed. 'I must try one!'

Louisa silently passed the cigarettes. She inclined her head demurely towards Laurence, acknowledging an unavoidable truth: the fact that three stubbed-out fat Bulgarian ends already lay in the ash-tray beside Mervyn Hogarth's chair.

Louisa sat passively witnessing Hogarth's performance as he affected to savour a hitherto untried brand of cigarette.

'My dear Louisa, how exotic! I don't think I could cope with many of these. So strong and so ... what shall I say?'

'Pungent,' said Louisa patiently, as one who has heard the same word said before by the same man in the same place.

'*Pungent*,' Mervyn repeated, as if she had hit on the one only precise word.

He continued, 'A flavour of – the Balkans, a tang as of – of –'

Louisa obliged him again, 'Goats' milk.'

'That's it! Goats' milk.'

Louisa's black shiny buttons of eyes turned openly on Laurence. He was watching the man's face; he glanced towards the ash-tray with its evidence of the pose, then looked at Mervyn again. Louisa began to giggle inaudibly as if she were gently shaking a bottle of cough-mixture within herself. Mr Webster caught her movement with the corner of his eye. From where he was seated, and his neck being stiff, he had to swivel round from the waist to get a better view of Louisa. At this sign, her face puckered slightly, but presently she composed herself like a schoolgirl.

Laurence said to Andrew, 'Do you live round here?'

Father and son replied simultaneously. Mervyn said, 'Oh, no'; Andrew said, 'Oh, yes.'

Louisa's mirth got the better of her, and though her lips were shut tight she whinnied through her nose like a pony. Mr Webster clicked his cup into his saucer as if the walls had spoken.

The Hogarths immediately attempted to rectify their blunder.

Both started together again – Mervyn: 'Well, we live in London mostly –' Andrew: 'I mean, we're here most of the time –' The father decided to let Andrew take over.

'And we sometimes go abroad,' he concluded limply.

Laurence looked at his watch, and said hastily to Andrew, 'Coming for a drink? There's about fifteen minutes to closing.' Then he saw his blunder. For the moment the boy had looked quite normal, not a cripple at all.

'Not tonight thanks. Another time, if you're staying,' Andrew said, unsurprised.

'Laurence is stopping till the end of the week,' said Louisa.

Laurence hurried out. They could hear his footsteps crossing the quiet road and down the village street towards the Rose and Crown.

Mr Webster spoke. 'Charming boy.'

Louisa said, 'Yes, and so clever.'

'Interesting lad,' Mervyn said.

'I was wondering . . .' said Andrew.

'What, dear?' Louisa asked him.

'Hadn't we better clear off till next week?'

Mr Webster twisted round to face the old lady. 'Mrs Jepp,' he said, 'I did not think you would permit your grandson meeting us. I understood he was to be out this evening. I trust he will not be upset in any way.'

'My!' said Louisa graciously. 'He won't be upset, Mr Webster. Young people are very democratic these days.'

That was not what had been meant. Mervyn spoke next.

'I think he will ask questions. It's only natural, Louisa, after all, what do you expect?' He lit one of the Bulgarian cigarettes.

'Whatever questions should he ask?'

'He is bound to wonder. . . .' said Andrew.

'He's bound to ask who we are, what we're doing here,' said Mervyn.

Mr Webster looked sadly at Mervyn, pained by some crudity in the other's words.

'My!' said Louisa. 'Laurence will certainly ask all about you. Would you care for another game, gentlemen?'

Mervyn looked at the clock.

Andrew said, 'He'll be back after the pub closes, won't he?'

Mr Webster smiled paternally at Louisa. 'The matter is not urgent,' he said, 'we can leave our business till the end of the week, if you know of an evening when your grandson will be out.'

'It can be discussed in front of Laurence,' she said. 'Laurence is a dear boy.'

'Of course,' said Mervyn.

'That's just what we mean,' said Andrew. 'The dear boy shouldn't be made to wonder –'

Louisa looked a little impatient. Something was defeating her. 'I did hope,' she said, 'that we could avoid making any difference between Laurence and ourselves. I assure you, with discretion we could say all we want to say in Laurence's presence. He has not got a suspicious nature.'

'Ah, discretion,' Mr Webster said, 'my dear Mrs Jepp, discretion is always desirable.'

Louisa beamed warmly at him, as at one who had come nearest to understanding her.

Mervyn spoke. 'I understand you, Louisa. You can't bear to participate in separated worlds. You have the instinct for unity, for coordinating the inconsistent elements of experience; you have the passion for picking up the idle phenomena of life and piecing them together. That is your ideal, it used to be mine. Reality, however, refuses to accommodate the idealist. It is difficult at your age to grasp a fact which you have never had occasion to recognize, but –'

'I don't know what you mean,' Louisa said, 'not at any age I wouldn't know.'

'Of course.'

'You are too far away,' she said, but then she perked up, 'Now Mervyn, if you feel I'm too old-fashioned in my ways I will quite understand. You may always withdraw from our arrangements.'

Mervyn, who had stood up, sat down again. Andrew gave an unsmiling laugh which caused Louisa to look at him with surprise.

Andrew responded: 'He spoke about doing detective work. He seems to be quite smart in the head.'

'Laurence is doing nicely on the wireless. He would never make a detective, nothing so low.'

'He would make a good informer,' Andrew said, and from the privilege of his invalid chair looked squarely at her.

'My, you need not continue with us, Andrew dear, if anything troubles you. In which case, of course, *we* shouldn't continue, should we?' She looked at Mervyn and Mr Webster, but they did not answer. They rose then, to leave. As he took her hand Mr Webster said, 'You see, Mrs Jepp, your dear grandson is exceedingly observant. That was the only reason I had for questioning the wisdom.'

Louisa laughed, 'Oh, he never misses anything. I've never met anyone like him for getting the details. But, you know, the dear boy can't put two and two together.'

'You mean,' said Mervyn, 'that he lacks the faculty of reflection?'

'I mean,' said Laurence's grandmother, 'that he could be more intelligent in some ways than he is. But he's clever enough to get on in the world, and he has a sweet nature, that's what matters.'

'And if he asks any questions . . .' said Andrew.

'Oh, he *will* ask questions,' Louisa answered him.

There was no doing anything with her.

'Oh, Mrs Jepp, you will be discreet won't you? I'm sure you will,' said Mr Webster.

'My grandson can't put two and two together – not so's to make four.' She looked rather amused so as to make them rather uncomfortable.

'He's leaving on Friday?' Mervyn asked.

'Yes, I'm afraid so.'

'Friday evening then?' said Mervyn.

'Yes,' she answered with melancholy.

'See you Friday,' said Andrew.

'Thank you, Mrs Jepp, for a most pleasant evening.' said Mr Webster.

Because Laurence had started writing a letter, resting the paper on a book on his knee, Louisa was clearing part of the table for him, saying, 'Come, love, sit up at the table, it's more comfortable.'

'No, I always write like this.'

Louisa spread a white cloth over the corner reserved for Laurence.

'Always put a white cloth under your papers when you write a letter. It's good for your eyes because it reflects back the light. Come, dear, sit up at the table.'

Laurence shifted to the table and continued writing. After a few minutes he said, 'The white cloth does make a difference. Much pleasanter.'

Louisa, lying full-length on the sofa by the little back window where she rested till tea-time in the afternoons, replied dozily, 'When I told Mervyn Hogarth of that little trick, he started working out in his head whether it could be effective or not, all about light-rays and optics. "Try it, Mervyn," I said, "just try it, then you'll know for certain that I'm right."'

'Of course,' Laurence reflected absently, 'it may be due to something psychological.'

'Oh, it's something psychological all right,' said Louisa surprisingly and imponderably. Then she closed her eyes.

She opened them again a few seconds later to say, 'If it's your mother you're writing to give her my love.'

'I'm writing to Caroline, actually.'

'Then give her my love and say I hope she feels better than she was at Easter. How has she been lately?'

'Miserable. She's gone away to some religious place in the north for a rest.'

'She won't get much of a rest in a religious place.'

'That's what I thought. But this is one of Mother's ideas. She gets together with her priests and builds these buildings. Then they dedicate them to a saint. Then Mother sends her friends to stay in them.'

'But Caroline isn't a Catholic.'

'She's just become one.'

'I *thought* she was looking thin. How does that affect you, dear?'

'Well, of course Caroline's left me, in a way. At least, she's gone to live somewhere else.'

'Well!' said the old woman, 'that's a nice thing!'

'We might get married some day.'

'Ah, and if not?' She looked at him with a reserved wonder as she added, 'Does Caroline know what she's doing? The one certain way for a woman to hold a man is to leave him for religion. I've known it happen. The man might get another girl, but he never can be happy with anyone else after a girl has left him for religious reasons. *She* secures him for good.'

'Is that really true?' Laurence said. 'How very jolly. I must tell Caroline.'

'Oh well, my love, it's all for the best. I hope you can marry her, soon. They wouldn't make you become a Catholic, you only have to promise to bring up the children Catholics. And after all, children these days make up their own minds when they grow up. And there's nothing wrong in being a Catholic if you want to be one.'

'It's a bit complicated,' Laurence said. 'Poor Caroline isn't well.'

'Poor Caroline. That's religion for you. Give her my love and tell her to come down here. I'll feed her up, I daresay everything will come out all right.'

'Grandmother has just dozed off again,' Laurence wrote, 'after looking up to inquire after you. The news of your conversion caused a serious expression, on her face. Made her look like one of Rembrandt's old women, but she rapidly regained her Louisa face. She wants you here, to give you things to eat.

'I hated seeing your train out at Euston and mooned off afterwards with thoughts of following you on the evening train. Met the Baron in Piccadilly Underground and walking back with him to the bookshop fell under his influence and decided against. He argued, "The presence of a non-believer in a Catholic establishment upsets them if the unbeliever is not interested in acquiring their faith. Those places always advertise their welcome to the faithless. However, if you go merely looking for Caroline, it will upset them, you will not be welcome. Moreover, they will have it in for Caroline, for being manifestly more desirable to you than their faith." On the whole, I decided it would be cloddish to barge in, just as well as it has turned out.

'I couldn't face the flat so went over to Hampstead. Father was in, Mother out. He let fall something that rather worries me. Apparently there's a woman by name of Hogg at the outfit you are staying at. She's a sort of manageress. Mother got her the job. God knows why. We all loathe her. That's why we've always gone out of our way for her really. She's that Georgina Hogg I think I've mentioned, the one who used to be a kind of nursery-governess before we went to school. She got married but her husband left her. Poor bastard, no wonder. We used to feel sorry for him. She suffers from chronic righteousness, exerts a sort of moral blackmail. Mother has a conscience about her –

about hating her so much I mean, is terrified of her but won't admit it. Father calls her Manders' Mortification. Of course she's harmless really if you don't let her get under your skin. I think I could handle the woman, at least I used to. But best to avoid her, darling. I hope you won't come across her. I confronted mother with her damned silliness in sending you to a place where Georgina is, at a time when you're feeling limp. She looked a bit guilty but said, "Oh, Caroline will put Georgina in her place." I do hope you will. If she upsets you, leave immediately and come down here to be plumped up. Such things are happening down here!

'Arrived on Sunday night. My little grandmother is a mighty woman, as I always knew. I've discovered such things! She runs a *gang*. I'm completely in the dark as to what sort of gang, but I should probably think they are Communist spies. Three men. A father and son. The son's a cripple, poor chap. The father has a decided air of one *manqué*. The third gangster is rather a love, like a retired merchant sailor, fairly old. He's sweet on Grandmother. He owns the local bakery and delivers the bread himself.

'I don't know how far Grandmother is implicated in their activities, but she's certainly the boss. She's handsomely well-off. I think she only draws her pension to avoid suspicion. Do you know where she keeps her capital? In the *bread*. She sticks diamonds in the bread. Without a word of exaggeration, I came across a loaf weirdly cut at both ends, and in one end diamonds, real ones. I wondered what the hell they were at first, and picked out one of the stones ever so carefully. Diamonds look so different when they aren't set in jewellery. When I saw what it was, I put the stone back in its place. Grandmother has no idea that I'm on to this, of course. Isn't she a wonder? I wonder what her racket is. I don't think seriously of course that they are spies, but criminals of some sort. The thing is, Grandmother isn't being used, she's running the show. The main thing is, Mother mustn't find out, so be most careful, my love, what you say.

'I intend to find everything out, even if it means taking an extra week and mucking up Christmas. I've started compiling a dossier.

'Any ideas on the subject, let me know. Personally, I think Grandmother is having the time of her life, but it might be serious for her if the men are caught. I can't begin to guess what they'd be caught at. They may be jewel thieves, but that doesn't fit in with the sweet naval old fellow's character. Anything fits G'mother's.

'Grandmother openly refers to them as "my gang", airy as a Soho slender. Says they come to play cards. I met them here the other night, since when I've been snooping. I wish you would come for a few days and help me "put two & two together" as G'mother says. I hope you don't get the jitters at St Philumena's. Take it from me, you have to pick and choose amongst Catholic society in England, the wrong sort can drive you nuts. Mother knows she's done the wrong thing in sending you there. It's her passion for founding "Centres" and peopling them, gets the better of her. Father swears she'll start a schism.

'I expect a letter from you tomorrow. Longing to hear that you have got Mrs Hogg under control. It would be rather fun in a way if you had a set-to with her. I'd like to be there if you did. *There*, but concealed.'

Louisa opened her eyes and said, 'Put the kettle on, dear.'

Laurence laid down his pen. He asked her, 'Who d'you think is in charge of that religious place Caroline's gone to?'

'Who, dear?'

'Mrs Hogg.'

'In charge! I thought it was a convent.'

'No, only a Centre. Georgina is housekeeper or something.'

'Does your mother know that?'

'Yes, she gave her the job.'

'I think something is happening to Helena's mind,' said Louisa.

'Mrs Hogg! Just think of her, Grandmother, worming in on Caroline.'

'Mrs Hogg,' said Louisa, as if she'd never heard the like. 'Mrs Hogg. Well, Caroline will fix her.'

Laurence went into the scullery to fill the kettle, and shouted from there,

'You haven't seen her lately?'

His grandmother was silent. But as he returned and placed the kettle on the black coal stove, Louisa told him,

'I haven't seen her for years. A few months ago your Mother wrote to suggest that Georgina Hogg should come and live here as a companion for me.'

Laurence chuckled.

'You said no bloody fear, I suppose.'

'I said that I would not wish to have that poisonous woman in my house for a five-second visit. It fairly puts you against Catholics, a person like that.'

Laurence took up his pen again.

'I detest that woman,' said Louisa.

'Grandmother is awake now,' Laurence wrote. 'She has been delivering herself of her views on Ma Hogg. "Poisonous" she says. It makes me rather sorry for the old Hogg being so dislikable. Truly, she has to be savoured to be believed.'

'Tell Caroline,' Louisa broke in, 'to be careful of Mrs Hogg. Say she's dangerous.'

'I've told her,' Laurence said.

He finished his letter, and read it over.

After tea he added to it, 'P.S. I forgot to mention Grandmother's cheque book. According to the stubs she donates the exact sum of her pension each week to the Prisoners' Aid Society.'

He sealed the letter, then went to post it.

TWO

A storm, fierce enough to hold up the shipping at the mouth of the Mersey, ranged far enough inland to keep Caroline Rose indoors, where she paced the pale green corridors. Not for exercise but in order to think. A thinking-place of green corridors. The Pilgrim Centre of St Philumena.

'Taking exercise.' This was Mrs Hogg tacking on to her, infuriating. Taking exercise. Not a question, a statement.

'Good afternoon,' said Caroline.

'And feeling lonely,' said Mrs Hogg with her sort of smile. Feeling lonely, taking exercise. Caroline made no answer. The small perfect idea which had been crystallizing in her mind went all to mist. All right, I am at your disposal. Eat me, bloodywell take the lot. I am feeling lonely. Rome has spoken.

'Another time,' said Mrs Hogg, 'you don't want to make a private Retreat. You want to come in the summer with one of the big pilgrimages for one of the big Feasts.'

'Do I?' Caroline said.

'Yes,' said Mrs Hogg. 'That's what you want to do. Please call me Georgina by the way. I'll call you Caroline. Sometimes we have as many as a hundred and thirty pilgrims to stay. And of course thousands for the day pilgrimages. Sir Edwin and Lady Manders and Father Ingrid had no idea what they started when they started St Philumena's. You must meet the Manders.'

'I know them,' said Caroline.

'Oh, you do. Are you one of their converts? They are always making converts.'

'Converts to what?' said Caroline in the imperative need to be difficult. Caroline vented in her mind her private formula: *You are damned. I condemn you to eternal flames. You are* caput, *as good as finished, you have had it, my dear.* More expressive, and therefore more satisfying than merely 'Go to hell', and only a little less functional than a small boy's 'Bang-bang, you're dead!'

'Converts to the Faith, of course,' Mrs Hogg was saying.

During her three days' stay at St Philumena's she had already observed Mrs Hogg. On her first evening Caroline overheard her:

'You have to take what's put before you here. Sometimes we have as many as a hundred and thirty pilgrims. Suppose a hundred and thirty people all wanted tea without milk –'

Her victim, a young lawyer who was recovering from dipsomania, had replied, 'But I only say don't *trouble* to put milk in mine.'

'It isn't what you say, it's what you get.'

They sat later at a polished oak refectory table silently eating a suet-laden supper which represented the monastic idea at St Philumena's. Their mouths worked silently, rhythmically, chew-pause-chew-pause-swallow-pause-chew. A sister from the convent next door was reading aloud the 'holy work' prescribed for mealtimes. Caroline recognized the Epistle of St John, and listened, fixing her eyes on the white blouse of Mrs Hogg opposite. Soon her mind was on Mrs Hogg, and the recent dispute about the tea. She began to take in the woman's details: an angular face, cropped white hair, no eyelashes, rimless glasses, a small fat nose of which the tip was twitching as she ate, very thin neck, a colossal bosom. Caroline realized that she had been staring at Mrs Hogg's breasts for some time, and was aware at the same moment that the woman's nipples were showing dark and prominent through her cotton blouse. The woman was apparently wearing nothing underneath. Caroline looked swiftly away, sickened at the sight, for she was prim; her sins of the flesh had been fastidious always.

That was the first evening.

And this was the third day. At the end of the long corridor they turned. Caroline looked at her watch. Mrs Hogg did not go away.

'The Manders converted you. They are always converting somebody.'

'No. Not in my case, they didn't.'

'The Manders are *very* nice people,' said Mrs Hogg defensively.

'Charming people.'

'*Very* good people,' Mrs Hogg insisted.

'I agree,' said Caroline.

'You couldn't possibly disagree. What made you a Catholic then?'

'Many reasons,' Caroline said, 'which are not too easy to define: and so I prefer not to discuss them.'

'Mm . . . I know your type,' Mrs Hogg said, 'I got your type the first evening you came. There's a lot of the Protestant about you still. You'll have to get rid of it. You're the sort that doesn't mix. Catholics are very good mixers. Why won't you talk about your conversion? Conversion's a wonderful thing. It's not *Catholic* not to talk about it.'

The woman was a funny old thing in her way. Caroline suddenly felt light-hearted. She giggled and looked again at her watch.

'I must be going.'

'Benediction isn't till three o'clock.'

'Oh, but I've come here for rest and quiet.'

'But you're not in Retreat.'

'Oh yes, you know, I *am* in retreat.' Then Caroline remembered that the popular meaning of 'retreat' in religious circles was an organized affair, not a private retiring from customary activities, so as to possess one's soul in peace. She added, 'I mean, I've retreated from London, and now I'm here for rest and quiet.'

'You were speaking plenty to that young lawyer this morning.'

In her private neurotic amusement Caroline decided to yield. Ten more minutes of Mrs Hogg. The rain pelted with sudden fury against the windows while she turned to the woman with a patronizing patience.

'Tell me about yourself, Mrs Hogg.'

Mrs Hogg had recently been appointed Catering Warden. 'If it wasn't for the Faith I couldn't hold down the job. On my feet from six till two, then on again at three and then two hours' break till supper and then there's the breakfast to think about. And I've got a great number of Crosses. That young lawyer you've got in with, the other night he said, "I don't take milk in my tea" – did you hear him? Sometimes we have as many as a hundred and thirty. Suppose a hundred and thirty people wanted tea without milk –'

'Well, that would be fairly easy,' said Caroline.

'Suppose they each wanted something different.'

'All at the same time?' said Caroline.

Seeing Mrs Hogg's expression at this moment, Caroline thought, 'Now it has struck her that I'm an enemy of the Faith.'

But Mrs Hogg righted herself; her mechanism was regulated for a chat.

'I'll tell you how I came here – it was a miracle. Our Lady sent me.'

But Caroline's mood had changed again. Her sophisticated forbearance departed and constriction took its place; a pinching irritated sense of being with something abominable, not to be tolerated. She had a sudden intense desire to clean her teeth.

'Oh tell me about the miracle,' Caroline said. Her tone was slightly menacing. 'Tell me all the details.' These scatty women with their miracles. Caroline thought, 'I hate all women and of all women Mrs Hogg. My nerves are starting up again. The next few eternal minutes are important. I must mind what I say. Keep aloof. Watch my manners at all costs.'

'Well,' Mrs Hogg was saying, 'I was of two minds whether to take a post in Bristol with a lady who was having her baby at home – I'm a registered midwife, you know, although most of my experience has been as a governess. One time I was housekeeper to a priest for two years. That was in Birmingham. He was sent to Canada in 1935, and when we said good-bye he said, "Well, Mrs Hogg –"'

'What about the miracle?' said Caroline, and to cover up her testiness overdid it and added, 'I can't hear enough about miracles.'

And, privately she consoled herself with the words, 'Little dear' – for that was how she spoke to herself on occasion – 'you will receive letters tomorrow morning from the civilized world.'

'Well, you know,' Mrs Hogg was saying, 'to *me* it was a miracle. I was debating whether to take the job in Bristol or a permanent place in the north with a deaf lady. A letter arrived, it was a Tuesday morning, to say that the lady in Bristol had gone to hospital because of some complications, and was having her baby there. The husband sent me a week's money. Then in the afternoon another letter arrived from the other place. No, I'm wrong, it was the next morning. The deaf lady had died. So there I was without a job. So I said to Our Lady, "What am I going to do now?" and Our Lady said, "Go back to St Philumena's and think it over." I'd already stayed at St Philumena's on one of the big Retreats –'

'Did you actually hear a voice?' Caroline inquired.

'A voice?'

'I mean, when you say, "Our Lady said", do you mean she spoke audibly to you?'

'Oh no. But that's how Our Lady always speaks to me. I ask a question and she answers.'

'How do you hear her answer, then?'

'The words come to me – but of course you won't know much about that. You have to be experienced in the spiritual life.'

'How do you know the words come from the Blessed Virgin?' Caroline persisted relentlessly. Mrs Hogg moved her upper lip into an indecent smile. Caroline thought: 'She desires the ecstasy of murdering me in some prolonged ritualistic orgy; she sees I am thin, angular, sharp, inquiring; she sees I am grisly about the truth; she sees I am well-dressed and good-looking. Perhaps she senses my weakness, my loathing of human flesh where the bulk outweighs the intelligence.'

Mrs Hogg continued: 'I know it was Our Lady's message because of what happened. I came to St Philumena's, and saw Lady Manders who was here just at that time. When I told her the position she said, "Now, there *is* a job for you here, if you like to try it. We want to get rid of the Catering Warden, she isn't strong enough for the job. It's hard work, but Our Lady would help you." So I came for a month's trial. That was in the autumn, and I'm loving it, every minute of it.'

'That was the miracle,' Caroline said.

'Oh, it *was* a miracle. My arriving here just when Lady Manders wanted to make a change in the staff. I only came, really, to think things over. But I can tell you, I don't have much chance to sit on my behind and think. It's hard work. And I always put duty first, before everything. And I don't mind the work; Our Lady helps me. When the kitchen girls grumble about the work, I always tell them, "Our Lady will do it for you." And she does.'

'In that case, there's no need for them to do it,' Caroline said.

'Now listen to me, Caroline,' said Mrs Hogg. 'You want to speak to a priest. You haven't really got the hang of the Catholic Faith. You want to speak to Father Ingrid.'

'You are wrong,' Caroline said. 'I've heard him speaking once from the pulpit. Once was enough. I must go now.'

The bell was ringing for Benediction. 'That's not the way to the chapel,' Mrs Hogg called after her as Caroline walked swiftly along the green-walled corridors.

Caroline did not reply. She went to her room and began to pack her things, neatly and calmly. St Philumena's was a dead loss, Caroline told herself; 'For one who demands much of life, there is always a certain amount of experience to be discarded as soon as one discovers its fruitlessness.'

She excelled at packing a suitcase. She told herself 'I'm good at packing a suitcase', forming these words in her mind to keep other words, other thoughts, from crowding in. The three days of St Philumena's were bleating to high heaven for formulation, but she kept them at bay as she muttered, 'Shoes there. Books here. The comb-bag in that corner. Blouses flat on the bed. Fold the arms. Like that. Then fold again. This way, that way. Hot-water bottle. Nothing rattling. Crucifix wedged in cotton wool. Catholic Truth Society pamphlet to read in the train. I am doing what I am doing.'

In this way, she subjugated St Philumena's for half an hour. She had devised the technique in the British Museum Reading Room almost a year ago, at a time when her brain was like a Guy Fawkes night, ideas cracking off in all directions, dark idiot-figures jumping round a fiery junk-heap in the centre.

In the train Caroline swung her case on to the rack and sat down. The case jutted out at an angle. Caroline got up and pushed it straight. She had the carriage to herself. After a while she rose again and moved the case to the middle of the rack, measuring by the mirror beneath until there was an equal space on either side. Then she sat down in her corner-seat facing it. She sat perfectly still while her thoughts became blind. Every now and then a cynical lucidity would overtake part of her mind, forcing her to comment on the fury of the other half. That was painful. She observed, 'The mocker is taking over.'

'Very funny, very funny,' said Caroline out loud. A woman just then passing in the corridor observed her talking to herself. Caroline thought, Good God, now my trouble is growing noticeable.

The shock of having been observed brought some relief. As her mental pain subsided, Caroline began to reflect. Am I justified?

I bloody well am. Carefully and intently she began to recollect what St Philumena's had been like.

On her second evening when she had joined the other residents in the recreation-room, 'I must remember they are called "pilgrims",' she thought. She had already made the blunder of referring to them as 'residents'.

Anyway, there were eight of them besides Caroline. She brought them one by one to mind as she sat, still as a telegraph post, in the train which carried her to London.

That evening she had looked very seldom at her fellow guests, but now revoking, she peered into their eyes, stared up and down at their clothes, scrutinized the very skin on their faces.

She recalled them, first singly, and then in a half-circle round the fireplace; she could even see herself.

And as the train chugged south, her memory dwelling continuously on the fireside group, while at the same time she repeated mentally the formula of the rosary, touched the beads imperceptibly in her pocket, which she did for its outward effect on her person, the automatic act of the rosary prevented her from fidgeting in her agitation, it stopped her talking aloud to herself, made her unnoticeable. For the group round St Philumena's fire inflamed her; after all, she was a most jumpy woman at the best of times.

Two nights ago that group were exchanging anecdotes about the treatment of Catholics in England by non-Catholics. It was their favourite theme.

'What do you think, they won't employ Catholics on the passenger transport where my mother lives.'

'Not one Catholic child got a scholarship. . . .'

'Forty per cent were Catholics, but not one . . .'

It was well known, said a large florid lady from the West of Ireland, that the University of Cambridge would not take Catholics.

'Oh no, that's not true,' Caroline said at once.

'And they do their best for to set the Catholics asunder,' the lady from the West of Ireland went on.

'Not noticeably,' Caroline said.

The young lawyer agreed with her, but his testimony was suspect. The lady from Ireland whispered aloud to her neighbour.

'He's curing from alcohol, poor lad.'

The lawyer added, 'Of course, there's always a prejudice in certain quarters,' which put him right with the company.

'My brother in the public library, when they found he was a Catholic ...'

As the atrocities mounted up, the lady from the West of Ireland continued to ply Caroline, 'What d'ye make of that? ... Isn't it awful? What d'ye think of it?'

At last, rising to leave, 'I think it very quaint,' Caroline answered.

Throughout, Mrs Hogg had been volubly present. She too had offered some relishes, had known what persecution was, and her eyes were frequently directed towards Caroline the suspect.

Recalling these proceedings, Caroline recalled too a similar fireside pattern, her family on the Jewish side with their friends, so long ago left behind her. She saw them again, nursing themselves in a half-circle as they indulged in their debauch of unreal suffering; 'Prejudice!' '... an outright insult!' Caroline thought, Catholics and Jews; the Chosen, infatuated with a tragic image of themselves. They are tragic only because they are so comical. But the thought of those fireside martyrs, Jews and Catholics, revolted Caroline with their funniness. She thought she might pull the emergency cord, halt the train, create a blinding distraction: and even while planning this action she reflected that she would not positively perform it.

But in her own rapacity for suffering, Caroline seized and held the images of the world she had left years ago and the world she had newly entered. She tugged and pulled the rosary in her pocket, while her thoughts, fine as teeth, went into action again and again with the fireside congregations of mock martyrs, their incongruity beside the real ones ... it was an insult.

It was in the dining-car that Caroline got round once more to Mrs Hogg. Mrs Hogg stuck in her mind like a lump of food on the chest which will move neither up nor down. Suddenly Caroline realized that she was bolting her lunch, and simultaneously the memory of mealtimes at St Philumena's returned, with the sight of Mrs Hogg chewing in rhythm with the reading from the Scriptures delivered in the sister's refined modulations: 'Beloved, let us love one another, love springs from God.... If a man boasts of loving God, while he hates his own brother, he is a liar ... the man who loves God must be one who loves his brother.'

Caroline thought, 'The demands of the Christian religion are exorbitant, they are outrageous. Christians who don't realize that from the start are not faithful. They are dishonest; their teachers are talking in their sleep. "Love one another ... brethren, beloved ... your brother, neighbours, love, love, love" – do they know what they are saying?'

She had stopped eating, was conscious of two things, a splitting headache and Mrs Hogg. These bemused patterers on the theme of love, had they faced Mrs Hogg in person? Returning to her carriage Caroline passed a married couple who had been staying at St Philumena's, on their way to the dining-car. They had been among the fireside company. She remembered that they were to have left today.

'Oh, it's you, Miss Rose! I didn't think you were leaving so soon.'

People were pressing to pass, which gave Caroline a chance to escape. 'I was called away,' she said, moving off.

The couple had been received into the Church two months ago, so they had told the company round the fire.

Their new-found faith was expressed in a rowdy contempt for the Church of England, in which the woman's father was a clergyman. 'Father was furious when we went over to Rome. Of course he's Anglo-Catholic; they have holy water and the saints; everything bar the Faith; too killing.' She was a large-boned and muscled woman in her mid-thirties. She had set in her final development, at the stage of athletic senior prefect. She had some hair on her face. Her lower lip had a minor pugilistic twist. Of the two, she made the more noise, but her husband, with his smooth thin face, high pink colouring, who looked as if he never needed to shave, was a good support for his wife as they sat round the fire at St Philumena's. He said, 'The wonderful thing about being a Catholic is that it makes life so easy. Everything easy for salvation and you can have a happy life. All the little things that the Protestants hate, like the statues and the medals, they all help us to have a happy life.' He finished there, as if he had filled up the required page of his school exercise book, and need state no more; he lay back in his chair, wiped his glasses, crossed his legs.

At this point the West of Ireland took over, warning them, 'Converts have a lot to learn. You can always tell a convert from a cradle Catholic. There's something different.'

The dipsomaniac lawyer, with his shiny blue suit, said, 'I like converts', and smiled weakly at Caroline. His smile faded away before Mrs Hogg's different smile.

At Crewe, Caroline got the compartment to herself again. She began to reflect that Mrs Hogg could easily become an obsession, the demon of that carnal hypocrisy which struck her mind whenever she came across a gathering of Catholics or Jews engaged in their morbid communal pleasures. She began to think of her life in London, her work, Laurence to whom she must send a wire; he would be amused by her account of St Philumena's. She began to giggle, felt drowsy, and, settling into her corner, fell asleep.

THREE

When Laurence returned to the cottage after posting his letter to Caroline his grandmother handed him a telegram.

He read it. 'It's from Caroline. She's back in London.'

'Yes, funny, I had a feeling it was from Caroline.' Louisa very often revealed a mild form of the gipsy's psychic faculties. 'Fancy, what a pity you've posted that letter to Liverpool.'

As Laurence set off to the post office again to telephone Caroline, he said, 'Shall I ask her to come down here?'

'Yes, certainly,' Louisa said with that inclination of her head which was a modified form of the regal gesture. When he was small she used to tell Laurence 'Don't just answer "Yes"; say "Yes, certainly", that's how Queen Mary always answers.'

'How do you know that, Grandmother?'

'A person told me.'

'Are you sure the person was telling the truth?'

'Oh yes, certainly.'

'Tell Caroline,' Louisa called after him, 'that I have some black-berries in my tins,' meaning by this to tell Laurence of her genuine desire for Caroline's visit.

'All right, I will.'

'And ask the post office to give you back the letter. There's no reason to send it all the way to Liverpool.'

'Oh, they won't fish it out without a fuss,' Laurence told her. 'They never give you back a letter, once it's posted. Not without a fuss.'

'Oh, what a pity!'

'It doesn't matter,' Laurence said. 'I'll be seeing Caroline. I wonder why she left so soon?'

'Yes, I wonder why.'

Caroline's number was engaged when he rang. The sky had cleared and the autumn sun, low in the sky, touched the countryside. He decided to go to Ladle Sands, a half-hour's walk, from where he could try Caroline's number again, and by which time the pubs would be open. He was impatient to talk to Caroline. His desire to get her interested and involved in the mystery surrounding his grandmother was almost a fulfilment of a more compelling desire to assert the continuing pattern of their intimacy.

Laurence had no success with Caroline's phone that night. He pursued the exchange with mounting insistence on the urgency of getting through; they continued to reply in benumbed and fatalistic tones that the phone was out of order, it had been reported.

A queer buzzing sound brought Caroline to the telephone just before midnight. 'Your receiver has been off. We've been trying to get a call through from Sussex.' They were extremely irate.

'It hasn't been off,' said Caroline.

'It must have been misplaced. Please replace your receiver.'

'And the call? Are you putting it through?'

'No. The caller has gone now.'

Caroline thought, 'Well, he will ring in the morning.' She lay on her divan staring out at the night sky beyond her balcony, too tired to draw the curtains. She was warmed by the knowledge that Laurence was near to hand, wanting to speak to her. She could rely on him to take her side, should there be any difficulty with Helena over her rapid departure from St Philumena's. On the whole she did not think there would be any difficulty with Helena.

Just then she heard the sound of a typewriter. It seemed to come through the wall on her left. It stopped, and was immediately followed by a voice remarking her own thoughts. It said: *On the whole she did not think there would be any difficulty with Helena.*

There seemed, then, to have been more than one voice: it was a recitative, a chanting in unison. It was something like a concurrent series of echoes. Caroline jumped up and over to the door. There was no one on the landing or on the staircase outside. She returned to her sitting-room and shut the door. Everything was quiet. The wall, from which direction the sounds had come, divided her sitting-room from the first-floor landing of a house converted into flats. Caroline's flat occupied the whole of this floor. She had felt sure the sounds had

come from the direction of the landing. Now she searched the tiny
flat. The opposite wall separated the bed-sitting-room from the
bathroom and kitchen. Everything was quiet there. She went out on
to the balcony from where she could see the whole length of Queen's
Gate. Two servicemen clattered up the street and turned into
Cromwell Road. The neighbouring balconies were dark and empty.
Caroline returned to the room, closed the windows, and drew the
curtains.

She had taken the flat four weeks ago. The house held six flats, most
of which were occupied by married couples or young men who went
out to their offices every day. Caroline knew the other tenants only by
sight, greeting them in passing on the staircase. There were occasional noises at night, when someone had a party, but usually the house
was quiet. Caroline tried to recall the tenants in the flat above hers.
She was not certain; they all passed her landing on their way upstairs
and she herself had never gone beyond the first floor.

A typewriter and a chorus of voices: What on earth are they up to at
this time of night? Caroline wondered. But what worried her were the
words they had used, coinciding so exactly with her own thoughts.

Then it began again. Tap-tappity-tap; the typewriter. And again,
the voices: Caroline ran out on to the landing, for it seemed quite
certain the sound came from that direction. No one was there. The
chanting reached her as she returned to her room, with these words
exactly:

What on earth are they up to at this time of night? Caroline wondered.
But what worried her were the words they had used, coinciding so exactly
with her own thoughts.

And then the typewriter again: tap-tap-tap. She was rooted. 'My
God!' she cried aloud. 'Am I going mad?'

As soon as she had said it, and with the sound of her own voice, her
mind was filled with an imperative need to retain her sanity. It was the
phrase 'Caroline wondered' which arrested her. Immediately then,
shaken as she was, Caroline began to consider the possibilities,
whether the sounds she had heard were real or illusory. While the
thought terrified her that she was being haunted by people – spirits or
things – beings who had read her thoughts, perhaps who could read
her very heart, she could not hope for the horrible alternative. She
feared it more; she feared that those sounds, so real that they seemed

to have come from the other side of the wall, were hallucinations sent forth from her own mind. Caroline sat for the next half-hour dazed and frightened, wondering what to do. She dreaded a repetition of the experience, yet prayed for some sign that her mind was not unhinged. The question began to appear as one on which she could herself decide; it was like being faced with a choice between sanity and madness.

She had already concluded that the noise could not have come from anyone in the house. The fact that her feelings and reflections were being recorded seemed to point to some invisible source, the issue being, was it objectively real or was it imaginary? If the sounds came from some real, invisible typewriter and voices, Caroline felt she was in danger, might go mad, but the experience was not itself a sign of madness. She was now utterly convinced that what she had heard was not the product of her own imagination. 'I am not mad. I'm not mad. See; I can reflect on the situation. I am being haunted. I am not haunting myself.' Meantime, she was trembling, frightened out of her wits, although her fear was not altogether blind.

Tap-click-tap. The voices again: *Meantime, she was trembling, frightened out of her wits, although her fear was not altogether blind.*

'Christ!' she said. 'Who *is* it there?' Although she had decided quite reasonably that no one in the house could be responsible for those sounds, none the less when she actually heard the voices again, so clear, just behind the wall, she sprang up and began to search every corner of the flat, even under the divan, which was too low to conceal a human body; even in the little cupboard where the gas meter was fixed. The activity took the edge off her panic, and although she knew she would not find her tormentors in this way, she put all her energy into the search, moving furniture, opening and shutting doors. She suspected everything, however improbable; even that the sound might be contained in some quite small object – a box with a machine inside, operated from a distance. She acted upon these suspicions, examining everything closely in case she should find something strange.

There was suddenly a knocking from the ceiling. Caroline propelled herself out of the flat and switched on the landing lights.

'Who's there?' she called up the stairs. 'Who is it?' Her voice was strained high with fear.

There was a movement above her, round the bend of the stair. A shuffle, and the opening of a door on the second landing. A woman's voice whispered fiercely, 'Keep quiet!'

Looking straight above her, Caroline saw the top half of a woman leaning over the banister, long wisps of grey hair falling over her face and her loose white garment showing between the banisters. Caroline screamed, was too late to stop herself when she recognized the woman as the occupant of the flat above.

'Are you drunk?' the angry tenant breathed at her. 'What do you mean by waking the house at this time of night? It's twenty-two minutes past one, and you've been banging about moving furniture and slamming doors for the last hour. I haven't slept a wink. I've got to go out to business in the morning.'

Another door opened on the second floor, and a man's voice said, 'Anything the matter? I heard a girl scream.' The woman scuttled back into her room, being undressed, and finished her complaint with her head only showing outside her door.

'It was that young woman downstairs. She's been making a disturbance for the past hour. Did you hear her?'

'I certainly heard a scream,' the man's voice said.

Caroline ran up a few steps so as to see the speakers from the bend in the staircase. 'I got a terrible fright when I saw you,' she explained to the woman. 'Was that you knocking?'

'Indeed it was,' said the woman. 'I'll complain about this in the morning.'

'Were *you* using a typewriter?' Caroline began to inquire. She was helpless and shaky. 'I heard a typewriter, and voices.'

'You're mad!' said the woman, as she withdrew and shut the door. The young man had also retreated.

Caroline returned to her rooms, and, rapidly and stealthily, began to pack a small suitcase. She wondered where she would spend the rest of the night. A lonely hotel room was unthinkable, it would have to be a friend's house. She moved about, jerkily snatching at the necessary articles as if she expected some invisible hand, concealed in each object, to close over hers before she had got possession of it. She was anxious to make as little sound as possible, but in her nervousness bumped into the furniture and knocked over a glass dish. To protect herself from the noises of her movements, she contracted a muscle somewhere behind her nose and throat, which produced the effect in her ears as of a rustling breeze – it dulled the sound of her footsteps, making the whole operation sound quieter than it was.

Caroline pressed down the lid of her small case. She had decided where to go for the night. The Baron; he was awake, or at least available, at all hours. She opened the case again, remembering that she had packed her money; she would need it for the taxi to the Baron's flat in Hampstead. She was absorbed by the pressing need to get out of her flat at the earliest possible moment, and as she searched among her clothes she did not even notice, with her customary habit of self-observation, that she had thrown her night-things together anyhow. The difference between this frenzied packing operation and the deliberate care she had taken, in spite of her rage, to fold and fit her possessions into place at St Philumena's less than a day ago failed to register.

Tap-tick-tap. Tap. She did not even notice Click-tappity with her customary habit of self-observation, that she had thrown her night-things together anyhow. The difference between this frenzied packing operation and the deliberate care she had taken, in spite of her rage, to fold and fit her possessions into place at St Philumena's less than a day ago failed to register. Tap.

Coat – hat – handbag – suitcase; Caroline grabbed them and hustled out of the door, slamming it to. She rattled downstairs and out of the front door, which she slammed behind her. At the top of Queen's Gate, turning in from Old Brompton Road, she got a taxi and secured herself inside it with a slam of the door.

'It is quite a common thing,' Willi Stock said. 'Your brain is overworked.' This was the Baron speaking. He stood by the electric fire with its flicking imitation coals, sipping Curaçao.

Caroline sipped hers, curled up on the sofa, and crying. Absorbing the warmth of the fire and of the liquor, she felt a warmth of gratitude towards the Baron. For the last hour he had been explaining her mental condition. She was consoled, not by the explanations, but by the fact of his recognizable face, by the familiar limitations of his mind, and by the reality of his warm flat and his bottle of Curaçao.

For the first time in her life, she felt that Willi Stock was an old friend. Regarding him in this category, she was able to secure her conscience in his company. For the Baron belonged to one of the half-worlds of Caroline's past, of which she had gradually taken leave; it was a society which she had half-forgotten, and of which she had come wholly to disapprove. It was over a year since she had last seen the Baron. But Laurence had kept up with him, had mentioned him from time to time, which confirmed Caroline in her feeling, that she was in the company of an old friend. She greatly needed the protection of an old friend till daylight.

He said, 'Eleanor is away on tour just now.'

Caroline said, 'I know, Laurence had a postcard.'

Eleanor Hogarth was the Baron's mistress.

'Did he?' said the Baron. 'When was that?'

'Oh, last week sometime. He merely mentioned it.'

They called him the Baron because he called himself Baron Stock. Caroline was not aware from what aristocracy he derived his title: nor had anyone inquired; she was sure it was not self-imposed as some suggested. He came originally from the Belgian Congo, had travelled in the Near East, loitered in Europe, and finally settled in England, a naturalized British subject. That was fifteen years ago, and he was now nearing fifty. Caroline had always felt that the Baron had native African blood, without being able to locate its traces in any one feature. She had been in Africa, and had a sense of these things. It was a matter of casual curiosity to her; but she had noticed, some years ago, when Africa's racial problems were being discussed in company with the Baron, he had denounced the blacks with ferocious bitter-ness, out of all proportion to the occasion. This confirmed Caroline's judgement; there was, too, an expression of pathos which at times appeared on the Baron's face, which she had seen in others of concealed mixed colour; and there was something about the whites of his eyes; what it was she did not know. And altogether, having observed these things, she did not much care.

The Baron had set up a bookshop in Charing Cross Road, one of those which keep themselves exclusively intellectual. 'Intellect-u-al,' the Baron pronounced it. He would say, 'Of course there are no intellect-u-als in England.'

It had been the delight of Caroline and Laurence to recall the day when they looked in on the Baron at Charing Cross Road, to find him being accosted by a tiny woman with the request:

'D'you have any railway books for children?'

The Baron reared high and thin on the central expanse of grey carpet and regarded her silently for half a second.

'Railway books for children,' she repeated. 'Books with pictures of trains and railways.'

The Baron said: 'Railway books for children, Madam? I do not think so, Madam.' His arm languidly indicated the shelves. 'We have Histor-ay, Biograph-ay, Theolog-ay, Theosoph-ay, Psycholog-ay, Religio-n, Poetr-ay, but railway books for children. . . . Try Foyles across the road, Madam.'

He raised his shoulders and eyebrows as he turned to Laurence and Caroline. 'My father,' he said, 'knew a man in the Belgian Diplomatic Service who was the author of a railway book for children. It was very popular and sold quickly. A copy was sent to a family in Yugoslavia. Of course, the book contained a code message. The author was revising the book for the second edition when he was arrested. That story is my total experience of railway books for children. Have you read this work on Kafka? – it has just come in, my darlings, my Laurence and my Caroline.'

In this way, Baron Stock was an old friend.

Caroline lay in the dark warm room on a made-up sofa bed. The Baron had left her just after four had struck. She had stopped crying. In case she should want them, the Baron had left a bottle of aspirins on a chair by the sofa. Caroline reached out for the bottle, unscrewed the cap and extracted the twist of cotton wool which she had hoped to find. She stuffed a piece in each ear. Now she was alone, it seemed to her that she had been playing a false role with the Baron. It was the inevitable consequence of her arrival at his flat in a panic, at a late hour; 'Willi! Let me in, I've been hearing voices!'

After that, she was forced to accept his protection, his friendliness; was glad of it. And when he had settled her by the fire:

'Caroline, *my* dear, how slender and febrile you've become! What kind of voices? How extremely interesting. Was it a religi-ous experience?'

She had begun to weep, to apologize.

'Caroline, *my* dear, as you know, I never go to bed. Seriously, I never go to bed unless it's the last possible alternative. I am delighted beyond words – Caroline, my dear, I am so honoured – your distress, my dear – if you can realize how I feel.'

And so she had to play the part. Now, alone in the dark, she thought, 'I should have faced it out at the flat. I shouldn't have run away.'

The Baron, of course, was convinced she was suffering from a delusion.

'It happens to many many people, my dear. It is quite nothing to worry about. If the experience should recur you will have a course of analysis or take some pills and the voices will go away. But I doubt that the phenomenon will recur. You have been under a considerable strain from what I hear of your severed relations with Laurence.'

'We haven't parted, really, you know.'

'But you now have separate establishments?'

'Yes, I've got rooms in Kensington. Laurence is keeping on the flat for the time being. He's away in the country. I must get in touch with him tomorrow, first thing.' She gave the deliberate impression of not wanting to talk any more.

'In Sussex? With Mrs Jepp?' – a genuine curiosity in his voice.

'Yes.'

'I met her one day about three years ago. Laurence introduced me. A fine old lady. Wonderful for her age. Quite excellent. Do you see much of her?'

'I saw her last Easter,' Caroline said, 'she was grand.'

'Yes, she is grand. She doesn't visit London, of course?'

'No,' Caroline said. 'That must have been her last trip when you met her. She hasn't been to London since.'

'She doesn't care for the Hampstead ménage?'

'Well, she's an independent soul,' said Caroline absently.

She had only half taken in the Baron's chatter, although he continued to speak of Louisa.

'I must get in touch with Laurence first thing,' Caroline repeated. 'Mrs Jepp isn't on the phone. I'll send a wire. Oh, Willi! – those voices, it was Hell!'

Now, lying awake in the dark, Caroline recalled the conversation, regretting that she had shown such a supine dependence on the Baron. More and more she thought, 'I should have stayed at home and faced whatever was to be faced.' She knew she had tough resources. And as she tormented herself, now, into confronting her weakness, painfully she recollected the past hour; some of the talk which she had let slip so drowsily through her mind came back to her. It had struck her in passing that the Baron had seemed extraordinarily interested in Laurence's grandmother. He was the last person one would expect to have remembered – and by name – an undistinguished old lady to whom he had been introduced casually three years ago. Mrs Jepp was not immediately impressive to strangers; was not at all the type to impress the Baron.

Through the darkness, from beside the fireplace, Caroline heard a sound. *Tap.* The typewriter. She sat up as the voices followed:

The Baron had seemed extraordinarily interested in Laurence's grandmother. He was the last person one would expect to have remembered – and by name – an undistinguished old lady to whom he had been introduced casually three years ago. Mrs Jepp was not immediately impressive to strangers.

Caroline yelled, 'Willi! Oh, my God, the voices. . . . Willi!'

Through the wall she heard him stir.

'Did you call, Caroline?'

Eventually he shuffled in and switched on the light.

Caroline pulled the bulky borrowed dressing-gown over her shoulders, her eyes blue and hard with fright. She had grasped the rosary which she had tucked under the cushion at her head. Her fingers clung shakily to the beads as a child clings to its abracadabra toy.

'*My* dear Caroline, what a charming picture you make! Don't move for a second, don't move: I am trying to recall – some moment, some scene in the past or a forgotten canvas – One of my sister's friends perhaps – or my nurse. Caroline, my dear, there is no more exquisite sight than that of a woman taken unawares with a rosary.'

Caroline slung the beads on the post of the chair. The thought flashed upon her, 'He is indecent.' She looked up at him sharply and caught him off his guard; his mouth and eyes drooped deadly tired, and he was resisting a yawn. She thought, 'After all, he is kind; it was only a pose.'

'Tell me about the voices,' he said. 'I heard nothing, myself. From what direction did they come?'

'Over there, beside the fireplace,' she answered.

'Would you like some tea? I think there is tea.'

'Oh, coffee. Could I have some coffee? I don't think I'm likely to sleep.'

'We shall both have some coffee. Stay where you are.'

Caroline thought, 'He means that he isn't likely to sleep, either.' She said, 'I'm awfully sorry about this, Willi. It sounds so foolish, but it really is appalling. And you must be dead tired.'

'Coffee and aspirins. *My* Caroline, you are not to apologize, I am delighted –'

But he could hardly conceal his sleepiness. As he returned bearing their coffee, with a bottle of brandy on a tray, he said, as one who keeps the conversation flowing, notwithstanding a tiger in the garden, 'You must tell me all about the voices.' He saw her removing the cottonwool plugs from her ears, but pretended not to notice. 'I have always believed that disembodied beings inhabit this room,' he went on, 'and now I'm sure. Seriously, I'm sure – indissuasibly convinced, Caroline, that you are in touch with something. I do so wish I had been able to give you some phenobarbitone, an excellent sedative; or something to make you sleep. But of course I shall sit up with you, it's nearly five already. . . .'

He said no more about hallucinations, by which Caroline understood that he now really believed that she was crazy. She sipped her coffee submissively and jerkily, weeping all the time. She told him to leave her.

'Of course not. I want to hear about the voices. It's most intriguing, really.'

She felt better for the effort to describe what had happened, although the fact gnawed at her that the Baron was finding the episode a strain and a nuisance. But ruthlessly, in her own interest, she talked on and on. And as she talked she realized that the Baron was making the best of it, had resigned himself, was attending to her, but as one who regards another's words, not as symbols but as symptoms.

He got out of her that the clicking of the typewriter always preceded the voices, and sometimes accompanied their speech. How many voices there were, she could not say. Male or female? Both, she told him. It was impossible to disconnect the separate voices, because they came in complete concert; only by the varying timbres could the chorus be distinguished from one voice. 'In fact,' she went on, wound-up and talking rapidly, 'it sounds like one person speaking in several tones at once.'

'And always using the past tense?'

'Yes. Mocking voices.'

'And you say this chorus comments on your thoughts and actions?'

'Not always,' said Caroline, 'that's the strange thing. It says "Caroline was thinking or doing this or that" – then sometimes it adds a remark of its own.'

'Give me an example, dear. I'm so stupid – I can never grasp –'

'Well,' said Caroline, unwhelming herself of a sudden access of confidence in the Baron's disinterestedness, 'take tonight. I was dropping off, and thinking over my conversation with you –

'– as one does –' she added,

'– and it drifted to my mind how you had remembered meeting Laurence's grandmother; I thought it strange you should do so. Next thing, I heard the typewriter and the voices. They repeated my thought, something like, "It came to her that the Baron" – you know we always call you the Baron, "– that the Baron had been extraordinarily interested in Laurence's grandmother." That's what the voices said. And then they added something to the effect that the Baron was the last person who would remember, and remember by name, an old woman like Mrs Jepp merely from a passing introduction three years ago. You see, Willi, the words are immaterial –'

'You're mad,' said the Baron abruptly.

Caroline felt relieved at these words, although, and in a way because, they confirmed her distress. It was a relief to hear the Baron speak his true mind, it gave her exactly what she had anticipated, what seemed to her a normal person's reaction to her story. Fearing this, she had been purposely vague when, earlier in the evening, she had explained her distress: 'A typewriter followed by voices. They speak in the past tense. They mock me.'

Now that she had been more explicit, and had been told she was mad, she felt a perverse satisfaction at the same time as a suffocating sense that she might never communicate the reality of what she had heard.

The Baron hastily recovered. 'I use "mad" of course in the colloquial sense. In the way that we're *all mad*, you know. A little crazy, you know. Amongst ourselves, I mean – the intelligentsia are all a little mad and, my dear Caroline, that's what makes us so nice. The sane are not worth noticing.'

'Oh, quite,' said Caroline. 'I know what you mean.' But she was wondering, now, why he had spoken so viciously: 'You're mad!' – like a dog snapping at a fly. She felt she had been tactless. She wished she had chosen to cite a different example of the voices.

'Someone is haunting me, that's what it is,' Caroline said, hoping to discard responsibility for offending the Baron.

He seemed to have forgotten his role as the intrigued questioner; his air of disinterested curiosity was suspended while he told Caroline exactly why and how Mrs Jepp had impressed him. 'You see, she is a character. So small and yet her strength – her aged yet vivid face. So dark, so small. I could never forget that face.'

With surprise, Caroline thought, 'He is defending himself.'

'And she looked so debonair, my dear, in a deep blue velvet hat. Her brown wrinkles. Quite a picture.'

'Three years ago, was it, Willi?'

'Almost three years – I remember it well. Laurence brought her into the shop, and she said, "What a lot of books!"'

He gave an affectionate chuckle, but Caroline did not join him. She was thinking of Louisa Jepp's last visit to London, three years ago. Certainly, she did not possess her blue hat at that time, Caroline was acquainted with all Louisa's hats. They were purchased at long intervals, on rare occasions. And only last Easter, Caroline had accompanied the old lady to Hayward's Heath where they had spent the afternoon, eventually deciding on that blue velvet hat which had so pleased Louisa that she had worn it on every occasion since.

'A blue hat?' said Caroline.

'My dear, believe it or not, a blue. I recall it distinctly. Blue velvet, curling close to her head, with a fluffy black feather at the side. I shall never forget that hat nor the face beneath it.'

That was the hat all right.

In the face of the Baron's apparent lie – to what purpose? – and the obvious fact that her account of the voices had somehow provoked it, Caroline began to gather her own strength. The glimmering of a puzzle distinct from her own problem was a merciful antidote to her bewilderment. She kept her peace and sipped her coffee, knowing that she was delivered at least from this second mockery, the Baron

posing as a credulous sympathizer, his maddening chatter about
psychic phenomena, while in reality he waited for the morning, when
he could hand her over to Laurence or someone responsible. The
Baron might think her mentally unhinged, but by a mercy she had
made it clear, though quite unintentionally, that her condition was
dangerous for him. In fact, she had forced him to take her seriously, to
the extent that he made excuses for himself and lied.

She considered this, but when she looked at him, saw him still
courteous in his extreme tiredness, her tears returned.

'Oh, Willi! How can I ever thank you? You are so kind.'

'So kind,' she repeated, she herself like a tired infant whose tongue
cannot extricate itself from a single phrase, 'So kind, so kind –' And
so, in her gratitude, she gave away what advantage she had gained and
became once more a distracted woman seeking the protection of an
old friend.

The Baron, as if he too would make a concession, and anxious to
place her in a less pathetic light, asked,

'What are you writing these days?'

'Oh, the same book. But I haven't done much lately.'

'The work on the twentieth-century novel?'

'That's right. *Form in the Modern Novel.*'

'How's it going so far?'

'Not bad. I'm having difficulty with the chapter on realism.'

Suddenly she felt furious with the voices for having upset her
arrangements. She had planned to start work that week; to put all her
personal troubles out of her mind. And now, this ghastly humiliating
experience.

She broke down again. 'It ought not to have happened to me! This
sort of thing shouldn't happen to an intelligent woman!'

'It is precisely to the intelligent that these things happen,' said the
Baron. Both he and Caroline were drinking brandy neat.

After a while the Baron made more coffee, and then, thank God, it
was dawn.

The Baron had put up a protest, but eventually he had let her leave his
flat. By daylight she had revived, with that unaccountable energy to
which nervous people have access, not only in spite of a sleepless and

harrowing night, but almost because of it. The Baron had put up a protest but he had let her go after she had promised to keep in touch with him during the day. She wanted to be out of his flat. She wanted to return to Kensington. And to contact Laurence; he would return to London. She would have to face the housekeeper at her flat; she was sure the other tenants must have complained of the last night's turmoil. 'The housekeeper is a brute, Willi,' Caroline had said, as she collected her things.

'Give her ten shill-ings,' said the Baron.

'It's a man.'

'Give him two pounds.'

'Perhaps a pound,' said Caroline. 'Well, Willi, I do thank you.'

'Two pounds would be on the safe side,' pursued the Baron.

'I'll make it thirty shillings,' said Caroline, seriously.

The Baron began to giggle quietly. Then Caroline, thinking it over, was taken with laughter too.

'I like to haggle.'

'All women do.'

On the way to Hampstead underground, she sent Laurence a wire. 'Come immediately something mysterious going on.'

'The voices may never come back,' she thought. In a way she hoped they would. Laurence might easily be the means of tracking them down by some sheer innocent remark. That was the sort of thing he could do. She did not think the voices would speak to her if she was with anyone else. But Laurence would investigate. She had almost a sense of adventure in her unnatural exhilaration. It was a sharp sunny day. In the train, she put a pound note and a ten-shilling note in a separate place in her handbag, and smiled; that was for the house-keeper. On the whole, she hoped the voices would return, would give her a chance to establish their existence, and to trace their source.

It was nearly nine-thirty when she reached Queen's Gate. A convenient time. The tenants had left for their offices, and the housekeeper had not yet emerged. She closed the door quietly and crept upstairs.

Laurence kept the door of the telephone box open to let in the sun and air of the autumn morning.

'Still no reply?'

'Sorry, no reply.'

'Sure you've got the right –?'

But the operator had switched off. He was sure she hadn't got the right number – at least – maybe – Caroline must have gone somewhere else for the night. Perhaps she had gone to Mass.

He rang his parents' home. There had been no word from Miss Rose. His mother was at Mass. His father had just left. He sent Caroline a wire from the village post office, and went for an exasperated walk, which turned cheerful as he anticipated Caroline's coming to stay at his grandmother's. He had arranged to prolong his holiday for another week. When he reached the cottage half an hour later, he found a wire from Caroline.

'There's been a mix-up at the post office,' he told Louisa.

'What, dear?'

'I sent Caroline a wire, and apparently Caroline has sent one to me. But they must have got the messages mixed up somehow. This is the message I sent to Caroline. The very words.'

'What dear? Read it out, I don't understand.'

'I'll go and speak to the post office,' Laurence said swiftly, leaving at once. He was anxious to avoid the appearance of concealing the wire from his grandmother, after admitting that it contained his own message. He read it again. 'Come immediately something mysterious going on.' It ended, 'love Caroline'.

At the post office, where a number of Louisa's neighbours were buying tea and other things, Laurence caused a slight stir. His outgoing message was compared with the one he had just received. He distinctly overheard the postmaster, in their little back office, say to his daughter, 'They've both used the exact same words. It's a code, or something fishy they've arranged beforehand.'

He came out and said to Laurence, 'The two telegrams are identical, sir.'

'Well, that's funny,' Laurence repeated the words, 'something mysterious going on'.

'Yes, it seems so,' said the man.

Laurence cleared off before the question could become more confused and public. He went into the phone box and asked for Caroline's number. It was ringing through. Immediately she answered.

'Caroline?'

'Laurence, is that you? Oh, I've just come home and found a wire. Did you send a wire?'

'Yes, did you?'

'Yes, how was it supposed to read? I'm so frightened.'

The little parlour in the Benedictine Priory smelt strongly of polish; the four chairs, the table, the floors, the window-frame gleamed in repose of the polish, as if these wooden things themselves had done some hard industry that day before dawn. Outside, the late October evening sun lit up the front garden strip, and Caroline while she waited in the parlour could hear the familiar incidence of birds and footsteps from the suburban street. She knew this parlour well, with its polish; she had come here weekly for three months to receive her instruction for the Church. She watched a fly alight on the table for a moment; it seemed to Caroline to be in a highly dangerous predicament, as if it might break through the glossy surface on which it skated. But it made off quite easily. Caroline jogged round nervily as the door opened. Then she rose as the priest came in, her friend, ageing Father Jerome. She had known him for so many years that she could not remember their first meeting. They had been in touch and out of touch for long periods. And when, after she had decided to enter the Church, and she went weekly to his Priory, her friends had said,

'Why do you go so far out of London for instruction? Why don't you go to Farm Street?' Caroline replied,

'Well, I know this priest.'

And if they were Catholics, her friends would say,

'Oh, it doesn't matter about the particular priest. The nearest priest is always the best one.'

And Caroline replied, 'Well, I know this priest.'

She wondered, now, if she did know him. He was, as usual, smiling with his russet face, limping with his bad leg, carrying a faded folder from which emerged an untidy sheaf of crumpled papers. 'I got two days off last week to copy parts of Lydgate's *Life of Our Lady* at the British Museum. I've got it here. Do you know it? I'll read you a bit presently. Glorious. What are you writing? You look tired, are you sleeping well? Are you eating proper food? What did you have for breakfast?'

'I haven't slept properly for a week,' said Caroline. Then she told him about the voices.

'This started after you got back from St Philumena's?'

'Yes. That's a week ago today. And it's been going on ever since. It happens when I'm alone during the day. Laurence came up from the country. He's moved into my flat. I can't bear to be alone at nights.'

'Sleeping there?'

'In the other room,' said Caroline. 'That's all right, isn't it?'

'For the time being,' said the priest absently.

He rose abruptly and went out. The thoughts shot through Caroline's brain, 'Perhaps he's gone to fetch another priest; he thinks I'm dangerous. Has he gone to fetch a doctor? He thinks I should be certified, taken away.' And she knew those thoughts were foolish, for Father Jerome had a habit of leaving rooms abruptly when he remembered something which had to be done elsewhere. He would be back presently.

He returned very soon and sat down without comment. He was followed almost immediately by a lay brother, bearing a tray with a glass of milk and a plate of biscuits which he placed before her. This brought back to her the familiarity of the monk and the parlour; only last winter in the early dark evenings after they had finished the catechism, Father Jerome would fetch Caroline the big editions of the Christian Fathers from the monastery library, for she had loved to rummage through them. Then, when he had left her in the warm parlour turning the pages and writing out her notes, he had used to send the lay brother to her with a glass of milk and biscuits.

Now, while she sipped the milk, Father Jerome read aloud a part of *The Life of Our Lady*. He had already started putting it into modern English, and consulted her on one or two points. Caroline felt her old sense of ease with the priest; he never treated her as someone far different from what she was. He treated her not only as a child; not only as an intellectual; not only as a nervy woman; not only as weird; he seemed to assume simply that she was as she was. When he asked, she told him more clearly about the voices.

'I think,' she said, 'that they are really different tones of one voice. I think they belong to one person.'

She also said, 'I think I am possessed.'

'No,' he said, 'you are not possessed. You may be obsessed, but I doubt it.'

Caroline said, 'Do you think this is a delusion?'

'How should I know?'

'Do you think I'm mad?'

'No. But you're ill.'

'That's true. D'you think I'm a neurotic?'

'Of course. That goes without saying.'

Caroline laughed too. There was a time when she could call herself a neurotic without a sense of premonition; a time when it was merely the badge of her tribe.

'If I'm not mad,' she said, 'I soon will be, if this goes on much longer.'

'Neurotics never go mad,' he said.

'But this is intolerable.'

'Doesn't it depend on how you take it?'

'Father,' she said, almost as if speaking to herself to clarify her mind, 'if only I knew where the voices came from. I think it is one person. It uses a typewriter. It uses the past tense. It's exactly as if someone were watching me closely, able to read my thoughts; it's as if the person was waiting to pounce on some insignificant thought or action, in order to make it signify in a strange distorted way. And how does it know about Laurence and my friends? And then there was a strange coincidence the other day. Laurence and I sent each other a wire with exactly the same words, at the same time. It was horrifying. Like predestination.'

'These things can happen,' said Father Jerome. 'Coincidence or some kind of telepathy.'

'But the typewriter and the voices – it is as if a writer on another plane of existence was writing a story about us.' As soon as she had said these words, Caroline knew that she had hit on the truth. After that she said no more to him on the subject.

As she was leaving he asked her how she had liked St Philumena's.

'Awful,' she said, 'I only stayed three days.'

'Well,' he said, 'I didn't think it was your sort of place. You should have gone to a Benedictine convent. They are more your sort.'

'But it was you recommended St Philumena's! Don't you

remember, that afternoon at Lady Manders', you were both so keen on my going there?'

'Oh sorry. Yes, I suppose we were. What didn't you like?'

'The people.'

He chuckled. 'Yes, the people. It's a matter of how you take them.'

'I believe it is,' said Caroline as though she had just thought of something.

'Well, God bless you. Get some sleep and keep in touch.'

She found Laurence in when she returned to the flat in Queen's Gate. He was fiddling about with a black box-like object which at first she took to be a large typewriter.

'What's that?' she said, when she saw it closer.

'Listen,' said Laurence.

He pressed a key. There was a whirring sound and the box began to talk with a male voice pitched on a peculiarly forced husky note. It said, 'Caroline darling, I have a suggestion to make.' Then it went on to say something funny but unprintable.

Caroline subsided with laughter and relief on to the divan.

Laurence did something to the instrument and the words rumbled forth again.

'I knew your voice right away,' Caroline said.

'I bet you didn't. I disguised it admirably. Listen again.'

'No!' said Caroline. 'Someone might overhear it. Dirty beast you are.'

He replayed the record and they both laughed helplessly.

'What have you brought that thing here for?' Caroline said. 'It might have given me a dreadful fright.'

'To record your spook-voices. Now see. I'm placing this disc in here. If you hear them again, you press that. Then it records any voice within hearing distance.'

He had placed it against the wall where the voices came from.

'Afterwards,' he explained, 'we can take out the disc and play it back.'

'Maybe those voices won't record,' Caroline said.

'They will if they're in the air. Any sound causes an occurrence. If the sound has objective existence it will be recorded.'

'This sound might have another sort of existence and still be real.'

'Well, let's first exhaust the possibilities of the natural order –'

'But we don't know all the possibilities of the natural order.'

'If the sound doesn't record, we can take it for granted that it either doesn't exist, or it exists in some supernatural order,' he explained.

She insisted, 'It does exist. I think it's a natural sound. I don't think that machine will record it.'

'Don't you want to try it?' He seemed disappointed almost.

'Of course. It's a lovely idea.'

'And better,' he said, 'than any ideas you've had so far.'

'I've got a good one now,' Caroline said. 'I'm sure it's the right one. It came to me while I was talking to Father Jerome.'

'Let's have it,' he said.

'Not yet. I want to assemble the evidence.'

Caroline was happy. Laurence looked at himself in the mirror, smiled, and told himself, 'She says I'm a dirty beast.'

The flat was untidy. Caroline loved to see her own arrangement of things upset by Laurence. It was a double habitation now. They had told the housekeeper that they had got married. He was only half satisfied with the story but he would put the other half on the bill, Laurence predicted. She was used to being called 'Mrs Manders': it was easy, as if they had never parted, except for the knowledge that this was an emergency set-up. Another week, at the most, and then something would have to be done. She regretted having disclosed her plight to the Baron. He had been pressing Laurence to get Caroline into a nursing home. She did not mind this suggestion, so much as the implication. 'A nursing home.' He meant a refined looney-bin. Laurence opposed it; he wanted to take her back with him to his grandmother. The Baron had carried the story to Helena, who offered to pay Caroline's expenses at a private nursing home for Catholics. Helena did not mean a looney-bin, however.

'I wouldn't mind a few weeks' rest in a nursing home,' Caroline had told Laurence. 'I don't think they could do away with the voices, but they might deafen me to them for a while. It would be a rest.'

Laurence had been altogether against this.

And he had a mystery of his own to solve. 'I wrote and told you all about it. I'd just posted a letter to St Philumena's when I got your first wire to say you'd returned to London. I daresay it will be forwarded.'

'Do tell me.' Caroline had half-expected to hear of a 'mystery' similar to her own.

'Well, the thing is, Grandmother is mixed up with some highly suspect parties. At first I thought she was running a gang, but now, all things considered, I think she may be their stooge.'

'No,' said Caroline. 'Quite definitely, your grandmother isn't anyone's stooge.'

'Now, d'you think that, honestly? – That's what I feel myself really. You must come and see for yourself.'

'I'll think about it,' Caroline had said.

Four times during the past week, while Laurence had been out, she had heard the typewriter and the voices.

Then she had told Laurence. 'I'll see Father Jerome. If he advises a nursing home, it's a nursing home. If he says go to your grand-mother's, I'll come. I could always go into a nursing home later on.'

But she had forgotten to put these alternatives to Father Jerome. And now, she did not feel it mattered.

'I'll come to Sussex,' she said.

'Really, will you? Is that what the holy pa advised?'

'No. I forgot to mention it. He advised food and sleep.'

Laurence knew Caroline's nervous responses to food and sleep at the best of times. But she didn't laugh with him. Instead, she said, 'I feel better. I think the worst of my trouble is over; I begin to see daylight.'

He was used to Caroline's rapid recoveries, but only from physical illness. In past years, he had known her prostrated by the chest complications to which she was subject; bronchitis, pleurisy, pneu-monia. Once or twice she had lain for several days, running a temperature, burning with fever. Then, overnight or in the course of an hour in the afternoon, or waking in the late morning after a kindling night, there would come a swift alteration, a lightning revival of her sick body; Caroline would say, 'I am better. I feel quite well.' She would sit up and talk. Her temperature would drop to normal. It was almost as though she was under a decision, as if her body, at such times, were only awaiting her word, and she herself submissively waiting for some secret go-ahead within her, permitting her at last to say, 'I am better. I feel well.' After such rapid reversals Caroline would feel depressed, would crave that attention due to an invalid which she had not cared about in her real danger. Frequently in the days that followed, she would say, 'I'm not better yet. I'm still weak.' But there was never any conviction in this. It became a joke eventually, for Laurence to say for months after her illnesses, 'You're still an invalid. You're not better yet', and Caroline, too, would tell him, 'You make breakfast today, dear. I'm still an invalid. I'm feeling *very unwell.*'

Laurence thought of these things when he heard Caroline, on her return from the Priory, tell him, 'I feel better.... I begin to see daylight.' He recognized this signal; he himself had nursed her through her illnesses over the past six years. Those were mostly times of poverty before his parents had accepted his irregular life with Caroline; before he got his job on the B.B.C.; before Caroline had got her literary reputation.

Caroline knew what he was thinking. He had not expected her to recover so abruptly from this sort of illness. He had seen it coming on for the past six months.

And now he was thinking – 'So she is better. She sees daylight. Is it just like that? Can she be right? No more melancholia. No more panic at the prospect of meeting strangers. No worry, no voices? Only the formal convalescence, the "invalid" period, and then the old Caroline again. Can it be so?'

Caroline saw on his face an expression which she remembered having seen before. It was a look of stumped surprise, the look of one who faces an altogether and irrational new experience; a look partly fearful, partly indignant, partly curious, but predominantly joyful. The other occasion on which she had seen this expression on Laurence's face was during an argument, when she told him of her decision to enter the Church, with the consequence that they must part. They were both distressed; they hardly knew what they were saying. In reply to some remark of Laurence she had rapped out, nastily, 'I love God better than you!' It was then she saw on his face that mixture of surprise and dismay, somehow revealing in its midst an unconscious alien delight, which she witnessed now once more when she told him, 'The worst is over. I see daylight.'

'But remember I'm still an invalid,' she added. He laughed quite a lot. She was sorry to have to disappoint him. She knew he would be expecting her 'recovery' to be something different from what it was going to be, and that he was wondering, 'How does she know she won't hear those voices again?'

He said, 'Do you really feel that everything's going to be all right now, darling?'

'Yes,' she said. 'I'm perfectly O.K. Only a bit tired, but now, you see, I know what the voices are. It's a creepy experience but I can cope with it. I'm sure I've discovered the true cause. I have a plan. I'll tell you something about it by and by.'

She lay on the divan and closed her eyes.

'I'm worried about you,' he said.

'You mean, the voices. You mean I can't be well if I go on hearing them.'

He thought for a moment. 'Let's see if this machine records anything.'

'All right,' said Caroline. 'But supposing it doesn't, what difference does that make?'

'Well, in that case, I think you should try to understand the experience in a symbolic light.'

'But the voices are voices. Of course they are symbols. But they are also voices. There's the typewriter too – that's a symbol, but it *is* a real typewriter. I hear it.'

'My Caroline,' he said, 'I hope you will hear it no more.'

'I don't,' Caroline said.

'Don't you? Now, why?'

'Because now I know what they are. I'm on the alert now,' Caroline said. 'You see, I really am quite better. Only tired.' She raised her voice a little, and said, 'And if anyone's listening, let them take note.'

Well, well!

'I bet they feel scared,' said Laurence quite merrily.

She slipped off her skirt, and slid between the sheets of the divan.

He thought, 'And yet, she does look better. Almost well again, only tired.'

She was dozing off when he left her; he had to run over to Hampstead to see his mother; she had telephoned to him rather urgently. He promised Caroline to be back in time to take her out to dinner. Before he went he reminded her of the tape-recorder.

'Don't forget to press that lever if anything should happen,' he said. 'Sure you'll be all right?'

'Perfectly O.K.,' said Caroline drowsily. 'I could sleep for a fortnight.'

'Good. Sleep well. And if you want anything, you know, just ring my mother. I'll be over there myself in about twenty minutes.'

Caroline was very quickly asleep. And even as she slept, she felt herself appreciating her sleep; told herself, this was the best sleep she had had for six months. She told herself to sleep on, for she would wake up presently, and then she would mean business.

At this point in the narrative, it might be as well to state that the characters in this novel are all fictitious, and do not refer to any living persons whatsoever.

Tap-tappity-tap. At this point in the narrative ... Caroline sprang up and pressed the lever on the dictaphone. Then she snatched the notebook and pencil which she had placed ready, and took down in shorthand the paragraph above; she did not start to tremble until after the chanting chorus had ended. She lay trembling in the darkening room, and considered the new form of her suffering, now that she was well again and committed to health.

FOUR

There were chrysanthemums and asters in the bowls, chrysanthemums and asters almost discernible on the faded loose upholstery in the drawing-room. They needed to be replaced, but Helena Manders had never replaced them, in order that the Knighthood, which had occurred when the covers were already past their best, should make no difference. The Manders put up with many discomforts so that the Knighthood should make no difference. The fire was lit because of Laurence coming. No fires till November, as a rule.

'Are you in a hurry?' Helena said, because now Laurence had arrived and was looking at his watch. He did this because he knew that when his mother wanted to see him about any particular business, she would usually forget the business until he was ready to go, causing him to stay for dinner or to stay the night; or she would forget the business until after he had gone, in which case she would ring him again and he would have to go again.

Laurence did not mind visiting his parents at Hampstead, he even enjoyed going there to stay for meals, or for days and weeks; only this had to be in his own time, when the time was ripe, when the time came round for him to say to himself, 'I would like to go over to Hampstead.' When he was summoned there, he couldn't be bothered greatly.

And so he looked at his watch. He said, 'I've only got an hour. I'm dining with Caroline. I would have brought her, only she's resting.'

'How is Caroline?'

'She says she's better. I think she is, really.'

'Do you? And the hallucinations, have they disappeared? Poor girl, she wouldn't tell me much.'

'I don't know,' said Laurence. 'I don't know if she's better. She says she feels better.'

'Not going into a nursing home? That would be best.'

'No. I'm taking her down to Grandmother's tomorrow, in fact.'

'I am worried, Laurence.'

She looked worried. Her face had no confidence. There was a ladder in her stocking. She had said she wanted to see him urgently, and within the first five minutes she was coming to the point. There were other signs that she was very worried.

'I asked you to come, Laurence, because I'm so worried.'

He sat on the arm of her chair, he put his arm round her shoulder, and said,

'Is it to do with Caroline and me?'

'No,' she said.

Laurence got up and poured himself a drink. His mother had not offered him a drink. She was worried.

'Georgina Hogg came to see me yesterday.'

'Oh! What did she want?'

'I don't know. She told me an extraordinary story. I'm so worried.'

'About Caroline? I told you Caroline had left St Philumena's on Georgina Hogg's account. Can you blame her?'

'No, of course not.'

'You shouldn't have sent Caroline to that place. You know what Georgina's like.'

'Well, Father Jerome agreed –'

'But he doesn't know Georgina Hogg. You should never have given her that job. What took you to do that? She's such a frightful advertisement for the Church.'

'I just thought,' said Helena. 'One tries to be charitable. I thought. She said a miracle seemed to have brought her back to me. I thought, "Perhaps she has changed." One never knows, in our Faith. Anything can happen to anyone.'

'Well, Georgina hasn't changed apparently. Still the same psychological thug as she always was. I think honestly she's to blame for Caroline's relapse. She must have touched a raw nerve.'

Helena said, 'Pour me a drink, Laurence.'

'What will you have?'

'Same as you.'

Laurence gave her a drink as strong as his own, which she didn't object to on this occasion.

'What's on your mind, darling? What does Georgina want now?'

'I don't know. She came to tell me something.'

'Felt it was her duty, as usual? What did she say about Caroline?'

'That's right, that's what she said, about it being her duty. She didn't say much about Caroline but she told me an extraordinary story about my mother going in for some terribly illegal business. She suggested that Mother was a receiver of stolen property.'

'My dear, what made her say that?'

Helena was apologetic. She didn't quite know how to tell Laurence what her protected servant had done.

'I don't quite know how to tell you, Laurence. I thought Georgina had changed. And of course she's got a justification, an excuse. Caroline didn't leave her address. She says a letter came for Caroline the day after she left. Georgina took upon herself to open it, just to see the address of the writer, she said, meaning to return it. Then she found the letter came from you. She read it, as she felt that was her duty to me. You see, Laurence, she has an excuse for everything.'

'But that's illegal. No one has any right to open a letter addressed to someone else. Only the Post Office can do that, when the person it's addressed to can't be traced. And even then, officially they only look at the signature and the address on the letter. No one *at all* has a right to read the substance of a letter addressed to someone else,' Laurence said. He was fairly raging.

'I told her that, Laurence. I'm worried, dear.'

'What did she mean, she felt it was her duty to you to read my letter to Caroline?'

'I don't know. Perhaps she thought there was something between you of which I wasn't aware. I put her right on that score.'

'Did you tell her it's a serious crime to do what she's done?' Laurence was on his third whisky.

'Hush, dear,' said his mother, forgetting his size, 'I don't know if we're in a position to talk about crime to Georgina Hogg. You must tell me all you know about Grandmother. You should have told me right away.'

'Did the Hogg show you my letter, or did she only tell you what I wrote?'

'She offered to let me read it. I refused.'

'Good,' said Laurence. 'That keeps our own standards up.'

His mother smiled a little and looked at him. But she returned to her anxiety. 'Georgina was very high-minded about what you wrote about *her*, whatever it was.'

'She didn't offer to return my letter to me, I suppose? It's my property.'

'No, she refused,' said Helena.

'And what's her excuse for *that*?'

'Feels it's her duty. She says that these things are too often hushed up.'

'Blackmail?' Laurence said.

'She didn't ask for anything,' said Helena. Then, as if these exchanges were so many tedious preliminaries, she said, as one getting down to business, 'Laurence, that was true wasn't it – what you wrote to Caroline about Grandmother?'

'Yes. But I don't think Grandmother's a criminal. I didn't say that. Possibly she's being used by a gang of criminals.' He did not sound very convinced of this.

Helena said, 'I've been blind. I've been simply inattentive these past four years since my father's death. I should have made it my business to look after my mother. I should have forced her to accept –'

'Where's Georgina now? Has she gone back?'

'No. She has given notice. I don't know where she's staying. I was too stunned to ask.'

'What is she going to do about the letter?'

'She said she would keep it, that's all.'

'What is she going to do about Grandmother?'

'She wouldn't say. Oh Laurence, I'm so worried about your grandmother. Tell me all about it. Tell me everything.'

'I don't know everything.'

'This about diamonds in the bread. I can't believe it and yet Georgina was so serious. I like to know where I am. Tell me what you discovered.'

'All right,' Laurence said. He knew that his mother had a peculiar faith that no evil could touch her. It made her adaptable to new ideas. Laurence had seen her coming round to one after another acceptance where his own vagaries were concerned. Especially now, when she sat worried in her shabby drawing-room, wearing her well-worn blue with the quite expensive pearls, a ladder in her stocking, Laurence thought, 'She could get through a jungle without so much as a scratch.'

When he had finished talking she said, 'When will you leave for Ladylees?'

'Tomorrow, as early as possible. By train; my car's going in for repair. I'll hire one at Hayward's Heath for the few days.'

'Don't take Caroline.'

'Why not?'

'She isn't strong enough, surely, to be mixed up in this?'

'I should say it would do her good.'

'She will be in your way, surely, if you intend making inquiries.'

'Not Caroline. She's too cute.'

'Tell Caroline to keep in touch with me, then. Ask her to phone every day and let me know what's happening. I can depend on Caroline.'

'Whisky makes you snooty,' he said. 'You can depend on me too.'

'Wheedle the truth out of your grandmother,' she pleaded.

As he started to leave, she said shyly in case there should be any offence, 'Try to find out how much it will cost us to get her out of the hands of these crooks.'

Laurence said, 'We don't know who's in whose hands, really. Better not mention it to Father just yet; it may turn out to be something quite innocent, a game of Grandmother's –'

'I won't trouble your father just yet,' she assured him abruptly. 'He does so admire my mother.' Then she added, 'To think that our old trusted servant should do a thing like this.'

He thought that a bit of hypocrisy – that 'old trusted servant' phrase.

'You think I'm a hypocrite, don't you?' his mother said.

'Of course not,' he replied, 'why should I?'

'Everything O.K.?'

Caroline woke at the sound of Laurence's voice. She was very sleepy still; this protracted waking up was also a sign that she was getting better. Muzzily, she was not sure if Laurence had said 'Everything O.K.?' or if this was something as yet unspoken, which it was her place to ask. So she said, all muzzed, sitting up, 'Everything O.K.?'

Laurence laughed.

She rose sleepily and went into the bathroom to wash and change, leaving the door open to talk through.

'Any incidents?' said Laurence.

She was awake now. 'Yes,' she told him. 'Lord Tom Noddy on the air.'

'Who?'

'Madame Butterfly.'

'And did you remember the tape-machine?'

'Um. I pressed the button. But I don't know if it's recorded anything.'

She sounded diffident. Laurence said:

'Shall I try?' He was afraid the experiment might upset her, might turn the luck of Caroline's health.

'Yes, do.'

He arranged the recording device, and pressed a lever. It gave a tiny whirr, then came the boom of Laurence's voice. 'Caroline darling . . .' followed by the funny, unprintable suggestion.

Caroline came out of the bathroom to listen, towel in hand. They were both eager for the next bit. It was a woman's voice. Laurence looked up sharply as it spoke: 'That's a damned lie. You're getting scared, I think. Why are you suddenly taking cover under that protestation?'

That was all. 'Good Christ!' said Laurence.

Caroline explained, rather embarrassed. 'That was my voice, answering back. It seems, my dear, that these visiting voices don't record. I didn't really think they would take.'

'What did they say to you? Why did you reply like that? What made you say "It's a lie"?'

She read him the shorthand notes she had taken.

'So you see,' she said with a hurt laugh, 'the characters are all fictitious.'

Laurence fiddled absently with the machine. When she stopped talking, he told her to hurry and get dressed. He kissed her as if she were a child.

As she made up her face she told him excitably, 'I have the answer. I know how to handle that voice.'

She expected him to ask, 'Tell me how.' But he didn't; he looked at her, still reckoning her in his regard as if she were a lovable child.

Then he said, 'Mother's worried. I'm afraid there's going to be a big shemozzle about Grandmother.'

It seemed to Laurence, then, that it was unsatisfactory for Caroline to be a child. He felt the need of her coordinating mind to piece together the mysterious facts of his grandmother's life. He felt helpless.

'You'll help me with my grandmother, won't you?' he said.

'Why?' she said gaily. 'What are you going to do to your grand-mother?' She looked mock-sinister. She was getting better. Laurence looked from her face to the shorthand notebook on the table, from the evidence of her normality to the evidence of her delusion. Perhaps, he thought, a person could go through life with one little crank and remain perfectly normal in every other respect. Perhaps it was only in regard to the imaginary aural impressions that Caroline was a child.

He said, 'Mrs Hogg read the letter I sent to you at St Philumena's.'

'You mean, she opened my letter and read it?'

'Yes, it's appalling. In fact, it's criminal.'

Caroline smiled a little at this. Laurence remembered the same sort of smile fleeting on his mother's face that afternoon in spite of her worry. He realized what it was the two women had smiled the same smile about.

'I admit that I've read other people's letters myself. I quite see that. But this is a different case. It's frightful, actually.'

Having established, with her smile, the fact that she considered him not altogether adult, Caroline said, 'On the level, is it serious?' And she began to question him as an equal.

They switched off the fires and light, still talking, and left the flat.

At about half past eleven, since they had decided to make a night of it, they went to dance at a place called the Pylon in Dover Street. There was hardly any light, and Caroline thought, Thank God for that.

For, after dinner at a restaurant in Knightsbridge, they had been to Soho. First, to a pub where some B.B.C. people were unexpectedly forgathered who called Laurence 'Larry'; and this was a washout so far as Laurence was concerned. His mind was on his grandmother, and the spoiling of his disinterestedness, his peace, by Mrs Hogg. He was on leave, moreover, and did not reckon to meet with his colleagues in those weeks. Next they had gone to a literary pub, where it rapidly became clear that the Baron had spread the story of Caroline and her hysterical night at his flat.

At the first pub, after they had left, a friend of Laurence had said, 'That's Larry's form of perversion – beautiful neurotic women. They have to be neurotic.'

It was understood that every close association between two people was a perversion. Caroline sensed the idea they had left behind them when they left this pub. Laurence, of course, knew it, but he didn't mind; he accepted that, for instance, 'perversion' was his friends' code-word for anyone's personal taste in love. While Caroline and Laurence were on their way to the second pub, this friend of Laurence's was saying, 'All Larry's girls have been neurotics.' This was true, as it happened.

Later, in the taxi, Caroline said to Laurence, 'Am I noticeably neurotic, do you think?'

Her eyes were huge and deep, unsettled, but she had the power of judgement in other features of her face.

He said, 'Yes, in a satisfactory way.' And he said presently, 'All my girls have been neurotics.'

Caroline knew this but was glad to hear it again from Laurence; his words made articulate her feeling of what was being said in the pub they had left. She knew most of Laurence's previous neurotic girls; she herself was the enduring one.

Presently again, and Laurence said,

'There are more interesting particulars about neurotic women. You never know what you mayn't find on their persons and in their general carry-on.'

In the second pub, where a fair fat poet said to Caroline, 'Tell me *all* about your visions, my dear'; and another poet, a woman with a cape and a huge mouth, said, 'Is there much Satanism going on within the Catholic Church these days?'; and another sort of writer, a man of over fifty, asked Caroline who was her psycho-analyst, and told her who was his – at this pub Caroline collected, one way and another, that the Baron had been mentioning this and that about her, to the ageless boys and girls who dropped in on him at his bookshop in Charing Cross Road.

The fat poet went steadily on about Caroline's 'visions'; he said they would be good for her publicity. Caroline and Laurence had been on short drinks, and both were rather lit up.

'Wonderful publicity,' they both agreed.

And the over-fifty, in his brown coat of fur-fabric, persisted,

'I could tell you of a psychiatrist who –'

'We know one,' Laurence said, 'who analyses crazy pavements.'

Caroline told the girl in the cape, did she know that Eleanor Hogarth had deserted the Baron?

'No!'

'Yes. He put me up for the night at his flat last week. All her things were gone. Not even a photograph. He only mentioned her once. He said she was away on tour, which was true; he said nothing about the break. Then Laurence found out definitely – he finds out everything, of course.'

'Gone off with someone else?'

'Don't know, really. But she's left him, not he her; I know that.'

'Poor Willi.'

'Oh, one can't blame her,' said Caroline, satisfied that the story would now spread.

The girl in the cape said, 'Have you tried to convert the Baron?'

'Me? No.'

'R.C.s usually try to convert everyone, however hopeless. I thought that was a sort of obligation.'

For good measure, Caroline quoted of the Baron what she heard said of someone else: 'He exhausted his capacity for conversion when he became an Englishman.'

Indeed, the Baron was rather scrupulous about his English observances and confident that he had the English idea, so that his contempt for the English, their intellect, their manners, arose from a vexation that they did not conform better to the idea. To this effect, Caroline exchanged her views on the Baron with the girl in the cape.

'But you know,' said the girl, 'there's another side to Willi Stock. He's an orgiast on the quiet.'

'A what?'

'Goes in for the Black Mass. He's a Satanist. Probably that's why Eleanor left him. She's so awfully bourgeois.'

Caroline suddenly felt oppressed by the pub and the people. That word 'bourgeois' had a dispiriting effect on her evening – it was part of the dreary imprecise language of this half-world she had left behind her more than two years since.

Laurence was talking to the blond fat poet who was inviting him to a party at someone else's house next week, describing the sort of people who would be present; and as Caroline got up, Laurence caught her eye just as this man was saying, 'You can't afford to miss it.'

Laurence piloted her out to the taxi, for she had been wobbly even when they arrived. But the momentary revulsion had sobered her.

They went to a coffee house, then on to the West End, to the Pylon, where, Caroline thought, thank God the lights are dim and the people not too distinguishable. The West End was another half-world of Caroline's past.

Eleanor Hogarth had a close look at the couple moving in the sleepy gloom before her. They had a square foot of floor-space, which they utilized with sweet skill, within its scope manoeuvring together like creatures out of natural history. This fascinated Eleanor; she was for a few moments incredulous at the sight of Caroline and Laurence in these surroundings, since she had never seen them before in a night-club, nor dancing.

Eleanor waved from her table; it was too far away from them to call, decently. Eventually Caroline saw. 'Oh, see, there's Eleanor.'

And there she was, with her business partner, white-haired young-faced Ernest Manders. This was Laurence's uncle, his father's youngest brother who had gone into ballet instead of Manders' Figs in Syrup.

When Laurence was quite little he had informed his mother,

'Uncle Ernest is a queer.'

'So he is, pet,' she answered happily, and repeated the child's words to several people before she learned from her husband the difference between being a queer and just being queer. After this, it became a family duty to pray for Uncle Ernest; it was understood that no occasion for prayers should pass without a mention of this uncle.

And with some success apparently, because in his fortieth year, when his relations with men were becoming increasingly violent, he gave them up for comfort's sake; not that he ever took to women as a substitute. Laurence had remarked to Caroline one day,

'I've gradually had to overcome an early disrespect for my Uncle Ernest.'

'Because he was a homosexual?'

'No. Because we were always praying specially for him.'

He was a religious man and likeable. Caroline got on well with him. She said he was her sort of Catholic, critical but conforming. Ernest always agreed with Caroline that the True Church was awful, though unfortunately, one couldn't deny, true.

She could not much bear Eleanor these days, though it was through Eleanor that she had first met Laurence. At one time these women were friends, exceedingly of a kind; that was at Cambridge, when, in their boxy rooms, they had leaned on the ignoble wooden fittings which were stained with rings from cocoa-mugs, and talked of this and that; mostly about the insolence of their fellow students and the insolence of their elders, for both girls had potential talents unrecognized. They were united in discontentment with the place as a place; its public-tiled wash-rooms, its bed-sitting-rooms, and other apartments so insolently designed. Eleanor left after a couple of terms to go into ballet. She might easily have gone to an art school, for she also had the art-school gift. It was Eleanor who had removed from one of the ground-floor corridors, and from its place on a wall, the portrait of a former Principal, keeping it for a whole night, in the course of which, by means of innumerable small touchings, she had made a subtle and important alteration in the portrait, which remains undetected to this day.

The thing about Eleanor, Caroline held, was that her real talent was for mimicry, and so she could have taken up any trade with ease, because all she had to do was to mimic the best that had already been done in any particular line, and that gave the impression of the expert.

Caroline was abroad during Eleanor's marriage; she did not know much about it, only that she had left her husband after the war, and under her married name had started a dancing school with a male partner. Ernest Manders. A few months later, Caroline and Laurence had set up together, by which time Eleanor's relationship with the

Baron was becoming established. What irritated Caroline now about her old friend was the fact that she had seemed not to change essentially in the years since their Cambridge days, and was apparently quite happy with herself as she was. Now Laurence was another like that. But Caroline could like in Laurence many characteristics which in others she could not tolerate. And she was aware of the irrationality and prejudice of all these feelings, without being able to stop feeling them.

But she said, so that her contempt for Eleanor should be concealed,

'Look at the band-leader. Who does he look like?' She mentioned a Cambridge don, with his rimless glasses and the sideways mouth. Eleanor laughed and laughed. She had been drinking more than Caroline that evening. 'So he does.' Then she told Caroline a story from which it emerged that this don was dead.

'I didn't know that,' said Caroline, being shocked then that Eleanor had laughed at her joke. When she saw Caroline involuntarily putting her face serious, Eleanor affirmed, 'But the band boy is the image of the man, just the same.'

Then Eleanor started picking out other members of the band, likening them to men they had agreed in despising during their friendship days. And she got Caroline to laugh, putting their meeting on a basis of workable humour, considering they were supposed to be enjoying themselves: and this was only possible by reference to the one kindly association between the two women, their college friendship. Caroline got over her annoyance at being caught out putting on a grave religious face when Eleanor had laughed at a dead man. And while she entered into Eleanor's amusement, she felt almost dumb about her suspicion that Eleanor was humouring her on account of her neurosis. She was right; this was exactly Eleanor's idea as she sat with her dark-brown head leaning over towards Caroline's much darker brown.

Two bottles of gin had appeared out of the gloom. Laurence, on his third drink from the first bottle, said,

'I've never felt more sober in my life. Some occasions, it just won't "take", you simply can't get drunk.'

Eleanor looked sorry for him, as if she knew he had worry on his mind from Caroline. This annoyed Caroline, because she knew he was worrying about his grandmother most of all.

While she danced with Ernest, who was weird to dance with, flexible, almost not there at all, so that she felt like a missile directed from a far distance, she saw Laurence examining Eleanor's cigarette case in his nosey way, and thought, 'He keeps trying to detect whatever it is he's looking for in life.' She admired his ability to start somewhere repeatedly; his courage; even if it was only in a cigarette case.

Soon, Laurence and Eleanor were dancing, then she saw that they sat down, and that Eleanor was talking in a confiding way; Eleanor was making small circular movements with her glass, stopping only to sigh reflectively into it before she drank, as often happens towards the end of a drinking night, when a woman confides in a man about another man.

Round the walls of the Pylon, so far as the walls could be discerned, were large gilt picture frames. Inside each, where the picture should be, was a square of black velvet, this being the Pylon's sort of effectiveness. As she smoothed her slight feet with Ernest, so limp, over their portion of dancing-floor, Caroline caught her view of Eleanor's head, described against one of the black squares of velvet in the background, just like a framed portrait, indistinct, in need of some touching-up.

FIVE

'I said, "Willi, this can't go on, it simply can not go on." ' Eleanor was getting maudlin. She was not a neurotic particularly, but that was not why Laurence didn't much care for her. It was only that he rather liked the Baron, and Eleanor, though her infidelities were her own affair, had never kept very quiet about them, except to the Baron himself who never suspected them.

Laurence, gazing intently at her small gold cigarette case as if it were the book of life itself, nodded his acknowledgement of her confidences.

'If he had been unfaithful,' she went on, 'I could have understood, I could have forgiven. But this obscenity – and apparently it's been going on for years – I never suspected. Of course I always knew he was interested in diabolism and that sort of thing, but I thought it was only theory. He had all the books, and I thought like a collector you know. But apparently it's been going on for years, the Black Masses, and they do frightful things, ask Caroline, she'll know all about the Black Mass. I feel it's a sort of personal insult to me personally, as if I'd found him out dabbling with a whore. And I said, "Willi, you've got to choose, it's either me or these foul practices – you can't have both." Because I tell you, Laurence, it was an insult to my intelligence apart from everything else. He said he was amused by my attitude. Amused. I'm not melodramatic, and further*more*, I'm not religious, but I do know that the Black Mass has a profoundly evil influence truly, Laurence. In fact, I wouldn't be surprised if he hasn't done something to Caroline.'

'How d'you mean, dear?'

'Well, I don't know if it's true, but I heard that she spent a night with Willi recently –'

'Yes, he was sweet to her really. She was ill at the time. But I think that was the climax, somehow. I think she's getting better now.'

'But I heard that she started hearing things after that night. I heard that and you can't help hearing things when people tell you, however unlikely.'

Laurence did not quite get the hang of this sentence, and while he was working it out Eleanor persisted,

'Hasn't Caroline been hearing things?'

'About you, dear?'

'No, voices. Spirits. Hearing –'

'Come and dance,' said Laurence.

This was their second attempt. She was even less steady than before, and it took him all his time to keep her upright. He said, 'Too many people, what d'you think?'

'Yes,' she said, 'let's sit down and drink.'

Ernest and Caroline were already returned. Eleanor said immediately, 'Caroline, what do you think of the Black Mass?'

Caroline's mood had become gay and physical; she was still jiggering about with her hands in time to the music. 'No idea,' she answered, 'but ask the Baron. He's the expert, so I'm told.' Then she remembered that Eleanor had left the Baron, so she said, 'Laurence, stop peering at Eleanor's cigarette case, like an old Jew looking for the carat mark.'

Laurence said, 'I'm trying to read the motto.'

On the front of the case was a tiny raised crest. Caroline poked her head in beside Laurence's with exaggerated curiosity. 'A wolf's head,' said Laurence. 'What's the motto? I can't read it.'

'*Fidelis et* – I can't remember, for the moment,' Eleanor said. 'I did know. It's the Hogarth crest. Only a Victorian rake-up, I imagine. My ex-husband gave me that case for a wedding present. He had a passion for putting his family crest on everything. Spoons, hair-brushes, you never saw the like. Caroline, seriously, don't you think the evil influence that's over us all is due to these Black Masses? I've found out about Willi. I suppose you've known all the time, but I didn't dream. And it takes place at Notting Hill Gate, as you probably know.'

Laurence had given her a weak drink, but now, sipping it, she noticed this, and said to Ernest reproachfully, 'I'm drinking lemon-ade, virtually. Don't be so mean with that gin, Ernest.'

Caroline was fascinated by Eleanor's performance. Indeed, it was only an act; the fascination of Eleanor was her entire submersion in whatever role she had to play. There did not seem to be any question of Eleanor's choosing her part, it was forced on her, she was enslaved by it. Just now, she appeared to be under the control of liquor; but she was also and more completely under the control of her stagey act: that of a scatty female who'd been drinking: wholeheartedly, her personality was involved, so that it was impossible to distinguish between Eleanor and the personality which possessed her during those hours; as well try to distinguish between the sea and the water in it.

Caroline was fascinated and appalled. In former days, Eleanor's mimicry was recognizable. She would change her personality like dresses according to occasion, and it had been fun to watch, and an acknowledged joke of Eleanor's. But she had lost her small portion of detachment; now, to watch her was like watching doom. As a child Caroline, pulling a face, had been warned, 'If you keep doing that it will stick one day.' She felt, looking at Eleanor, that this was actually happening to the woman. Her assumed personalities were beginning to cling; soon one of them would stick, grotesque and ineradicable.

'She's got the Black Mass on the brain,' Ernest was sighing.

'So would you if you'd been living with a diabolist,' said Eleanor, contorting her face according to her role of the moment. And she drawled, placing a hand on Caroline's hand, looking intensely into her eyes,

'Caroline, my poor Caroline. You're haunted by spirits, aren't you? And you know who's behind it, don't you?'

The performance was becoming more and more corny. Caroline tried to revert to their earlier farce about the band and their Cambridge friends.

'But she's haunted,' said Eleanor, still gazing at Caroline.

Caroline had never felt less haunted. She was almost shocked to find how she seemed to derive composure from the evidence of her friend's dissolution.

'I've never felt less haunted,' Caroline said.

'*I'm* haunted,' said Ernest, 'by the fact that we're nearly bankrupt, and Eleanor has abandoned our only form of security.'

'Willi can't withdraw financially. But he'll ruin us all another way. I know it. I feel it. He's working a tremendous power against us,' Eleanor drivelled.

'What was your husband's name?' Laurence asked her.

'You *are* haunted, my dear girl,' Eleanor insisted, still gazing upon Caroline's face.

'Hogarth.' It was Ernest who supplied the name, smiling like a conjurer who has produced the rabbit.

'Mervyn,' said Eleanor belatedly.

'I believe I've met him. Does he live at Ladle Sands in Sussex by any chance?'

'Yes,' said Eleanor. 'Don't remind me *please*. He ought to be in prison. I've had a tragic life, Laurence. Ernest, haven't I had a tragic life?'

'Desperately,' said Ernest.

'And the tragedy of that poor cripple boy,' said Eleanor. 'Caroline, I've never told you about my marriage. What a mess. He had a son by a former marriage, quite helpless. What could I do? These tragedies occur everywhere through influences of evil spirits, that I do believe. You've given me sheer *lemonade*, Ernest, don't be mean with the gin.'

'You're getting tight,' said Ernest.

'Can you blame me? Caroline, do you realize the sheer potency of the Black Mass? It's going on all the time.'

'I shouldn't worry,' said Caroline. 'It's only an infantile orgy. It can't do much harm.'

'Have you ever been to a Black Mass?'

'No. It takes me all my time to keep up with the white Mass on Sundays.'

'What's the white Mass? Ernest, tell me what's the white Mass?'

'She means the Mass, dear. The ordinary Catholic Mass,' Ernest said.

'Oh, but this is different. The Black Mass has tremendous power. It can actually make objects move. Nobody touches them. They move. I've read heaps about it. There are naked girls, and they say everything backward. And obscenity. Ernest, you don't take me seriously, but you just go to a Black Mass, and see. I challenge you. *I* wouldn't dare go. I'd die.'

Caroline and Laurence spoke simultaneously, 'Catholics can't go to Black Masses.'

'Not allowed,' Ernest explained.

'They treat you like kids,' said Eleanor, 'don't they, Laurence?'

she said, for she knew he had lapsed from religion.

'That's right,' he said agreeably.

'Why is the Black Mass forbidden, if there isn't some tremendous evil in it?' she persisted, her hand on Caroline's.

'I don't say there isn't great evil in it,' Caroline replied, 'I only say it's a lot of tomfoolery.'

'I wouldn't dismiss it so lightly as that,' Ernest argued.

'It depends on how you regard evil,' Caroline said. 'I mean, as compared with the power of goodness. The effectuality of the Black Mass, for instance, must be trivial so long as we have the real Mass.'

'I wouldn't dismiss the power of evil lightly,' Ernest insisted. 'It does exist, obviously.'

'I thought,' said Eleanor, 'that Catholics all believed the same thing. But I can see you don't.'

'Caroline is being mystical,' Ernest said.

'Caroline is a mystic,' said Eleanor. 'I've always said so. She's a mystic, isn't she, Laurence?'

'Every time,' said Laurence, very pleasantly.

'And the trouble with these mystics, they theorise on the basis of other people's sufferings, and in the end they belittle suffering. Caroline, if you'd suffered as much as I've suffered, you wouldn't be talking like something out of this world.'

'I won't compete with you on the question of suffering,' Caroline spoke acidly, for, after all, she rather fancied herself as a sufferer.

'Poor girl, you are haunted by the evil ones,' Eleanor said, which was maddening just at that moment.

'I shouldn't have much to do with Willi,' Eleanor continued. 'Take my advice and keep clear.'

'Poor Willi!' Caroline said with a happy laugh, though meaning malice.

'The Baron is charming, bless him,' said Laurence, in an absent way, for he was conferring with Ernest over paying their bill.

'Willi makes his money out of the Black Mass,' Eleanor stated. 'That's where he gets it from, I'm sure.'

'Oh, surely it can't be a business matter?' Laurence put in again.

'They do quite a trade in consecrated wafers,' said Eleanor.

'In *what*?' Caroline said, seriously disturbed for the first time since the subject was mentioned.

Laurence said, 'I doubt if they make a point of the wafers being consecrated.'

'I believe they do,' Ernest said. 'I'm afraid that seems to be the whole point of the Black Mass.'

'It's a very rare thing these days,' Caroline said. 'Satanism fizzled out in the twenties.'

'Oh, did it?' Eleanor said, getting ready to argue the point.

Laurence interrupted with, 'Why did you say your ex-husband should be in prison?'

'Mind y'r own business, lovey.' Eleanor screwed up her face into an inebriate smile.

'Is there a relation of his, do you know, called Georgina Hogg?'

'I can see,' said Caroline, 'we've reached the stage where each one discourses upon his private obsession, regardless –'

'I just wondered,' Laurence explained, 'because that crest on Eleanor's cigarette case is the same as the one on some of Georgina's possessions.'

Eleanor did not reply. She had a look of drunken incoherence which may have covered any emotion.

'Possibly derived from the same name, originally,' Caroline suggested. '"Hogg" and "Hogarth".'

When they went to get their coats Caroline had to take Eleanor's arm to keep her steady, although she felt a slight electricity singing in her own limbs. In the cloakroom Eleanor revived a little, and putting on her lipstick shifted over her attitude to the woman-to-woman basis. 'Men are clods.

'And keep away, Caroline, do, from the Baron.

'And Laurence said something about a woman called Hogg? I couldn't quite catch – I'm so sleepy, so tight.' In evidence, she yawned with her mouth all over her face.

Caroline replied with exaggerated precision, annoyed at having to repeat what Eleanor already knew.

'Yes. She was a nursemaid or governess with the Manders years ago. Laurence thought there might be some connexion between her and your husband because the crest on your cigarette case is the same as the crest on Mrs Hogg's possessions, apparently.'

'A nursemaid with a family crest?'

'Apparently. It's quite possible,' said Caroline.

'There may be some original connexion between the names "Hogg" and "Hogarth",' Eleanor said, as if she had not heard Caroline's remark to this effect, and had just thought of it herself.

'Quite,' said Caroline, and noticed that this abrupt finality did not have a satisfying effect on Eleanor.

As they waited for their coats Eleanor asked,

'Where are you living now?'

'In Queen's Gate, quite near our old flat.'

'And Laurence?'

'Laurence is still in the old flat.'

'Officially, that is?' said Eleanor.

'What d'you mean?'

'Well, dear Carrie, I heard that Laurence couldn't tear himself away from you, and was stopping over at your new place.'

'Oh, that's only a temporary arrangement. I haven't been well.'

'A temporary arrangement! You Roman Catholics can get away with anything. You just nip into the confessional in between temporary arrangements, so to speak.'

'We sleep in separate rooms, as it happens.' Then Caroline was furious with herself for making this defence where none was due. Laurence wouldn't like it, either. 'I rate friendship infinitely higher than erotic love,' she added, trying to improve matters, but making them worse.

They found Laurence and Ernest outside with a taxi.

'Let's walk a little way and get some air,' Caroline said to Laurence.

'Oh, then we'll walk with you. That would be nice,' said Eleanor.

But Ernest, with his tact, got her into the cab. Before they said good night, Eleanor, slurred and mouthy, declared, 'Now, Laurence, take care of Caroline. She's just been telling me that you both sleep in separate rooms. It's a good story if you stick to it. And it must be a frightful strain either way. No wonder Caroline's haunted.'

They left London next day by car, though Laurence's M.G. was overdue for repair, instead of going by train. This was owing to their getting up late and frittering the day in talk, first about poor Eleanor, as they agreed she was, then about themselves.

Caroline had not slept much that night. To start with it was after four o'clock by the time she parted from Laurence who was sleeping on a camp bed in the kitchen. She lay awake for about half an hour and then she was visited by the voices, preceded by the typewriter. This was the first time it had happened while Laurence was in the flat.

As soon as she heard the familiar tapping she called softly to Laurence; he was quite near, only a few yards away through the open door.

'Are you awake?'

He was instantly awake. 'Yes?'

'Don't come. Only listen. Here's that noise again. Keep quiet.'

It had already started its chanting. She switched on the light and grabbed her notebook and pencil. She missed the first bit, but she got:

'... *next day by car, though Laurence's M.G. was due for repair, instead of going by train. This was owing to their getting up late and frittering the day in talk, first about poor Eleanor, as they agreed she was, then about themselves. Click. Click.*

'Did you hear that?' Caroline then called out to Laurence.

'No, my dear, I didn't hear a thing.'

He had got out of bed and now came in, looking anxious. 'Are you all right?'

She was sitting up, gazing at her shorthand notes.

'I can't make this out,' she said. 'I can't make it out at all.'

She read it to him.

'You're thinking ahead. Don't worry about tomorrow. We can sleep late and catch an afternoon train.'

'I didn't imagine these words. They were told me,' she stated, but unprotesting factually.

'Shall I come in beside you?'

'Make some tea first.'

He did this, while Caroline continued gazing at the notebook.

When he brought their tea, he said, 'I'll come in beside you.'

It was a three-quarter divan and so there was just room. Caroline considered the situation as she drank her tea, then she said,

'I'll be all right by myself, really I will.'

'It's cold in the kitchen,' said Laurence.

He began to snuggle down.

'I'll put a pillow down the middle,' Caroline said.

'Wouldn't a bread-knife and a prayer book do instead?'

'Clear off,' said Caroline.

'All I want is a beautiful night's sleep.'

'Same here,' she said.

Eventually they brought in the camp bed from the kitchen and settled down alongside. He reflected how strangely near impracticable sexual relations would be between them, now that Caroline thought them sinful. She was thinking the same thing.

It was past eleven when they woke next morning.

It was while they cooked their omelettes for lunch that she told Laurence, as if it were an undeniable fact, of her theory about the author making a book out of their lives.

Laurence knew that people with obsessions could usually find evidence to fit their craziest convictions. From the time he had learned about the voices, he had been debating within himself what this might mean to his relationship with Caroline. He had hoped that the failure of the tape-machine to record the sounds would prove her delusion to her. And when this failed to impress her he wondered whether it would be possible for him to humour her fantasy indefinitely, so that she could be the same Caroline except for this one difference in their notions of reality; or whether reality would force them apart, and the time arrive when he needs must break with, 'Caroline, you are wrong, mistaken, mad. There are no voices; there is no typewriter; it is all a delusion. You must get mental treatment.'

It was on his tongue to tell her so when, standing in her dressing-gown cooking the eggs and bacon, she told him, 'I've discovered the truth of the matter'; the truth of the matter being, it transpired, this fabulous idea of themselves and their friends being used as characters in a novel.

'How do you know it's a novel?'

'"The characters in this novel are all fictitious,"' she quoted with a truly mad sort of laugh.

'In fact,' she continued, 'I've begun to study the experience objectively. That's a sign, isn't it, that I'm well again?'

He thought not. He went so far to suggest, 'Your work on the novel form – isn't it possible that your mind –'

'It's convenient that I know something of the novel form,' Caroline said.

'Yes,' he said.

He argued a little, questioned her. Was the author disembodied? –
She didn't know. If so, how could he use a typewriter? How could she
overhear him? How could one author chant in chorus? – That she
didn't know, that she didn't know. Was the author human or a spirit,
and if so –

'How can I answer these questions? I've only begun to ask them
myself. The author obviously exists in a different dimension from
ours. That will make the investigation difficult.'

He realized, then, that he was arguing madness upon madness, was
up against a private revelation. He almost wished he were still a
believer, so that he could the more forcefully use some Catholic
polemic against her privacy.

'From the Catholic point of view, I should have thought there were
spiritual dangers in holding this conviction.'

'There are spiritual dangers in everything. From the Catholic point
of view the chief danger about a conviction is the temptation to deny
it.'

'But you ought to subject it to reason.'

'I'm doing so,' Caroline said. 'I have started investigations,' and
she was becoming delighted with this talk.

He said then, 'Don't you think the idea of an invisible person
tuning in to your life might possibly upset your faith?'

'Of course,' she said. 'That's why he ought to be subjected to
reason!'

'Well,' he said wearily, 'I've never heard of a Catholic being
allowed to traffic with the unknown like this.'

'The author is doing all the trafficking,' she explained. 'But I'm
going to make it difficult for him, you'll see.'

'The whole thing is far too gnostic,' he said.

That did amuse her. 'That does amuse me,' she said; 'you expressing yourself so orthodox.'

'It makes damn all difference to me if you're a heretic, darling,
because you're sweet. But sooner or later you'll come bump against
authority. Did you tell Father Jerome about this idea?'

'I mentioned the possibility. I had only just realized it.'

'Didn't he object?'

'No, why should he? It isn't a sin to be a little cracked in the head.'
She added, 'I know that I am slightly insane.'

'No,' he said gently, 'you are quite sane, Caroline.'

'From your point of view,' she insisted, 'I am out of my senses. It would be a human indignity to deny it.'

He thought, How cunning of her to get round it that way, and he remembered that with madness comes cunning.

'You have a mild nervous disorder,' he said.

'I have what you ought to call a delusion. In any normal opinion that's a fact.'

'Caroline, don't distress yourself, dear.'

'The normal opinion is bound to distress me because it's a fact like the fact of the author and the facts of the Faith. They are all painful to me in different ways.'

'What can I do?' he said, as he had said many times in the past days. 'What can I do to help you?'

'Will you be able to make an occasional concession to the logic of my madness?' she asked him. 'Because that will be necessary between us. Otherwise, we shall be really separated.' She was terrified of being entirely separated from Laurence.

'Haven't I always tried to enter your world?'

'Yes, but this is a very remote world I'm in now.'

'Not really,' he said. 'You're as good as normal in every other way.'

He wondered if she was hurt by this. He wondered he had not courage enough to make her see a mental doctor.

She said, 'We shall have to keep this secret. I don't want the reputation of being crackers more than necessary. The Baron has broadcast enough already.'

It was a pact. But less than a couple of hours later he saw how irksome it could be.

They had already frittered the best part of the day, and it was past four when Laurence, after telephoning the station about the trains, said,

'We'd better go by car. It's O.K. for the one trip, and I can get it seen to at Hayward's Heath quite quickly. Then we can have the use of it, much more convenient.'

'Oh, you can hire a car at Hayward's Heath,' Caroline said quickly. 'I want to go by train. We must go by train.'

'Don't be awkward. Get dressed, and I'll get the car out. Trains are hateful if you have the alternative of a car.'

'Awkward is just what I'm going to be,' Caroline said.

She started hunting for her notebook.

'I've just jerked up to the fact,' she said, 'that our day is doing what the voices said it would. Now, we chatted about Eleanor. Then about ourselves. All right. We've frittered the day. The narrative says we went by car; all right, we must go by train. You do see that, don't you, Laurence? It's a matter of asserting free will.'

He quite saw. He thought, 'Why the hell should we be enslaved by her secret fantasy?'

'I don't see,' he said, 'why we should be inconvenienced by it one way or another. Let's act naturally.'

But he saw that Caroline had it very much on the brain that her phantom should be outwitted in this one particular.

'Very well,' he said. He felt his honesty under threat of strangling. He desired their relationship to continue with the least possible change, but ever since her conversion it had been altering. Laurence could not feel that they were further apart than before, but he felt, now, that Caroline was on shifting ground, liable to be swept beyond his reach at any moment. He was not sure if he was agile enough to keep contact with her, nor that the effort would be worth it beyond a point at which Caroline might become unrecognizable.

These misgivings nearly choked him while he said to Caroline,

'All right, we'll go by train.'

But when, at this, she turned gay, he thought predominantly, 'She will help me with Grandmother in spite of her illness. The holiday will be good for Caroline. We still need each other.' Also he thought, 'I love the girl.' And his excitement at the thought of unravelling his grandmother's mysteries somehow made Caroline more lovable.

She was dressed and had packed for them both, to make up to Laurence for his concession. It was half past five. Laurence was telephoning a wire to his grandmother, to expect them about eight o'clock.

'She probably prepared lunch,' he said, as he put down the receiver.

'Laurence, that's too bad of us.'

'But she'll be so happy when we arrive, she won't say a word. Are you ready?'

Standing by her desk when he had finished phoning, Laurence had torn a few outdated pages off the calendar.

'That brings you up to date,' he said.

She remarked ruefully, 'I tear off the weeks automatically, when I'm sitting at the desk. It's a reproach when the calendar gets behind the times. Really, I must get down to my book soon.'

They were ready to leave. Laurence lifted the suitcases. But she was still staring at the calendar.

'What's today?' she asked. 'It isn't November the first, is it?'

'That's right. November already. Do make haste.'

'All Saints' Day,' she continued, 'you know what that means?'

Like most people who are brought up in the Catholic faith, Laurence was quick in recollecting such things. 'A Holiday of Obligation,' he said.

'And I haven't been to Mass!'

'Oh, it can't be helped. Don't worry. It isn't considered a mortal sin if you genuinely forgot.'

'But I'm obliged to attend a Mass if there's an opportunity, since I have remembered. There's probably a late Mass at the Oratory. Probably at six-thirty. I'll have to go to that. You do see that, don't you, Laurence?'

'Yes, I quite see that.' So he did; he found it easy to see the obligations of the Catholic religion; it was part of his environment. He found it much easier to cope with Caroline's new-found Catholicism than her new-found psychicism. He also found it easy to say,

'We can't let Grandmother down again. Wouldn't that be a valid excuse for missing Mass?'

And he quite expected her reply,

'You go ahead by car, and I'll come by a later train.'

And therefore, happy at regaining his liberty on the question of taking his car, he said with ease,

'It would be more fun if we both went by car after your Mass. We could make it by eight o'clock.'

She felt relieved on the whole. Her great desire to travel by train was dispersed by the obvious necessities of going to Mass, and of not messing Laurence around any further.

Presently he said, 'Sure you won't mind,' for he understood the question was safely settled for her, and he did not wish to play the tyrant. So he had the luxury of asking her several times, 'Quite sure, dear, it's all right? You don't mind coming by car?'

'After all,' she told him, 'it isn't a moral defeat. The Mass is a proper obligation. But to acquiesce in the requirements of someone's novel would have been ignoble.'

He gave academic consideration to this statement and observed, 'The acquiescence is accidental, in which sense the nobility must oblige.'

She thought, 'The hell of it, he understands that much. Why isn't he a Catholic, then?' She smiled at him over her drink, for their immediate haste was over and Laurence had fished out the bottle which she had packed in his suitcase, very carefully in its proper corner.

Brompton Oratory oppressed her when it was full of people, such a big monster of a place. As usual, when she entered, the line from the Book of Job came to her mind, 'Behold now Behemoth which I made with thee.'

Before the Mass started, this being the Feast of All Saints, there was a great amount of devotion going on before the fat stone statues. The things worth looking at were the votive candles, crowds of these twinklers round every altar; Caroline added her own candle to the nearest cluster. It occurred to her that the Oratory was the sort of place which might become endeared in memory, after a long absence. She could not immediately cope with this huge full-blown environment, for it antagonized the diligence with which Caroline coped with things, bit by bit.

Having been much in Laurence's company for the fortnight past, and now alone in this company of faces, in the midst of the terrifying collective, she remembered more acutely than ever her isolation by ordeal. She was now fully conscious that she was under observation intermittently by an intruder. And presently her thoughts were away, dwelling on the new strangeness of her life, and although her eyes and ears had been following the Mass throughout, it was not until the Offertory verse that she collected her wits;

Justorum animae ... from sheer intelligence, the climax of the Mass approaching, she had to let her brood of sufferings go by for the time being.

'You're always bad-tempered after Mass,' Laurence observed as they cruised through the built-up areas.

'I know,' she said. 'It's one of the proofs of the Faith so far as I'm concerned. It's evidence of the truth of the Mass, don't you see? The flesh despairs.'

'Pure subjectivism,' he said. 'You're something of a Quietist, I think. And quite Manichaean. A Catharist.' He had been schooled in the detection of heresies.

'Anything else?'

'Scribe and Pharisee,' he said, 'alternately according to mood.'

'The decor of Brompton Oratory makes me ill,' she told him, as another excuse. For when he had met her after the Mass she had turned most sour.

'You don't refer to the "decor" of a church,' he said – 'at least, I think not.'

'What is it then?'

'I'm not sure of the correct term. I've never heard it called a "decor".'

'Very useful, your having been brought up a Catholic,' said Caroline. 'Converts can always rely on your kind for instruction in the non-essentials.'

Eventually, they had clear road. Caroline pulled their spare duffle from the back seat and arranged it over her head and shoulders, so that she was secluded inside this tent, concealed from Laurence; then he guessed she was trying to suppress her irritable mood. In fact, it was getting on her nerves more and more that the eyes of an onlooker were illicitly upon them. Her determination to behave naturally in face of that situation made her more self-conscious.

Laurence was thinking about his grandmother, and as he did so he speeded up.

Two days had passed since Mrs Hogg had paid her bleak visit to Helena. Strangely, when Caroline had heard of this, she had seemed incredulous: and now, when he reverted to the subject:

'No. Helena must be mistaken. I can't conceive Mrs Hogg as a blackmailer.'

'But you've seen what she's like.'

'I don't think that particular vice is quite in her line. Opening your letter – that I do visualize. I got the impression that she's a type who acts instinctively: she'd do any evil under the guise of good. But she wouldn't engage in deliberate malice. She's too superstitious. In fact, Mrs Hogg is simply a Catholic atrocity, like the tin medals and bleeding hearts. I don't see her as a cold-blooded blackmailer. Helena must have imagined those insinuated threats.' And so Caroline rattled on, overtaken by an impulse to talk, to repeat and repeat any assertion as an alternative to absolute silence. For in such a silence Caroline kept her deepest madness, a fear void of evidence, a suspicion altogether to be distrusted. It stuck within her like something which would go neither up nor down, the shapeless notion that Mrs Hogg was somehow in league with her invisible persecutor. She would not speak of this nor give it verbal form in her mind.

Laurence could not see her face, it was behind the duffle coat. He felt exasperated by Caroline's seeming to take Mrs Hogg's part, if only that little bit.

'We've known her for twenty-odd years. We know her better than you do, dear. She's vicious.'

She snapped back at him. And so, in his need for their relations to return to a nice normal, he said peaceably,

'Yes, I suppose old Georgina means well. But she's done a lot of harm one way and another, and this time she's gone too far. We can't have Grandmother tormented at her time of life, no matter what mischief the old lady's up to. We can't, can we?' So Laurence tried to calm her testiness and engage her sympathy.

Caroline did soften down. But she surprised him when she declared vehemently, 'I don't know that Mrs Hogg wants to torment your grandmother. I don't really think your grandmother is involved in any suspicious activity. I think you're imagining it all, on the strength of a few odd coincidences.'

It was strange. Normally, Laurence's concession, his 'Yes, I suppose old Georgina means well' should have evoked something quite agreeable from Caroline.

So he tried again. 'There's something else to be considered. That clue I got from Eleanor's cigarette case. I'm sure the crest is the same as Georgina's. There is some connexion between Georgina and this Hogarth couple, I'm convinced of it.'

She did not reply.

'Strange, wasn't it, my discerning that crest, quite by chance?'

'By chance.' Caroline repeated the words on a strained pitch.

'I mean,' said Laurence obligingly, but misunderstanding her, 'that God led me to it, God bless him. Well, it's a small world. We just bump into Eleanor and –'

'Laurence,' said Caroline, 'I don't think I'm going to be much help to you at Ladylees. I've had enough holiday-making. I'll stay for a couple of days but I want to get back to London and do some work, actually. Sorry to change my mind but –'

'Go to hell,' Laurence said. 'Kindly go to hell.'

After that they stopped at a pub. When they resumed their journey Caroline began patiently to state her case. They had lost half an hour, and Laurence drove swiftly into Sussex.

'From my point of view it's clear that you are getting these ideas into your head through the influence of a novelist who is contriving some phoney plot. I can see clearly that your mind is working under the pressure of someone else's necessity, and under the suggestive power of some irresponsible writer you are allowing yourself to become an amateur sleuth in a cheap mystery piece.'

'How do you know the plot is phoney?' he said, which was rather sweet of him.

'I haven't been studying novels for three years without knowing some of the technical tricks. In this case it seems to me there's an attempt being made to organize our lives into a convenient slick plot. Is it likely that your grandmother is a gangster?'

Just ahead of them two girls in a shining black open racer skimmed the wet road. Automatically Laurence put on speed, listening intently to Caroline at the same time, for it was difficult to grasp her mind at this fantastic level.

'That's a Sunbeam Alpine,' he remarked.

'Are you listening to what I'm saying, dear?'

'I am, truly,' he said.

'Your grandmother being a gangster, it's taking things too far. She's an implausible character, don't you see?'

'She's the most plausible person I know. She'd take in anyone. That's the difficulty.'

'I mean, as a character, don't you see? She's unlikely. So is Mrs Hogg. Is it likely that the pious old cow is a blackmailer?'

'I think it likely that she's done *you* a lot of harm. She must have got properly on your nerves. She's an evil influence. You haven't been the same since you met her.'

Above the throb and tapping of the engine and the rain, he heard her, 'You don't know what you're talking about!'

'No,' he said.

'Do you really think, Laurence, that the coincidence of the crest on Eleanor's cigarette case with the one on Mrs Hogg's hairbrushes is plausible?'

'Well,' he said, 'I didn't invent the coincidence. There it was.'

'Quite,' she said.

They were losing on the Sunbeam Alpine. Laurence put on speed, so that the noise of the engine made conversation impossible. But when he had regained his ground, doing an easy fifty over the bright wet road, she asked him,

'Do you want to understand my point of view, Laurence?'

'Yes, darling, I do. Try to be reasonable.'

'It's a question of what you choose,' she said. 'If you hadn't been on the look-out for some connexion between the Hogarths and poor Mrs Hogg you wouldn't have lit on that crest. And you wouldn't have been looking for it if you hadn't been influenced in that direction. I nearly fell for the trick myself, that night I stayed with the Baron. He happened to let fall a remark; it seemed to point to the suspicion that he'd been seeing your grandmother secretively during the past year, and quite often. But personally, I reject the suspicion – I refuse to have my thoughts and actions controlled by some unknown, possibly sinister being. I intend to subject him to reason. I happen to be a Christian. I happen –'

'You think the Baron's been seeing Grandmother?' Laurence pressed her. 'How did you come to think that? It's very important, dear, do tell me.'

The Sunbeam Alpine was still ahead of them. The girl at the wheel said something to her companion, who looked round. They obviously expected a race. Laurence accelerated.

'No,' Caroline said. 'That's just the point. I won't be involved in this fictional plot if I can help it. In fact, I'd like to spoil it. If I had my way I'd hold up the action of the novel. It's a duty.'

'Do tell me what the Baron said about my grandmother,' Laurence said. 'That would be the reasonable thing, my dear.'

'No, it would involve me. I intend to stand aside and see if the novel has any real form apart from this artificial plot. I happen to be a Christian.'

She said a good deal more against the plot. Laurence thought in his misery, 'She really is mad, after all. There's no help for it, Caroline is mad.' And he thought of the possibility of the long months and perhaps years ahead in which he might have to endure the sight of Caroline, his love, a mental chaos, perhaps in an asylum for months, years.

She said a great deal more about the artificial plot. Once she broke off to warn him.

'Laurence, don't try to chase those girls. They've got a supercharger.'

But he took no notice, and she continued to assure him of her resolution not to be involved in any man's story.

It was all very well for Caroline to hold out for what she wanted and what she didn't want in the way of a plot. All very well for her to resolve upon holding up the action. Easy enough for her to criticize. Laurence speeded up and touched seventy before they skidded and crashed. The Sunbeam Alpine slowed down and turned back. Laurence was still conscious, though the pain in his chest was fierce, when he saw the girls get out of their shiny racer and come towards his, where he lay entangled in his wreckage.

He saw Caroline too, her face covered with blood beside him, one of her legs bent back beneath her body most unnaturally, a sight not to be endured after he had noted her one faint moan and one twist.

PART TWO

SIX

A woman came in three days a week to do housework for Louisa Jepp. It was on one of these days that Mrs Hogg called at the cottage.

Mrs Jepp, keeping her on the doorstep, said,

'I cannot ask you to come inside, Mrs Hogg. My woman is all over the floors. Is it anything in particular?'

'Perhaps this afternoon,' Mrs Hogg said, and she was looking over Louisa's shoulder into the interior, right through to the green back garden.

'No. This afternoon I'm going to see my grandson in hospital. Master Laurence has had an accident. Is it anything in particular, Mrs Hogg?'

'I would like to inquire for Laurence.'

'That's kind of you. Master Laurence is progressing *and* Miss Caroline, though she's more serious. I shall say you inquired.' Louisa did not for the world suggest that Mrs Hogg might have anything further to say.

'I have a message for Laurence. That's why I came personally.'

'All the way from the North of England,' stated Louisa.

Mrs Hogg said, 'I'm here for the day. From London.'

'Come round to the back and we shall sit in the garden.'

It was a day of mild November light and sun. Louisa led the way among her pigeons across the small green patch to the bench in front of her loganberry bush.

Mrs Hogg sat down beside her, fished into her carrier bag, and pulled out an old yellow fox cape which she arranged and patted on her shoulders.

'This time of year,' she said.

Louisa thought, 'My charwoman is turned out more ladylike, and yet this woman is of good family.' She said, 'Is it anything special, your message for Master Laurence?' And while there was time she added on second thoughts,

'He is quite able to read although not sitting up yet, if you would care to write a note.'

'Oh no,' said Mrs Hogg.

Louisa thought, 'I thought not.'

'No, I shouldn't trouble him with a letter, poor Laurence, letters can cause trouble,' Mrs Hogg said. She seemed glad of the rest after the up-hill walk from the station. Observably, she gathered strength while Louisa sat beside her expressly making no reply.

'I learn,' said Mrs Hogg, 'that you call me a poisonous woman.'

'One is always learning,' Louisa said, while her black eyes made a rapid small movement in her thinking head. Mrs Hogg saw only the small hands folded on the brown lap.

'Do you not think it is time for you,' said Mrs Hogg, 'to take a reckoning of your sins and prepare for your death?'

'You spoke like that to my husband,' said Louisa. 'His death was a misery to him through your interference.'

'I nursed Mr Jepp day and night –'

'No,' said Louisa, 'only night. And then only until I discovered your talk.'

'He should have seen a priest, as I said.'

'Mrs Hogg, what is your message for Master Laurence?'

'Only that he is not to worry. I shall take no legal action against *him*. He will understand what I mean. And, Mrs Jepp,' she continued, 'you are lonely here living by yourself.'

'I am lonely by no means. I shall give no such foolish message to Master Laurence. If you have any grievance against him, I suggest you write to Sir Edwin. My grandson is not to be troubled at present.'

'There is the matter of slander. In my position my character in the world is very important.'

'You have got hold of Master Laurence's letter to Miss Caroline,' Louisa said in a voice she sometimes used when she had played a successful hand at rummy through guesswork.

'You really must remember your age,' said Mrs Hogg. 'No good carrying on as if you were in your prime.'

'I will not have you to stay with me,' Louisa said.

'You need a companion.'

'I am not feeble. I trust I shall never be so feeble as to choose you for a companion.'

'Why do you keep diamonds in the bread?'

Louisa hardly moved nor paused at all. Indeed it entered her mind: how like Laurence to have found the hiding place!

'I will not deny, that is my habit.'

'You are full of sin.'

'Crime,' said Louisa. 'I would hardly say "full"....'

Mrs Hogg rose then, her lashless eyes screwed on Louisa's brown hands on her brown lap. Was the woman really senile, then?

'Wait. Sit down,' Louisa said, 'I should like to tell you all about the crime.' She looked up, her black old eyes open to Mrs Hogg. The appealing glance was quite convincing.

Thus encouraged, 'You must see a priest,' said Mrs Hogg. None the less, she sat down to hear Louisa's confession.

'I am in smuggling,' said Louisa. 'I shan't go into the whys and hows because of my memory, but I have a gang of my own, my dear Georgina, what do you think of that?' Louisa peered at Mrs Hogg from the corner of her eye and pursed her lips as if she were kissing the breeze. Mrs Hogg stared. Was she drunk perhaps? But at seventy-eight, after all –

'A *gang?*' said Mrs Hogg at last.

'A gang. We are four. I am the leader. The other three are gentlemen. They smuggle diamonds from abroad.'

'In loaves of bread?'

'I won't go into the ways and whats. Then I dispose of the diamonds through my contact in London.'

Mrs Hogg said, 'Your daughter doesn't know this. *If* it's true.'

'You have been to see Lady Manders, of course? You have told her what was in that letter you stole?'

'Lady Manders is very worried about you.'

'Ah yes. I will put that right. Well, let me tell you the names of the parties involved in my smuggling arrangements. If you know everything I'm sure you won't want to worry my daughter any more.'

'You can trust me,' said Mrs Hogg.

'I'm sure. There is a Mr Webster, he is a local baker. A real fine person, he doesn't go abroad himself. I had better not say what part he plays in my smuggling arrangements. Then there's a father and son –

such a sad affair, the boy's a cripple but it does him so much good the trips abroad, the father too. Their name is Hogarth. Mervyn is the father and Andrew is the son. That is my gang.'

But Mrs Hogg looked in a bad way just then. The dreadful fluffy fur slipped awry on her shoulder. Violently she said, 'Mervyn and Andrew!'

'That is correct. Hogarth they call themselves.'

'You are evil,' said Mrs Hogg.

'You won't be needing that letter,' said Louisa, 'but you may keep it just the same.'

Mrs Hogg gathered her fur cape around her huge breasts, and speaking without a movement of her upper lip in a way that fascinated Louisa by its oddity, she said, 'You're an evil woman. A criminal evil old, a wicked old', and talking like that, she made off. Louisa climbed to her attic, from where she could see the railway station set in a dip of the land, and, through her father's old spyglass, Mrs Hogg eventually appeared like a shady yellow wasp on the platform.

When Louisa came downstairs, she said to her charwoman, 'That visitor I had just now.'

'Yes, Mrs Jepp?'

'She wanted to come and look after me as I'm getting so old.'

'Coo.'

Louisa opened a drawer in the kitchen dresser, took out a folded white cloth, placed it carefully at the window end of the table. She brought out her air-mail writing paper and her fountain pen and wrote a note of six lines. Next she folded the letter and laid it on the dresser while she replaced the white cloth in the drawer. She put away her fountain pen, then the writing paper, took up the note and went out into her garden. There she sat in the November mildness, uttering repeatedly and softly 'Coo, Coo-oo!' Soon a pigeon flashed out from its high loft and descended to the seat beside her. She folded the thin paper into a tiny pellet, fixed it into the band on the silver bird's leg, stroked its bill with her brown fingers, and let it go. Off it flew, in the direction of Ladle Sands.

It is possible for a man matured in religion by half a century of punctilious observance, having advanced himself in devotion the slow and exquisite way, trustfully ascending his winding stair, and, to make assurance doubly sure, supplementing his meditations by deep-breathing exercises twice daily, to go into a flat spin when faced with some trouble which does not come within a familiar category. Should this occur, it causes dismay in others. To anyone accustomed to respect the wisdom and control of a contemplative creature, the evidence of his failure to cope with a normal emergency is distressing. Only the spiritual extremists rejoice – the Devil on account of his crude triumph, and the very holy souls because they discern in such behaviour a testimony to the truth that human nature is apt to fail in spite of regular prayer and deep breathing.

But fortunately that situation rarely happens. The common instinct knows how to gauge the limits of a man's sanctity, and anyone who has earned a reputation for piety by prayer, deep breathing and one or two acceptable good works has gained this much for his trouble, that few people bring him any extraordinary problem.

That is why hardly anyone asked Sir Edwin Manders for a peculiar favour or said weird things to him.

He had coped, it was true, with the shock of the car accident; Laurence and Caroline were seen into safe hands. He floated over Helena's anxiety on the strength of his stout character. He might have managed to do something suave and comforting about Helena's other worry – her mother's suspected criminal activities. He might have turned this upset of his social tranquillity to some personal and spiritual advantage, but then he might not. Helena instinctively did not try him with this problem. She did not know what Louisa was up to, but she understood that the difficulty was not one which the Manders' cheque book could solve. Helena would not have liked to see her husband in a state of bewilderment. He went to Mass every morning, confession once a week, entertained Cardinals. He would sit, contemplating deeply, for a full hour in a silence so still you could hear a moth breathe. And Helena thought, 'No, simply no' when she tried to envisage the same Edwin grappling also with the knowledge that his mother-in-law ran a gang, kept diamonds in the bread – stolen diamonds possibly. Helena took her troubles to his brother Ernest who sailed through life wherever the fairest wind should waft him, and for whom she had always prayed so hard.

'I feel I ought not to worry Edwin about this. He has a certain sanctity. You understand, don't you, Ernest?'

'Yes, of course, dear Helena, but I'm the last person, as you know, to cope with Louisa's great gangsters. If I could invite them to lunch at my club –'

'I'm sure you could if they are my mother's associates,' Helena said.

A week later, Helena went to the flat at Queen's Gate where Caroline had lodged. It was the job of packing up the girl's possessions. Caroline's fracture would keep her in hospital for another month at least. The housekeeper, a thin ill-looking man, who, on Helena's delicate inquiries, proved not to be ill but merely a retired lightweight boxer, let her in. Nice man, she thought, telling herself that she had a way with people: Laurence and Caroline had said he was frightful.

Helena was expecting Ernest to join her. She sat for a moment on Caroline's divan; then, it was so restful, she decided to put her feet up and recline among the piled-up cushions until he should arrive. The room had been tidied up, but it was clear that Laurence and Caroline had made a sort of home of the place. The realization did not really shock Helena, it quickly startled her, it was soon over. Years ago she had come to a reckoning with the business between Laurence and Caroline and when they had parted, even while she piously rejoiced, she had felt romantically sad, wished they could be married without their incomprehensible delay. But still it was a little startling to see the evidence of what she already knew, that Laurence had been sharing the flat with Caroline, innocently but without the externals of innocence. The housekeeper had asked her, 'How are Mr and Mrs Manders? What a shame, so newly married.' Helena had kept herself collected, revealed nothing. That sort of remark – and this place with Laurence's tie over the back of the chair – caused the little startles, soon over.

'I was resting. I'm so tired running backwards and forwards to the country,' she told Ernest when he was shown up by that nice little man.

For the first few days after the accident, till Caroline was out of her long bruised sleep, Helena had stayed intermittently at a local hotel and at Ladylees with her mother. She had been watchful, had said nothing to upset the old lady. Once in the night she had turned it over in her mind to have it out with Louisa – Mother, I'm driven mad with anxiety over this accident, I can't be doing with worry on your account as well. Laurence told me ... his idea ... your gang ... diamonds in the bread ... tell me, is it true or not? What's your game ... what's your source of income ...?

But supposing there was nothing in it. Seventy-eight, the old woman. Helena considered and considered between her sleeps. Suppose she has a stroke! She had refrained often from speaking her mind to Louisa in case she caused the old lady a stroke, it was an old fear of Helena's.

So she said nothing to upset her, had been more than ever alert when, on returning to the cottage one evening after her hospital visiting, Louisa told her, 'Your Mrs Hogg has been here.'

Then Helena could not conceal her anxiety.

'But I sent her away,' said Louisa, 'and I don't think I shall see her again.'

'Oh, Mother, what did she want?'

'To be my companion, dear. I am able to get about very nicely.'

'Nothing worrying you, Mother? Oh, I wish you would let us help you!'

'My!' said Louisa. 'I vow, you are all a great comfort to me, and once the children are recovered we shall all be straight with the world.'

'Well,' said Helena, 'I brought you a present from Hayward's Heath, I was so happy to see Laurence looking better.'

It was a tin-opening gadget. The old woman got out the tomato basket in which she kept a few handy tools. Helena held the machine against the scullery door while her mother screwed it in place, the old fingers manipulating the screwdriver but without a tremor.

'It's a great life if you don't weaken,' Louisa remarked as she twisted the screws in their places.

'That will be handy for you,' said Helena, 'won't it?'

'Yes, certainly,' Louisa said. 'Let's try it now.' They opened a tin of gooseberries. 'It was just what I wanted to open my cans,' said Louisa. 'You must have guessed. You have a touch of our gipsy insight in you, dear. The only thing, you don't cultivate it.'

'Now that's an exaggeration, really, Mother. Buying you a can-opener doesn't prove anything specially psychic, now does it?'

'Not when you put it that way,' said Louisa.

Helena had already taken advantage of one of her mother's outings to search the bread bin. There were no diamonds anywhere evident, neither in the bread nor in the rice and sugar tins, nor nestling among the tea nor anywhere on the shelves of the little pantry. There Louisa also kept the sealed bottles and cans of food, neatly labelled, which she canned and bottled herself from season to season.

'Georgina wasn't horrid to you, or anything?' This was Helena's last try.

'She is not a pleasant woman by nature. I can't think why you ever took up with her. I would never have had her in my house.'

'She's had a hard life. We felt sorry for her. I don't think she can do any harm. At least . . . well, I think not, do you?'

'Everyone can do harm, and do whether they mean it or not. But Mrs Hogg is not a decent woman.'

Everything stood so quiet, Helena wondered if perhaps Laurence had been mistaken, his foolish letter useless in Mrs Hogg's hands.

And that was what she told Ernest when he was shown up to Caroline's flat. She had allowed this hope to grow on her during the weeks following the accident when, sometimes alone, sometimes with her husband, she had motored back and forth between London and the country hospital. Laurence was a case of broken ribs, he could be moved home very soon. Caroline had come round, her head still bandaged, her leg now caged in its plaster and slung up on its scaffold. She had started to make a fuss about the pain, which was a good sign. Everything could have been worse.

'I doubt very much that there was anything in that suspicion of Laurence's. It caused me a lot of worry and the accident on top of it. Everything could have been worse but I'm worn out.'

'Do you know,' said Ernest, 'my dear, so am I.'

Those revelatory tones and gestures! – she watched Ernest as he picked up Caroline's blue brocade dressing-gown with the intention of folding it, helping Helena to pack, but there – before he knew what he was doing he had posed himself before the long mirror, draping the blue stuff over one hip. 'Sumptuous material!'

Helena surprised herself by the mildness of her distaste.

'The room is full of Caroline,' she remarked. 'I feel that I am seeing things through Caroline's eyes, d'you know?'

'So do I,' said he, 'now you come to mention it.'

Helena knelt by the large suitcase she had brought. Her fair skin was drawn under its frail make-up.

'We could make a pot of tea, Ernest. The meter may need a shilling.'

He put on the kettle while she considered his predicament in life. Caroline had always been able to accept his category. It was easier, Helena thought, to accept his effeminacy now that he had given up his vice and had returned to the Church, but even before that Caroline had declared, on one occasion of discussing Ernest, 'I should think God would say, "Don't dare despise My beloved freak, My homosexual."'

Helena had replied, 'Of course. But if it goes against one's very breathing to respect the man –? Oh, love is very difficult.'

'I have my own prejudices,' Caroline had said, 'so I understand yours. Ernest doesn't happen to be one of mine, that's all.'

Helena, adrift in these recollections, caught herself staring at Ernest. She lifted the phone, spoke in reply to the housekeeper's 'Yes, what number?' – 'May we have a little milk, please? We've just made some tea and we have no milk.'

Whatever he said caused Helena to exclaim when she had put down the receiver.

'Rather beastly abrupt that man! I thought him so nice before.'

She apologized for the trouble when the man brought the milk, to which he made no reply at all.

'The man's a brute, Ernest,' she said. 'He knows the sad circumstances of our being here.'

But she settled down with Ernest now, observing the peculiar turn of his wrist – he showed a lot of wrist – as he poured out their tea. Caroline with her sense of mythology would see in him a beautiful hermaphrodite, she thought, and came near to realizing this vision of Ernest herself.

'I managed to see Laurence yesterday,' Ernest said, 'remarkably well, isn't he, considering?'

'Thank God,' Helena said.

'He gave me this' – a red pocket notebook – 'and told me what he knew about your mother's friends.'

'D'you know, Ernest, I don't think there's anything to fear. I kept my eyes open those few days I spent at the cottage, but I noticed nothing suspicious. Laurence must have been mistaken, I can't help thinking. And apparently Mrs Hogg has come to the same conclusion; she actually descended on my mother while I was out. Mother was very calm about it – simply sent her away. I've no doubt – though Mother didn't say so – that Mrs Hogg came about Laurence's letter.'

'That's exactly what I should have thought. Exactly that.' Ernest was now folding Caroline's blue dressing-gown, very meticulously. 'But,' he said, 'I happen to know vaguely one of the men in Mrs Jepp's gang.'

'Oh, who's that?'

'Mervyn Hogarth. Eleanor used to be married to him. Now, *he's* most odd. Laurence thinks Mrs Hogg may be related to him.'

Helena said it was unlikely. 'I've never heard her mention the name Hogarth.' She took the notebook from him and turned its pages. The meagre dossier Laurence had prepared had a merciless look of reality. It revived Helena's fears. She was happiest when life could be reduced to metaphor, but life on its lofty literal peaks oppressed her. She peered at the stringent notes in Laurence's hand.

'What do you think of this, Ernest? Is my mother involved or not?'

'Why don't you ask her?'

'Oh, she would never say.'

Ernest said, 'Laurence thinks we should investigate. I promised him we would, in fact.'

Helena read aloud one of the unbearable pages of the notebook:

'Mervyn Hogarth: The Green House, Ladle Sands. Lives with crippled son (see Andrew Hogarth). No servants. Ex-library workshop. Bench tools. Mending (?) broken plaster statuettes. St Anthony. S. Francis. Immac. Concept. – others unrecognizable. No record in S.H. Ex Eleanor.'

'I can't make this out,' she said, 'broken plaster and the saints – are they Catholics, the Hogarths?'

'I think not,' Ernest said.

'What does "S.H." stand for?'

'Somerset House. There's apparently no record of them there. They may have been born abroad. I shall ask Eleanor, she'll know.'

'Laurence has explained all these notes to you?'

'More or less. Please don't upset yourself, Helena.'

'Oh, I did hope there was nothing more to be feared. Explain all this to me, please.'

She kept turning the pages, hoping for some small absurdity to prove the whole notion absurd that her aged mother should be involved in organized crime. She had a strong impulse to tear up the book.

'There wasn't time to go through the whole of it with Laurence. He wants me to go and stay nearby for a couple of weeks, so that I can investigate under his supervision and consult him on my daily visits.'

'No,' Helena said, 'that won't do. We can't weary Laurence in his state. I want him moved to London at the first opportunity.'

Ernest agreed. 'It would be very inconvenient for me to leave London at this time of the year. But Laurence was keen. Perhaps there's some other way –'

Helena looked at Ernest reclining now on Caroline's divan in such a hollowed-out sort of way. Shifting sand, we must not build our houses on it. But Helena was not sure whether he didn't possess some stable qualities in spite of the way the family regarded him. She realized her inexperience of Ernest: Caroline had a more lucid idea of him.

'Of course,' Helena said, 'it would cheer Laurence up tremendously, someone visiting him every day. Now that they're out of danger I can only manage twice a week. Caroline too, you would visit Caroline too?'

'I'm not sure that I can get away.'

'Ernest, I will pay your expenses of *course*.' She was almost glad of his resistance, it proved him to be ever so slightly substantial.

'If you would,' he said, 'it would be a help. But I shall have to talk to Eleanor. This time of year is difficult, and we aren't doing so well just now.'

'Please,' she said, 'don't confide in Eleanor.'

'Oh, I shouldn't mention any family business.'

They talked back and forth until it became needful to Helena that Ernest should go to reside at Hayward's Heath for two weeks.

'We must get to the bottom of this intrigue without upsetting my mother,' she declared. 'Laurence understands that perfectly. I'm sure his recovery depends on our doing something active. We must be *doing*. I know you are discreet, Ernest. I don't want Mother to have a stroke, Ernest. And we must pray.'

'I'll try to see Hogarth,' he promised. 'Maybe I can get him to meet me in London.'

He was pouring out their second cups, with that wrist, of which there was a lot showing, poised in a woman's fashion which nibbled at Helena's trust in him.

'I have no misgivings,' she declared, 'I have implicit trust in you, Ernest.'

'Dear me,' said Ernest. She thought how Caroline with her aptitude for 'placing' people in their correct historical setting had once placed Ernest in the French Court of the seventeenth century. 'He's born out of his time,' Caroline had explained, 'that's part of his value in the present age.' Laurence had said placidly, and not long ago, 'Ernest never buys a tie, he has them made. Five-eighths of an inch wider than anyone else's.'

Parents learn a lot from their children about coping with life. It is possible for parents to be corrupted or improved by their children. Through Laurence, and also of later years through Caroline, Helena's mental organization had been recast. She was, at least, prepared for the idea that Ernest was not only to be tolerated in a spirit of what she understood as Christian charity, but valued for himself, his differences from the normal. Helena actually admired him a little for what she called his reform. But when he gave up his relations with men she had half expected an external change in Ernest; was disappointed and puzzled that his appearance and attitudes remained so infrangibly effeminate, and she understood that these mannerisms were not offensive to people like Laurence and Caroline. Helena possessed some French china, figurines of the seventeenth century which she valued, but the cherishing of Ernest while he was in her presence came hard enough to present her with an instinctive antagonism; something to overcome.

Ernest had folded while she packed nearly everything. What couldn't be packed was ready to be carried to the car. 'Let's have a cigarette, we've worked hard.'

'I suppose,' she said, 'that machine belongs to Caroline. We had better have the man up to make sure we haven't left anything of ours, or taken away what's theirs.'

Ernest, curling himself on a low footstool, lifted the cover off the machine. 'It's a tape-recorder. Caroline probably used it for her work.'

'I have implicit trust in you, Ernest. I've come to you before anyone. I don't want to inconvenience you of course, and if it's a question of expense –'

'Thank you, Helena. But I can't promise – I'll try of course – this time of year we have our bookings, our classes. Maybe Hogarth will agree to come to London.'

'I'm so grateful to you, Ernest.'

He fiddled with the tape machine, pressed the lever. It gave a faint whirr and the voice came with an exaggerated soppy yak: 'Caroline, darling. . . .'

Within a few seconds Helena had recognized Laurence's voice; a slight pause and it was followed by Caroline's. The first speech was shocking and the second was nonsense.

Ernest said, 'Hee, silly little dears.'

Helena lifted her coat, let Ernest help her on with it.

'Will you send for the man, Ernest? Give him a pound and ask if everything's all right. I'll take some of the loose things down to the car. No, ten shillings will do.'

She felt almost alone in the world, wearily unfit for the task of understanding Laurence and Caroline. These new shocks and new insights, this perpetual obligation on her part to accept what it went against her to accept. . . . She wanted a warm soft bath in her own home; she was tired and worried and she didn't know what.

Just as she was leaving, Ernest phoning for the housekeeper said,

'Look, there's something. A notebook, that's Caroline's I'm sure.'

A red pocket notebook was lying on the lower ledge of the telephone table. He picked it up and handed it to Helena.

'What a good thing you saw it. I'd quite forgotten. Caroline was asking specially for this. A notebook with shorthand notes, she asked for it.' Helena flicked it open to make sure. Most of it was in shorthand, but on one of the pages was a list in longhand. She caught the words: 'Possible identity.'

'This must be connected with Laurence's investigations,' Helena said.

She turned again to that page while she sat in the car waiting for Ernest with the bags, but she could make nothing of it. Under 'Possible identity' were listed

Satan
a woman
hermaphrodite
a Holy Soul in Purgatory

'I don't know what,' said Helena, as she put it away carefully among Caroline's things. 'I really don't know what.'

SEVEN

Just after two in the mild bluish afternoon a tall straight old man entered the bookshop. He found Baron Stock alone and waiting for him.

'Ah, Mr Webster, how punctual you are, how very good of you to make the journey. Come right through to the inside, come to the inside.'

Baron Stock's large personal acquaintance – though he had few intimate friends – when they dropped in on the Baron in his Charing Cross Road bookshop were invariably greeted with this request, 'Come to the inside.' Customers, travellers and the trade were not allowed further than the large front show-place; the Baron was highly cagey about 'the inside', those shabby, comfortable, and quite harmless back premises where books and files piled and tumbled over everything except the three old armchairs and the square of worn red carpet, in the centre of which stood a foreign-looking and noisy paraffin stove. Those admitted to the inside, before they sat down and if they knew the Baron's habits, would wait while he placed a sheet of newspaper on the seat of each chair. 'It is exceedingly dusty, my dears, I never permit the cleaners to touch the inside.' When the afternoons began to draw in, the Baron would light a paraffin lamp on his desk: the electricity had long since failed here in these back premises, 'and really,' said the Baron, 'I can't have electricians coming through to the inside with their mess.' Occasionally one of his friends would say, 'It looks a simple job, I think I could fix your lights, Willi.' 'How very obliging of you.' 'Not at all, I'll do it next week.' But no one ever came next week to connect up the electricity.

'And how,' said the Baron when he had settled Mr Webster on a fresh piece of newspaper, 'is Mrs Jepp?'

Mr Webster sat erect and stiff, turning his body from the waist to answer the Baron.

'She is well I am pleased to say, but worried about her grandson I am sorry to say.'

'Yes, a nasty accident. I've known Laurence for years of course. A bad driver. But he's coming home next week, I hear.'

'Yes, he had a handsome escape. The poor young lady's leg is fractured, but she too might be worse, they tell us.'

'Poor Caroline, I've known her for years. Her forehead was cut quite open, I hear.'

'Slight abrasions, I understand, nothing serious.'

'Such a relief. I hear everything in this shop but my informants always exaggerate. They are poets on the whole or professional liars of some sort, and so one has to make allowances. I'm glad to know that Caroline's head has no permanent cavity. I've known her for years. I am going to visit her next week.'

'If you will pardon my mentioning, Baron, if you intend to be in our part of the country, I think at the moment you should not make occasion to call on Mrs Jepp. The Hogarths have had to cancel their trip to the Continent and they frequently call at the cottage.'

'What was the trouble? Why didn't they go?'

'Mrs Jepp had the feeling that the Manders were about to investigate her concerns. She thinks there should be no further trips till the spring. The Hogarths were ready to leave, but she stopped them at the last minute. She is not at all worried.'

'It sounds fairly worrying to me. The Hogarths do not suspect that I am involved in your arrangements?'

'I don't think you need fear that. Mrs Jepp and I are very careful about mentioning names. You are simply Mrs Jepp's "London connexion". They have never shown further curiosity.'

'And the Manders? I suppose Laurence has put them up to something, he is so observant, it's terrifying. I am never happy when he goes to that cottage.'

'Mrs Jepp is very fond of him.'

'Why, of course. *I* am very fond of Laurence, I've known the Manders for years. But Laurence is most inquisitive. Do you think the Manders are likely to suspect my part in the affair?'

'If anything, their interest would reside in myself and the Hogarths. I do not think you need worry, Baron.'

'I will tell you why I'm anxious. There is no risk of exposure either from the Hogarths or from the Manders. In the one case they themselves are involved. In the other case the old lady is involved and the Manders would of course wish to hush up anything they found out. But it happens that I am interested in Mervyn Hogarth in another connexion. I have arranged to be introduced to him, and I do not wish to confuse the two concerns.'

Mr Webster thought, Ah, to do with the woman, Hogarth's former wife, but he was wrong.

'Hogarth is up in London today,' he informed the Baron, 'I saw him on the train, but I thought best to remain unseen.'

'Sure he didn't see you? No chance of his having followed you here out of curiosity?'

'No, in fact I kept *him* in sight until he disappeared into a club in Piccadilly. Ho, ho, Baron.'

He handed the Baron a small neat package. 'I had better not forget to give you this,' he said, still chuckling in an old man's way.

The Baron opened it carefully, taking out a tin marked in Louisa Jepp's clear hand, 'Soft herring roes.'

'Mrs Jepp was particularly anxious that you should eat the actual herring roes,' Mr Webster said. 'She bade me say that they are very nourishing and no contamination can possibly arise from the other contents of the tin.'

'I shall,' said the Baron, 'I shall.'

He slid the tin into his brief case, then opening a double-locked drawer took out a bundle of white notes. These he counted. He took another bunch and did likewise, then a third; from a fourth lot he extracted a number of notes which he added to the three bundles. He replaced the remainder of the notes in his drawer and relocked it before handing the bundles to Mr Webster. Then he wrote three cheques and handed them over.

'They are dated at three-weekly intervals. Please check the amount,' he said, 'and then I will give you this good strong envelope to put them in.'

'Much the safest way,' said Mr Webster as he always did, referring, not to the envelope but to the method of payment. 'Much the safest in case of inquiries,' he added as always.

When this business was done, and the notes packed into their envelope and locked away in Mr Webster's bag, the Baron said,

'Now, a cigar, Mr Webster, and a sip of Curaçao.'

'Very well, thank you. But I mustn't delay long because of the time of year.'

The shop door tinkled. 'Tinkle,' said the Baron, and rising, he peered through a chink in the partition that separated the grey-carpeted front shop from the warm and shabby inside. 'A barbarian wanting a book,' the Baron remarked as he went forth to serve his customer.

Returning within a few seconds, he said,

'Do you know anything of diabolism?'

'I've seen witchcraft practised, many times in the olden days; that was before your time, Baron; mostly in South American ports.'

'You are a sail-or,' said the Baron. 'I have always thought you were a sail-or.'

'I was a merchant seaman. I have seen witchcraft, Baron. In those countries it can be fearful, I can tell you.'

'I am interested in diabolism. In a detached way, I assure you.'

'Ho, I am sure, Baron. It isn't a thing for a temperate climate.'

'That is why,' said the Baron, 'I am interested in Mervyn Hogarth. You would call him a mild and temperate man?'

'Well, Baron, he doesn't say much though he talks a lot. Myself I don't care for him. But Mrs Jepp tolerates, she tolerates. She is thinking perhaps of the poor son. This *trading* of ours, it gives him something in life. Poor lad, poor lad.'

'Would it surprise you, Mr Webster, to know that Mervyn Hogarth is the foremost diabolist in these islands?'

'I should never have thought of the man as being foremost in anything.'

'How does he strike you, tell me?'

'Between ourselves, Baron, he strikes me, between ourselves, as a cynic, as they say, and a misanthropist. A tedious fellow.'

'Devoted to his son, though?'

'I don't know, I do not. He behaves well to the lad. Mrs Jepp believes, and this is between ourselves, Baron, that he only sticks to the boy in order to spite his former wife. At least that was her impression when she first met them.'

'This diamond trading was Mrs Jepp's idea, wasn't it?'

'Oh yes. Oh, and she enjoys it, Mrs Jepp would be the last to deny it.'

'They don't need money, the Hogarths?'

'No. Hogarth himself is comfortable. The unfortunate young man does so enjoy evading the customs, Baron.'

The Baron put a finger to his lips with a smile. Mr Webster lowered his voice as he thanked his host for the replenishment of his glass.

'Evading the customs has made a great difference to young Andrew Hogarth. It has given him confidence,' Mr Webster said in low tones.

'When Mrs Jepp first suggested this arrangement to me – for it was she, you know, who approached me with the scheme, she came straight in to the shop here a few days after I had met her with Laurence and stated her proposition most admirably; I could see her quality. Well, when she put it to me she added that if I should agree to come in with her, I must undertake not to inquire into the *methods* used by the more active agents. When I had thought over her suggestion and had satisfied myself that the plan was genuinely and well conceived – allowing for the usual risk which I do not find unpleasurable – I agreed exactly to Mrs Jepp's terms. I mention this, because frankly I would not be within my rights if I asked you by what means the Hogarths convey their valuables. Up to the past few months I have not been greatly interested in that side of the transactions, but now I am greatly inter*ested* because of my interest in the actions of Mervyn Hogarth.'

'I do not know their method,' said Mr Webster, and the Baron could not tell if he were speaking the truth or not, so unaltered were his sharp blue eyes.

'Hogarth is a diabolist. I am intensely inter*ested* in Hogarth for the reason that I am *inter*ested in the psychology of diabolism. You do not know the madness of scholarly curiosity, Mr Webster. To be interested and at the same time disinterested. . . .'

'I can well understand it, Baron. But I should not have thought the elder Mr Hogarth indulged in any exotic practices. He seems to me a disillusioned man, far from an enthusiast.'

'That is the interesting factor,' said the Baron excitedly. 'From all I have discovered of the man's personality, he is drenched in disillusionment, an intelligent man, a bored man; an unsuccessful man with women, indifferent to friendships. Yet, he is a fanatical diabolist. You will keep my confidence, Mr Webster.'

'Baron, of course. And now I must be going.'

'A fanatic,' said the Baron as he escorted Mr Webster from the inside to the outside. 'A pity the Hogarths did not go abroad. I would have called on Mrs Jepp. She may have been persuaded to tell me more of Mervyn Hogarth. However, I shall be meeting him myself very soon, I believe.'

'Good day to you, Baron.'

'My regards to Mrs Jepp.' And he added, 'Be assured, Mr Webster, the risk is neglig-ible.'

'Oh, Hogarth is not dangerous.'

'I do not mean Hogarth. I mean our happy trade. We are amateurs. There is a specially protective providence for amateurs. How easily the powerful and organized professionals come to grief! They fall like Lucifer –'

'Quite so, Baron.'

'But we innocents are difficult to trip up.'

'I shouldn't call us *innocents*. Ho!' said Mr Webster stepping forth.

'That's the point. . . .' But by this time the old man had gone out of hearing.

'I don't pretend to understand women,' Mervyn Hogarth stated over the brandy. He looked at his host as if he were not sure he had said the right thing, for there was a touch of the woman, a musing effect in the baby-faced, white-haired man.

'The lamb was not right or else the sauce, I fear,' Ernest Manders mused. After all, he had not gone to Sussex. He had contrived a better plan.

'I take it you are speaking in good faith?' Mervyn Hogarth was saying.

'The lamb –?'

'No, no, the subject we were discussing, I take it –'

'Do let's take it that way, Mr Hogarth.'

'Manders, I meant no offence. I wanted to make my mind clear – only that. It seems to me a definitely odd suggestion to come from Eleanor, she knows my position, definitely.'

'It was only, you see, that we're temporarily in a tight place. Baron Stock has withdrawn his support. Naturally Eleanor thought of you. It was a kind of compliment.'

'Oh, definitely.'

'And if you can't, you can't, that is quite understood,' said Ernest.

'Have you approached your brother?'

'Yes. My brother Edwin is a mystic. He is not interested in dancing and will only invest in that which interests him. But he gave us fifty pounds. Eleanor bought a dress.'

'I can imagine Eleanor would.'

'I am myself very detached from money,' Ernest remarked, 'that is why I need so much of it. One simply doesn't notice the stuff; it slithers away.'

He sat back in his chair as if he had the whole afternoon. His guest had discovered that the business proposition for which he had been summoned was an unprofitable one.

'A quarter to three,' said Mervyn Hogarth. 'My word, the time does fly. I have one or two things to do this afternoon. People to see. Bore.'

'There *was* something else,' Ernest said, 'but if you're rushed, perhaps another time.'

'Perhaps another time' – but Mervyn Hogarth did a little exercise in his head which took no time at all, but which, had it been laboured out, would have gone like this:

Fares 13s. but had to come to London anyway; dreariness of food but it was free; disappointment at subject of discussion (Ernest had invited him to discuss 'matters of interest to you') but satisfaction about Eleanor's break with Stock and consequent money difficulties; annoyance at being touched for money but satisfaction in refusing; waste of time but now Manders wants to say something further, which might possibly redeem the meeting or on the other hand confirm it as a dead loss.

The process passed through his mind like a snap of the fingers and so, when Ernest said, 'There *was* something else, but if you're rushed –'

'Something else?' Hogarth replied.

'Perhaps another time,' Ernest said.

'Oh, I'm not rushed for the next half-hour. Do carry on.'

'Well,' said Ernest, 'it may interest you or it may not. I feel, you know, I've brought you up to London on a disappointing inducement – I did think honestly it would please you to be substantially connected with the dancing school – and Eleanor was sure you would – I hope you don't feel it impertinent on our part.'

'He is like a woman,' Mervyn thought. 'It's just like lunching with a woman.' And he assured Ernest that he hadn't minded a bit: 'only too sorry I can't spare a penny. What was the other question you wanted to mention?'

'Yes, well, that may be of interest and it may not. It's just as you feel. The lamb was most peculiar, I must apologize. It's the worst club lunch I do ever remember. I would send a complaint, only I did fire watching with the chef, who is most really nice and almost never has an off day like this.'

'A very good lunch,' said Mervyn sadly.

'*Sweet* of you to say so,' said Ernest.

'This further question –?'

'Truly you've time? I should so like to say a few words, something which you might be interested in. You know my brother Edwin?'

'I haven't met Sir Edwin Manders.'

'He is very rich. You know Helena?'

'His wife, that is? I know *of* her.'

'She's rather sweet. You've met her mother?'

'As a matter of fact I do know Mrs Jepp.'

'Mrs Jepp,' said Ernest.

'Fine old lady. Lives quite near my place,' said Mervyn.

'Yes, I know that,' said Ernest. 'You visit regularly, I hear.'

'I hear,' said Mervyn, 'that her grandson had an accident.'

'Only a broken rib. He's recovering rapidly.'

'Ah, these young people. I met the grandson.'

'I know,' said Ernest.

It was creeping on three o'clock and their glasses had been twice filled. Ernest thought he was doing rather well. Mervyn was hoping against time, but really there was no excuse for prolonging the afternoon. Ernest had made it clear, in the soft mannerly style of pertinacity, that the Manders family had started to smell out the affairs of Louisa Jepp. Mervyn would have liked to hit Ernest for his womanly ways, and he said,

'I must say, Manders, I can't reveal any of Mrs Jepp's confidences.'

'Certainly not. Are you going abroad soon?'

'I take it this farce of asking me to lunch in order to ask me for a loan was really intended to create an opportunity to ask –'

'Oh dear, I can't possibly,' said Ernest, 'cope. I am so – am so sorry about the lunch. "Farce" is the word exactly. I do wish I had made you take duck. Most distressing, I did so think you'd be interested in Eleanor's academy, it is top-ranking absolutely if she only had the capital. How dire for you, how frightful my dear man, for me.'

'Your questions about Mrs Jepp, I can't possibly answer them,' said Mervyn, looking at his watch but unpurposed, settling into his chair, so that Ernest in his heart shook hands with himself: 'He is waiting for more questions, more clues towards how much I'm in the know.' He said to his guest, 'I mustn't keep you, then. It's been charming.'

Mervyn rose. He said, 'Look here,' and stopped.

'Yes?'

'Nothing, nothing.' But as he stood on the top doorstep taking his leave from Ernest he said, 'Tell Eleanor I shall think over her proposition. Perhaps after all I shall think it over and scrape up a little to help her out. But it's very grim these days, you realize, and I have my poor boy. He's a heavy expense.'

'Don't think of it,' said Ernest. 'Please don't dream.'

'Tell Eleanor I shall do what I can.'

For about four minutes after his guest's departure Ernest was truly puzzled by these last-minute remarks. Then he sat back in a cushiony chocolate-coloured chair and smiled all over his youthful face, which made his forehead rise in lines right up to his very white hair.

He was in Kensington within half an hour, and at the studio. He saw Eleanor in one of the dressing cubicles off the large upper dancing floor, and pirouetted beautifully to attract her attention.

She sleeked her velvet jeans over her hips, pulled the belt tight as she did always when she wanted to pull her brains together.

'How did you get on? Anything doing?'

'I think so,' he said.

'He'll put up the money?'

'I think so,' he said.

'Ernest, what charm you must have with men. I would have sworn you wouldn't get an old bit of macaroni out of Mervyn, especially seeing I'm to benefit by it. He's so mean as a rule. What did he say? How did you do it?'

'Blackmail,' Ernest said.

'How did you do it, dear?'

'I told you. It isn't certain yet, of course. And yet – I'm pretty sure you'll get the money, my dear.'

'How did you manage it?'

'Blackmail by mistake.'

'What can you mean? Tell me all.'

'I gave him lunch. I explained your difficulties. Asked for a loan. He said no. Then I asked him some other questions about something else, which he took to be a form of blackmail. Then, as he was leaving, he succumbed.'

'What questions – the ones he thought were a blackmailing effort? – What were they?'

'Sorry, can't say, my dear. Something rather private.'

'Concerning me?' said Eleanor.

'No, nothing at all to do with you, honestly.'

'Nothing honestly to do with me?'

'Honestly.'

Then she was satisfied. Ernest left her intent on her calculations, anticipating the subsidy from Mervyn Hogarth. She sat cross-legged on a curly white rug with pen and paper, adding and multiplying, as if the worries of the past had never been, as if not even yesterday had been a day of talking and thinking about bankruptcy. Before he left she said to Ernest, 'Don't forget to draw on expenses for the lunch.'

'Helena?'

'Hold the line a minute.'

'Helena?'

'Who's that? Oh, it's you, Ernest.'

'I saw Hogarth.'

'Already? Where?'

'At my club. For lunch. Frightful serious little man with a Harris-tweed jacket.'

'Ernest, you are a marvel. You will let me pay for it of course.'

'I thought you might like to know how things went. Such a glum little fellow.'

'Tell me all. I'm on edge to know.'

'Laurence is right. There is certainly something going on between your mother and Hogarth.'

'*What's* going on?'

'He wouldn't say, of course. But it's something important enough to make him most unhappy, most eager to appease us. A bleak little bodikin actually. We had such unfortunate food, lamb like tree-bark, no exaggeration. He thinks we know more than we do. That's one up for us, I feel.'

'Certainly it is. Can you come right over, Ernest? You could take a taxi.'

'It would cost ten bob.'

'Where are you speaking from?'

'South Kensington underground.'

'Oh well, come by tube if you like. But take a taxi *if* you like.'

'I'll be with you presently.'

While Ernest was telephoning to Helena that afternoon Mervyn Hogarth climbed the steps of a drab neglected house at Chiswick. He pressed the bell. He could hear no sound, so pressed again, keeping his finger on it for a long time. Presumably out of order. Just as he was peering through the letter-box to see if anything was doing inside, the door opened so that Mervyn nearly stumbled over the threshold into the body of the blue-suited shady-looking man with no collar, who opened it.

'Is Mrs Hogg living here at present?' Mervyn said.

He was acquainted with the place, Georgina's habitual residence when in London. He had been to the place before and he did not like it.

On that day Caroline Rose in hospital heard the click of a typewriter, she heard those voices,

He was acquainted with the place, Georgina's habitual residence when in London. He had been to the place before and he did not like it.

It is not easy to dispense with Caroline Rose. At this point in the tale she is confined in a hospital bed, and no experience of hers ought to be allowed to intrude. Unfortunately she slept restlessly. She never did sleep well. And during the hours of night, rather than ring for the nurse and a sedative, she preferred to savour her private wakefulness, a luxury heightened by the profound sleeping of seven other women in the public ward. When her leg was not too distracting, Caroline among the sleepers turned her mind to the art of the novel, wondering and cogitating, those long hours, and exerting an undue, unreckoned, influence on the narrative from which she is supposed to be absent for a time.

Tap-tick-click. Caroline among the sleepers turned her mind to the art of the novel, wondering and cogitating, those long hours, and exerting an undue, unreckoned, influence on the narrative from which she is supposed to be absent for a time.

Mrs Hogg's tremendous bosom was a great embarrassment to her – not so much in the way of vanity, now that she was getting on in life – but in the circumstance that she didn't know what to do with it.

When, at the age of thirty-five she had gone to nursery-govern the Manders' boys, Edwin Manders remarked to his wife,

'Don't you think, rather buxom to have about the house?'

'Don't be disagreeable, please, Edwin. She has a fine character.'

Laurence and Giles (the elder son, killed in the war) were overjoyed at Georgina's abounding bosom. Giles was the one who produced the more poetic figures to describe it; he declared that under her blouse she kept pairs of vegetable marrows, of infant whales, St Paul's Cathedrals, goldfish bowls. Laurence's interest in Georgina's bulging frontage was more documentary. He acquired knowledge of her large stock of bust-bodices, long widths of bright pink or yellow-white materials, some hard as canvas, some more yielding in texture, from some of which dangled loops of criss-cross straps, some with eyelets for intricate tight-lacing, some with much-tried hooks and eyes. He knew exactly which one of these garments Georgina was wearing at any given time; one of them gave her four breasts, another gave her the life-jacket look which Laurence had seen in his danger-ous sea-faring picture books. He knew the day when she wore her made-to-measure brassiere provided at a costly expense by his mother. That was about the time Georgina was leaving to get married. The new garment was a disappointment to the children, they felt it made her look normal, only, of course, far more so. And they knew their mother was uneasy about these new shapely protrusions which did so seem to proceed heraldically far in advance of Georgina herself; the old bust-bodices were ungainly, but was this new contraption decent?

'I will lift up mine eyes to the hills,' little Giles chanted for the entertainment of the lower domestics.

The boys did not share their mother's view of Georgina's character. They were delighted when she was to leave to marry her cousin.

'What's wrong with her cousin, then?'

'Be quiet, Laurence, Miss Hogg will hear you.'

They had found her to be a sneak, a subtle tyrant. Prep school, next year, was wonderfully straightforward in comparison.

Her pale red-gold hair, round pale-blue eyes, her piglet 'flesh-coloured' face: Georgina Hogg had certain attractions at the time of her marriage. Throughout the 'tragic' years which followed (for when misfortune occurs to slightly absurd or mean-minded people it is indeed tragic for them – it falls with a thud which they don't expect, it does not excite the pity and fear of the onlooker, it excites revulsion more likely; so that the piece of bad luck which happened to Georgina Hogg was not truly tragic, only pathetic) – throughout those years since her marriage, Mrs Hogg had sought in vain for an effectual garment to harness her tremendous and increasing bosom. She spent more money than she could afford in the effort – it was like damming up the sea. By that time of her life when she met Caroline Rose at St Philumena's she had taken to wearing nothing regardless beneath her billowing blouses. 'As God made me,' she may have thought in justification, and in her newfound release.

... 'As God made me,' she may have thought in justification, and in her newfound release.

'Bad taste,' Caroline commented. 'Revolting taste.' She had, in fact, 'picked up' a good deal of the preceding passage, all about Mrs Hogg and the breasts.

'Bad taste' – typical comment of Caroline Rose. Wasn't it she in the first place who had noticed with revulsion the transparent blouse of

Mrs Hogg, that time at St Philumena's? It was Caroline herself who introduced into the story the question of Mrs Hogg's bosom.

Tap-tap. It was Caroline herself who introduced into the story the question of Mrs Hogg's bosom.

Caroline Rose sighed as she lay in hospital contemplating her memory of Mrs Hogg. 'Not a real-life character,' she commented at last, 'only a gargoyle.'

Mervyn Hogarth, when he was admitted to Georgina's lodgings by the lazy dog-racing son of her landlady, was directed to Georgina's room. As he mounted the stairs towards it, he heard the swift scamper of mice, as if that part of the house was uninhabited. He knocked and jerked open the door. He saw her presently, her unfortunate smile, her colossal bust arranged more peculiarly than he had ever seen it before – and he had seen it in many extraordinary shapes – all lopsided, one side heaving up and the other one rolling down, for, possibly in the flurry of confronting him, the right shoulder strap of her bodice had snapped.

He took in her appearance without being fully aware of it, so anxious was he to speak his mind, give her warning, and be at peace.

Mrs Hogg said, collecting herself though lopsided,

'You're late, Mervyn.'

He sidled into an easy chair while she made to light the gas-ring under the kettle.

'No tea for me,' he said. 'Tell me,' he said, 'why you have started interfering. You've been to see Mrs Jepp. What's your game?'

'I know what yours is,' she said. 'Smuggling.' She sat down in her chair by the window so that the side where her bust-bodice had burst was concealed from him.

'Mrs Jepp told you that.'

'Yes, and it's true. She can afford to be truthful.'

'Andrew is involved,' he said.

'Ah yes, it's all in keeping, you have ruined Andrew already. It's only to be expected that you're making a criminal of him.'

'Why exactly did you go to Mrs Jepp?'

'I know I can do her some good if I have the chance. She's a wicked old woman. But I didn't know she had got thick with you and Andrew. When she told me "Mervyn and Andrew Hogarth" I was stabbed, stabbed to the heart.' And taking her handkerchief she stabbed each eye.

Mervyn Hogarth, looking at her, thought, I never pity myself. A weaker mind would be shattered by the perversity of my life. There would be plenty to pity if I were a man who indulged in self-pity.

Georgina was speaking. 'Bigamy and now diamond smuggling. Diamond smuggling' – she repeated this crowning iniquity with dramatic contempt, upturning her profile. She looked very like Mervyn in profile.

He determined to frighten her, though he had intended only to warn.

Georgina Hogg had no need to worry about her odd appearance that afternoon, for Mervyn, though he looked straight at her, could not see her accurately. She had stirred in him, as she always did, a brew of old troubles, until he could not see Georgina for her turbulent mythical dimensions, she being the consummation of a lifetime's error, she in whom he could drown and drown if he did not frighten her.

There was no need for him to fear that the woman profiled in the window would ever denounce him openly for his bigamous marriage with Eleanor.

In their childhood he had watched his cousin Georgina's way with the other cousins – Georgina at ten, arriving at the farm for the summer holidays with her bloodless face, reddish hair, lashless eyes, her greediness, would tell the cousins,

'I can know the thoughts in your head.'

'You don't know what I'm thinking just now, Georgina.'

'Yes I do.'

'What then?'

'I shan't say. But I know because I go to school at a convent.'

There was always something in her mouth: grass – she would eat grass if there was nothing else to eat.

'Georgina, greedy guts.'

'Why did you swing the cat by its tail, poor creature, then?'

She discovered and exploited their transgressions, never told on them. She ruined their games.

'I'm to be queen of the Turks.'

'Ya Georgina lump of a girl, queen of the fairies!'

Even Mervyn, though a silent child, would mimic, 'I'm to be queen of the turkeys!'

'You stole two pennies,' and in making this retort Georgina looked as pleased as if she were eating a thick sandwich. Mervyn, the accused, was overpowered by the words, he thought perhaps they were true and eventually, as the day wore on, believed them.

He had married her in his thirty-second year instead of carving her image in stone. It was not his first mistake and her presence, half-turned to the window, dabbing each eye with her furious handker-chief, stabbed him with an unwanted knowledge of himself.

'I have it in me to be a sculptor if I find the right medium . . . the right environment . . . the right climate . . . terrific vision of the female form if I could find the right model . . . the right influences', and by the time he was forty it became,

'I had it in me . . . if only I had found the right teachers.'

By that time he had married Georgina instead of hacking out her image in stone. A *mistake*. She turned out not at all his style, her morals were as flat-chested as her form was sensuous; she conversed in acid drops while her breasts swelled with her pregnancy. He left her at the end of four months. Georgina refused to divorce him: that was the mistake of marrying a Catholic. Wouldn't let him see the son; a mistake to marry a first cousin, the child was crippled from birth, and Georgina moved him from hospitals to convents, wherever her various jobs took her. In her few letters to Mervyn, she leered at him out of her martyrdom. He sent her money, but never a message in reply.

At intervals throughout the next twenty years Georgina would put in appearances at the Manders' house in Hampstead, there to chew over her troubles. Helena hardly ever refused to see her, although she could hardly abide Georgina's presence. As the years passed, Helena would endure these sessions with her distasteful former servant, she would express banal sympathies, press small gifts into Georgina's hand and, when the woman had gone, 'offer up' the dreary interview for the Holy Souls in Purgatory. Sometimes Helena would find her a job, recommending her to individuals and institutes with an indiscri-minate but desperate sense of guilt.

'I am sure you are better off without Mr Hogg,' Helena would say often when Georgina bemoaned her husband's desertion.

'It is God's will, Georgina,' Helena would say when Georgina lamented her son's deformity.

Georgina would reply, 'Yes, and better he should be a cripple than a heathen like Master Laurence.'

That was the sort of thing Helena put up with, partly out of weakness and partly strength.

One day after a long absence Georgina had arrived as of old with her rampant wounded rectitude. On this occasion she kicked the Manders' cat just as Helena entered the room. Helena pretended not to notice but sat down as usual to hear her story.

'Lady Manders,' said Georgina, dabbing her eyes, 'my son has gone.'

Helena thought at first he must be dead.

'Gone?' she said.

'Gone to live with his father,' Mrs Hogg said. 'Imagine the deception. That vile man has been seeing my boy in the hostel, behind my back. It's been going on for months, a great evil, Lady Manders. The father has money you know, and my poor boy, a good Catholic –'

'The father has taken him away?'

'Yes. Andrew has gone to live with him.'

'But surely Mr Hogg has no right. You can demand him back. What were the authorities thinking of? I shall look into this, Georgina.'

'Andrew is of age. He went of his own free will. I wrote to him, begged him to explain or to see me. He won't, he just won't.'

'Were you not informed by the authorities before Andrew was removed?' Helena asked.

'No. It was very sudden. All in an afternoon. They say they had no power to prevent it, and I was in Bristol at the time in that temporary post. It's a shocking thing, a tragedy.'

Later Helena said to her husband,

'Poor Mrs Hogg. She had reason to be distressed about it. I wish I could like the woman, but there's something so unwholesome about her.'

'Isn't there!' he said. 'The children never cared for her, remember.'

'I wonder if her son disliked her.'

'Shouldn't be surprised.'

'Perhaps he's better off with Mr Hogg.'

'Shouldn't be surprised.'

There was only one disastrous event which Georgina Hogg omitted to tell the Manders. That was the affair of Mervyn's bigamous
marriage under the assumed name 'Hogarth'.

Mrs Hogg shifted from the window to turn up the gas fire.

She said to Mervyn,

'Making a criminal out of Andrew.'

'He likes the game.'

'Bigamy,' she said, 'and now smuggling. You may get a surprise
one day. I'm not going to sit by and watch you ruining Andrew.'

But he knew, she would never dissipate, in open scandal, the
precious secret she held against him. He counted always and accurately on the moral blackmailer in Georgina, he had known in his
childhood her predatory habits with other people's seamy secrets.
Most of all she cherished those offences which were punishable by
law, and for this reason she would jealously keep her prey from the
attention of the law. Knowledge of a crime was safe with her, it was
the criminal himself she was after, his peace of mind if she could get it.
And so Mervyn had exploited her nature without fear of her disclosing to anyone his bigamy (another 'mistake' of his), far less his
smuggling activities. It was now three years since Mrs Hogg had
made her prize discovery of the bigamy. She had simply received an
anonymous letter. It informed her that her husband, under the name
of Hogarth, had undergone a form of marriage in a register office with
the woman who had since shared his home. Georgina thought this
very probable – too probable for her even to confide in Helena who
might have made investigations, caused a public fuss.

Instead, Georgina made her own investigations. The letter, to start
with: on close examination, obviously written by Andrew. She
rejoiced at this token of disloyalty as much as the contents agitated her
with a form of triumph.

They were true. Georgina turned up at Ladle Sands, Sussex, where
the couple were established, and made a scene with Eleanor.

'You have been living with my husband for some years.'

'Quite right,' said Andrew who was present.

'I must ask you to leave,' Eleanor had kept repeating, very uncertain of her ground.

It was as banal as that.

Eleanor left Mervyn Hogg, now Hogarth, shortly after this revelation of his duplicity. She re-enacted the incident many times to the Baron. She made the most of it but her acting ability was inferior to her power of dramatic invention; what Eleanor added to the scene merely detracted from the sharp unambiguous quality of the original which lingered now only in the memories of Andrew and Georgina, exultant both, distinct though their satisfactions, and separated though they were. All the same, the Baron was impressed by Eleanor's repeated assertion, 'Mrs Hogg is a *witch*!'

Georgina wielded the bigamy in terrified triumph. Her terror lest Eleanor should take public action against the bigamist was partly mitigated by the fact that Eleanor had a reputation to keep free of scandal.

'But my name would suffer more than hers. I've always been respectable whereas she's a dancer,' Georgina declared on one of her unwelcome visits to Ladle Sands. On the strength of the bigamy she had made free of Mervyn's house.

'Moreover,' she declared, 'the affair must be kept quiet for Andrew's sake.'

'I'm not fussy,' Andrew said.

'Imagine if my friends the Manders got to hear,' Georgina said as she propped a post-card picture of the Little Flower on the mantelpiece.

For a year she made these visits frequently, until at length Mervyn threatened to give himself up to the police. 'Six to twelve months in jail would be worth it for a little peace,' he declared.

'Good idea,' said Andrew.

'You are possessed by the Devil,' his mother told him as she departed for the last time with a contemptuous glance at some broken plaster statuettes lying on a table. 'Mervyn has taken up modelling, no doubt!'

Mervyn continued to tell himself, as he sat in that room in Chiswick late in the afternoon, that if he were a man given to indulge in self-pity he would have plenty of scope. It was one mistake after another. It came to mind that on one occasion, during his matrimonial years with Eleanor, he had slipped while crossing her very polished dancing floor. Polished floors were a mistake, he had broken an eye-tooth, and in consequence, so he maintained, he had lost his sense of smell. Other calamities, other mistakes came flooding back.

It was not any disclosure of his crimes that he feared from Georgina, he was frightened of the damage she could do to body and soul by her fanatical moral intrusiveness, so near to an utterly primitive mania.

Georgina was speaking. 'Repent and be converted, Mervyn.'

He shuddered, all hunched in the chair as he was, penetrated by the chill of danger. Georgina's lust for converts to the Faith was terrifying, for by the Faith she meant herself. He felt himself shrink to a sizable item of prey, hovering on the shores of her monstrous mouth to be masticated to a pulp and to slither unrecognizably down that abominable gully, that throat he could almost see as she smiled her smile of all-forgetting. 'Repent, Mervyn. Be converted.' And in case he should be converted perhaps chemically into an intimate cell of her great nothingness he stood up quickly and shed a snigger.

'Change your evil life,' said she. 'Get out of the clutches of Mrs Jepp.'

'You don't know what evil is,' he said defensively, 'nor the difference between right and wrong . . . confuse God with the Inland Revenue and God knows what.' And he recalled at that moment several instances of Georgina's muddled morals, and he thought again of his mistakes in life, his lost art and skill, his marriages, the slippery day when he broke the eye-tooth and another occasion not long ago when he had missed his travellers' cheques after spending half an hour in Boulogne with an acquaintance of his youth whom he had happened to meet. Added to this, he had a stomach ulcer, due to all these mistakes. He thought of Ernest Manders, the hush money. He sat down again and set about to defy Georgina.

'I'll tell you what has happened thanks to your interference in my affairs. The Manders are on our trail.'

'The Manders? They dare not act. When I saw Lady Manders about my suspicions she was very very frightened about her mother.'

'You told Lady Manders? You've been busy. No wonder the affair is almost common property.'

'She was more frightened than grieved, I'm sorry to say,' Georgina said. 'She dare not act because of the mother being involved.'

'The old woman takes a very minor part in our scheme. Do you suppose we put ourselves in the hands of that senile hag?'

'She isn't senile, that one.'

'Mrs Jepp has very little to do with us. Almost nothing. The Manders are after us; they intend to make a big fuss. You see their line? – Preying on a defenceless old lady. That was the line Ernest Manders took when I met him today.'

'Ernest Manders,' Georgina said, 'you've been seeing that pervert.'

'Yes, he's blackmailing us. Thanks to your interference. But I won't be intimidated. A few years in prison wouldn't worry me after all I've been through. Andrew will get off, I daresay, on account of his condition. A special probationary home for him, I reckon. He wouldn't care a damn. Our real name would come out of course and you would be called as witness. Andrew doesn't care. Only the other day he said, "I don't care a damn".'

'You've ruined Andrew,' she declared, as she always did.

He replied: 'I was just about to take Andrew on a pilgrimage to the shrine at Einsiedeln, but we've had to cancel it thanks to your interference.'

'*You* go on a pilgrimage!' she said. 'I don't believe you would go on a holy pilgrimage, I don't believe that.'

Sir Edwin Manders had been in retreat for two weeks.

'Edwin has been in retreat for two weeks,' said Helena.

Ernest, dining with her, noticed that she had said this three times since his arrival, speaking almost to herself. 'I suppose,' he thought, 'she must love him,' and he was struck by the strangeness of this love, whatever its nature might be; not that his brother was unlovable in the great magnanimous sense, but it was difficult to imagine wifely affection stretching out towards Edwin of these late years, for he had grown remote to the world though always amiable, always amiable, with a uniform amiability.

For himself, trying to approach his brother was an unendurable embarrassment. Ernest had decided that his last attempt was to remain the last.

'A temporary difficulty, Edwin. We had expensive alterations carried out at the studio. Unfortunately Eleanor has no head for business. She was under the impression that Baron Stock's financial interests in the school were secure from any personal – I mean to say any personal – you see, whereas in fact the Baron's commitments were *quite* limited, a mere form of patronage. Do you think yourself it would be a worth-*while* venture, for yourself, to satisfy your desire to promote what Eleanor and I are trying to do?' and so on.

Edwin had said, all amiable, 'To be honest now, Ernest, I have no real attraction to investing in dancing schools. But look, I'll write you a cheque. You are not to think of repayment. I am sure that is the best way to solve your problem.'

He handed Ernest the slip he had signed and folded neatly and properly. He was obviously at ease in his gesture; nothing *in* the transaction to cause reasonable resentment but Ernest was in horrible discomfort, he was unnerved, no one could know why.

Ernest began to effuse. 'I can't begin to thank you, Edwin, I can't say how pleased Eleanor . . .' What he had meant to say was: 'We don't want a gift – this is a business proposition', but the very sight of his smiling brother blotted out the words.

'Why, don't think of it,' – Edwin looked surprised, as if he had written the cheque a long-forgotten twenty years ago.

Ernest fumbled the gift into his pocket and in his nervousness exaggerated his effeminate movements. Blandly the brother spoke of the ballet, of the famous dancers he had seen; this for goodwill; Ernest knew that his brother had withdrawn for many years since into a life of interior philosophy, as one might say. The arts had ceased to nourish Edwin. It was sweet of him to talk of ballet, but it put Ernest out dreadfully, and altogether he had to go home to bed. Next day he remembered the cheque, looked at it, took it to Eleanor.

'Fifty pounds! How mean! Your brother is rich enough to *invest*!' Ernest was vexed at her tone.

'Do modify your exclamation marks,' he said. 'He doesn't want to invest in the school, don't you see? He tried so hard to be nice. Fifty pounds is a generous gift.'

Eleanor bought a dress, black grosgrain with a charming backward

swish which so suited her lubricious poise that Ernest felt better.
With the money left over from the dress Eleanor paid down a deposit
for an amber bracelet.

'Wouldn't your brother be dismayed if he knew how his sacred
money was being spent?'

'No, he would not be angry at all,' Ernest said, 'not even surprised.'

For the fourth time Helena murmured,

'Edwin has been in retreat for two weeks.'

'When he returns,' Ernest said, 'you must tell him the whole story,
much the best way.'

'First we shall settle the business. I never tell Edwin my troubles
until they are over.'

'I feel there is nothing more to worry about. Hogarth was really
scared, poor bilious little bloke he was. I pulled a gorgeous bluff.'

'If he was scared there must be something in our suspicions.
Laurence was right.'

'Does it matter if we never know exactly what your mother's been
doing, so long as we put an effective stop to it?'

'I should like to know a little more,' said Helena. 'But Mother is
very deep, Ernest. So deep, and yet in her way so innocent. I must say
I feel it a shortcoming on my part that I can't accept her innocence
without wondering how it *works*. I mean, those diamonds in the
bread, and where she gets her income from. It's a great defect in me,
Ernest, but I'm bound to wonder, it's natural.'

'Perfectly natural, dear,' said Ernest, 'and I shouldn't reproach
myself.'

'Oh *you* have nothing to reproach yourself about, Ernest dear.'

Ernest had meant to imply, 'I shouldn't reproach myself *if I were
you*', but he did not correct her impression. A light rain had started to
pat the windows.

'Let's employ a firm of private detectives and be done with it,' he
suggested.

'Oh no, they might find out something,' she said quite seriously.

Ernest, who hated getting wet, departed soon after dinner in case
the shower should turn into a steady drencher.

He had been gone nearly half an hour and it was nine-thirty, Helena thinking of saying her rosary, and of bed with a hot-water bottle since it was chilly, when the doorbell rang. Presently the middle-aged housekeeper put her head round the drawing-room door.

'Who is it, Eileen?'

'Mrs Hogg. I've sat her in the hall. She wants to see you. She said she saw the drawing-room light.' This Eileen knew Mrs Hogg; she was the one whose marriage was long ago precipitated by Laurence, his reading of her love letters. Though she had only recently returned to the Manders' service after much lively knocking about the world, she retained sufficient memory of her kitchen-girl days and especially of Mrs Hogg to resent that woman's appearances at the house, her drawing-room conferences with Lady Manders.

'I was just going to bed, Eileen. I thought an early night –'

'I'll tell her,' said Eileen, disappearing.

'No, send her up,' Helena called out.

Eileen put her head round the door again with the expression of one who demands a final clear decision.

'Send her up,' Helena said, 'but tell her I was just going to bed.'

An absurd idea came into Helena's mind while she heard the tread of footsteps ascending the stairs. She thought, 'How exhilarating it is to be myself', and the whole advantage of her personality flashed into her thoughts as if they were someone else's – her good manners and property, her good health, her niceness and her modest sense and charity; and she felt an excitement to encounter Mrs Hogg. She felt her strength; a fine disregard, freedom to take sides with her mother absolutely if necessary.

It was hardly necessary. Mrs Hogg was docile. She began by apologizing for her previous visit about Laurence's letter. 'My nerves were upset. I'd been overdoing things at St Philumena's. Some days as many as a hundred and thirty pilgrims –'

'Of course, Georgina,' Helena said.

Georgina went on to explain that she'd been thinking things over. Clearly, she had misread that letter from Master Laurence. It was all a joke, she could see that now.

'You never should have read it in the first place. It wasn't addressed to you.'

'I did it for the best,' said Mrs Hogg dabbing her eyes. And she handed the letter to Helena.

'What's this?' Helena said.

'Laurence's letter. You can see for yourself how I was misled.'

Helena tore it in two and tossed it on the fire.

'I hope you will do nothing more about it,' Georgina said.

'About what? The letter is burned. What more should I do about it?'

'I mean, about your mother. Poor old lady, I'm sure she's a holy soul,' Georgina said, adding, as she watched Helena's face, 'at heart.'

The interview continued for half an hour before Helena realized how desperately anxious the woman was to put a stop to all investigations. It was barely a month since Mrs Hogg had descended upon her mother at the cottage. Helena was puzzled by this change of attitude and yet her suspicions were allayed by the sight of Mrs Hogg dabbing her tearful eyes.

'I'm glad you have come to your senses, Georgina.'

'I meant everything for the best, Lady Manders.'

'I understand you called to see my mother. Why was that?'

Georgina was startled. Helena was made aware of one of her suspicions being confirmed: something more than she knew had passed between her mother and Mrs Hogg.

'I thought she might want a companion,' Mrs Hogg said feebly. 'You yourself suggested it not long ago.'

Helena felt her courage surge up. 'You mean to say that you offered your services to Mrs Jepp at a time when you believed her to be a criminal?'

'A Catholic can do a lot of good amongst wicked people.'

'My mother is not a wicked person, Georgina.'

'Yes, I quite see that.'

A knock at the door, and 'Your bottle is in your bed, Lady Manders.'

'Thank you, Eileen.'

Mrs Hogg rose. She said, 'I can take it, then, that the matter is closed.'

'What on earth are you worrying about? Of course there is no more to be done,' said Helena.

'Thank God! Now I shall feel easy in my mind.'

'Where are you placed now? Have you got a job?' Helena said as if by habit.

'No, Lady Manders.'

'Have you anything in mind?'

'No. It's a worry.'

'Come and see me tomorrow at five.'

Before she went to bed Helena rang Ernest.

'Are you up, Ernest?'

'No, in bed.'

'Oh, I've woken you up, I'm sorry.'

'No, I was awake.'

'Just to say, Ernest, that Mrs Hogg came here after you left. For some reason she's highly anxious to stop all inquiries. She apologized for her suspicions.'

'Well, that's all to the good, isn't it?'

'Yes, I know. But don't you see this sudden change is rather odd, just at this time?'

'Are you sure she has nothing to do with Hogarth?' Ernest said in a more wakeful voice.

'Well, I've never heard her mention the name. Is he a Catholic?'

'Shouldn't think so.'

'Then definitely she wouldn't be *friendly* with the man in any way. She's got a religious kink.'

'You don't think she means to attempt blackmail? These blackmailers beetle round in a curious way, you know.'

'No. She actually brought me Laurence's letter. I burned it in front of her. I carried the thing off well, Ernest.'

'Of course. Well, we've nothing more to worry about from Mrs Hogg's direction.'

She was grateful for that 'we'. 'Perhaps we haven't. I told her to come and see me tomorrow about a job. I want to keep my eye on her.'

'Good idea.'

'But personally,' said Helena, 'I am beginning to think that Georgina is not all there.'

At that hour Mr Webster lay in his bed above the bakery turning over in his mind the satisfaction of the day. In spite of his tiredness on his return from London he had gone straight to Mrs Jepp, had repeated with meticulous fidelity his conversation with the Baron, and together they had reckoned up the payment and their profits as they always did.

'I am glad I sent herring roes,' Louisa said. 'I nearly sent fruit but the herring roes will be a change for Baron Stock. Herrings make brains.'

'What a day it's been!' said Mr Webster, smiling round at the walls before he took his leave.

For Baron Stock it had also been 'a day'. He hated the business of money-making, but one had to do it. The bookshop, if it had not been a luxurious adjunct to his personality, would have been a liability.

After sweet old Webster had gone the Baron closed his bookshop for the day and, taking with him Louisa Jepp's tin of herring roes, went home. There he opened the can, and tipping the contents into a dish, surveyed the moist pale layers of embryo fish. He took a knife and lifting them one by one he daintily withdrew from between each layer a small screw of white wax paper; and when he had extracted all of these he placed the paper pellets on a saucer. These he opened when he was seated comfortably before his fire. The diamonds were enchanting, they winked their ice-hard dynamics at him as he moved over to the window to see them better.

'Blue as blue,' he said, an hour later when he sat in the back premises of a high room in Hatton Garden.

The jeweller said nothing in reply. He had one eye screwed up and the other peering through his glass at the gems, each little beauty in turn. The Baron thought afterwards, as he always did, 'I must make a new contract. This man swindles me.' But then he remembered how terse and unexcitable the jeweller was, so different from those gem-dealers who, meeting with each other on the pavements at Hatton Garden, could not contain for two seconds their business verve, nor refrain from displaying there and then their tiny precious wares, produced out of waistcoat pockets and wrapped in tissue paper. It was inconceivable that the Baron's silent dealer should ever be seen on the street; possibly he never went home, possibly had no home, but sat in vigilance and fasting from dawn to dawn, making laconic bargains with such people who arrived to sell diamonds.

Later that evening the Baron sipped Curaçao in his flat and decided that doing business was exhausting. Once every three months, this trip to Hatton Garden and the half-hearted haggle with the jeweller exhausted him. He reclined as in a hammock of his thoughts, shifting gently back and forth over the past day, and before he went to bed he began to write a letter to Louisa.

'The herring roes, my dear Mrs Jepp, have provided the most exquisite light supper for me after a most *exhausting* (but satisfying) day. I put them on toast under the grill – delicious! I admire your preservative process. The contents of your tin were more delicate than oysters, rarer than ...' But his mind drifted to other delicacies, mysterious Mervyn Hogarth, the inter-esting black arts.

What a day it had been, also, for Mervyn Hogarth, who had returned to Ladle Sands to find Andrew in one of his ugly moods. When he was in such moods Andrew would literally spit on everyone. Andrew had been left in charge of a village woman whom he had spat at so much she had gone home long before the arranged time, leaving the young cripple alone as darkness fell. When Mervyn at last got to bed he tried to read himself to sleep, but the 'mistakes' of the day started tingling; he lay in darkness fretting about the cunning of Ernest Manders, the tasteless lunch, the blackmail; and he murmured piteously to himself 'What a day, what a day', far past midnight.

And what a day for Mrs Hogg, that gargoyle, climbing to her mousy room at Chiswick where, as she opened the door, two mice scuttled one after the other swiftly down their hole beside the gas meter.

However, as soon as Mrs Hogg stepped into her room she disappeared, she simply disappeared. She had no private life whatsoever. God knows where she went in her privacy.

EIGHT

It is very much to be doubted if Mervyn Hogarth had ever in his life given more than a passing thought to any black art or occult science. Certainly he was innocent of prolonged interest in, let alone any practice of, diabolism, witchcraft, demonism, or such cult. Nevertheless Baron Stock believed otherwise.

It was not till the New Year that the Baron was able to assemble his evidence. He confided often in Caroline, for since her return to London they met as frequently, almost, as in earlier days. She lived now in a flat in Hampstead, quite near the Baron, with only a slight twinge in her leg before rainy weather to remind her of the fracture, and in reminding her, to bring the surprise of having had a serious accident.

'It is strange,' said the Baron, 'how Eleanor left me, her reasons. Did you ever hear?'

Caroline said, 'I know she had suspicions of your participating in Black Masses and what not.'

'I'm not surprised,' the Baron said. 'A woman of Eleanor's limited intellig-ence is incapable of distinguishing between interest in an activity and participation in it. I am interested, for instance, in relig-ion, poetr-ay, psycholog-ay, theosoph-ay, the occult, and of course demonolog-ay and diabolism, but I participate in none of them, practise none.'

'And your chief interest is diabolism,' Caroline observed.

'Oh yes, utterly my chief. As I tried to explain to Eleanor at the time, I regard these studies of mine as an adult pursuit; but to actually take part in the absurd rituals would be childish.'

'Quite,' said Caroline.

'I have, of course, attended a few Black Masses and the ceremonies of other cults, but purely as an observer.'

Caroline said, 'Um.'

It was a gusty day, and from the windows of Caroline's top-floor flat, only the sky was visible with its little hurrying clouds. It was a day when being indoors was meaningful, wasting an afternoon in superior confidences with a friend before the two-barred electric heater.

'Eleanor would not be reasoned with,' the Baron went on. 'And for some reason the idea of living with a man whose spare-time occupation was black magic appalled her. Now the curious thing is, I've since discovered that her former husband Mervyn Hogarth is a *raging* diabolist, my dear Caroline. That is obviously why she deserted him.'

'Never mind, Willi. You're as well apart from Eleanor, and she from you.'

'I've got over it. And you,' he said, 'are as well without Laurence.'

'Our case is different,' she said snappily. 'There's love saved up between Laurence and me, but no love lost between you and Eleanor.'

'No love lost,' he said, 'but still it hurts when I think of her.'

'Of course,' she said nicely.

'But not enough, my Caroline,' said he, 'to induce me to give up these investigations. People are unaccountable. One finds barbarity and superstition amongst the most unlikely. The subject, the people, excite me in-tensely. At present my attention is almost entirely on this Mervyn Hogarth. He is, I assure you, Caroline, the foremost diabolist in the kingdom. I go so far as to employ agents. I have him watched.'

'Oh, come!' Caroline said.

'Truly,' said the Baron. 'I have him watched. I get reports. I have compiled a dossier. I spend a fortune. The psychology of this man is my main occupation.'

'Dear me. You must miss Eleanor more than I thought.'

'What d'you mean?'

'Obviously your obsession with Eleanor's former lover is a kind of obsession with Eleanor. You are looking in him for something concealed in her, don't you see! Obviously you are following the man because you can't follow Eleanor, she has eluded you, don't you see? Obviously –'

'Physician, heal thyself,' said the Baron with what he thought was aptness.

'Oh, I may be wrong,' said Caroline mildly. The indoor afternoon idea went limp and she was reminded of her imprudence when, in hospital, she had begun to confide her state of mind to the Baron on the occasion of his visits. She knew he would not keep her confidences any more than she his.

But unable to leave well alone she said, 'Why really does it trouble you even if Hogarth is a diabolist? I could understand your fanaticism if you had any religion to defend. Perhaps unawares you are very religious.'

'I have no religion,' he said. 'And I don't disapprove of diabolism. For my part, it is not a moral interest; simply an intellectual passion.'

She teased him, but did not watch her words. 'You remind me of an African witch-doctor on the trail of a witch. Perhaps you picked up the spirit of the thing in the Congo – weren't you born there?' Then she saw her mistake, and the strange tinge in the whites of his eyes that had made her wonder at times if the Baron had native blood. He was extremely irritated by her remark.

'At least,' articulated he, 'I pursue an intelligible objective. Diabolism exists; the fact can be proved by the card index of any comprehensive library. Diabolism is practised: I can prove it to you if you care to accompany me to Notting Hill Gate on certain nights – unless, of course, you are too bound by the superstitious rules of your Church. Mervyn Hogarth exists. He practises diabolism; that fact is available to anyone who cares to instigate private inquiries into his conduct. You on the other hand,' he said, 'assert a number of unascertainable facts. That chorus of voices,' he said, 'who but yourself has heard them? Your theories – your speculations about the source of the noises? I think, Caroline *my* dear, that you yourself are more like a witch-doctor than I am.'

This upset Caroline, whereupon she busied herself with tea-cups, quick movements, tiny clatters of spoons and saucers. As she did this she protested nebulously.

'The evidence will be in the book itself.'

Now Caroline, one day when the Baron had visited her in hospital, had told him,

'Those voices, Willi – since I've been in hospital I have heard them. But one thing I'm convinced of' – and she indicated her leg which had swollen slightly within the plaster case so that it hurt quite a lot – 'this physical pain convinces me that I'm not wholly a fictional character. I have independent life.'

'Dear me,' said the Baron, 'were you ever in doubt of it?'

So she told him, confidentially, of her theory. He was intrigued. She warmed to the sense of conspiracy induced by the soft tones of their conversation, for it was an eight-bed ward.

'Am I also a charact-er in this mysterious book, Caroline?' he asked.

'Yes you are, Willi.'

'Is everyone a character? – Those people for instance?' He indicated the seven other beds with their occupants and visiting relatives and fuss.

'I don't know,' Caroline said. 'I only know what the voices have hinted, small crazy fragments of a novel. There may be characters I'm unaware of.'

The Baron came to see her every week-end. On each occasion they discussed Caroline's theory. And although, profoundly, she knew he was not to be trusted with a confidence, she would tell herself as he arrived and after he had gone, 'After all, he is an old friend.'

One day she informed him, 'The Typing Ghost has not recorded any lively details about this hospital ward. The reason is that the author doesn't know how to describe a hospital ward. This interlude in my life is not part of the book in consequence.' It was by making exasperating remarks like this that Caroline Rose continued to interfere with the book.

The other patients bored and irritated her. She longed to be able to suffer her physical discomforts in peace. When she experienced pain, what made it intolerable was the abrasive presence of the seven other women in the beds, their chatter and complaints, and the crowing and clucking of the administering nurses.

'The irritant that comes between us and our suffering is the hardest thing of all to suffer. If only we could have our sufferings clean,' Caroline said to the Baron.

A visiting priest on one occasion advised her to 'offer up' her sufferings for the relief of some holy soul in Purgatory.

'I do so,' Caroline declared, 'with the result that my pain is intensified, not at all alleviated. However, I continue to do so.'

'Come, come,' said the priest, youthful, blue-eyed behind his glasses, fresh from his seminary.

'That is a fact, as far as my experience goes,' said Caroline.

He looked a trifle scared, and never stopped for long at Caroline's bedside after that.

On those Saturday afternoons the Baron had seemed to bring to Caroline her more proper environment, and for the six weeks of her confinement in the country hospital she insulated herself by the phrase 'he is an old friend' against the certainty that the Baron would, without the slightest sense of betrayal, repeat and embellish her sayings and speculations for the benefit of his Charing Cross Road acquaintance. Much was the psycho-analysing of Caroline that went on in those weeks at the back of the Baron's bookshop, while she lay criticizing the book in the eight-bed ward. Which was an orthopaedic ward, rather untidy as hospital wards go, owing to the plaster casts which were lying here and there, the cages humping over the beds and the trolley at the window end on which was kept the plaster-of-Paris equipment, also a huge pair of plaster-cutting scissors like gardening shears, all of which were covered lumpily with a white sheet; and into which ward there came, at certain times, physiotherapists to exercise, exhort, and manipulate their patients.

The Baron, it is true, while he discussed 'the book' with her, had no thought for the Monday next when he should say to this one and that,

'Caroline is embroiled in a psychic allegory which she is trying to piece together while she lies with her leg in that dreary, dreary ward. I told you of her experience with the voices and the typewriter. Now she has developed the idea that these voices represent the thoughts of a disembodied novelist, if you follow, who is writing a book on his typewrite-r. Caroline is apparently a character in this book and so, my dears, am I.'

'Charming notion. She doesn't believe it literally though?'

'Quite literally. In all other respects her reason is unimpaired.'

'Caroline, of all people!'

'Oh it's absol-utely the sort of thing that happens to the logical mind. I am so fond of Caroline. I think it all very harmless. At first I thought she was on the verge of a serious disorder. But since the accident she has settled down with the fantasy, and I see no reason why she shouldn't cultivate it if it makes her happy. We are all a little mad in one or other particular.'

'Aren't we just, Willi!'

Laurence was out of hospital some weeks before Caroline.

'I can't think what possesses you,' he said, when at last he was able to see her, 'to confide in the Baron. You asked me to keep your wild ideas a secret and naturally I've been denying all the rumours. It's embarrassing for me.'

'What rumours?'

'They vary. Roughly, it goes that you've dropped Catholicism and taken up a new religion.'

'What new religion?'

'Science Fiction.'

She laughed then winced, for the least tremble hurt her leg.

'Sorry,' said Laurence who had promised not to make her laugh.

'I never expected the Baron to keep his peace on any subject,' she said. 'I rather like talking to him, it amuses me. I've been lonely here, sick as well.'

She could see that Laurence was more niggled by the Baron's attentiveness than by her actual conversations with him.

To return to that afternoon in the New Year when Caroline unwittingly hurt the Baron by comparing him to an African witch-doctor.

After tea, which she made in two pots: green for the Baron and plain Ceylon for herself, the Baron attempted to compensate for his anger. He told her a story in strictest confidence which, however, she repeated to Laurence before the day was out.

'Once, on Eleanor's behalf – shortly after her divorce from her daemonical Hogarth, and in connexion with a financial settlement, I went to call on him at his house in Ladle Sands. I had not informed him previously of my intention to call, believing that if I did so he would refuse to see me. I hoped to catch him by chance – Many were such services, I assure you, Caroline, that I performed for Eleanor. Well, I called at the house. It is fairly large with some elegance of frontage, Queen Anne; set well back from the road and concealed by a semi-circle of plane trees within a high hedge that had not been trimmed for months. The garden was greatly neglected. The house was empty. Peering through the letter-box I could see a number of circular letters lying on the hall table. From this I assumed that the Hogarths had been absent for some weeks, having arranged for their personal letters to be forwarded. I went round to the back of the house. I was curious. At that time, you must understand, I was greatly in love with Eleanor, and the house where she had lived with Hogarth inter-ested me in the sense that it gave me a physical contact with a period of Eleanor's past which I knew only from what she had chosen to tell me.

'The back premises were even more untidy than the front. The kitchen garden gone to seed and stalk, and an important thing that I am going to tell you is this. At the door of an outhouse lay a pile of junk. Empty boxes, rusty broken gardening tools, old shoes. And amongst these a large number of broken plaster statuettes – religious objects of the more common kind that are sold by the thousand in the repositories attached to the Christian shrines. These were hacked about in a curious way. The heads were severed from many of them, and in some cases the whole statue had been reduced to fragments. There were far too many of these plaster pieces to be accounted for by accidental breakage. Even at that time – I knew nothing of Hogarth's occult activities then – I assumed that there had been a wholesale orgy of deliberate iconoclasm. In cases where the body was intact, only the head or limbs being severed, I noticed how cleanly the cleavage occurred, as if cut by an instrument, certainly not smashed by a fall, not that.

'Then I must tell you, Caroline, what happened while I was engaged in examining these extraordinary bits of clay. The back premises were skirted by a strip of woodland. This was about thirty yards from the outhouse where I was standing. The sound of a dog growling caused me to turn and observe this direction, and soon I saw the dog emerge from the wood towards me. It was a black spaniel, very well cared for. I picked up a stick in case it should attack me. It approached with its horrid growling. However, it did not make straight for me. As soon as it got within five yards it started to walk round me in a circle. *It encircled me three times*, Caroline. Then it bounded towards the heap of broken statues and sat, simply sat, in front of the heap as though defying me to touch them.

'Of course I went away, walking casually in case the dog should leap. But what I am trying to tell you, Caroline, is that the black dog was Mervyn Hogarth.'

'What did you say?' said Caroline.

'I did not realize at the time,' said the Baron, stirring his green tea, 'I merely thought it an uncommonly behaved dog. Of course I am speaking to you confidentially, it is not the sort of thing one can tell one's acquaintances, however intimate. But I feel you have an understanding of such things, especially as you yourself are super-normal, clairaudient and –'

'What was that you said,' Caroline said, 'just now, about the dog?'

'The dog was Mervyn Hogarth. Magically transformed, of course. It is not unknown –'

'You're mad, Willi,' said Caroline amiably.

'Indeed,' said the Baron, 'I am not.'

'Oh, I don't mean *mad*, you know,' Caroline said. 'Just a little crazy, just a little crazy. I think of course it's a lovely tale, it has the makings of a shaggy dog.'

'I wouldn't have expected you to be incredu-lous of all people.'

'Well, Willi, I ask you!'

He was serious. 'What,' he said, 'do you make of the broken saints?'

'Maybe they had a house-full and then got fed up with them and chucked them out. Maybe they break up the statues for pleasure. After all, most of those plaster saints are atrocious artistically, one can well understand the urge.'

'For pleasure,' the Baron repeated. 'And how do you account for the dog?'

'Dogs are. One doesn't have to account for dogs. It must have been the Hogarths' dog –'

'It wasn't the Hogarths' dog. I inquired. They possess no dog.'

'It must have been a neighbour's dog. Or a stray, looking for something to eat.'

'What do you say to its having encircled me *three times*?'

'My dear Willi, I'm speechless.'

'True,' said the Baron, 'you have no answer to *that*. Not that I have formed my opinion that Hogarth is a black magician solely from the experience which I have just described to you. I haven't told you yet about the carrier-pigeons, and many subsequent pheno-mena. Are you free to dine with me tonight? If you are I can tell you the whole story, and then, my Caroline, you will no longer say Willi's mad.'

'We're all a little mad, Willi. That's what makes us so nice, dear. No, I'm not free tonight, I'm sorry to say. It would have been pleasant really. . . .'

He planted a friendly kiss on her cheek when he said good-bye. As soon as Caroline heard him descending in the shaky lift she went into her bathroom and taking out a bottle of Dettol poured rather a lot into a beaker of warm water. She saturated a piece of cotton wool with this strong solution; she dabbed that area on her face where the Baron had deposited his kiss.

'The Baron is crackers.'

It gave Laurence pleasure to hear Caroline say these words, for he had been lately put out by the renewed friendship between Caroline and the Baron.

'The Baron,' she declared, 'is clean gone. He came to tea this afternoon. He related the most bats tale I've ever heard.'

So she told Laurence the Baron's story. At first it amused him. Then suddenly his mild mirth changed to a real delight. 'Good for the Baron!' he said. 'He's actually stumbled on a clue, a very important one, I feel.'

'Clue to what?' she said.

'My grandmother.'

'What has the black dog to do with your grandmother?'

'The clue is in the broken statues. Why didn't I think of it before?'

'Your grandmother wouldn't break anything whatsoever. What's the matter with you, dear man?'

'No, but Hogarth would.'

'You're as bad as the Baron,' she said, 'with your obsession about Hogarth.'

Since their motor accident Laurence had been reticent with Caroline. She saw that, because he was partly afraid, he could not keep away from her, but it was not at all to her taste to nourish the new kind of power by which she attracted him. Laurence's fear depressed her. For that reason she stopped altogether discussing with him the private mystique of her life. Only when she was taken off-guard in conversation did she reveal her mind to Laurence, as when he innocently inquired,

'How is your book going?' meaning her work on the structure of the modern novel.

'I think it is nearing the end,' she answered.

He was surprised, for only a few days since she had announced that the work was slow in progress.

Another thing had surprised him.

They had planned a holiday together abroad, to take place in the last two weeks in March.

At first Caroline had objected that this was too early in the year. Laurence, however, was fixed on this date, he had already applied for leave before consulting Caroline. She thought it rather high behaviour, too, when he announced that they would go to Lausanne.

'Lausanne in March! No fear.'

'Do trust me,' he said. 'Have I been your good friend?'

'Yes, yes, but Lausanne in March.'

'Then believe that I have my reasons. Do, please.'

She suspected that his choice of time and place was connected with his intense curiosity about his grandmother's doings. Ernest and Helena had come to believe that the danger was over. Any illicit enterprise the old woman had been engaged in was squashed by Ernest's interference and bluff. They hardly cared to think there had been any cause for anxiety. But Laurence, who had made several week-end trips to the cottage during the past winter, seemed convinced that his grandmother's adventures were still in hearty progress. Arriving unexpectedly one recent week-day evening Laurence had found her little 'gang' assembled as before, the cards in play as before, Louisa unconcerned as always. From her own lips he learned that the Hogarths had twice been abroad since January.

For his failure to pull off a dramatic swift solution of his grandmother's mystery Laurence blamed the car accident. He bitterly blamed the accident. At the same time he felt stimulated by his discovery that Ernest and Helena had between them succeeded only in putting the gang on its guard. It still remained for him to search out the old woman's craftiness. That was what he mostly desired, and not content merely to put an end to her activities, Laurence wanted to know them.

Throughout the winter his brief trips to the cottage tantalized him. He snooped round Ladylees and Ladle Sands with blank results; he had a mounting certainty that the gang was lying low. Ernest had bungled the quest. Most of all Laurence felt up against his grandmother's frankness. She was never secretive in her talk or manner, but decidedly she refrained from disclosing her secret. All he had gained was the information that the Hogarths planned a trip to Lausanne in the last two weeks of March.

'The Hogarths go abroad a great deal, Grandmother.'

'They do like travelling, my, don't they!'

He got no more out of Louisa. He applied for a fortnight's leave to start on 15 March.

Helena had been so far emancipated by her son that she saw nothing offensive in suggesting to him,

'Why not take Caroline with you? She needs a holiday and, poor girl, she can't afford one. I'll pay her expenses.'

It was then Laurence was faced with Caroline's objection, 'Lausanne in March! Why Lausanne? It will be so bleak.'

But when he said, 'Haven't I been your good friend? Do please agree with me this once,' she agreed.

That was in the middle of February. Two weeks later she disagreed.

'I've been to the Priory to see Father Jerome,' she began.

'Jolly good!' said Laurence. She had observed lately with some amusement that Laurence displayed himself keen to promote all her contacts with religion, the more as he himself continued to profess his merry scepticism. One recent Sunday when she had decided to miss church because of a sore throat, he had shown much concern, in the suggestion of a warm scarf, the providing of a gargle, and transport to and from the church in his new car, to see that she did not evade the obligation. 'Jolly good!' said Laurence, when he heard that she had visited the old monk whom he had known since his boyhood.

'He says,' Caroline announced, 'that I ought not to go to Lausanne with you.'

'But he knows me! Surely he knows we can be trusted together, that it's simply a companionable holiday. My goodness, it's done continually by the deadliest proper couples. My goodness, I always thought he was a reasonable broad-minded priest.'

'He said that in view of our past relationship, we ought not to appear in circumstances which might give rise to scandal.'

'But there's no question of sin. Even I know that. I was indoctrinated in the Catholic racket, don't forget.'

'No question of sin, but he said it would disedify,' Caroline said.

'We needn't tell anyone we're going together. And we're hardly likely to be seen by anyone at all in Lausanne in March.'

'A furtive trip would be worse than an open one. More disedifying still. I can't go. Awfully sorry.'

Her withdrawal upset Laurence more than she expected. He had not told her that, as she had guessed, his determination to visit Lausanne in March was in some way connected with his passion to play the sleuth on his grandmother. She had not reckoned with his need for her participation, and the more he argued with her the more she conceived herself well out of the affair. It reminded her too much of the pattern of events preceding the car-smash.

Laurence did not press her very far. He accepted her decision with that strange fear he now had of approaching close enough to Caroline to precipitate a row. It was on this occasion that, suppressing his disappointedness, he asked her amicably,

'How is your book going?' and she, her mind brooding elsewhere, answered, 'I think it is nearing the end.'

'Really? You were saying only the other day that you still had a lot to write.'

Swiftly she realized her mistake, and so did Laurence. He looked rather helpless, as if enmeshed. She hated to think of herself as a spiritual tyrant, she longed to free him from those complex familiars of her thoughts which were to him so foreign.

'Naturally, I look forward to the end of the book,' she said, 'in a manner of speaking to get some peace.'

'I meant,' said Laurence with a burst of irritation, 'of course, the book that you are writing, not the "book" in which you think you are participating.'

'I know,' she said meekly, 'that is what you meant.' And to lift the heavy feeling between them she gave him her pretty, civilized smile and said, 'Do you remember that passage in Proust where he discusses the ambiguous use of the word "book", and he says –?'

'To hell with Proust,' said Laurence.

'Look,' she said, 'I don't inquire into your fantastic affairs. Leave mine alone. And look,' she said, 'we have nothing to say to each other this evening. I'm going home. I'll walk.'

They were dining in a small restaurant only a few minutes' walk from Caroline's flat, and so her 'I'll walk', falling short of its intended direness, tickled Laurence.

'I find it difficult to keep up with you these days.' And to pacify her he added, 'Why do you say that the "book" is nearing the end?'

She was reluctant to answer, but his manner obliged her.

'Because of incidents which have been happening within our orbit of consciousness, and their sequence. Especially this news about your grandmother's friend.'

'Which friend?' said Laurence.

'Haven't you heard about it? Helena rang me this morning, very excited, and from what I can gather it's most remarkable –'

'Which friend?'

'One of those concerning whom you entertain your daft suspicions. Andrew Hogarth. Apparently he was paralysed, and his father took him off to some little shrine of Our Lady in the French Alps. Well, he was brought back yesterday and he's actually started to move his paralysed limb. Helena says it's a miracle. I don't know about that but it seems the sort of incident which winds up a plot and brings a book to a close. I shan't be sorry.'

'But they haven't been abroad since January. They hadn't planned to leave until the middle of March, at least so I understood. I have reason to believe the Hogarths are diamond smugglers, don't you understand?'

'Ask your mother,' Caroline said. 'She knows all about it. She's brimming full of it.'

'I don't see,' said Laurence, 'much point, now, in going to Lausanne in March.'

'Absolutely perfect ... A pass back there – a foul tackle and the whistle ... the sun has come out, everything looks *absolutely perfect* with the red coats of the band ... that feeling of – of tenseness ... and now again for the second half ... the first dramatic ... absolutely perfect ... it's a *corner*, a goal to Manchester City ... a beautiful, absolutely ...'

Louisa Jepp sat beside the wireless cuddled in the entranced caress of Laurence's voice.

Much later in the day, after he had braked up loudly outside the cottage in his new car, and had settled into a chair by the stove with a newly opened bottle of beer, he said,

'Is it true about young Hogarth?'

'He is receiving physiotherapeutic treatment,' she said, with correctness, for she used and pronounced her words, however unlikely, accurately, or not at all.

'And he has actually started to use his legs?'

'Yes. He totters a little. It's too soon to say "he walks".'

'He was absolutely paralysed before.'

'My, yes. The trips abroad did him good. I always knew they would.'

'I suppose,' said Laurence, 'that the Hogarths have cancelled their holiday in Lausanne?'

'Oh yes. There's no need for them to go wandering in March. It's very chilly. Much better at home. Andrew is getting his treatment.'

'I suppose,' said Laurence, 'they will be off again in the early summer?'

'Not abroad,' said the old lady. 'Somerset or Cornwall I should say, if the boy's fit enough.'

'I suppose that means,' said Laurence, 'that your game is up, Grandmother?'

'Why, dear,' she said, 'I was thinking, as I listened to you on the wireless today, how much I wished for your sake, dear, that you could have caught us red-handed. It must be a disappointment, love. But never mind, we all have our frustrations and you were lovely on the wireless, you were *absolutely perfect*.'

'I had every clue, Grandmother. I only needed the time. If I hadn't had the smash I'd have got you last autumn, Grandmother.'

'There, never mind.'

'But you're in danger. An acquaintance of ours is on your trail. I heard by chance through Caroline. His name's Willi Stock, a phoney Baron —'

'No, he is quite authentic a Baron.'

'You know Baron Stock, then?'

'I have met the Baron,' she said.

'Well, do you know,' he said, 'Caroline told me last November, just before the smash, that the Baron had been seeing you last year. He described a hat you wore. Caroline recognized it, and inferred –'

'That was very stupid of the Baron, but typical, though he is nice –'

'But I didn't,' said Laurence, 'place much faith in what Caroline said. I thought she was sort of dreaming.'

'Why, you can't be clever at everything.'

'It was a good clue,' said Laurence. 'I ought to have followed it up. I might have got you right away. Have you any fears of the Baron? – Because if so –'

'No, no. He's my London party. Or was.'

'The *Baron* has been in with you! I thought there were only the four of you.'

'There are only four of us. Baron Stock was only our London agent.'

'You've packed up the game, then?'

'Now, which game?' she said, puckering a smile as if to encourage him to recite a lesson.

'Smuggling diamonds through the customs,' he said, 'concealed in plaster figures.'

'And rosary beads at times,' said Louisa. Her whole body seemed to perk with delight, and to further signify her sense of occasion she passed Laurence a glass and a bottle of stout to open for her. She watched him pour the brown liquid and she watched the high self-controlled froth as one who watches a scene to be preserved in memory.

'You took a risk, Grandmother.'

'There was very small risk,' she said. 'What there was, the Hogarths took, as I see it.'

She drew up to the stove and sipped warmly.

'I had many a smile,' she said, 'considering how they came through with the merchandise.'

'Several times a year,' said Laurence, 'at a guess.'

'It has varied,' she said, 'over four years and eight months. Some trips were better than others. It depended so much on our continental parties. It was difficult for that end to get the right moulds for the statues. The beads were easier. But Andrew preferred the statues.'

'I should have thought the customs would have got suspicious with all that coming and going. Very risky,' Laurence said.

'Everything's risky,' she said. 'Many a laugh I had to myself when Mervyn told me about the customs men passing remarks. *Mervyn* didn't laugh, he didn't like that part of it. You see they went as pilgrims looking for a cure, Andrew in his invalid chair, you can picture him, hugging his statues with a long churchy face. So as to deceive the customs, don't you see. Each time they went to some shrine of the Virgin Mary and our contact would meet them in the town, who was a gentlemanly party I believe. But I made Mervyn and Andrew visit the shrines properly, in case they were watched. You can't be too careful with the continental police, they are very deceitful and low.'

'Are the Hogarths Catholics?'

'Oh, no. Not religious at all. That was the pose, you see. Many an entertainment I had, love.'

'Mother has heard about Andrew Hogarth's recovery,' Laurence said.

'Yes, I wrote and told her. I thought it would be of interest to her that the young man, being a neighbour of mine, had got a cure at a Roman Catholic shrine. She likes those stories.'

'Do you think it was a miracle, then?'

'Oh yes,' she said, 'I do believe in lucky places if your luck is in. Indeed Andrew was unlucky before. He got a cold in the bladder at Lourdes two years back, but Myans has brought him luck, where there's a *black* Madonna, I believe. And indeed I once knew a gentleman very up in history and fond of the olden days who had a stammer which he lost in the Tower of London.'

'That sounds psychological,' said Laurence.

'Oh, it's all what I call luck,' Louisa said.

'You don't think Andrew's case is clearly a miracle, then?'

'Oh, quite clear a miracle, as I see him now. He can move his legs from the knees, sitting in his chair. He couldn't do that before.'

'What do the doctors say?'

'They say he has to have physiotherapy. He's improving already.'

'How do they explain it?'

'They say it's a marvel but they don't make mention of miracles. They brought a great crowd of students to look at Andrew up at the hospital. Andrew put an end to it, though, by swearing and spitting. He has such a temper.'

'Good for him!' Laurence said. 'I suppose he's thrilled to be able to move his legs?'

'I think so. But he has a temper,' she said, and passing a box of cigarettes, 'Have a Bulgarian.'

Laurence smiled, comparing this account of Andrew with the picture in his mother's imagination of the young man miraculously cured. In Helena's eyes, the event entirely justified the Hogarths' shady activities. It justified her mother. She was content to remain vague about Louisa's late intrigues, and convinced that Ernest, through his strong hand with Mervyn Hogarth last year in the course of a luncheon, had been successful in ending the troubles, whatever they were.

When she told Laurence of Andrew's cure at the Alpine shrine, he remarked,

'They're still at the game, then.'

'Nonsense,' Helena replied. 'At the very worst, the Hogarths might have been winding up their business, whatever it was. I expect they will both become Catholics. The young man will, surely.'

'Helena wants to make a Church thing of it,' Louisa told Laurence. 'But she won't be able to. I'm sorry for her sake, but the Hogarths aren't interested at all in churches.'

'Like me,' said Laurence.

'No, not at all. They aren't interested in quite a different way from you.'

The old woman had sipped from her glass only at long intervals. Even so, Laurence was fascinated to notice how little she had drunk, while giving the companionable appearance of keeping pace with him.

'I suppose,' he said, 'you made a packet between you.'

'Yes. I meant to retire this year in any case.'

Helena had developed a firm new theory about her mother's motives. 'I am sure she involved herself in all that unpleasantness, whatever it was, simply to help the young man. My mother is extremely secretive. She is quite capable of *planning* to send him to the holy shrines, using the financial reward as a bribery.'

Laurence reported this to his grandmother. She wrinkled her nose and sipped from her glass. 'Of course I knew the trips would be good for Andrew. Psychologically. It gave him a job to do and a change now and then. The business side was good for me too. Psychologically. I shall miss it, dear, it was sport. Helena is sentimental, my!'

'What was Mr Webster's role, Grandmother?'

'Oh, the good fellow baked the bread, and he sometimes went to London for me.'

'Now tell me where the bread comes in,' said Laurence.

'You found diamonds in the bread, and you wrote to tell Caroline of it. That caused a lot of trouble.' – Laurence, feeling sleepy from his day's work, the warmth and the beer, was not quite sure whether he heard or imagined these words.

'What did you say, Grandmother?'

The glass was at her lips. 'Nothing, dear,' she said when she had sipped.

'Tell me about the bread. Who transferred the diamonds to the bread? You know I saw them once.'

'Mr Webster,' she said. 'Because I desired to have my merchandise quickly, as soon as the Hogarths brought it in. For the sake of the London end. Sometimes, at first, there was a little delay owing to Andrew being poorly after the journey and leading Mervyn a dance. So we arranged that Mervyn should break up his saints and rosaries and extract the stones as soon as he returned from the trips, which was always in the morning. Mervyn would telephone Mr Webster, because they use telephones, I stick to my pigeons. And then Mr Webster called at the Hogarths to deliver the bread.'

'Ostensibly,' said Laurence.

Louisa closed her eyes. 'He called to deliver the bread as it might seem. You can't be too careful. And he took the money for it.'

'Along with the diamonds.'

'Yes, you are clever, dear. Mr Webster has been invaluable. He would bring the merchandise to me on the following morning in my bread. I didn't think it would be nice to let him slip the little goods into my hand as if there were some mystery or anything shady going on.'

'Wonderfully ingenious,' Laurence said.

'It was sport,' said Louisa.

'But totally unnecessary, the bread part of it,' Laurence said.

'No, that was necessary. I never liked to have the diamonds carried loose.'

'I can guess why,' Laurence put in suddenly. 'The police.'

'Of course,' she said. 'I don't trust the police. Our local constable is a nice fellow, but the police all stick together if it comes to the bit, the world over.'

Laurence laughed. Louisa's dislike of the police was a family joke. 'It's the gipsy in her,' Helena would explain.

'I should have thought,' Laurence said, 'that if you got the goods safely into the country, there would be no need for elaborate precautions.'

'You never can tell. It was sport,' Louisa said.

After a while Laurence said, 'I believe Mrs Hogg gave you some trouble.'

'None at all,' she said, 'nor will she.'

'You think she's likely to turn up again? Has she any evidence against you, Grandmother?'

'I don't know about that. But she won't trouble me, that I know. She might try, but I shan't be troubled.' She added, 'There are things about Mrs Hogg which you don't know.'

At a later time when Laurence learned of the relationship between Mrs Hogg and the Hogarths, he recalled this remark of his grandmother's, and thought that was what she must have meant.

'And at a side altar, I do assure you, Caroline,' said the Baron, 'robed in full liturgical vestments, was Mervyn Hogg alias Hogarth serving cocktails.' Thus he ended his description of the Black Mass he had recently attended at Notting Hill Gate.

'It sounds puerile,' Caroline said, lapsing unawares into that Catholic habit of belittling what was secretly feared.

'You as a Catholic,' he said, 'must think it evil. I myself do not judge good and evil. I judge by interesting or otherwise.'

'It sounds otherwise to me,' said Caroline.

'In fact you are right. This was a poor effort from the sinister point of view. For a really effective Black Mass you need a renegade priest.

They are rare in these days, when the Faith is so thin. But Hogg is the one who inter*ests* me. He assumes the name of Hogg on the dark side of his life and Hogarth by daylight so to speak. I am preparing a monograph on the psychology of diabolism and black magic.

'And my informants tell me that Hogarth has recently un-bewitched his son, a man in his early twenties who since infancy has suffered from paralysis in the lower part of his body due to a spell. This proves that Hogarth's magical powers are not exclusively bent towards evil, it proves –'

'Tell me,' said Caroline, 'have you ever spoken to Mervyn Hogarth?'

'Not in his natural flesh. But I shall shortly. A private meeting is to be arranged. Unofficially, I believe, he has been into the bookshop, transformed into a woman.'

'I'm sure, Willi,' said Caroline, 'that you are suffering from the emotional effects of Eleanor's leaving you. I am sure, Willi, that you should see a psychiatrist.'

'If what you say were true,' he said, 'it would be horribly tactless of you to say it. As it is I make allowances for your own disorder.'

'Is the world a lunatic asylum then? Are we all courteous maniacs discreetly making allowances for everyone else's derangement?'

'Largely,' said the Baron.

'I resist the proposition,' Caroline said.

'That is an intolerant attitude.'

'It's the only alternative to demonstrating the proposition,' Caroline said.

'I don't know,' said the Baron,' really why I continue to open my mind to you.'

At various times the Baron had described to Caroline the stages by which he had reached the conclusion that Mervyn Hogarth was a diabolist and magician. The first hint had come to him from Eleanor. 'She told me he had previously been through a form of marriage with a witch. Eleanor had seen the witch, a repulsive woman. In fact, it was when she began to frequent the house in Ladle Sands that Eleanor left Hogarth.'

'I shouldn't take much account of what Eleanor says. She dramatizes a lot,' said Caroline, and barely refrained from adding the information that Eleanor, in her college days, had been wont to send love-letters to herself. Caroline only refrained because she was not too sure if this were true.

'My subsequent experience has borne out her allegations. My subsequent investigations have proved that Hogarth is the foremost diabolist in the kingdom. One must speak as one experiences and as one finds. You, Caroline, are no exception. Your peculiar experiences are less explicable than mine: I have the evidence. The broken plaster images: a well-known diabolic practice: the black dog. If you would only enter*tain* the subject a little more you would see that I am right.'

So he attempted to extort sympathy from Caroline. He appeared to her more and more in the nature of a demanding creditor. 'The result,' she told herself, 'of going to him with my troubles last autumn. He acted the old friend and now he wants me to do the same, which is impossible.'

And she told him, 'You are asking me to entertain impossible beliefs: what you claim may be true or not; I have doubts, I can't give assent to them. For my own experiences, however, I don't demand anyone's belief. You may call them delusions for all I care. I have merely registered my findings.'

Caroline had been reflecting recently on the case of Laurence and his fantastic belief that his grandmother had for years been the leader of a gang of diamond-smugglers. She had considered, also, the case of the Baron and his fantastic belief in the magical powers of Mervyn Hogarth. The Baron was beginning to show a sickly resemblance to Eleanor. She thought of Eleanor with her habit of giving spontaneous utterance to stray and irresponsible accusations. Caroline found the true facts everywhere beclouded. She was aware that the book in which she was involved was still in progress. Now, when she speculated on the story, she did so privately, noting the facts as they accumulated. By now, she possessed a large number of notes, transcribed from the voices, and these she studied carefully. Her sense of being written into the novel was painful. Of her constant influence on its course she remained unaware and now she was impatient for the story to come to an end, knowing that the narrative could never become coherent to her until she was at last outside it, and at the same time consummately inside it.

Eventually she told the Baron that she simply wasn't interested in black magic. She forbade the subject.

'It gets on my nerves, Willi. I have no sympathy with your occult interests. Talk about something else in future.'

'You are lost,' he said sadly, 'to the world of ideas. You had the makings of an inter-esting mind, I do assure you, Caroline. Ah, well!'

One morning Caroline had an unexpected caller. She had opened the door of her flat unguardedly, expecting the parcel post. For a second Caroline got the impression that nobody was there, but then immediately she saw the woman standing heavily in the doorway and recognized the indecent smile of Mrs Hogg just as she had last seen it at St Philumena's.

'May I have a word with you, Miss Rose?' Already the woman was in the small square hall, taking up most of it.

'I'm busy,' Caroline said. 'I work in the mornings. Is it anything urgent?'

Mrs Hogg glared with her little eyes. 'It's important,' she said.

'Will you come inside, then?'

She seated herself in Caroline's own chair and cast her eyes on the notebook in which Caroline had been writing. It was lying on a side table. Caroline leant forward and snapped the book shut.

'There is a Baron Stock,' said Mrs Hogg. 'He was in your flat till after one o'clock this morning. He was in your flat till after two on Wednesday morning. You were in his flat till after midnight twice the week before last. If you think you are going to catch Laurence Manders with this carry-on –'

'You are insolent,' Caroline said. 'You'll have to leave.'

'Till after two on Wednesday morning. Baron Stock is more attractive than Laurence Manders, I don't doubt, but I think it low behaviour and so would everyone –'

'Take yourself off,' said Caroline.

She left, pathetic and lumpy as a public response. Caroline seized the phone angrily and rang Helena.

'Would you mind calling off your Mrs Hogg. She's just been round here making wild insinuations about my private life, citing Willi Stock. She must have been watching my flat for weeks. Haven't you any control over the woman? I do think, Helena, you are far too soft with that woman. She's a beast. If there's any more trouble I shall simply call the police, tell her that.'

'Dear me. I haven't seen Mrs Hogg for months. I *am* sorry, Caroline. Won't you come round to lunch? I recommended Mrs Hogg for a job in a place at Streatham last autumn. I haven't heard from her since. We've got a new sort of risotto, quite simple, and heaps to spare. Edwin won't be in to lunch. Have you seen Laurence lately?'

'You ought not to recommend Mrs Hogg for jobs. She's quite vile.'

'Oh, one tries to be charitable. I shall speak severely. Did she upset you seriously, Caroline?'

'No, she did not. I mean, she did, yes. But it's not what she says, it's what she is.'

'She's not all there,' said Helena.

Presently, Caroline sprayed the room with a preparation for eliminating germs and insects.

NINE

'Wonderful to have a whole day unplanned,' Caroline said. 'It's like a blank sheet of paper to be filled in according to inspiration.'

It was summer, on a day which Laurence described as absolutely perfect for a riverside picnic. They chose their spot and got the luncheon boxes out of the car. It was Laurence's day off. Helena too had decided to have a day off.

'I've been working so hard on the committees, and Edwin is in retreat – I should love a day in the country,' she admitted when Laurence invited her to join them. 'But I hate intruding. You and Caroline enjoy yourselves together, do.'

But she yielded easily when Caroline too insisted on her coming.

'All right. But you two go ahead. I'll join you before lunch, if you tell me where to find you.'

They described the area where they intended to park on the banks of the Medway where it borders Kent and Sussex.

There they were at midday sunning themselves lusciously and keeping an intermittent look-out for Helena's car.

She arrived at half past twelve, and they could see as she bumped down the track towards them that she had brought two people with her, a man beside her in the front and a woman with a black hat at the back.

The couple turned out to be the Baron and Mrs Hogg.

Helena, uncertain of her welcome, and unusually nervous, began immediately,

'Such fun. Willi phoned me just after you'd left and d'you know what, he's been meaning to come down here the first opportunity. He wants to look at an Abbey in these parts, don't you, Willi? So I made him come. And I've brought poor Mrs Hogg, I made her come. It was a lovely ride, wasn't it? Poor Georgina's had neuralgia. She called round to the house by chance just after you'd left, so I made her come.

A day in the country will do you a world of good, Georgina. We shan't interfere with your plans, Laurence. We've brought extra lunch and you can go off by yourselves if you like while we sit in the sun.'

Helena looked a trifle shaky. While they prepared lunch she made the opportunity of a private word with Caroline,

'I hope you don't mind dreadfully, dear, about my bringing Georgina. She turned up so desolate, and there was I so obviously preparing the picnic basket. I asked her on impulse and of course she jumped to it – I was rather sorry afterwards, remembering how much you dislike her. Do try to ignore her and if she says anything funny to you just shake her off. I know how you feel about Georgina for I can't bear the sight of her at times, but one tries to be charitable.'

'Don't you think,' Caroline said, 'that you misconstrue charity?'

'Well, charity,' said Helena, 'begins at home. And Georgina *has* been part of our household.'

'Mrs Hogg is not home,' Caroline said.

'Oh dear, I wish I hadn't asked her to come. It was foolish of me, I've spoiled your day.'

'The day isn't over yet,' said Caroline cordially, for the weather was glorious really.

'But still I wish I hadn't brought her, for another reason. Something happened on the way here, Caroline. It was disturbing.' Caroline saw she was distressed.

'Come over here and help me to take out the bottles,' Caroline said, 'and tell me what happened.'

'I gave Georgina a tablet for her neuralgia before we set off,' Helena said, 'and sat her comfortably at the back of the car. Before we were out of London I said over my shoulder, "Are you all right, Georgina?" She replied that she was feeling sleepy. I went on chatting to Willi and thought no more of Georgina at the back. I assumed she had fallen asleep for I could hear her breathing heavily.'

'She snores,' Caroline said. 'I remember at St Philumena's I could hear her snoring six doors away.'

'Well, yes, she was snoring,' Helena said. 'And I thought the sleep would do her good. After a while she stopped snoring. I said to Willi, "She's dead asleep." Then Willi's cigarette lighter gave out and he asked for some matches. I thought there were some at the back of the car, but I didn't want to wake Georgina. So I pulled up. And when I turned to reach for the matches, I couldn't see Georgina.'

'Why, what had happened?'

'She simply wasn't there,' Helena declared. 'I said to Willi, "Heavens, where's Georgina?" and Willi said, "My God! she's gone!" Well, just as he said this, we saw Georgina again. She suddenly appeared before our eyes at the back of the car, sitting in the same position and blinking, as if she'd just then woken up. It was as if there'd been a black-out at the films. I would have thought I'd been dreaming the incident, but Willi apparently had the same experience. He said, "Where have you been, Mrs Hogg? You vanished, didn't you?" She looked really surprised, she said, "I've been asleep, sir."'

'It may have been some telepathic illusion shared by you and Willi,' Caroline said. 'I shouldn't worry.'

'Maybe it was. I haven't had an opportunity to discuss this privately with Willi. It was a most strange affair; truly I wish I hadn't brought Georgina. Sometimes I feel I can handle her, but at other times she seems to get the better of me.'

'Maybe when she goes to sleep she disappears as a matter of course,' Caroline said with a dry laugh so that Helena would not take her too seriously.

'What a gruesome idea. Well, I swear that she did apparently vanish. All I saw when I first looked round was the empty seat.'

'Maybe she has no private life whatsoever,' Caroline said, and she giggled to take the grim edge off her words.

'Oh, she has no private life, poor soul,' Helena agreed, meaning that the woman had no friends.

Mrs Hogg ate heartily at lunch. Caroline sat as far away from her as possible to avoid the sight of her large mouth chewing, and the memory of that sight, when at St Philumena's, she had first observed Mrs Hogg sitting opposite to her at the refectory table, chew – pause – chew – pause. Mrs Hogg spoke little, but she was very much present.

After lunch, Caroline was stacking an empty food box in the boot of Helena's car some distance from the rest of the party, when the Baron approached her.

'Summer suits you, my Caroline,' he said. 'Your sun dress is charming. Green suits you, and you are plumper. I thought you a delightful picture at lunch, so secluded within your proud personality as you always seem to be and with such a watchful air.'

Caroline appreciated flattery, the more so when it was plainly excessive and well laid on, for then she felt that the flatterer had really taken pains to please. So she smiled languidly and waited for the rest, not at all surprised that these remarks were a prelude to one of those 'confidences' which the Baron so greatly longed to make. For, since she had forbidden the subject of black magic, the Baron had been manifestly unhappy. She realized that he had chosen her as a repository for his secret enthusiasm because of that very edginess and snap with which she responded. If like his other friends, she could have been merely sociable about his esoteric interests, making a gay palaver of them – 'Do describe the formula, Willi, for changing oneself into a fly. One could watch all one's friends. . . . Suppose one got stuck in a pot of jam' – if only she could have played buoyant and easy with the Baron, he never would have plagued her with his 'confidences'.

Having lubricated the way with his opening speech he proceeded instantly,

'I must tell you, Caroline, such a strange thing happened in the car as we came down. This woman, Mrs Hogg –'

Caroline tried to be pleasant. 'Helena has already told me of the incident. Obviously, Willi, you've been infecting Helena with your fancies. Obviously –'

'I do assure you, Caroline, I have never discussed any occult subject with Helena. I am very careful in whom I confide these matters. There is no other way of accounting for the strange pheno-menon in the car but to accept the fact that this woman Hogg is a witch.'

'Not necessarily,' Caroline said, 'even if she did disappear. I think she's too ignorant to be a witch.' And she added, 'Not that I believe in witches particularly.'

'And I have made a curious discovery,' the Baron continued relentlessly. 'Don't you see – this woman Hogg is, I am certain, the witch to whom Mervyn Hogarth was married. The facts meet together – he *has* been known to use the name Hogg, as I told you. My informants say he always used it in his younger days. This Georgina Hogg is his witch-wife.'

'Nonsense. She's an old servant of the Manders. I believe she married a cousin. She has a crippled son somewhere.'

'Has she? – Then it is certain she is the one, the witch, the wife! It is her son who was cured a few months ago by Hogarth's magic. It must be the same young man!'

'Awfully far-fetched,' Caroline said. 'And, Willi, all this bores me.' In fact it agitated her, as he could see. 'That Hogarth crest,' she was thinking, 'on Eleanor's cigarette case. Laurence identified it, the same as Mrs Hogg's. . . .' She decided to speak of this to Laurence later on.

Just then Helena shouted,

'Caroline, will you fetch my book – I threw it in at the back of the boot with my little head cushion. Will you fetch that too?'

'Hell!' Caroline breathed.

It meant unloading the entire contents of the boot. The Baron helped Caroline to ease them out of the tiny space, while he talked as fast as he could, as if to get in as much as possible of his precious confidences in the next few moments.

'It is the same young man,' he said, 'and you will see that I am right.'

'You must be wrong,' said Caroline, out of breath with the effort of shifting the boxes, old petrol cans, and other clutter. She was reminding herself that only the other day Helena had said, 'Fancy, I told Mrs Hogg about that wonderful miracle that happened to the Hogarth boy. I thought it might give her some hope for her own son who's a cripple. But do you know, she wouldn't believe it was a miracle – she said if it had been a real miracle the young man would have become a Catholic. Unfortunately this Hogarth boy has gone off with some woman – a rich Theosophist, I understand. Perhaps I shouldn't have told Georgina that bit.'

'You must be wrong,' Caroline told the Baron. 'Helena knows Georgina Hogg's affairs. Ask Helena, she'll confirm that Mrs Hogg has nothing to do with Hogarth.' Again, she wondered about that crest.

'Helena does *not* know,' said the Baron. 'And another thing, Caroline. So exciting, Caroline. I am going to see Mervyn Hogarth this afternoon. I have been informed that he is staying at an Abbey a few miles from this spot. Now why should he be staying at a religious house? He must be posing as a Catholic retreatant. I daresay that these are the means he uses for stealing the consecrated elements for use in the Black Mass. After all, he must get them from somewhere –'

Caroline caught his sleeve and nodded towards the hedgerow a few yards from where the car was parked. He looked in that direction. The black hat had just bobbed out of sight.

'Mrs Hogg has been listening,' Caroline said in a loud voice.

'Did you call me, Miss Rose?'

Mrs Hogg came out of hiding as if she had never been in it.

'Lovely round here,' she said with her smile. 'Did you call? I thought you called "Mrs Hogg".'

Caroline walked away quickly, followed by the Baron, while Mrs Hogg made off along the towpath.

Caroline handed Helena the book. 'It had slipped down at the very back,' she said, 'I had to move everything. I feel as exhausted as if I'd done a hard day's work.'

'Oh, you shouldn't have – I thought Willi was doing all the heaving. Willi, why didn't you do all the heaving?'

'I did so, my Helena,' said the Baron.

'Mrs Hogg was bent behind the hedge listening to our conversation,' Caroline said.

'I take an oriental view of manual labour myself,' said Laurence. He was stretched in the dappling shade of a tree.

'She has nothing in her life,' Helena said, 'that's her trouble. She always has been a nosey type. Simply because she hasn't any life of her own. I'm sorry I brought her. I dread taking her back.'

Laurence gurgled. 'I think that's sweet.' Helena had not told him of their creepy experience with Georgina that morning.

'I've sent her off for a walk,' said Helena, looking round. 'I wonder if she'll be all right.' Georgina was nowhere in sight.

'Georgina is nowhere in sight,' she said anxiously.

'You've sent her off; well, she's gone off,' Laurence said. 'Stop jittering. Relax. Read your book. There's too much talking.'

'Which way did she go?' Helena said.

'Downstream, by the towpath,' said Caroline.

'Silence,' said Laurence. 'Let nothing disturb thee,' he chanted, 'nothing affright thee, all things are passing. . . .'

'God never changeth,' Helena continued, surprised that he had remembered the words.

The Baron was examining a map. 'I should be back just after four,' he said. 'Will that do?'

'Perfectly,' said Laurence. 'Kindly depart.'

'The Abbey is on the other side of the river,' said the Baron, 'but there's a bridge two miles down. I shall be back just after four.'

He set off with his jacket trailing over his arm. Lazily, they watched him until he was out of sight round a bend.

'I wonder why he wants to see the Abbey,' said Helena, 'it isn't an exceptional place, nothing architecturally speaking.'

'He's looking for a man he believes is staying at the Abbey. A man called Mervyn Hogarth,' Caroline said deliberately.

Helena looked startled. 'Mervyn Hogarth! Does Willi know him then?'

'By hearsay,' Caroline said.

'That's the father of the young man who was cured,' Helena said. 'Has Mr Hogarth become a Catholic, I wonder?'

'The Baron thinks,' Caroline said, 'that he is a magician. The Baron believes that Mervyn Hogarth is the leader of a Black Mass circle and that he's staying at the Abbey under the guise of a retreatant, but really on purpose to steal the consecrated Host.'

'Oh how frightful, oh how frightful!'

'The Baron has a kink,' Laurence put in.

'Exactly,' said Caroline.

'It does sound a far-fetched story,' Helena said. 'There's nothing in it, you think?'

'Nothing at all,' Caroline said. 'I should be surprised if he found Mervyn Hogarth at the Abbey. And more surprised if his suspicions were true.'

'It would be dreadful if they were true,' Helena said. 'But why should Willi Stock be troubled if they were; does he intend to expose the man?'

'No, he intends to write a monograph.'

Caroline put the palms of her hands out to the sun to get them browned.

'He thinks he is aloof from the subject of black magic, merely interested. Whereas he is passionately attracted to it. "My nature,"' she quoted, '"is subdued to what it works in, like the dyer's hand. Pity me then...."'

'Willi always has been eccentric,' Helena remarked.

'Part of his cultivated Englishness,' said Laurence.

'It will be interesting,' Helena said, 'to hear what he says when he comes back.'

'Don't mention what I've told you,' Caroline said, 'he's touchy, poor Willi.'

She felt a sweet pleasure in her words, 'Poor Willi!' They soothed her resentment of the Baron's 'Poor Caroline!' with which he must have ended many an afternoon's session at Charing Cross Road. Especially with Helena was she pleased to discredit the Baron. Sometimes Helena would inquire gently of Caroline if she was quite happy – nothing worrying her? From which Caroline was sensitive to assume that the Baron had been talking. In fact, Helena had discouraged the Baron's gossip. One day in the early spring he had asked her plainly,

'Is it all off between Laurence and Caroline?'

'No, I don't think so. They are waiting.'

'For what? My dear, they are not chicks,' said the Baron.

'I suppose Caroline wants to get her book off her hands. But I don't know their business at all really. I wish they would do something definite, but there it is.'

'Caroline's "book",' he said; 'do you mean the book she is writing or the one in which she lives?'

'Now, Willi! Caroline is not a silly girl. She did have a little upset and imagined things, I know. And then there was the accident. But since that time she's recovered wonderfully.'

'*My* dear Helena, I do assure you that Caroline has been receiving communications from her Typing Spooks continuously since that time.'

'Nonsense. Caroline is perfectly sane. What's going to win the Lincoln, do you think, Willi?'

And so, occasionally, when Helena asked Caroline, 'Quite happy now, dear?' or 'Nothing worrying you?' Caroline would be unhappy and worrying about these inquiries.

So, on the day of the picnic she was especially happy to discuss the Baron's latest fantasy with Helena.

'He must have built up a theory,' said Helena, 'on rumours and suspicions. I hate,' she said with unusual force, 'doubt and suspicion.'

Caroline thought, 'She is worried about Mrs Hogg. The affair in

the car is pressing on her mind. Poor Helena! Perhaps she would not
at all like to know things clearly.'

Laurence lay listening to their voices, contentedly oblivious of what
they said. He was too somnolent in the warmth of the sun to take part
in the conversation and too enchanted by his sense of the summer day
to waste it in sleep. He watched the movements of a young fat woman
on a houseboat moored nearby. Every now and then she would
disappear into the cabin to fetch something. First a bright scarf to
protect her head from the sun. Then a cushion. Next she went below
for so long a time, as it seemed to Laurence, that he thought she was
never coming back. But she did emerge again, with a cup of tea. She
drank it propped tubbily on the tiny bridge of the boat. Laurence
spent his pleasurable idleness of long meaningless moments in
following every sip. He wished the houseboat were his. He wondered
where the man of the house could be, for he was sure there must be a
man, referred to by Tubby as 'my friend'. Laurence wished it were
possible for him to go on lying drowsily by the river and at the same
time to poke about in the cabin of the boat, to pry into the cooking
arrangements, the bunks, the engine. A little rowing boat which lay
alongside caught Laurence's fancy.

It came home to him that Caroline was saying, 'I'll start the kettle
for tea.'

She had lit the spirit stove when Helena said,

'Thunder.'

'No,' said Laurence. 'Couldn't be. I was just thinking,' he said, 'we
might be able to borrow that little boat and row over to the other side.'

'*I* thought I heard a rumble,' Caroline said.

'No.'

'It's quarter past four,' Helena said. 'I wonder where Georgina has
got to?'

'Spirited away,' said Laurence remarkably.

Helena roused him to scout round for Georgina.

'I'm sure it's going to rain,' she said.

The sky had clouded, and in spite of Laurence's protests the
barking of distant thunder was undeniable.

'The thunder's miles away over the downs,' Laurence said, 'it will miss the valley.' Nevertheless, he went off in search of Mrs Hogg, pausing on the way to look more closely at the houseboat. The plump girl had gone inside.

Caroline and Helena started to move their rugs and tea-cups into the cars.

'Even if we miss the storm,' Helena said, 'it will certainly set in to rain within the next ten minutes.'

Suddenly they caught sight of the Baron on the opposite bank. He shouted something, but he was too far from them to be heard. With his hands describing a circuit he conveyed that he was coming back by the bridge.

'He'll get soaked,' Caroline said. 'Poor Willi!' But before he set off again she waved him to stop.

'I'll ask for the boat,' she said, 'and row him over.'

'That *would* be nice,' Helena said. 'Sure you can manage it?'

But Caroline, with Laurence's raincoat over her shoulders, was away to the houseboat. The Baron stood perplexed for a moment. He saw Caroline bend down and knock at the little window. He understood the plan, then, and waited. In a few minutes Caroline signed to him that she had the owner's permission to use the boat.

The rain had started, but it was light and the river calm. Caroline reached him within a few moments. He climbed into the boat and took the oars from her.

'I got a sight of Hogarth,' he said immediately, 'alias Hogg, but he was in disguise. Quite a different appearance from the man I saw conducting the Black Mass. In the circumstances I did not address him, it was too frightening.'

'How did you know it was Mervyn Hogarth, then?'

'I asked one of the lay-brothers. He confirmed that Mervyn Hogarth was staying there, and pointed him out. *They* believe he is come to the Abbey for the fishing.'

'What fishing?'

'Apparently the Abbey rents out a strip of fishing ground. They put up the anglers in the Abbey,' said the Baron. 'Little do they know whom they are harbouring. Hogarth alias Hogg,' he said.

'I think you are mixed up, Willi.' Caroline pulled the raincoat over her head and patted her hair beneath it. 'The man at the Black Mass must have been a different Hogarth.'

'Oh no, *he* was named Hogg. Hogarth is the daytime name. I know for a fact that Mervyn Hogarth was born Mervyn Hogg.'

'The man at the Black Mass must have been a different Hogg.'

'I have the whole picture, which you have not,' the Baron said. 'This afternoon, as I was leaving the Abbey grounds I saw the witch, Mrs Hogg, entering them. I turned back and followed her. I *saw* – actually saw, Caroline – Mrs Hogg approaching Hogarth. He was doing something to a fishing rod at the time. He recognized her of course. He looked very miserable. They exchanged a few words. Soon, he walked away and left her. The couple are clearly known to each other.'

They had landed. Caroline thanked the woman while the Baron tied up the boat.

'There's no sign of Georgina,' Helena said as they reached her car. 'Laurence has been back and he's gone off again to search for her. What a nuisance.'

'She was over at the Abbey,' said the Baron. 'I left her there half an hour ago.'

'How vexing. Well, we shall have to wait. Let's try and continue some tea in the back of the car.'

The thunder was still distant. The storm that was raging some miles away seemed unlikely to reach them, but now the rain was heavy.

'Which way did Laurence go?' the Baron said.

'Towards the bridge.'

'I'll take his car and meet him. I daresay I shall pick up Mrs Hogg on her way back. She must be at the bridge by now.'

He drove off. Every few minutes Helena poked her head out of the back window of her car. 'I hope they don't miss each other,' she said, 'Laurence only has his jacket. Oh, there's Georgina!'

Mrs Hogg was coming down to the riverside by a track through the trees on the opposite bank. She saw Helena and raised her hand in recognition.

Helena made a frantic dumb-show at her. Mrs Hogg stood waiting and stupid-looking.

'Caroline,' said Helena, 'be an angel.'

'You want me to fetch her in the boat,' Caroline stated.

'Put the mac over your head, do.' Helena was nervy. 'We shall be kept waiting here for ages if she has to plod round by the bridge. It's two miles each way. I'm dying to get home.'

When Caroline did not reply, Helena seemed aware of having asked more than an ordinary favour.

'I'll go, dear,' said Helena at once. 'Give me the mac. I'm sure I can manage the boat.'

Caroline was sure she couldn't. She jumped out of the car and was off like someone taking a plunge against nature.

In spite of the rain, with only a cardigan over her summer dress, Helena followed. She caught up Caroline at the houseboat, and added her gracious thanks to the owner. As Caroline unmoored she said,

'This really is charitable, Caroline. Poor Georgina would be drenched if she had to walk round to cross the bridge.'

Caroline gave her an amiable smile, for she was too proud to reveal her neurotic dread. Her dread was on account of a very small thing. She knew she would have to give Mrs Hogg a hand into the boat. The anticipation of this physical contact, her hand in Mrs Hogg's only for a moment, horrified Caroline. It was a very small thing, but it was what she constitutionally dreaded.

'Step down here, Mrs Hogg. On to that stone. Give me your hand. Take care, the river's deep here.'

The bank had grown muddy but there were several firm footholds. Caroline, standing astride in the boat, reached out and grasped Mrs Hogg's hand firmly. Step there, now there. 'I'm doing fine,' Caroline thought, gripping the woman's hand tightly in her own. She was filled with the consciousness of hand.

Mrs Hogg had rubber-soled shoes which had picked up a good deal of mud. In spite of all her care she slipped on her heels, she tottered backwards with her hand still gripped in Caroline's so that the boat rocked wildly. In an instant she was loudly in the water and Caroline, still grasping the hand by the first compulsive need to overcome her horror of it, went with her. Mrs Hogg lashed about her in a screaming panic. Caroline freed herself and gripped the side of the boat. But she was wrenched away, the woman's hands were on her neck – 'I can't swim!'

Caroline struck her in the face. 'Hold on to my shoulders,' she shouted. 'I can swim.' But the woman in her extremity was intent on Caroline's throat. Caroline saw the little boat bobbing away downstream. Then her sight became blocked by one of Mrs Hogg's great hands clawing across her eyes, the other hand tightening on her throat. Mrs Hogg's body, and even legs, encompassed Caroline so that her arms were restricted. She knew then that if she could not free herself from Mrs Hogg they would both go under.

They were under water and out of sight for a while. Helena said later that it was only a matter of seconds before Caroline's head emerged. But in that space of time it was a long breath-holding contest between them. Caroline had practised underwater swimming. Not so, Mrs Hogg. The woman clung to Caroline's throat until the last. It was not until Mrs Hogg opened her mouth finally to the inrush of water that her grip slackened and Caroline was free, her lungs aching for the breath of life. Mrs Hogg subsided away from her. God knows where she went.

Caroline had the sense of being hauled along a bumpy surface, of being landed with a thud like a gasping fish, before she passed out.

'Jolly good luck I had my friend here. I can't swim myself.'

Caroline lay in the bunk of the houseboat, without a sense or even a care of where she was. She recognized Helena, then the plump woman of the houseboat and a strange man who was taking off all his dripping wet clothes. Caroline had a sense of childhood, and she closed her eyes.

'There was no sign of the other,' the man was saying. 'She's had it. Any relation?'

'No,' said Helena's voice.

'She gave this one a rough time,' said the man. 'Just look at her face. I'll bet she's been trained to hold her breath under water. If she hadn't, she'd have had it too, this one.'

The woman of the houseboat helped Caroline to sip from a warm beaker.

'Have you anything to put on the scratches?' That was Helena.

Presently Caroline felt something soft being smoothed over her face and throat. Her neck was hurting. And again she was sipping something warm and sweet, her shoulders supported by Helena.

The man said, 'I had a look for the other, best I could. It's deep in that spot. I daresay we'll get the body. There was a tragedy five summers back and we got the body two days after.'

Helena murmured, 'You've been marvellous.'

Before she went off to sleep, Caroline heard Laurence's voice from somewhere outside, then the Baron's, then Helena again,

'Here they are with the doctor.'

Sir Edwin Manders was making his autumn retreat. October 24th, the Feast of St Raphael the Archangel; he had arrived at the monastery during the afternoon in time for Benediction.

The window of his room looked down on a green courtyard over which the leaves were scattering. Fixing his eye on this sunlit square of leaves and grass, he gave himself to think about his surprising family affairs.

Usually when he was in retreat this man would give his time, under a spiritual director, to regarding the state of his soul. In the past few months he had been given cause to wonder if he did not make his retreats too frequently. Amazing things occurred at home; extraordinary events which he never heard of till later.

'Why didn't you inform me at the time, Helena?'

'You were in retreat, Edwin.'

He had misgivings then, about his retreats. He told his spiritual director. 'I might have done better to spend the time at home. My family have had to cope with difficulties ... my son ... my brother ... my mother-in-law ... one of our old servants ... I might have done better had I not made so many retreats.'

'You might have done worse,' said the shrewd old priest, and sounded as if he meant it. It was a humiliating thought, which in turn was good for the soul.

'They manage admirably without me,' Edwin Manders admitted.

And so he was in retreat again. Really on this occasion he had not wanted to come. But Helena insisted. Ernest even, in his shy way, had said, 'Someone has got to pray for us, Edwin.' Laurence had said, 'Cancel your autumn retreat? Oh you can't do that,' without giving any reasons. Caroline Rose had driven him to the station.

For years he had felt drawn to the contemplative life. To partake more fully of it he had retired, all but nominally, from Manders' Figs. Helena took pride in his frequent recourse to monasteries. In fact he was embarrassed at this moment to realize how effectively she had fostered the legend of his 'certain sanctity'. More and more he had felt attracted by the ascetic formalities. Only this autumn, in his hesitation before leaving home, did he feel he was being pushed into it.

He had no more qualms after his arrival at the monastery. The charm began to work on him. His austere cell was like a drug. The rise and fall of plain-song from the Chapel invited him into its abiding pure world. The noiseless, timeless lay-brothers moved amenably about their business, causing Edwin Manders to feel pleasurably humble in the presence of this profound elect. The fact that there was a big upset going on in the monastic quarters of the buildings due to half the bedrooms being flooded by a burst pipe, that one of the lay-brothers was sick to death of his life, that the Abbot was worried about an overdraft, was mercifully concealed from Edwin at that moment. And so he was sufficiently unhampered by material distractions to see his spiritual temptation plain, which being so, he found it after all resistible, that luxurious nostalgia, that opium daze of devotion, for he knew, more or less, that he never would have made a religious. He gave his mind to reviewing his family affairs.

There were two items in the embarrassing category, for both had reached the newspapers. He was in doubt which was the more distressing, Louisa Jepp's case or Georgina Hogg's. He decided, on the whole, Georgina's. And for a good half-hour he concentrated on Georgina, now lodged, it was believed, in the mud of the Medway, for her body was never recovered. There was a piece in the London evening papers, mentioning by name Helena, Laurence, Caroline, Baron Stock, and the couple on the houseboat. There was an inquest. Poor Helena. In former days, he recalled, their name for Georgina in the household was Manders' Mortification.

As he heard afterwards, for he was in retreat at the time, Helena got Laurence to make inquiries for poor Mrs Hogg's son. He turned out to be an unfortunate person. The father a bigamist. Helena dropped her inquiries as soon as she learned that Eleanor Hogarth was involved in the bigamy; innocently no doubt, but she was in partnership with his brother Ernest, another embarrassment ... Helena hushed it up. Helena was marvellous.

'We had a sort of forewarning of Mrs Hogg's death. Willi Stock and I were on our way to the picnic, with Georgina at the back. . . .'

Women were rather fanciful, of course. Edwin often wondered if

there was any truth in the story that Mrs Hogg's son was miraculously cured. Helena was convinced of it. There had been nothing
official on the subject. The man in question had been taken under
the wing of a wealthy woman, a Theist or Theosophist, something like that. Anyway, the later news was that he had left that
woman's house and departed for Canada to lecture there about his
cure.

'In spite of which,' Edwin thought, 'young Hogarth may be a
worthier man than me.'

Likewise, when he turned to Baron Stock, he murmured, '*Miserere
mei, Deus.*' The Baron, probably a better man than himself, was
having treatment in a private mental home and, according to
accounts, loving it. He thought of his brother Ernest, so worldly and
yet so short of money and not perhaps really keen on that dancing girl.
He forced himself to consider Eleanor.... 'All these people have
suffered while I have fattened on fasting.' He meant what he said, and
so truly he was not as limited as he seemed.

And to think of his mother-in-law! He reflected, now, unflinch-
ingly on the question of Louisa Jepp. There again he could not quite
grasp ... smuggling diamonds, a gang, it sounded like an adventure
story. Then there was Louisa's real folly and it was quite embarrassing. Heroically he forced his mind to that moment in September
when, at breakfast, Helena limply passed him a letter. The letter was
from Louisa. With it was a press cutting from a local paper. The press
cutting was headed 'Sunset Wedding'. It was a long piece. It began
'In the sunset of their lives two of the old folks of Ladylees have come
together in Holy Matrimony. At All Saints' on Saturday last, Mrs
Louisa Jepp, 78, of Smugglers' Retreat, Ladylees, gave her hand in
marriage to Mr J. G. L. Webster, 77, of the Old Mill, Ladylees....
The bride promised to "obey"....' This was followed by a substantial account of Webster and his career in the Merchant Navy, and the
column ended, 'Mrs Jepp (now Webster) has one daughter, Lady
Manders, wife of Sir Edwin Manders, head of the famous firm
Manders' Figs in Syrup. The Rev. R. Socket who conducted the
ceremony stated, "This is a very happy and unique occasion. Though
not a regular churchgoer, Mrs Jepp is a figure much loved and
respected in the district."'

The accompanying letter was brief. In it Louisa remarked, 'It is not strictly accurate to say that I am not a regular churchgoer as I go to church regularly on Remembrance Day.'

'It isn't for us to judge her wisdom,' Helena said glumly.

Edwin stared out at the green quadrangle, the blown leaves. *Miserere nobis.*... Have mercy.

Laurence and Caroline had been high-spirited about Louisa's marriage. That was to be expected of Laurence. He had always adored his grandmother; and indeed she was charming, indeed.

Edwin wondered if Caroline herself was really interested in marriage.

'She's waiting for Laurence to return to the Church,' Helena said.

He wondered. Caroline was an odd sort of Catholic, very little heart for it, all mind.

'That dreadful experience with poor Georgina in the river hasn't had any harmful effects on Caroline,' Helena said. 'She must have a strong constitution. In fact, since then she's been much more lighthearted. She seems to be amused by something, I don't know what.'

Caroline had finished her book about novels. Now she announced she was going away on a long holiday. She was going to write a novel.

'I don't call that a holiday,' said Helena, 'not if you mean to spend it writing a novel.'

'This is a holiday of obligation,' Caroline replied.

'What is the novel to be about?'

Caroline answered, 'Characters in a novel.'

Edwin himself had said, 'Make it a straight old-fashioned story, no modern mystifications. End with the death of the villain and the marriage of the heroine.'

Caroline laughed and said, 'Yes, it would end that way.'

A few weeks later the character called Laurence Manders was snooping around in Caroline Rose's flat. She was away in Worcestershire writing her novel, and he had gone to the flat to collect some books which she had asked to be sent to her.

He took his time. In fact, the books were the last things he looked for.

He thought, What am I looking for? and flicked the dresses in her wardrobe.

He found the books that Caroline wanted, but before he left he sat down at Caroline's desk and wrote her a letter.

I have spent 2 hours 28 mins. in your flat [he wrote]. I have found those books for you, and had a look round. Why did you lock the right-hand drawer in the wall cupboard? I had difficulty in getting it open, and then the hair curlers in one box and the scarves in another, and the white gloves were all I found. I can't lock it again. I have just found myself wondering what I was looking for.

I found an enormous sheaf of your notes for your novel in the cupboard in that carton marked Keep in a Cool Place. Why did you leave them behind? What's the point of making notes if you don't use them while you are writing the book?

Do you want me to send the notes to you?

I wonder if you left them on purpose, so that I should read them?

But I remember your once saying you always made a lot of notes for a book, then never referred to them. I feel very niggled.

I will tell you what I think of your notes:

(1) You misrepresent all of us.
(2) Obviously you are the martyr-figure. 'Martyrdom by misunderstanding.' But actually you yourself understand nobody, for instance the Baron, my father, myself, we are martyred by your misunderstanding.
(3) I love you. I think you are hopelessly selfish.
(4) I dislike being a character in your novel. How is it all going to end?

Laurence wrote a long letter, re-read it, then folded and sealed it. He put it in his pocket, stacked away Caroline's notes in their place in the carton in the cupboard.

The autumn afternoon was darkening as he turned into Hampstead Heath. Religion had so changed Caroline. At one time he had thought it would make life easier for her, and indirectly for himself. 'You have to be involved personally,' Caroline had said on one occasion, infuriating him by the know-all assumption of the words. At least, he thought, I am honest; I misunderstand Caroline. His letter had failed to express his objections. He took it out of his pocket and tore it up into small pieces, scattering them over the Heath where the wind bore them away. He saw the bits of paper come to rest, some on the scrubby ground, some among the deep marsh weeds, and one piece on a thorn-bush; and he did not then foresee his later wonder, with a curious rejoicing, how the letter had got into the book.

THE
ONLY PROBLEM

Surely I would speak to the Almighty,
and I desire to reason with God.

Book of Job, 13,3.

PART ONE

ONE

He was driving along the road in France from St Dié to Nancy in the district of Meurthe; it was straight and almost white, through thick woods of fir and birch. He came to the grass track on the right that he was looking for. It wasn't what he had expected. Nothing ever is, he thought. Not that Edward Jansen could now recall exactly what he had expected; he tried, but the image he had formed faded before the reality like a dream on waking. He pulled off at the track, forked left and stopped. He would have found it interesting to remember exactly how he had imagined the little house before he saw it, but that, too, had gone.

He sat in the car and looked for a while at an old green garden fence and a closed gate, leading to a piece of overgrown garden. There was no longer a visible path to the stone house, which was something like a lodgekeeper's cottage with loose tiles and dark, neglected windows. Two shacks of crumbling wood stood apart from the house. A wider path, on Edward's side of the gate, presumably led to the château where he had no present interest. But he noticed that the car-tracks on the path were overgrown, very infrequently used, and yet the grass that spread over that path was greener than on the ground before him, inside the gate. If his wife had been there he would have pointed this out to her as a feature of Harvey Gotham, the man he had come to see; for he had a theory, too unsubstantiated to be formulated in public, but which he could share with Ruth, that people have an effect on the natural greenery around them regardless of whether they lay hands on it or not; some people, he would remark, induce fertility in their environment and some the desert, simply by psychic force. Ruth would agree with him at least in this case, for she didn't seem to like Harvey, try as she might. It had already got to the point that everything Harvey did and said, if it was only good night, to her mind made him worse and worse. It was true there are ways and ways of saying good night. Yet Edward wondered if there wasn't something of demonology in those confidences he shared with Ruth about Harvey; Ruth didn't know him as well as Edward did. They had certainly built up a case against Harvey between themselves which they wouldn't have aired openly. It was for this reason that Edward had thought it fair that he should come alone, although at first he expected Ruth to come with him. She had said she couldn't face it. Perhaps, Edward had thought, I might be more fair to Harvey.

And yet, here he was, sitting in the car before his house, noting how the grass everywhere else was greener than that immediately surrounding the cottage. Edward got out and slammed the door with a bang, hoping to provoke the dark front door of the house or at least one of the windows into action. He went to the gate. It was closed with a rusty wire loop which he loosened. He creaked open the gate and walked up the path to the door and knocked. It was ten past three, and Harvey was expecting him; it had all been arranged. But he knocked and there was silence. This, too, was typical. He walked round the back of the house, looking for a car or a motor-cycle, which he supposed Harvey had. He found there a wide path, a sort of drive which led away from the back door, through the woods; this path had been hidden from the main road. There was no motor-cycle, but a newish small Renault, light brown, under a rush-covered shelter. Harvey, then, was probably at home. The back door was his front door, so Edward banged on that. Harvey opened it immediately and stood with that look of his, to the effect that he had done his utmost.

'You haven't cut your hair,' he said.

Edward had the answer ready, heated-up from the pre-cooking, so many times had he told Harvey much the same thing. 'It's my hair, not your hair. It's my beard, not your beard.' Edward stepped into the house as he said this, so that Harvey had to make way for him.

Harvey was predictable only up to a point. 'What are you trying to prove, Edward,' he said, 'wearing that poncho at your age?' In the living room he pushed some chairs out of the way. 'And your hair hanging down your back,' he said.

Edward's hair was in fact shoulder-length. 'I'm growing it for a part in a film,' he said then wished he hadn't given any excuse at all since anyway it was his hair, not Harvey's hair. Red hair.

'You've got a part?'

'Yes.'

'What are you doing here, then? Why aren't you rehearsing?'

'Rehearsals start on Monday.'

'Where?'

'Elstree.'

'Elstree.' Harvey said it as if there was a third party listening – as if to draw the attention of this third party to that definite word, Elstree, and whatever connotations it might breed.

Edward wished himself back in time by twenty minutes, driving along the country road from St Dié to Nancy, feeling the spring weather. The spring weather, the cherry trees in flower, and all the budding green on the road from St Dié had supported him, while here inside Harvey's room there was no outward support. He almost said, 'What am I doing here?' but refrained because that would be mere rhetoric. He had come about his sister-in-law Effie, Harvey's wife.

'Your wire was too long,' said Harvey. 'You could have saved five words.'

'I can see you're busy,' said Edward.

Effie was very far from Edward's heart of hearts, but Ruth worried about her. Long ago he'd had an affair with beautiful Effie, but that was a thing of the past. He had come here for Ruth's sake. He reminded himself carefully that he would do almost anything for Ruth.

'What's the act?' said Harvey. 'You are somehow not yourself, Edward.'

It seemed to Edward that Harvey always suspected him of putting on an act.

'Maybe I can speak for actors in general; that, I don't know,' Edward said. 'But I suppose that the nature of my profession is mirrored in my own experience; at least, for certain, I can speak for myself. That, I can most certainly do. In fact I know when I'm playing a part and when I'm not. It isn't every actor who knows the difference. The majority act better off stage than on.'

Edward went into the little sitting room that Harvey had put together, the minimum of stuff to keep him going while he did the job he had set himself. Indeed, the shabby, green plush chairs with the stuffing coming out of them and the quite small work-table with the papers and writing materials piled on it (he wrote by hand) seemed out of all proportion to the project. Harvey was only studying a subject, preparing an essay, a thesis. Why all this spectacular neglect of material things? God knows, thought Edward, from where he has collected his furniture. There was a kitchen visible beyond the room, with a loaf of bread and a coffee mug on the table. It looked like a nineteenth century narrative painting. Edward supposed there were habitable rooms upstairs. He sat down when Harvey told him to. From where he sat he could see through a window a washing-line with baby clothes on it. There was no sign of a baby in the house, so Edward presumed this washing had nothing to do with Harvey; maybe it belonged to a daily help who brought along her child's clothes to wash.

Harvey said, 'I'm awfully busy.'

'I've come about Effie,' Edward said.

Harvey took a long time to respond. This, thought Edward, is a habit of his when he wants an effect of weightiness.

Then, 'Oh, Effie,' said Harvey, looking suddenly relieved; he actually began to smile as if to say he had feared to be confronted with some problem that really counted.

Harvey had written Effie off that time on the Italian *autostrada* about a year ago, when they were driving from Bologna to Florence – Ruth, Edward, Effie, Harvey and Nathan, a young student-friend of Ruth's. They stopped for a refill of petrol; Effie and Ruth went off to the Ladies', then they came back to the car where it was still waiting in line. It was a cool, late afternoon in April, rather cloudy, not one of those hot Italian days where you feel you must have a cold drink or an ice every time you stop. It was sheer consumerism that made Harvey – or maybe it was Nathan – suggest that they should go and get something from the snack-bar; this was a big catering monopoly with huge windows in which were arranged straw baskets and pottery from Hong Kong and fantastically shaped bottles of Italian liqueurs. It was, 'What shall we have from the bar?' – 'A sandwich, a coffee?' – 'No, I don't want any more of those lousy sandwiches.' Effie went off to see what there was to buy, and came back with some chocolate. –

'Yes, that's what I'd like.' – She had two large bars. The tank was now full. Edward paid the man at the pump. Effie got in the front with him. They were all in the car and Edward drove off. Effie started dividing the chocolate and handing it round. Nathan, Ruth and Harvey at the back, all took a piece. Edward took a piece and Effie started eating her piece.

With her mouth full of chocolate she turned and said to Harvey at the back, 'It's good, isn't it? I stole it. Have another piece.'

'You what?' said Harvey. Ruth said something, too, to the same effect. Edward said he didn't believe it.

Effie said, 'Why shouldn't we help ourselves? These multinationals and monopolies are capitalising on us, and two-thirds of the world is suffering.'

She tore open the second slab, crammed more chocolate angrily into her mouth, and, with her mouth gluttonously full of stolen chocolate, went on raving about how two-thirds of the world was starving.

'You make it worse for them and worse for all of us if you steal,' Edward said.

'That's right,' said Ruth, 'it really does make it worse for everyone. Besides, it's dishonest.'

'Well, I don't know,' Nathan said.

But Harvey didn't wait to hear more. 'Pull in at the side,' he said. They were going at a hundred kilometres an hour, but he had his hand on the back door on the dangerous side of the road. Edward pulled in. He forgot, now, how it was that they reasoned Harvey out of leaving the car there on the *autostrada*; however, he sat in silence while Effie ate her chocolate inveighing, meanwhile, against the capitalist system. None of the others would accept any more of the chocolate. Just before the next exit Harvey said, 'Pull in here, I want to pee.' They waited for him while he went to the men's lavatory. Edward was suspicious all along that he wouldn't come back and when the minutes went by he got out of the car to have a look, and was just in time to see Harvey get up into a truck beside the driver; away he went.

They lost the truck at some point along the road, after they reached Florence. Harvey's disappearance ruined Effie's holiday. She was furious, and went on against him so much that Ruth made that always infuriating point: 'If he's so bad, why are you angry with him for leaving you?' The rest of them were upset and uneasy for a day or two but after that they let it go. After all, they were on holiday. Edward refused to discuss the subject for the next two weeks; they were travelling along the Tuscan coast stopping here and there. It would have been a glorious trip but for Effie's fury and unhappiness.

Up to the time Edward went to see Harvey in France on her behalf, she still hadn't seen any more of him. They had no children and he had simply left her life, with all his possessions and the electricity bills and other clutter of married living on her hands. All over a bit of chocolate. And yet, no.

Ruth thought, and Edward agreed with her, that a lot must have led up to that final parting of Harvey from Effie.

Edward deeply envied Harvey, he didn't know exactly what for. Or rather, perhaps he had better not probe deeply enough into the possibility that if Ruth wasn't Ruth, and if they weren't always so much in agreement, he would have liked to walk off, just like that. When Harvey talked of his marriage it was always as if he were thinking of something else, and he never talked about it unless someone else did first. And then, it was as if the other person had mentioned something quite irrelevant to his life, provoking from him a puzzled look, then a frown, an effort of concentration, it seemed, then an impatient dismissal of the apparently alien subject. It seemed, it seemed, Edward thought; because one can only judge by appear-ances. How could Edward know Harvey wasn't putting on an act, as he so often implied that Edward did? To some extent we all put on acts.

Harvey began to be more sociable, for he had somehow dismissed the subject of Effie. He must have known Edward would bring up Effie later, that in fact all he had come for was to talk about her. Well, perhaps not all. Edward was an old friend. Harvey poured him a drink, and, for the moment Edward gave up trying to get on to the subject of Effie.

'Tell me,' said Harvey, 'about the new film. What's it called? What sort of part are you playing?'

'It's called *The Love-Hate Relationship*. That's only provisional as a title. I don't think it'll sell as a film on that title. But it's based on a novel called *The Love-Hate Relationship*. And that's what the film is about. There's a married couple and another man, a brother, in the middle. I'm playing the other man, the brother.' (Was Harvey listening? He was looking round into the other room.)

'If there's anything I can't stand it's a love-hate relationship,' Harvey said, turning back to Edward at last. 'The element of love in such a relation simply isn't worthy of the name. It boils down to hatred pure and simple in the end. Love comprises among other things a desire for the well-being and spiritual freedom of the one who is loved. There's an objective quality about love. Love-hate is obsessive, it is possessive. It can be evil in effect.'

'Oh well,' Edward said, 'love-hate is a frequent human problem. It's a very important problem, you can't deny it.'

'It's part of the greater problem,' said Harvey after a while. Edward knew what Harvey was coming round to and was pleased, now that he was sitting here with his drink and his old friend. It was the problem of suffering as it is dealt with in the biblical *Book of Job*. It was for this, in the first place, that Harvey had come to study here in the French countryside away from the environment of his family business and his friends.

Harvey was a rich man; he was in his mid-thirties. He had started writing a monograph about the *Book of Job* and the problem it deals with. For he could not face that a benevolent Creator, one whose charming and delicious light descended and spread over the world, and being powerful everywhere, could condone the unspeakable sufferings of the world; that God did permit all suffering and was therefore by logic of his omnipotence, the actual author of it, he was at a loss how to square with the existence of God, given the premise that God is good.

'It is the only problem,' Harvey had always said. Now, Harvey believed in God, and this was what tormented him. 'It's the only problem, in fact, worth discussing.'

It was just under a year after Harvey had disappeared that Effie traced him to St Dié. She hadn't been to see him herself, but she had written several times through his lawyer asking him what was the matter. She described to him the process by which she had tracked him down;

when she read Edward the letter before she posted it he felt she could have left that part out, for she had traced him quite simply, but by trickery, of which Harvey would not see the charm; furthermore, her revelation of the trick compromised an innocent, if foolish, person, and this fact would not be lost on Harvey. His moral sense was always intensified where Effie was concerned.

'Don't tell him, Effie,' Edward said, 'how you got his address. He'll think you unprincipled.'

'He thinks that already,' she said.

'Well, this might be the finishing touch. There's no need to tell.'

'I don't want him back.'

'You only want his money,' Edward said.

'Oh, God, Edward, if you only knew what he was like to live with.'

Edward could guess. But he said, 'What people are like to live with . . . It isn't a good test to generalise on.'

'He's rich,' said Effie. 'He's spoilt.' Effie had a lover, Ernie Howe, an electronics expert. Effie was very good-looking and it was hardly to be expected that she would resist, year after year, the opportunities for love affairs that came her way all the time; she was really beautiful. Ernie Howe was a nice-looking man, too, but he lacked the sort of money Harvey had and Effie was used to. Ernie had his job, and quite a good one; Edward supposed that Effie, who herself had a job with an advertising firm, might have been content with the simpler life with him, if she was in love with Ernie. It was only that now she was expecting a baby she felt she might persuade Harvey to divorce her with a large settlement. Edward didn't see why this should not be.

Harvey had never replied to any of Effie's letters. She continued to write, care of his lawyer. She told him of her love-affair and mentioned a divorce.

Finally she managed to find his actual whereabouts in St Dié, in a quite unpremeditated way. She had in fact visited the lawyer to try to persuade him to reveal the address. He answered that he could only forward a letter. Effie went home and wrote a letter, calling with it at the lawyer's office the next day to save the extra time it would have taken in the post. She gave it to the receptionist and asked that it be forwarded. There were two or three letters on the girl's desk, in a neat pile, already stamped. Acting on a brainwave Effie said, casually, 'If you like, as I'm passing the post box, I'll pop them all in.'

'Oh, thanks,' said the foolish girl, 'I have to go beyond the bus stop to post letters.' So she hastily filled in Harvey's address and handed the letters to Effie with a smile. And although Edward said to Effie, 'You shouldn't tell Harvey how you got his address. It'll put him right off. Counter-productive. And rather unfair on the poor girl at the lawyer's office,' she went ahead and wrote to Harvey direct, telling him of her little trick. 'He'll realise all the more how urgent it is,' she said.

But still Harvey didn't reply.

That was how Edward came to be on this errand to Harvey on her behalf. Incidentally, Edward also hoped for a loan. He was short of money till he got paid under his contract with the film people.

Edward used to confide in Harvey, and he in Edward, during their student life together. Harvey had never, to Edward's knowledge, broken any of these confidences in the sense of revealing them to other people; but he had a way of playing them back to Edward at inopportune moments; it was disconcerting, it made Edward uncomfortable, especially as Harvey chose to remind him of things he had said which he would rather have forgotten. Harvey seemed especially to choose the negative remarks he made all those years ago, ten, twelve, years ago, such as when he had said something unfavourable about Ruth, something that sounded witty, perhaps, at the time, but which he probably didn't mean. Scarcely ever did Harvey remind him of the praise he devoted in sincere abundance to others, Ruth included. So many sweet things seemed to have spilled out of his ears as soon as they entered them; so many of the sour and the sharp, the unripe and frivolously carping observations he made, Harvey had saved up in his memory-bank at compound interest; it seemed to Edward that he capitalised on these past confidences at a time when they were likely to have the most deflating effect on him; he called this a breach of confidence in a very special sense. Harvey would deny this, of course; he would claim that he had a clear memory, that his reminders were salutary, that Edward was inclined to fool himself, and that the uncomfortable truths of the past were always happier in their outcome than convenient illusions.

And undoubtedly Harvey was often right. That he had a cold side was no doubt a personal matter. In Edward's view it wasn't incompatible with Harvey's extremely good mind and his occasional flashes of generosity. And indeed his moral judgment. Perhaps a bit too much moral judgment.

Edward always spoke a lot about himself and Harvey as they were in their young days, even to people who didn't know them. But few people listen carefully to the reminiscences of someone who has achieved nothing much in life; the end-product of a personal record has somehow to justify the telling. What did come across to Edward's friends was that he had Harvey more or less on his mind. Edward wished something to happen in his own life to make him forget Harvey, get his influence out of his system. Only some big change in my life could do that, Edward thought. Divorce from Ruth, which was unthinkable (then how did I come to think it?). Or great success as an actor; something I haven't got.

Eventually Edward said, as he sat in Harvey's cottage in France, 'I've come about Effie, mainly. Ruth's anxious about her, very anxious. I've come here for Ruth's sake.'

'I recall,' Harvey said, 'how you told me once, when you first married Ruth, "Ruth is a curate's wife and always will be."'

Edward was disconcerted. 'Oh, I was only putting on an act. You know how it was in those days.'

In those days Edward had been a curate, doing so well with church theatricals that he was in demand from other parishes up and down the country. It wasn't so very long before he realised he was an actor, not a curate, not a vicar in bud. Only his sermons interested him and that was because he had his own little stage up there in the pulpit, and an audience. The congregation loved his voice and his delivery. When he resigned, what they said mostly in their letters was 'You were always so genuine in your sermons,' and 'One knew you felt every word.' Well, in fact Edward was and did. But in fact he was more involved in the delivery of his sermons than in the substance. He said good-bye to the fund-raising performances of *The Admirable Crichton* and *The Silver Box*, not to mention *A Midsummer Night's Dream* on the one chilly midsummer night when he was a curate.

He had played parts in repertory theatre, then that principal part (in *The Curate's Egg*) on the West End, and was well launched in his film career, spasmodic and limited though it was, by the time he sat talking to Harvey on Effie's behalf, largely for Ruth's sake. To himself, Edward now described his acting career as 'limited' in the sense that too often he had been cast as a clergyman, an unfrocked priest or a welfare worker. But, at present, in the film provisionally entitled *The Love-Hate Relationship*, he had been cast in a different role, to his great pleasure; he was playing a sardonic scholar, a philosopher. Thinking himself into the part had made him feel extraordinarily equal to his discussion with Harvey; and he returned, with the confidence of the part, to the subject of Effie.

'She wants a divorce,' he said, and waited the inevitable few seconds for Harvey's reply.

'Nothing to stop her.'

'She wants to get married, she's expecting a baby by Ernie Howe. And you know very well she's written to you about it.'

'What she wrote to me about was money. She wants money to get married with. I'm a busy man with things to do. Money; not enough money, but a lot. That's what Effie boils down to.'

'Oh, not entirely. I should have thought you wanted her to be happy. After all, you left her. You left Effie abruptly.'

Harvey waited a while. Time was not of an essence, here. 'Well, she soon found consolation. But she can get a divorce quite easily. Ernie Howe has a job.'

Edward said, 'I don't know if you realise how hateful you can be, Harvey. If it wasn't for your money you wouldn't speak like that.' For it struck him that, since Harvey had recently come into a vast share of a Canadian uncle's fortune, he ought not to carry on as if he were the moderately well-off Harvey of old. This treatment of Effie was brutal.

'I don't know what you mean,' said Harvey, in his time. 'I really don't care what you mean, what you say. I'll give you a letter to Stewart Cowper, my lawyer in London, with suitable instructions.' Harvey got up and reached on a bookshelf for a block of writing paper and one envelope. He said, 'I'll write it now. Then you can go away.'

He wrote without much reflection, almost as if he had come to an earlier decision about the paying off of Effie, and by how much, and had just been waiting for the moment Edward arrived to make a settlement. He addressed the envelope, put in the folded letter, then sealed it down. He handed it to Edward. 'You can take it straight to him yourself. Quicker than posting it.'

Edward was astonished that Harvey had sealed the letter since he was to be the bearer. Bloody indelicate. He wondered why Harvey was trying to diminish him.

'Harvey,' he said, 'are you putting on an act? Are you playing the part of a man who's a swine merely because he can afford to be?'

Harvey took a lot of thought. Then, 'Yes,' he said.

'Well, it doesn't suit you. One meets that sort of character amongst the older generation of the motion picture and theatre world. I remember hearing a producer say to a script writer, "It's the man who writes the cheque who has the final say in the script. And I'm the man who writes the cheque." One still hears that sort of thing. He had yellow eye-balls.'

Harvey sat with folded arms staring at his loaded work-table.

'I suppose you're playing this part to relieve your feelings?' Edward said.

'I imagine you are relieving yours, Edward.'

'I suppose you're fairly disgusted with things,' Edward said. 'With Effie and so on. I know you left her that day in disgust when she was eating her stolen chocolate and talking about the sufferings of the hungry. All that. But Effie has some good points, you know. Some very good points.'

'If you want a loan why don't you ask for it?' Harvey said, staring at his papers as if nostalgic for their lonely company.

Anxiety, suffering, were recorded in his face; that was certain. Edward wasn't sure that this was not self-induced. Harvey had once said, 'There can be only one answer to the question of why people suffer, irrespective of whether they are innocent or guilty; to the question of why suffering has no relation to the moral quality of the individual, of the tribe or of the nation, one way or another. If you believe that there is a Creator, a God, and that he is good, the only logical answer to the problem of suffering is that the individual soul has made a pact with God before he is born, that he will suffer during his lifetime. We are born forgetful of this pact, of course; but we have made it. Sufferers would, in this hypothesis, be pre-conscious volunteers. The same might apply to tribes or nations, especially in the past.'

Edward had been very impressed by this, by then the latest, idea of Harvey's. (How many ideas about *Job* they had formulated in the past!) But he had said he still couldn't see the need for suffering.

'Oh, development involves suffering,' Harvey had said.

'I wonder if I made that agreement with God before I was born,' said Edward at that time, 'for I've suffered.'

'We have all suffered,' said Harvey, 'but I'm talking about the great multitudes who are starving to death every year, for instance. The glaze-eyed infants.'

'Could your theory be borne out by science?'

'I think possibly there might be a genetic interpretation of it. But I'm talking theologically.'

When, now, Edward looked at his friend's face and saw stress on it, rich and authoritative as Harvey was, swine as he could be, he envied him for the detachment with which he was able to set himself to working on the problem through the *Book of Job*. It was possible for a man like Harvey to be detached and involved at the same time. As an actor, Edward envied him. He also envied the ease with which he could write to his lawyer about his divorce from Effie without a thought for the money involved. As for Edward's loan, Harvey had already written a cheque without a word, knowing, of course, that Edward would pay it back in time. And then, although Harvey wasn't consistently generous, and had ignored Effie's letters, Edward remembered how only a few months ago he had arranged bail through his ever-ready lawyer for Effie and Ruth's student, Nathan, when they were arrested during a demonstration, and been had up for riot and affray. Effie didn't need the bail money, for her lover came to the rescue first, but Nathan did. They were both bound over to keep the peace. Harvey's money was so casual. Edward envied him that, and felt guilty, glimpsing again, for that sharp unthinkable instant, the possibility that he might like to part from Ruth as abruptly and as easily. Edward closed the subject in his mind quickly, very quickly. It had been established that Ruth and Edward always thought alike. Edward didn't want to dwell on that thought, either.

*

As a theological student Edward had spent many an hour lying with Harvey Gotham on the grass in the great green university square if the weather was fine in the early summer, while the croquet mallets clicked on another part of the green, and the croquet players' voices made slight exclamations, and together he and Harvey discussed the *Book of Job*, which they believed was not only as important, as amazing, a poem as it was generally considered to be, but also the pivotal book of the Bible.

Edward had always maintained that the link – or should he say fetter? – that first bound him to Harvey was their deep old love of marvellous Job, their studies, their analyses, their theories. Harvey used to lie on his back on the grass, one leg stretched out, the other bent at the knee, while Edward sat by his side sunning his face and contemplating the old castle, while he listened with another part of his mind to Harvey's talk. 'It is the only problem. The problem of suffering is the only problem. It all boils down to that.'

'Did you know,' Edward remembered saying, 'that when Job was finally restored to prosperity and family abundance, one of his daughters was called Box of Eye-Paint? Can we really imagine our tormented hero enjoying his actual reward?'

'No,' said Harvey. 'He continued to suffer.'

'Not according to the Bible.'

'Still, I'm convinced he suffered on. Perhaps more.'

'It seems odd, doesn't it,' Edward had said, 'after he sat on a dung-heap and suffered from skin-sores and put up with his friends' gloating, and lost his family and his cattle, that he should have to go on suffering.'

'It became a habit,' Harvey said, 'for he not only argued the problem of suffering, he suffered the problem of argument. And that is incurable.'

'But he wanted to argue with God.'

'Yes, but God as a character comes out badly, very badly. Thunder and bluster and I'm Me, who are you? Putting on an act. Behold now Leviathan. Behold now Behemoth. Ha, ha among the trumpets. Where wast thou when I laid the foundations of the earth? And Job, insincerely and wrongly, says, "I am vile." And God says, All right, that being understood, I give you back double your goods, you can have fourteen thousand sheep and six thousand camels and a thousand yoke of oxen, and a thousand she-asses. And seven sons and three daughters. The third daughter was Kerenhappuch – that was Eye-Paint.'

Towards evening, on the day when Edward visited Harvey at his place near St Dié, Harvey went out and brought in the baby clothes. He didn't fold them; he just dumped them on a chair in the little scullery at the back of the kitchen. He seemed to forget that he was impatient for Edward to leave. He brought out some wine, some glasses, cheese and bread. In fact, Edward could see that Harvey didn't want him to leave, lest he should feel lonely afterwards. Edward had been feeling rather guilty at interrupting what was probably a fairly contented solitude. Now, it was not that he regretted imposing his presence, but that by doing so he must impose the absence to follow. For Harvey more and more seemed to want him to remain. Edward said something about catching a night ferry. He thought, Surely Harvey's involved with the mother of the baby whose clothes he's just brought in off the line. They must be the clothes of an infant not more than a year old. Where are the mother and child?

There was no sign of any mother or child apart from the clothes Harvey had dumped on a chair. Edward was envious, too. He was envious of Harvey's woman and his child. He wanted, at that moment, to be free like Harvey and to have a girl somewhere, but not visible, with a baby.

Harvey said, 'It's fairly lonely here.' By which Edward knew for certain that Harvey was suddenly very lonely indeed at the thought of his leaving. The mother and child were probably away for the night.

'Stay the night,' said Harvey. 'There's plenty of room.'

Edward wanted to know where Harvey had been and what he'd been doing since he disappeared on the *autostrada*. But they did not talk of that. Harvey told him that Effie was writing a thesis on child-labourers in the Western democracies, basing much of it on Kingsley's *The Water Babies*. She hadn't told Edward this. Harvey seemed pleased that he had a bit more news of her than Edward had. But then they had a laugh over Effie and her zeal in the sociological industry.

Harvey made up a bed for him in a sort of cupboard-room upstairs.

It was nearly four in the morning when he pulled the extra rough covers over a mattress and piled two cushions for a pillow. From the doorway into Harvey's bedroom Edward could see that the bed was narrow, the furniture quite spare in a cheap new way. He said, 'Where's the baby?'

'What baby?' Harvey said.

'The baby whose washing was out on the line.'

'Oh that,' said Harvey; 'that's only my safeguard. I put baby clothes out on the line every day and bring them in at night. I change the clothes every other day, naturally.'

Edward wondered if Harvey had really gone mad.

'Well, I don't understand,' Edward said, turning away as if it didn't matter.

'You see,' said Harvey, 'the police don't break in and shoot if there's likely to be a baby inside. Otherwise they might just break in and shoot.'

'Go to hell,' Edward said.

'Well, if I told you the truth you wouldn't understand.'

'Thanks,' he said.

'You wouldn't believe,' said Harvey.

'All right, I don't want to know.'

'When I settled here I strung up the clothes-line. I have a sure system of keeping away the well-meaning women who always come round a lone man, wanting to cook and launder and mend socks and do the shopping; they love a bachelor; even in cities – no trouble at all getting domestic help for a single man. In my wanderings since I left Effie I've always found that a line of baby clothes, varying from day to day, keeps these solicitous women away; they imagine without thinking more of it, that there's already a woman around.'

But Edward knew him too well; it was surely one of those demonstrative acts by which Harvey attempted to communicate with a world whose intelligence he felt was away behind his own. Harvey was always in a state of exasperation, and, it was true, always ten thoughts ahead of everybody around him. Always likely to be outrageous. The baby clothes probably belonged to his girl.

Edward left three hours later before Harvey was up. He still felt envious of Harvey for his invisible and probably non-existent girl and her baby.

TWO

Nathan Fox was sitting up with Ruth when Edward got back to
London. It was a Sunday, a Pimlico Sunday with vacant parking
spaces and lights in some of the windows.

Nathan had graduated in English literature, at the university where
Ruth was now teaching, over a year before. He couldn't get a job.
Ruth looked after him most of the time. Edward always said he
himself would do almost anything for Ruth; they saw eye to eye. So
Nathan was quite welcome. But just that night on his return from
France, very tired, and needing to get to bed for an early rise the next
morning – he was due at the studio at seven – just that night Edward
wished Nathan Fox wasn't there. Edward was not at all sure how they
would manage without Nathan. Nathan wasn't ashamed of calling
himself an intellectual, which, for people like themselves, made life so
much easier; not that he was, in fact, an intellectual, really; he was
only educated. But they could talk to Nathan about anything; and at
the same time he made himself useful in the house. Indeed, he was a
very fair cook. To a working couple like Ruth and Edward he was an
invaluable friend.

It was just that night, and on a few previous occasions, Edward
wished he wasn't there. Edward wanted to talk to Ruth, to get to bed
early. Nathan sat there in his tight jeans and his T-shirt with 'Poetry
Is Emotion Recollected In Tranquillity' printed on it. He was a good-
looking boy, tall, with an oval face, very smooth and rather silvery-
green in colour – really olive. His eyebrows were smooth, black and
arched, his hair heavy and sleek, quite black. But he wasn't vain at all.
He got up in the morning, took a shower, shaved and dressed, all in
less than seven minutes. It seemed to Edward that the alarm in their
room had only just gone off when he could smell the coffee brewing in
the kitchen, and hear Nathan already setting the places for breakfast.
Ruth, too, wondered how he managed it. His morning smile was

313

delightful; he had a mouth like a Michelangelo angel and teeth so good, clear, strong and shapely it seemed to Edward, secretly, that they were the sexiest thing about him.

The only problem with Nathan was how to explain what he saw in them. They paid him and fed him as well as they could, but it was supposed to be only a fill-in job. They were together as on a North Sea oil platform. It wasn't that Nathan wouldn't leave them, it now seemed he couldn't. Edward thought, He is hankering after Effie, and we are the nearest he can get to her. Edward often wondered whether Effie would really marry Ernie Howe when she got her divorce from Harvey.

When Edward got back from France they had supper; he told Nathan and Ruth what had happened at Harvey's cottage, almost from start to finish. Ruth wanted actually to see with her eyes the sealed letter to the lawyer; so that Edward got up from the table and fished it out of his duffel bag.

She turned it over and over in her hand; she examined it closely; she almost smelt it. She said, 'How rude to seal down a letter you were to carry by hand.'

'Why?' said Nathan.

'Because one doesn't,' Ruth piped primly, 'seal letters that other people are to carry.'

'What about the postman?'

'Oh, I mean one's friends.'

'Well, open it,' said Nathan.

Edward had been rather hoping he would suggest this, and he knew Ruth had the same idea in mind. If they'd been alone, neither of them would have suggested it out loud, although it would certainly have occurred to them, so eager were they to know what Harvey had settled on Effie in this letter to his solicitors. They would have left the letter and their secret desires unopened. They were still somewhat of the curate and his wife, Ruth and himself.

But Nathan seemed to serve them like a gentleman who takes a high hand in matters of form, or an unselfconscious angel. In a way, that is what he was there for, if he had to be there. He often said things out of his inexperience and cheerful ignorance that they themselves wanted to say but did not dare.

'Open it?' said Ruth.

'Oh, we can't do that,' said Edward.

'You can steam it open,' suggested Nathan, as if they didn't know. 'You only need a kettle.'

'Really?' said Ruth.

Nathan proceeded, very know-all: 'It won't be noticed. You can seal it up again. My mother steamed open my aunt's letters. Only wanted to know what was in them, that's all. Then later my aunt would tell a lot of lies about what was in the letters, but my mother knew the truth, of course. That was after my father died, and my mother and my auntie were living together.'

'I don't know that we have the right,' said Ruth.

'It's your duty,' Nathan pronounced. He turned to Edward, appealing: 'In my mother's case it wasn't a duty, although she said it was. But in your case it's definitely a duty to steam open that letter. It might be dynamite you've been carrying.'

Edward said, 'He should have left it open. It might be really offensive or something. It was ill-mannered of Harvey. I noticed it at the time, in fact.'

'You should have objected,' Nathan said. Edward was now delighted that Nathan was there with them that evening.

'It's difficult to object,' Ruth said. 'But I think we have a right to know what's in it. At least you do, Edward, since you're the bearer.'

They steamed open the letter in the kitchen and stood reading it together.

Dear Stewart,

This letter is being brought to you by Edward Jansen, an old friend of mine from university days. I don't know if you've met him. He's a sort of actor but that is by the way. My wife Effie is his sister-in-law. He came to see me about Effie's divorce. As you know I'm not contesting it. She wants a settlement. Let her go on wanting, let her sue.

The object of this letter is to tell you that I agree the date of *Job* is post-exile, that is, about 500 BC, but it could be the middle of the 5th century. It could easily be contemporaneous with the *Prometheus Bound* of Aeschylus. (The *Philoctetes* of Sophocles, another *Job*-style work, is dated I think about 409.)

Yours,
Harvey

'I won't deliver it,' Edward said.

'Oh, you must,' said Nathan. 'You mustn't let him think you've opened it.'

'There's something fishy about it,' Edward said. He was greatly annoyed.

'Calling you a sort of actor,' Ruth said, in a soothing voice that made him nearly choleric.

'It's Effie's fault,' said Ruth. 'She's brought out this quality in Harvey.'

'Well, I'm too busy tomorrow to go in person to Gray's Inn,' Edward said.

'I'll deliver it,' said Nathan.

THREE

It was October. Harvey sat at his writing-table, set against the wall of the main room in his little house.

'*Job* 37, 5,' he wrote, 'God thundereth marvellously with his voice ...'

'I think we'll have to send to England for some more cretonne fabric,' said Ruth, looking over his shoulder.

It was at the end of August that Ruth had moved in, bringing with her Effie's baby, a girl. The baby was now asleep for a merciful moment, upstairs.

Harvey looked up from his work. 'I try to exude goodwill,' he said.

'You positively try to sweat it,' Ruth said, kindly. And she wondered how it was that she had disliked and resented Harvey for so many years. It still amazed her to find herself here with him. That he was perfectly complacent about the arrangement, even cheerful and happy, did not surprise her so much; everything around him, she knew – all the comings and goings – were really peripheral to his preoccupation with the *Book of Job*. But her being there, with Effie's baby, astonished her sometimes to the point of vertigo. This was not at all what she had planned when she decided to turn up at the cottage with Effie's baby daughter.

Once, after she had settled in, she said to Harvey, 'I didn't plan this.'

'It wasn't a plan,' said Harvey, 'it was a plot.'

'I suppose it looks like that from the outside,' Ruth said. To her, what she had wanted was justice. Given Effie's character, it was not to be expected that she would continue to live with Ernie Howe on his pay in a small house. Ruth had offered to take the baby when Effie decided she wasn't in love with Ernie any more. Harvey's money would perhaps not have made much difference to Effie's decision. At any rate, Ruth had known that, somehow, in the end, she would have to take on Effie's baby. It rather pleased her.

Effie was trying to sue Harvey for alimony, so far without success. 'The lawyers are always on the side of the money,' she said. Harvey continued to ignore her letters.

The baby, named Clara, had been born toward the end of June. Effie went back to her job in advertising for a short while after she had left Ernie Howe. Then she took a job with an international welfare organisation in Rome. Ernie wasn't at all happy, at first, with Ruth's plan to take the baby Clara to visit Harvey. They sat in the flat in Pimlico where Ernie often came, now, for consolation, as much as to see his daughter.

'He doesn't sound the sort of man to have any *sent-y-ments*,' Ernie said.

Edward wanted very much to give Ernie some elocution lessons to restore his voice to the plain tones of his origins. 'He hasn't any sentimentality, but of course he has sentiments,' said Edward.

'Especially about his wife's baby by a, well, a lover.'

'As to that,' said Edward, 'he won't care who the father is. He just won't have any sentimental feelings, full stop.'

'It's a matter of justice,' Ruth said.

'How do you work that out?' said Nathan.

'Well, if it hadn't been for Harvey leaving Effie she would never have had a baby by Ernie,' Ruth said. 'Harvey should have given her a child. So Harvey's responsible for Clara; it's a question of justice, and with all his riches it would be the best thing if he could take responsibility, pay Effie her alimony. He might even take Effie back.'

'Effie doesn't want to go back to Harvey Gotham,' said Ernie.

'Harvey won't take her back,' Edward said. 'He believes that Effie boils down to money.'

'Alas, he's right,' said Ernie.

'Why can't Clara go on living with us?' said Nathan, who already knew how to prepare the feeds and bath the baby.

'I'm only taking her for a visit,' Ruth said. 'What's wrong with that? You went to see Harvey, Edward. Now I'll have a try.'

'Be sure to bring her back, Ree-uth,' said Ernie. 'The legal position –'

'Do you still want to marry Effie?' Edward asked him.

'No, quite frankly, I don't.'

'Effie's so beautiful,' Nathan said. He got up to replenish the drinks. 'What a beautiful girl she is!'

'A matter of justice. A balancing of accounts.' This was how Ruth put it to Harvey. 'I'm passionate about justice,' she said.

'People who want justice,' Harvey said, 'generally want so little when it comes to the actuality. There is more to be had from the world than a balancing of accounts.'

She supposed he was thinking of his character Job, as in fact he was. She was used to men answering her with one part of their mind on religion. That was one of the reasons why Edward had become so unsatisfactory after he had ceased to be a curate and become an actor.

Ruth and Effie grew up in a country rectory that to-day is converted into four commodious flats. The shabbiness of the war still hung over it in the late fifties, but they were only aware of the general decay by the testimony of their elders as to how things were 'in the old days', and the evidence of pre-war photographs of garden parties where servants and trees stood about, well-tended, and the drawing room chintzes were well-fitted and new. Otherwise, they simply accepted that life was a muddle of broken barrows, tin buckets in the garden sheds, overgrown gardens, neglected trees. They had an oak of immense girth; a mulberry tree older than the house, to judge from early sketches of the place. The graveyard had a yew the circumference and shape of their oval dining-table; the tree was hollow inside and the bark had formed itself into the shape of organ pipes. Yews were planted in graveyards, originally, because they poisoned cattle, and as they were needed for long-bows they were planted in a place where cattle didn't go. All this Ruth picked up from God knows where; the air she breathed informed her. House-martins nested under the eaves outside Ruth's room and used to make a dark-and-white flash almost up to the open window as they came and fled in the morning.

There was a worn carpet on the staircase up to the first landing.

After that, bare wood. Most of the rooms were simply shut for ever. They had been civil servants' bedrooms in war-time before Ruth was born, and she never knew what it was like to see the houseful of people that the rectory was made for.

For most of Ruth's life, up to the time Edward became an actor, religion was her bread and butter. Her father was what Edward at one time called a career-Christian; she assumed he was a believer too, as was her mother; but she never got the impression that either had time to think about it.

Effie was three years younger than Ruth. The sisters were very close to each other all their schooldays and in their early twenties. Ruth often wondered when exactly they had separated in their attitude to life. It was probably after Ruth's return from Paris where she had spent a year with a family. Shortly afterwards Effie, too, went off to be an *au pair* in France.

If you are the child of a doctor or a butcher you don't have to believe in your father's occupation. But, in their childhood, they had to believe in their father's job as a clergyman in a special way. Matins and Sunday services and Evensong were part of the job; the family was officially poor, which was to say they were not the poor in the streets and cottages, but poor by the standards of a country rector. Ruth's mother was a free-lance typist and always had some work in hand. She could do seventy words a minute on her old pre-war typewriter. Before her marriage she had done a hundred and thirty words a minute at Pitman's shorthand. Ruth used to go to sleep on a summer night hearing the tap-tapping of the typewriter below, and wake to the almost identical sound of the woodpecker in the tree outside her window. Ruth supposed this was Effie's experience too, but when she reminded her sister of it many years later Effie couldn't recall any sound effects.

Effie went to a university on her return from France and left after her first year about the time that Ruth graduated and married Edward. Ruth worked with and for Edward and the parish, organising a live crib at Christmas with a real baby, a real cow and a real virgin; she wrote special prayers to the Holy Spirit and the Trinity for the parish magazine (which she described as Prayers to the HS etc.) and she arranged bring-and-pay garden lunches. She lectured and made bedspreads, and she taught child-welfare and jam preserving.

Ruth was very much in the business. Effie, meanwhile, went off the rails, and when this was pointed out to her in so many words, she said, 'What rails? Whose rails?' It was Effie who first called Edward an actor more than a man of God, and she probably put the idea in his mind.

Effie was doing social work when Ruth got married. The sisters looked very much alike in their separate features; it was one of those cases where the sum total of each came out with a difference, to the effect that Effie was extremely beautiful and Ruth was nothing remarkable; perhaps it was a question of colouring and complexion. Whatever the reason, everyone looked at Effie in a special way. Both sisters were fair with the fair-lashed look and faint eyebrows of some Dutch portraits.

It was Edward who introduced Effie to Harvey Gotham. Effie was in the habit of despising the rich, but she married him. They had a small house in Chelsea and at first they travelled everywhere together.

When Edward became an actor Ruth got a job in a university, teaching twentieth century history. Edward had a television part which came to an end about the time Ruth discerned that Effie and Harvey were not getting on. Effie's young men-friends from her days of welfare-work were always in her house, discussing their social conscience. Harvey was often away.

'You're sleeping around,' Ruth said to Effie.

'What do you mean?' she said.

'I know,' Ruth said.

'What do you know?'

Ruth said, 'I know all about it.' What she meant was that she knew Effie.

'You must be guessing,' said Effie, very shaken.

'I know,' Ruth said, 'that you're having affairs. Not one only. Plural.'

Edward was still out of a job. They hadn't any prospect of a holiday that year, but Effie and Harvey had planned a motoring trip in Italy.

Ruth said, 'Why don't you get Harvey to invite us to join you on your holiday in Italy?'

'He wouldn't like that,' she said. 'Four in the car.'

'It's a big car.'

'You couldn't afford your share,' said Effie, 'could you?'

'No, not all of it. '

'What all this has to do with my love affairs, real or imagined,' said Effie, 'I really do not know.'

'Don't you?' said Ruth.

'Ruth,' she said, 'you're a blackmailer, aren't you?'

'Only in your eyes. In my eyes it is simply that we're going to come to Italy with you. Harvey won't mind the money.'

'Oh, God,' she said, 'I'd rather you went ahead and told him all you know. Think of all the suffering in the world, the starving multitudes. Can't you sacrifice a pleasure? Go ahead and tell Harvey what you know. Your sordid self-interest, your —'

'You shock me,' Ruth said. 'Stick to the point. Is it likely that I would go to your husband and say . . .?'

They went on holiday with Effie and Harvey, and they took Ruth's student, Nathan, as well. Effie stole two bars of chocolate from the supermarket on the *autostrada* and Harvey left them abruptly. It was the end of their marriage. Fortunately Effie had enough money on her to pay for the rest of the trip. It was a holiday of great beauty. Effie tried to appreciate the pictures in the art galleries, the fountains in the squares, the ancient monuments and the Mediterranean abundance, but even basking on the beach she was uneasy.

Harvey saw Effie's features in Ruth; it struck him frequently that she was what Effie should have been. It had been that situation where the visitor who came to stay remained to live. (Harvey had heard of an author who had reluctantly granted an interview to a young critic, who then remained with him for life.) The arrangement was not as uncomfortable as it might have been, for Ruth had claimed and cleared one of the shacks outside the house, where she spent most of the daytime with the baby. She was careful to make the changes unobtrusively. Delivery vans drove up with rugs or with an extra stove, but it was all done in a morning. Harvey paid for the things. When the baby cried it upset him, but that was seldom, for Ruth drove off frequently with the child, no doubt to let it cry elsewhere She took it with her when she went shopping.

It was three weeks after she had arrived that Ruth said, 'I'm going to write to Edward.'

'I have written,' said Harvey.

'I know,' she said, and he wondered how she knew, since he had posted the letter himself. 'But I'll write myself. I couldn't be the wife of an actor again.'

'If he was a famous actor?'

'Well, he isn't a famous actor. A part here, a part there, and sometimes a film. So full of himself when he has a part. It was a much better life for me when he was a curate.'

But she had no nostalgia even for those days of church fêtes, evening lectures and sewing classes. She already had a grip of her new life, dominated as it was by the *Book of Job*.

'You feel safer when you're living with someone who's in the God-business,' Harvey said. 'More at home.'

'Perhaps that's it,' she said.

'And a steadier income.'

'Such as it is,' she said, for she asked little for herself. 'But,' she said, 'I was bored. He always agreed with me, and you don't.'

'That's because you're one of my comforters,' Harvey said. 'Job had his comforters to contend with; why shouldn't I?'

'Do you think of yourself as Job?'

'Not exactly, but one can't help sympathising with the man.'

'I don't know about that,' said Ruth. 'Job was a very rich man. He lost all his goods, and all his sons and daughters, and took it all very philosophically. He said, "The Lord gave, the Lord taketh away, blessed be the name of the Lord." Then he gets covered with boils; and it's only then that his nerve gives way, he's touched personally. He starts his complaint against God at that point only. No question of why his sons should have lost their lives, no enquiries of God about the cause of their fate. It's his skin disease that sets him off.'

'Maybe it was shingles,' Harvey said. 'A nervous disease. Anyway, it got on his nerves.'

Ruth said, 'He had to be touched himself before he would react. Touched in his own body. Utterly selfish. He doesn't seem to have suffered much or he wouldn't have been able to go into all that long argument. He couldn't have had a temperature.'

'I don't agree. I think he had a high temperature all through the argument,' Harvey said. 'Because it's high poetry. Or else, maybe you're right; maybe it was the author who had the temperature. Job himself just sat there with a long face arguing against the theories of his friends.'

'Make a note of that,' Ruth commanded.

'I'll make a note.' He did so.

'Someone must have fed him,' said Ruth. 'Someone must have brought him meals to eat as he sat on the dung-hill outside the town.'

'I'm not sure he sat on a dung-hill outside the town. That is an assumption based on an unverified Greek version of the text. He is merely said to have sat in the ashes on the ground. Presumably at his own hearth. And his good wife, no doubt, brought him his meals.'

Ruth had proved to be an excellent cook, cramped in the kitchen with that weird three-tiered kerosene stove of hers.

'What do you mean, "his good wife"?' Ruth said. 'She told him, "Curse God and die."'

'That was a way of expressing her exasperation. She was tired of his griping and she merely wanted him to get it off his chest quickly, and finish.'

'I suppose the wife suffered,' said Ruth. 'But whoever wrote the book made nothing of her. Job deserved all he got.'

'That was the point that his three friends tried to get across to him,' Harvey said. 'But Job made the point that he didn't deserve it. Suffering isn't in proportion to what the sufferer deserves.'

Ruth wrote in September:

Dear Edward,

I suppose you have gathered by now that I've changed my mind about Harvey. I don't know what he's written to you.

He really is a most interesting man. I believe I can help Harvey.

I can't return to face the life we had together, ever again. My dear, I don't know how I could have thought I would. My plan was, as you know, entirely different. I feel Harvey needs me. I am playing a role in his life. He is serious. Don't imagine I'm living in luxury. He never mentions his wealth. But of course I am aware that if there is anything I require for myself or Clara, I can have it.

You may have heard from Ernie Howe that he is coming to visit Clara. She's well and pretty, and full of life.

I'm sure you have heard from Harvey how things are between him and me. It's too soon to talk of the future.

This has been a difficult letter to write. I know that you'll agree with what I say. You always do.

Ruth

She gave Harvey the letter to read, watching him while he read it. He looked younger than Edward, probably because of Edward's beard, although he was a little older. Harvey was lean and dark, tall, stringy.

'It's a bit dry,' Harvey said.

'It's all I can do. Edward knows what I'm like.'

'I suppose,' said Harvey, 'he'll be hurt.'

'He doesn't love me,' Ruth said.

'How do you know?'

'How does one know?'

'Still, he won't want to lose his property.'

'That's something else.'

Now, in October, Ruth was talking about sending to England for cretonne fabric. 'One can't get exactly what I want in France,' she said.

Harvey wrote:

Dear Edward,

Thanks for yours.

The infant is cutting a tooth and makes a din at night. Ruth has very disturbed nights. So do I. It's been raining steadily for three days. Ernie Howe came. We had a chat. He seems to feel fraternal towards me because we both had to do with Effie. He wants to talk about Effie. I don't. Afterwards, in the place next door that Ruth has fixed up for herself and Clara, Ernie asked her if she would go home and live with him and bring the baby. Ruth said no. I think he's after Ruth because she reminds him of Effie. He said he wouldn't take the child away from Ruth if she doesn't want to part with it, which she doesn't.

I'm sorry to hear that you don't miss Ruth. You ought to.

Cheque enclosed. I know you're not 'selling your wife'. Why should I think you are? You took money before I was sleeping with Ruth, so where's the difference?

I don't agree the comforters just came to gloat. They relieved Job's

suffering by arguing with him, keeping him talking. In different ways
they keep insinuating that Job 'deserved' his misfortunes; he must
have done something wrong. While Job insists that he hasn't, that the
massed calamities that came on him haven't any relation to his own
actions. He upsets all their theology. Those three friends of his are
very patient and considerate, given their historical position. But Job
is having a nervous crisis. He can't sleep. See 7, 13–16.

> When I say, My bed shall
> comfort me, my couch shall ease
> my complaint;
> Then thou scarest me with
> dreams, and terrifiest me through
> visions:
> So that my soul chooseth
> strangling, and death rather than
> my life.
> I loathe it; I would not
> live alway: let me alone . . .

So I say, at least the three comforters kept him company. And they
took turns as analyst. Job was like the patient on the couch.

Ruth doesn't sympathise with Job. She sees the male pig in him.
That's a point of view.

The baby has started to squawk. I don't know what I'm going to do
about the noise.

Yours,
Harvey

Ruth came in, jogging in her arms the baby Clara who had a whole fist
in her mouth and who made noises of half-laughing, half-crying.
Soon, she would start to bawl. Ruth's hair fell over her face, no longer
like that of a curate's wife.

'Did you know that they want to sell the château?' she said.

The château was half a mile up the grassy pathway which led away
from the cottage. Harvey knew the owner and had seen the house; that
was when he first rented the cottage. He knew it was up for sale, and
had been for some years.

'It's falling to bits,' he said to Ruth.

'What a pity to neglect it like that!' Ruth said. 'It's a charming house. It reminds me of something from my childhood, I don't know quite what. Perhaps somewhere we visited. I think something could be done to it.'

She brought the fretful child close to Harvey so that he could make an ugly face. He showed his teeth and growled, whereupon Clara temporarily forgot her woes. She smelt of sour milk.

FOUR

Up at the château where the neglected lawns were greener than the patch round Harvey's house, and where the shrubberies were thick and very dark evergreen, the workmen were putting in the daylight hours of the last few days before the Christmas holidays. She had already reclaimed one wing for habitation. The roof had been secured in that part, but most of the rooms were cold. Ruth had arranged one sitting room, however, with a fire, and two bedrooms with oil stoves. A good start.

What a business it had been to persuade Harvey to buy the château! And now he was enchanted. Once he agreed to buy – and that was the uphill work – it was simple. Harvey sent for his London lawyer, Stewart Cowper, and for his French lawyer, Martin Deschamps, to meet in Nancy and discuss the deal with the family who owned the château. Ruth had gone with Harvey to this meeting, in October, with Clara in her folding pram. When the hotel room got too boring for the baby, Ruth hushed her, put her in her pram and took her for a walk in Place Stanislas. It was not long before Ruth saw through the splendid gilt gates the whole business group, with Harvey, trooping out to take the sun and continue the deal in the glittering square. Harvey, his two lawyers, and the three members of the de Remiremont family, which comprised a middle-aged man, his daughter and his nephew, came and joined Ruth. The daughter put her hand on the handle of the pram. They all ambled round in a very unprofessional way, talking of notaries and tax and the laws governing foreigners' property in France. You could see that this was only a preliminary.

Harvey said, 'We have to leave you. I'm writing a book on the *Book of Job.*'

It was difficult to get across to them what the *Book of Job* was. Harvey's French wasn't at fault, it was their knowledge of the Bible of which, like most good Catholics, they had scant knowledge. They stood around, the father in his old tweed coat and trousers, the daughter and nephew in their woollen jumpers and blue jeans, puzzling out what was *Job*. Finally, the father remembered. It all came back to him. 'You shouldn't be in a hurry, then,' he said. 'Job had patience, isn't that right? One says, "the patience of Job".'

'In fact,' said Harvey, 'Job was the most impatient of men.'

'Well, it's good to know what it is you're writing in that wretched little cottage,' said the elder man. 'I often wondered.'

'I hope we'll soon have the house,' said Ruth.

'So do we,' said the owner. 'We'll be glad to get rid of it.' The young man and the girl laughed. The lawyers looked a little worried about the frankness and the freedom, suspecting, no doubt, some façade covering a cunning intention.

Ruth and Harvey left them then. It was all settled within a month except for the final bureaucracy, which might drag on for years. Anyhow, Harvey had paid, and Ruth was free to order her workmen to move in.

'Instead of disabusing myself of worldly goods in order to enter the spirit of *Job* I seem to acquire more, ever more and more,' was all that Harvey said.

Ruth wrote to Effie with her letter-pad on her knee, beside the only fireplace, while the workmen hammered away, a few days before Christmas.

Dear Effie,

I really am in love with Harvey and you have no reason to say I am not. The lovely way he bought the house – so casual – we just walked round the *Place* with Clara and the family who used to own the château – and Harvey shook hands and that was all. The lawyers are working it out, but the house is ours.

I can't make out your letter. You don't want Clara, at least not the bother of her. You despise Harvey. What do you mean, that I have stolen your husband and your child? Be civilised.

Ruth stopped, read what she had written, and tore it up. Why should I reply to Effie? What do I owe her? She stole a bit of chocolate, on principle. I stole her husband, not on principle. As for her child, I haven't stolen her, she has abandoned her baby. All right, Effie is young and beautiful, and now has to work for her living. Possibly she's broke.

Dear Effie,

What attracted me most about the château was the woodpecker in the tree outside the bedroom window. Why don't you come and visit Clara?

Love,
Ruth

She sealed it up and put it on the big plate in the hall to be posted, for all the world as if the château was already a going concern. The big plate on a table by the door was all there was in the huge dusty hall, but it was a beginning.

Now she took sleeping Clara in her carry-cot and set her beside the driver's seat in the car. She put a basket in the back containing bread, pâté, a roast bantam hen and a bottle of Côte du Rhône, and she set off down the drive to Harvey's house for lunch. The tired patch of withered shrubbery round Harvey's cottage was still noticeably different from the rest of the château's foliage, although Ruth had dug around a few bushes to improve them, and planted some bulbs. As soon as she pushed open the door she saw he had a visitor. She dumped the food basket and went back for the baby, having glimpsed the outline of a student, a young man, any student, with those blue jeans of such a tight fit, they were reminiscent of Elizabethan women's breasts, in that you wondered, looking at their portraits, where they put their natural flesh. The student followed her out to the car. It was Nathan. 'Nathan! It's you, – you here. I didn't recognise . . .' He woke Clara with his big kiss, and the child wailed. He picked her up and pranced up and down with the wakened child. Harvey's studious cottage was a carnival. Harvey said to Ruth, 'I've told Nathan there will be room for him up at the house.'

Nathan had brought some food, too. He had been skilful as ever in finding the glasses, the plates; everything was set for lunch. Ruth got Clara back to sleep again, but precariously, clutching a ragged crust.

Harvey said very little. He had closed the notebook he was working on, and unnaturally tidied his papers; his pens were arranged neatly, and everything on his writing-table looked put-away. He sat looking at the floor between his feet.

Nathan announced, 'I just had to come. I had nothing else to do. It's a long time since I had a holiday.'

'And Edward, how's Edward?' Ruth said.

'Don't you hear from Edward?'

'Yes of course,' said Ruth, and Harvey said the same.

Nathan opened his big travel pack and brought out yet more food purchases that he had picked up on the way: cheese, wine, pâté and a bottle of Framboise. He left the pack open while he took them to the table. Inside was a muddle of clothes and spare shoes, but Harvey noticed the edges of Christmas-wrapped parcels sticking up from the bottom of the pack. My God, he has come for Christmas. Harvey looked at Ruth: did she invite him? Ruth fluttered about with her thanks and her chatter.

'Are you off to Paris for Christmas?' Harvey enquired. This was his first meeting with Nathan since the holiday in Italy when Harvey had abandoned his party on the *autostrada*; he felt he could be distant and impersonal without offence.

'I've come mainly to visit Clara for Christmas,' said Nathan. He was lifting the baby out of the carry-cot.

'Let her sleep,' Harvey said.

'Oh, Nathan must stay over Christmas,' Ruth said. 'Paris will be crowded. And dreadfully expensive.' She added, 'Nathan is a marvellous cook.'

'So I have heard.'

Ruth didn't notice, or affected not to notice, a look of empty desperation on Harvey's face; a pallor, a cornered look; his lips were parted, his eyes were focusing only on some anguished thought. And he was, in fact, suddenly aghast: What am I doing with these people around me? Who asked this fool to come and join us for Christmas? What do I need with Christmas, and Ruth, and a baby and a bloody little youth who needs a holiday? Why did I buy that château if not for Ruth and the baby to get out of my way? He looked at his writing-table, and panicked.

'I'm going out, I'll just fetch my coat,' he said, thumping upstairs two at a time.

'Harvey, what's the matter?' said Ruth when he appeared again with his sheepskin jacket, his woollen hat. Rain had started to splash down with foul eagerness.

'Don't you want lunch?' she said.

'Excuse me. I'm studious,' said Harvey, as he left the cottage. The car door slammed. The starter wouldn't work at first try. The sound of Harvey working and working at the starter became ever more furious until finally he was off.

When he came back in the evening the little house was deserted, all cleaned up. He poured himself a whisky, sat down and started to think of Effie. She was different from Ruth, almost a race apart. Ruth was kind, or comparatively so. Effie wasn't comparatively anything, certainly not kind. She was absolutely fascinating. Harvey remembered Effie at parties, her beauty, part of which was a quick-witted merriment. How could two sisters be so physically alike and yet so totally different? At any moment Ruth might come in and reproach him for not having the Christmas spirit. Effie would never do that. Ruth was thoroughly bourgeois by nature; Effie, anarchistic, aristocratic. I miss Effie, I miss her a lot, Harvey told himself. The sound of Ruth's little car coming down the drive, slowly in the mist, chimed with his thought as would the stroke of eight if there was a clock in the room. He looked at his watch, eight o'clock precisely. She had come to fetch him for dinner; three dinner-places set out on the table of the elegant room in the château, and the baby swinging in a hammock set up in a corner.

Ruth came in. 'You know, Harvey,' she said, 'I think you might be nicer to Nathan. After all, it's Christmas time. He's come all this way, and one should have the Christmas spirit.'

Nathan was there, at the château, settled in for Christmas. Harvey thought: I should have told him to go. I should have said I wanted Ruth and the baby to myself for Christmas. Why didn't I? – Because I don't want them to myself. I don't want them enough; not basically.

Ruth looked happy, having said her say. No need to say any more. I can't hold these women, Harvey thought. Neither Effie nor Ruth. My mind isn't on them enough, and they resent it, just as I resent it when they put something else before me, a person, an idea. Yes, it's understandable.

He swallowed down a drink and put on his coat.

'Nathan thinks it was marvellous of you to buy the château just to make me comfortable with Clara,' said Ruth.

'I bought it for myself, too, you know. I always thought I might acquire it.'

'Nathan has been reading the *Book of Job*, he has some ideas.'

'He did his homework, you mean. He must think I'm some sort of monster. In return for hospitality he thinks he has to discuss my subject.'

'He's polite. Besides, it's my subject too, now,' said Ruth.

'Why?' said Harvey. 'Because I've put you in the château?'

He thought, on the way through the misty trees that lined the long drive, They think I'm such a bore that I have to bribe them to come and play the part of comforters.

He made himself cheerful at the château; he poured drinks. In his anxiety to avoid the subject of *Job*, to be normal, to make general conversation, Harvey blurted out the other thing he had on his mind: 'Any news of Effie?'

God, I've said the wrong thing. Both Nathan and Ruth looked, for a moment, startled, uncomfortable; both, discernibly, for different reasons. Nathan, Harvey supposed, had been told to avoid the subject of Effie. Ruth didn't want to bring Effie into focus; it was enough that she was still Harvey's wife, out there vaguely somewhere else, out of sight.

'Effie?' said Ruth.

'I heard from her,' said Nathan. 'Only a postcard, after she got out.'

'Out from where?'

'From prison in Trieste. Didn't you hear about it?'

'Harvey never discusses Effie,' said Ruth. 'I've only just heard about it. She wrote to me last week from London, but she didn't mention prison.'

'What happened?' said Harvey.

'She was caught shop-lifting in a supermarket in Trieste. She said she did it to obtain an opportunity to study a women's prison at first-hand. She got out after three days. There was a small paragraph about it in the *Telegraph*, nothing in the other papers; it was about a month ago,' Ruth said. 'Nathan just told me.'

'All she said on the card was that she was going to Munich,' said Nathan.

'I wish her well of Munich,' said Harvey.

'I thought it was a beautiful town,' Ruth said.

'You thought strangely. There is a carillon clock with dancers coming out of the clock-tower twice a day. That's all there is in Munich.'

'She has friends there,' Nathan said. 'She said on the card she was joining friends in Munich. She seems to be getting around.'

'Well, I'm glad, for Effie, there is something else in Munich besides the carillon clock. Who made this soup?'

'Nathan did,' said Ruth.

'It's great.' He wondered why Stewart Cowper hadn't told him about Effie being arrested. He felt over-protected. How can you deal with the problem of suffering if everybody conspires to estrange you from suffering? He felt like the rich man in the parable: it is easier for a camel to go through the eye of a needle than for him to enter the Kingdom of Heaven.

'One must approach these things with balanced thought,' Ruth was saying, alarmingly. Harvey bent his mind to take in what they were discussing. It emerged that they were talking about the huge price Nathan had paid for the taxi from the airport to the château.

'There's a train service,' Harvey said.

'I've just been telling him that,' said Ruth. 'Spending all that money, as much as the air fare. He could have phoned me from the airport.'

'I don't have the number,' said Nathan.

'Oh, yes, I forgot,' said Ruth. 'No-one gets the number. Harvey has to be protected; in his position everyone wants him for something. He's here to study an important subject, write a thesis, get away from it all. You have to realise that, Nathan.'

Nathan turned to Harvey. 'Maybe I shouldn't have told you about Effie.'

'Oh, that's all right. I asked you about her, after all.'

'Yes, you did,' said Ruth. She had served veal, delicately cooked in white wine. 'You did bring up the subject, Harvey.'

'A beautiful girl, Effie,' said Nathan. 'What a lovely girl she is!'

Harvey wondered how much he knew about how beautiful Effie was. He looked at Nathan and thought, He has barged into my peace, he's taking his place for Christmas, he's discussing my wife as if she was everybody's girl (which she is), and he's going to get together again with Ruth; they will conspire how to protect me. Finally, he will ask me for a loan.

'Will you be all right up here alone in the château tonight?' Harvey said with determination. 'Ruth and I always shack down in my cottage; Ruth brings the baby back here immediately after early breakfast so that I can start on my work at about seven-thirty.'

'If you'll leave Clara with me I won't feel lonely,' said Nathan.

'Not at all,' said Harvey. 'We have a place for her. She's teething.'

'Nathan's used to Clara,' said Ruth. 'He's known her and looked after her since she was born.'

'I don't think we need ask our guests to baby-sit for us.' Don't think, Harvey said within himself, that you are one of the family here; you are one of 'our guests' in this house.

'Well, as she's teething,' said Ruth, 'I'd better take her with me. I really do think so, Nathan.'

'We'll move up here to the château for Christmas,' Harvey said, now that Ruth was winding up the feast with a cheese *soufflé* as light as could be. He fetched the brandy glasses.

FIVE

Dear Edward,

Happy New Year. Thanks for yours.

The day before Christmas Eve he turned up. After dinner he sat up late discussing his ideas on *Job* – he'd done some reading (for my benefit, which I suppose is a compliment). I don't agree with you that he seems 'positively calculating', I don't agree at all. I think he wanted to spend Christmas with Ruth and the baby. He would have preferred to spend Christmas with Effie. He didn't want to spend Christmas alone with you; that's why you're sour. You should get a lot of friends and some of your colleagues, pretty young actresses, have parties. Nathan would like that.

We went to Midnight Mass at the local church. Nathan carried Clara in a sling on his back and she slept throughout. There was a great crowd.

He hasn't left yet. He shows no sign of leaving.

I agree that Job endlessly discusses morals but there is nothing moral about the *Book of Job*. In fact it is shockingly amoral.

God has a wager with Satan that Job will not lose faith, however much he is afflicted. Job never knows about this wager, neither do his friends. But the reader knows. Satan finally makes the explicit challenge (2,5):

> But put forth thy hand
> now, and touch his bone and
> his flesh, and he will
> curse thee to thy face.

And God says, Go ahead ('Behold, he is in thine hand; but save his life.')

Consequently Job, having lost his sons and his goods, is now covered with sores. He is visited by his bureaucratic friends who tell him he must have deserved it. The result is that Job has a sort of nervous breakdown. He demands an explanation and he never gets it.

Do you know that verse of Kipling's?

> The toad beneath the harrow knows
> Exactly where each tooth-point goes;
> The butterfly upon the road
> Preaches contentment to that toad.

I think this expresses Job's plight. The boils are personal, they loosen his tongue, they set him off. He doesn't reproach God in so many words, but he does by implication.

I must tell you that early in the New Year we started to be bothered by people hanging around the house. Some 'tourists' (at this time of year!) went to the château and asked if they could see round the house – a couple of young men. Nathan got rid of them. Ruth says she heard there were 'strangers' in the village shop asking questions about me the other day. A suspicious-looking workman came to my cottage, saying he'd been sent to test the electricity (not to read the meter, but to test). He showed me his card, it looked all right. But the electricity department hadn't heard of him. We suspect that Effie is putting in some private detectives. I've written to Stewart Cowper. Where would she get the money?

Why didn't you tell me that Effie had been arrested for shop-lifting in Trieste?

I hope you get that part in the play you write about in your letter. You must know by now.

Yours,
Harvey

Please check the crocodiles for me at the London Zoo. Their eyelids are vertical, are they not? Leviathan in *Job* is generally supposed to be the crocodile. It is written of Leviathan, 'his eyes are like the eyelids of the morning.' None of the commentaries is as yet satisfactory on this. You may remember they never were.

PART TWO

SIX

The village shop, about two kilometres from Harvey's cottage, was normally busy when, about nine in the morning, Harvey stopped to buy a newspaper and cigarettes. He remembered this clearly later, when the day had developed and in the later profusion of events he set about to decipher them, starting from this, the beginning of his day.

The shop was divided into two parts, one leading into the other. The owner, a large man in his forties, wearing a dark grey working apron the colour of his hair, looked after the part which sold groceries, detergents, ham, pâté, sausage, cheese, fruit, vegetables, all well laid-out; and also a large stock of very good Vosges wines stacked in rows and arranged according to types and prices. The other part of the shop was presided over by the wife, plump, ruddy-cheeked, with short black curly hair, in her mid-thirties. She looked after the coffee machine, the liquor bar, the pre-wrapped buns and sweets, the newspapers and cigarettes, some stationery and other conveniently saleable goods.

That morning Harvey took an espresso coffee, his packet of cigarettes and the Vosges local paper which he scarcely glanced at. He looked around as he drank his coffee; the suspect people were not there to-day; it was not to be expected that they would always be at the bar, it would have been too obvious had they been hanging around all day and every day: two young Belgians, touring forests and caves, students, campers, the shopkeepers had said. It seemed unlikely; they were too old for students. There had been another man and woman, older still, in their forties; they looked like a couple of *concierges* from Paris. Harvey was convinced these were Effie's detectives, getting enough evidence for Effie's huge alimonial scoop. The owners of the shop had seemed to take them for granted as they walked up and down in the road. The so-called Belgians had a dormobile with a Lyons registration number – that meant nothing, they had probably hired it.

The middle-aged couple, both of them large and solid, came and went in a sad green Citroën Dyane 6. Harvey, having got such a brisk reply to his casual enquiries about the Belgians, had not ventured to enquire about the second couple. Maybe the shopkeepers were in their pay.

This morning, the strangers were not in sight. Only two local youths were at the bar; some countrywomen queued up at the counter on the grocery side. Harvey drank his coffee, paid, took up his paper and cigarettes and left. As he went out he heard behind him the chatter of the women, just a little more excited and scandalised than usual. '*Les supermarchés, les supermarchés . . .*' was the phrase he took in most, and assumed there was a discussion in progress about prices and food.

He put down the paper beside him and as he drove off his eye caught a picture on the front page. It was a group of three identikits, wanted people, two men and a girl. The outlines of the girl's face struck him as being rather like Ruth's. He must remember to let her see it. He turned at the end of the road towards Epinal, the town he was bound for.

After about two kilometres he ran into a road-block; two police motor cycles, three police cars, quite a lot. It was probably to do with the identikits. Harvey produced his papers and sat patiently while the policeman studied them, gave a glance at the car, and waved him on. While waiting, Harvey looked again at the newspaper on the seat by his side. The feature with the identikits was headed 'Armed Robberies in the Vosges'. Undoubtedly the police were looking for the gang. At Epinal he noticed a lot of police actively outside the commissariat on the banks of the Moselle, and, above that, at the grand prefecture. There, among the fountains and flags, he could see in the distance flashes of blue and white uniforms, blue, red and white police cars, a considerable display. He noticed, and yet took no notice. He had come to look once more, as he had often done before, at the sublime painting, *Job Visited by His Wife* at the *Musée* of Epinal. He parked his car and went in.

He was well known to the receptionist who gave him a sunny greeting as he passed the desk.

'No schoolchildren to-day,' she said. Sometimes when there were school-groups or art-college students in the gallery Harvey would turn away, not even attempting to see the picture. But very often there were only one or two visitors. Sometimes, he had the museum to himself; he was already half-way up the stairs when the receptionist told him so; she watched him approvingly, even admiringly, as he ran up the staircase, as if even his long legs, when they reached the first turning of the stairs, had brought a touch of pleasure into her morning. The dark-blue custodian with his hands behind his back as he made his stately round, nodded familiarly as Harvey reached the second floor; as usual the man went to sit patiently on a chair at the other end of the room as Harvey took his usual place on a small bench in front of the picture.

The painting was made in the first part of the seventeenth century by Georges de La Tour, a native of Lorraine. It bears a resemblance to the Dutch candlelight pictures of the time. Its colours and organisation are superb. It is extremely simple, and like so much great art of the past, surprisingly modern.

Job visité par sa femme: To Harvey's mind there was much more in the painting to illuminate the subject of Job than in many of the lengthy commentaries that he knew so well. It was eloquent of a new idea, and yet, where had the painter found justification for his treatment of the subject?

Job's wife, tall, sweet-faced, with the intimation of a beautiful body inside the large tent-like case of her firm clothes, bending, long-necked, solicitous over Job. In her hand is a lighted candle. It is night, it is winter; Job's wife wears a glorious red tunic over her dress. Job sits on a plain cube-shaped block. He might be in front of a fire, for the light of the candle alone cannot explain the amount of light that is cast on the two figures. Job is naked except for a loin-cloth. He clasps his hands above his knees. His body seems to shrink, but it is the shrunkenness of pathos rather than want. Beside him is the piece of broken pottery that he has taken to scrape his wounds. His beard is thick. He is not an old man. Both are in their early prime, a couple in their thirties. (Indeed, their recently-dead children were not yet married.) His face looks up at his wife, sensitive, imploring some favour, urging some cause. What is his wife trying to tell him as she bends her sweet face towards him? What does he beg, this stricken man, so serene in his faith, so accomplished in argument?

The scene here seemed to Harvey so altogether different from that suggested by the text of *Job*, and yet so deliberately and intelligently contemplated that it was impossible not to wonder what the artist actually meant. Harvey stared at the picture and recalled the verses that followed the account of Job's affliction with boils:

And he took him a potsherd to scrape himself withal; and he sat down among the ashes.

Then said his wife unto him, Dost thou still retain thine integrity? curse God, and die.

But he said unto her, Thou speakest as one of the foolish women speaketh. What? shall we receive good at the hand of God, and shall we not receive evil? In all this did not Job sin with his lips.

But what is she saying to him, Job's wife, in the serious, simple and tender portrait of Georges de La Tour? The text of the poem is full of impatience, anger; it is as if she is possessed by Satan. 'Dost thou still retain thine integrity?' She seems to gloat, 'Curse God and die.' Harvey recalled that one of the standard commentators has suggested a special interpretation, something to the effect, 'Are you still going to be so righteous? If you're going to die, curse God and get it off your chest first. It will do you good.' But even this, perhaps homely, advice doesn't fit in with the painting. Of course, the painter was idealising some notion of his own; in his dream, Job and his wife are deeply in love.

Some people had just arrived in the museum; Harvey could hear voices downstairs and footsteps mounting. He continued to regard the picture, developing his thoughts: Here, she is by no means the carrier of Satan's message. She comes to comfort Job, reduced as he is to a mental and physical wreck. 'You speak,' he tells her, 'as one of the foolish women;' that is to say, he doesn't call her a foolish woman, he rather implies that she isn't speaking as her normal self. And he puts it to her, 'Shall we receive good at the hand of God, and shall we not receive evil?' That domestic 'we' is worth noticing, thought Harvey; he doesn't mean to abandon his wife, he has none of the hostility towards her that he has, later, for his friends. In order to have a better look at Job's wife's face, Harvey put his head to one side. Right from the first he had been struck by her resemblance to Effie in profile. She was like Ruth, too, but more like Effie, especially about the upper part of her face. Oh, Effie, Effie, Effie.

There were people behind Harvey. He glanced round and was amazed to see four men facing towards him, not looking at the other pictures as he had expected. Nor were they looking at the painting of Job. They were looking at him, approaching him. At the top of the staircase two other men in police uniform appeared. The keeper looked embarrassed, bewildered. Harvey got up to face them. He realised that, unconsciously, he had been hearing police sirens for some time. With the picture of Job still in his mind's eye, Harvey had time only to form an abrupt impression before they moved in on him, frisked him, and invited him to descend to the waiting police cars.

Harvey had time to go over again all the details of the morning, later, in between interrogations. He found it difficult to get the rest of his life into focus; everything seemed to turn on the morning: the time he had stopped at the village shop; the drive to Epinal; the thoughts that had gone through his mind in front of the painting, *Job visité par sa femme*, at the museum; the moment he was taken to the police car, and driven over the bridge to the commissariat for questioning.

He answered the questions with lucidity so long as they lasted. On and off, he was interrogated for the rest of the day and half the night.

'No, I've never heard of the FLE.'

'*Fronte de la Libération de l'Europe*. You haven't heard of it?'

'No, I haven't heard of it.'

'You know that your wife belongs to this organisation?'

'I don't know anything about it.'

'There was an armed robbery in a supermarket outside Epinal this morning. You were waiting here to join your wife.'

'I'm separated from my wife. I haven't seen her for nearly two years.'

'It was a coincidence that you were in Epinal this morning visiting a museum while your estranged wife was also in Epinal engaged in an armed robbery?'

'If my wife was in Epinal, yes, it was a coincidence.'

'Is that your English sense of humour?'

'I'm a Canadian.'

'Is it a coincidence that other supermarkets and a jeweller's shop in the Vosges have been robbed by this gang in the last two weeks? Gérardmer, La Bresse, Baccarat; this morning, Epinal.'

'I don't read the papers.'

'You bought one this morning.'

'I give no weight to local crimes.' If Effie's involved, thought Harvey, plainly she's in this district to embarrass me. It was essential that he shouldn't suggest this, for at the same time it would point to Effie's having directive authority over the gang.

'I still can't believe that my wife's involved,' said Harvey. He partly meant it.

'Three of them, perhaps four. Where are they?'

'I don't know. You'd better look.'

'You recently bought the château. Why?'

'I thought I might as well. It was convenient.'

'You've been a year at the cottage?'

'About a year and a half.'

'How did you find it?'

'I've already explained —'

'Explain again.'

'I found the cottage,' recited Harvey, 'because I was in the Vosges at that time. I had come here to Epinal expressly to look at the painting *Job Visited by His Wife* by Georges de La Tour. I had heard through some friends that the château was for sale. I went to look it over. I said I'd think about it, but I was struck by the suitability of the cottage to my needs, and took that on in the meantime. The owner, Claude de Remiremont, let me have it.'

'How much rent do you pay?'

'I have no idea,' Harvey said. 'Very little. My lawyer attends to that.'

(The rich!)

This interrogator was a man of about Harvey's age, not more than forty, black hair, blue eyes, a good strong face, tall. A chief-inspector, special branch; no fool. His tone of voice varied. Sometimes he put his questions with the frank lilt of a query at the end; at other times he simply made a statement as if enunciating a proved fact. At the end of the table where they sat facing each other, was a hefty policeman in uniform, older, with sandy hair growing thin and faded. The door of the room opened occasionally, and other men in uniform and ordinary clothes came and went.

'Where did you learn French?'

'I have always spoken French.'

'You have taken part in the French-Canadian liberation movement.'

'No.'

'You don't believe in it?'

'I don't know anything about it,' said Harvey. 'I haven't lived in Canada since I was eighteen.'

'You say that your wife's sister has been living with you since last October.'

'That's right.'

'With a baby.'

'Yes. My wife's baby daughter.'

'But there was a woman with a baby in your house for a year before that.'

'Not at all. The baby was only born at the end of June last year.'

'There was another infant in your house. We have evidence, M. Gotham, that there was a small child's washing on the line outside your house at least from April of last year.'

'That is so. But there wasn't any baby, there wasn't any woman.'

'Look, M. Gotham, it is a simple trick for terrorists to take the precaution, in the case of discovery, to keep a woman and a child in the house in order to avoid a shoot-out. Rather a low and dangerous trick, using a baby as a cover, but people of that nature –'

'There was no baby at all in my house, nobody but myself,' Harvey explained patiently. 'It was a joke – for the benefit of my brother-in-law who came to visit me. I brought some baby clothes and put them out on the line. He obviously thought I had a girl living with me. I only put them out a few times after that. I told my brother-in-law that I did it to keep women from bothering me with offers of domestic care. As they do. They would assume, you see, that there was a woman. I suppose I'm an eccentric. It was a gesture.'

'A gesture.'

'Well, you might say,' said Harvey, thinking fast how to say it, 'that it was a surrealistic gesture.'

The inspector looked at Harvey for rather a long time. Then he left the room and came back with a photograph in his hand. Effie, in half-profile, three years ago, with her hair blowing around.

'Is that your wife?'

'Yes,' said Harvey. 'Where did you get this photograph?'

'And the woman you are living with, Ruth, is her sister?'

'Mme Jansen is her sister. Where did you get this photograph of my wife? Have you been ransacking through my papers?'

The inspector took up the photograph and looked at it. 'She resembles her sister,' he said.

'Did you have a search warrant?' said Harvey.

'You will be free to contact a lawyer as soon as you have answered our questions. I presume you have a lawyer in Paris? He will explain the law to you.'

'I have, of course, a French lawyer,' Harvey said. 'But I don't need him at the moment. Waste of money.'

Just then a thought struck him: Oh, God, will they shoot Ruth in mistake for Effie?

'My sister-in-law, Ruth Jansen, is, as you say, very like her sister. She's caring for the baby of nine months. Be very careful not to confuse them should you come to a confrontation. She has the baby there in the château.'

'We have the baby.'

'What?'

'We are taking care of the baby.'

'Where is she?'

The sandy-faced policeman spoke up. He had a perfectly human smile: 'I believe she is taking the air in the courtyard. Come and see out of the window.'

Down in the courtyard among the police cars and motor-bicycles, a large policeman in uniform, but without his hat, whom Harvey recognised as one of those who had escorted him from the museum, was holding Clara in his arms, wrapped up in her woollies; he was jogging her up and down while a young policewoman was talking to her. Another, younger policeman, in civilian clothes, was also attempting to curry favour with her. Clara had her chubby arms round the large man's neck, enjoying the attention, fraternising with the police all round.

'Is she getting her feeds?' said Harvey. 'I believe she has some special regular feeds that have to be –'

'Mme Jansen is seeing to all that, don't worry. Let's proceed.'

'I want to know where Ruth Jansen is,' said Harvey.

'She's downstairs, answering some questions. The sooner we proceed with the job the sooner you will be able to join her. Why did you explain your baby clothes to your brother-in-law Edward Jansen in the words, "The police won't shoot if there's a baby in the house"?'

'Did I say that?' said Harvey.

'Mme Jansen has admitted it,' said the inspector.

Admitted it. What had Edward told Ruth, what was Ruth telling them downstairs? But 'admitted' was not the same as 'volunteered' the information.

'You probably suggested the phrase to her,' said Harvey. The old police trick: Is it true that he said 'The police won't shoot . . .'?

'Did you or did you not say those words last April when M. Jansen came to see you?'

'If I did it was a joke.'

'Surrealism?'

'Yes, call it that.'

'You are a man of means?'

'Oh, yes.'

'Somebody is financing the FLE,' said the inspector.

'But I am not financing it.'

'Why do you live in that shack?'

'It doesn't matter to me where I work. I've told you. All I want is peace of mind. I'm studious.'

'Scholarly,' said the inspector dreamily.

'No, studious. I can afford to study and speculate without achieving results.'

The inspector raised his shoulders and exchanged a glance with the sandy-haired policeman. Then he said, 'Studious, scholarly . . . Why did you buy the château?'

'It was convenient for me to do so. Mme Jansen thought it desirable for her to have a home for herself and the baby.'

'It isn't your child.'

It was Harvey's turn to shrug. 'It's my wife's child. It makes no difference to me who the father is.'

'The resemblance between your wife and her sister might be very convenient,' said the inspector.

'I find them quite distinct. The resemblance is superficial. What do you mean – "convenient"?' Harvey, not quite knowing what the man was getting at, assumed he was implying that an exchange of lovers would be easy for him, the two sisters being, as it were, interchangeable. 'They are very different,' said Harvey.

'It would be convenient,' said the inspector, 'for two women who resemble each other to be involved in the same criminal organisation. I am just hypothesising, you understand. A question of one being able to provide an alibi for the other; it's not unknown . . .'

'My papers are in order,' Harvey said now, for no reason that was apparent, even to himself.

The inspector was very polite. 'You maintain your wife financially, of course.'

'I've given her no money since I left her. But if I had, that wouldn't signify that I was financing a terrorist organisation.'

'Then you know that your wife is an active member of the FLE, and consequently have refused to supply money.'

'I never knew of the existence of the FLE until now. I don't at all know that my wife is a member of the group.'

'And you give your wife no money,' the policeman said.

'No money.'

'You knew that she was arrested in Trieste.'

'I didn't know until the other day. Nobody told me.'

'Nobody told you,' stated the inspector.

'That's right. Nobody told me. I'm studious, you see. I have arranged for people not to bother me, and they don't; rather to excess. I think someone should have told me. Not that it would have made any difference.'

'Your wife knows where you live?'

'Yes.'

'You have written to her?'

'No. I left her two years ago. Eventually she found out where I lived.'

'How did she find out?'

'I suppose she got it out of someone. She's an intelligent woman. I doubt very much she's mixed up with a terrorist group.'

'You must have had some reason to abandon her. Why are you so eager to protect her?'

'Look, I just want to be fair, to answer your questions.'

'We know she's an activist in the FLE.'

'Well, what exactly have they done?'

'Armed robbery and insurrection in various places. Of recent weeks they've been operating in the Vosges. Where are their headquarters?'

'Not in my house. And if my wife is involved in these incidents – which I don't admit she is – isn't it possible she has been kidnapped and forced to join this FLE? It's happened before. The Hearst case in the United States . . .'

'Do you have reason to believe she has been kidnapped?'

'I don't know. I have no idea. Has anyone been killed, injured, by this group?'

'Injured? But they are armed. They've collected a good deal of money, wounded twelve, damaged many millions of francs' worth of property. They are dangerous. Three men and a girl. The girl is your wife. Who are the others?'

'How should I know? I've never heard of the –'

'Nobody told you.'

'Correct.'

'It's time for lunch,' said the inspector, looking at his watch; and, as he got up, he said, 'Can you explain why Nathan Fox disappeared from the château last night?'

'Nathan Fox. Disappeared?'

'Nobody told you.'

'No. I left my cottage at nine this morning.'

'Where is Nathan Fox?' said the inspector, still standing.

'I have no idea. He's free to come and go . . . I don't really know.'

'Well, think it over.' The inspector left the room.

Harvey's cottage was in darkness when he drove back at four in the morning. He was tempted to go in and see what had happened to his papers, his work; had they been careful or had they turned everything upside down? Later, he found everything more or less intact with hardly a sign of a search; he had suspected that at least half the time he was kept for questioning had been for the purpose of giving the police leisure to continue their search at the cottage and the château; much good it had done them.

He didn't stop at the cottage that early morning, but drove up to the château. A police car was parked at a bend in the drive. Harvey tooted twice, softly and quickly, as he passed it. Friendly gesture. The light was on in the porch. He let himself in. Ruth came out of the living room in her dressing gown; she had been sleeping on a sofa, waiting for him. 'They brought us back at half-past six,' she said. She came to hug him, to kiss him. 'Are you all right?' they both said at the same time. Clara was sleeping in her carry-cot.

The first thing that struck him was the colour in the room. There was nothing new, but after the grey and neutral offices, hour after hour, at the police headquarters, the blue of Ruth's dressing gown, the flower-patterned yellow sofa, green foliage arranged in a vase, the bright red tartan rug folded over Clara's cot, made a special impact on his senses. He smiled, almost laughed.

'Do you want to go to bed? Aren't you tired?' Ruth said.

'No. I'm wide awake.'

'Me, too.'

They poured whiskies and sodas. 'I simply told them the truth,' Ruth said. She decided she couldn't face her whisky and took orange juice.

'Me, too. What else could one say?'

'Oh, I know you told them everything,' Ruth said, 'I could guess by the questions.'

Harvey quoted, '"The police won't shoot if there's a baby in the house."'

'Yes, why did you bring that up?' said Ruth. 'Was it necessary? They're suspicious enough –'

'I didn't suggest it to them.'

'Well, neither did I,' said Ruth. 'The inspector asked me if it was true you'd made that remark. I said I believed so. Edward told me, of course –'

'They're quite clever,' Harvey said. 'How did they treat you?'

'Very polite. They were patient about my *au pair* French.'

'How many?'

'Two plain-clothes men and a glamorous policewoman. Did you see the policewoman?' said Ruth.

'I saw one, from the window, playing with Clara.'

'They were very decent about Clara.'

Harvey's interrogators had been three, one after the other, then starting in the late afternoon with the first again.

Ruth and Harvey described and identified their respective policemen, and in a euphoric way compared a great many of their experiences of the day, questions and answers. Finally Ruth said, 'Do you really think Effie's in it?'

'Up to the neck,' said Harvey.

'Can you blame them for suspecting us?'

'No. I think, in fact, that Effie has chosen this district specifically to embarrass me.'

'So do I.'

He sat on the sofa beside her, relaxed, with his arm round her. She said, 'You know, I'm more afraid of Effie than the police.'

'Did you tell them that?'

'No.'

'Did they come and look round the château while you were at the headquarters?'

'I don't think so, because when they brought me back they asked if they might have a look round. I said, of course. They went all over, attics, cellars, and both towers. Actually, I was quite relieved that they didn't find anything, or rather anyone. It would be easy to hide in this house, you know.'

'Did you tell them you were relieved?'

'No.'

'Now tell me about Nathan.'

'It's a long story,' said Ruth. 'He's in love with Effie. He'd do anything she asked him.' Her voice had changed to a mumble.

Harvey said, 'But when did you know –' Then he stopped. 'My God,' he said, 'I'm becoming another interrogator. I expect you've had enough.'

'Quite enough.'

It was he who had the idea to go and make breakfast, which he brought in on a tray. 'I had a lousy pizza for supper,' he said.

She said, 'Nathan must have left last night. He didn't sleep here. He wasn't here when I came up from the cottage this morning. His bed wasn't slept in.'

'Did Anne-Marie see him?' Anne-Marie was a local woman who had been coming daily to help in the house for the past two weeks.

'No, he wasn't here when she arrived at eight. He'd taken nothing special that I could see. But he had a phone call yesterday. He said it was from London. I was annoyed at the time, because I'd told him not to give anyone your number.'

The telephone at the château operated through an exchange for long distance. 'One could easily find out if it came from London,' Harvey said.

'The police say there was no call from London,' Ruth said.

'Then it might have been a national call. He could have been in touch with Effie.'

'Exactly,' she said.

'How much did you tell them about Nathan?'

'Everything I know.'

'Quite right.'

'And another thing,' Ruth said, 'I told them –'

'Let's forget it and go to bed.'

Clara woke up just then. They shoved a piece of toast into her hand, which seemed to please her mightily.

It was nine-fifteen when the telephone rang. This time it was from London. At the same time the doorbell rang. Harvey had been dreaming that his interrogator was one of those electric typewriters where the typeface can be changed by easy manipulation; the voice of the interrogator changed like the type, and in fact was one and the same, now roman, now élite, now italics. In the end, bells on the typewriter rang to wake him up to the phone and the doorbell.

He looked out of the window while Ruth went to answer the phone. Reporters, at least eight, some with cameras, some with open umbrellas or raincoats over their heads to shield them from the pouring rain. Up the drive came a television van. Behind him, through the door of the room, Ruth called to him, 'Harvey, it's urgent for you, from London.'

'Get dressed,' Harvey said. 'Don't open the door. Those are reporters out there. Keep them in the rain for a while, at least.'

Clara began to wail. The doorbell pealed on. From round the side of the château someone was banging at another door.

On the phone was Stewart Cowper from London.

'What's going on there?' said Stewart.

Harvey thought he meant the noise.

'There's been a bit of trouble. Reporters are at the doors of the house and the baby's crying.'

'There are headlines in all the English papers. Are you coming back to England?'

'Not at the moment,' Harvey said. 'I don't know about Ruth and the child; but we haven't discussed it. What are the headlines?'

'Headlines and paras, Harvey. Hold on, I'll read you a bit:

Millionaire's religious sect possibly involved in French terrorist activities. Wife of English actor involved . . .

And here's another:

Playboy Harvey Gotham, 35, with his arsenal of money from Gotham's Canadian Salmon, whose uncles made a fortune in the years before and during the second world war, has been questioned by the *gendarmes d'enquêtes* of the Vosges, France, in connection with hold-ups and bombings of supermarkets and post offices in that area. It is believed that his wife, Mrs Effie Gotham, 25, is a leading member of FLE, an extreme leftist terrorist movement. Mr Gotham, who has recently acquired a base in that area, denies having in any way financed the group or having been in touch with his estranged wife. He claims to be occupied with religious studies. Among his circle are his sister-in-law, Ruth, 28, sister of the suspected terrorist, and Nathan Fox, 25, who disappeared from the Gotham château on the eve of the latest armed robbery at Epinal, capital of the Vosges.

There's a lot more,' said Stewart. 'If you're not coming back to England I'd better come there. Have you got hold of Martin Deschamps?'

'Who the hell is he?'

'Your Paris lawyer.'

'Oh, him. No. I don't need lawyers. I'm not a criminal. Look, I've got to get rid of these reporters. By the way,' Harvey continued, partly for the benefit of the police who had undoubtedly tapped the phone, and partly because he meant it, 'I must tell you that the more I look at La Tour's "Job" the more I'm impressed by the simplicity, the lack of sentimentality above all. It's a magnificent —'

'Don't get on the wrong side of the press,' shouted Stewart.

'Oh, I don't intend to see them. Ruth and I have had very little sleep.'

'Make an appointment for a press conference, late afternoon, say five o'clock,' said Stewart. 'I'll send you Deschamps.'

'No need,' said Harvey, and hung up.

None the less, he managed to mollify the soaking pressmen outside his house, speaking to them from an upstairs window, by making an appointment with them for five o'clock that afternoon. They didn't all go away, but they stopped battering at the doors.

Then, to Ruth's amazement their newly-engaged, brisk domestic help, Anne-Marie, arrived, with a bag of provisions. It was her second week on the job. She managed to throw off the reporters who crowded round her with questions, by upbraiding them for disturbing the baby, and by pushing her way through. Inside the front door, Harvey stood ready to open it quickly, admitting her and nobody else.

'The police,' Anne-Marie said, 'were at my house yesterday for hours. Questions, questions.' But she seemed remarkably cheerful about the questions.

SEVEN

A long ring at the front doorbell. Outside in the pouring rain a police car waited. From the upper window Harvey saw the interrogator he had left less than twelve hours ago in the headquarters at Epinal.

'Ah,' said Harvey from the window. 'I've been missing you dreadfully.'

'Look,' said the man, 'I'm not enjoying this, am I? Just one or two small questions to clarify –'

'I'll let you in.'

The policeman glanced through the open door at the living room as he passed. Harvey conducted him to a small room at the back of this part of the château. The room had a desk and a few chairs; it hadn't been furnished or re-painted; it was less smart and new than the police station at Epinal, but it was the next best thing.

'You have no clue, absolutely no idea where your wife is?'

'No. Where do you yourselves think she is?'

'Hiding out in the woods. Or gone across into Germany. Or hiding in Paris. These people have an organisation,' said the inspector.

'If she's in the woods she would be wet,' said Harvey, glaring at the sheet rain outside the window.

'Is she a strong woman? Any health complications?'

'Well, she's slim, rather fragile. Her health's all right so far as I know,' Harvey said.

'If she contacts you, it would be obliging if you would invite her to the house. The same applies to Nathan Fox.'

'But I don't want my wife in the house. I don't want to oblige her. I don't need Nathan Fox,' Harvey said.

'When things quieten down she might try to contact you. You might oblige us by offering her a refuge.'

'I should have thought you had the house surrounded.'

'We do. We mean to keep it surrounded. You know, these people are heavily armed, they have sophisticated weapons. It might occur to them to take you hostages, you and the baby. Of course, they would be caught before they could get near you. But you might help us by issuing an invitation.'

'It's all a supposition,' Harvey said. 'I'm not convinced that this woman-terrorist is my wife, nor that my wife is a terrorist. As for Nathan Fox, he's a mystery to me, but I wouldn't have thought he'd draw attention to himself by going off and joining an armed band at the very moment when they were active.'

'If your wife is a fascinating woman –'

'I hope,' said Harvey, 'that you're taking special precautions to protect the baby.'

'You admit that the baby might be in danger?'

'With an armed gang around, any baby might be in danger.'

'But you admit that your wife's baby might be an object of special interest to your wife.'

'She has taken no interest in the child.'

'Then why are you suggesting that we specially protect this child?'

'I hope you have made arrangements to do so,' said Harvey.

'We have your house and grounds surrounded.'

'The baby,' said Harvey, 'must be sent back to England. My sister-in-law will take her.'

'A good idea. We can arrange for them to leave, quietly, with every protection. But it would be advisable for you to keep the move as secret as possible. I mean the press. We don't want this gang to know every move. I warn you to be careful what you say to the press. The examining magistrate –'

'The press! They've already –'

The man spread his hands helplessly. 'This wasn't my fault. These things leak out. After all, it's a matter of national concern. But not a word about your plans to send the child away.'

'The maid will know. They talk –'

'Anne-Marie is one of our people,' said the inspector.

'You don't say! We rather liked her.'

'She'd better stay on with you, then. And hang out baby clothes on the line, as you always want to do. I might look in again soon.'

'Don't stand on ceremony.'

*

'How is it possible,' Ruth said, 'that the police think the gang might turn up here, now that this story's all over the papers, on the radio, the television? It's the last place they would come to. Clara's safer here than anywhere. How can they think –'

'The police don't think so, they only say they think so.'

'Why?'

'How do I know? They suspect me strongly. They want the baby out of France. Maybe it's got something to do with their public image.'

'I don't want to go,' said Ruth.

'I don't want you to go,' said Harvey, 'but I think you should. It's only for a while. I think you must.'

'Are you free to come, too? Harvey, let's both get away.'

'On paper, I'm free to go. In fact, they might detain me. The truth is, I don't want to leave just at this moment. Just bloody-mindedness on my part.'

'I can be stubborn, too,' said Ruth; but she spoke with a fluidity that implied she was giving way. 'But, after all,' she went on, 'I suppose you didn't ask me to come here in the first place.'

Harvey thought, I don't love her, I'm not in the least in love with her. Much of the time I don't even like her very much.

Anne-Marie had put some soup on the table. Harvey and Ruth were silent before her, now that she wasn't a maid but a police auxiliary. When she had left, Ruth said, 'I don't know if I'll be able to keep this down. I'm pregnant.'

'How did that happen?' Harvey said.

'The same as it always happens.'

'How long have you known?'

'Three weeks.'

'Nobody tells me anything,' Harvey said.

'You don't want to know anything.'

Had Ruth stopped taking the pill? Was it his child or Nathan's? She didn't guess his first thought, but she did his second. 'I never slept with Nathan, ever,' she said. 'His mind's on Effie – That's one thing I didn't mention to the police.'

'Take some bread with your soup. You'll keep it down better.'

'You know, I'd rather not go back to England. Now that Edward's having this amazing success –'

'What success?'

'He's having an astonishing success on the West End. That play –'

'Well, how long have you known about this?'

'Three weeks. It's been in the papers, and he wrote –'

'Nobody tells me anything.'

'I think it funny Edward hasn't rung us up to-day. He must have seen the papers,' Ruth said. 'Maybe it scared him. A scandal.'

'Where would you like to go?' Harvey said.

'Have you got anyone in Canada I could take Clara to?'

'I have an aunt and I have an uncle in Toronto. They're married but they live in separate houses. You could go to either. I'll ring up.'

'I'll go to the uncle,' said Ruth. She started to smile happily, but she was crying at the same time.

'There's nothing to worry about,' Harvey said.

'Yes there is. There's Effie. There's Edward.'

'What about Edward?'

'He's a shit. He might have wanted to know if I was all right. He's been writing all the time I've been here, and phoning every day since we got the telephone put in. Up to now.'

Anne-Marie came in with a splendid salad, a tray of cheeses.

'Shall I help Madame to pack after lunch?' she said.

'How did she know I was leaving?' Ruth said when the maid had gone out.

'Somebody told her. Everyone knows everything,' said Harvey, 'except me.'

Ruth was in the bedroom, packing, and Harvey was pushing the furniture here and there to make a distance between the place where he intended to sit to receive the reporters, and the part of the room reserved for them. Ruth, Harvey thought as he did so, has been crying a lot over the past few weeks, crying and laughing. I noticed, but I didn't notice. I wonder if she cried under the interrogation, and laughed? Anyway, it isn't this quite unlooked-for event that's caused her to cry and laugh, it started earlier. Did she tell the police she was pregnant? Probably. Maybe that's why they want to get rid of her. Is she really pregnant? Harvey plumped up a few cushions. Yellow chintzes, lots of yellow; at least, the chintzes had a basis of yellow, so that you saw yellow when you came into the room. New chintzes: all right, order new chintzes. Curtains and cushions and cosiness: all right, order them; have them mail my lawyer the bill. You say you need a château: all right, have the château, my lawyers will fix it. Harvey kicked an armchair. It moved smoothly on its castors into place. Ruth, he thought, is fond of the baby. She adores Clara. Who wouldn't? But Clara belongs to me, that is, to my wife, Effie. No, Clara belongs to Ruth and depends on Ruth. It's good-bye, good-bye, to Clara. He looked at his watch. Time to telephone Toronto, it's about ten in the morning there. The story of playboy Harvey Gotham and his terrorist connections are certainly featured in the Canadian press, on the radio, the television.

Anne-Marie had come in, shiny black short hair, shiny black eyes, clear face. She had a small waist, stout hips. She carried a transistor radio playing rock music softly enough not to justify complaint.

'Do you know how to get a number on the telephone, long-distance to Toronto?' Harvey said.

'Of course,' said the policewoman.

He thought, as he gave her the number, She doesn't look like a police official, she looks like a maid. Bedworthy and married. She's somebody's wife. Every woman I have to do with is somebody's wife. Ruth, Job's wife, and Effie who is still my wife, and who is shooting up the supermarkets. Twelve people hurt and millions of francs' theft and damage. If the police don't soon get the gang there will be deaths; housewives, policemen, children murdered. Am I responsible for my wife's debts? Her wounded, her dead?

Anne-Marie had left the transistor while she went to telephone; the music had been interrupted and the low murmur of an announcement drew Harvey's attention; he caught the phrases: terrorist organisation ... errors of justice ...; he turned the volume up. It was a bulletin from FLE issued to a Paris news agency, vindicating its latest activities. The gang was going to liberate Europe from its errors. 'Errors of society, errors of the system.' Most of all, liberation from the diabolical institution of the *gendarmerie* and the brutality of the *Brigade Criminelle*. It was much the same as every other terrorist announcement Harvey had ever read. 'The multinationals and the forces of the reactionary imperialist powers ...' It was like an alarm clock that ceases to wake the sleeper who, having heard it morning after morning, simply puts out a hand and switches it off without even opening his eyes.

The bulletin was followed by an announcement that fifty inspectors of the *Brigade Criminelle* were now investigating FLE's activities in the Vosges where the terrorists were still believed to be hiding out. End of announcement: on with the music.

'Your call to Toronto,' said Anne-Marie.

Ruth was to go to Paris and leave next morning, with Clara, for Canada. A Volvo pulled up at the door. When he had finished his call, Harvey saw two suitcases already packed in the hall. Those people work fast. 'Not so fast,' Harvey said to Anne-Marie. 'The child's father might not agree to her going to Canada. We must get his permission.'

'We have his permission. Mr Howe will call you to-night. He has agreed with Scotland Yard.'

'The press will be here any minute,' said Harvey. 'They'll see Madame and the baby driving off.'

'No, the police have the road cordoned off. Madame and the child will leave by a back door, anyway.' She went out and gave instructions to the driver of the Volvo, who took off, round to the back of the house. Anne-Marie lifted one of the suitcases and gestured to Harvey to take the other. He followed her, unfamiliar with all the passages of his château, through a maze of grey kitchens, dairies and wash-houses as yet unrestored. By a door leading to a vast and sad old plantation which must have once been a kitchen garden, Ruth stood, huddled in her sheepskin coat, crying, cuddling the baby.

'Is it to be Toronto?' she said.

'Oh, yes, you'll be met. Do you have the money with you?' Harvey had given her charge of a quantity of cash long before the trouble started.

'I've taken most of it.'

'You'll be all right once you're at my uncle Joe's.'

'Who did you say I was?' she said.

'My sister-in-law.'

'And Clara?'

'Your niece. Ernie Howe has given his permission –'

'Oh, I know. I spoke to him myself,' she said.

'Nobody tells me anything,' Harvey said.

'Will I like your Uncle Joe?'

'I hope so. If not, you can go to my Auntie Pet.'

'What is "Pet" short for?' said Ruth.

'I really don't know.' He could see she wanted to delay the parting. 'Ring me to-night from Paris,' he said. He kissed Ruth and he kissed Clara, and practically pushed them towards Anne-Marie who had already seen the suitcases into the car, and was waiting for Ruth, almost taking her under arrest. With a hand under Ruth's arm she led her along the little path towards the wider path where the car waited. They were off, Ruth and Clara in the front seat beside the driver. They were like an affluent married couple and child. Anne-Marie came back to the house, closed and locked the back door. Harvey said, 'You lead the way back. I'll follow you. I don't know my way about this place.' She laughed.

Twenty minutes later the press were let in. 'Quiet!' said Anne-Marie. 'We have a baby in the house. You mustn't wake her.'

Harvey, freshly and acutely aware of Clara's innocent departure, was startled for an instant, then remembered quickly that Ruth and Clara were gone in secret.

'Madame is resting, too,' announced Anne-Marie, 'please, gentlemen, ladies, no noise.'

There were eighteen men, five women; the rest were at the road-block outside the house arguing vainly with the police. This, Harvey learned from the reporters themselves, who crowded into the living room. There was a predominance of French, British and Americans among them. Harvey scrutinised them, as best he could trying to guess which one of them was a police agent. A wiry woman of about fifty with a red face, broken-veined, and thin grey hair fluffed out and falling all over her face as if to make the most of it, seemed to him a possible *flic*, if only for the reason that unlike the others she seemed to have no-one to talk to.

'Mr Gotham, when did you last see –'

'I will answer no questions,' Harvey said, 'until you stop these flash-photographs.' He sat back in his chair with folded arms. 'Stop,' he said, 'just stop. I'll answer questions first, if they're reasonable. Then you can take some photos. But not all at once. Kindly keep your voices down; as you've heard, there's a baby sleeping upstairs and a lady who needs a lot of rest.' One of the reporters, slouching by the door, a large fair middle-aged man, was already taking notes. What of? The man's face seemed familiar to Harvey but he couldn't place it.

The French journalists were the most vociferous. 'Do you know where your wife is?' – 'How long has she been a member – ?' – 'Your wife Effie's terrorist activities, do you ascribe them to a reaction against her wealthy matrimonial experience, with all the luxury and boredom that capitalism produces?' – 'What exactly are the creed and aims of your religious group, Mr Gotham?'

Harvey said, 'One at a time, please.'

'With all your prospects and holdings, you still believe in God, is that right?' – 'Are you asking us to believe that you have come to this château to study the Bible?' – 'Isn't it so that you originally lived in that little lodge at the end of the drive?'

'Yes,' said Harvey, 'I went to work down there.'

'Where does your wife get the money for her terrorist activities?'

'I don't know that my wife is engaged in terrorist activities.'

'But the police have identified her. Look, Mr Gotham, those people of the FLE get their money from someplace.' This came from a fat young American who spoke like a machine-gun.

'Would you mind speaking French so that we all know where we are?' said Harvey. A Frenchman swiftly came to his American colleague's aid, and repeated the question in French.

'Apparently they bomb supermarkets and rob the cash. Haven't you read the papers?' Harvey said.

'If your wife came in here with a sub-machine-gun right now – ?'

'That is a hypothetical question,' Harvey said. The question was asked by a timid young Asiatic type with fine features and a sad pallor, who had evidently been let in to the conference on a quota system. He looked puzzled. 'Your question is all theory,' Harvey said, to help him. The young man nodded wisely and made some notes. What notes? – God knows.

'Didn't you hear a registration in the police station of your wife's voice on a loudspeaker warning the people to leave the supermarket before the bombing? – Surely you recognised your wife's voice?' said an American.

'I heard no registration. But if my wife should happen to give a warning to anyone in danger at any time, that would be very right of her, I think,' Harvey said.

Most of the reporters were younger than Harvey. One, a bearded Swede, was old, paunchy. He alone seemed to know what the *Book of Job* was. He asked Harvey, 'Would you say that you yourself are in the position of Job, in so far as you are a suspicious character in the eyes of the world, yet feel yourself to be perfectly innocent?'

Harvey saw his chance and took it: 'I am hardly in the position of Job. He was covered with boils, for one thing, which I am not. And his friends, merely on the basis of his suffering, accused him of having sinned in some way. What Job underwent was tantamount to an interrogation by the Elders of his community. I intend no personal analogy. But I am delighted to get down at last to the subject of this conference: what was the answer to Job's question? Job's question was, why does God cause me to suffer when I've done nothing to deserve it? Now, Job was in no doubt whatsoever that his sufferings came from God and from no other source. The very rapidity with which one calamity followed upon another, shattering Job's world, leaving him destitute, bereft and sick all in a short space of time, gave dramatic evidence that the cause was not natural, but supernatural. The supernatural, with power to act so strongly and disastrously, could only, in Job's mind, be God. And we know he was right in the context of the book, because in the Prologue you read specifically that it was God who brought up the subject of Job to Satan; it was God, in fact, who tempted Satan to torment Job, not Satan who tempted God. I'm afraid my French version of the scriptures isn't to hand, it's down in my study in the cottage, or I'd quote you the precise passage. But –'

'Mr Gotham,' said a young Englishwoman dressed entirely in dark grey leather, 'I'm sorry to interrupt but I have to file my story at six. Is it true that Nathan Fox is your wife's lover?'

'Please stick to French if you can. Anyway, I am addressing this gentleman,' said Harvey, indicating the elderly Swede, 'on a very important subject and –'

'Oh, no, Mr Gotham. Oh, no.' This was a tough pressman, indeterminately British or American, who spoke with a loud, fierce voice. 'Oh, no, Mr Gotham. You're here to answer our questions.'

'Keep your voice down, please. The fact is that I am here because it is my home. You are here to listen to me. The subject is the *Book of*

Job to which I have dedicated many years of my life. This gentleman,'
said Harvey, nodding to the grave and rather flattered Swede, 'has
asked me an interesting question on the subject. I have answered his
question and I am elaborating on it. Your chance, and that of your
colleagues, to put further questions will come in due course. As I was
about to remark, Job's problem was partly a lack of knowledge. He
was without access to any system of study which would point to the
reason for his afflictions. He said specifically, "I desire to reason with
God," and expected God to come out like a man and state his case.'

'Mr Gotham –'

'Mr Gotham, can you state if you would side with your wife in any
sense if she came up for trial? Do you yourself feel politically that the
FLE have something to offer the young generation?' – This was from
a lanky French journalist with bright eyes and a wide smile. He was
rather a sympathetic type, Harvey thought, probably new to his trade.

'I'm really sorry to disappoint you,' said Harvey with some charm,
'but I'm giving you a seminar on *Job* without pay.'

A hubbub had now started to break out. Protests and questions
came battering in on Harvey from every side.

'Quiet!' bawled Harvey. 'Either you listen to me in silence or you all
go. Job's problem, as I was saying, was partly a lack of knowledge.
Everybody talked but nobody told him anything about the reason for
his sufferings. Not even God when he appeared. Our limitations of
knowledge make us puzzle over the cause of suffering, maybe it is the
cause of suffering itself. Quiet, over there! The baby's asleep. And I
said, no photographs at present. As I say, we are plonked here in the
world and nobody but our own kind can tell us anything. It isn't
enough. As for the rest, God doesn't tell. No, I've already told you
that I don't know where my wife is. How the *Book of Job* got into the
holy scriptures I really do not know. That's the greatest mystery of
all. For it doesn't –'

'Mr Gotham,' said the tough pressman, 'the FLE have held up
supermarkets, jewellers and banks at Gérardmer, La Bresse, Ram-
bervillers, Mirecourt and Baccarat. Your wife is –'

'You've left out Epinal,' said Harvey. Cameras flashed. 'Will you
allow me to continue to answer the question put to me, or will you go?'

'Your wife –' . . . 'Your background, Mr Gotham –' . . . 'Your wife's
sister –'

'Conference over,' said Harvey.

'Oh, no.' – 'No, Mr Gotham.' – 'Wait a minute.'

Some were swearing and cursing; some were laughing.

But Harvey got up and made for the door. Most of the reporters were on their feet, very rowdy. The wiry red-faced woman, the possible police agent, sat holding her tape-recorder modestly on her lap. The large fair man at the door had grabbed a belt as if from nowhere and was fastening it rapidly round his waist. Harvey saw that it was packed neatly with cartridges and that a revolver hung from a holster, with the man's hand on it. He recognised him now as the sandy-haired policeman who, in uniform, had sat at the table throughout his interrogation at Epinal.

Harvey said, 'I must tell you that there is a policeman in the room.'

'What police? *La Brigade antigang?*'

'I have no idea what variety. Kindly leave quietly and in order, and don't wake the baby.'

They left without order or quietness.

'Why don't you get out while you can? Get back to Canada,' said a girl. – 'We'll be seeing you in the courtroom,' said another. Some joked as they left, some overturned chairs as they went. From everywhere came the last-minute flashes of the cameras recording the policeman, the overturned chairs, and recording Harvey standing in the middle of it, an image to be reproduced in one of next morning's papers under the title, 'Don't Wake the Baby'. But at last they had gone. The wiry red-faced woman said sadly to Harvey as she passed him, 'I'm afraid you'll get a very bad press.'

The policeman followed them out and chivied them down the drive from his car. Before he shut the door Harvey noticed something new in the light cast from the hall: a washing-line had been slung well in evidence of the front portico. Anne-Marie had just finished taking baby clothes from it, had evidently been photographed doing so. She came towards him.

'Not very convincing,' Harvey said. 'Nobody hangs washing within sight of the approach to a château.'

'Nobody used to,' Anne-Marie said. 'They do now. We, for example, are doing it. Nobody will find it in the least suspect.'

*

'Didn't she tell you the hotel where she was going to in Paris?' Harvey said.

'Not me,' said Anne-Marie. 'I think she'll ring you if she said she would. In any case, the inspector is sure to know where she's staying.'

It was nine-thirty, and Anne-Marie was leaving for the night, anxious about being extraordinarily late in returning home; she lived several miles away. A car driven by a plain-clothes policeman was waiting at the door. She hurried away, banged the car door, and was off.

Stewart Cowper had arrived about an hour before, full of travel-exasperation and police-harassment; he had been frisked and questioned at the entrance to the house; he had been travelling most of the day and he was cold. At present he was having a shower.

Harvey and Anne-Marie had together put the living room to rights. Ruth had not yet rung him from Paris as she had promised. Where was she? Harvey then noticed something new in the room, a large bowl of early spring flowers, professionally arranged, beautiful. Irises, jonquils, lilies, daffodils; all too advanced to be local products; they must have come from an expensive shop in Nancy. Anne-Marie must have put them there at some time between the clearing up of the mess and her leaving, but Harvey hadn't noticed them. They stood on a low round table, practically covering it as the outward leaves of the arrangement bent gracefully over the edge of the bowl. Harvey hadn't noticed them, either, while he was sitting having a drink with Stewart, trying to calm him down, nor while Anne-Marie, anxious about the time, laid out a cold supper that was still sitting on the small dining-table, waiting for Stewart to wash and change. Where did those flowers come from? Who brought them, who sent them? Anne-Marie hadn't left the house. And why should she order flowers?

Stewart came in and went to get himself another drink. He was a man of medium height, in his mid-forties with a school-boy's round face and round blue eyes; but this immature look was counteracted by a deep and expressive quality in his voice, so that as soon as he spoke the total effect was of a certain maturity and intelligence, cancelling that silly round-eyed look.

'Did you bring these flowers?' said Harvey.

'Did I bring what?'

'These flowers – I don't know where they've come from. The maid – and by the way she's a policewoman – must have put them there some time this evening. But why?'

Stewart brought his drink to the sofa and sat sipping it.

Harvey's mind was working fast, and faster. 'I think I know why they're there. Have you ever heard of a vase of flowers being bugged?'

'Rather an obvious way to plant a bug if the flowers weren't there already,' said Stewart.

But Harvey was already pulling the flower-arrangement to bits. He shook each lily, each daffodil; he tore at the petals of the irises. Stewart drank his drink and told Harvey to calm down; he watched Harvey with his big blue eyes and then took another sip. Harvey splashed the water from the bowl all over the table and the floor. 'I don't see anything,' he said.

'From what I understand the police have had every opportunity to plant bugs elsewhere in the house; they need not introduce a bunch of flowers for the purpose,' Stewart said. 'What a mess you've made of a lovely bunch of flowers.'

'I'd take you out to dinner,' said Harvey. He sat on the sofa with his dejected head in his hands. He looked up. 'I'd take you out to eat but I've got to wait in for a call from Ruth. She's in Paris but I don't know where. I've got to let my uncle in Toronto know the time of her arrival and her flight number. Did I tell you that she's taking the baby to my Uncle Joe's?'

'No,' said Stewart.

'Well, she is. I've got to arrange for her to be met, and get through to Toronto and give them reasonable notice. And I've got to have a call from Ernie Howe, I think. At least he said he'd ring.'

'How many other things have you got to do?'

'I don't know.'

'Why don't you relax? You're in a hell of a state.'

'I know. What are you supposed to be doing here?'

'Giving you some advice,' Stewart said. 'Of course, I can't act for you here in France.'

'I don't need anyone. I've got what's-his-name in Paris if necessary.'

'Martin Deschamps? – I've been in touch with him. He can't act for you in a case like this. No-one in his firm can, either. That means they won't. Terrorism is too unladylike for those fancy lawyers. I'm hungry.'

'Let's sit down, then,' said Harvey; they sat at the table to eat the cold supper. Harvey's hand shook as he started to pour the wine. He stopped and looked at his hand. 'I'm shaking,' he said. 'I wonder why Ruth hasn't rung?'

Stewart took the bottle from him and poured out the wine. 'Your nerves,' he said.

'She must have had her dinner and put the baby to bed by now,' Harvey said. 'I'll give it another hour, then I'm going to ring the police and find out where she is. Ernie Howe should have rung, too.'

'Maybe she didn't stop over in Paris. Perhaps she went straight to the airport.'

'She should have rung. She could have been taken ill. She's pregnant.'

'Is she?'

'So she says.'

The telephone rang. An inspector of police, 'M. Gotham? – I want to let you know that Mme. Ruth Jansen has arrived in London.'

'In London? I thought she was going to stop overnight in Paris. I've arranged for her to go to Canada to my –'

'She changed her mind.'

'Where is she in London?'

'I can't tell you. Good night.'

'If she didn't ring you as promised,' said Stewart the next morning, 'and Ernie Howe didn't ring you as promised, and if, in addition, it transpires she went to London, I should have thought you would suspect that the two were together.'

'You think she has gone to Ernie Howe? Why should she go to him? She is pregnant by me.'

'She has Ernie Howe's baby in her arms. It would be natural to take her to the father. You can't possess everything, Harvey.'

'Do you know more than you say?' said Harvey.

'No, it's only a supposition.'

'I'll ring Ernie Howe's flat as soon as my call to Canada has come through. It's hard on my uncle, mucking him about like this. He's not so young. I've just put through a call.'

'It's the middle of the night in Toronto,' said Stewart.

'I don't care.'

Anne-Marie arrived in her thick coat, scarves and boots. 'Good morning,' she said, and then gave a pained wail. Her eyes were on the flowers that she had left in such a formal display the night before, now all pulled to pieces, even the petals torn to bits.

'I was looking for an electronic bug,' Harvey said.

'I think you are not human,' said Anne-Marie. She was now in tears, aimlessly lifting a daffodil, putting it down, then a blue, torn iris.

'Who ordered them, who sent them?' said Harvey.

Stewart said, 'I'll help to clear the mess. Leave it to me.'

'I had them sent myself,' said Anne-Marie. 'To give you some joy after your ordeal with the press and your loss of the baby. My sister-in-law has a flower shop and I made a special-messenger arrangement with her for the most beautiful flowers; a personal present. I thought that with the loss of Madame and Clara you would enjoy those lovely spring flowers.'

Stewart had his arm round the police agent's shoulders. 'His nerves gave way,' said Stewart. 'That's all.'

The telephone rang; Harvey's call to Canada. It was a sleepy manservant who answered, as Harvey had counted on. He was able to explain, without having to actually talk to his uncle, that Ruth and the baby were probably not coming after all, and that any references to him in the newspapers and on the television were probably false.

He put down the receiver. The telephone rang: 'Hallo, Harvey!' The telephone rang off. Again it rang: 'Harvey, it's Ruth.' She was speaking in a funny way. She was calling herself Ree-uth, although definitely the voice was hers. It must be the London influence, Harvey registered all in a moment. But she was going on. 'I changed my mind, Harvey. I had to bring Clara (pronounced Clah-rah) to her father (pronounced fah-thar).'

'What are you saying?' said Harvey. 'You mean you're not going to my Uncle Joe in Toronto. You've decided to shack down with Ernie Howe, is that it?'

'That's it,' said Ruth.

'Then I think you might have had enough consideration for my Uncle Joe – he's seventy-eight – to let me know.'

'Oh, I was busy with Clah-rah.'

'Pass me Ernie,' said Harvey.

'Ernie, do you mind?' said Ruth's voice, apart.

'Hallo,' said the other voice.

'Ernie Howe?'

'That's me.'

'What are you doing with Ruth?'

'We've just had a tunah-fish salad. We fed Clah-rah.'

Harvey then remembered Ernie's voice (that's where Ruth got the Clah-rah).

'I make a good fah-thah,' said Ernie; 'and I don't like your tone of superiority.'

After a great many more hot words, Harvey began to recollect, at the back of his mind, that he really had no rights in the matter; not much to complain of at all. He said good night, hung up, and returned to the sitting room hoping for some consolation from his friend.

His friend was sitting on the sofa holding hands with Anne-Marie. Harvey was in time to hear him say, 'May I fall in love with you?'

'She's married,' said Harvey in English.

'Not at all,' said Anne-Marie in her most matter-of-fact voice. 'I live with my married brother.'

'Well, I thought you were married,' said Harvey.

'That's when you thought I was a maid.'

'If you're not a maid then what are you doing here?' said Harvey.

'He's exasperated,' said Stewart. 'Don't mind him.'

Anne-Marie took a long glance at the disorderly table of ruined flowers and said, 'I have to remain here on duty. I'm going to make the coffee.'

When she had left, Harvey said, 'You're behaving like an undergraduate who's just put foot on the Continent for the first time, meeting his first Frenchwoman.'

'What was the news from England?'

'Ruth is with Ernie Howe.'

'What do the newspapers say?'

'I don't know. Find out; it's your job.'

'Is it?' said Stewart.

'If it isn't, what are you doing here?'

'I suppose I'm just a comforter,' Stewart said.

'I suppose you are.'

EIGHT

'Is it possible,' said Harvey, 'for anyone to do something perfectly innocent but altogether unusual, without giving rise to suspicion?'

Stewart said, 'Not if his wife is a terrorist.'

'Assume that she is not.'

'All right, I assume. But here you were in a small hamlet in France, a rich man living in primitive conditions. Well, nobody bothered you until the police began to suspect a link between you and the FLE a certain time ago, and even then they only had you under surveillance, from a distance; they didn't haul you in immediately or harass you so that your life was uncomfortable. You weren't even aware of their presence till lately. And now you've been questioned, grilled; it's only natural. It might have been worse. Much worse. You don't know the police.'

'My papers have been scrutinised, all my work, my private things –'

'I can't sympathise too much, Harvey. I can't say you've really suffered. These police obviously are going carefully with you. They're protecting you from the mob, the phone calls. They probably believe you; they know by now, I should think, that you have no contact with Effie. I think they're right to watch out in case she has any contact with you.'

'You are wrong,' said Harvey, 'to say that I haven't suffered. Did you hear the press round-up on the radio this morning? – My name's worse than Effie's in the eyes of the press.'

The local newspaper, the only one so far to arrive in his hands, was on the coffee-table in front of them, with the front page uppermost. The headline, 'The Guru of the Vosges' stretched above a picture of Harvey, distraught, in his sitting room of final disorder at the press conference. Under the picture was the title-paragraph of the subsequent article:

Harvey Gotham, the American 'prophet', inveighing against God, who he claims has unjustly condemned the world to suffering. *God is a Shit* was one of the blasphemies preached at an international press conference held yesterday in his 40-roomed château recently acquired by this multimillionaire husband of the gangster-terrorist Effie Gotham, leading activist of FLE.

In the article, the writer of it reflected on the influence of Harvey on a girl like Effie 'from the poorer classes of London', and on her sister and an infant, Clara, still under his control at the château.

Harvey said to Stewart, 'I never once said "*Dieu est merde.*"'

'Maybe you implied it.'

'Perhaps I did. But I did not speak as a prophet; I discussed some aspects of *Job* in an academic sense.'

'For a man of your intelligence, you are remarkably stupid,' said Stewart. 'It's Effie they wanted news of. Failing that, they made the best of what they got. You should have let Effie divorce you with a huge settlement a long time ago. She can get a divorce any time; it's the money she wanted.'

'To finance FLE?'

'You asked me to assume she isn't involved.'

'I don't want to divorce Effie. I don't want a divorce.'

'Are you still in love with Effie?'

'Yes.'

'Then you're an unhappy man. Why did you leave her?'

'I couldn't stand her sociological clap-trap. If she wanted to do some good in the world she had plenty of opportunity. There was nothing to stop her taking up charities and causes; she could have had money for them, and she always had plenty of time. But she has to rob super-markets and banks and sleep with people like *that*.' He pointed to a row of photographs in the paper. Three young men and Effie. The photograph of Effie was that which the police had found among his papers. Harvey told Stewart this, and said, 'They don't seem to have any other picture of Effie. I wonder how they got photos of her friends.'

'In the same way that they got Effie's, I expect. Through rummaging in the homes of their families, their girl-friends.'

'What can she see in them?' Harvey said. Stewart turned the paper round to see it better. One of the men was dressed in a very padded-shouldered coat, a spotted bow tie and hair falling down past the point where the picture ended, which was just above his elbow; the second man was a blond, blank-faced boy with thick lips; the third seemed to be positively posing as the criminal he was alleged to be, being sneery, narrow-eyed and double-chinned, and bearing a two-day stubble beard. There was Effie amongst them, looking like Effie. The men were identified by French names, Effie by the name of Effie Gotham, wife of the millionaire guru.

'What does she see in them?' demanded Harvey. 'It's not so much that I'm jealous as that I'm intellectually insulted by the whole thing. I always have been by Effie's attitude to life. I thought she'd grow out of it.'

'I am to assume that Effie is not involved,' said Stewart.

'Well, there's her picture along with the others. It's difficult for me to keep up the fiction,' Harvey said.

'Do you mean that the photograph convinces you?' Stewart said. 'You know where the police got the photograph. Out of a drawer in your desk.'

'It wasn't exactly out of a drawer in a desk,' Harvey said. 'It was out of a box. I keep things in boxes down there in my working cottage. I'll take you to see it. I haven't been back to the cottage since I was arrested in Epinal three days ago.'

'Were you really arrested?'

'Perhaps not technically. I was definitely invited to come along to the commissariat. I went.'

'I wonder,' said Stewart, 'why there's been so little in the press about Nathan Fox. I only heard on the radio that he'd disappeared suddenly from your house. And they don't include him in the gang. Maybe they couldn't find a photograph of him. A photo makes a gangster real.'

'There was an identikit of Effie in the papers the day I was hauled in,' said Harvey.

'Did it look like Effie?'

'I'm afraid so. In fact it looked like Ruth. But it would pass for Effie. It looked like Job's wife, too. You know, it was a most remarkable thing, Stewart, I was sitting in the museum at Epinal reflecting on that extraordinary painting of Job and his wife by Georges de La Tour, when suddenly the police –'

'You told me that last night,' said Stewart.

'I know. I want to talk about it.'

'Don't you think,' said Stewart, 'that it would be odd if Effie wanted alimony from you simply to finance the FLE, when she could have sold her jewellery?'

'Hasn't she done that?'

'No, it's still in the safety-box at the bank. I hold the second key. There's still enough money in her bank to meet the standing orders for insurances and charities. Nothing's changed.'

'Well, why did she want to fleece me?'

'I don't see why she shouldn't have tried to get maintenance of some sort from you. It's true that her child by Ernie Howe damaged her case. But you walked out on her. She behaved like a normal woman married to a man in your position.'

'Effie is not a normal woman,' said Harvey.

'Oh, if you're talking in a basic sense, what woman is?'

'Women who don't get arrested in Trieste for shoplifting are normal,' said Harvey. 'Especially women with her kind of jewellery in the bank. Whose side are you on, anyway, mine or Effie's?'

'In a divorce case, that is the usual question that the client puts, sooner or later. It's inevitable,' said the lawyer.

'But this is something different from a divorce case. Don't you realise what's happened?'

'I'm afraid I do,' said Stewart.

Next day was a Saturday. They sat in Harvey's cottage, huddling over the stove because the windows had been opened to air the place. There had been a feeling of spring in the early March morning, but this had gone by eleven o'clock; it was now winter again, bleak, with a slanting rain. As Harvey unlocked the door of his little house Stewart said, 'Lousy soil you've got here. Nothing much growing.'

'I haven't bothered to cultivate it.'

'It's better up at the château.'

'Oh, yes, it's had more attention.'

This was Harvey's first visit to the cottage since the police had pounced. He looked round carefully, opening the windows upstairs and downstairs, while Stewart lit the stove. 'They haven't changed the décor,' Harvey said. 'But a few bundles of papers are not in the places I left them in. Shifted, a matter of inches – but I know, I know.'

'Have they taken any of your papers, letters, business documents?'

'What letters and business papers? You have the letters and the business papers. All I have are my notes, and the manuscript of my little book, so far as it goes – it's to be a monograph, you know. I don't know if they've subtracted the few files, but they could have photographed them; much good might it do them. Files of notes on the *Book of Job*. They did take the photograph of Effie; that, they did take. I want it back.'

'You're entitled to ask for it,' said Stewart.

From the window, a grey family Citroën could be seen parked round a bend in the path, out of sight of the road; in it were two men in civilian clothes occupying the front seats. The rain plopped lazily on to the roof of the car and splashed the windscreen. 'Poor bastards,' Harvey said. 'They do it in three- or four-hour shifts.'

'Well, it's a protection for you, anyway. From the press if not from the terrorists.'

'I wish I was without the need for protection, and I wish you were in your office in London.'

'I don't go to the office on Saturday,' Stewart said.

'What do you do at the week-ends?'

'Fuck,' said Stewart.

'Do you mean, fuck the question or that on Saturdays and Sundays you fuck?'

'Both.'

'Don't you ever go to a concert or a film on Sundays? Never go to Church?'

'Sometimes I go to a concert. I go away for the week-ends, often. I do the usual things.'

'Well, you're wasting your time here,' Harvey said.

'No, because first you're my most valuable client. That's from a practical point of view. And secondly, I'm interested in your *Book of Job*; it just beats me how a man of your scope should choose to hide himself away in this hole. And thirdly, of course, I'm a friend; I want to see you out of this mess. I strongly advise you to come back to London here and now. Do you have your passport?'

'Yes, they gave me back my passport.'

'Oh, they took it away?'

'Yes, they took the stuff out of my pockets,' Harvey said. 'They gave it all back. I'm not leaving.'

'Why?'

'Well, all my books and things are here. I don't see why I should run away. I intend to go on as usual. Besides, I'm anxious about Effie.'

'Maybe Effie would move to another field of action if you weren't in the Vosges,' said Stewart. 'You see, I don't want you to become an unwilling accomplice.'

'Effie follows the gang,' said Harvey.

'Doesn't she lead it?'

'Oh, I don't know. I don't even know for certain that she's in it. It's all mere allegation on the part of the police.'

Stewart walked about the little room, with his scarf wound round his neck. 'It's chilly,' he said. He was looking at the books. 'Does Anne-Marie cook for you?' he said.

'Yes, indifferently. She's a police agent by profession.'

'Oh, that doesn't mean much,' said Stewart, 'when you know that she is.'

'I used to love mealtimes with Effie,' said Harvey. 'I enjoyed the mealtimes more than the meals.'

'Let's go out somewhere for lunch,' said Stewart.

'We can go in to Nancy. Undoubtedly we'd be followed.'

'That doesn't mean much if you know you are being followed,' said Stewart.

Harvey stood in the middle of the room watching with an irritated air while Stewart fingered his books.

'There's nothing of interest,' said Harvey, 'unless you're interested in the subject.'

'Well, you know I am. I still don't see why you can't write your essay elsewhere.'

'I've got used to it here.'

'Would you like to have Ruth back?' said Stewart.

'Not particularly. I would like to have Clara back.'

'With Effie?'

'No, Effie isn't a motherly type.'

'Ruth is a mother?'

'She is a born children's nurse.'

'But you would like to have Effie back?' Stewart said, and he made light of this, as of all his questions, by putting them simultaneously with a flicking-through of the pages of Harvey's books.

'Yes, I would; in theory,' said Harvey. 'That is the *New English Bible*. The translation is godforsaken.'

'Then you'd be willing to take Ruth back if she brought Clara. But you'd prefer to have Effie to make love to?'

'That is the unattainable ideal. The *New English Bible*'s version of *Job* makes no distinction between Behemoth and Leviathan. They translate the two as "the crocodile", which has of course some possibility as a theory, but it simply doesn't hold in the context.'

'I thought Behemoth was the hippopotamus,' said Stewart.

'Well, that's the general view, not necessarily correct. However, the author of *Job* turns God into a poet at that point, proclaiming wonderful hymns to his own creation, the buffalo, the ostrich, the wild ass, the horse, the eagle; then there's the sparrow-hawk. And God says, Consider this, look at that, reflect on their ways, how they live and survive; I did it all; where were you when I did it? Finally come Behemoth and Leviathan. Well, if you are going to translate both Behemoth and Leviathan as the crocodile, it makes far too long a passage, it gives far more weight to the crocodile as one of God's marvels than is obviously intended. As for the features of Behemoth, they fit in with the hippopotamus or some large and similar creature equally as well as with the crocodile. Why should God be so proud of his crocodile that he devotes thirty-eight verses to it, and to the horse only seven?'

'There must be some good arguments in favour of Behemoth and Leviathan both being the crocodile, though,' Stewart said.

'Of course there are arguments. The scholars try to rationalise *Job* by rearranging the verses where there is obviously no sense in them. Sometimes, of course, the textual evidence irresistibly calls for a passage to be moved from the traditional place to another. But moving passages about for no other reason than that they are more logical is no good for the *Book of Job*. It doesn't make it come clear. The *Book of Job* will never come clear. It doesn't matter; it's a poem. As for Leviathan and Behemoth, Lévêque who is the best

modern scholar on *Job* distinguishes between the two.' Harvey
was apparently back in his element. He seemed to have forgotten
about the police outside his house, and that Effie was a criminal at
large.

Stewart said, 'You amaze me.'

'Why?'

'Don't you want to know the facts about Effie?'

'Oh, Effie.'

Harvey had in his hands one of Lévêque's volumes. 'He accepts
Leviathan as the crocodile and Behemoth as the hippopotamus. He
takes Behemoth to be a hippopotamus or at least a large beast.'

'What about these other new Bibles?' said Stewart, pointing to a
couple of new translations. He wondered if perhaps Harvey was not
so guileless as he seemed. Stewart thought perhaps Harvey might
really be involved with Effie and her liberation movement. There was
something not very convincing about Harvey's cool-headedness.

'Messy,' said Harvey. 'They all try to reach everybody and end by
saying nothing to anybody. There are no good new Bibles. The 1945
Knox wasn't bad but still obscure – it's a Vulgate translation, of
course; the *Jerusalem Bible* and this *Good News Bible* are not much
improvement on the old *Moffat*.'

'You stick to the *Authorised* then?'

'For my purpose, it's the best English basis. One can get to know
the obvious mistakes and annotate accordingly.'

Harvey poured drinks and handed one to Stewart.

'I think I can see,' said Stewart, 'that you're happy here. I didn't
realise how much this work meant to you. It has puzzled me slightly; I
knew you were dedicated to the subject but didn't understand how
much, until I came here. You shouldn't think of marriage.'

'I don't. I think of Effie.'

'Only when you're not thinking of *Job*?'

'Yes. What can I do for her by thinking?'

'Your work here would make a good cover if you were in with
Effie,' said the lawyer.

'A very bad cover. The police aren't really convinced by my story.
Why should you be?'

'Oh, Harvey, I didn't mean –'

Anne-Marie arrived with a grind of brakes in the little Renault. She left the car with a bang of the door and began to proclaim an urgency before she had opened the cottage gate.

'Mr Gotham, a phone call from Canada.'

Harvey went to open the door to her. 'What is it from Canada?' he said.

'Your aunt on the telephone. She'll ring you back in ten minutes.'

'I'll come up to the house right away.'

To Stewart, he said, 'Wait for me. I'll be back shortly and we'll go out to lunch. You know, there could have been an influence of *Prometheus* on *Job*; the dates could quite possibly coincide. But I find vast differences. Prometheus wasn't innocent, for one thing. He stole fire from Heaven. Job was innocent.'

'Out to lunch!' said Anne-Marie. 'I'm preparing lunch at the château.'

'We'll have it cold for dinner,' thundered Harvey as he got into the car. Anne-Marie followed him; looking back at Stewart who gave her a long smile full of what looked like meaning, but decidedly so unspecific as to mean nothing.

As they whizzed up the drive to the château Anne-Marie said, 'You think because you are rich you can do anything with people. I planned a lunch.'

'You should first have enquired whether we would be in for lunch,' said Harvey.

'Oh, no,' she said, with some point. 'It was for you to say you would be out.'

'I apologise.'

'The apologies of the rich. They are cheap.'

Half an hour went by before the telephone rang again. The police were vetting the calls, turning away half the world's reporters and others who wanted to speak to the terrorist's guru husband. Harvey therefore made no complaint. He sat in patience reading all about himself once more in the local morning newspaper, until the telephone rang.

'Oh, it's you, Auntie Pet. It must be the middle of the night with you; how are you?'

'How are *you*?'

'All right.'

'I saw you on the television and it's all in the paper. How could you blaspheme in that terrible way, saying those things about your Creator?'

'Auntie Pet, you've got to understand that I said nothing whatsoever about God, I mean our Creator. What I was talking about was a fictional character in the *Book of Job*, called God. I don't know what you've seen or read, but it's not yet proved finally that Effie, my wife, is a terrorist.'

'Oh, Effie isn't involved, it goes without saying. I never said Effie was a terrorist, I know she isn't, in fact. What I'm calling about is this far more serious thing, it's a disgrace to the family. I mean, this is to blaspheme when you say that God is what you said he was.'

'I never said what they said I said he was,' said Harvey. 'How are you, Auntie Pet? How is Uncle Joe?'

'Uncle Joe, I never hear from. But I get to know.'

'And yourself? I haven't heard from you for ages.'

'Well, I don't write much. The prohibitive price of stamps. My health is everything that can be expected by a woman who does right and fears the Lord. Your Uncle Joe just lives on there with old Collier who is very much to blame, too. Neither of them has darkened the door of the church for as long as I can remember. They are unbelievers like you.'

'On the contrary, I have abounding faith.'

'You shouldn't question the Bible. Job was a good man. There is a Christian message in the *Book of Job*.'

'But Job didn't know that.'

'How do you know? We have a lovely Bible, there. Why do you want to change it? You should look after your wife and have a family, and be a good husband, with all your advantages, and the business doing so well. Your Uncle Joe refused the merger.'

'Well, Auntie Pet, it's been a pleasure to talk to you. I have to go out with my lawyer for lunch, now. I'm glad you managed to get my number so you could put your mind at rest.'

'I got your number with the utmost difficulty.'

'Yes, I was wondering how you got it, Auntie Pet.'

'Money,' said Auntie Pet.

'Ah,' said Harvey.

'I'll be in touch again.'

'Keep well. Don't take the slightest notice of what the newspapers and the television say.'

'What about the radio?'

'Also, the radio.'

'Are you starting a new religion, Harvey?'

'No.'

Stewart and Harvey crossed the Place Stanislas at Nancy. The rain had stopped and a silvery light touched the gilded gates at the corners of the square, it glittered on the lamp-posts with their golden garlands and crown-topped heads, and on the bright and lacy iron-work of all the balconies of the *hôtel de ville*.

'The square always looks lovely out of season,' said Stewart.

'It's supposed to have crowds,' Harvey said. 'That's what it was evidently made for.'

Two police cars turned into the square and followed them at a crawl.

'The bistro I had in mind is down a narrow street,' said Harvey. 'Let them follow us there. The police have to eat, too.'

But they had a snack-lunch in the police station at Nancy, two policemen having got out of their car and invited Harvey and Stewart to join them.

'What's the matter, now?' Harvey had said when the police approached them.

Stewart said, 'I require an explanation.'

The explanation was not forthcoming until they were taken later in the afternoon to the police headquarters in Epinal.

'A policeman has been killed in Paris.'

NINE

Stewart Cowper, having invoked the British Consul, was allowed to leave the police headquarters the same afternoon that he was detained with Harvey. He refused to answer any questions at all, and his parting advice to Harvey was to do likewise. They were alone in a corridor.

'The least I can do,' said Harvey, 'is to defend Effie.'

'Understandable,' said Stewart, and left to collect his luggage from the château and get a hired car to Paris, and a plane to London.

Harvey got home later that night, having failed to elicit, from the questions he was asked by an officer who had come to Epinal for the purpose – the same old questions – what had exactly happened in Paris that morning, and where Effie was supposed to fit into the murder of the policeman.

'Did you hear about the killing on the radio, M. Gotham?'

'No. I've only just learned of it from you. I wasn't in the château this morning. I was in the cottage with my English lawyer, Stewart Cowper.'

'What did you discuss with your lawyer?'

'The different versions of the *Book of Job* in various recent English translations of the Bible.'

Harvey's interrogator looked at him with real rage. 'One of our policemen has been killed,' he said.

'I'm sorry to hear it,' said Harvey.

They escorted him to pick up his car at Nancy, and followed him home.

Next day the Sunday papers had the same photograph of Effie. There was also a photograph of the policeman, lying in the street beside a police car, covered by a sheet, with some police standing by. Effie had been recognised by eye-witnesses at the scene of the killing, in the eighteenth *arrondissement*. A blonde, longhaired girl with a gun. She was the killer. Her hair was drawn back in a pony-tail at the time of the commando-raid; she was wearing blue jeans and a grey pullover. The Paris security police and the *gendarmerie* were now operating jointly in the search for FLE and its supporters, and especially for the Montmartre killers.

That was the whole of the news, though it filled several pages of the newspapers. The volume of printed words was to be explained by the length of the many paragraphs ending with a question mark, by numerous interpolations about Harvey and his Bible-sect, his wealth, his château, and by details of the unfortunate policeman's family life.

It was not till after lunch on Monday that he was invited to the commissariat at Epinal once more. Two security men from Paris had arrived to interrogate him. Two tall men, one of them in his late forties, robust, with silvering sideburns, the other fair and skinny, not much over thirty, with gilt-rimmed glasses, an intellectual. Harvey thought, if he had seen them together in a restaurant, he would have taken the older man for a business-man, the younger for a priest.

Later, when he chewed over their questions, he was to find it difficult to distinguish between this second interrogation and the first one of a few days ago. This was partly because the older man, who introduced himself by the name of Chatelain, spent a lot of time going over Harvey's previous deposition.

'My house is surrounded by your men,' said Harvey. 'You have your young woman auxiliary in my house. What are you accusing me of?' (Stewart Cowper had advised him: If they question you again, ask them what they have against you, demand to know what is the charge.)

'We are not accusing, Mr Gotham, we are questioning.'

'Questions can sound like accusations.'

'A policeman has been shot dead.'

And their continual probe into why he had settled in France: Harvey recalled later.

'I liked the house,' said Harvey, 'I got my permit to stay in France. I'm regular with the police.'

'Your wife has been in trouble before.'

'I know,' said Harvey.

'Do you love your wife?'

'That's rather a personal question.'

'It was a personal question for the policeman who was killed.'

'I wonder,' said Harvey, conversationally. He was suddenly indignant and determined to be himself, thoughtfully in charge of his reasoning mind, not any sort of victim. 'I wonder . . . I'm not sure that death is personal in the sense of being in love. So far as we know, we don't feel death. We know the fear of death, we know the process of dying. From the outside it looks the most personal of phenomena. But isn't death the very negation of the personal, therefore strictly speaking impersonal? A dead body is the most impersonal thing I can think of. Unless one believes in the continuity of personality in its terrestrially recognisable form, as opposed to life-after-death which is something else. Many disbelieve in life after death, of course, but –'

'*Pardon?* Are you trying to tell me that the death of one of our men is trivial?'

'No. I was reflecting on a remark of yours. Philosophising, I'm afraid. I meant –'

'Kindly don't philosophise,' said Chatelain. 'This is not the place. I want to know where your wife is. Where is Effie?'

'I don't know where Mme Gotham is.'

And again:

'A policeman has been killed by the FLE gang. Two men and a girl, all armed. In the eighteenth *arrondissement* in Paris.'

'I'm sorry that a policeman has been shot,' said Harvey. 'Why in the eighteenth *arrondissement*?'

'That's what we're asking you,' said Chatelain.

'I have no idea. I thought these terrorists acted mainly in popular suburbs.'

'Was your wife ever before in the eighteenth *arrondissement*, do you know?'

'Of course,' said Harvey. 'Who hasn't been in the eighteenth? It's Montmartre.'

'Have you and your wife any friends there?'

'I have friends there and I suppose my wife has, too.'

'Who are your friends?'

'You should know. Your colleagues here went through my address book last week and checked all my friends.'

In the middle of the afternoon Chatelain became more confidential. He began to melt, but only in resemblance to a refrigerator which thaws when the current is turned off. True warmth, thought Harvey at the time, doesn't drip, drip, drip. And later, in his cottage, when he reconstituted the scene he thought: And I ask myself, why was he a refrigerator in the first place?

'Don't think I don't sympathise with you, Mr Gotham,' said Chatelain, on the defreeze. 'Not to know where one's wife is can not be a pleasant experience.'

'Don't think I don't sympathise with you,' said Harvey. 'I know you've lost one of your men. That's serious. And I sympathise, as everyone should, with his family. But you offer no proof that my wife, Effie, is involved. You offer only a photograph that you confiscated from a box on my table.'

'We confiscated . . .?' The man consulted Harvey's thick file which lay on the desk. 'Ah, yes. You are right. The Vosges police obtained that photograph from your house. Witnesses have identified that photograph as the girl in the gang. And look – the identikit, constructed with the help of eye-witnesses to a bank robbery and supermarket bombings, some days prior to our obtaining the photograph. Look at it – isn't that your wife?'

Harvey looked at the drawing.

'When I first saw it in the paper I thought it resembled my wife's sister, Ruth, rather than my wife,' he said. 'Since it couldn't possibly refer to Ruth it seems to me even more unlikely that it refers to Effie.'

'Mme Gotham was arrested in Trieste.'

Harvey was still looking at the identikit. It reminded him, now, of Job's wife in La Tour's painting even though the drawing was full-face and the painting showed a profile.

'She was arrested for shop-lifting,' said Harvey.

'Why did she do that?'

Harvey put down the identikit and gave Chatelain his attention. 'I don't know that she did it. If she did, it does not follow that she bombs supermarkets and kills policemen.'

'If I was in your place,' said Chatelain, 'I would probably speak as you do. But if you were in my place, you would press for some indication, any indication, any guess, as to where she is. I don't blame you for trying to protect your wife. You see,' he said, leaning back in his chair and looking away from Harvey, towards the window, 'a policeman has been shot dead. His wife is in a shop on the outskirts of

Paris where they live, a popular quarter, with her twelve-year-old daughter who has a transistor radio. The lady is waiting her turn at the cash-desk. The child draws her mother's attention to a flash item of news that has interrupted the music. A policeman has been shot and killed in the eighteenth *arrondissement*; the name is being withheld until the family can be informed. The assassins, two men and a girl, have escaped. The terrorist gang FLE have immediately telephoned the press to claim the crime. The main points of the news flash are repeated: a policeman killed, leaving a wife and two daughters aged fourteen and twelve respectively. Now this lady, the policeman's wife, is always worried when she hears of the death or wounding of a policeman. In this case the description is alarmingly close. The eighteenth *arrondissement* where her husband is on duty; the ages of their daughters. She hurries home and finds a police car outside her block of flats. It is indeed her husband who has been killed. Did she deserve this?'

'No,' said Harvey. 'Neither did the policeman. We do not get what we merit. The one thing has nothing to do with the other. Your only course is to prevent it happening again.'

'Depend on us,' said the policeman.

'If I may say so,' said Harvey, 'you are wasting efforts on me which might profitably be directed to that end.'

'Any clue, any suggestion ...' said Chatelain, with great patience. He almost pleaded. 'Are there any houses in Paris that you know of, where they might be found?'

'None,' said Harvey.

'No friends?'

'The few people I know with establishments in Paris are occupied with business affairs in rather a large, multinational way. I don't believe they would like the FLE.'

'Nathan Fox is a good housekeeper?'

'I believe he can be useful in a domestic way.'

'He could be keeping a safe house for the gang in Paris.'

'I don't see him as the gangster type. Honestly, you know, I don't think he's in it.'

'But your wife ... She is different?'

'I didn't say so.'

'And yourself?'

'What about myself? What are you asking?' Harvey said.

'You have a connection with the gang?'

'No.'

'Why did you hang baby clothes on the line outside your cottage as early as last spring?' said Chatelain next.

Harvey was given a break at about seven in the evening. He was accompanied to a café for a meal by the tall young Parisian inspector with metal-rimmed glasses, Louis Pomfret by name.

Pomfret spoke what could be described as 'perfect English', that awful type of perfect English that comes over Radio Moscow. He said something apologetic, in semi-disparagement of the police. Harvey couldn't now remember the exact words. But he recalled Pomfret remarking, too, on the way to the café, 'You must understand that one of their men has been killed.' ('Their' men, not 'our' men, Harvey noted.)

At the café table the policeman told Harvey, 'A Canadian lady arrived in Paris who attempted to reach you on the telephone, and we intercepted her. She's your aunt. We've escorted her safely to the château where she desired to go.'

'God, it's my Aunt Pet. Don't give her any trouble.'

'But, no.'

If you think you'll make me grateful for all this courtesy, thought Harvey, you are mistaken. He said, 'I should hope not.'

The policeman said, 'I'm afraid the food here is ghastly.'

'They make a good omelette. I've eaten here before,' said Harvey.

Ham omelettes and wine from the Vosges.

'It's unfortunate for you, Gotham,' said Pomfret, 'but you appreciate, I hope, our position.'

'You want to capture these members of the FLE before they do more damage.'

'Yes, we do. And of course, we will. Now that a member of the police has been killed ... You appreciate, his wife was shopping in a supermarket with her son of twelve, who had a transistor radio. She was taking no interest in the programme. At one point the boy said –'

'Are you sure it was a boy?' Harvey said.

'It was a girl. How do you know?'

'The scene has been described to me by your colleague.'

'You're very observant,' Pomfret smiled, quite nicely.

'Well, of course I'm observant in a case like this,' said Harvey. 'I'm hanging on your lips.'

'Why?'

'To hear if you have any evidence that my wife is involved with a terrorist gang.'

'We have a warrant for her arrest,' said Pomfret.

'That's not evidence.'

'I know. But we don't put out warrants without reason. Your wife was arrested in Trieste. She was definitely lodging there with a group which has since been identified as members of the FLE gang. When the police photograph from the incident at Trieste noticeably resembled the photograph we obtained from you, and also resembled the identikit made up from eyewitnesses of the bombings and incursions here in France, we call that sufficient evidence to regard your wife as a suspect.'

'I would like to see the photograph from Trieste,' said Harvey. 'Why haven't I been shown it?'

'You are not investigating the case. We are.'

'But I'm interested in her whereabouts,' Harvey said. 'What does this photograph from the police at Trieste look like?'

'It's an ordinary routine photograph that's taken of all people under arrest. Plain and flat, like a passport photograph. It looks like your wife. It's of no account to you.'

'Why wasn't I shown it, told about it?'

'I think you can see it if you want.'

'Your people at the commissariat evidently don't believe me when I say I don't know where Effie is.'

'Well, I suppose that's why you've been questioned. You've never been officially convoked.'

'The English word is summoned.'

'Summoned; I apologise.'

'Lousy wine,' said Harvey.

'It's what you get in a cheap café,' said Pomfret.

'They had better when I ate here before,' said Harvey. 'Look, all you've got to go on is an identikit made in France which resembles two photographs of my wife.'

'And the address she was residing at in Trieste. That's most important of all.'

'She is inclined to take up with unconventional people,' said Harvey.

'Evidently, since she married yourself.'

'Do you know,' said Harvey, 'I'm very conventional, believe it or not.'

'I don't believe it, of course.'

'Why?'

'Your mode of life in France. For an affluent man to establish himself in a cottage and study the *Book of Job* is not conventional.'

'Job was an affluent man. He sat among the ashes. Some say, on a dung-heap outside the city. He was very conventional. So much so that God was bored with him.'

'Is that in the scriptures?' said the policeman.

'No, it's in my mind.'

'You've actually written it down. They took photocopies of some of your pages.'

'I object to that. They had no right.'

'It's possible they had no right. Why have you never brought in a lawyer?'

'What for?'

'Exactly. But it would be the conventional thing to do.'

'I hope you're impressed,' said Harvey. 'You see, if I were writing a film-script or a pornographic novel, you wouldn't find it so strange that I came to an out-of-the-way place to work. It's the subject of *Job* you can't understand my giving my time to.'

'More or less. I think, perhaps, you've been trying to put yourself in the conditions of Job. Is that right?'

'One can't write an essay on *Job* sitting round a swimming pool in a ten-acre park, with all that goes with it. But I could just as well study the subject in a quiet apartment in some city. I came to these parts because I happened to find the cottage. There is a painting of Job and his wife here in Epinal which attracts me. You should see it.'

'I should,' said Pomfret. 'I shall.'

'Job's wife looks remarkably like my wife. It was painted about the middle of the seventeenth century so it can't be Effie, if that's what you're thinking.'

'We were discussing Job, not Mme Effie.'

'Then what am I doing here,' said Harvey, 'being interrogated by you?'

Pomfret remained good-natured. He said something about their having a supper and a talk, not an interrogation. 'I am genuinely interested,' said Pomfret, 'speaking for myself. You are isolated like Job. But you haven't lost your goods and fortune. Any possibility of that?'

'No, but I'm as good as without them here. More so before I took the château.'

'Oh, I was forgetting the château. I've only seen your cottage, from the outside. It looks impoverished enough.'

'It was the boils that worried Job.'

'*Pardon*? The boils?'

'Boils. Skin-sores. He was covered with them.'

'Ah, yes, that is correct. Don't you, like Job, feel the need of friends to talk to in your present troubles?'

'One thing that the *Book of Job* teaches us,' Harvey said, 'is the futility of friendship in times of trouble. That is perhaps not a reflection on friends but on friendship. Friends mean well, or make as if they do. But friendship itself is made for happiness, not trouble.'

'Is your aunt a friend?'

'My Aunt Pet, who you tell me has arrived at the château? – I suppose she thinks of herself as a friend. She's a bore, coming at this moment. At any moment. – You don't suppose this is anything but an interrogation, do you? Any more questions?'

'Would you like some cheese?'

Harvey couldn't help liking the young man, within his reservation that the police had, no doubt, sent him precisely to be liked. Soften me up as much as you please, Harvey thought, but it doesn't help you; it only serves to release my own love, my nostalgia, for Effie. And he opened his mouth and spoke in praise of Effie, almost to his own surprise describing how she was merry at parties, explaining that she danced well and was fun to talk to. 'She's an interesting woman, Effie.'

'Intellectual?'

'We are all more intellectual than we know. She doesn't think of herself as an intellectual type. But under a certain stimulus, she is.'

They were walking back to the commissariat. Harvey had half a mind to go home and let them come for him with an official summons, if they wanted. But it was only half a mind; the other half, mesmerised and now worked up about Effie, propelled him on to the police station with his companion.

'She tried some drugs, I suppose,' said Pomfret.

'You shouldn't suppose so,' said Harvey. 'Effie is entirely anti-drug. It would be extraordinary if she's taken to drugs in the last two years.'

'You must recognise,' said Pomfret, 'that she is lively and vital enough to be a member of a terrorist gang.'

'Lively and vital,' said Harvey, 'lively and vital – one of those words is redundant.'

Pomfret laughed.

'However,' said Harvey, 'it's out of the question that she could be a terrorist.' He had a suspicion that Pomfret was now genuinely fascinated by the images of Effie that Harvey was able to produce, Effie at a party, Effie an interesting talker, a rich man's wife; his imagination was involved, beyond his investigator's role, in the rich man's mechanism, his free intellectual will, his casual purchase of the château; Pomfret was fascinated by both Effie and Harvey.

'A terrorist,' said Pomfret. 'She obviously has an idealistic motive. Why did you leave her?'

The thought that Effie was a member of a terrorist band now excited Harvey sexually.

'Terrorist is out of the question,' he said. 'I left her because she seemed to want to go her own way. The marriage broke up, that's all. Marriages do.'

'But on a hypothesis, how would you feel if you knew she was a terrorist?'

Harvey thought, I would feel I had failed her in action. Which I have. He said, 'I can't imagine.'

At the police station Pomfret left him in a waiting-room. Patiently sitting there was a lean-faced man with a dark skin gone to a muddy grey, bright small eyes and fine features. He seemed to be a Balkan. What was he doing there? It was after nine in the evening. Surely it was in the morning that he would come about his papers. Perhaps he had been picked up without papers? What sort of work was he doing in Epinal? He wore a black suit, shiny with wear; a very white shirt open at the neck; brown, very pointed shoes; and he had with him a brown cardboard brief-case with tinny locks, materials such as Harvey had only seen before in the form of a suitcase on a train in a remote part of Sicily. The object in Sicily had been old and battered, but his present companion's brief-case had a new-bought look. It was not the first time Harvey had noticed that poor people from Eastern Europe resembled, not only in their possessions and clothes, but in their build and expression, the poor of Western Europe years ago. Who he was, where he came from and why, Harvey was never to know, for he was just about to say something when the door opened and a policeman in uniform beckoned the man away. He followed with nervous alacrity and the door closed again on Harvey. Patience, pallor and deep anxiety: there goes suffering, Harvey reflected. And I found him interesting. Is it only by recognising how flat would be the world without the sufferings of others that we know how desperately becalmed our own lives would be without suffering? Do I suffer on Effie's account? Yes, and perhaps I can live by that experience. We all need something to suffer about. But *Job*, my work on *Job*, all interrupted and neglected, probed into and interfered with: that is experience, too; real experience, not vicarious, as is often assumed. To study, to think, is to live and suffer painfully.

Did Effie really kill or help to kill the policeman in Paris whose wife was shopping in the suburbs at the time? Since he had left the police station on Saturday night he had recurrently put himself to imagine the scene. An irruption at a department store. The police arrive. Shots fired. Effie and her men friends fighting their way back to their waiting car (with Nathan at the wheel?). Effie, lithe and long-legged, a most desirable girl, and quick-witted, unmoved, aiming her gun with a good aim. She pulls the trigger and is away all in one moment. Yes, he could imagine Effie in the scene; she was capable of that, capable of anything.

'Will you come this way, please, Mr Gotham?'

There was a stack of files on Chatelain's desk.

The rest of that night Harvey remembered as a sort of roll-call of his visitors over the past months; it seemed to him like the effect of an old-fashioned village policeman going his rounds, shining his torch on name-plates and door-knobs; one by one, each name surrounded by a nimbus of agitated suspicion as his friends' simple actions, their ordinary comings and goings came up for questioning. It was strange how guilty everything looked under the policeman's torch, how it sounded here in the police headquarters. Chatelain asked Harvey if he would object to the conversation being tape-recorded.

'No, it's a good thing. I was going to suggest it. Then you won't have to waste time asking me the same questions over and over again.'

Chatelain smiled sadly. 'We have to check.' Then he selected one of the files and placed it before him.

'Edward Jansen,' he said, 'came to visit you.'

'Yes, he's the husband of my wife's sister, Ruth, now separated. He came to see me last April.'

Chatelain gave a weak smile and said, 'Your neighbours seem to remember a suspicious-looking character who visited you last spring.'

'Yes, I daresay that was Edward Jansen. He has red hair down to his shoulders. Or had. He's an actor and he's now famous. He is my brother-in-law through his marriage to my wife's sister, but he's now separated from his wife. A lot can happen in less than a year.'

'He asked you why there were baby clothes on the line?'

'I don't remember if he actually asked, but he made some remark about them because I answered, as you know, "The police won't shoot if there's a baby in the house."'

'Why did you say that?'

'I can't answer precisely. I didn't foresee any involvement with the police, or I wouldn't have said it.'

'It was a joke?'

'That sort of thing.'

'Do you still hear from Edward Jansen?' Chatelain opened one of the files.

'I haven't heard for some time.'

Chatelain flicked through the file.

'There's a letter from him waiting for you at your house.'

'Thanks. I expect you can tell me the contents.'

'No, we can't.'

'That could be taken in two senses,' Harvey said.

'Well, you can take it in one sense: we haven't opened it. The name and address of the sender is on the outside of the envelope. As it happens, we know quite a lot about Mr Jansen, and he doesn't interest us at the moment. He's also been questioned.' Chatelain closed the file, evidently Edward's dossier; it was rather thin compared with some of the others. Chatelain took up another and opened it, as if starting on a new subject. Then, 'What did you discuss with Edward Jansen last April?'

'I can't recall. I know his wife, Ruth, was anxious for me to make a settlement on her sister and facilitate a divorce. I am sure we didn't discuss that very much, for I had no intention of co-operating with my wife to that end. I know we discussed the *Book of Job*.'

'And about Ruth Jansen. Did you invite her to stay?'

'No, she came unexpectedly with her sister's baby, about the end of August.'

'Why did she do that?'

'August is a very boring month for everybody.'

'You really must be serious, Mr Gotham.'

'It's as good a reason as any. I can't analyse the motives of a woman who probably can't analyse them herself.'

Chatelain tapped the file. 'She says here that she brought the baby, hoping to win you over to her view that the child would benefit if you made over a substantial sum of money to its mother, that is, to your wife Effie.'

'If that's what Ruth says, I suppose it is so.'

'She greatly resembles your wife.'

'Yes, feature by feature. But of course, to anyone who knows them they are very different. Effie is more beautiful, really. Less practical than Ruth.'

Pomfret came in and sat down. He was less free of manner in the presence of the other officer. He peered at the tape-recording machine as if to make sure everything was all right with it.

'So you had a relation with Mrs Jansen.'

'Yes.'

'Your sister-in-law and wife of your friend.'

'Yes, I grew fond of Ruth. I was particularly taken by the baby. Of course, by this time Ruth and Edward had parted.'

'Things happen fast in your set.'

'Well, I suppose the parting had been working up for a long time. Is there any point in all these questions?'

'Not much. We want to check, you see, against the statements made in England by the people concerned. Did Ruth seem surprised when she heard that Effie was involved in the terrorist attacks?'

What were these statements of Ruth, of Edward, of others? Harvey said firmly, even as he felt his way, 'She was very much afraid of the police, coming into our lives as they did. It was quite unforeseen. She could no more blame her sister for it than she could blame her for an earthquake. I feel the same, myself.'

'She did not defend her sister?'

'She had no need to defend Effie to me. It isn't I who accuse Effie of being a terrorist. I say there is a mistake.'

'Now, Nathan Fox,' said the officer, reaching for a new file. 'What do you know about him?'

'Not very much. He made himself useful to Ruth and Edward when they were living in London. He's a graduate but can't find a job. He came to my house, here, to visit Ruth and the baby for Christmas.'

'He is a friend of your wife?'

'Well, he knows her, of course.'

'He is a weak character?'

'No, in fact I think it shows a certain strength of character in him to have turned his hand to domestic work since he can't find anything else to do. He graduated at an English university, I have no idea which one.'

'What about his friends? Girls or boys?'

'I know nothing about that.'

'Why did he disappear from your house?'

'I don't know. He just left. Young people do.'

'He had a telephone call and left overnight without saying good-bye.'

'I believe so,' said Harvey.

'He said the telephone call was from London. It wasn't.'

'So I understand. I was working in my cottage that night. You must understand I'm very occupied, and all these questions of yours, and all these files, have nothing whatever to do with me. I've agreed to come here simply to help you to eliminate a suspect, my wife.'

'But you have no idea why he should say he got a phone call from London, when he didn't. It must have been an internal call.'

'Perhaps some girl of his turned up in France; maybe in Paris, and called him. And he skipped.'

'Some girl or some boy?'

'Your question is beyond me. If I hear from him I'll ask him to get in touch with you. Perhaps he's come down with influenza.'

Pomfret now spoke: 'Why do you suggest that?' He was decidedly less friendly in French.

'Because people do come down with 'flu. They stay in bed. This time of year is rather the time for colds. Perhaps he's gone back to England to start a window-cleaning business. I believe I heard him speculating on the idea. There's always a need for window-cleaners.'

'Anything else?' said Chatelain.

'The possibilities of Nathan Fox's whereabouts are such that I could go on all night and still not exhaust them.'

'Would he go to join your wife if she asked him?'

Harvey considered. 'That's also a possibility; one among millions.'

'What are his political views?'

'I don't know. He never spoke of politics to me.'

'Did he ask you for money?'

'After Christmas he asked me for his pay. I told him that Ruth had the housekeeping money, and kept the accounts.'

'Then Mrs Jansen did give him money?'

'I only suppose,' said Harvey, 'that she paid him for his help. I really don't know.'

'Do you think Ruth Jansen is a calculating woman? She left her husband, came to join you with the baby, induced you to buy the château –'

'She wanted the château because of a tree outside the house with a certain bird – how do you say "woodpecker"?' – Harvey put the word to Pomfret in English.

Pomfret didn't recognise the word.

'It makes a sound like a typewriter. It pecks at the wood of the tree.'

'*Pic*', said Pomfret.

'Well, she liked the sound of it,' said Harvey.

'Are you saying that is why you bought the château?'

'I'd already thought of buying it. And now, with Ruth and the baby, it was convenient to me.'

'Ernest L. Howe,' said Chatelain. 'He came to see you, didn't he?'

'Yes, some time last autumn. He came to see his baby daughter. He wanted Ruth to go back to London with the baby and live with him. Which, in fact, she has now done. You see, he doesn't think of what's best for the child; he thinks of what's most pleasant for himself. To console his hurt pride that Effie walked out on him – and I don't blame her – he's persuaded her sister to go and live with him, using the child as an excuse. It's contemptible.'

Harvey was aware that the two men were conscious of a change in his tone, that he was loosening up. Harvey didn't care. He had nothing, Effie had nothing, to lose by his expressing himself freely on the subject of Ernie Howe. He was tired of being what was so often called civilised about his wife's lover. He was tired of the questioning. He was tired, anyway, and wanted a night's sleep. He deliberately gave himself and his questioners the luxury of his true opinion of Ernie.

'Would you care for a drink?' said Pomfret.

'A double scotch,' said Harvey, 'with a glass of water on the side. I like to put in the water myself.'

Chatelain said he would have the same. Pomfret disappeared to place the orders. Chatelain put a new tape in the recording machine while Harvey talked on about Ernie.

'He sounds like a shit,' said Chatelain. 'Let me tell you in confidence that even from his statement which I have in front of me here, he sounds like a shit. He stated categorically that he wasn't at all surprised that Effie was a terrorist, and further, he says that you know it.'

'He's furious that Effie left him,' Harvey said. 'He thought she would get a huge alimony from me to keep him in comfort for the rest of his life. I'm sure she came to realise what he was up to, and that's why she left him.'

Pomfret returned, followed by a policeman with a tray of drinks. It was quite a party. Harvey felt easier.

'I'm convinced of it,' he said, and for the benefit of Pomfret repeated his last remarks.

'It's altogether in keeping with the character of the man, but he was useful,' said Chatelain. He said to Pomfret, 'I have revealed to M. Gotham what Ernest Howe stated about Effie Gotham.'

And what Chatelain claimed Ernie had said was evidently true, for Pomfret quite spontaneously confirmed it: 'Yes, I'm afraid he was hardly gallant about her. He is convinced she's a terrorist and that you know it.'

'When did you get these statements?' said Harvey.

'Recently. Ernest Howe's came through from Scotland Yard on Sunday.'

'You've got Scotland Yard to help you?'

'To a certain degree,' said Chatelain, waving his right hand lightly, palm-upward.

Was he softening up these men, Harvey wondered, or they him?

'It would interest me,' said Harvey, 'to see the photograph of my wife that was taken of her by the police in Trieste, when she was arrested for shoplifting.'

'You may see it, of course. But it isn't being handed out to the newspapers. It has been useful for close identification purposes by eye-witnesses. You will see it looks too rigid – like all police photos – to be shown to the public as the girl we are actually looking for. She is quite different in terrorist action, as they all are.' He turned to Pomfret. 'Can you find the Trieste photograph?'

Pomfret found it. The girl in the photo was looking straight ahead of her, head uplifted, eyes staring, against a plain light background. Her hair was darker than Effie's in real life, but that might be an effect of the flash-photography. It looked like Effie, under strain, rather frightened.

'It looks like a young shop-lifter who's been hauled in by the police,' said Harvey.

'Do you mean to say it isn't your wife?' said Pomfret. 'She gave her name as Signora Effie Gotham. Isn't it her?'

'I think it is my wife. I don't think it looks like the picture of a hardened killer.'

'A lot can happen in a few months,' said Chatelain. 'A lot has happened to that young woman. Her battle-name isn't Effie Gotham, naturally. It is Marion.'

In the meantime Pomfret had extracted from his papers the photograph of Effie that the police had found in Harvey's cottage. 'You should have this back,' said Pomfret. 'It is yours.'

'Thank you. You've made copies. I see this photo in every newspaper I open.'

'It is the girl we are looking for. There is movement and life in that photograph.'

'I think you should publish the police-photo from Trieste,' said

Harvey. 'To be perfectly fair. They are both Effie. The public might not then be prejudiced.'

'Oh, the public is not so subtle as to make these nice distinctions.'

'Then why don't you publish the Trieste photograph?'

'It is the property of the Italian police. For them, the girl in their photograph is a kleptomaniac, and in need of treatment. They had put the treatment in hand, but she skipped off, as they all do.'

'I thought she went to prison.'

'She had a two weeks' sentence. That is a different thing from imprisonment. It was not her first offence, but she was no more than three days in prison. She agreed to treatment. She was supposed to register with the police every day, but of course –'

'Look,' said Harvey. 'My wife is suffering from an illness, klepto-mania. She needs treatment. You are hounding her down as a terrorist, which she isn't. Effie couldn't kill anyone.'

'Why did you leave her on the motorway in Italy?' said Pomfret. 'Was it because she stole a bar of chocolate? If so, why didn't you stand by her and see that she had treatment?'

'She has probably told Ernie Howe that story, and he has told you.'

'Correct,' said Chatelain.

'Well, if I'd given weight to a bar of chocolate, I would have stood by her. I didn't leave her over a bar of chocolate. To be precise, it was two bars.'

'Why did you leave her?'

'Private reasons. Incompatibility, mounting up. A bar of chocolate isn't a dead policeman.'

'We know,' said Chatelain. 'We know that only too well. We are not such fools as to confuse a shop-lifter with a dangerous assassin.'

'But why,' said Pomfret, 'did you leave her? We think we know the answer. She isn't a kleptomaniac at all. Not at all. She stole, made the easy gesture, on ideological grounds. They call it proletarian reappro-priation. You must already have perceived the incipient terrorist in your wife; and on this silly occasion, suddenly, you couldn't take it. Things often happen that way.'

'Let me tell you something,' said Harvey. 'If I'd thought she was a terrorist in the making, I would not have left her. I would have tried to reason her out of it. I know Effie well. She isn't a terrorist. She's a simple shop-lifter. Many rich girls are.'

'Is she rich?'

'She was when she was with me.'

'But afterwards?'

'Look, if she needed money, she could have sold her jewellery. But she hasn't. It's still in the bank. My lawyer told me.'

'Didn't you say – I think you said –' said Pomfret, 'that you only discussed the recent English translations of the Bible with your lawyer?'

'I said that was what we were discussing on Saturday morning, instead of listening to the news on the radio. I haven't said that I discussed nothing else with him. You see, I, too, am anxious to trace the whereabouts of my wife. She isn't your killer in Paris. She's somewhere else.'

'Now, let us consider,' said Chatelain, 'her relations with Ernest Howe. He has stated that he knows her character. She is the very person, according to him, who would take up with a terrorist group. The Irish terrorists had her sympathy. She was writing a treatise on child-labour in England in the nineteenth century. She often –'

'Oh, I know all that,' Harvey said. 'The only difficulty is that none of her sympathies makes her a terrorist. She shares these sympathies with thousands of people, especially young people. The young are very generous. Effie is generous in spirit, I can say that.'

'But she has been trying to get money out of you, a divorce settlement.'

'That's understandable. I'm rich. But quite honestly, I hoped she'd come back. That's why I refused the money. She could have got it through the courts, but I thought she'd get tired of fighting for it.'

'What do you mean, "come back"?' said Pomfret. 'It was you who left her.'

'In cases of desertion in marriage, it is always difficult to say who is the deserter. There is a kind of constructional desertion, you know. Technically, yes, I left her. She also had left me. These things have to be understood.'

'I understand,' said Chatelain. 'Yes, I understand your point.'

Pomfret said, 'But where is she getting the money from?'

'I suppose that the girl who calls herself Marion has funds from the terrorist supporters,' said Harvey. 'They are never short of funds. It has nothing whatsoever to do with my wife, Effie.'

'Well, let us get back to your visitors, M. Gotham.' said Chatelain. 'Has there been anyone else besides those we have mentioned?'

'The police, and Anne-Marie.'

'No-one else?'

'Clara,' said Harvey. 'Don't you want to hear about Clara?'

'Clara?'

'Clara is the niece of my wife's sister.'

Chatelain was getting tired. He took a long moment to work out Harvey's representation, and was still puzzling while Pomfret was smiling. 'The niece?' said Chatelain. 'Whose daughter is she?'

'My wife's.'

'You mean the infant?'

'That's right. Don't you have a dossier on Clara?' Harvey asked the security men.

'M. Gotham, this is serious. A man has been fatally shot. More deaths may follow. We are looking for a political fanatic, not a bar of chocolate. Can you not give us an idea, a single clue, as to where your wife can be hiding? It might help us to eliminate her from the enquiry.

'I wish I could find her, myself.'

TEN

'I brought you some English mustard,' said Auntie Pet. 'They say English mustard in France is a prohibitive price even compared to Canadian prices.'

Harvey had slept badly after his late return from the session with the security police at Epinal. He hadn't shaved.

'You got home late,' said Auntie Pet. Already, the château was her domain.

'I was with the police,' said Harvey.

'What were you doing with them?' she said.

'Oh, talking and drinking.'

'I shouldn't hob-nob too close with them,' she said, 'if I were you. Keep them in their place. I must say those plain-clothes officers who escorted me here were very polite. They were useful with the suitcases, too. But I kept them in their place.'

'I should imagine you would,' Harvey said.

They were having breakfast in the living room which the presence of Auntie Pet somehow caused to look very shabby. She was large-built, with a masculine, military face; grey eyes which generally conveyed a warning; heavy, black brows and a head of strong, wavy, grey hair. She was sewing a piece of stuff; some kind of embroidery.

'When I arrived,' she said, 'there was a crowd of reporters and photographers on the road outside the house. But the police soon got rid of them with their cars and motor-cycles. No problem.' Her eyes rose from her sewing. 'Harvey, you have let your house go into a state of dilapidation.'

'I haven't had time to put it straight yet. Only moved in a few months ago. It takes time.'

'I think it absurd that your maid brings her baby's washing to do in your house every day. Hasn't she got a house of her own? Why are you taking a glass of scotch with your breakfast?'

'I need it after spending half the night with the police.'

'They were all right to me. I was glad of the ride. The prohibitive price of fares,' said his aunt, as one multimillionaire to another.

'I can well believe they were civil to you. I should hope they would be. Why shouldn't they be?' He looked at her solid, irreproachable shape, her admonishing face; she appeared to be quite sane; he wondered if indeed the police had been half-afraid of her. Anne-Marie was already tip-toeing around in a decidedly subdued way. Harvey added, 'You haven't committed any offence.'

'Have you?' she said.

'No.'

'Well, I should have said you have. It's certainly an offence if you're going to attack the Bible in a foreign country.'

'The French police don't care a damn about the Bible. It's Effie. One of their policemen has been shot, killed, and they think she's involved.'

'Oh, no, not Effie,' said Auntie Pet. 'Effie is your wife. She is a Gotham as of now, unfortunately, whatever she was before. No Gotham would stoop to harm a policeman. The police have always respected and looked up to us. And you're letting yourself go, Harvey. Just because your wife is not at home, there isn't any reason to neglect to shave.'

Harvey escaped to go and shave, leaving Auntie Pet to quarrel with Anne-Marie, and walk about the grounds giving orders to the plain-clothes police, whom she took for gardeners and woodsmen, for the better upkeep of shrubs and flower-beds, for the cultivation of vegetables and the felling of over-shady trees. From his bathroom window Harvey saw her finding cigarette-ends on the gravel path, and chiding the men in full spate of Canadian French. Prompted by Anne-Marie, they took it fairly well; and it did actually seem to Harvey, as he found it did to Anne-Marie, that they were genuinely frightened of her, armed though they were to the full capacity of their leather jackets.

When Harvey came down he found in the living room a batch of press-cuttings which he at first presumed to be about himself and Effie; Stewart Cowper had left them behind. But a glance at the top of the bundle showed him Edward's face, now beardless. The cuttings were, in reality, all reviews of the play Edward had made such an amazing success in; they were apparently full of lavish praise of the new star, but Harvey put them aside for a more serene moment. Amongst some new mail, a letter from Edward was lying on the table. Edward's name and address was written on the back of the envelope. Maybe the police hadn't read it; maybe they had. Harvey left this aside, too, as Auntie Pet came back into the room.

'I have something to tell you,' she said. 'I have come all the way from Toronto to say it. I know it is going to hurt you considerably. After all, you are a Gotham, and must feel things of a personal nature, a question of your honour. But say it I had to. Not on the telephone. Not through the mail. But face to face. Your wife, Effie, is consorting with a young man in a commune, as they call it, in the mountains of California, east of Santa Barbara if I recall rightly. I saw her myself on the television in a documentary news-supplement about communes. They live by Nature and they have a sort of religion. They sleep in bags. They –'

'When did you see this?'

'Last week.'

'Was it an old film – was it live?'

'I guess it was live. As I say, it was a news item, about a drug-investigation by the police, and they had taken this commune by surprise at dawn. The young people were all scrambling out of their bags and into their clothes. And I am truly sorry to tell you this, Harvey, but I hope you'll take it like a man: Effie was sleeping in a double bag, a double sleeping-bag, do you understand; there was a young man right in there with her, and they got out of that bag sheer, stark naked.'

'Are you sure it was Effie? Are you sure?'

'I remember her well from the time she came when you were engaged, and then from the wedding, and I have the wedding-photo of you both on my piano, right there in the sitting room where I go every day. I ought to recognise Effie when I see her. She was naked, with her hair hanging down her shoulders, and laughing, and then pulling her consort after her out of the extramarital bag, without shame; I am truly sorry, Harvey, to be the bearer of this news. To a Gotham. Better she killed a policeman. It's a question of honour. Mind you, I always suspected she was unvirtuous.'

'You always suspected?'

'Yes, I did. All along I feared the worst.'

'Are you sure,' said Harvey, very carefully, 'that perhaps your sus-picions have not disposed you to imagine that the girl you saw on the television was Effie, when in fact it was someone who resembled her?'

'Effie is not like anybody else,' said Auntie Pet.

'She resembles her sister,' said Harvey.

'How could it be Ruth? Ruth is not missing, is she?'

'No. I don't say it could have been Ruth. I only say that there is one case where Effie looks like somebody else. I know of another.'

'Who is that?'

'Job's wife, in a painting.'

'Job's wife it could not be. She was a foolish woman but she never committed adultery in a sack. You should read your Bible, Harvey, before you presume to criticise it.'

Harvey poured himself a drink.

'Don't get over-excited,' said Auntie Pet. 'I know this is a blow.'

'Look, Auntie Pet, I must know the details, every detail. I have to know if you're absolutely sure, if you're right. Would you mind describing the man to me?'

'I hope you're not going to cite him as co-respondent, Harvey. You would have to re-play that news item in court. It would bring ridicule on our heads. You've had enough publicity.'

'Just describe the young man she was with, please.'

'Well, this seems like an interrogation. The young man looked like a Latin-Mediterranean type, maybe Spanish, young, thin. I didn't look closely, I was looking at Effie. She had nothing on.'

Auntie Pet had not improved with the years. Harvey had never known her so awful. He thought, She is mistaken but at least, sincere. He said, 'I must tell the police.'

'Why?' said Auntie Pet.

'For many reasons. Not the least of which is that, if Effie and her friend are in California and decide to leave, – they might come here, for instance, here to France, or here to see me; if they do that, they could be shot at sight.'

'That's out of the question. Effie wouldn't dare come to your house, now. But if you tell the police how I saw them, the story will go round the world. And the television picture, too. Think of your name.'

*

Harvey got through to the commissariat. 'My wife has been seen in California within the last few days.'

'Who saw her?'

'My aunt.'

'Ah, the aunt,' said the police inspector.

'She says she saw her in a youth-documentary on the television.'

'We had better come and talk to your aunt.'

'It isn't necessary.'

'Do you believe your aunt?'

'She's truthful. But she might be mistaken. That's all I have to say.'

'I would like to have a word with her.'

'All right,' said Harvey. 'You'll find her alone because I'm going down to my cottage to work.'

He then rang Stewart Cowper in London but found he was out of the office. 'Tell him,' said Harvey to the secretary, 'that I might want him to go to the United States for me.'

He had been in his cottage half-an-hour when he saw the police car going up the drive, with the two security men from Paris. He wished them well of Auntie Pet.

Harvey had brought his mail with him, including Edward's letter.

In his old environment, almost smiling to himself with relief at being alone again, he sat for a while sorting out his thoughts.

Effie and Nathan in a commune in California: it was quite likely. Effie and Nathan in Paris, part of a band of killers: not unlikely.

He began to feel uneasy about Auntie Pet, up there at the house, being questioned by the security men. He was just getting ready to go and join them, and give his aunt a show of support, when the police car with the two men inside returned, passed his cottage, and made off. Either they had made short work of Auntie Pet or she of them. Harvey suspected the latter. Auntie Pet had been separated from Uncle Joe for as long as Harvey could remember. They lived in separate houses. There was no question of a divorce, no third parties, no lovers and mistresses. 'I had to make a separate arrangement,' Uncle Joe had once confided to Harvey. 'She would have made short work of me if I'd stayed.'

Harvey himself had never felt in danger of being made short work of by his aunt. Probably there was something in his nature, a self-sufficiency, that matched her own.

He wondered how much to believe of what she had told him. He began to wonder such things as why a news supplement from California should be shown on a main network in Toronto. Auntie Pet wasn't likely to tune in to anything but a main network. He wondered why she had felt it necessary to come to France to give him these details; and at the same time he knew that it was quite reasonable that she should do so. It would certainly be, for her, a frightful tale to tell a husband and a Gotham.

And to his own amazement, Harvey found himself half-hoping she was wrong. Only half-hoping; but still, the thought was there: he would rather think of Effie as a terrorist than laughing with Nathan, naked, in a mountain commune in California. But really, thought Harvey, I don't wish it so. In fact, I wish she wasn't a terrorist; and in fact, I think she is. Pomfret was right; I saw the terrorist in Effie long ago. Even if she isn't the killer they're looking for, but the girl in California, I won't live with her again.

He decided to get hold of Stewart Cowper later in the day, when he was expected back at his office. Stewart would go to California and arrange to see a re-play of the programme Auntie Pet had seen. Stewart would find out if Effie was there. Or he would go himself; that would be the decent thing to do. But he knew he wouldn't go himself. He was waiting here for news of Effie. He was writing his monograph on the *Book of Job* as he had set himself to do. ('Live? – Our servants can do it for us.') He wouldn't even fight with Ernie Howe himself; if necessary, Stewart would do it for him.

He opened Edward's letter.

Dear Harvey,

The crocs at the zoo have rather lack-lustre eyes, as can be expected. Perhaps in their native habitat their eyes are 'like the eyelids of the dawn' as we find in *Job*, especially when they're gleefully devouring their prey. Yes, their eyes are vertical. Perhaps Leviathan is not the crocodile. The zoo bores me to a degree.

I wish you could come over and see the play before it closes. My life has changed, of course. I don't feel that my acting in this play, which has brought me so much success, is really any different from my previous performances in films, plays, tv. I think the psychic forces, the influences around me have changed. Ruth wasn't good for me. She made me into a sort of desert. And now I'm fertile. (We are the best of friends, still. I saw her the other day. I don't think she's happy with Ernie Howe. She's only sticking to him because of Clara, and as you know she's pregnant herself at long last. She claims, and of course I believe her, that she's preg by you. – Congratulations!) Looking back – and it seems a long time to look back although it's not even a year – I feel my past life had a drabness that I wasn't fully aware of at the time. It lies like a shabby old pair of trousers that I've let fall on the bedroom floor: I'll never want to wear *those* again. It isn't only the success and the money, although I don't overlook that aspect of things – I don't want to crow about them, esp to you. It's simply a new sense of possibility. One thing I do know is when I'm playing a part and when I'm not. I used to 'play a part' most of the time. Now I only do it when I'm onstage. You should come over and see the play. But I suspect that possibly you can't. The police quizzed me and I made a statement. What could I say? Very little. Fortunately the public is sympathetic towards my position – brother-in-law, virtually *ex*-brother-in-law of a terrorist. (Our divorce is going through.) It isn't a close tie.

I've almost rung you up on several occasions. But then I supposed your phone was bugged, and felt it better not to get involved. Reading the papers – of course you can't trust them – it seems you're standing by Effie, denying that she's the wanted girl, and so on. Now, comes this ghastly murder of the policeman. I admire your stance, but do you feel it morally necessary to protect her? I must say, I find it odd that having left her as you did, you now refuse to see (or admit?) how she developed. To me (and Ruth agrees with me) she has always had this criminal streak in her. I know she is a beautiful girl, but there are plenty of lovely girls like Effie. You can't have been so desperately in love with her. Quite honestly, when you were together, I never thought you were really crazy about her. I don't like giving advice, but you should realise that something tragic has happened to Effie. She is a fanatic – she always had that violent, reckless streak. There is nothing, Harvey, nothing at all that anyone can do for her. You shouldn't try. Conclude your work on *Job*, then get away and start a new life. If your new château is as romantic and grand as Ruth says it is, I'd love to see it. I'll come, if you're still there, when the play closes. It'll be good to see you.

Affectionately,
Edward

Harvey's reply:

Dear Edward,

That was good of you to go to the zoo for me. You say the zoo bores you to a degree. What degree?

I congratulate you on your success. It was always in you, so I'm not surprised. No, I can't leave here at present. Ruth would be here still if it were not that the place is bristling with the police – no place for Clara whom I miss terribly.

As to your advice, do you remember how Prometheus says, 'It's easy for the one who keeps his foot on the outside of suffering to counsel and preach to the one who's inside'? I will just say that I'm not taking up Effie's defence. I hold that there's no proof that the girl whom the police are looking for is Effie. A few people have 'identified' her from a photograph.

Auntie Pet has arrived from Toronto wearing those remarkable clothes that so curiously bely her puritanical principles. This morning she was wearing what appeared to be the wallpaper. Incidentally, she recognised Effie in a recent television documentary about a police-raid on a mountain commune in California. She was with a man whose description could fit Nathan Fox.

I've been interrogated several times. What they can't make out is why I'm here in France, isolated, studying *Job*. The last time it went something like this:

Interrogator – You say you're interested in the problem of suffering?

Myself – Yes.

Interrogator – Are you interested in violence?

Myself – Yes, oh, yes. A fascinating subject.

Interrogator – *Fascinating*?

Almost anything you answer is suspect. At the same time, super-markets have been bombed, banks robbed, people terrorised and a policeman killed. They are naturally on edge.

There is a warrant of arrest out for my wife. The girl in the gang, whoever she is, could be killed.

But 'no-one pities men who cling wilfully to their sufferings.' (*Philoctetes* – speech of Neoptolemus). I'm not even sure that I suffer, I only endure distress. But why should I analyse myself? I am analysing the God of *Job*.

I hope the mystery of Effie can be cleared up and when your show's over you can come and see Château Gotham. Ruth will undoubtedly come.

I'm analysing the God of *Job*, as I say. We are back to the Inscrutable. If the answers are valid then it is the questions that are all cock-eyed.

> *Job* 38, 2–3: Who is this that
> darkeneth counsel by words
> without knowledge?
>   Gird up now thy loins like
> a man; for I will demand of thee,
> and answer thou me.

I find that the self-styled friends and comforters in *Job* are distinguished one from the other only by their names. Otherwise, they are identical in their outlook. I now suspect they are the criminal-investigation team of their time and place. They were sent in, one after the other, it now seems to me, to interrogate Job, always on the same lines, trying to trip him up. He could only insist on his innocence. They acted as the representatives of the God of the Old Testament. They were the establishment of that theocratic society.

It is therefore first God's representatives and finally God himself who ask the questions in Job's book.

Now I hope you'll tell Ruth she can come here with Clara when the trouble's over, and have her baby. I'm quite willing to take on your old trousers, Edward, and you know I wish you well in your new pair, your new life.

Yours,
Harvey

PART THREE

ELEVEN

'So the Lord blessed the latter end of Job more than his beginning.' It was five days since Stewart Cowper had left for California. He had telephoned once, to say he had difficulty in getting the feature identified which Auntie Pet had seen, but he felt he was on the track of it now. There definitely had been a news item of that nature.

'Ring me as soon as you know,' said Harvey.

Meantime, since he was near the end of his monograph on *Job*, he finished it. The essay had taken him over three years to complete. He was sad to see his duty all ended, his notes in the little room of the cottage now neatly stacked, and his manuscript, all checked and revised, ready to be photocopied and mailed to the typist in London (Stewart Cowper's pretty secretary).

The work was finished and the Lord had blessed the latter end of Job with precisely double the number of sheep, camels, oxen and she-asses that he had started out with. Job now had seven sons and three daughters, as before. The daughters were the most beautiful in the land. They were called Jemima, Kezia and Kerenhappuch which means Box of Eye-Paint. Job lived another hundred and forty years. And Harvey wondered again if in real life Job would be satisfied with this plump reward, and doubted it. His tragedy was that of the happy ending.

He took his manuscript to St Dié, had it photocopied and sent one copy off to London to be typed. He was anxious to get back to the château in case Stewart should ring with news. He hadn't told Auntie Pet of Stewart's mission, but somehow she had found out, as was her way, and had mildly lamented that her story should be questioned.

'You're just like the police,' she said. 'They didn't actually say they didn't believe me, but I could see they didn't.'

He got back to the château just in time to hear the telephone. It was from the police at Epinal.

'You have no doubt heard the news, M. Gotham.'

'No. What now?'

'The FLE gang were surrounded and surprised an hour ago in an apartment in Paris. They opened fire on our men. I regret to say your wife has been killed. You will come to Paris to identify the body.'

'I think my wife is in California.'

'We take into account your state of mind, Monsieur, but we should be obliged if –'

Anne-Marie was standing in the doorway with her head buried in her hands.

L'Institut Médico-Légal in Paris. Her head was bound up, turban-wise, so that she looked more than ever like Job's wife. Her mouth was drawn slightly to the side.

'You recognise your wife, Effie Gotham?'

'Yes, but this isn't my wife. Where is she? Bring me my wife's body.'

'M. Gotham, you are overwrought. It displeases us all very much. You must know that this is your wife.'

'Yes, it's my wife, Effie.'

'She opened fire. One of our men was wounded.'

'The boy?'

'Nathan Fox. We have him. He was caught while trying to escape.'

Harvey felt suddenly relieved at the thought that Nathan wasn't in California with Effie.

The telephone rang when, finally, he got back to the château. It was from Stewart. 'I've seen a re-play of the feature, Harvey,' he said. 'It looks like Effie but it isn't.'

'I know,' said Harvey.

He said to Auntie Pet, 'Did you really think it was Effie in that mountain commune? How could you have thought so?'

'I did think so,' said Auntie Pet. 'And I still think so. That's the sort of person Effie is.'

Anne-Marie said, 'I'll be saying good-bye, now.'

TWELVE

Edward drives along the road between Nancy and St Dié. It is the end of April. All along the way the cherry trees are in flower. He comes to the grass track that he took last year. But this time he passes by the cottage, bleak in its little wilderness, and takes the wider path through a better-tended border of foliage, to the château.

Ruth is there, already showing her pregnancy. Clara staggers around her play-pen. Auntie Pet, wrapped in orange and mauve woollens, sits upright on the edge of the sofa, which forms a background of bright yellow and green English fabrics for her. Harvey is there, too.

'You've cut your hair,' says Harvey.

'I had to,' says Edward, 'for the part.'

It is later, when Clara has gone to bed, that Edward gives Harvey a message he has brought from Ernie Howe.

'He says if you want to adopt Clara, you can. He doesn't want the daughter of a terrorist.'

'How much does he want for the deal?'

'Nothing. That amazed me.'

'It doesn't amaze me. He's a swine. Better he wanted money than for the reason he gives.'

'I quite agree,' says Edward. 'What will you do now that you've finished *Job*?'

'Live another hundred and forty years. I'll have three daughters, Clara, Jemima and Eye-Paint.'

THE
DRIVER'S SEAT

ONE

'And the material doesn't stain,' the salesgirl says.

'Doesn't stain?'

'It's the new fabric,' the salesgirl says. 'Specially treated. Won't mark. If you spill like a bit of ice-cream or a drop of coffee, like, down the front of this dress it won't hold the stain.'

The customer, a young woman, is suddenly tearing at the fastener at the neck, pulling at the zip of the dress. She is saying, 'Get this thing off me. Off me, at once.'

The salesgirl shouts at the customer who, up to now, has been delighted with the bright coloured dress. It is patterned with green and purple squares on a white background, with blue spots within the green squares, cyclamen spots within the purple. This dress has not been a successful line; other dresses in the new stainless fabric have sold, but this, of which three others, identical but for sizes, hang in the back storeroom awaiting the drastic reductions of next week's sale, has been too vivid for most customers' taste. But the customer who now steps speedily out of it, throwing it on the floor with the utmost irritation, had almost smiled with satisfaction when she had tried it on. She had said, 'That's my dress.' The salesgirl had said it needed taking up at the hem. 'All right,' the customer had said, 'but I need it for tomorrow.' 'We can't do it before Friday, I'm sorry,' the salesgirl had said. 'Oh, I'll do it myself, then,' the customer had said, and turned round to admire it sideways in the long mirror. 'It's a good fit. Lovely colours,' she said.

'And it doesn't stain,' the salesgirl had said, with her eye wandering to another unstainable and equally unsaleable summer dress which evidently she hoped, now, to offer the satisfied customer.

'Doesn't stain?'

The customer has flung the dress aside.

The salesgirl shouts, as if to assist her explanation. 'Specially treated fabric . . . If you spill like a drop of sherry you just wipe it off. Look, Miss, you're tearing the neck.'

'Do you think I spill things on my clothes?' the customer shrieks. 'Do I look as if I don't eat properly?'

'Miss, I only remarked on the fabric, that when you tell me you're going abroad for your vacation, there is always the marks that you pick up on your journey. Don't treat our clothes like that if you please. Miss, I only said stain-resisting and then you carry on, after you liked it.'

'Who asked you for a stain-resisting dress?' the customer shouts, getting quickly, with absolute purpose, into her own blouse and skirt.

'You liked the colours, didn't you?' shouts the girl. 'What difference does it make, so it resists stains, if you liked the fabric before you knew?'

The customer picks up her bag and goes to the door almost at a run, while two other salesgirls and two other customers gasp and gape. At the door she turns to look back and says, with a look of satisfaction at her own dominance over the situation with an undoubtable excuse, 'I won't be insulted!'

She walks along the broad street, scanning the windows for the dress she needs, the necessary dress. Her lips are slightly parted; she, whose lips are usually pressed together with the daily disapprovals of the accountants' office where she has worked continually, except for the months of illness, since she was eighteen, that is to say, for sixteen years and some months. Her lips, when she does not speak or eat, are normally pressed together like the ruled line of a balance sheet, marked straight with her old-fashioned lipstick, a final and a judging mouth, a precision instrument, a detail-warden of a mouth; she has five girls under her and two men. Over her are two women and five men. Her immediate superior had given her the afternoon off, in kindness, Friday afternoon. 'You've got your packing to do, Lise. Go home, pack and rest.' She had resisted. 'I don't need a rest. I've got all this work to finish. Look – all this.' The superior, a fat small man, looked at her with frightened eyeglasses. Lise smiled and bent her head over her desk. 'It can wait till you get back,' said the man, and when she looked up at him he showed courage and defiance in his rimless spectacles. Then she had begun to laugh hysterically. She finished laughing and started crying all in a flood, while a flurry at the other desks, the jerky backward movements of her little fat superior, conveyed to her that she had done again what she had not done for five years. As she ran to the lavatory she shouted to the whole office who somehow or other were trying to follow or help her. 'Leave me alone! It doesn't matter. What does it matter?' Half an hour later they said, 'You need a good holiday, Lise. You need your vacation.' 'I'm going to have it,' she said, 'I'm going to have the time of my life,' and she had looked at the two men and five girls under her, and at her quivering superior, one by one, with her lips straight as a line which could cancel them all out completely.

Now, as she walks along the street after leaving the shop, her lips are slightly parted as if to receive a secret flavour. In fact her nostrils and eyes are a fragment more open than usual, imperceptibly but thoroughly they accompany her parted lips in one mission, the sensing of the dress that she must get.

She swerves in her course at the door of a department store and enters. Resort Department: she has seen the dress. A lemon-yellow top with a skirt patterned in bright V's of orange, mauve and blue. 'Is it made of that stain-resisting material?' she asks when she has put it on and is looking at herself in the mirror. 'Stain-resisting? I don't know, Madam. It's a washable cotton, but if I were you I'd have it dry-cleaned. It might shrink.' Lise laughs, and the girl says, 'I'm afraid we haven't anything really stain-resisting. I've never heard of anything like that.' Lise makes her mouth into a straight line. Then she says, 'I'll have it.' Meanwhile she is pulling off a hanger a summer coat with narrow stripes, red and white, with a white collar; very quickly she tries it on over the new dress. 'Of course, the two don't go well together,' says the salesgirl. 'You'd have to see them on separate.'

Lise does not appear to listen. She studies herself. This way and that, in the mirror of the fitting room. She lets the coat hang open over the dress. Her lips part, and her eyes narrow; she breathes for a moment as in a trance.

The salesgirl says, 'You can't really see the coat at its best, Madam, over that frock.'

Lise appears suddenly to hear her, opening her eyes and closing her lips. The girl is saying, 'You won't be able to wear them together, but it's a lovely coat, over a plain dress, white or navy, or for the evenings ...'

'They go very well together,' Lise says, and taking off the coat she hands it carefully to the girl. 'I'll have it; also, the dress. I can take up the hem myself.' She reaches for her blouse and skirt and says to the girl, 'Those colours of the dress and the coat are absolutely right for me. Very natural colours.'

The girl, placating, says, 'Oh, it's how you feel in things yourself, Madam, isn't it? It's you's got to wear them.' Lise buttons her blouse disapprovingly. She follows the girl to the shop-floor, pays the bill, waits for the change and, when the girl hands her first the change then the large bag of heavy paper containing her new purchases, she opens the top of the bag enough to enable her to peep inside, to put in her hand and tear a corner of the tissue paper which enfolds each garment. She is obviously making sure she is being handed the right garments. The girl is about to speak, probably to say, 'Everything all right?' or 'Thank you, Madam, goodbye,' or even, 'Don't worry; everything's there all right.' But Lise speaks first; she says, 'The colours go together perfectly. People here in the North are ignorant of colours. Conservative; old-fashioned. If only you knew! These colours are a natural blend for me. Absolutely natural.' She does not wait for a reply; she does not turn towards the lift, she turns, instead, towards the down escalator, purposefully making her way through a short lane of dresses that hang in their stands.

She stops abruptly at the top of the escalator and looks back, then smiles as if she sees and hears what she had expected. The salesgirl, thinking her customer is already on the escalator out of sight, out of hearing, has turned to another black-frocked salesgirl. 'All those colours together!' she is saying. 'Those incredible colours! She said they were perfectly natural. Natural! Here in the North, she said ...' Her voice stops as she sees that Lise is looking and hearing. The girl affects to be fumbling with a dress on the rack and to be saying something else without changing her expression too noticeably. Lise laughs aloud and descends the escalator.

'Well, enjoy yourself Lise,' says the voice on the telephone. 'Send me a card.'

'Oh, of course,' Lise says, and when she has hung up she laughs heartily. She does not stop. She goes to the wash-basin and fills a glass of water, which she drinks, gurgling, then another, and still nearly choking she drinks another. She has stopped laughing, and now breathing heavily says to the mute telephone, 'Of course. Oh, of course.' Still heaving with exhaustion she pulls out the hard wall-seat which adapts to a bed and takes off her shoes, placing them beside the bed. She puts the large carrier-bag containing her new coat and dress in a cupboard beside her suitcase which is already packed. She places her hand-bag on the lamp-shelf beside the bed and lies down.

Her face is solemn as she lies, at first staring at the brown pinewood door as if to see beyond it. Presently her breathing becomes normal. The room is meticulously neat. It is a one-room flat in an apartment house. Since it was put up the designer has won prizes for his interiors, he has become known throughout the country and far beyond and is now no longer to be obtained by landlords of moderate price. The lines of the room are pure; space is used as a pattern in itself, circumscribed by the dexterous pinewood outlines that ensued from the designer's ingenuity and austere taste when he was young, unknown, studious and strict-principled. The company that owns the apartment house knows the worth of these pinewood interiors. Pinewood alone is now nearly as scarce as the architect himself, but the law, so far, prevents them from raising the rents very much. The tenants have long leases. Lise moved in when the house was new, ten years ago. She has added very little to the room; very little is needed, for the furniture is all fixed, adaptable to various uses, and stackable. Stacked into a panel are six folding chairs, should the tenant decide to entertain six for dinner. The writing desk extends to a dining table, and when the desk is not in use it, too, disappears into the pinewood wall, its bracket-lamp hingeing outward and upward to form a wall-lamp. The bed is by day a narrow seat with overhanging bookcases; by night it swivels out to accommodate the sleeper. Lise has put down a patterned rug from Greece. She has fitted a hopsack covering on the seat of the divan. Unlike the other tenants she has not put unnecessary curtains in the window; her flat is not closely overlooked and in summer she keeps the venetian blinds down over the windows and slightly opened to let in the light. A small pantry-kitchen adjoins this room. Here, too, everything is contrived to fold away into the dignity of unvarnished pinewood. And in the bathroom as well, nothing need be seen, nothing need be left lying about. The bed-supports, the door, the window frame, the hanging cupboard, the storage space, the shelves, the desk that extends, the tables that stack – they are made of such pinewood as one may never see again in a modest bachelor apartment. Lise keeps her flat as clean-lined and clear to return to after her work as if it were uninhabited. The swaying tall pines among the litter of cones on the forest floor have been subdued into silence and into obedient bulks.

Lise breathes as if sleeping, deeply tired, but her eye-slits open from time to time. Her hand moves to her brown leather bag on the lamp-shelf and she raises herself, pulling the bag towards her. She leans on one elbow and empties the contents on the bed. She lifts them one by one, checking carefully, and puts them back; there is a folded envelope from the travel agency containing her air ticket, a powder compact, a lipstick, a comb. There is a bunch of keys. She smiles at them and her lips are parted. There are six keys on the steel ring, two Yale door-keys, a key that might belong to a functional cupboard or drawer, a small silver-metal key of the type commonly belonging to zip-fastened luggage, and two tarnished car-keys. Lise takes the car-keys off the ring and lays them aside; the rest go back in her bag. Her passport, in its transparent plastic envelope, goes back in her bag. With straightened lips she prepares for her departure the next day. She unpacks the new coat and dress and hangs them on hangers.

Next morning she puts them on. When she is ready to leave she dials a number on the telephone and looks at herself in the mirror which has not yet been concealed behind the pinewood panels which close upon it. The voice answers and Lise touches her pale brown hair as she speaks. 'Margot, I'm just off now,' Lise says. 'I'll put your car-keys in an envelope and I'll leave them downstairs with the door-keeper. All right?'

The voice says, 'Thanks. Have a good holiday. Have a good time. Send me a card.'

'Yes, of course, Margot.'

'Of course,' Lise says when she has replaced the receiver. She takes an envelope from a drawer, writes a name on it, puts the two car-keys in it and seals the envelope. Then she telephones for a taxi, lifts her suitcase out to the landing, fetches her hand-bag and the envelope, and leaves the flat.

When she reaches the street floor, she stops at the windows of the porter's wood-lined cabin. Lise rings the bell and waits. No one appears, but the taxi has pulled up outside. Lise shouts to the driver, 'I'm just coming!' and indicates her suitcase which the taxi-driver fetches. While he is stacking it in the front of the cab a woman with a brown overall comes up behind Lise. 'You want me, Miss?'

Lise turns quickly to face the woman. She has the envelope in her hand and is about to speak when the woman says, 'Well, well, my goodness, what colours!' She is looking at Lise's red and white striped coat, unbuttoned, and the vivid dress beneath, the purple, orange and blue V-patterns of the skirt and the yellow top. The woman laughs hugely as one who has nothing to gain by suppressing her amusement, she laughs and opens the pinewood door into the porter's office; there she slides open the window panel and laughs aloud in Lise's face. She says, 'Are you going to join a circus?' Then again she throws back her head, looking down through half-closed lids at Lise's clothes, and gives out the high, hacking cough-like ancestral laughter of the streets, holding her breasts in her hands to spare them the shake-up. Lise says, with quiet dignity, 'You are insolent.' But the woman laughs again, now no longer spontaneously but with spiteful and deliberate noise, forcing the evident point that Lise habitually is mean with her tips, or perhaps never tips the porter at all.

Lise walks quietly out to the cab, still holding in her hand the envelope which contains the car-keys. She looks at this envelope as she goes, but whether she has failed to leave it at the door-keeper's desk by intention, or whether through the distraction of the woman's laughter, one could not tell from her serene face with lips slightly parted. The woman comes to the street door emitting noise like a brown container of laughing-gas until the taxi is out of her scope.

TWO

Lise is thin. Her height is about five-foot-six. Her hair is pale brown, probably tinted, a very light streaked lock sweeping from the middle of her hair-line to the top of her crown; her hair is cut short at the sides and back, and is styled high. She might be as young as twenty-nine or as old as thirty-six, but hardly younger, hardly older. She has arrived at the airport; she has paid the taxi-driver quickly and with an expression of abstract eagerness to be somewhere else. Likewise, with the porter, while he takes her bag and follows her to the desk to have it weighed-in. She seems not to see him.

There are two people in front of her. Lise's eyes are widely spaced, blue-grey and dull. Her lips are a straight line. She is neither good-looking nor bad-looking. Her nose is short and wider than it will look in the likeness constructed partly by the method of identikit, partly by actual photography, soon to be published in the newspapers of four languages.

Lise looks at the two people in front of her, first a woman and then a man, swaying to one side and the other as she does so, either to discern in the half-faces visible to her someone she might possibly know, or else to relieve, by these movements and looks, some impatience she might feel.

When it comes to her turn she heaves her luggage on to the scale and pushes her ticket to the clerk as quickly as possible. While he examines it she turns to look at a couple who are now waiting behind her. She glances at both faces, then looks back to the clerk, regardless of their returning her stares and their unanimous perception of her bright-coloured clothes.

'Any hand-luggage?' says the clerk, peering over the top of the counter.

Lise simpers, placing the tips of her upper teeth over her lower lip, and draws in a little breath.

'Any hand-luggage?' The busy young official looks at her as much as to say, 'What's the matter with *you*?' And Lise answers in a voice different from the voice in which she yesterday spoke to the shop assistant when buying her lurid outfit, and has used on the telephone, and in which early this morning she spoke to the woman at the porter's desk; she now speaks in a little-girl tone which presumably is taken by those within hearing to be her normal voice even if a nasty one. Lise says, 'I only have my hand-bag with me. I believe in travelling light because I travel a lot and I know how terrible it is for one's neighbours on the plane when you have great huge pieces of hand-luggage taking up everybody's foot-room.'

The clerk, all in one gesture, heaves a sigh, purses his lips, closes his eyes, places his chin in his hands and his elbow on the desk. Lise turns round to address the couple behind her. She says, 'When you travel as much as I do you have to travel light, and I tell you, I nearly didn't bring any luggage at all, because you can get everything you want at the other end, so the only reason I brought that suitcase there is that the customs get suspicious if you come in and out without luggage. They think you're smuggling dope and diamonds under your blouse, so I packed the usual things for a holiday, but it was all quite unnecessary, as you get to understand when you've travelled about as you might say with experience in four languages over the years, and you know what you're doing –'

'Look, Miss,' the clerk says, pulling himself straight and stamping her ticket, 'you're holding up the people behind you. We're busy.'

Lise turns away from the bewildered-looking couple to face the clerk as he pushes her ticket and boarding card towards her. 'Board-ing card,' says the clerk. 'Your flight will be called in twenty-five minutes' time. Next please.'

Lise grabs the papers and moves away as if thinking only of the next formality of travel. She puts the ticket in her bag, takes out her passport, slips the boarding card inside it, and makes straight towards the passport boxes. And it is almost as if, satisfied that she has successfully registered the fact of her presence at the airport among the July thousands there, she has fulfilled a small item of a greater purpose. She goes to the emigration official and joins the queue and submits her passport. And now, having received her passport back in her hand, she is pushing through the gate into the departure lounge.

She walks to the far end, then turns and walks back. She is neither good-looking nor bad-looking. Her lips are slightly parted. She stops to look at the departures chart, then walks on. The people around her are mostly too occupied with their purchases and their flight-numbers to notice her, but some of those who sit beside their hand-luggage and children on the leather seats waiting for their flights to be called look at her as she walks past, noting without comment the lurid colours of her coat, red and white stripes, hanging loose over her dress, yellow-topped, with its skirt of orange, purple and blue. They look, as she passes, as they look also at those girls whose skirts are specially short, or those men whose tight-fitting shirts are patterned with flowers or are transparent. Lise is conspicuous among them only in the particular mixture of her colours, contrasting with the fact that her hem-line has been for some years an old-fashioned length, reaching just below her knees, as do the mild dresses of many other, but dingy, women travellers who teem in the departure lounge. Lise puts her passport into her hand-bag, and holds her boarding card.

She stops at the bookstall, looks at her watch and starts looking at the paperback stands. A white-haired, tall woman who has been looking through the hardback books piled up on a table, turns from them and, pointing to the paperbacks, says to Lise in English, 'Is there anything there predominantly pink or green or beige?'

'Excuse me?' says Lise politely, in a foreignly accented English, 'what is that you're looking for?'

'Oh,' the woman says, 'I thought you were American.'

'No, but I can speak four languages enough to make myself understood.'

'I'm from Johannesburg,' says the woman, 'and I have this house in Jo'burg and another at Sea Point on the Cape. Then my son, he's a lawyer, he has a flat in Jo'burg. In all our places we have spare bedrooms, that makes two green, two pink, three beige, and I'm trying to pick up books to match. I don't see any with just those pastel tints.'

'You want English books,' Lise says. 'I think you find English books on the front of the shop over there.'

'Well, I looked there and I don't find my shades. Aren't these English books here?'

Lise says 'No. In any case they're all very bright-coloured.' She smiles then, and with her lips apart starts to look swiftly through the paperbacks. She picks out one with bright green lettering on a white background with the author's name printed to look like blue lightning streaks. In the middle of the cover are depicted a brown boy and girl wearing only garlands of sunflowers. Lise pays for it, while the white-haired woman says, 'Those colours are too bright for me. I don't see anything.'

Lise is holding the book up against her coat, giggling merrily, and looking up to the woman as if to see if her purchase is admired.

'You going on holiday?' the woman says.

'Yes. My first after three years.'

'You travel much?'

'No. There is so little money. But I'm going to the South now. I went before, three years ago.'

'Well, I hope you have a good time. A very good time. You look very gay.'

The woman has large breasts, she is clothed in a pink summer coat and dress. She smiles and is amiable in this transient intimacy with Lise, and not even sensing in the least that very soon, after a day and a half of hesitancy, and after a long midnight call to her son, the lawyer in Johannesburg, who advises her against the action, she nevertheless will come forward and repeat all she remembers and all she does not remember, and all the details she imagines to be true and those that are true, in her conversation with Lise when she sees in the papers that the police are trying to trace who Lise is, and whom, if anyone, she met on her trip and what she had said. 'Very gay,' says this woman to Lise, indulgently, smiling all over Lise's vivid clothes.

'I look for a gay time,' Lise is saying.

'You got a young man?'

'Yes, I have my boy-friend!'

'He's not with you, then?'

'No. I'm going to find him. He's waiting for me. Maybe I should get him a gift at the duty-free shop.'

They are walking towards the departures chart. 'I'm going to Stockholm. I have three-quarters of an hour wait,' says the woman.

Lise looks at the chart as the amplified voice of the announcer hacks its way through the general din. Lise says, 'That's my flight. Boarding at Gate 14.' She moves off, her eyes in the distance as if the woman

from Johannesburg had never been there. On her way to Gate 14 Lise
stops to glance at a gift-stall. She looks at the dolls in folk-costume
and at the corkscrews. Then she lifts up a paper-knife shaped like a
scimitar, of brass-coloured metal with inset coloured stones. She
removes it from its curved sheath and tests the blade and the point
with deep interest. 'How much?' she asks the assistant who is at that
moment serving someone else. The girl says impatiently aside to
Lise, 'The price is on the ticket.'

'Too much. I can get it cheaper at the other end,' Lise says, putting
it down.

'They're all fixed prices at the duty-free,' the girl calls after Lise as
she walks away towards Gate 14.

A small crowd has gathered waiting for embarkation. More and
more people straggle or palpitate, according to temperament, towards the group. Lise surveys her fellow-passengers, one by one, very
carefully but not in a manner to provoke their attention. She moves
and mingles as if with dreamy feet and legs, but quite plainly, from
her eyes, her mind is not dreamy as she absorbs each face, each dress,
each suit of clothes, all blouses, blue-jeans, each piece of hand-
luggage, each voice which will accompany her on the flight now
boarding at Gate 14.

THREE

She will be found tomorrow morning dead from multiple stab-wounds, her wrists bound with a silk scarf and her ankles bound with a man's necktie, in the grounds of an empty villa, in a park of the foreign city to which she is travelling on the flight now boarding at Gate 14.

Crossing the tarmac to the plane Lise follows, with her quite long stride, closely on the heels of the fellow-passenger whom she appears finally to have chosen to adhere to. This is a rosy-faced, sturdy young man of about thirty; he is dressed in a dark business suit and carries a black briefcase. She follows him purposefully, careful to block the path of any other traveller whose aimless hurry might intervene between Lise and this man. Meanwhile, closely behind Lise, almost at her side, walks a man who in turn seems anxious to be close to her. He tries unsuccessfully to catch her attention. He is bespectacled, half-smiling, young, dark, long-nosed and stooping. He wears a check shirt and beige corduroy trousers. A camera is slung over his shoulders and a coat over his arm.

Up the steps they go, the pink and shiny business man, Lise at his heels, and at hers the hungrier-looking man. Up the steps and into the plane. The air-hostess says good morning at the door while a steward farther up the aisle of the economy class blocks the progress of the staggering file and helps a young woman with two young children to bundle their coats up on the rack. The way is clear at last. Lise's business man finds a seat next to the right-hand window in a three-seat row. Lise takes the middle seat next to him, on his left, while the lean hawk swiftly throws his coat and places his camera up on the rack and sits down next to Lise in the end seat.

Lise begins to fumble for her seat-belt. First she reaches down the right-hand side of her seat which adjoins that of the dark-suited man. At the same time she takes the left-hand section. But the right-hand buckle she gets hold of is that of her neighbour. It does not fit in the left-hand buckle as she tries to make it do. The dark-suited neighbour, fumbling also for his seat-belt, frowns as he seems to realize that she has the wrong part, and makes an unintelligible sound. Lise says, 'I think I've got yours.'

He fishes up the buckle that properly belongs to Lise's seat-belt. She says, 'Oh yes. I'm so sorry.' She giggles and he formally smiles and brings his smile to an end, now fastening his seat-belt intently and then looking out of the window at the wing of the plane, silvery with its rectangular patches.

Lise's left-hand neighbour smiles. The loudspeaker tells the passengers to fasten their seat-belts and refrain from smoking. Her admirer's brown eyes are warm, his smile, as wide as his forehead, seems to take up most of his lean face. Lise says, audibly above the other voices on the plane, 'You look like Red Riding-Hood's grandmother. Do you want to eat me up?'

The engines rev up. Her ardent neighbour's widened lips give out deep, satisfied laughter, while he slaps her knee in applause. Suddenly her other neighbour looks at Lise in alarm. He stares, as if recognizing her, with his brief-case on his lap, and his hand in the position of pulling out a batch of papers. Something about Lise, about her exchange with the man on her left, has caused a kind of paralysis in his act of fetching out some papers from his brief-case. He opens his mouth, gasping and startled, staring at her as if she is someone he has known and forgotten and now sees again. She smiles at him; it is a smile of relief and delight. His hand moves again, hurriedly putting back the papers that he had half drawn out of his brief-case. He trembles as he unfastens his seat-belt and makes as if to leave his seat, grabbing his brief-case.

On the evening of the following day he will tell the police, quite truthfully, 'The first time I saw her was at the airport. Then on the plane. She sat beside me.'

'You never saw her before at any time? You didn't know her?'

'No, never.'

'What was your conversation on the plane?'

'Nothing. I moved my seat. I was afraid.'

'Afraid?'

'Yes, frightened. I moved to another seat, away from her.'

'What frightened you?'

'I don't know.'

'Why did you move your seat at that time?'

'I don't know. I must have sensed something.'

'What did she say to you?'

'Nothing much. She got her seat-belt mixed with mine. Then she was carrying on a bit with the man at the end seat.'

Now, as the plane taxis along the runway, he gets up. Lise and the man in the aisle seat look up at him, taken by surprise at the abruptness of his movements. Their seat-belts fasten them to their seats and they are unable immediately to make way for him, as he indicates that he wants to pass. Lise looks, for an instant, slightly senile, as if she felt, in addition to bewilderment, a sense of defeat or physical incapacity. She might be about to cry or protest against a pitiless frustration of her will. But an air-hostess, seeing the standing man, has left her post by the exit-door and briskly comes up the aisle to their seat. She says. 'The aircraft is taking off. Will you kindly remain seated and fasten your seat-belt?'

The man says, in a foreign accent, 'Excuse me, please. I wish to change.' He starts to squeeze past Lise and her companion.

The air-hostess, evidently thinking that the man has an urgent need to go to the lavatory, asks the two if they would mind getting up to let him pass and return to their seats as quickly as possible. They unfasten their belts, stand aside in the aisle, and he hurries up the plane with the air-hostess leading the way. But he does not get as far as the toilet cubicles. He stops at an empty middle seat upon which the people on either side, a white-haired fat man and a young girl, have dumped hand-luggage and magazines. He pushes himself past the woman who is seated on the outside seat and asks her to remove the luggage. He himself lifts it, shakily, his solid strength all gone. The air-hostess turns to remonstrate, but the two people have obediently made the seat vacant for him. He sits, fastens his seat-belt, ignoring the air-hostess, her reproving, questioning protests, and heaves a deep breath as if he had escaped from death by a small margin.

Lise and her companion have watched the performance. Lise smiles bitterly.

The dark man by her side says, 'What's wrong with him?'

'He didn't like us,' Lise says.

'What did we do to him?'

'Nothing. Nothing at all. He must be crazy. He must be nutty.'

The plane now comes to its brief halt before revving up for the take-off run. The engines roar and the plane is off, is rising and away. Lise says to her neighbour, 'I wonder who he is?'

'Some kind of a nut,' says the man. 'But it's all the better for us, we can get acquainted.' His stringy hand takes hers; he holds it tightly. 'I'm Bill,' he says. 'What's your name?'

'Lise.' She lets him grip her hand as if she hardly knows that he is holding it. She stretches her neck to see above the heads of the people in front, and says, 'He's sitting there reading the paper as if nothing had happened.'

The stewardess is handing out copies of newspapers. A steward who has followed her up the aisle stops at the seat where the dark-suited man has settled and is now tranquilly scanning the front page of his newspaper. The steward inquires if he is all right now, sir?

The man looks up with an embarrassed smile and shyly apologizes. 'Yes, fine. I'm sorry . . .'

'Was there anything the matter, sir?'

'No, really. Please. I'm fine here, thanks. Sorry . . . it was nothing, nothing.'

The steward goes away with his eyebrows mildly raised in resignation at the chance eccentricity of a passenger. The plane purrs forward. The no-smoking lights go out and the loudspeaker confirms that the passengers may now unfasten their seat-belts and smoke.

Lise unfastens hers and moves to the vacated window seat.

'I knew,' she says. 'In a way I knew there was something wrong with him.'

Bill moves to sit next to her in the middle seat and says, 'Nothing wrong with him at all. Just a fit of puritanism. He was unconsciously jealous when he saw we'd hit it off together, and he made out he was outraged as if we'd been doing something indecent. Forget him; he's probably a clerk in an insurance brokers' from the looks of him. Nasty little bureaucrat. Limited. He wasn't your type.'

'How do you know?' Lise says immediately as if responding only to Bill's use of the past tense, and, as if defying it by a counter-demonstration to the effect that the man continues to exist in the present, she half-stands to catch sight of the stranger's head, eight rows forward in a middle seat, at the other side of the aisle, now bent quietly over his reading.

'Sit down,' Bill says. 'You don't want anything to do with that type. He was frightened of your psychedelic clothes. Terrified.'

'Do you think so?'

'Yes. But I'm not.'

The stewardesses advance up the aisle bearing trays of food which they start to place before the passengers. Lise and Bill pull down the table in front of their seats to receive their portions. It is a mid-morning compromise snack composed of salami on lettuce, two green olives, a rolled-up piece of boiled ham containing a filling of potato salad and a small pickled something, all laid upon a slice of bread. There is also a round cake, swirled with white and chocolate cream, and a corner of silver-wrapped processed cheese with biscuits wrapped in cellophane. An empty plastic coffee cup stands by on each of their trays.

Lise takes from her tray the transparent plastic envelope which contains the sterilized knife, fork and spoon necessary for the meal. She feels the blade of the knife. She presses two of her fingers against the prongs of her fork. 'Not very sharp,' she says.

'Who needs them, anyway?' says Bill. 'This is awful food.'

'Oh, it looks all right. I'm hungry. I only had a cup of coffee for my breakfast. There wasn't time.'

'You can eat mine too,' says Bill. 'I stick as far as possible to a very sensible diet. This stuff is poison, full of toxics and chemicals. It's far too Yin.'

'I know,' said Lise. 'But considering it's a snack on a plane –'

'You know what Yin is?' he says.

She says, 'Well, sort of . . .' in a vaguely embarrassed way, 'but it's only a snack, isn't it?'

'You understand what Yin is?'

'Well, something sort of like this – all bitty.'

'No, Lise,' he says.

'Well it's a kind of slang, isn't it? You say a thing's a bit too yin . . .'; plainly she is groping.

'Yin,' says Bill, 'is the opposite of Yang.'

She giggles and, half-rising, starts searching with her eyes for the man who is still on her mind.

'This is serious,' Bill says, pulling her roughly back into her seat. She laughs and begins to eat.

'Yin and Yang are philosophies,' he says. 'Yin represents space. Its colour is purple. Its element is water. It is external. That salami is Yin and those olives are Yin. They are full of toxics. Have you ever heard of macrobiotic food?'

'No, what is it?' she says cutting into the open salami sandwich.

'You've got a lot to learn. Rice, unpolished rice is the basis of macrobiotics. I'm going to start a centre in Naples next week. It is a cleansing diet. Physically, mentally and spiritually.'

'I hate rice,' she says.

'No, you only think you do. He who hath ears let him hear.' He smiles widely towards her, he breathes into her face and touches her knee. She eats on with composure. 'I'm an Enlightenment Leader in the movement,' he says.

The stewardess comes with two long metal pots. 'Tea or coffee?' 'Coffee,' says Lise, holding out her plastic cup, her arm stretched in front of Bill. When this is done, 'For you, sir?' says the stewardess.

Bill places his hand over his cup and benignly shakes his head.

'Don't you want anything to eat, sir?' says the stewardess, regarding Bill's untouched tray.

'No, thank you,' says Bill.

Lise says, 'I'll eat it. Or at least, some of it.'

The stewardess passes on to the next row, unconcerned.

'Coffee is Yin,' says Bill.

Lise looks towards his tray. 'Are you sure you don't want that open sandwich? It's delicious. I'll eat it if you don't want it. After all, it's paid for, isn't it?'

'Help yourself,' he says. 'You'll soon change your eating habits, though, now that we've got to know each other.'

'Whatever do you eat when you travel abroad?' Lise says, exchanging his tray for hers, retaining only her coffee.

'I carry my diet with me. I never eat in restaurants and hotels unless I have to. And if I do, I choose very carefully. I go where I can get a little fish, maybe, and rice, and perhaps a bit of goat's cheese. Which are Yang. Cream cheese – in fact butter, milk, anything that comes from the cow – is too Yin. You become what you eat. Eat cow and you become cow.'

A hand, fluttering a sheet of white paper, intervenes from behind them.

They turn to see what is being offered. Bill grasps the paper. It is the log of the plane's flight, informing the passengers as to the altitude, speed and present geographical position, and requesting them to read it and pass it on.

Lise continues to look back, having caught sight of the face behind her. In the window seat, next to a comfortably plump woman and a young girl in her teens, is a sick-looking man, his eyes yellow-brown and watery, deep-set in their sockets, his face pale green. It was he who had handed forward the chart. Lise stares, her lips parted slightly, and she frowns as if speculating on the man's identity. He looks away, first out of the window, then down towards the floor, embarrassed. The woman does not change her expression, but the young girl, understanding Lise to be questioning by her stare the man behind, says, 'It's only the flight chart.' But Lise stares on. The sick-looking man looks at his companions and then down at his knees, and Lise's stare does not appear to be helping his sickness.

A nudge from Bill composes her so far that she turns and faces forward again. He says, 'It's only the flight chart. Do you want to see it?' And since she does not reply he thrusts it forward to bother it about the ears of the people in front until they receive it from his hand.

Lise starts to eat her second snack. 'You know, Bill,' she says, 'I think you were right about that crazy man who moved his seat. He wasn't my type at all and I wasn't his type. Just as a matter of interest, I mean, because I didn't take the slightest notice of him and I'm not looking to pick up strangers. But you mentioned that he wasn't my type and, of course, let me tell you, if he thought I was going to make up to him he made a mistake.'

'I'm your type,' Bill says.

She sips her coffee and looks round, glimpsing through the partition of the seats the man behind her. He stares ahead with glazed and quite unbalanced eyes, those eyes far too wide open to signify anything but some sort of mental distance from reality; he does not see Lise now, as she peers at him, or, if so, he appears to have taken a quick turn beyond caring and beyond embarrassment.

Bill says, 'Look at me, not at him.'

She turns back to Bill with an agreeable and indulgent smile. The stewardesses come efficiently collecting the trays, cluttering one upon the other. Bill, when their trays are collected, puts up first Lise's table and then his own. He puts his arm through hers.

'I'm your type,' he says, 'and you're mine. Are you planning to stay with friends?'

'No, but I have to meet somebody.'

'No chance of us meeting some time? How long are you planning to stay in the city?'

'I have no definite plans,' she says. 'But I could meet you for a drink tonight. Just a short drink.'

'I'm staying at the Metropole,' he says. 'Where will you be staying?'

'Oh, just a small place. Hotel Tomson.'

'I don't think I know Hotel Tomson.'

'It's quite small. It's cheap but clean.'

'Well, at the Metropole,' Bill says, 'they don't ask any questions.'

'As far as I'm concerned,' Lise says, 'they can ask any questions they like. I'm an idealist.'

'That's exactly what I am,' Bill says. 'An idealist. You're not offended, are you? I only meant that if we get acquainted, I think, somehow, I'm your type and you're my type.'

'I don't like crank diets,' Lise says. 'I don't need diets. I'm in good form.'

'Now, I can't let that pass, Lise,' Bill says. 'You don't know what you're talking about. The macrobiotic system is not just a diet, it's a way of life.'

She says, 'I have somebody to meet some time this afternoon or this evening.'

'What for?' he says. 'Is it a boy-friend?'

'Mind your own business,' she says. 'Stick to your yin and your yang.'

'Yin and Yang,' he says, 'is something that you've got to understand. If we could have a little time together, a little peaceful time, in a room, just talking, I could give you some idea of how it works. It's an idealist's way of life. I'm hoping to get the young people of Naples interested in it. I should think there would be many young people of Naples interested. We're opening a macrobiotic restaurant there, you know.'

Lise peers behind her again at the staring, sickly man. 'A strange type,' she says.

'With a room behind the public dining hall, a room for strict observers who are on Regime Seven. Regime Seven is cereals only, very little liquid. You take such a very little liquid that you can pee only three times a day if you're a man, two if you're a woman. Regime Seven is a very elevated regime in macrobiotics. You become like a tree. People become what they eat.'

'Do you become a goat when you eat goat's cheese?'

'Yes, you become lean and stringy like a goat. Look at me, I haven't a spare piece of fat on my body. I'm not an Enlightenment Leader for nothing.'

'You must have been eating goat's cheese,' she says. 'This man back here is like a tree, have you seen him?'

'Behind the private room for observers of Regime Seven,' Bill says, 'there will be another little room for tranquillity and quiet. It should do well in Naples once we get the youth movement started. It's to be called the Yin-Yang Young. It does well in Denmark. But middle-aged people take the diet too. In the States many senior citizens are on macrobiotics.'

'The men in Naples are sexy.'

'On this diet the Regional Master for Northern Europe recommends one orgasm a day. At least. In the Mediterranean countries we are still researching that aspect.'

'He's afraid of me,' Lise whispers, indicating with a jerk of her head the man behind her. 'Why is everybody afraid of me?'

'What do you mean? I'm not afraid of you.' Bill looks round, impatiently, and as if only to oblige her. He looks away again. 'Don't bother with him,' he says. 'He's a mess.'

Lise gets up. 'Excuse me,' she says, 'I have to go and wash.'

'See you come back,' he says.

She passes across him to the aisle, holding in her hand both her hand-bag and the paperback book she bought at the airport, and as she does so she takes the opportunity to look carefully at the three people in the row behind, the ill-looking man, the plump woman and the young girl, who sit without conversing, as it seems unconnected with each other. Lise stands for a moment in the aisle, raising the arm on which the hand-bag is slung from the wrist, so that the paperback, now held between finger and thumb, is visible. She seems to display it deliberately, as if she is one of those spies one reads about who effect recognition by pre-arranged signals and who verify their contact with another agent by holding a certain paper in a special way.

Bill looks up at her and says, 'What's the matter?'

She starts moving forward, at the same time answering Bill: 'The matter?'

'You won't need that book,' Bill says.

She looks at the book in her hand as if wondering where it came from and with a little laugh hesitates by his side long enough to toss it on to her seat before she goes up the plane towards the toilets.

Two people are waiting in line ahead of her. She takes her place abstractedly, standing in fact almost even with the row where her first neighbour, the business man, is sitting. But she does not seem to be aware of him or to care in the slightest that he glances up at her twice, three times, at first apprehensively and then, as she continues to ignore him, less so. He turns a page of his newspaper and folds it conveniently for reading, and reads it without looking at her again, settling further into his seat with the slight sigh of one whose visitor has left and who is at last alone.

It has turned out that the sick-looking man is after all connected with the plump woman and the young girl who sat beside him on the plane. He is coming out of the airport building, now, not infirmly but with an air of serious exhaustion, accompanied by the woman and the girl.

Lise stands a few yards away. By her side is Bill; their luggage is on the pavement beside them. She says, 'Oh there he is!' and leaves Bill's side, running up to the sick-eyed man. 'Excuse me!' she says.

He hesitates, and makes an awkward withdrawal: two steps backward, and with the steps he seems to withdraw even more his chest, shoulders, legs and face. The plump woman looks at Lise inquiringly while the girl just stands and looks.

Lise addresses the man in English. She says, 'Excuse me, but I wondered if you wanted to share a limousine to the centre. It works out cheaper than a taxi, if the passengers agree to share, and it's quicker than the bus, of course.'

The man looks at the pavement as if inwardly going through a ghastly experience. The plump woman says, 'No, thank you. We're being met.' And touching the man on the arm, moves on. He follows, as if bound for the scaffold while the girl stares blankly at Lise before walking round and past her. But Lise quickly moves with the group, and once again confronts the man. 'I'm sure we've met somewhere before,' she says. The man rolls his head slightly as if he has toothache or a headache. 'I would be so grateful,' Lise says, 'for a lift.'

'I'm afraid –' says the woman. And just then a man in a chauffeur's uniform comes up. 'Good morning, m' lord,' he says. 'We're parked over there. Did you have a good trip?'

The man has opened his mouth wide but without making a sound; now he closes his lips tight.

'Come along,' says the plump woman, while the girl turns in an unconcerned way. The plump woman says sweetly to Lise, while brushing past her, 'I'm sorry, we can't stop at the moment. The car's waiting and we have no extra room.'

Lise shouts, 'But your luggage – you've forgotten your luggage.'

The chauffeur turns cheerily and says over his shoulder, 'No luggage, Miss, they don't bring luggage. Got all they need at the villa.' He winks and breezes about his business.

The three follow him across the street to the rows of waiting cars and are followed by other travellers who stream out of the airport building.

Lise runs back to Bill. He says, 'What are you up to?'

'I thought I knew him,' Lise says. She is crying, her tears fall heavily. She says, 'I was sure he was the right one. I've got to meet someone.'

Bill says, 'Don't cry, don't cry, people are looking. What's the matter? I don't get it.' At the same time he grins with his wide mouth as if to affirm that the incomprehensible needs must be a joke. 'I don't get it,' he says, pulling out of his pocket two men's-size paper handkerchiefs, and, selecting one, handing it to Lise. 'Who did you think he was?'

Lise wipes her eyes and blows her nose. She clutches the paper handkerchief in her fist. She says, 'It's a disappointing start to my holidays. I was sure.'

'You've got me for the next few days if you like,' Bill says. 'Don't you want to see me again? Come on, we'll get a taxi, you'll feel better in a taxi. You can't go on the bus, crying like that. I don't get it. I can give you what you want, wait and see.'

On the pavement, further up, among a cluster of people waiting for a taxi is the sturdy young man in his business suit, holding his brief-case. Lise looks listlessly at Bill, then beyond Bill, and just as listlessly takes in the man whose rosy face is turned towards her. He lifts his suitcase immediately he catches sight of her and crosses the road amongst the traffic, moving quickly away and away. But Lise is not watching him any more, she does not even seem to have remembered him.

In the taxi she laughs harshly when Bill tries to kiss her. Then she lets him kiss her, emerging from the contact with raised eyebrows as who should say, 'What next?' 'I'm your type,' Bill says.

The taxi stops at the grey stone downtown Hotel Tomson. She says, 'What's all that on the floor?' and points to a scatter of small seeds. Bill looks at them closely and then at his zipper-bag which has come unzipped by a small fraction.

'Rice,' he says. 'One of my sample packs must have burst and this bag isn't closed properly.' He zips up the bag and says, 'Never mind.'

He takes her to the narrow swing doors and hands her suitcase to the porter. 'I'll look for you at seven in the hall of the Metropole,' he says. He kisses her on the cheek and again she raises her eyebrows. She pushes the swing door and goes with it, not looking back.

FOUR

At the hotel desk she seems rather confused as if she is not quite sure where she is. She gives her name and when the concierge asks for her passport she evidently does not immediately understand, for she asks him what he wants first in Danish, then French. She tries Italian, lastly English. He smiles and responds to Italian and English, again requesting her passport in both languages.

'It is confusing,' she says in English, handing over her passport.

'Yes, you left part of yourself at home,' the concierge says. 'That other part, he is still en route to our country but he will catch up with you in a few hours' time. It's often the way with travel by air, the passenger arrives ahead of himself. Can I send you to your room a drink or a coffee?'

'No, thank you.' She turns to follow the waiting page-boy, then turns back. 'When will you be finished with my passport?'

'Any time, any time, Madam. When you come down again. When you go out. Any time.' He looks at her dress and coat, then turns to some other people who have just arrived. While the boy waits, dangling a room-key, to take her up, Lise pauses for a moment to have a good look at them. They are a family: mother, father, two sons and a small daughter all speaking German together volubly. Lise is meanwhile gazed back at by the two sons. She turns away, impatiently gesturing the page-boy towards the lift, and follows him.

In her room she gets rid of the boy quickly, and without even taking her coat off lies down on the bed, staring at the ceiling. She breathes deeply and deliberately, in and out, for a few minutes. Then she gets up, takes off her coat, and examines what there is of the room.

It is a bed with a green cotton cover, a bedside table, a rug, a dressing-table, two chairs, a small chest of drawers; there is a wide tall window which indicates that it had once formed part of a much larger room, now partitioned into two or three rooms in the interests of hotel economy; there is a small bathroom with a bidet, a lavatory, a wash-basin and a shower. The walls and a built-in cupboard have been a yellowish cream but are now dirty with dark marks giving evidence of past pieces of furniture now removed or rearranged. Her suitcase lies on a rack-table. The bedside light is a curved chromium stand with a parchment shade. Lise switches it on. She switches on the central light which is encased in a mottled glass globe; the light flicks on, then immediately flickers out as if, having served a long succession of clients without complaint, Lise is suddenly too much for it.

She tramps heavily into the bathroom and first, without hesitation, peers into the drinking-glass as if fully expecting to find what she does indeed find: two Alka-Seltzers, quite dry, having presumably been put there by the previous occupant who no doubt had wanted to sober up but who had finally lacked the power or memory to fill the glass with water and drink the salutary result.

By the side of the bed is a small oblong box bearing three pictures without words to convey to clients of all languages which bell-push will bring which room attendant. Lise examines this with a frown, as it were deciphering with the effort necessary to those more accus-tomed to word-reading the three pictures which represent first a frilly maid with a long-handled duster over her shoulder, next a waiter carrying a tray and lastly a man in buttoned uniform bearing a folded garment over his arm. Lise presses the maid. A light goes on in the box illuminating the picture. Lise sits on the bed and waits. Then she takes off her shoes and, watching the door for a few seconds more, presses the buttoned valet who likewise does not come. Nor does room-service after many more minutes. Lise lifts the telephone, demands the concierge and complains in a torrent that the bell-pushes bring no answer, the room is dirty, the tooth-glass has not been changed since the last guest left, the central light needs a new bulb, and that the bed, contrary to the advance specifications of her travel agency, has a too-soft mattress. The concierge advises her to press the bell for the maid.

Lise has started reciting her list over again from the beginning, when the maid does appear with a question-mark on her face. Lise puts down the receiver rather loudly and points to the light which the maid tries for herself, then, nodding her understanding of the case, makes to leave. 'Wait!' says Lise, first in English then in French, to neither of which the maid responds. Lise produces the glass with its Alka-Seltzers nestled at the bottom. 'Filthy!' Lise says in English. The maid obligingly fills the glass from the tap and hands it to Lise. 'Dirty!' Lise shouts in French. The maid understands, laughs at the happening, and this time makes a quick getaway with the glass in her hand.

Lise slides open the cupboard, pulls down a wooden hanger and throws it across the room with a clatter, then lies down on the bed. Presently she looks at her watch. It is five past one. She opens her suitcase and carefully extracts a short dressing-gown. She takes out a dress, hangs it in the cupboard, takes it off the hanger again, folds it neatly and puts it back. She takes out her sponge-bag and bedroom slippers, undresses, puts on her dressing-gown and goes into the bathroom, shutting the door. She has reached the point of taking a shower when she hears voices from her room, a scraping sound, a man's and a girl's. Putting forth her head from the bathroom door, she sees a man in light brown overalls with a pair of steps and an electric light bulb, accompanied by the maid. Lise comes out in her dressing-gown without having properly dried herself in the evident interest of protecting her hand-bag which lies on the bed. Her dressing-gown clings damply to her. 'Where is the tooth-glass?' Lise demands. 'I must have a glass for water.' The maid touches her head to denote forgetfulness and departs with a swish of her skirt, never to return within Lise's cognizance. However, Lise soon makes known her need for a drinking-glass on the telephone to the concierge, threatening to leave the hotel immediately if she doesn't get her water-glass right away.

While waiting for the threat to take effect Lise again considers the contents of her suitcase. This seems to present her with a problem, for she takes out a pink cotton dress, hangs it in the cupboard, then after hesitating for a few seconds she takes it off the hanger again, folds it carefully and lays it back in her case. It may be that she is indeed contemplating an immediate departure from the hotel. But when another maid arrives with two drinking-glasses, apologies in Italian and the explanation that the former maid had gone off duty, Lise continues to look through her belongings in a puzzled way, taking nothing further out of her suitcase.

This maid, seeing laid out on the bed the bright-coloured dress and coat in which Lise had arrived, inquires amiably if Madam is going to the beach.

'No,' says Lise.

'You American?' says the maid.

'No,' Lise says.

'English?'

'No.' Lise turns her back to continue her careful examination of her clothes in the suitcase, and the maid goes out with an unwanted air, saying, 'Good day.'

Lise is lifting the corners of her carefully packed things, as if in absent-minded accompaniment to some thought, who knows what? Then, with some access of decision, she takes off her dressing-gown and slippers and starts putting on again the same clothes that she wore on her journey. When she is dressed she folds the dressing-gown, puts the slippers back in their plastic bag, and replaces them in her suitcase. She also puts back everything that she has taken out of her sponge-bag, and packs this away.

Now she takes from an inside pocket of her suitcase a brochure with an inset map which she spreads out on the bed. She studies it closely, finding first the spot where the Hotel Tomson is situated and from there traces with her finger various routes leading into and away from the centre of the town. Lise stands, bending over it. The room is dark although it is not yet two in the afternoon. Lise switches on the central light and pores over her map.

It is marked here and there with tiny pictures which denote historic buildings, museums and monuments. Eventually Lise takes a ball-point pen from her bag and marks a spot in a large patch of green, the main parkland of the city. She puts a little cross beside one of the small pictures which is described on the map as 'The Pavilion'. She then folds up the map and replaces it in the pamphlet which she then edges in her hand-bag. The pen lies, apparently forgotten, on the bed. She looks at herself in the glass, touches her hair, then locks her suitcase. She finds the car-keys that she had failed to leave behind this morning and attaches them once more to her key-ring. She puts the bunch of keys in her hand-bag, picks up her paperback book and goes out, locking the door behind her. Who knows her thoughts? Who can tell?

She is downstairs at the desk where, behind the busy clerks, numbered pigeon-holes irregularly contain letters, packages, the room-keys, or nothing, and above them the clock shows twelve minutes past two. Lise puts her room-key on the counter and asks for her passport in a loud voice causing the clerk whom she addresses, another clerk who sits working an adding machine, and several other people who are standing and sitting in the hotel lobby, to take notice of her.

The women stare at her clothes. They, too, are dressed brightly for a southern summer, but even here in this holiday environment Lise looks brighter. It is possibly the combination of colours – the red in her coat and the purple in her dress – rather than the colours themselves which drags attention to her, as she takes her passport in its plastic envelope from the clerk, he looking meanwhile as if he bears the whole of the eccentricities of humankind upon his slender shoulders.

Two girls, long-legged, in the very brief skirts of the times, stare at Lise. Two women who might be their mothers stare too. And possibly the fact that Lise's outfit comes so far and unfashionably below her knees gives an extra shockingness to her appearance that was not even apparent in the less up-to-date Northern city from which she set off that morning. Skirts are worn shorter here in the South. Just as, in former times, when prostitutes could be discerned by the brevity of their skirts compared with the normal standard, so Lise in her knee-covering clothes at this moment looks curiously of the street-prostitute class beside the mini-skirted girls and their mothers whose knees at least can be seen.

So she lays the trail, presently to be followed by Interpol and elaborated upon with due art by the journalists of Europe for the few days it takes for her identity to be established.

'I want a taxi,' Lise says loudly to the uniformed boy who stands by the swing door. He goes out to the street and whistles. Lise follows and stands on the pavement. An elderly woman, small, neat and agile in a yellow cotton dress, whose extremely wrinkled face is the only indication of her advanced age, follows Lise to the pavement. She, too, wants a taxi, she says in a gentle voice, and she suggests to Lise that they might share. Which way is Lise going? This woman seems to see nothing strange about Lise, so confidently does she approach her. And in fact, although this is not immediately apparent, the woman's eyesight is sufficiently dim, her hearing faint enough, to eliminate, for her, the garish effect of Lise on normal perceptions.

'Oh,' says Lise, 'I'm only going to the Centre. I've no definite plans. It's foolish to have plans.' She laughs very loudly.

'Thank you, the Centre is fine for me,' says the woman, taking Lise's laugh for acquiescence in the sharing of the taxi.

And, indeed, they do both load into the taxi and are off.

'Are you staying here long?' says the woman.

'This will keep it safe,' says Lise, stuffing her passport down the back of the seat, stuffing it down till it is out of sight.

The old lady turns her spry nose towards this operation. She looks puzzled for an instant, but soon complies with the action, moving forward to allow Lise more scope in shoving the little booklet out of sight.

'That's that,' says Lise, leaning back, breathing deeply, and looking out of the window. 'What a lovely day!'

The old lady leans back too, as if leaning on the trusting confidence that Lise has inspired. She says, 'I left my passport in the hotel, with the Desk.'

'It's according to your taste,' Lise says opening the window to the slight breeze. Her lips part blissfully as she breathes in the air of the wide street on the city's outskirts.

Soon they run into traffic. The driver inquires the precise point at which they wish to be dropped.

'The Post Office,' Lise says. Her companion nods.

Lise turns to her. 'I'm going shopping. It's the first thing I do on my holidays. I go and buy the little presents for the family first, then that's off my mind.'

'Oh, but in *these* days,' says the old lady. She folds her gloves, pats them on her lap, smiles at them.

'There's a big department store near the Post Office,' Lise says. 'You can get everything you want there.'

'My nephew is arriving this evening.'

'The traffic!' says Lise.

They pass the Metropole Hotel. Lise says, 'There's a man in that hotel I'm trying to avoid.'

'Everything is different,' says the old lady.

'A girl isn't made of cement,' Lise says, 'but everything is different now, it's all changed, believe me.'

At the Post Office they pay the fare, each meticulously contributing the unfamiliar coins to the impatient, mottled and hillocky palm of the driver's hand, adding coins little by little, until the total is reached and the amount of the tip equally agreed between them and deposited; then they stand on the pavement in the centre of the foreign city, in need of coffee and a sandwich, accustoming themselves to the lay-out, the traffic crossings, the busy residents, the ambling tourists and the worried tourists, and such of the unencumbered youth who swing and thread through the crowds like antelopes whose heads, invisibly antlered, are airborne high to sniff the prevailing winds, and who so appear to own the terrain beneath their feet that they never look at it. Lise looks down at her clothes as if wondering if she is ostentatious enough.

Then, taking the old lady by the arm, she says, 'Come and have a coffee. We'll cross by the lights.'

All perky for the adventure, the old lady lets Lise guide her to the street-crossing where they wait for the lights to change and where, while waiting, the old lady gives a little gasp and a jerk of shock; she says, 'You left your passport in the taxi!'

'Well, I left it there for safety. Don't worry,' Lise says. 'It's taken care of.'

'Oh, I see.' The old lady relaxes, and she crosses the road with Lise and the waiting herd. 'I am Mrs Fiedke,' she says. 'Mr Fiedke passed away fourteen years ago.'

In the bar they sit at a small round table, place their bags, Lise's book and their elbows on it and order each a coffee and a ham-and-tomato sandwich. Lise props up her paperback book against her bag, as it were so that its bright cover is addressed to whom it may concern. 'Our home is in Nova Scotia,' says Mrs Fiedke, 'where is yours?'

'Nowhere special,' says Lise waving aside the triviality. 'It's written on the passport. My name's Lise.' She takes her arms out of the sleeves of her striped cotton coat and lets it fall behind her over the back of the chair. 'Mr Fiedke left everything to me and nothing to his sister,' says the old lady, 'but my nephew gets everything when I'm gone. I would have liked to be a fly on the wall when she heard.'

The waiter comes with their coffee and sandwiches, moving the book while he sets them down. Lise props it up again when he has gone. She looks around at the other tables and at the people standing up at the bar, sipping coffee or fruit-juice. She says, 'I have to meet a friend, but he doesn't seem to be here.'

'My dear, I don't want to detain you or take you out of your way.'

'Not at all. Don't think of it.'

'It was very kind of you to come along with me,' says Mrs Fiedke, 'as it's so confusing in a strange place. Very kind indeed.'

'Why shouldn't I be kind?' Lise says, smiling at her with a sudden gentleness.

'Well, I'll be all right just here after we've finished our snack. I'll just take a look round and do a bit of shopping. I won't keep you, my dear.'

'You can come shopping with me,' Lise says, very genially. 'Mrs Fiedke, it's a pleasure.'

'How very kind you are!'

'One should always be kind,' Lise says, 'in case it might be the last chance. One might be killed crossing the street, or even on the pavement, any time, you never know. So we should always be kind.' She cuts her sandwich daintily and puts a piece in her mouth.

Mrs Fiedke says, 'That's a very, very beautiful thought. But you mustn't think of accidents. I can assure you, I'm terrified of traffic.'

'So am I. Terrified.'

'Do you drive an automobile?' says the old lady.

'I do, but I'm afraid of traffic. You never know what crackpot's going to be at the wheel of another car.'

'These days,' says Mrs Fiedke.

'There's a department store not far from here,' Lise says. 'Want to come?'

They eat their sandwich and drink their coffee. Lise then orders a rainbow ice while Mrs Fiedke considers one way or another whether she really wants anything more, and eventually declines.

'Strange voices,' says the old lady looking round. 'Look at the noise.'

'Well, if you know the language.'

'Can you speak the language?'

'A bit. I can speak four.'

Mrs Fiedke marvels benevolently while Lise bashfully plays with crumbs on the tablecloth. The waiter brings the rainbow ice and while Lise lifts the spoon to start Mrs Fiedke says, 'It matches with your outfit.'

Lise laughs at this, longer than Mrs Fiedke had evidently expected. 'Beautiful colours,' Mrs Fiedke offers, as one might offer a cough-sweet. Lise sits before the brightly streaked ice-cream with her spoon in her hand and laughs on. Mrs Fiedke looks frightened, and more frightened as the voices of the bar stop to watch the laughing one; Mrs Fiedke shrinks into her old age, her face dry and wrinkled, her eyes gone into a far retreat, not knowing what to do. Lise stops suddenly and says, 'That was funny.'

The man behind the bar, having started coming over to their table to investigate a potential disorder, stops and turns back, muttering something. A few young men round the bar start up a mimic laugh-laugh-laugh but are stopped by the barman.

'When I went to buy this dress,' Lise says to Mrs Fiedke, 'do you know what they offered me first? A stainless dress. Can you believe it? A dress that won't hold the stain if you drop coffee or ice-cream on it. Some new synthetic fabric. As if I would want a dress that doesn't show the stains!'

Mrs Fiedke, whose eager spirit is slowly returning from wherever it had been to take cover from Lise's laughter, looks at Lise's dress and says, 'Doesn't hold the stains? Very useful for travelling.'

'Not this dress,' Lise says, working her way through the rainbow ice; 'it was another dress. I didn't buy it, though. Very poor taste, I thought.' She has finished her ice. Again the two women fumble in their purses and at the same time Lise gives an expert's glance at the two small tickets, marked with the price, that have been left on the table. Lise edges one of them aside. 'That one's for the ice,' she says, 'and we share the other.'

'The torment of it,' Lise says. 'Not knowing exactly where and when he's going to turn up.'

She moves ahead of Mrs Fiedke up the escalator to the third floor of a department store. It is ten minutes past four by the big clock, and they have had to wait more than half an hour for it to open, both of them having forgotten about the southern shopping hours, and in this interval have walked round the block looking so earnestly for Lise's

friend that Mrs Fiedke has at some point lost the signs of her initial
bewilderment when this friend has been mentioned, and now shows
only the traces of enthusiastic cooperation in the search. As they were
waiting for the store to open, having passed the large iron-grated
shutters again and again in their ambles round the block, Mrs Fiedke
started to scan the passers-by.

'Would that be him, do you think? He looks very gaily dressed like
yourself.'

'No, that's not him.'

'It's quite a problem, with all this choice. What about this one? No
this one, I mean, crossing in front of that car? Would he be too fat?'

'No, it isn't him.'

'It's very difficult, my dear, if you don't know the cast of person.'

'He could be driving a car,' Lise had said when they at last found
themselves outside the shop at the moment the gates were being
opened.

They go up, now, to the third floor where the toilets are, skimming
up with the escalator from which they can look down to see the
expanse of each floor as the stairs depart from it. 'Not a great many
gentlemen,' Mrs Fiedke remarks. 'I doubt if you'll find your friend
here.'

'I doubt it too,' says Lise. 'Although there are quite a few men
employed here, aren't there?'

'Oh, would he be a shop assistant?' Mrs Fiedke says.

'It depends,' says Lise.

'These days,' says Mrs Fiedke.

Lise stands in the ladies' room combing her hair while she waits for
Mrs Fiedke. She stands at the basin where she has washed her hands,
and, watching herself with tight lips in the glass, back-combs the
white streak, and with great absorption places it across the darker
locks on the crown of her head. At the basins on either side of her two
other absorbed young women are touching up their hair and faces.
Lise wets the tip of a finger and smooths her eyebrows. The women
on either side collect their belongings and leave. Another woman,
matronly with her shopping, bustles in and swings into one of the
lavatory cubicles. Mrs Fiedke's cubicle still remains shut. Lise has
finished tidying herself up; she waits. Eventually she knocks on Mrs
Fiedke's door. 'Are you all right?'

She says again, 'Are you all right?' And again she knocks. 'Mrs Fiedke, are you all right?'

The latest comer now bursts out of her cubicle and makes for the wash-basin. Lise says to her, while rattling the handle of Mrs Fiedke's door, 'There's an old lady locked in here and I can't hear a sound. Something must have happened.' And she calls again, 'Are you all right, Mrs Fiedke?'

'Who is she?' says the other woman.

'I don't know.'

'But you're with her, aren't you?' The matron takes a good look at Lise.

'I'll go and get someone,' Lise says, and she shakes the handle one more time. 'Mrs Fiedke! Mrs Fiedke!' She presses her ear to the door. 'No sound,' she says, 'none at all.' Then she grabs her bag and her book from the wash-stand and dashes out of the ladies' room leaving the other woman listening and rattling at the door of Mrs Fiedke's cubicle.

Outside, the first department is laid out with sports equipment. Lise walks straight through, stopping only to touch one of a pair of skis, feeling and stroking the wood. A salesman approaches, but Lise has walked on, picking her way among the more populated area of School Clothing. Here she hovers over a pair of small, red fur-lined gloves laid out on the counter. The girl behind the counter stands ready to serve. Lise looks up at her. 'For my niece,' she says. 'But I can't remember the size. I think I won't risk it, thank you.' She moves across the department floor to Toys, where she spends some time examining a nylon dog which, at the flick of a switch attached to its lead, barks, trots, wags its tail and sits. Through Linen, to the down escalator goes Lise, scanning each approaching floor in her descent, but not hovering on any landing until she reaches the ground floor. Here she buys a silk scarf patterned in black and white. At a gadgets counter a salesman is demonstrating a cheap electric food-blender. Lise buys one of these, staring at the salesman when he attempts to include personal charm in his side of the bargain. He is a thin, pale man of early middle age, eager-eyed. 'Are you on holiday?' he says. 'American? Swedish?' Lise says, 'I'm in a hurry.' Resigned to his mistake, the salesman wraps her parcel, takes her money, rings up the till and gives her the change. Lise then takes the wide staircase leading to the basement. Here she buys a plastic zipper-bag in which she places her packages. She stops at the Records and Record-Players department and loiters with the small group that has gathered to hear a new pop-group disc. She holds her paperback well in evidence, her hand-bag and the new zipper-bag slung over her left arm just above the wrist, and her hands holding up the book in front of her chest like an identification notice carried by a displaced person.

> Come on over to my place
> For a sandwich, both of you,
> Any time . . .

The disc comes to an end. A girl with long brown pigtails is hopping about in front of Lise, continuing the rhythm with her elbows, her blue-jeans, and apparently her mind, as a newly beheaded chicken continues for a brief time, now squawklessly, its panic career. Mrs Fiedke comes up behind Lise and touches her arm. Lise says, turning to smile at her, 'Look at this idiot girl. She can't stop dancing.'

'I think I fell asleep for a moment,' Mrs Fiedke says. 'It wasn't a bad turn. I just dropped off. Such kind people. They wanted to put me in a taxi. But why should I go back to the hotel? My poor nephew won't be there till 9 o'clock tonight or maybe later; he must have missed the earlier plane. The porter was so kind, ringing up to find out the time of the next plane. All that.'

'Look at her,' Lise says in a murmur. 'Just look at her. No, wait! – She'll start again when the man puts on the next record.'

The record starts, and the girl swings. Lise says, 'Do you believe in macrobiotics?'

'I'm a Jehovah's Witness,' says Mrs Fiedke. 'But that was after Mr Fiedke passed on. I have no problems any more. Mr Fiedke cut out his sister you know, because she had no religion. She questioned. There are some things which you can't. But I know this, if Mr Fiedke was alive today he would be a Witness too. In fact he was one in many ways without knowing it.'

'Macrobiotics is a way of life,' Lise says. 'That man at the Metropole, I met him on the plane. He's an Enlightenment Leader of the macrobiotics. He's on Regime Seven.'

'How delightful!' says Mrs Fiedke.

'But he isn't my type,' Lise says.

The girl with the pigtails is dancing on by herself in front of them, and as she suddenly steps back Mrs Fiedke has to retreat out of her way. 'Is she what they call a hippy?' she says.

'There were two others on the plane. I thought they were my type, but they weren't. I was disappointed.'

'But you are to meet your gentleman soon, won't you? Didn't you say?'

'Oh, *he's* my type,' Lise says.

'I must get a pair of slippers for my nephew. Size nine. He missed the plane.'

'This one's a hippy,' says Lise, indicating with her head a slouching bearded youth dressed in tight blue-jeans, no longer blue, his shoulders draped with an assortment of cardigans and fringed leather garments, heavy for the time of year.

Mrs Fiedke looks with interest and whispers to Lise, 'They are hermaphrodites. It isn't their fault.' The young man turns as he is touched on the shoulder by a large blue-suited agent of the store. The bearded youth starts to argue and gesticulate, but this brings another, slighter, man to his other shoulder. They lead him protesting away towards the emergency exit stairway. A slight disturbance then occurs amongst the record-hearing crowd, some of whom take the young man's part, some of whom do not. 'He wasn't doing any harm!' 'He smelt awful!' 'Who do *you* think you are?'

Lise walks off towards Televisions, followed anxiously by Mrs Fiedke. Behind them the pigtailed girl is addressing her adjacent crowd: 'They think they're in America where if they don't like a man's face they take him out and shoot him.' A man's voice barks back: 'You couldn't see his face for the hair. Go back where you came from, little whore! In this country, we . . .'

The quarrel melts behind them as they come to the television sets where the few people who have been taking an interest in the salesman appear now to be torn between his calm rivulet of words and the incipient political uprising over at Records and Record-Players. Two television screens, one vast and one small, display the same pro-gramme, a wild-life documentary film which is now coming to an end; a charging herd of buffalo, large on one screen and small on the other, cross the two patches of vision while music of an unmistakably finale nature sends them on their way with equal volume from both machines. The salesman turns down the noise from the larger set, and continues to address his customers, who have now dwindled to two, meanwhile keeping an interested eye on Lise and Mrs Fiedke who hover behind.

'Would that be your gentleman?' Mrs Fiedke says, while the screens give a list of names responsible for the film, then another and another list of names. Lise says, 'I was just wondering myself. He looks a respectable type.'

'It's up to you,' says Mrs Fiedke. 'You're young and you have your life in front of you.'

A well-groomed female announcer comes on both televisions, small and large, to give out the early evening headlines, first stating that the time is 17.00 hours, then that a military coup has newly taken place in a middle-eastern country details of which are yet unknown. The salesman, abandoning his potential clients to their private deliberations, inclines his head towards Mrs Fiedke and inquires if he can help her.

'No thank you,' Lise replies in the tongue of the country. Whereupon the salesman comes close up and pursues Mrs Fiedke in English. 'We have big reductions, Madam, this week.' He looks winningly at Lise, eventually approaching to squeeze her arm. Lise turns to Mrs Fiedke. 'No good,' she says. 'Come on, it's getting late,' and she guides the old lady away to Gifts and Curios at the far end of the floor. 'Not my man at all. He tried to get familiar with me,' Lise says. 'The one I'm looking for will recognize me right away for the woman I am, have no fear of that.'

'Can you credit it?' says Mrs Fiedke looking back indignantly in the direction of Televisions. 'Perhaps we should report him. Where is the Office?'

'What's the use?' Lise says. 'We have no proof.'

'Perhaps we should go elsewhere for my nephew's slippers.'

'Do you really want to buy slippers for your nephew?' Lise says.

'I thought of slippers as a welcome present. My poor nephew – the hotel porter was so nice. The poor boy was to have arrived on this morning's flight from Copenhagen. I waited and I waited. He must have missed the plane. The porter looked up the timetable and there's another arriving tonight. I must remember not to go to bed. The plane gets in at ten-twenty but it may be eleven-thirty, twelve, before he gets to the hotel, you know.'

Lise is looking at the leather notecases, embossed with the city's crest. 'These look good,' Lise says. 'Get him one of these. He would remember all his life that you gave it to him.'

'I think slippers,' says Mrs Fiedke. 'Somehow I feel slippers. My poor nephew has been unwell, we had to send him to a clinic. It was either that or the other, they gave us no choice. He's so much better now, quite well again. But he needs rest. Rest, rest and more rest is what the doctor wrote. He takes size nine.'

Lise is playing with a corkscrew, then with a ceramic-handled cork. 'Slippers might make him feel like an invalid,' she says. 'Why don't you buy him a record or a book? How old is he?'

'Only twenty-four. It comes from the mother's side. Perhaps we should go to another shop.'

Lise leans over the counter to inquire which department is men's slippers. Patiently she translates the answer to Mrs Fiedke. 'Foot-wear on the third floor. We'll have to go back up. The other stores are much too expensive, they charge you what they like. The travel-folder recommends this place as they've got fixed prices.'

Up they go, once more, surveying the receding departments as they rise; they buy the slippers; they descend to the ground floor. There, near the street door, they find another gift department with a miscellany of temptations. Lise buys another scarf, bright orange. She buys a striped man's necktie, dark blue and yellow. Then, glimpsing through the crowd a rack from which dangles a larger assortment of men's ties, each neatly enfolded in transparent plastic, she changes her mind about the coloured tie she has just bought. The girl at the counter is not pleased by the difficulties involved in the refund of money, and accompanies Lise over to the rack to see if an exchange can be effected.

Lise selects two ties, one plain black knitted cotton, the other green. Then, changing her mind once more, she says, 'That green is too bright, I think.' The girl conveys exasperation, and in a manner of vexed resignation Lise says, 'All right, give me two black ties, they're always useful. Please remove the prices.' She returns to the counter where she had left Mrs Fiedke, pays the difference and takes her package. Mrs Fiedke appears from the doorway where she has been examining, by daylight, two leather notecases. A shopman, who has been hovering by, in case she should be one of those who make a dash for it, goods in hand, follows her back to the counter. He says, 'They're both very good leather.'

Mrs Fiedke says, 'I think he has one already.' She chooses a paper-knife in a sheath. Lise stands watching. She says, 'I nearly bought one of those for my boy-friend at the airport before I left. It was almost the same but not quite.' The paper-knife is made of brassy metal, curved like a scimitar. The sheath is embossed but not, like the one Lise had considered earlier in the day, jewelled. 'The slippers are enough,' Lise says.

Mrs Fiedke says, 'You're quite right. One doesn't want to spoil them.' She looks at a key-case, then buys the paper-knife.

'If he uses a paper-knife,' Lise says, 'obviously he isn't a hippy. If he were a hippy he would open his letters with his fingers.'

'Would it be too much trouble,' she says to Lise, 'to put this in your bag? And the slippers – oh, where are the slippers?'

Her package of slippers is lost, is gone. She claims to have left it on the counter while she had been to the door to compare the two leather notecases. The package has been lifted, has been taken away by somebody. Everyone looks around for it and sympathizes, and points out that it was her own fault.

'Maybe he has plenty of slippers, anyway,' Lise says. 'Is he my type of man, do you think?'

'We ought to see the sights,' says Mrs Fiedke. 'We shouldn't let this golden opportunity go by without seeing the ruins.'

'If he's my type I want to meet him,' Lise says.

'Very much your type,' says Mrs Fiedke, 'at his best.'

'What a pity he's coming so late,' Lise says. 'Because I have a previous engagement with my boyfriend. However, if he doesn't turn up before your nephew arrives I want to meet your nephew. What's his name did you say?'

'Richard. We never called him Dick. Only his mother, but not us. I hope he gets the plane all right. Oh – where's the paper-knife?'

'You put it in here,' says Lise, pointing to her zipper-bag. 'Don't worry, it's safe. Let's get out of here.'

As they drift with the outgoing shoppers into the sunny street, Mrs

Fiedke says, 'I hope he's on that plane. There was some talk that he would go to Barcelona first to meet his mother, then on here to meet up with me. But I wouldn't play. I just said No! No flying from Barcelona, I said. I'm a strict believer, in fact, a Witness, but I never trust the airlines from those countries where the pilots believe in the afterlife. You are safer when they don't. I've been told the Scandinavian airlines are fairly reliable in that respect.'

Lise looks up and down the street and sighs. 'It can't be long now. My friend's going to turn up soon. He knows I've come all this way to see him. He knows it, all right. He's just waiting around somewhere. Apart from that I have no plans.'

'Dressed for the carnival!' says a woman, looking grossly at Lise as she passes, and laughing as she goes her way, laughing without possibility of restraint, like a stream bound to descend whatever slope lies before it.

'It is in my mind,' says Mrs Fiedke; 'it is in my mind and I can't think of anything else but that you and my nephew are meant for each other. As sure as anything, my dear, you are the person for my nephew. Somebody has got to take him on, anyhow, that's plain.'

'He's only twenty-four,' considers Lise. 'Much too young.'

They are descending a steep path leading from the ruins. Steps have been roughly cut out of the earthy track, outlined only by slats of wood which are laid at the edge of each step. Lise holds Mrs Fiedke's arm and helps her down one by one.

'How do you know his age?' says Mrs Fiedke.

'Well, didn't you tell me, twenty-four?' Lise says.

'Yes, but I haven't seen him for quite a time you know. He's been away.'

'Maybe he's even younger. Take care, go slowly.'

'Or it could be the other way. People age when they've had unpleasant experiences over the years. It just came to me while we were looking at those very interesting pavements in that ancient temple up there, that poor Richard may be the very man that you're looking for.'

'Well, it's your idea,' says Lise, 'not mine. I wouldn't know till I'd seen him. Myself, I think he's around the corner somewhere, now, any time.'

'Which corner?' The old lady looks up and down the street which runs below them at the bottom of the steps.

'Any corner. Any old corner.'

'Will you feel a presence? Is that how you'll know?'

'Not really a presence,' Lise says. 'The lack of an absence, that's what it is. I know I'll find it. I keep on making mistakes, though.' She starts to cry, very slightly sniffing, weeping, and they stop on the steps while Mrs Fiedke produces a trembling pink face-tissue from her bag

466

for Lise to dab her eyes with and blow her nose on. Sniffing, Lise throws the shredded little snitch of paper away and again takes Mrs Fiedke's arm to resume their descent. 'Too much self-control, which arises from fear and timidity, that's what's wrong with them. They're cowards, most of them.'

'Oh, I always believe *that*,' says Mrs Fiedke. 'No doubt about it. The male sex.'

They have reached the road where the traffic thunders past in the declining sunlight.

'Where do we cross?' Lise says, looking to right and left of the overwhelming street.

'They are demanding equal rights with us,' says Mrs Fiedke. 'That's why I never vote with the Liberals. Perfume, jewellery, hair down to their shoulders, and I'm not talking about the ones who were born like that. I mean, the ones that can't help it should be put on an island. It's the others I'm talking about. There was a time when they would stand up and open the door for you. They would take their hat off. But they want their equality today. All I say is that if God had intended them to be as good as us he wouldn't have made them different from us to the naked eye. They don't want to be all dressed alike any more. Which is only a move against us. You couldn't run an army like that, let alone the male sex. With all due respects to Mr Fiedke, may he rest in peace, the male sex is getting out of hand. Of course, Mr Fiedke knew his place as a man, give him his due.'

'We'll have to walk up to the intersection,' Lise says, guiding Mrs Fiedke in the direction of a distant policeman surrounded by a whirlpool of traffic. 'We'll never get a taxi here.'

'Fur coats and flowered poplin shirts on their backs,' says Mrs Fiedke as she winds along, conducted by Lise this way and that to avoid the oncoming people in the street. 'If we don't look lively,' she says, 'they will be taking over the homes and the children, and sitting about having chats while we go and fight to defend them and work to keep them. They won't be content with equal rights only. Next thing they'll want the upper hand, mark my words. Diamond earrings, I've read in the paper.'

'It's getting late,' says Lise. Her lips are slightly parted and her nostrils and eyes, too, are a fragment more open than usual; she is a stag scenting the breeze, moving step by step, inhibiting her stride to accommodate Mrs Fiedke's pace, she seems at the same time to search for a certain air-current, a glimpse and an intimation.

'I clean mine with toothpaste when I'm travelling,' confides Mrs Fiedke. 'The better stuff's in the bank back home, of course. The insurance is too high, isn't it? But you have to bring a few bits and pieces. I clean them with my toothbrush and ordinary toothpaste, then I rub them with the hand-towel. They come up very nicely. You can't trust the jewellers. They can always take them out and replace them with a fake.'

'It's getting late,' says Lise. 'There are so many faces. Where did all the faces come from?'

'I ought to take a nap,' says Mrs Fiedke, 'so that I won't feel too tired when my nephew arrives. Poor thing. We have to leave for Capri tomorrow morning. All the cousins, you know. They've taken such a charming villa and the past will never be mentioned. My brother made that clear to them. I made it clear to my brother.'

They have reached the circular intersection and turn into a side-street where a few yards ahead at the next corner there is a taxi-rank occupied by one taxi. This one taxi is taken by someone else just as they approach it.

'I smell burning,' says Mrs Fiedke as they stand at the corner waiting for another taxi to come along. Lise sniffs, her lips parted and her eyes moving widely from face to face among the passers-by. Then she sneezes. Something has happened to the people in the street, they are looking round, they are sniffing too. Somewhere nearby a great deal of shouting is going on.

Suddenly round the corner comes a stampede. Lise and Mrs Fiedke are swept apart and jostled in all directions by a large crowd composed mainly of young men, with a few smaller, older and grimmer men, and here and there a young girl, all yelling together and making rapidly for somewhere else. 'Tear-gas!' someone shouts and then a lot of people are calling out, 'Tear-gas!' A shutter on a shop-front near Lise comes down with a hasty clatter, then the other shops start closing for the day. Lise falls and is hauled to her feet by a tough man who leaves her and runs on.

Just before it reaches the end of the street which joins the circular intersection the crowd stops. A band of grey-clad policemen come running towards them, in formation, bearing tear-gas satchels and with their gas-masks at the ready. The traffic on the circular intersection has stopped. Lise swerves with her crowd into a garage where some mechanics in their overalls crouch behind the cars and others take refuge underneath a car which is raised on a cradle in the process of repair.

Lise fights her way to a dark corner at the back of the garage where a small red Mini-Morris, greatly dented, is parked behind a larger car. She wrenches at the door, forcefully, as if she expects it to be locked. It opens so easily as to throw her backwards, and as soon as she regains her balance she gets inside, locks herself in and puts her head down between her knees, breathing heavily, drawing in the smell of petrol blended faintly with a whiff of tear-gas. The demonstrators form up in the garage and are presently discovered and routed out by the police. Their exit is fairly orderly bar the shouting.

Lise emerges from the car with her zipper-bag and her hand-bag, looking to see what damage has been done to her clothes. The garage men are vociferously commenting on the affair. One is clutching his stomach proclaiming himself poisoned and vowing to sue the police for the permanent damage caused him by tear-gas. Another, with his hand to his throat, gasps that he is suffocating. The others are cursing the students whose gestures of solidarity, they declare in the colourful derisive obscenities of their mother-tongue, they can live without. They stop when Lise limps into view. There are six of them in all, including a young apprentice and a large burly man of middle age, without overalls, wearing only a white shirt and trousers and the definite air of the proprietor. Apparently seeing in Lise a tangible remnant of the troubles lately visited upon his garage, this big fellow turns on her to vent his fury with unmastered hysteria. He advises her to go home to the brothel where she came from, he reminds her that her grandfather was ten times cuckolded, that she was conceived in some ditch and born in another; after adorning the main idea with further illustrations he finally tells her she is a student.

Lise stands somewhat entranced; by her expression she seems almost consoled by this outbreak, whether because it relieves her own tensions after the panic or whether for some other reason. However, she puts a hand up to her eyes, covering them, and in the language of the country she says, 'Oh please, please. I'm only a tourist, a teacher from Iowa, New Jersey. I've hurt my foot.' She drops her hand and looks at her coat which is stained with a long black oily mark. 'Look at my clothes,' Lise says. 'My new clothes. It's best never to be born. I wish my mother and father had practised birth-control. I wish that pill had been invented at the time. I feel sick, I feel terrible.'

The men are impressed by this, one and all. Some are visibly cheered up. The proprietor turns one way and another with arms outstretched to call the whole assembly to witness his dilemma. 'Sorry, lady, sorry. How was I to know? Pardon me, but I thought you were one of the students. We have a lot of trouble from the students. Many apologies, lady. Was there something we can do for you? I'll call the First Aid. Come and sit down, lady, over here, inside my office, take a seat. You see the traffic outside, how can I call the ambulance through the traffic? Sit down, lady.' And, having ushered her into a tiny windowed cubicle, he sits Lise in its only chair beside a small sloping ledger-desk and thunders at the men to get to work.

Lise says, 'Oh please don't call anyone. I'll be all right if I can get a taxi to take me back to my hotel.'

'A taxi! Look at the traffic!'

Outside the archway that forms the entrance to the garage, there is a dense block of standing traffic.

The proprietor keeps going to look up and down the street and returning to Lise. He calls for benzine and a rag to clean Lise's coat. No rag clean enough for the purpose can be found and so he uses a big white handkerchief taken from the breast pocket of his coat which hangs behind the door of the little office. Lise takes off her black-stained coat and while he applies his benzine-drenched handkerchief to the stain, making it into a messy blur, Lise takes off her shoes and rubs her feet. She puts one foot up on the slanting desk and rubs. 'It's only a bruise,' she says, 'not a sprain. I was lucky. Are you married?'

The big man says, 'Yes, lady, I'm married,' and pauses in his energetic task to look at her with new, appraising and cautious eyes. 'Three children – two boys, one girl,' he says. He looks through the office at his men who are occupied with various jobs and who, although one or two of them cast a swift glance at Lise with her foot up on the desk, do not give any sign of noticing any telepathic distress signals their employer might be giving out.

The big man says to Lise, 'And yourself? Married?'

'I'm a widow,' Lise says, 'and an intellectual. I come from a family of intellectuals. My late husband was an intellectual. We had no children. He was killed in a motor accident. He was a bad driver, anyway. He was a hypochondriac, which means that he imagined that he had every illness under the sun.'

'This stain,' said the man, 'won't come out until you send the coat to the dry-cleaner.' He holds out the coat with great care, ready for her to put on; and at the same time as he holds it as if he means her, temptress in the old-fashioned style that she is, to get out of his shop, his eyes are shifting around in an undecided way.

Lise takes her foot off the desk, stands, slips into her shoes, shakes the skirt of her dress and asks him, 'Do you like the colours?'

'Marvellous,' he says, his confidence plainly diminishing in confrontation with this foreign distressed gentlewoman of intellectual family and conflicting appearance.

'The traffic's moving. I must get a taxi or a bus. It's late,' Lise says, getting into her coat in a business-like manner.

'Where are you staying, lady?'

'The Hilton,' she says.

He looks round his garage with an air of helpless, anticipatory guilt. 'I'd better take her in the car,' he mutters to the mechanic nearest him. The man does not reply but makes a slight movement of the hand to signify that it isn't for him to give permission.

Still the owner hesitates, while Lise, as if she had not overheard his remarks, gathers up her belongings, holds out her hand and says 'Good-bye. Thank you very much for helping me.' And to the rest of the men she calls 'Good-bye, good-bye, many thanks!'

The big man takes her hand and holds on to it tightly as if his grasp itself was a mental resolution not to let go this unforeseen, exotic, intellectual, yet clearly available treasure. He holds on to her hand as if he was no fool, after all. 'Lady, I'm taking you to your hotel in the car. I couldn't let you go out into all this confusion. You'll never get a bus, not for hours. A taxi, never. The students, we have the students only to thank.' And he calls sharply to the apprentice to bring out his car. The boy goes over to a brown Volkswagen. 'The Fiat!' bellows his employer, whereupon the apprentice moves to a dusty cream-coloured Fiat 125, passes a duster over the outside of the windscreen, gets into it and starts to manoeuvre it forward to the main ramp.

Lise pulls away her hand and protests. 'Look, I've got a date. I'm late for it already. I'm sorry, but I can't accept your kind offer.' She looks out at the mass of slowly-moving traffic, the queues waiting at the bus-stops, and says, 'I'll have to walk. I know my way.'

'Lady,' he says, 'no argument. It's my pleasure.' And he draws her to the car where the apprentice is now waiting with the door open for her.

'I really don't know you,' Lise says.

'I'm Carlo,' says the man, urging her inside and shutting the door. He gives the grinning apprentice a push that might mean anything, goes round to the other door, and drives slowly towards the street, slowly and carefully finding a gap in the line of traffic, working his way in to the gap, blocking the oncoming vehicles for a while until finally he joins the stream.

It is also getting dark, as big Carlo's car alternately edges and spurts along the traffic, Carlo meanwhile denouncing the students and the police for causing the chaos. When they come at last to a clear stretch Carlo says, 'My wife I think is no good. I heard her on the telephone and she didn't think I was in the house. I heard.'

'You must understand,' Lise says, 'that anything at all that is overheard when the speaker doesn't know you're listening takes on a serious note. It always sounds far worse than their actual intentions are.'

'This was bad,' mutters Carlo. 'It's a man. A second cousin of hers. I made a big trouble for her that night, I can tell you. But she denied it. How could she deny it? I heard it.'

'If you imagine,' Lise says, 'that you are justifying any anticipations you may have with regards to me, you're mistaken. You can drop me off here, if you like. Otherwise, you can come and buy me a drink at the Hilton Hotel, and then it's good night. A soft drink. I don't take alcohol. I've got a date that I'm late for already.'

'We go out of town a little way,' says Carlo. 'I know a place. I brought the Fiat, did you see? The front seats fold back. Make you comfortable.'

'Stop at once,' Lise says. 'Or I put my head out of the window and yell for help. I don't want sex with you. I'm not interested in sex. I've got other interests and as a matter of fact I've got something on my mind that's got to be done. I'm telling you to stop.' She grabs the wheel and tries to guide it into the curb.

'All right, all right,' he says, regaining control of the car which has swerved a little with Lise's interference. 'All right. I'm taking you to the Hilton.'

'It doesn't look like the Hilton road to me,' Lise says. The traffic lights ahead are red but as there is very little traffic about on this dark, wide residential boulevard, he chances it and skims across. Lise puts her head out of the window and yells for help.

He pulls up at last in a side lane where, back from the road, there are the lights of two small villas; beyond that the road is a mass of stony crevices. He embraces her and kisses her mightily while she kicks him and tries to push him off, gurgling her protests. When he stops for breath he says, 'Now we put back the seats and do it properly.' But already she has jumped out of the car and has started running towards the gate of one of the houses, wiping her mouth and screaming, 'Police! Call the police!' Big Carlo overtakes her at the gate. 'Quiet!' he says. 'Be quiet, and get into the car. Please. I'll take you back, I promise. Sorry, lady, I haven't done any harm at all to you, have I? Only a kiss, what's a kiss.'

She runs and makes a grab for the door of the driver's seat, and as he calls after her, 'The other door!' she gets in, starts up, and backs speedily out of the lane. She leans over and locks the other door just in time to prevent him from opening it. 'You're not my type in any case,' she screams. Then she starts off, too quickly for him to be able to open the back door he is now grabbing at. Still he is running to catch up, and she yells back at him, 'If you report this to the police I'll tell them the truth and make a scandal in your family.' And then she is away, well clear of him.

She spins along in expert style, stopping duly at the traffic lights. She starts to sing softly as she waits:

> Inky-pinky-winky-wong
> How do you like your potatoes done?
> A little gravy in the pan
> For the King of the Cannibal Islands.

Her zipper-bag is on the floor of the car. While waiting for the lights to change she lifts it on to the seat, unzips it and looks with a kind of satisfaction at the wrapped-up objects of different shape, as it might be they represent a good day's work. She comes to a crossroad where some traffic accumulates. Here, a policeman is on duty and as she passes at his bidding she pulls up and asks him the way to the Hilton.

He is a young policeman. He bends to give her the required direction.

'Do you carry a revolver?' Lise says. He looks puzzled and fails to answer before Lise adds, 'Because, if you did, you could shoot me.'

The policeman is still finding words when she drives off, and in the mirror she can see him looking at the retreating car, probably noting the number. Which in fact he is doing, so that, on the afternoon of the following day, when he has been shown her body, he says, 'Yes, that's her. I recognize the face. She said, "If you had a revolver you could shoot me."' Which is to lead to many complications in Carlo's private life when the car is traced back to him, he being released by the police only after six hours of interrogation. A photograph of Carlo and also a picture of his young apprentice who holds a lively press conference of his own, moreover will appear in every newspaper in the country.

But now, at the Hilton Hotel her car is held up just as it enters the gates in the driveway. There is a line of cars ahead, and beyond them a group of policemen. Two police cars are visible in the parking area on the other side of the entrance. The rest of the driveway is occupied by a line of four very large limousines each with a uniformed driver standing by.

The police collect on either side of the hotel doorway, their faces picked out by the bright lights, while there emerge down the steps from the hotel two women who seem to be identical twins, wearing black dresses and high-styled black hair, followed by an important-looking Arabian figure, sheikh-like in his head-dress and robes, with a lined face and glittering eyes, who descends the steps with a floating motion as if his feet are clearing the ground by an inch or two; he is flanked by two smaller bespectacled, brown-faced men in business-like suits. The two black-dressed women stand back with a respectful housekeeperly bearing while the robed figure approaches the first limousine; and the two men draw back too, as he enters the recesses of the car. Two black-robed women with the lower parts of their faces veiled and their heads shrouded in drapery then make their descent, and behind them another pair appear, menservants with arms raised, bearing aloft numerous plastic-enveloped garments on coat-hangers. Still in pairs, further components of the retinue appear, each two moving in such unison that they seem to share a single soul or else two well-rehearsed parts in the chorus of an opera by Verdi. Two men wearing western clothes but for their red fezes are duly admitted to one of the waiting limousines and, as Lise gets out of her car to join the watchers, two ramshackle young Arabs with rumpled grey trousers and whitish shirts end the procession, bearing two large baskets, each one packed with oranges and a jumbo-sized vacuum-flask which stands slightly askew among the fruit, like champagne in an ice-bucket.

A group of people who are standing near Lise on the driveway, having themselves got out of their held-up taxis and cars, are discussing the event: 'He was here on vacation. I saw it on the television. There's been a coup in his country and he's going back.' – 'Why should he go back?' – 'No, he won't go back, believe me. Never.' – 'What country is it? I hope it doesn't affect us. The last time there was a coup my shares regressed so I nearly had a breakdown. Even the mutual funds . . .'

The police have gone back to their cars, and escorted by them the caravan goes its stately way.

Lise jumps back into Carlo's car and conducts it as quickly as possible to the car park. She leaves it there, taking the keys. Then she leaps into the hotel, eyed indignantly by the doorman who presumably resents her haste, her clothes, the blurred stain on her coat, the rumpled aspect that she has acquired in the course of the evening and whose built-in computer system rates her low on the spending scale.

Lise makes straight for the ladies' toilets and while there, besides putting her appearance to rights as best she can, she takes a comfortable chair in the soft-lit rest-room and considers, one by one, the contents of her zipper-bag which she lays on a small table beside her. She feels the outside of the box containing the food-blender and replaces it in her bag. She also leaves unopened a soft package containing the neckties, but, having rummaged in her hand-bag for something which apparently is not there, she brings forth her lipstick and with it she writes on the outside of the soft package, 'Papa'. There is an unsealed paper bag which she peers into; it is the orange scarf.

She puts it back into place and takes out another bag containing the black and white scarf. She folds this back and with her lipstick she traces on the outside of the bag in large capitals, 'Olga'. Another package seems to puzzle her. She feels round it with half-closed eyes for a moment, then opens it up. It contains the pair of men's slippers which Mrs Fiedke had mislaid in the shop having apparently in fact put them in Lise's bag. Lise wraps them up again and replaces them. Finally she takes out her paperback book and an oblong package which she opens. This is a gift-box containing the gilded paper-opener in its sheath, also Mrs Fiedke's property.

Lise slowly returns the lipstick to her handbag, places the book and the box containing the paperknife on the table beside her, places the zipper-bag on the floor, then proceeds to examine the contents of her hand-bag. Money, the tourist folder with its inset map of the city, the bunch of six keys that she had brought with her that morning, the keys of Carlo's car, the lipstick, the comb, the powder compact, the air ticket. Her lips are parted and she leans back in a relaxed attitude but that her eyes are too wide open for restfulness. She looks again at the contents of her hand-bag. A notecase with paper money, a purse with loose change. She gathers herself together in such an abrupt manner that the toilet attendant who has been sitting vacantly in a corner by the wash-basins starts to her feet. Lise packs up her belongings. She puts the paper-knife box back in the zipper-bag, carefully tucking it down the side, and zips the bag up. Her hand-bag is also packed tidily again, except for the bunch of six keys that she had brought on her travels. She holds the book in her hand, and, placing the bunch of six keys with a clatter on the plate left out for the coins, the attendant's reward, she says to the woman, 'I won't be needing these now.' Then, with her zipper-bag, her book, her hand-bag, her hair combed and her face cleaned up, she swings out of the door and into the hotel lounge. The clock above the reception desk says nine thirty-five. Lise makes for the bar, where she looks round. Most of the tables are occupied by chattering groups. She sits at a vacant but rather out-of-the-way table, orders a whisky, and bids the tentative waiter hurry. 'I've got a train to catch.' She is served with the drink together with a jug of water and a bowl of peanuts. She drenches the whisky with water, sips a small part of it and eats all the peanuts. She takes another small sip from her glass, and, leaving it nearly full, stands up and motions the waiter to bring her bill. She pays for this high-priced repast with a note taken from her bag and tells the waiter to keep the change, which amounts to a very high tip. He accepts it with incredulous grace and watches her as she leaves the bar. He, too, will give his small piece of evidence to the police on the following day, as will also the toilet attendant, trembling at the event which has touched upon her life without the asking.

Lise stops short in the hotel lounge and smiles. Then without further hesitation she goes over to a group of armchairs, only one of which is occupied. In it sits a sickly-looking man. Bending over him deferentially to listen to something the man is saying is a uniformed chauffeur who presently turns to go, waved away by the seated man, just as Lise approaches.

'There you are!' says Lise. 'I've been looking for you all day. Where did you get to?'

The man shifts to look at her. 'Jenner's gone to have a bite. Then we're off back to the villa. Damn nuisance, coming back in to town all this way. Tell Jenner he's got half-an-hour. We must be off.'

'He'll be back in a minute,' Lise says. 'Don't you remember we met on the plane?'

'The Sheikh. Damn rotters in his country have taken over behind his back. Now he's lost his throne or whatever it is he sits on. I was at school with him. Why did he ring me up? He rang me up. On the telephone. He brings me back to town all this way and when we get here he says he can't come to the villa after all, there's been a coup.'

'I'll take you back to the villa,' Lise says. 'Come on, get in the car with me. I've got a car outside.'

The man says, 'Last time I saw the Sheikh it was '38. He came on safari with me. Rotten shot if you know anything about big game. You've got to wait for the drag. They call it the drag, you see. It kills its prey and drags it into the bush then you follow the drag and when you know where it's left its prey you're all right. The poor bloody beast comes out the next day to eat its prey, they like it high. And you only have a few seconds. You're here and there's another fellow there and a third over here. You can't shoot from here, you see, because there's another hunter there and you don't want to shoot him. You have to shoot from over here or over there. And the Sheikh, I've known him for years, we were at school together, the bloody fool shot and missed it by five feet from a fifteen-foot range.'

His eyes look straight ahead and his lips quiver.

'You're not my type after all,' Lise says. 'I thought you were, but I was away out.'

'What? Want a drink? Where's Jenner?'

She gathers up the handles of her bags, picks up her book and looks at him and through him as if he were already a distant memory and leaves without a good-bye, indeed as if she had said good-bye to him long ago.

She brushes past a few people at the vestibule who look at her with the same casual curiosity with which others throughout the day have looked at her. They are mainly tourists; one exceptional sight among so many others does not deflect their attention for very long. Outside, she goes to the car park where she has left Carlo's car, and does not find it.

She goes up to the doorman. 'I've lost my car. A Fiat 125. Have you seen anyone drive off with a Fiat?'

'Lady, there are twenty Fiats an hour come in and out of here.'

'But I parked it over there less than an hour ago. A cream Fiat, a bit dirty, I've been travelling.'

The doorman sends a page-boy to find the parking attendant who presently comes along in a vexed mood since he has been called from conversation with a more profitable client. He owns to having seen a cream-coloured Fiat being driven away by a large fat man whom he had presumed to be the owner.

'He must have had extra keys,' says Lise.

'Didn't you see the lady drive in with it?' the doorman says.

'No, I didn't. The royalty and the police were taking up all my time, you know that. Besides, the lady didn't say anything to me, to look after her car.'

Lise says, opening her bag, 'Well, I meant to give you a tip later. But I'll give you one now.' And she holds out to him the keys of Carlo's car.

The doorman says, 'Look, lady, we can't take responsibility for your car. If you want to see the porter at the desk he can ring the police. Are you staying at the hotel?'

'No,' says Lise. 'Get me a taxi.'

'Have you got your licence?' says the parking attendant.

'Go away,' Lise says. 'You're not my type.' He looks explosive. Another of tomorrow's witnesses.

The porter is meanwhile busy helping some newcomers out of a taxi. Lise calls out to the taxi-driver, who nods his agreement to take her on.

As soon as the passengers are out, Lise leaps into the taxi.

The parking attendant shouts, 'Are you sure it was your own car, lady?'

She throws Carlo's keys out of the window on to the gravel and directs the taxi to the Hotel Metropole with tears falling over her cheeks.

'Anything the matter, lady?' says the driver.

'It's getting late,' she says, weeping. 'It's getting terribly late.'

'Lady, I can't go faster. See the traffic.'

'I can't find my boy-friend. I don't know where he's gone.'

'You think you'll find him at the Metropole?'

'There's always a chance,' she says. 'I make a lot of mistakes.'

SIX

The chandeliers of the Metropole, dispensing a vivid glow upon the just and unjust alike, disclose Bill the macrobiotic seated gloomily by a table near the entrance. He jumps up when Lise enters and falls upon her with a delight that impresses the whole lobby, and in such haste that a plastic bag that he is clutching, insufficiently sealed, emits a small trail of wild rice in his progress towards her.

She follows him back to his seat and takes a chair beside him. 'Look at my coat,' she says. 'I got mixed up in a student demonstration and I'm still crying from the effect of tear-gas. I had a date at the Hilton for dinner with a very important Sheikh but I was too late, as I went to buy him a pair of slippers for a present. He'd gone on safari. So he wasn't my type, anyway. Shooting animals.'

'I'd just about given you up,' says Bill. 'You were to be here at seven. I've been desperate.' He takes her hand, smiling with glad flashes of teeth and eyes. 'You wouldn't have been so unkind as to have dinner with someone else, would you? I'm hungry.'

'And my car got stolen,' she says.

'What car?'

'Oh, just a car.'

'I didn't know you had a car. Was it a hired car?'

'You know nothing whatsoever about me,' she says.

'Well I've got a car,' he says. 'A friend has lent me it. I'm taking it to Naples as soon as possible to get started on the Yin-Yang Young Culture Centre. I'm opening with a lecture called "The World – Where is it Going?" That will be a general introduction to the macrobiotic way of life. It'll bring in the kids, all right.'

'It's getting late,' she says.

'I was nearly giving you up,' he says, squeezing her hand. 'I was just about to go out and look for another girl. I'm queer for girls. It has to be a girl.'

'I'll have a drink,' she says. 'I need one.'

'Oh no, you won't. Oh no, you won't. Alcohol is off the diet. You're coming to supper with me at a house I know.'

'What kind of a house?' she says.

'A macrobiotic family I know,' he says. 'They'll give us a good supper. Three sons, four daughters, the mother and father, all on macrobiotics. We'll have rice with carrots followed by rice biscuits and goat's cheese and a cooked apple. No sugar allowed. The family eat at six o'clock, which is the orthodox system, but the variation that I follow lets you eat late. That way, we'll get through to the young. So we'll go there and heat up a meal. Come on!'

She says, 'That tear-gas is still affecting me.' Tears brim in her eyes. She gets up with him and lets him, trailing rice, lead her past every eye of the Metropole lobby into the street, up the road, and into a small black utility model which is parked there.

'It's wonderful,' says Bill as he starts up the car, 'to think we're together again at last.'

'I must tell you,' says Lise, sniffing, 'that you're not my type. I'm sure of it.'

'Oh, you don't know me! You don't know me at all.'

'But I know my type.'

'You need love,' he says with a hand on her knee.

She starts away from him. 'Take care while you're driving. Where do your friends live?'

'The other side of the park. I must say, I feel hungry.'

'Then hurry up,' she says.

'Don't you feel hungry?'

'No, I feel lonely.'

'You won't be lonely with me.'

They have turned into the park.

'Turn right at the end of this road,' she says. 'There should be a road to the right, according to the map. I want to look at something.'

'There are better places farther on.'

'Turn right, I say.'

'Don't be nervy,' he says. 'You need to relax. The reason why you're so tense, you've been eating all the wrong things and drinking too much. You shouldn't have more than three glasses of liquid a day.

You should pass water not more than twice a day. Twice for a woman, three times for a man. If you need to go more than that it means you're taking in too much fluid.'

'Here's the road. Turn right.'

Bill turns right, going slowly and looking about him. He says, 'I don't know where this leads to. But there's a very convenient spot farther up the main road.'

'What spot?' she says. 'What spot are you talking about?'

'I haven't had my daily orgasm. It's an essential part of this particular variation of the diet, didn't I tell you? Many other macrobiotic variations have it as an essential part. This is one of the main things the young Neapolitans must learn.'

'If you think you're going to have sex with me,' she says, 'you're very much mistaken. I have no time for sex.'

'Lise!' says Bill.

'I mean it,' she says. 'Sex is no use to me, I assure you.' She gives out her deep laughter.

The road is dimly lit by lamps posted at far intervals. Bill is peering to right and left.

'There's a building over there,' she says. 'That must be the Pavilion. And the old villa behind – they say in the brochure that it's to be restored and turned into a museum. But it's the famous Pavilion that I want.'

At the site of the Pavilion several cars and motor bicycles are parked. Another road converges, and a band of teenaged boys and girls are languidly leaning against trees, cars and anything else that can prop them up, looking at each other.

'There's nothing doing here,' says Bill.

'Stop, I want to get out and look around.'

'Too many people. What are you thinking of?'

'I want to see the Pavilion, that's all.'

'Why? You can come by daylight. Much better.'

Some iron tables are scattered on the ground in front of the Pavilion, a graceful three-storey building with a quaint gilded frieze above the first level of the façade.

Bill parks the car near the others, some of which are occupied by amorous couples. Lise jumps out as soon as the car stops. She takes with her the hand-bag leaving the zipper-bag and her book in the car. He runs after her, putting an arm round her shoulders, and says, 'Come on, it's getting late. What do you want to see?'

She says, 'Will your rice be safe in the car? Have you locked it?'

He says, 'Who's going to steal a bag of rice?'

'I don't know,' says Lise, making her way along the path which leads to the Pavilion. 'Maybe those young people might feel very intensely about rice.'

'The movement hasn't got started yet, Lise,' says Bill. 'And red beans are also allowed. And sesame-flour. But you can't expect people to know about it till you tell them.'

The ground floor of the Pavilion is largely glass-fronted. She goes up to it and peers in. There are bare café tables and chairs piled high in the classic fashion of restaurants closed for the night. There is a long counter and a coffee machine at the far end, with an empty glass sandwich-bar. There is nothing else except an expanse of floor, which in the darkness can only be half-seen, patterned in black-and-white chequered pavements. Lise cranes and twists to see the ceiling which obscurely seems to be painted with some classical scene; the hind-leg of a horse and one side of a cupid are all that is visible.

Still she peers through the glass. Bill tries to draw her away, but again she starts to cry. 'Oh,' she says, 'the inconceivable sorrow of it, those chairs piled up at night when you're sitting in a café, the last one left.'

'You're getting morbid, dear,' says Bill. 'Darling, it's all a matter of chemistry. You've been eating toxic foods and neglecting the fact that there are two forces in the world, centrifugal which is Yin and centripetal which is Yang. Orgasms are Yang.'

'It makes me sad,' she says. 'I want to go home, I think. I want to go back home and feel all that lonely grief again. I miss it so much already.'

He jerks her away and she calls out, 'Stop it! Don't do that!' A man and two women who are passing a few yards away turn to look, but the young group pays no attention.

Bill gives a deep sigh. 'It's getting late,' he says, pinching her elbow.

'Let me go, I want to look round the back. I've got to see how things are round here, it's important.'

'You'd think it was a bank,' Bill says, 'that you were going to do a stick-up in tomorrow. Who do you think you are? Who do you think I am?' He follows her as she starts off round the side of the building, examining the track. 'What do you think you're doing?'

She traverses the side of the building and turns round to the back where five large dust-bins stand waiting for tomorrow's garbage-men, who will also find Lise, not far off, stabbed to death. At this moment, a disturbed cat leaves off its foraging at one of the half-closed dust-bins and flows into an adjacent blackness.

Lise surveys the ground earnestly.

'Look,' says Bill, 'Lise, darling, over by the hedge. We're all right.'

He pulls her towards a hedge separating the back yard of the Pavilion from a foot-path which can be seen through a partly-open iron gate. A band of very tall fair young men all speaking together in a Scandinavian-sounding language passes by and stops to watch and comment buoyantly on the tussle that ensues between Bill and Lise, she proclaiming that she doesn't like sex and he explaining that if he misses his daily orgasm he has to fit in two the next day. 'And it gives me indigestion,' he says, getting her down on the gravel behind the hedge and out of sight, 'two in one day. And it's got to be a girl.'

Lise now shrieks for help in four languages, English, French, Italian and Danish. She throws her hand-bag into the hedge; then, 'He's taken my purse!' she cries in four languages. 'He's gone off with my hand-bag!' One of the onlookers tries to creak open the stiff iron gate, but meantime another has started to climb it, and gets over.

'What's going on?' he says to Lise in his own language. 'We're Swedes. What's wrong?'

Bill who has been kneeling to hold her down gets up and says, 'Go away. Clear off. What do you think's going on?'

But Lise has jumped to her feet and shouts in English that she never saw him before in her life, and that he is trying to rob her, and rape her. 'I just got out of my car to look at the Pavilion, and he jumped on me and dragged me here,' she screams, over and over again in four languages. 'Get the police!'

The other men have come into the yard. Two of them take hold of Bill who grins, trying hard to convince them that this turmoil is Lise's joke. One of them says he is going to find a policeman. Lise says, 'Where's my bag? He's got rid of it somewhere. What has he done with it?' Then, in a burst of spontaneous composure she says, quietly, 'I'm going to find a policeman, too,' and walks off to the car. Most of the other parked cars have gone, as have also the young loiterers. One of the Swedes runs after her, advising her to wait till his friend brings a policeman.

'No, I'm going to the police-station right away,' she says in a calm voice as she gets in and shuts the door. She has already made off, already thrown the bag of wild rice out of the window, when the police arrive on the scene. They hear the Swedes' account, they listen to Bill's protests, they search for Lise's bag, and find it. Then they ask Bill what the girl's name was since she was, as he claims, a friend of his. 'Lise,' he says. 'I don't know her other name. We met on the plane.'

They take Bill into custody anyway, mercifully for him as it turns out, since in the hours logically possible for the murder of Lise on that spot Bill is safely in a police cell, equally beyond suspicion and the exercise of his diet.

SEVEN

It is long past midnight when she arrives at the Hotel Tomson which stands like the only living thing in the shuttered street. Lise parks the little black car in a spot near the entrance, takes her book and her zipper-bag and enters the hall.

At the desk the night-porter is on duty, the top three buttons of his uniform unfastened to reveal his throat and the top of his under-vest, a sign that the deep night has fallen and the tourists have gone to bed. The porter is talking on the desk telephone which links with the bedrooms. Meanwhile the only other person in the hall, a youngish man in a dark suit, stands before the desk with a brief-case and a tartan hold-all by his side.

'Please don't wake her. It isn't at all necessary at this late hour. Just show me my room —'

'She's on her way down. She says to tell you to wait, she's on her way.'

'I could have seen her in the morning. It wasn't necessary. It's so late.' The man's tone is authoritative and vexed.

'She's wide awake, sir,' says the porter. 'She was very definite that we were to let her know as soon as you arrived.'

'Excuse me,' Lise says to the porter, brushing against the dark-suited man as she comes up to the desk beside him. 'Would you like a book to read?' She holds out her paperback. 'I don't need it any more.'

'Oh, thanks, Miss,' says the porter, good-naturedly taking the book and holding it at arm's length before his eyes the better to see what the book is all about. Meanwhile the new arrival, having been jostled by Lise, turns to look at her. He starts, and bends to pick up his bags.

Lise touches him on the arm. 'You're coming with me,' she says.

'No,' he says, trembling. His round face is pink and white, his eyes are wide open with fear. He looks neat in his business suit and white shirt, as he did this morning when Lise first followed and then sat next to him on the plane.

'Leave everything,' says Lise. 'Come on, it's getting late.'

She starts propelling him to the door.

'Sir!' calls the porter. 'Your aunt's on her way –'

Lise, still holding her man, turns at the door and calls back, 'You can keep his luggage. You can have the book as well; it's a whydunnit in q-sharp major and it has a message: never talk to the sort of girls that you wouldn't leave lying about in your drawing-room for the servants to pick up.' She leads her man towards the door.

There, he puts up some resistance: 'No, I don't want to come. I want to stay. I came here this morning, and when I saw you here I got away. I want to get away.' He pulls back from her.

'I've got a car outside,' says Lise, and pushes open the narrow swing-door. He goes with her as if he is under arrest. She takes him to the car, lets go of his arm, gets into the driver's seat and waits while he walks round the front of the car and gets in beside her. Then she drives off with him at her side.

He says, 'I don't know who you are. I never saw you before in my life.'

'That's not the point,' she says. 'I've been looking for you all day. You've wasted my time. What a day! And I was right first time. As soon as I saw you this morning I knew that you were the one. You're my type.'

He is trembling. She says, 'You were in a clinic. You're Richard. I know your name because your aunt told me.'

He says, 'I've had six years' treatment. I want to start afresh. My family's waiting to see me.'

'Were the walls of the clinic pale green in all the rooms? Was there a great big tough man in the dormitory at night, patrolling up and down every so often, just in case?'

'Yes,' he says.

'Stop trembling,' she says. 'It's the madhouse tremble. It will soon be over. Before you went to the clinic how long did they keep you in prison?'

'Two years,' he said.

'Did you strangle or stab?'

'I stabbed her, but she didn't die. I never killed a woman.'

'No, but you'd like to. I knew it this morning.'

'You never saw me before in your life.'

'That's not the point,' Lise says. 'That's by the way. You're a sex maniac.'

'No, no,' he says. 'That's all over and past. Not any more.'

'Well you won't have sex with me,' Lise says. She is driving through the park and turns right towards the Pavilion. Nobody is in sight. The wandering groups are null and void, the cars have gone away.

'Sex is normal,' he says. 'I'm cured. Sex is all right.'

'It's all right at the time and it's all right before,' says Lise, 'but the problem is afterwards. That is, if you aren't just an animal. Most of the time, afterwards is pretty sad.'

'You're afraid of sex,' he says, almost joyfully, as if sensing an opportunity to gain control.

'Only of afterwards,' she says. 'But that doesn't matter any more.'

She pulls up at the Pavilion and looks at him. 'Why are you shaking?' she says. 'It will soon be over.' She reaches for her zipper-bag and opens it. 'Now,' she says, 'let's be lucid about this. Here's a present from your aunt, a pair of slippers. You can pick them up later.' She throws them on the back seat and pulls out a paper bag. She peers into it. 'This is Olga's scarf,' she says, putting it back in the bag.

'A lot of women get killed in the park,' he says, leaning back; he is calmer now.

'Yes, of course. It's because they want to be.' She is searching in the bag.

'Don't go too far,' he says quietly.

'I'll leave that to you,' she says and brings out another paper bag. She peers in and takes out the orange scarf. 'This is mine,' she says. A lovely colour by daylight.' She drapes the scarf round her neck.

'I'm getting out,' he says, opening the door on his side. 'Come on.'

'Wait a minute,' she says. 'Just wait a minute.'

'A lot of women get killed,' he says.

'Yes, I know, they look for it.' She brings out the oblong package, tears off the wrapping and opens the box that contains the curved paper-knife in its sheath. 'Another present for you,' she says. 'Your aunt bought it for you.' She takes the knife from the box which she throws out of the window.

He says, 'No, they don't want to be killed. They struggle. I know that. But I've never killed a woman. Never.'

Lise opens the door and gets out with the paperknife in her hand. 'Come on, it's getting late,' she says. 'I know the spot.'

The morning will dawn, and by the evening the police will place in front of him the map marked with an X at the point where the famous Pavilion is located, the little picture.

'You made this mark.'

'No I didn't. She must have made it herself. She knew the way. She took me straight there.'

They will reveal, bit by bit, that they know his record. They will bark, and exchange places at the desk. They will come and go in the little office, already beset by inquietude and fear, even before her identity is traced back to where she came from. They will try soft speaking, they will reason with him in their secret dismay that the evidence already coming in seems to confirm his story.

'The last time you lost control of yourself didn't you take the woman for a drive in the country?'

'But this one took me. She made me go. She was driving. I didn't want to go. It was only by chance that I met her.'

'You never saw her before?'

'The first time was at the airport. She sat beside me on the plane. I moved my seat. I was afraid.'

'Afraid of what? What frightened you?'

Round and round again will go the interrogators, moving slowly forward, always bearing the same questions like the whorling shell of a snail.

Lise walks up to the great windows of the Pavilion and presses close to look inside, while he follows her. Then she walks round the back and over to the hedge.

She says, 'I'm going to lie down here. Then you tie my hands with my scarf; I'll put one wrist over the other, it's the proper way. Then you'll tie my ankles together with your necktie. Then you strike.' She points first to her throat. 'First here,' she says. Then, pointing to a place beneath each breast, she says, 'Then here and here. Then anywhere you like.'

'I don't want to do it,' he says, staring at her. 'I didn't mean this to happen. I planned everything to be different. Let me go.'

She takes the paper-knife from its sheath, feels the edge and the point, and says that it isn't very sharp but it will do. 'Don't forget,' she says, 'that it's curved.' She looks at the engraved sheath in her hand and lets it fall carelessly from her fingers. 'After you've stabbed,' she says, 'be sure to twist it upwards or it may not penetrate far enough.' She demonstrates the movement with her wrist. 'You'll get caught, but at least you'll have the illusion of a chance to get away in the car. So afterwards, don't waste too much time staring at what you have done, at what you have done.' Then she lies down on the gravel and he grabs at the knife.

'Tie my hands first,' she says, crossing her wrists. 'Tie them with the scarf.'

He ties her hands, and she tells him in a sharp, quick voice to take off his necktie and bind her ankles.

'No,' he says, kneeling over her, 'not your ankles.'

'I don't want any sex,' she shouts. 'You can have it afterwards. Tie my feet and kill, that's all. They will come and sweep it up in the morning.'

All the same, he plunges into her, with the knife poised high.

'Kill me,' she says, and repeats it in four languages.

As the knife descends to her throat she screams, evidently perceiving how final is finality. She screams and then her throat gurgles while he stabs with a turn of his wrist exactly as she instructed. Then he stabs wherever he likes and stands up, staring at what he has done. He stands staring for a while and then, having started to turn away, he hesitates as if he had forgotten something of her bidding. Suddenly he wrenches off his necktie and bends to tie her ankles together with it.

He runs to the car, taking his chance and knowing that he will at last be taken, and seeing already as he drives away from the Pavilion and away, the sad little office where the police clank in and out and the typewriter ticks out his unnerving statement: 'She told me to kill her and I killed her. She spoke in many languages but she was telling me to kill her all the time. She told me precisely what to do. I was hoping to start a new life.' He sees already the gleaming buttons of the policemen's uniforms, hears the cold and the confiding, the hot and the barking voices, sees already the holsters and epaulets and all those trappings devised to protect them from the indecent exposure of fear and pity, pity and fear.

MEMENTO MORI

What shall I do with this absurdity –
O heart, O troubled heart – this caricature,
Decrepit age that has been tied to me
As to a dog's tail?

W.B. YEATS, *The Tower*

O what Venerable and Reverend Creatures
did the Aged seem! Immortal Cherubims!

THOMAS TRAHERNE, *Centuries of Meditation*

Q. What are the four last things to be ever
     remembered?
A. The four last things to be ever remembered
     are Death, Judgement, Hell, and Heaven.

The Penny Catechism

ONE

Dame Lettie Colston refilled her fountain-pen and continued her letter:

One of these days I hope you will write as brilliantly on a happier theme. In these days of cold war I *do* feel we should soar above the murk & smog & get into the clear crystal.

The telephone rang. She lifted the receiver. As she had feared, the man spoke before she could say a word. When he had spoken the familiar sentence she said, 'Who is that speaking, who is it?'

But the voice, as on eight previous occasions, had rung off.

Dame Lettie telephoned to the Assistant Inspector as she had been requested to do. 'It has occurred again,' she said.

'I see. Did you notice the time?'

'It was only a moment ago.'

'The same thing?'

'Yes,' she said, 'the same. Surely you have some means of tracing –'

'Yes, Dame Lettie, we will get him, of course.'

A few moments later Dame Lettie telephoned to her brother Godfrey.

'Godfrey, it has happened again.'

'I'll come and fetch you, Lettie,' he said. 'You must spend the night with us.'

'Nonsense. There is no danger. It is merely a disturbance.'

'What did he say?'

'The same thing. And quite matter-of-fact, not really threatening. Of course the man's mad. I don't know what the police are thinking of, they must be sleeping. It's been going on for six weeks now.'

'Just those words?'

'Just the same words – *Remember you must die* – nothing more.'

'He must be a maniac,' said Godfrey.

Godfrey's wife Charmian sat with her eyes closed, attempting to put her thoughts into alphabetical order which Godfrey had told her was better than no order at all, since she now had grasp of neither logic nor chronology. Charmian was eighty-five. The other day a journalist from a weekly paper had been to see her. Godfrey had subsequently read aloud to her the young man's article:

> . . . By the fire sat a frail old lady, a lady who once set the whole of the literary world (if not the Thames) on fire . . . Despite her age, this legendary figure is still abundantly alive . . .

Charmian felt herself dropping off, and so she said to the maid who was arranging the magazines on the long oak table by the window, 'Taylor, I am dropping off to sleep for five minutes. Telephone to St Mark's and say I am coming.'

Just at that moment Godfrey entered the room holding his hat and wearing his outdoor coat. 'What's that you say?' he said.

'Oh, Godfrey, you made me start.'

'*Taylor* . . .' he repeated, 'St Mark's . . . Don't you realize there is no maid in this room, and furthermore, you are not in Venice?'

'Come and get warm by the fire,' she said, 'and take your coat off'; for she thought he had just come in from the street.

'I am about to go *out*,' he said. 'I am going to fetch Lettie who is to stop with us tonight. She has been troubled by another of those anonymous calls.'

'That was a pleasant young man who called the other day,' said Charmian.

'Which young man?'

'From the paper. The one who wrote –'

'That was five years and two months ago,' said Godfrey.

'Why can't one be kind to her?' he asked himself as he drove to Lettie's house in Hampstead. 'Why can't one be more gentle?' He himself was eighty-seven, and in charge of all his faculties. Whenever he considered his own behaviour he thought of himself not as 'I' but as 'one'.

'One has one's difficulties with Charmian,' he told himself.

'Nonsense,' said Lettie. 'I have no enemies.'

'*Think*,' said Godfrey. 'Think hard.'

'The red lights,' said Lettie. 'And don't talk to me as if I were Charmian.'

'Lettie, if you please, I do not need to be told how to drive. I observed the lights.' He had braked hard, and Dame Lettie was jerked forward.

She gave a meaningful sigh which, when the green lights came on, made him drive all the faster.

'You know, Godfrey,' she said, 'you are wonderful for your age.'

'So everyone says.' His driving pace became moderate; her sigh of relief was inaudible, her patting herself on the back, invisible.

'In your position,' he said, 'you must have enemies.'

'Nonsense.'

'I say *yes*.' He accelerated.

'Well, perhaps you're right.' He slowed down again, but Dame Lettie thought, I wish I hadn't come.

They were at Knightsbridge. It was only a matter of keeping him happy till they reached Kensington Church Street and turned into Vicarage Gardens where Godfrey and Charmian lived.

'I have written to Eric,' she said, 'about his book. Of course, he has something of his mother's former brilliance, but it did seem to me that the subject-matter lacked the joy and hope which was the mark of a good novel in those days.'

'I couldn't *read* the book,' said Godfrey. 'I simply could not go on with it. A motor salesman in Leeds and his wife spending a night in a hotel with that communist librarian . . . Where does it all lead you?'

Eric was his son. Eric was fifty-six and had recently published his second novel.

'He'll never do as well as Charmian did,' Godfrey said. 'Try as he may.'

'Well, I can't quite agree with that,' said Lettie, seeing that they had now pulled up in front of the house. 'Eric has a hard streak of realism which Charmian never –'

Godfrey had got out and slammed the door. Dame Lettie sighed and followed him into the house, wishing she hadn't come.

'Did you have a nice evening at the pictures, Taylor?' said Charmian.

'I am not Taylor,' said Dame Lettie, 'and in any case, you always called Taylor "Jean" during her last twenty or so years in your service.'

Mrs Anthony, their daily housekeeper, brought in the milky coffee and placed it on the breakfast table.

'Did you have a nice evening at the pictures, Taylor?' Charmian asked her.

'Yes, thanks, Mrs Colston,' said the housekeeper.

'Mrs Anthony is not Taylor,' said Lettie. 'There is no one by name of Taylor here. And anyway you used to call her Jean latterly. It was only when you were a girl that you called Taylor Taylor. And, in any event, Mrs Anthony is not Taylor.'

Godfrey came in. He kissed Charmian. She said, 'Good morning, Eric.'

'He is not Eric,' said Dame Lettie.

Godfrey frowned at his sister. Her resemblance to himself irritated him. He opened *The Times*.

'Are there lots of obituaries today?' said Charmian.

'Oh, don't be gruesome,' said Lettie.

'Would you like me to read you the obituaries, dear?' Godfrey said, turning the pages to find the place in defiance of his sister.

'Well, I should like the war news,' Charmian said.

'The war has been over since nineteen forty-five,' Dame Lettie said. 'If indeed it is the last war you are referring to. Perhaps, however, you mean the First World War? The Crimean perhaps . . .?'

'Lettie, please,' said Godfrey. He noticed that Lettie's hand was unsteady as she raised her cup, and the twitch on her large left cheek was pronounced. He thought in how much better form he himself was than his sister, though she was the younger, only seventy-nine.

Mrs Anthony looked round the door. 'Someone on the phone for Dame Lettie.'

'Oh, who is it?'

'Wouldn't give a name.'

'Ask who it is, please.'

'Did ask. Wouldn't give –'

'I'll go,' said Godfrey.

Dame Lettie followed him to the telephone and overheard the male voice. 'Tell Dame Lettie,' it said, 'to remember she must die.'

'Who's there?' said Godfrey. But the man had hung up.

'We must have been followed,' said Lettie. 'I told no one I was coming over here last night.'

She telephoned to report the occurrence to the Assistant Inspector.

He said, 'Sure you didn't mention to anyone that you intended to stay at your brother's home?'

'Of course I'm sure.'

'Your brother actually heard the voice? Heard it himself?'

'Yes, as I say, he took the call.'

She told Godfrey, 'I'm glad you took the call. It corroborates my story. I have just realized that the police have been doubting it.'

'Doubting your word?'

'Well, I suppose they thought I might have imagined it. Now, perhaps, they will be more active.'

Charmian said, 'The police ... what are you saying about the police? Have we been robbed?'

'I am being molested,' said Dame Lettie.

Mrs Anthony came in to clear the table.

'Ah, Taylor, how old are you?' said Charmian.

'Sixty-nine, Mrs Colston,' said Mrs Anthony.

'When will you be seventy?'

'Twenty-eighth November.'

'That will be splendid, Taylor. You will then be one of us,' said Charmian.

TWO

There were twelve occupants of the Maud Long Medical Ward (aged people, female). The ward sister called them the Baker's Dozen, not knowing that this is thirteen, but having only heard the phrase; and thus it is that a good many old sayings lose their force.

First came a Mrs Emmeline Roberts, seventy-six, who had been a cashier at the Odeon in the days when it was the Odeon. Next came Miss or Mrs Lydia Reewes-Duncan, seventy-eight, whose past career was uncertain, but who was visited fortnightly by a middle-aged niece, very bossy towards the doctors and staff, very uppish. After that came Miss Jean Taylor, eighty-two, who had been a companion-maid to the famous authoress Charmian Piper after her marriage into the Colston Brewery family. Next again lay Miss Jessie Barnacle who had no birth certificate but was put down as eighty-one, and who for forty-eight years had been a newsvendor at Holborn Circus. There was also a Madame Trotsky, a Mrs Fanny Green, a Miss Doreen Valvona, and five others, all of known and various careers, and of ages ranging from seventy to ninety-three. These twelve old women were known variously as Granny Roberts, Granny Duncan, Granny Taylor, Grannies Barnacle, Trotsky, Green, Valvona, and so on.

Sometimes, on first being received into her bed, the patient would be shocked and feel rather let down by being called Granny. Miss or Mrs Reewes-Duncan threatened for a whole week to report anyone who called her Granny Duncan. She threatened to cut them out of her will and to write to her M.P. The nurses provided writing-paper and a pencil at her urgent request. However, she changed her mind about informing her M.P. when they promised not to call her Granny any more. 'But,' she said, 'you shall never go back into my will.'

'In the name of God that's real awful of you,' said the ward sister as she bustled about. 'I thought you was going to leave us all a packet.'

'Not now,' said Granny Duncan. 'Not now, I won't. You don't catch me for a fool.'

Tough Granny Barnacle, she who had sold the evening paper for forty-eight years at Holborn Circus, and who always said, 'Actions speak louder than words', would send out to Woolworth's for a will-form about once a week; this would occupy her for two or three days. She would ask the nurse how to spell words like 'hundred' and 'ermine'.

'Goin' to leave me a hundred quid, Granny?' said the nurse. 'Goin' to leave me your ermine cape?'

The doctor on his rounds would say, 'Well, Granny Barnacle, am I to be remembered or not?'

'You're down for a thousand, Doc.'

'My word, I must stick in with you, Granny. I'll bet you've got a long stocking, my girl.'

Miss Jean Taylor mused upon her condition and upon old age in general. Why do some people lose their memories, some their hearing? Why do some talk of their youth and others of their wills? She thought of Dame Lettie Colston who had all her senses intact, and yet played a real will-game, attempting to keep the two nephews in suspense, enemies of each other. And Charmian ... Poor Charmian, since her stroke. How muddled she was about most things, and yet perfectly sensible when she discussed the books she had written. Quite clear on just that one thing, the subject of her books.

A year ago, when Miss Taylor had been admitted to the ward, she had suffered misery when addressed as Granny Taylor, and she thought she would rather die in a ditch than be kept alive under such conditions. But she was a woman practised in restraint; she never displayed her resentment. The lacerating familiarity of the nurses' treatment merged in with her arthritis, and she bore them both as long as she could without complaint. Then she was forced to cry out with pain during a long haunted night when the dim ward lamp made the beds into grey-white lumps like terrible bundles of laundry which muttered and snored occasionally. A nurse brought her an injection.

'You'll be better now, Granny Taylor.'

'Thank you, nurse.'

'Turn over, Granny, that's a good girl.'

'Very well, nurse.'

The arthritic pain subsided, leaving the pain of desolate humiliation, so that she wished rather to endure the physical nagging again.

After the first year she resolved to make her suffering a voluntary affair. If this is God's will then it is mine. She gained from this state of mind a decided and visible dignity, at the same time as she lost her stoical resistance to pain. She complained more, called often for the bed-pan, and did not hesitate, on one occasion when the nurse was dilatory, to wet the bed as the other grannies did so frequently.

Miss Taylor spent much time considering her position. The doctor's 'Well, how's Granny Taylor this morning? Have you been making your last will and test –' would falter when he saw her eyes, the intelligence. She could not help hating these visits, and the nurses giving her a hair-do, telling her she looked like sixteen, but she volunteered mentally for them, as it were, regarding them as the Will of God. She reflected that everything could be worse, and was sorry for the youngest generation now being born into the world, who in their old age, whether of good family or no, educated or no, would be forced by law into Chronic Wards; she dared say every citizen in the Kingdom would take it for granted; and the time would surely come for everyone to be a government granny or grandpa, unless they were mercifully laid to rest in their prime.

Miss Doreen Valvona was a good reader, she had the best eyes in the ward. Each morning at eleven she read aloud everyone's horoscopes from the newspaper, holding it close to her brown nose and – behind her glasses – to the black eyes which came from her Italian father. She knew by heart everyone's Zodiacal sign. 'Granny Green – Virgo,' she would say. '*A day for bold measures. Close partnerships are beneficial. A wonderful period for entertaining.*'

'Read us it again. My hearing aid wasn't fixed.'

'No, you'll have to wait. Granny Duncan's next. Granny Duncan – Scorpio. *Go all out for what you want today. Plenty of variety and gaiety to keep you on your toes.*'

Granny Valvona remembered everyone's horoscope all the day, checking up to see the points where it came true, so that, after Dame Lettie Colston had been to visit Granny Taylor the old family servant, a cry arose from Granny Valvona: 'What did I tell you in your horoscope? Listen while I read it out again. Granny Taylor –

Gemini. *You are in wonderful form today. Exceptionally bright social potents are indicated.'*

'*Portents,*' said Miss Taylor. 'Not potents.'

Granny Valvona looked again. She spelt it out. 'Potents,' she said. Miss Taylor gave it up, murmuring, 'I see.'

'Well?' said Granny Valvona. 'Wasn't that a remarkable forecast? *You are in wonderful form today. Exceptionally bright social* ... Now isn't that your visitor foretold, Granny Taylor?'

'Yes indeed, Granny Valvona.'

'Some dame!' said the littlest nurse, who could not make out why Granny Taylor had so seriously called her visitor 'Dame Lettie'. She had heard of dames as jokes, and at the pictures.

'Wait, nurse, I'll read your horoscope. What's your month?'

'I've to go, Granny Valvoni. Sister's on the hunt.'

'Don't call my name Valvoni, it's Valvon*a*. It ends with an *ah*.'

'*Ah*,' said the little nurse, and disappeared with a hop and a skip.

'Taylor was in wonderful form today,' Dame Lettie told her brother.

'You've been to see Taylor? You are really very good,' said Godfrey. 'But you look tired, I hope you haven't tired yourself.'

'Indeed, I felt I could have changed places with Taylor. These people are so fortunate these days. Central heating, everything they want, plenty of company.'

'Is she in with nice people?'

'Who – Taylor? Well, they all look splendid and clean. Taylor always says she is perfectly satisfied with everything. So she should be.'

'Got all her faculties still?' Godfrey was obsessed by the question of old people and their faculties.

'Certainly. She asked for you and Charmian. She cries a little of course at the mention of Charmian. Of course she was fond of Charmian.'

Godfrey looked at her closely. 'You look ill, Lettie.'

'Utter nonsense. I'm in wonderful form today. I've never felt more fit in my life.'

'I don't think you should return to Hampstead,' he said.

'After tea. I've arranged to go home after tea, and after tea I'm going.'

'There was a telephone call for you,' said Godfrey.

'Who was it?'

'That chap again.'

'Really? Have you rung the C.I.D.?'

'Yes. In fact, they're coming round tonight to have a talk with us. They are rather puzzled about some aspects of the case.'

'What did the man say? What did he say?'

'Lettie, don't upset yourself. You know very well what he said.'

'I go back to Hampstead after tea,' said Lettie.

'But the C.I.D. –'

'Tell them I have returned to Hampstead.'

Charmian came unsteadily in. 'Ah, Taylor, have you enjoyed your walk? You look in wonderful form today.'

'Mrs Anthony is late with tea,' said Dame Lettie, moving her chair so that her back was turned to Charmian.

'You must not sleep alone at Hampstead,' said Godfrey. 'Call on Lisa Brooke and ask her to stop with you for a few days. The police will soon get the man.'

'Lisa Brooke be damned,' said Dame Lettie, which would have been an alarming statement if intended seriously, for Lisa Brooke was not many moments dead, as Godfrey discovered in *The Times* obituary the next morning.

THREE

Lisa Brooke died in her seventy-third year after her second stroke. She had taken nine months to die, and in fact it was only a year before her death that, feeling rather ill, she had decided to reform her life, and reminding herself how attractive she still was, offered up the new idea, her celibacy to the Lord to whom no gift whatsoever is unacceptable.

It did not occur to Godfrey as he marched into a pew in the crematorium chapel that anyone else present had ever been Lisa's lover except himself. It did not even come to mind that he had been Lisa's lover, for he had never been her lover in any part of England, only Spain and Belgium, and at the moment he was busy with statistics. There were sixteen people present. On first analysis it emerged that five were relatives of Lisa. Next, among the remaining eleven, Godfrey elicited Lisa's lawyer, her housekeeper, the bank manager. Lettie had just arrived. Then there was himself. That left six, only one of whom he recognized, but all of whom were presumably Lisa's hangers-on, and he was glad their fountain of ready cash had dried up. All those years of daylight robbery; and many a time he had told Lisa, 'A child of six could do better than that,' when she displayed one of the paintings, outrages, committed by one of her pets. 'If he hasn't made his way in the world by now,' he had said, time and again, of old Percy Mannering the poet, 'he never will. You are a fool, Lisa, letting him drink your gin and shout his poetry in your ears.'

Percy Mannering, almost eighty, stood with his lean stoop as the coffin was borne up the aisle. Godfrey stared hard at the poet's red-veined hatchet cheek-bones and thin nose. He thought, 'I bet he's regretting the termination of his income. They've all bled poor Lisa white . . .' The poet was, in fact, in a state of excitement. Lisa's death had filled him with thrilling awe, for though he knew the general axiom that death was everyone's lot he could never realize the

particular case; each new death gave him something fresh to feel. It
came to him as the service began that within a few minutes Lisa's
coffin would start sliding down into the furnace, and he saw as in a
fiery vision her flame-tinted hair aglow as always, competing with the
angry tresses of the fire below. He grinned like an elated wolf and shed
tears of human grief as if he were half-beast, half-man, instead of half-
poet, half-man. Godfrey watched him and thought, 'He must be
senile. He has probably lost his faculties.'

The coffin began to slide slowly down the slope towards a gap in the
wall while the organ played something soft and religious. Godfrey,
who was not a believer, was profoundly touched by this ensemble,
and decided once and for all to be cremated when his time came.
'There goes Lisa Brooke,' he said to himself as he saw the last tilt of
the coffin. The prow, thought the poet, lifts, and the ship goes under
with the skipper on board . . . No, that's too banal, Lisa herself as the
ship is a better idea. Godfrey looked round him and thought, 'She
should have been good for another ten years, but what can you expect
with all that drink and all these spongers?' So furiously did he glare
about him that he startled the faces which caught his eye.

Tubby Dame Lettie caught up with her brother in the aisle as he
moved with the others to the porch. 'What's the matter with you,
Godfrey?' Lettie breathed.

The chaplain was shaking doleful hands with everyone at the door.
As Godfrey gave his hand he said over his shoulder to Lettie, 'The
matter with *me*? What d'you mean what's the matter with me? What's
the matter with *you*?'

Lettie, as she dabbed her eyes, whispered, 'Don't talk so loud.
Don't glare so. Everyone's looking at you.'

On the floor of the long porch was a muster of flowers done up,
some in tasteful bunches, one or two in old-fashioned wreaths. These
were being inspected by Lisa's relatives, her middle-aged nephew
and his wife, her parched elder sister Janet Sidebottome who had
been a missionary in India at a time when it *was* India, her brother
Ronald Sidebottome who had long since retired from the City, and
Ronald's Australian wife who had been christened Tempest. Godfrey
did not immediately identify them, for he saw only the row of their
several behinds as they stooped to examine the cards attached to each
tribute.

'Look, Ronald, isn't this sweet? A tiny bunch of violets – oh, see, it says, "Thank you, Lisa dear, for all those wonderful times, with love from Tony."'

'Rather odd words. Are you sure –'

'Who's Tony, I wonder?'

'See, Janet, this huge yellow rose wreath here from Mrs Pettigrew. It must have cost her a fortune.'

'What did you say?' said Janet who did not hear well.

'A wreath from Mrs Pettigrew. It must have cost a fortune.'

'Sh-sh-sh,' said Janet, looking round. True enough, Mrs Pettigrew, Lisa's old housekeeper, was approaching in her well-dressed confident manner. Janet, cramped from the card-inspection, straightened painfully and turned to meet Mrs Pettigrew. She let the woman grip her hand.

'Thank you for all you have done for my sister,' said Janet sternly.

'It was a pleasure.' Mrs Pettigrew spoke in a surprisingly soft voice. It was understood Janet was thinking of the will. 'I loved Mrs Brooke, poor soul.'

Janet inclined her head graciously, firmly withdrew her hand and rudely turned her back.

'Can we see the ashes?' loudly inquired Percy Mannering as he emerged from the chapel. 'Is there any hope of *seeing* them?' At the noise he made, Lisa's nephew and his wife jumped nervily and looked round.

'I want to see those ashes if possible.' The poet had cornered Dame Lettie, pressing his hungry demand. Lettie felt there was something unhealthy about the man. She moved away.

'That's one of Lisa's artists,' she whispered to John Sidebottome, not meaning to prompt him to say 'Oh!' and lift his hat in Percy's direction, as he did.

Godfrey stepped backwards and stood on a spray of pink carnations. 'Oh – sorry,' he said to the carnations, stepping off them quickly, and then was vexed at his folly, and knew that in any case no one had seen him after all. He ambled away from the trampled flowers.

'What's that fellow want with the ashes?' he said to Lettie.

'He wants to see them. Wants to see if they've gone grey. He is quite disgusting.'

'Of course they will be grey. The fellow must have lost his faculties. *If* he ever had any.'

'I don't know about faculties,' said Lettie. 'Certainly he has no feelings.'

Tempest Sidebottome, blue-haired and well corseted, was saying in a voice which carried away out to the Garden of Remembrance, 'To some people there's just nothing that's sacred.'

'Madam,' said Percy, baring his sparse green teeth in a smile, 'the ashes of Lisa Brooke will always be sacred to me. I desire to see them, kiss them if they are cool enough. Where's that cleric? – He'll have the ashes.'

'Do you see over there – Lisa's housekeeper?' Lettie said to Godfrey.

'Yes, yes, I wonder –'

'That's what *I'm* wondering,' said Lettie, who was wondering if Mrs Pettigrew wanted a job, and if so would agree to undertake the personal care of Charmian.

'But I think we would need a younger woman. That one must be getting on,' said Godfrey, 'if I remember aright.'

'Mrs Pettigrew has a constitution like a horse,' said Dame Lettie, casting a horse-dealer's glance over Mrs Pettigrew's upright form. 'And it is impossible to get younger women.'

'Has she got all her faculties?'

'Of course. She had poor Lisa right under her thumb.'

'I hardly think Charmian would want –'

'Charmian needs to be bullied. What Charmian needs is a firm hand. She will simply go to pieces if you don't keep at her. Charmian needs a firm hand. It's the only way.'

'But what about Mrs Anthony?' said Godfrey. 'The woman might not get on with Mrs Anthony. It would be tragic if we lost her.'

'If you don't find someone soon to look after Charmian you will certainly lose Mrs Anthony. Charmian is too much of a handful for Mrs Anthony. You will lose Mrs Anthony. Charmian keeps calling her Taylor. She is bound to resent it. Who are you staring at?'

Godfrey was staring at a short bent man walking with the aid of two sticks round a corner of the chapel. 'Who is that man?' said Godfrey. 'He looks familiar.'

Tempest Sidebottome fussed over to the little man who beamed up at her with a fresh face under his wide black hat. He spoke in a shrill boyish tone. 'Afraid I'm late,' he said. 'Is the party over? Are you all Lisa's sinisters and bothers?'

'That's Guy Leet,' said Godfrey, at once recognizing him, for Guy had always used to call sisters and brothers sinisters and bothers. 'The little rotter,' said Godfrey, 'he used to be after Charmian. It must be thirty-odd years since last I saw him. He can't be more than seventy-five and just see what he's come to.'

Tables at a tea-shop near Golders Green had been reserved for Lisa's post-crematorial party. Godfrey had intended to miss the tea party but the arrival of Guy Leet had changed his mind. He was magnetized by the sight of the clever little man doubled over his sticks, and could not keep his eyes off the arthritic hobbling of Guy making his way among the funeral flowers.

'Better join them for tea,' he said to Lettie, 'hadn't we?'

'What for?' said Lettie, looking round the company. 'We can have tea at home. Come back with me for tea, we can have it at home.'

'I think we'd better join them,' said Godfrey. 'We might have a word with Mrs Pettigrew about her taking on Charmian.

Lettie saw Godfrey's gaze following the hunched figure of Guy Leet who, on his sticks, had now reached the door of his taxi. Several of the party helped Guy inside, then joined him. As they drove off, Godfrey said, 'Little rotter. Supposed to be a critic. Tried to take liberties with all the lady novelists, and then he was a theatre critic and he was after the actresses. You'll remember him, I dare say.'

'Vaguely,' said Lettie. 'He never got much change out of *me*.'

'He was never after you,' said Godfrey.

At the tea-shop Dame Lettie and Godfrey found the mourners being organized into their places by Tempest Sidebottome, big and firm in her corsets, aged seventy-five, with that accumulated energy which strikes despair in the hearts of jaded youth, and which now fairly intimidated even the two comparative youngsters in the group, Lisa's nephew and his wife who were not long past fifty.

'Ronald, sit down here and stay put,' Tempest said to her husband, who put on his glasses and sat down.

Godfrey was casting about for Guy Leet, but in the course of doing so his sight was waylaid by the tables on which were set silver-plate cakestands with thin bread and butter on the bottom tier, cut fruit cake above that, and on the top, a pile of iced cakes wrapped in Cellophane paper. Godfrey began to feel a passionate longing for his tea, and he pushed past Dame Lettie to stand conspicuously near the organizer, Tempest. She did notice him right away and allotted him a seat at a table. 'Lettie,' he called then, 'come over here. We're sitting here.'

'Dame Lettie,' said Tempest over his head, 'you must come and sit with us, my dear. Over here beside Ronald.'

'Damned snob,' thought Godfrey. 'I suppose she thinks Lettie is somebody.'

Someone leant over to offer him a cigarette which was a filter-tip. However, he said, 'Thanks, I'll keep it for after tea.' Then looking up, he saw the wolf grin on the face of the man who was offering him the packet with a trembling hand. Godfrey plucked out a cigarette and placed it beside his plate. He was angry at being put beside Percy Mannering, not only because Percy had been one of Lisa's spongers, but also because he must surely be senile with that grin and frightful teeth, and Godfrey felt the poet would not be able to manage his teacup with those shaking hands.

He was right, for Percy spilled a lot of his tea on the cloth. 'He ought to be in a home,' thought Godfrey. Tempest glanced at their table every now and then and tut-tutted a lot, but she did this all round, as if it were a children's beanfeast. Percy was oblivious of the mess he was making or of anyone's disapproval. Two others sat at their table, Janet Sidebottome and Mrs Pettigrew. The poet had taken it for granted that he was the most distinguished and therefore the leader of conversation.

'One time I fell out with Lisa,' he roared, 'was when she took up Dylan Thomas.' He pronounced the first name Dyelan. 'Dylan Thomas,' he said, 'and Lisa was good to him. Do you know, if I was to go to Heaven and find Dylan Thomas there, I'd prefer to go to HELL. *And* I wouldn't be surprised if Lisa hasn't gone to Hell for aiding and abetting him in his poetry so-called.'

Janet Sidebottome bent her ear closer to Percy. 'What did you say about poor Lisa? I don't hear well.'

'I say,' he said, 'I wonder if Lisa's gone to Hell because of her –'

'From respect to my dear sister,' said Janet with a hostile look, 'I don't think we will discuss –'

'Dye-lan Thomas died from D.T.' said the old poet, becoming gleeful. 'You see the coincidence? – His initials were D.T. and he *died* from D.T. Hah!'

'In respect for my late sister –'

'Poetry!' said Percy. 'Dylan Thomas didn't know the meaning of the word. As I said to Lisa, I said, "You're making a bloody fool of yourself supporting that charlatan. It isn't poetry, it's a leg-pull." She didn't see it, nobody saw it, but I'm telling you his verse was all a HOAX.'

Tempest turned round in her chair. 'Hush, Mr Mannering,' she said, tapping Percy on the shoulder.

Percy looked at her and roared, 'Ha! Do you know what you can tell Satan to do with Dye-lan Thomas's poetry?' He sat back to observe, with his two-fanged gloat, the effect of this question, which he next answered in unprintable terms, causing Mrs Pettigrew to say, 'Gracious!' and to wipe the corners of her mouth with her handkerchief. Meanwhile various commotions arose at the other tables and the senior waitress said, 'Not in *here*, sir!'

Godfrey's disgust was arrested by fear that the party might now break up. While everyone's attention was still on Percy he hastily took up a couple of the Cellophane-wrapped cakes from the top tier of the cakestand, and stuffed them into his pocket. He looked round and felt sure no one had noticed the action.

Janet Sidebottome leaned over to Mrs Pettigrew. 'What did he say?' she said.

'Well, Miss Sidebottome,' said Mrs Pettigrew, meanwhile glancing at herself sideways in a glass on the wall, 'as far as I could comprehend, he was talking about some gentleman indelicately.'

'Poor Lisa,' said Janet. Tears came to her eyes. She kissed her relatives and departed. Lisa's nephew and his wife sidled away, though before they had reached the door they were summoned back by Tempest because the nephew had left his scarf. Eventually, the couple were permitted to go. Percy Mannering remained grinning in his seat.

To Godfrey's relief Mrs Pettigrew refilled his cup. She also poured one for herself, but when Percy passed his shaking cup she ignored it. Percy said, 'Hah! That was strong meat for you ladies, wasn't it?' He reached for the teapot. 'I hope it wasn't me made Lisa's sister cry,' he said solemnly. 'I'd be sorry to have made her cry.' The teapot was too heavy for his quivering fingers and fell from them on to its side, while a leafy brown sea spread from the open lid over the tablecloth and on to Godfrey's trousers.

Tempest rose, pushing back her chair as if she meant business. She was followed to the calamitous table by Dame Lettie and a waitress. While Godfrey was being sponged, Lettie took the poet by the arm and said, 'Please go.' Tempest, busy with Godfrey's trousers, called over her shoulder to her husband, 'Ronald, you're a man. Give Dame Lettie a hand.'

'What? Who?' said Ronald.

'Wake up, Ronald. Can't you see what has to be done? Help Dame Lettie to take Mr Mannering outside.'

'Oh,' said Ronald, 'why, someone's spilt their tea!' He ogled the swimming tablecloth.

Percy shook off Dame Lettie's hand from his arm, and grinning to right and left, buttoning up his thin coat, departed.

A place was made for Godfrey and Mrs Pettigrew at the Sidebottomes' table. 'Now we shall have a fresh pot of tea,' said Tempest. Everyone gave deep sighs. The waitresses cleaned up the mess. The room was noticeably quiet.

Dame Lettie started to question Mrs Pettigrew about her future plans. Godfrey was anxious to overhear this conversation. He was not sure that he wanted Lisa Brooke's housekeeper to look after Charmian. She might be too old or too expensive. She looked a smart woman, she might have expensive ideas. And he was not sure that Charmian would not have to go into a home.

'There's no definite offer, of course,' he interposed.

'Well, Mr Colston, as I was saying,' said Mrs Pettigrew, 'I can't make any plans, myself, until things are settled.'

'What things?' said Godfrey.

'Godfrey, please,' said Lettie, 'Mrs Pettigrew and I are having a chat.' She slumped her elbow on the table and turned to Mrs Pettigrew, cutting off her brother from view.

'What is your feeling about the service?' said Tempest.

Godfrey looked round at the waitresses. 'Very satisfactory,' he said. 'That older one handled that Mannering very well, I thought.'

Tempest closed her eyes as one who prays for grace. 'I mean,' she said, 'poor Lisa's last rites at the crematorium.'

'Oh,' said Godfrey, 'you should have said funeral service. When you said the service, naturally I thought –'

'What do you feel about the cremation service?'

'First rate,' said Godfrey. 'I've quite decided to be cremated when my time comes. Cleanest way. Dead bodies under the ground only contaminate our water supplies. You should have said cremation service in the first place.'

'I thought it was cold,' said Tempest. 'I do wish the minister had read out poor Lisa's obituary. The last cremation I was at – that was Ronald's poor brother Henry – they read out his obituary from the *Nottingham Guardian*, all about his war service and his work for SSAFA and Road Safety. It was so very moving. Now why couldn't they have read out Lisa's? All that in the papers about what she did for the Arts, he should have read it out to us.'

'I quite agree,' said Godfrey. 'It was the least he could have done. Did you make a special request for it?'

'No,' she sighed. 'I left the arrangements to Ronald. Unless you do everything yourself . . .'

'They always get very violent about other poets,' said Ronald. 'You see, they feel very personal about poetry.'

'Whatever is he talking about?' said Tempest. 'He's talking about Mr Mannering, that's what he's on about. We aren't talking about Mr Mannering, Ronald. Mr Mannering's left, it's a thing of the past. We've gone on to something else.'

As they rose to leave Godfrey felt a touch on his arm. Turning round he saw Guy Leet behind him, his body crouched over his sticks and his baby face raised askew to Godfrey's.

'Got your funeral baked meats all right?' said Guy.

'What?' said Godfrey.

Guy nodded his head towards Godfrey's pocket which bulged with the cakes. 'Taking them home to Charmian?'

'Yes,' said Godfrey.

'And how is Charmian?'

Godfrey had partly regained his poise. 'She's in wonderful form,' he said. 'I'm sorry,' he said, 'to see you having such a difficult time. Must be terrible not being able to get about on your own pins.'

Guy gave a high laugh. He came close to Godfrey and breathed into his waistcoat, 'But I *did* get about, dear fellow. At least I did.'

On the way home Godfrey threw the cakes out of his car window. Why did one pocket those damned things? he thought. One doesn't need them, one could buy up every cake-shop in London and never miss the money. Why did one do it? It doesn't make sense.

'I have been to Lisa Brooke's funeral,' he said to Charmian when he got home, 'or rather, cremation.'

Charmian remembered Lisa Brooke, she had cause to remember her. 'Personally, I'm afraid,' said Charmian, 'that Lisa was a little spiteful to me sometimes, but she had her better side. A generous nature when dealing with the right person, but –'

'Guy Leet was there,' said Godfrey. 'He's nearly finished now, bent over two sticks.'

Charmian said, 'Oh, and what a clever man he was!'

'Clever?' said Godfrey.

Charmian, when she saw Godfrey's face, giggled squeakily through her nose.

'I have quite decided to be cremated when my time comes,' said Godfrey. 'It is the cleanest way. The cemeteries only pollute our water supplies. Cremation is best.'

'I do so agree with you,' said Charmian sleepily.

'No, you do *not* agree with me,' he said. 'R.C.s are not allowed to be cremated.'

'I mean, I'm sure you are right, Eric dear.'

'I am not Eric,' said Godfrey. 'You are not sure I'm right. Ask Mrs Anthony, she'll tell you that R.C.s are against cremation.' He opened the door and bawled for Mrs Anthony. She came in with a sigh.

'Mrs Anthony, you're a Roman Catholic, aren't you?' said Godfrey.

'That's right. I've got something on the stove.'

'Do you believe in cremation?'

'Well,' she said, 'I don't really much like the idea of being shoved away quick like that. I feel somehow it's sort of –'

'It isn't a matter of how you feel, it's a question of what your Church says you've not got to do. Your Church says you must not be cremated, that's the point.'

'Well, as I say, Mr Colston, I don't really fancy the idea –'

'*Fancy the idea* . . . It is not a question of what you fancy. You have no choice in the matter, do you see?'

'Well, I always like to see a proper burial, I always like –'

'It's a point of discipline in your Church,' he said, 'that you mustn't be cremated. You women don't know your own system.'

'I see, Mr Colston. I've got something on the stove.'

'*I* believe in cremation, but you don't – Charmian, you disapprove of cremation, you understand.'

'Very well, Godfrey.'

'And you too, Mrs Anthony.'

'O.K., Mr Colston.'

'On principle,' said Godfrey.

'That's right,' said Mrs Anthony and disappeared.

Godfrey poured himself a stout whisky and soda. He took from a drawer a box of matches and a razor blade and set to work, carefully splitting the slim length of each match, so that from one box of matches he would eventually make two boxfuls. And while he worked he sipped his drink with satisfaction.

FOUR

The reason Lisa Brooke's family arranged her post-funeral party at a tea-shop rather than at her small brick studio-house at Hampstead was this. Mrs Pettigrew, her housekeeper, was still in residence there. The family had meanwhile discovered that Lisa had bequeathed most of her fortune to Mrs Pettigrew whom they had long conceived as an unfortunate element in Lisa's life. They held this idea in the way that people often are obscurely right, though the suspicions that lead up to their conclusions are faulty. Whatever they suspected was the form that Mrs Pettigrew's influence over Lisa took, they hoped to contest Lisa's will if possible, on the grounds that Lisa, when she made it, was not in her right mind, and probably under undue influence of Mrs Pettigrew.

The very form of the will, they argued, proved that Lisa had been unbalanced when she made it. The will had not been drafted by a lawyer. It was a mere sheet of writing paper, witnessed by the charwoman and her daughter a year before Lisa's death, bequeathing her entire fortune 'to my husband if he survives me and thereafter to my housekeeper, Mabel Pettigrew'. Now Lisa, so her relatives believed, had no husband alive. Old Brooke was long dead, and moreover Lisa had been divorced from him during the Great War. She must have been dotty, they argued, even to mention a husband. The sheet of paper, they insisted, must be invalid. Alarmingly, their lawyers saw nothing invalid on the face of it; Mrs Pettigrew was apparently the sole beneficiary.

Tempest Sidebottome was furious. 'Ronald and Janet,' she said, 'should inherit by rights. We'll fight it. Lisa would never have mentioned a husband had she been in her right mind. Mrs Pettigrew must have had a hold on Lisa.'

'Lisa was always liable to say foolish things,' Ronald Sidebottome remarked.

'You're a born obstructionist,' Tempest said.

Hence, they had felt it cautious to avoid the threshold of Harmony Studio for the time being, and had felt it equally cautious to invite Mrs Pettigrew to the tea-shop.

Dame Lettie was explaining this to Miss Taylor, who had seen much in her long service with Charmian. Dame Lettie had, unawares, in the past few months, slipped into the habit of confiding in Miss Taylor. So many of Lettie's contemporaries, those who knew her world and its past, had lost their memories or their lives, or were away in private homes in the country; it was handy having Miss Taylor available in London to discuss things with.

'You see, Taylor,' said Dame Lettie, 'they never did like Mrs Pettigrew. Now, Mrs Pettigrew is an admirable woman. I was hoping to persuade her to take on Charmian. But of course with Lisa's money in prospect, she does not intend to work any longer. She must be over seventy, although of course she says ... Well, you see, with Lisa's money –'

'She would never do for Charmian,' said Miss Taylor.

'Oh really, I feel Charmian needs a firm hand if we are to keep her at home. Otherwise she will have to go into a nursing home. Taylor, you have no conception how irritated poor Godfrey gets. He tries his best.' Dame Lettie lowered her voice. 'And then, Taylor, there is the lavatory question. Mrs Anthony can't be expected to take her every time. As it is, Godfrey attends to the chamber pots in the morning. He isn't used to it, Taylor, he's not used to that sort of thing.'

In view of the warm September afternoon Miss Taylor had been put out on the balcony of the Maud Long Ward where she sat with a blanket round her knees.

'Poor Charmian,' she said, 'darling Charmian. As we get older these affairs of the bladder and kidneys do become so important to us. I hope she has a commode by her bedside, you know how difficult it is for old bones to manage a pot.'

'She has a commode,' said Dame Lettie. 'But that doesn't solve the daytime problem. Now Mrs Pettigrew would have been admirable in that respect. Think what she did for poor Lisa after the first stroke. However, Mrs Pettigrew is out of the question because of this inheritance from Lisa. It was ridiculous of Lisa.'

Miss Taylor looked distressed. 'It would be tragic,' she said, 'for

Mrs Pettigrew to go to the Colstons. Charmian would be most unhappy with the woman. You must not think of such a thing, Dame Lettie. You don't know Mrs Pettigrew as I do.'

Dame Lettie's yellow-brown eyes focused as upon an exciting scene as she bent close to Miss Taylor. 'Do you think,' she inquired, 'there was anything peculiar, I mean not right, between Mrs Pettigrew and Lisa Brooke?'

Miss Taylor did not pretend not to know what she meant. 'I cannot say,' she said, 'what were the habits of their relationship in former years. I only know this, and you yourself know, Dame Lettie, Mrs Pettigrew was very domineering towards Mrs Brooke in the last eight or nine years. She is not suitable for Charmian.'

'It is precisely because she is domineering,' said Lettie, 'that I wanted her for Charmian. Charmian *needs* a bully. For her own good. But anyway, that's beside the point, Mrs Pettigrew does not desire the job. I understand Lisa has left her practically everything. Now Lisa was very comfortable as you know, and –'

'I would not be sure that Mrs Pettigrew will in fact inherit,' insisted Miss Taylor.

'No, Taylor,' said Dame Lettie, 'I'm afraid Lisa's family do not stand a chance. I doubt if their advisers will let them take it to court. There is no case. Lisa was perfectly sane to the day she died. It is true Mrs Pettigrew had an undesirable influence over Lisa, but Lisa was in her right mind to the end.'

'Yes, it is true Mrs Pettigrew had a hold on her.'

'I wouldn't say a hold, I would say an influence. If Lisa was fool enough –'

'Quite, Dame Lettie. Was Mr Leet at the funeral, by any chance?'

'Oh, Guy Leet was there. I shouldn't think he will last long. Rheumatoid arthritis with complications.' Dame Lettie recalled, as she spoke, that rheumatoid arthritis was one of Miss Taylor's afflictions, but, she thought, after all she must face the facts. 'Very advanced case,' said Dame Lettie, 'he was managing with great difficulty on two sticks.'

'It is like wartime,' Miss Taylor remarked.

'What do you say?'

'Being over seventy is like being engaged in a war. All our friends are going or gone and we survive amongst the dead and the dying as on a battlefield.'

She is wandering in her mind and becoming morbid, thought Dame Lettie.

'Or suffering from war nerves,' Miss Taylor said.

Dame Lettie was annoyed, because she had intended to gain some advice from Miss Taylor.

'Come now, Taylor,' she said. 'You are talking like Charmian.'

'I must,' said Miss Taylor, 'have caught a lot of her ways of thought and speech.'

'Taylor,' Lettie said, 'I want to ask your advice.' She looked at the other woman to see if she was alert. 'Four months ago,' she said, 'I began to receive anonymous telephone calls from a man. I have been receiving them ever since. On one occasion when I was staying with Godfrey, the man, who must have traced me there, gave a message for me to Godfrey.'

'What does he say?' said Miss Taylor.

Dame Lettie leant to Miss Taylor's ear and, in a low tone, informed her.

'Have you told the police?'

'Of course we have told the police. They are useless. Godfrey had an interview with them too. Useless. They seem to think we are making it up.'

'You will have thought of consulting Chief Inspector Mortimer who was such a fan of Charmian's?'

'Of course I have not consulted Mortimer. Mortimer is retired, he is close on seventy. Time passes, you know. You are living in the past, Taylor.'

'I only thought,' said Miss Taylor, 'that Inspector Mortimer might act privately. He might at least be helpful in some way. He always struck me as a most unusual –'

'Mortimer is out of the question. We want a young, active detective on the job. There is a dangerous lunatic at large. I know not how many people besides myself are endangered.'

'I should not answer the telephone, Dame Lettie, if I were you.'

'My dear Taylor, one can't be cut off perpetually. I still have my Homes to consider, I am not entirely a back number, Taylor. One must be on the phone. But I confess, I am feeling the strain. Imagine for yourself every time one answers the telephone. One never knows if one is going to hear that distressing sentence. It *is* distressing.'

'Remember you must die,' said Miss Taylor.

'Hush,' said Dame Lettie, looking warily over her shoulder.

'Can you not ignore it, Dame Lettie?'

'No, I can not. I have tried, but it troubles me deeply. It *is* a troublesome remark.'

'Perhaps you might obey it,' said Miss Taylor.

'What's that you say?'

'You might, perhaps, try to remember you must die.'

She is wandering again, thought Lettie. 'Taylor,' she said, 'I do not wish to be advised how to think. What I hoped you could suggest is some way of apprehending the criminal, for I see that I must take matters into my own hands. Do you understand telephone wires? Can you follow the system of calls made from private telephone boxes?'

'It's difficult,' said Miss Taylor, 'for people of advanced years to start remembering they must die. It is best to form the habit while young. I shall think of some plan, Dame Lettie, for tracing the man. I did once know something about the telephone system, I will try to recall what I knew.'

'I must go.' Lettie rose, and added, 'I expect you are keeping pretty well, Taylor?'

'We have a new ward sister here,' said Miss Taylor. 'She is not so pleasant as the last. I have no complaint personally, but some of my companions are inclined to be touchy, to imagine things.'

Lettie cast her eye along the sunny veranda of the Maud Long Ward where a row of old women sat out in their chairs.

'They are fortunate,' said Dame Lettie and uttered a sigh.

'I know it,' said Miss Taylor. 'But they are discontented and afraid.'

'Afraid of what?'

'The sister in charge,' said Miss Taylor.

'But what's wrong with her?'

'Nothing,' said Miss Taylor, 'except that she is afraid of these old people.'

'*She* is afraid? I thought you said the patients were afraid of *her*.'

'It comes to the same thing,' said Miss Taylor.

She is wandering, thought Lettie, and she said, 'In the Balkan countries, the peasants turn their aged parents out of doors every summer to beg their keep for the winter.'

'Indeed?' said Miss Taylor. 'That is an interesting system.' Her hand, when Dame Lettie lifted it to say good-bye, was painful at the distorted joints.

'I hope,' said Miss Taylor, 'you will think no more of employing Mrs Pettigrew.'

Dame Lettie thought, She is jealous of anyone else's having to do with Charmian.

Perhaps I am, thought Miss Taylor who could read Dame Lettie's idea.

And as usual after Dame Lettie had left, she pondered and understood more and more why Lettie came so frequently to visit her and seemed to find it pleasant, and at the same time seldom spoke or behaved pleasantly. It was the old enmity about Miss Taylor's love affair in 1907 which in fact Dame Lettie had forgotten – had dangerously forgotten; so that she retained in her mind a vague fascinating enmity for Jean Taylor without any salutary definition. Whereas Miss Taylor herself, until quite recently, had remembered the details of her love affair, and Dame Lettie's subsequent engagement to marry the man, which came to nothing after all. But recently, thought Miss Taylor, I am beginning to feel as she does. Enmity is catching. Miss Taylor closed her eyes and laid her hands loosely on the rug which covered her knees. Soon the nurses would come in to put the grannies to bed. Meanwhile she thought with a sleepy pleasure, I enjoy Dame Lettie's visits, I look forward to them, in spite of which I treat her with my asperity. Perhaps it is because I have now so little to lose. Perhaps it is because these encounters have an exhilarating quality. I might sink into a torpor were it not for fat old Lettie. And perhaps, into the bargain, I might use her in the matter of the ward sister, although that is unlikely.

'Granny Taylor – Gemini. *Evening festivities may give you all the excitement you want. A brisk day for business enterprises,*' Granny Valvona read out for the second time that day.

'There,' said Miss Taylor.

The Maud Long Ward had been put to bed and was now awaiting supper.

'It comes near the mark,' said Miss Valvona. 'You can always know by your horoscope when your visitors are coming to see you, Granny Taylor. Either your Dame or that gentleman that comes; you can always tell by the stars.'

Granny Trotsky lifted her wizened head with low brow and pug nose, and said something. Her health had been degenerating for some weeks. It was no longer possible to hear exactly what she said. Miss Taylor was the quickest in the ward at guessing what Granny Trotsky's remarks might be, but Miss Barnacle was the most inventive.

Granny Trotsky repeated her words, whatever they were.

Miss Taylor replied, 'All right, Granny.'

'What did she say?' demanded Granny Valvona.

'I am not sure,' said Miss Taylor.

Mrs Reewes-Duncan, who claimed to have lived in a bungalow in former days, addressed Miss Valvona. 'Are you aware that the horoscope you have just read out to us specifies evening festivities, whereas Granny Taylor's visitor came at three-fifteen this afternoon?'

Granny Trotsky again raised her curiously shaped head and spoke, emphasizing her statement with vehement nods of this head which was so fearfully and wonderfully made. Whereupon Granny Barnacle ventured, 'She says festivities my backside. What's the use of the stars foretell with that murderous bitch of a sister outside there, she says, waiting to finish off the whole ward in the winter when the lot goes down with pneumonia. You'll be reading your stars, she says, all right when they need the beds for the next lot. That's what she says – don't you, Granny Trotsky?'

Granny Trotsky, raising her head, made one more, and very voluble effort, then dropped exhausted on her pillow, closing her eyes.

'That's what she said,' said Granny Barnacle. 'And right she is, too. Come the winter them that's made nuisances of theirselves don't last long under that sort.'

A ripple of murmurs ran up the rows of beds. It ceased as a nurse walked through the ward, and started again when she had gone.

Miss Valvona's strong eyes stared through her spectacles into the past, as they frequently did in the autumn, and she saw the shop door open on a Sunday afternoon, and the perfect ices her father manufactured, and heard the beautiful bellow of his accordion after night had fallen, on and on till closing time. 'Oh, the parlour and the sundaes and white ladies we used to serve,' she said, 'and my father with the Box. The white ladies stiff on your plate, they were hard, and made from the best-quality products. And the fellows would say to me, "How do, Doreen," even if they had another girl with them after the pictures. And my father got down the Box and played like a champion. It cost him fifty pounds, in those days, mind you, it was a lot.'

Granny Duncan addressed Miss Taylor, 'Did you ask that Dame to do something for us, at all?'

'Not exactly,' said Miss Taylor, 'but I mentioned that we were not so comfortable now as we have been previously.'

'She goin' to *do* something for us?' demanded Granny Barnacle.

'She is not herself on the management committee,' Miss Taylor explained. 'It is a friend of hers who is on the committee. Now, it will take time. I can't, you know, press her. She is very easily put off. And then, you know, in the meantime, we must try to make the best of this.' The nurse walked back through the ward among the grannies, all sullen and silent but for Granny Trotsky who had now fallen noisily asleep with her mouth open.

It was true, thought Miss Taylor, that the young nurses were less jolly since Sister Burstead had taken over the ward. Of course it was but two seconds before she had become 'Sister Bastard' on the lips of Granny Barnacle. The associations of her name, perhaps, in addition to her age – Sister Burstead was well over fifty – had affected Granny Barnacle with immediate hostile feelings. 'Over fifty they got the workhouse mind. You can't never trust a ward sister over fifty. They don't study that there's new ways of goin' on since the war by law.' These sentiments in turn had affected the other occupants of the ward. But the ground had been prepared the week before by their knowledge of the departure of the younger sister: 'A change, hear that? – there's to be a change. What's the stars say, Granny Valvona?' Then, on the morning that Sister Burstead took over, she being wiry, bespectacled, and middle-aged with a bad-tempered twitch at one side of her face between lip and jaw, Granny Barnacle declared she had absolutely placed her. 'The workhouse mind. You see what'll happen now. Anyone that's a nuisance or can't contain themselves like me with Bright's disease, they won't last long in this ward. You get pneumonia in the winter, can't help but do, and that's her chance.'

'What you think she'll do, Granny Barnacle?'

'Do? It's what she won't do. You wait to the winter, you'll be lyin' there and nothin' done for you. Specially if you got no relations or that to raise inquiries.'

'The other nurses is all right, Granny, though.'

'You'll see a difference in *them*.'

There had been a difference. The nurses were terrified of their new superior, that was all. But as they became more brisk and efficient so did the majority of the grannies behold them with hostile thoughts and deadly suspicions. When the night staff came on duty the ward relaxed, and this took the form of much shouting throughout the night. The grannies shouted in their sleep and half-waking restlessness. They accepted their sedative pills fearfully, and in the morning would ask each other, 'Was I all right last night?' not quite remembering whether they or another had made the noise.

'It all goes down in the book,' said Granny Barnacle. 'Nothing happens during the night but what it goes into the book. And Sister Bastard sees it in the morning. You know what that'll mean, don't you, when the winter comes?'

At first, Miss Taylor took a frivolous view of these sayings. It was true the new sister was jittery and strict, and over fifty years of age, and frightened. It will all blow over, thought Miss Taylor, when both sides get used to the change. She was sorry for Sister Burstead and her fifty-odd years. Thirty years ago, thought Miss Taylor, I was into my fifties, and getting old. How nerve-wracking it is to be getting old, how much better to be old! It had been touch and go, in those days, whether she would leave the Colstons and settle down with her brother in Coventry while she had the chance. It was such a temptation to leave them, she having been cultivated by twenty-five years' association with Charmian. By the time she was fifty it really seemed absurd for her to continue her service with Charmian, her habits and tastes were so superior to those of the maids she met on her travels with Charmian, so much more intelligent. She had been all on edge for the first two years of her fifties, not knowing whether to go to look after the widowed brother in Coventry and enjoy some status or whether to continue waking Charmian up every morning, and observing in silence Godfrey's infidelities. For two years while she made up her mind she had given Charmian hell, threatening to leave every month, folding Charmian's dresses in the trunk so that they were horribly creased, going off to art galleries while Charmian rang for her in vain.

'You're far worse now,' Charmian would tell her, 'than when you were going through the menopause.'

Charmian plied her with bottles of tonic medicine which she had poured down the lavatory with a weird joy. At last, after a month's holiday with her brother in Coventry, she found she could never stand life with him and his ways, the getting him off to his office in the morning, the keeping him in clean shirts, and the avaricious whist parties in the evening. At the Colstons' there was always some exotic company, and Charmian's sitting-room had been done out in black and orange. All the time she was at Coventry Miss Taylor had missed the exciting scraps of conversation which she had been used to hearing on Charmian's afternoons.

'Charmian darling, don't you think, honestly, I should have Boris bumped off?'

'No, I rather like Boris.'

And those telephone messages far into the nights.

'Is that you, Taylor darling? Get Charmian to the phone, will you? Tell her I'm in a state. Tell her I want to read her my new poem.' That was thirty years ago.

Ten years before that, the telephone messages had been different again, 'Taylor, tell Mrs Colston I'm in London. Guy Leet. Not a word, Taylor to *Mr* Colston.' These were messages which Miss Taylor sometimes did not deliver. Charmian herself was going through her difficult age at that time, and was apt to fly like a cat at any man who made approaches to her, even Guy who had previously been her lover.

At the age of fifty-three Miss Taylor had settled down. She could even meet Alec Warner without any of the old feelings. She went everywhere with Charmian, sat for hours while Charmian read aloud her books, while still in manuscript, gave judgement. As gradually the other servants became difficult and left, so Jean Taylor took charge. When Charmian had her hair bobbed so did Miss Taylor.

When Charmian entered the Catholic Church Miss Taylor was received, really just to please Charmian.

She rarely saw her brother from Coventry, and when she did, counted herself lucky to have escaped him. On one occasion she told Godfrey Colston to watch his step. The disappointed twitch at the side of her mouth which had appeared during her forties, now gradually disappeared.

So it will be, thought Miss Taylor, in the case of Sister Burstead, once she settles down. The twitch will go.

Presently, however, Miss Taylor began to feel there was very little chance of the new sister's twitch disappearing. The grannies were so worked up about her, it would not be surprising if she did indeed let them die of pneumonia should she ever get the chance.

'You must speak to the doctor, Granny Barnacle,' said Miss Taylor, 'if you really feel you aren't getting the right treatment.'

'The doctor my backside. They're hand-in-glove. What's an old woman to them I ask you?'

The only good that could be discerned in the arrival of the new sister was the fact that the ward was now more alert. Everyone's wits had improved, as if the sister were a sort of shock treatment. The grannies had forgotten their will-making, and no longer threatened to disinherit each other or the nurses.

Mrs Reewes-Duncan, however, made the great mistake of threatening the sister with her solicitor one dinner-time when the meat was tough or off, Miss Taylor could not recall which. 'Fetch the ward sister to me,' Mrs Reewes-Duncan demanded. 'Fetch her here to me.'

The sister marched in purposefully when thus summoned.

'Well, Granny Duncan, what's the matter? Hurry up now, I'm busy. What's the matter?'

'This meat, my good woman . . .' The ward felt at once that Granny Duncan was making a great mistake. 'My niece will be informed . . . My solicitor . . .'

For some reason, the word 'solicitor' set fire to Sister Burstead. That one word did the trick. You could evidently threaten the doctor, the matron, or your relations, and she would merely stand there glaring angrily with her twitch, she would say no more than, 'You people don't know you're born,' and, 'Fire ahead, tell your niece, *my dear*.' But the word solicitor fairly turned her, as Granny Barnacle recounted next day, arse over tip. She gripped the bedrail and yelled at Granny Duncan for a long time, it might have been ten minutes. Words, in isolation and grouped in phrases, detached themselves like sparks from the fiery scream proceeding from Sister Burstead's mouth. 'Old beast . . . dirty old beast . . . food . . . grumble and grouse . . . I've been on since eight o'clock this morning . . . I've been on and on . . . work, work, work, day after day, for a lot of useless old, filthy old . . .'

Sister Burstead went off duty immediately assisted by a nurse. If only, thought Miss Taylor, we could try to be sweet old ladies, she would be all right. It's because we aren't sweet old things . . .

'Scorpio,' Granny Valvona had declared four hours later, although like everyone else in the ward she was shaken up. 'Granny Duncan – Scorpio. *You can sail ahead with confidence. The success of another person could affect you closely.*' Granny Valvona put down the paper. 'You see what I mean?' she said. 'The stars never let you down. *The success of another person* . . . A remarkable forecast.'

The incident was reported to the matron and the doctor. The former made inquiries next morning of a kind which clearly indicated she was hoping against hope Sister Burstead could be exonerated, for she would be difficult to replace.

The matron bent over Miss Taylor and spoke quietly and exclusively. 'Sister Burstead is having a rest for a few days. She has been overworking.'

'Evidently,' said Miss Taylor, whose head ached horribly.

'Tell me what you know of the affair. Sister Burstead was provoked, I believe?'

'Evidently,' said Miss Taylor, eyeing the bland face above her and desiring it to withdraw.

'Sister Burstead was cross with Granny Duncan?' said the matron.

'She was nothing,' said Miss Taylor, 'if not cross. I suggest the sister might be transferred to another ward where there are younger people and the work is lighter.'

'All the work in this hospital,' said the matron, 'is heavy.'

Most of the grannies felt too upset to enjoy the few days' absence from duty of Sister Burstead, for whenever the general hysteria showed signs of waning, Granny Barnacle applied the bellows: 'Wait till the winter. When you get pneumonia . . .'

During those days it happened that Granny Trotsky had her second stroke. An aged male cousin was summoned to her bedside, and a screen was put round her bed. He emerged after an hour still wearing the greenish-black hat in which he had arrived, shaking his head and hat, and crying all over his blotchy foreign face.

Granny Barnacle, who was up in her chair that day, called to him, 'Pssst!'

Obediently he came to her side.

Granny Barnacle flicked her head towards the screened-in bed.

'She gone?'

'Nah. She breathe, but not speak.'

'D'you know who done it?' said Granny Barnacle. 'It was the sister that brought it on.'

'She have no sister. I am next of kin.'

A nurse came and hurried him away.

Granny Barnacle declared once more to the ward, 'Sister Bastard done for Granny Trotsky.'

'Ah but Granny, it was her second stroke. There's always a second, you know.'

'Sister done it with her bad temper.'

On learning that Sister Burstead had neither been dismissed nor transferred to another ward but was to return on the following day, Granny Barnacle gave notice to the doctor that she refused further treatment, was discharging herself next day, and that she would tell the world why.

'I know my bloody rights as a patient,' she said. 'Don't think I don't know the law. *And* what's more, I can get the phone number of the newspaper. I only got to ring up and they come along and want to know what's what.'

'Take it easy, Granny,' said the doctor.

'If Sister Bastard comes back, I go,' said Granny Barnacle.

'Where to?' said the nurse.

Granny Barnacle glared. She felt that the nurse was being sarcastic, must know that she had spent three months in Holloway prison thirty-six years ago, six months twenty-two years ago, and subsequently various months. Granny Barnacle felt the nurse was referring to her record when she said 'Where to?' in that voice of hers.

The doctor frowned at the nurse and said to Granny Barnacle,

'Take it easy, Granny. Your blood pressure isn't too good this morning. What sort of a night did you have? Pretty restless?'

This speech unnerved Granny Barnacle who had indeed had a bad night.

Granny Trotsky, who had so far recovered that the bedscreen had been removed, had been uttering slobbery mutters. The very sight of Granny Trotsky, the very sound of her trying to talk as she did at this moment, took away Granny Barnacle's nerve entirely.

She looked at the doctor's face, to read it. 'Ah, doc, I don't feel too bloody good,' she said. 'And I just don't feel easy with that bitch in charge. I just feel anything might happen.'

'Come, come, the poor woman's overworked,' he recited. 'We all like to be of help if we can and in any way we can. We are trying to help you, Granny.'

When he had gone Granny Barnacle whispered over to Miss Taylor, 'Do I look bad, love?'

'No, Granny, you look fine.' In fact, Granny Barnacle's face was blotched with dark red.

'Did you hear what the doc said about my blood pressure? Do you think it was a lie, just so's I wouldn't make a fuss?'

'Perhaps not.'

'For two pins, Granny Taylor, I'd be out of that door and down them stairs if it was the last thing I did and –'

'I shouldn't do that,' said Miss Taylor.

'Could they certify me, love?'

'I don't know,' said Miss Taylor.

'I'll tell the priest.'

'You know what he'll say to you,' said Miss Taylor.

'Offer it bloodywell up for the Holy Souls.'

'I daresay.'

'It's a hard religion, Granny Taylor. If it wasn't that my mother was R.C. I would never of –'

'I know a lady –' It was then Miss Taylor had said, rashly, 'I know a lady who knows another lady who is on the management committee of this hospital. It may take some time but I will see what I can do to get them to transfer Sister Burstead.'

'God bless you, Granny Taylor.'

'I can't promise. But I'll try. I shall have to be tactful.'

'You hear that?' said Granny Barnacle to everyone in the ward. 'You hear what Granny Taylor's goin' to do?'

Miss Taylor was not very disappointed with her first effort at sounding Dame Lettie. It was a beginning. She would keep on at Dame Lettie. There was also, possibly, Alec Warner. He might be induced to speak to Tempest Sidebottome who sat on the management committee of the hospital. It might even be arranged without blame to dreary Sister Burstead.

'Didn't your Dame promise nothing definite then?' said Granny Barnacle.

'No, it will take time.'

'Will it be done before the winter?'

'I hope so.'

'Did you tell her what she done to Granny Duncan?'

'Not exactly.'

'You should of. Strikes me you're not on our side entirely, Granny Taylor. I seem to remember that face somehow.'

'Whose face?'

'That Dame's face.'

The difficulty was, Miss Taylor reflected, she could not feel the affair to be pre-eminently important. Sometimes she would have liked to say to the grannies, 'What if your fears were correct? What if we died next winter?' Sometimes she did say to them, 'Some of us may die next winter in any case. It is highly probable.' Granny Valvona would reply, 'I'm ready to meet my God, any time.' And Granny Barnacle would stoutly add, 'But not before time.'

'You must keep on at your friend, Granny Taylor,' said Granny Duncan, who, among all the grannies, most irritated Sister Burstead. Granny Duncan had cancer. Miss Taylor often wondered if the sister was afraid of cancer.

'I seem to remember that Dame's face,' Granny Barnacle kept on. 'Was she ever much round Holborn way of an evening?'

'I don't think so,' said Miss Taylor.

'She might be an old customer of mine,' said Granny Barnacle.

'I think she had her papers sent.'

'Did she go out to work, this Dame?'

'Well, not to a job. But she did various kinds of committee work. That sort of thing.'

Granny Barnacle turned over the face of Dame Lettie in her mind. 'Was it charity work you said she did?'

'That kind of thing,' said Miss Taylor. 'Nothing special.'

Granny Barnacle looked at her suspiciously, but Miss Taylor would not be drawn, nor say that Dame Lettie had been a Prison Visitor at Holloway from her thirtieth year until it became too difficult for her, with her great weight and breathlessness, to climb the stairs.

'I will keep on at Dame Lettie,' she promised.

It was Sister Burstead's day off, and a nurse whistled as she brought in the first supper tray.

Granny Barnacle commented in a hearty voice,

> 'A whistling woman, a crowing hen,
> Is neither fit for God nor man.'

The nurse stopped whistling and gave Granny Barnacle a close look, dumped the tray, and went to fetch another.

Granny Trotsky attempted to raise her head and say something.

'Granny Trotsky wants something,' said Granny Duncan.

'What you want, Granny?'

'She is saying,' said Miss Taylor, 'that we shouldn't be unkind to the nurses just because –'

'Unkind to the nurses! What they goin' to do when the winter –'

Miss Taylor prayed for grace. Is there no way, she thought, for them to forget the winter? Can't they go back to making their wills every week?

In the course of the night Granny Trotsky died as the result of the bursting of a small blood-vessel in her brain, and her spirit returned to God who gave it.

FIVE

Mrs Anthony knew instinctively that Mrs Pettigrew was a kindly woman. Her instinct was wrong. But the first few weeks after Mrs Pettigrew came to the Colstons to look after Charmian she sat in the kitchen and told Mrs Anthony of her troubles.

'Have a fag,' said Mrs Anthony, indicating with her elbow the packet on the table while she poured strong tea. 'Everything might be worse.'

Mrs Pettigrew said, 'It couldn't very well be worse. Thirty years of my life I gave to Mrs Lisa Brooke. Everyone knew I was to get that money. Then this Guy Leet turns up to claim. It wasn't any marriage, that wasn't. Not a proper marriage.' She pulled her cup of tea towards her and, thrusting her head close to Mrs Anthony's, told her in what atrocious manner and for what long-ago reason Guy Leet had been incapable of consummating his marriage with Lisa Brooke.

Mrs Anthony swallowed a large sip of her tea, the cup of which she held in both hands, and breathed back into the cup while the warm-smelling steam spread comfortingly over her nose. 'Still,' she said, 'a husband's a husband. By law.'

'Lisa never recognized him as such,' said Mrs Pettigrew. 'No one knew about the marriage with Guy Leet, until she died, the little swine.'

'I thought you says she was all right,' said Mrs Anthony.

'Guy Leet,' said Mrs Pettigrew. 'He's the little swine.'

'Oh, I see. Well, the courts will have something to say to that, dear, when it comes up. Have a fag.'

'You're making me into a smoker, Mrs Anthony. Thanks, I will. But you should try to cut them down, they aren't too good for you.'

'Twenty a day since I was twenty-five and seventy yesterday,' said Mrs Anthony.

'Seventy! Gracious, you'll be –'

'Seventy years of age yesterday.'

'Oh, seventy. Isn't it time you had a rest then? I don't envy you with this lot,' Mrs Pettigrew indicated with her head the kitchen door, meaning the Colstons residing beyond it.

'Not so bad,' said Mrs Anthony. '*He's* a bit tight, but *she's* nice. I like *her*.'

'He's tight with the money?' said Mrs Pettigrew.

Mrs Anthony said, 'Oh very,' swivelling her eyes towards her companion to fix the remark.

Mrs Pettigrew patted her hair which was thick, dyed black and well cut, as Lisa had made her wear it. 'How old,' she said, 'would you say I was, Mrs Anthony?'

Mrs Anthony, still sitting, pushed back in her chair the better to view Mrs Pettigrew. She looked at the woman's feet in their suede black shoes, her tight good legs – no veins, her encased hips and good bust. Mrs Anthony then put her head sideways to regard, from an angle of fifteen degrees, Mrs Pettigrew's face. There were lines from nose to mouth, a small cherry-painted mouth. Only the beginnings of one extra chin. Two lines across the brow. The eyes were dark and clear, the nose firm and broad. 'I should say,' said Mrs Anthony, folding her arms, 'you was sixty-four abouts.'

The unexpectedness of Mrs Pettigrew's gentle voice was due to her heavily-marked appearance. It was gentler still as she said to Mrs Anthony, 'Add five years.'

'Sixty-nine. You don't look it,' said Mrs Anthony. 'Of course you've had the time and money to look after yourself and powder your face. You should of been in business.'

In fact, Mrs Pettigrew was seventy-three, but she did not at all look the age under her make-up.

She drew her hand across her forehead, however, and shook her head slowly. She was worried about the money, the court case which would probably drag on and on. Lisa's family were claiming their rights too.

Mrs Anthony had started washing up.

'Old Warner still in with *her*,' she said, 'I suppose?'

'Yes,' said Mrs Pettigrew. 'He is.'

'It takes her off my hands for a while,' said Mrs Anthony.

'I must say,' Mrs Pettigrew said, 'when I was with Lisa Brooke I used to be asked in to meet the callers. I mixed with everyone.'

Mrs Anthony started peeling potatoes and singing.

'I'm going in,' said Mrs Pettigrew, rising and brushing down her neat skirt. 'Whether she likes it or whether she doesn't, I'd better keep my eye on her in any case, that's what I'm here for.'

When Mrs Pettigrew entered the drawing-room she said, 'Oh, Mrs Colston, I was just wondering if you were tired.'

'You may take the tea-things away,' said Charmian.

Instead Mrs Pettigrew rang for Mrs Anthony, and, as she piled plates on the tray for the housekeeper to take away, she knew Charmian's guest was looking at her.

Charmian said to Mrs Anthony, 'Thank you, Taylor.'

Mrs Pettigrew had met Alec Warner sometimes at Lisa Brooke's. He smiled at her and nodded. She sat down and took a cigarette out of her black suède bag. Alec lit it. The clatter of Mrs Anthony's tray faded out as she receded to the kitchen.

'You were telling me ...?' Charmian said to her guest.

'Oh yes.' He turned his white head and grey face to Mrs Pettigrew. 'I was explaining the rise of democracy in the British Isles. Do you miss Mrs Brooke?'

'Very much,' said Mabel Pettigrew, blowing out a long puff of smoke. She had put on her social manner. 'Do continue about democracy,' she said.

'When I went to Russia,' said Charmian, 'the Tsarina sent an escort to –'

'Now, Mrs Colston, just a moment, while Mr Alec Warner tells us about democracy.'

Charmian looked about her strangely for a moment, then said, 'Yes, continue about democracy, Eric.'

'Not Eric – Alec,' said Mrs Pettigrew.

Alec Warner soothed the air with his old, old steady hand.

'The real rise of democracy in the British Isles occurred in Scotland by means of Queen Victoria's bladder,' he said. 'There had, you know, existed an idea of democracy, but the real thing occurred through this little weakness of Queen Victoria's.'

Mabel Pettigrew laughed with a backward throw of her head.

Charmian looked vague. Alec Warner continued slowly as one filling in the time with his voice. His eyes were watchful.

'Queen Victoria had a little trouble with the bladder, you see. When she went to stay at Balmoral in her latter years a number of privies were caused to be built at the backs of little cottages which had not previously possessed privies. This was to enable the Queen to go on her morning drive round the countryside in comfort, and to descend from her carriage from time to time, ostensibly to visit the humble cottagers in their dwellings. Eventually, word went round that Queen Victoria was exceedingly democratic. Of course it was all due to her little weakness. But everyone copied the Queen and the idea spread, and now you see we have a great democracy.'

Mrs Pettigrew laughed for a long time. Alec Warner was gazing like a bird-watcher at Charmian, who plucked at the rug round her knees, waiting to tell her own story.

'When I went to Russia,' said Charmian, looking up at him like a child, 'the Tsarina sent an escort to meet me at the frontier, but did not send an escort to take me back. That is so like Russia, they make resolutions then get bored. The male peasants lie on the stove all winter. All the way to Russia my fellow-passengers were opening their boxes and going over their belongings. It was spring and . . .'

Mrs Pettigrew winked at Alec Warner. Charmian stopped and smiled at him. 'Have you seen Jean Taylor lately?' she said.

'Not for a week or two. I have been away to Folkestone on my research work. I shall go to see her next week.'

'Lettie goes regularly. She says Jean is very happy and fortunate.'

'Lettie is –' He was going to say she was a selfish fool, then remembered Mrs Pettigrew's presence. 'Well, you know what I think of Lettie's opinions,' he said and waved away the topic with his hand.

And as if the topic had landed on Charmian's lap, she stared at her lap and continued, 'If only you had discovered Lettie's character a little sooner. If only . . .'

He rose to leave, for he knew how Charmian's memory was inclined to wake up in the past, in some arbitrary year. She would likely fix on those events, that year 1907, and bring them close up to her, as one might bring a book close to one's eyes. The time of his love-affair with Jean Taylor when she was a parlour-maid at the Pipers' before Charmian's marriage, would be like last week to

Charmian. And her novelist's mind by sheer habit still gave to those disjointed happenings a shape which he could not accept, and in a way which he thought dishonest. He had been in love with Jean Taylor, he had decided after all to take everyone's advice. He had therefore engaged himself to Lettie. He had broken the engagement when he came to know Lettie better. These were the facts in 1907. By 1912 he had been able to contemplate them without emotion. But dear Charmian made the most of them. She saw the facts as a dramatic sequence reaching its fingers into all his life's work. This interested him so far as it reflected Charmian, though not at all so far as it affected himself. He would, nevertheless, have liked to linger in his chair on that afternoon, in his seventy-ninth year, and listen to Charmian recalling her youth. But he was embarrassed by Mrs Pettigrew's presence. Her intrusion had irritated him, and he could not, like Charmian, talk on as if she were not present. He looked at Mrs Pettigrew as she helped him on with his coat in the hall, and thought, 'An irritating woman.' Then he thought, 'A fine-looking woman,' and this was associated with her career at Lisa's as he had glimpsed it at intervals over twenty-six years. He thought about Mabel Pettigrew all the way home across two parks, though he had meant to think about Charmian on that walk. And he reflected upon himself, amazed, since he was nearly eighty and Mrs Pettigrew a good, he supposed, sixty-five. 'Oh,' he said to himself, 'these erotic throes that come like thieves in the night to steal my High Church-manship!' Only, he was not a High Churchman – it was no more than a manner of speaking to himself.

He returned to his rooms – which, since they were officially described as 'gentlemen's chambers', he always denied were a flat – off St James's Street. He hung his coat, put away his hat and gloves, then stood at the large bow window gazing out as at an imposing prospect, though in reality the window looked down only on the side entrance to a club. He noted the comings and goings of the club porter. The porter of his own chambers came up the narrow street intently reading the back page of an evening paper. With his inward eye, Dr Warner, the old sociologist, at the same time contemplated Old Age which had been his study since he had turned seventy. Nearly ten years of inquisitive work had gone into the card indexes and files encased in two oak cabinets, one on either side of the window. His approach to the subject was unique; few gerontologists had the ingenuity or the freedom to conduct their investigations on the lines he had adopted. He got about a good deal; he employed agents; his work was, he hoped, valuable; or would be, one day.

His wide desk was bare, but from a drawer he took a thick bound notebook and sat down to write.

Presently he rose to fetch the two boxes of index cards which he used constantly when working at his desk. One of these contained the names of those of his friends and acquaintances who were over seventy, with details of his relationship to them, and in the case of chance encounters, the circumstances of their meeting. Special sections were devoted to St Aubrey's Home for mental cases in Folkestone where, for ten years, he had been visiting certain elderly patients by way of unofficial research.

Much of the information on this first set of cards was an aid to memory, for, although his memory was still fairly good, he wished to ensure against his losing it: he had envisaged the day when he might take up a card, read the name and wonder, for instance, 'Colston – Charmian, who is Charmian Colston? Charmian Colston . . . I know the name but I can't for the moment think who . . .' Against this possibility was inscribed 'Née Piper. Met 1907. Vide Ww page . . .' 'Ww,' stood for *Who's Who*. The page number was inserted in pencil, to be changed every four years when he acquired a new *Who's Who*. Most of the cards in this category were filled in with small writing on both sides. All of them were, by his instruction, to be destroyed at his death. At the top left-hand corner of each card was a reference letter and number in red ink. These cross-referred to a second set of cards which bore pseudonyms invented by Dr Warner for each person. (Thus, Charmian was, in the second set of cards, 'Gladys'.) All these cards in the second set were his real working cards, for these bore the clues to the case-histories. On each was marked a neat network of codes and numbers relating to various passages in the books around the walls, on the subjects of gerontology and senescence, and to the ten years' accumulation of his thick note-books.

Alec Warner lifted the house phone and ordered grilled turbot. He sat to his desk, opened a drawer and extracted a notebook; this was his current diary which would also be destroyed at his death. In it he noted his afternoon observations of Charmian, Mrs Pettigrew and himself. 'Her mind,' he wrote, 'has by no means ceased to function, as her husband makes out. Her mind works associatively. At first she went off into a dream, making plucking movements at the rug on her knees. She appeared to be impatient. She did not follow my story at all, but apparently the words "Queen Victoria" had evoked some other regal figure. As soon as I had finished she embarked upon a reminiscence (which is likely to be true in detail) of her visit to St Petersburg to see her father in 1908. (As she spoke, I myself recalled, for the first time since 1908, Charmian's preparations for her journey to Russia. This has been dormant in my memory since then.) I observed that Charmian did not, however, mention the meeting with her father nor the other diplomat whose name I forget, who later committed suicide on her account. Nor did she mention that she was accompanied by Jean Taylor. I have no reason to doubt the accuracy of her memory on the habits of Russian travellers. So far as I recall her actual words were . . .'

He wrote on till his turbot came up.

My Aunt Marcia, he reflected as he ate, was ninety-two, that is seven years older than Charmian, and was still playing a brilliant game of chess to the time of her death. Mrs Flaxman, wife of the former Rector of Pineville, was seventy-three when she lost her memory completely; twelve years younger than Charmian. Charmian's memory is not completely gone, it is only erratic. He rose from the table and went to his desk to make a note in the margin of his diary where he had written his day's account of Charmian: 'Vide Mrs Flaxman.'

He returned to his turbot. Ninon de Lenclos of the seventeenth century died at ninety-nine, in full reason and reputed for wit, he reflected.

His wine-glass rested a moment on his lip. Goethe, he mused, was older than me when he was writing love poems to young girls. Renoir at eighty-six . . . Titian, Voltaire. Verdi composed *Falstaff* at the age of eighty. But artists are perhaps exceptions.

He thought of the Maud Long Ward where Jean Taylor lay, and wondered what Cicero would make of it. He looked round his shelves. The great Germans on the subject: they were either visionaries or pathologists, largely. To understand the subject, one had to befriend the people, one had to use spies and win allies.

He ate half of what he had been sent. He drank part of half a bottle of wine. He read over what he had written, the account of the afternoon from the time of his arrival at the Colstons' to his walk back across the park with the thoughts, which had taken him by surprise, of Mrs Pettigrew whose intrusive presence, as he had noted in his diary, had excited him with both moral irritability and erotic feelings. The diary would go into the fire, but his every morning's work was to analyse and abstract from it the data for his case-histories, entering them in the various methodical notebooks. There Charmian would become an impersonal, almost homeless 'Gladys', Mabel Pettigrew 'Joan', and he himself 'George'.

Meantime he put away his cards and his journal and read, for an hour, from one of the fat volumes of Newman's *Life and Letters*. Before he put it down he marked a passage with a pencil:

I wonder, in old times what people died of. We read, 'After this, it was told Joseph that his father was sick.' 'And the days of David drew nigh that he should die.' What were they sick, what did they die, of? And so of the great Fathers. St Athanasius died past seventy – was his a paralytic seizure? We cannot imitate the Martyrs in their death – but I sometimes feel it would be a comfort if we could associate ourselves with the great Confessor Saints in their illnesses and decline: Pope St Gregory had the gout, St Basil had a liver complaint, but St Gregory Naziazen? St Ambrose? St Augustine and St Martin died of fevers, proper to old age . . .

At half past nine he took a packet of ten cigarettes from a drawer and went out. He turned into Pall Mall where the road was up and a nightwatchman on duty whom Alec Warner had been visiting each night for a week past. He hoped to get sufficient consistent answers to construct a history. 'How old are you? Where do you live? What do you eat? Do you believe in God? Any religion? Did you ever go in for sport? How do you get on with your wife? How old is she? Who? What? Why? How do you feel?'

'Evening,' said the man as Alec approached. 'Thanks,' he said, as he took the cigarettes. He shifted up on the plank by the brazier to let Alec sit down beside him.

Alec warmed his hands.

'How are you feeling tonight?' he said.

'Not so bad! How's yourself, guv?'

'Not so bad. How old did you say . . .?'

'Seventy-five. Sixty-nine to the Council.'

'Of course,' said Alec.

'Doesn't do to let on too much.'

'I'm seventy-nine,' coaxed Alec.

'Don't look a day over sixty-five.'

Alec smiled into the fire knowing the remark was untrue, and that he did not care how old he looked, and that most people cared. 'Where were you born?' said Alec.

A policeman passed and swivelled his eyes towards the two old men without changing the rhythm of his tread. He was not surprised to see the nightwatchman's superior-looking companion. He had seen plenty of odd old birds.

'That young copper,' said Alec, 'is wondering what we're up to.'

The watchman reached for his bottle of tea, and pulled out the cork.

'Got any tips for tomorrow?'

'Gunmetal for the two-thirty. They say Out of Reach for the four-fifteen. Tell me –'

'Gunmetal's even money,' said the watchman. 'Not worth your trouble.'

'How long,' said Alec, 'do you sleep during the day?'

Charmian had been put to bed. Rough physical handling made her mind more lucid in some ways, more cloudy in others. She knew quite well at this moment that Mrs Anthony was not Taylor, and Mabel Pettigrew was Lisa Brooke's former housekeeper, whom she disliked.

She lay and resented, and decided against, Mrs Pettigrew. The woman had had three weeks' trial and had proved unsatisfactory.

Charmian also lay and fancied Mrs Pettigrew had wronged her, long ago in the past. This was not the case. In reality, it was Lisa Brooke who had blackmailed Charmian, so that she had been forced to pay and pay, although Lisa had not needed the money; she had been forced to lie awake worrying throughout long night hours, and in the end she had been forced to give up her lover Guy Leet, while Guy had secretly married Lisa to satisfy and silence her for Charmian's sake. All this Charmian blamed upon Mrs Pettigrew, forgetting for the moment that her past tormentor had been Lisa; so bitter was the particular memory and so vicious was her new tormentor. For Mrs Pettigrew had wrenched Charmian's arm while getting her dress off, had possibly bruised the arm with her hard impatient grasp. 'What you need,' Mrs Pettigrew had said, 'is a nurse. I am not a nurse.'

Charmian felt indignant at the suggestion that she needed a nurse.

She decided to give Mrs Pettigrew a month's money in the morning and tell her to go. Before Mrs Pettigrew had switched out the light, Charmian had spoken sharply. 'I think, Mrs Pettigrew –'

'Oh, do call me Mabel and be friendly.'

'I think, Mrs Pettigrew, it will not be necessary for you to come in to the drawing-room when I have visitors unless I ring.'

'Good *night*,' said Mrs Pettigrew and switched out the light.

Mrs Pettigrew descended to her sitting-room and switched on the television which had been installed at her request. Mrs Anthony had gone home. She took up her knitting and sat working at it while watching the screen. She wanted to loosen her stays but was not sure whether Godfrey would look in to see her. During the three weeks of her stay at the Colstons' he had been in to see her on five evenings. He had not come in the night. Perhaps he would come tonight, and she did not wish to be caught untidy-looking. There was indeed a knock at the door, and she bade him come in.

On the first occasion it had been necessary for him to indicate his requirements to her. But now, she perfectly understood. Godfrey, with his thin face outstanding in the dim lamplight, and his excited eyes, placed on the low coffee table a pound note. He then stood, arms dangling and legs apart, like a stage rustic, watching her. Without shifting her posture she raised the hem of her skirt at one side until the top of her stocking and the tip of her suspender were visible. Then she went on knitting and watching the television screen. Godfrey gazed at the stocking-top and the glittering steel of the suspender-tip for the space of two minutes' silence. Then he pulled back his shoulders as if recalling his propriety, and still in silence, walked out.

After the first occasion Mrs Pettigrew had imagined, almost with alarm, that his request was merely the preliminary to more daring explorations on his part, but by now she knew with an old woman's relief that this was all he would ever desire, the top of her stocking and the tip of her suspender. She took the pound note off the table, put it in her black suède handbag and loosened her stays. She had plans for the future. Meantime a pound was a pound.

SIX

Miss Jean Taylor sat in the chair beside her bed. She never knew, when she sat in her chair, if it was the last time she would be able to sit out of bed. Her arthritis was gradually spreading and digging deep. She could turn her head slowly. So, and with difficulty, she did. Alec Warner shifted his upright chair a little to face her.

She said, 'Are you tormenting Dame Lettie?'

The thought crossed his mind, among other thoughts, that Jean's brain might be undergoing a softening process. He looked carefully at her eyes and saw the grey ring round the edge of the cornea, the *arcus senilis*. Nevertheless, it surrounded the main thing, a continuing intelligence amongst the ruins.

Miss Taylor perceived his scrutiny and thought, it is true he is a student of the subject but he is in many ways the same as the rest. How we all watch each other for signs of failure!

'Come, Alec,' she said, 'tell me.'

'Tormenting Lettie?' he said.

She told him about the anonymous telephone calls, then said, 'Stop *studying* me, Alec. I am not soft in the brain as yet.'

'Lettie must be so,' he said.

'No, she isn't, Alec.'

'And supposing,' he said, 'she really has been receiving those telephone calls. Why do you suggest I am the culprit? I ask as a matter of interest.'

'It seems to me likely, Alec. I may be wrong, but it is the sort of thing, isn't it, that you would do for purposes of study? An experiment –'

'It is the sort of thing,' he said, 'but in this case I doubt if I am the culprit.'

'You *doubt*.'

'Of course, I doubt. In a court of law, my dear, I would with

543

complete honesty deny the charge. But you know, I can't affirm or deny anything that is within the range of natural possibility.'

'Alec, are you the man, or not?'

'I don't know,' he said. 'If so, I am unaware of it. But I may be a Jekyll and Hyde, may I not? There was a recent case –'

'Because,' she said, 'if you are the culprit the police will get you.'

'They would have to prove the deed. And if they proved it to my satisfaction I should no longer be in doubt.'

'Alec,' she said, 'are you the man behind those phone calls?'

'Not to my knowledge,' he said.

'Then,' she said, 'you are not the man. Is it someone employed by you?'

He did not seem to hear the question, but was watching Granny Barnacle like a naturalist on holiday. Granny Barnacle accepted his attention with obliging submission, as she did when the doctor brought the medical students round her bed, or when the priest brought the Blessed Sacrament.

'Ask her how she is keeping,' said Miss Taylor, 'since you are staring at her.'

'How are you keeping?' said Alec.

'Not too good,' said Granny Barnacle. She jerked her head to indicate the ward dispensaries just beyond the door. 'Time there was a change of management,' she said.

'Indeed yes,' said Alec, and, inclining his head in final acknowledgement, which included the whole of the Maud Long Ward, returned his attention to Jean Taylor.

'Someone,' she said, 'in your employ?'

'I doubt it.'

'In that case,' she said, 'the man is neither you nor your agent.'

When she had first met him, nearly fifty years ago, she had been dismayed when he had expressed these curious 'doubts'. She had thought him perhaps a little mad. It had not occurred to her till many years later that this was a self-protective manner of speech which he used exclusively when talking to women whom he liked. He never spoke so to men. She had discerned, after these many years, that his whole approach to the female mind, his only way of coping with it, was to seem to derive amusement from it. When Miss Taylor had made this discovery she was glad they had never been married. He was too much masked behind his mocking, paternal attitude – now become a habit – for any proper relationship with a grown woman.

She recalled an afternoon years ago in 1928 – long after the love affair – when she had been attending Charmian on a week-end party in the country and Alec Warner was a fellow-guest. One afternoon he had taken Jean Taylor off for a walk – Charmian had been amused – 'to question her, as Jean was so reliable in her evidence.' Most of their conversation she had forgotten, but she recalled his first question.

'Do you think, Jean, that other people exist?'

She had not at once understood the nature of the question. For a moment she had wondered if his words might in some way refer to that love affair twenty-odd years earlier, and his further words, 'I mean, Jean, do you consider that people – the people around us – are real or illusory?' had possibly some personal bearing. But this did not fit with her knowledge of the man. Even at the time of their love relationship he was not the type to proffer the conceit: there is no one in the world but we two; we alone exist. Besides, she who was now walking beside this middle-aged man was herself a woman in her early fifties.

'What do you mean?' she said.

'Only what I say.' They had come to a beech wood which was damp from a last night's storm. Every now and then a little succession of raindrops would pelt from the leaves on to his hat or her hat. He took her arm and led her off the main path, so that for all her sober sense, it rapidly crossed her mind that he might be a murderer, a maniac. But she had, the next instant, recalled her fifty years and more. Were they not usually young women who were strangled in woods by sexual maniacs? No, she thought again, sometimes they were women of fifty-odd. The leaves squelched beneath their feet. Her mind flashed messages to itself back and forth. But I know him well, he's Alec Warner. Do I know him, though? – he is odd. Even as a lover he was strange. But he is known everywhere, his reputation ... Still, some eminent men have secret vices. No one ever finds them out; their very eminence is a protection.

'Surely,' he was saying, as he continued to draw her into the narrow, dripping shadows, 'you see that here is a respectable question. Given that you believe in your own existence as self-evident, do you believe in that of others? Tell me, Jean, do you believe that I for instance, at this moment, exist?' He peered down at her face beneath the brim of her brown felt hat.

'Where are you taking me?' she said, stopping still.

'Out of these wet woods,' he said, 'by a short cut. Tell me, now, surely you understand what I am asking? It's a plain question ...'

She looked ahead through the trees and saw that their path was indeed a short cut to the open fields. She realized at once that his question was entirely academic and he was not contemplating murder with indecent assault. And what reason, after all, had she to suspect this? How things do, she thought, come and go through a woman's mind. He was an unusual man.

'I agree,' she then said, 'that your question can be asked. One does sometimes wonder, perhaps only half-consciously, if other people are real.'

'Please,' he said, 'wonder more than half-consciously about this question. Wonder about it with as much consciousness as you have, and tell me what is your answer.'

'Oh,' she said, 'I think in that case, other people do exist. That's my answer. It's only common sense.'

'You have made up your mind too quickly,' he said. 'Take time and think about it.'

They had emerged from the wood and took a path skirting a ploughed field which led to the village. There the church with its steep sloping graveyard stood at the top of the street. Miss Taylor looked over the wall at the graveyard as they passed it. She was not sure now if his words had been frivolous or serious or both; for, even in their younger days – especially during that month of July 1907 at the farmhouse – she had never really known what to make of him, and had sometimes felt afraid.

She looked at the graveyard and he looked at her. He noted dispassionately that her jaw beneath the shade of the hat was more square than it had ever been. As a young woman she had been round-faced and soft; her voice had been extremely quiet, like the voice of an invalid. In middle age she had begun to reveal, in appearance, angular qualities; her voice was deeper; her jaw-line nearly masculine. He was interested in these factors; he supposed he approved of them; he liked Jean. She stopped and leaned over the low stone wall looking at the gravestones.

'This graveyard is a kind of evidence,' she said, 'that other people exist.'

'How do you mean?' he said.

She was not sure. Having said it, she was not sure why. The more she wondered what she had meant the less she knew.

He tried to climb over the wall, and failed. It was a low wall, but still he was not up to it. 'I am going on fifty,' he said to her without embarrassment, not even with a covering smile, and she remembered how, at the farmhouse in 1907, when he had chanced to comment that they were both past their prime, he being twenty-eight and she thirty-one, she had felt hurt and embarrassed till she realized he meant no harm by it, meaning only to point a fact. And she, catching this habit and tone, had been able to state quite levelly, 'We are not social equals,' before the month was over.

He brushed the dust of the graveyard wall from his trousers. 'I am going on fifty. I should like to look at the gravestones. Let's go in by the gate.'

And so they had walked among the graves, stooping to read the names on the stones.

'They are, I quite see, they are,' he said, 'an indication of the existence of others, for there are the names and times carved in stone. Not a proof, but at least a large testimony.'

'Of course,' she said, 'the gravestones might be hallucinations. But I think not.'

'There is that to be considered,' he said, so courteously that she became angry.

'But the graves are at least reassuring,' she said, 'for why bother to bury people if they don't exist?'

'Yes, oh precisely,' he said.

They ambled up the short drive to the house where Lettie, who sat writing at the library window, glanced towards them and then away again. As they entered, Lisa Brooke with her flaming bobbed head came out. 'Hallo, you two,' she said, looking sweetly at Jean Taylor. Alec went straight to his room while Miss Taylor went in search of Charmian. On the way, various people encountered and said 'Hallo' to her. This party was composed of a progressive set; they would think nothing of her walk with Alec that summer of 1928 even though some remembered the farmhouse affair of 1907 which had been a little scandal in those days. Only a brigadier, a misfit in the party who had been invited because the host wanted his advice on dairy herds, and who had passed the couple on their walk, later inquired of Lettie in Miss Taylor's hearing, 'Who was that lady I passed with Alec? Has she just arrived?' And Lettie, loathing Jean as she did, but wishing to be broad-minded, replied, 'Oh, she's Charmian's maid.'

'Say what you like about that sort of thing, the other domestics won't like it,' commented the brigadier, which was, after all, true.

And yet, Jean Taylor reflected as she sat with Alec in the Maud Long Ward, perhaps it was not all mockery. He may have half-meant the question.

'Be serious,' she said, looking down at her twisted arthritic hands.

Alec Warner looked at his watch.

'Must you be going?' she said.

'Not for another ten minutes. But it'll take me three quarters of an hour across the parks. I have to keep fairly strictly to my times, you know. I am going on eighty.'

'I'm relieved it's not you, Alec – the telephone calls ...'

'My dear, this has come from Lettie's imagination, surely that is obvious.'

'Oh no. The man has twice left a message with Godfrey. "Tell Dame Lettie," he said, "to remember she must die."'

'Godfrey heard it too?' he said. 'Well, I suppose, in that case, it must be a lunatic. How did Godfrey take it? Did he get a fright?'

'Dame Lettie didn't say.'

'Oh, do find out what their reactions were. I hope the police don't catch the fellow too soon. One might get some interesting reactions.' He rose to leave.

'Oh, Alec – before you go – there was something else I wanted to ask you.'

He sat down again and replaced his hat on her locker.

'Do you know Mrs Sidebottome?'

'Tempest? Ronald's wife. Sister-in-law of Lisa Brooke. Now in her seventy-fifth year. I first met her on a boat entering the Bay of Biscay in 1930. She was –'

'That's right. She is on the Management Committee of this hospital. The sister in charge of this ward is unsuitable. We all here desire her to be transferred to another ward. Do you want me to go into details?'

'No,' he said. 'You wish me to talk to Tempest.'

'Yes. Make it plain that the nurse in question is simply overworked. There was a fuss about her some time ago, but nothing came of it.'

'I cannot speak to Tempest just yet. She went into a nursing home for an operation last week.'

'A serious one?'

'A tumour on the womb. But at her age it is, in itself, less serious than in a younger woman.'

'Oh well, then you can't do anything for us at present.'

'I shall think,' he said, 'if I know anyone else. Have you approached Lettie on the subject?'

'Oh, yes.'

He smiled, and said, 'Approach her no more. It is a waste of time. You must seriously think, Jean, of going to that home in Surrey. The cost is not high. Godfrey and I can manage it. I think Charmian would be joining you there soon. Jean, you should have a room of your own.'

'Not now,' said Miss Taylor. 'I shan't move from here. I've made friends here, it's my home.'

'See you next Wednesday, my dear,' he said, taking his hat and looking round the ward, sharply at each of the grannies in turn.

'All being well,' she said.

Two years ago, when she first came to the ward, she had longed for the private nursing home in Surrey about which there had been too much talk. Godfrey had made a fuss about the cost, he had expostulated in her presence, and had quoted a number of their friends of the progressive set on the subject of the new free hospitals, how superior they were to the private affairs. Alec Warner had pointed out that these were days of transition, that a person of Jean Taylor's intelligence and habits might perhaps not feel at home among the general aged of a hospital.

'If only,' he said, 'because she is partly what we have made her, we should look after her.'

He had offered to bear half the cost of keeping Jean in Surrey. But Dame Lettie had finally put an end to these arguments by coming to Jean with a challenge, 'Would you not really, my dear, *prefer* to be independent? After all, you are the public. The hospitals are yours. You are entitled ...' Miss Taylor had replied, 'I prefer to go to hospital, certainly.' She had made her own arrangements and had left them with the daily argument still in progress concerning her disposal.

Alec Warner had not liked to see her in this ward. The first week he had wanted her to move. In misery she had vacillated. Her pains were increasing, she was not yet resigned to them. There had been further consultations and talking things over. Should she be moved to Surrey? Might not Charmian join her there eventually?

Not now, she thought, after Alec Warner had departed. Granny Valvona had put on her glasses and was searching for the horoscopes. Not now, thought Miss Taylor. Not now that the worst is over.

At first, in the morning light, Charmian forgave Mrs Pettigrew. She was able, slowly, to walk downstairs by herself. Other movements were difficult and Mrs Pettigrew had helped her to dress quite gently.

'But,' said Mabel Pettigrew to her, 'you should get into the habit of breakfast in bed.'

'No,' said Charmian cheerfully as she tottered round the table, grasping the backs of chairs, to her place. 'That would be a bad habit. My morning cup of tea in bed is all that I desire. Good morning, Godfrey.'

'Lydia May,' said Godfrey, reading from the paper, 'died yesterday at her home in Knightsbridge six days before her ninety-second birthday.'

'A Gaiety Girl,' said Charmian. 'I well remember.'

'You're in good form this morning,' Mrs Pettigrew remarked. 'Don't forget to take your pills.' She had put the bottle beside Charmian's plate. She now unscrewed the cap and extracted two pills which she laid before Charmian.

'I have had my pills already,' said Charmian. 'I had them with my morning tea, don't you remember?'

'No,' said Mrs Pettigrew, 'you are mistaken, dear. Take your pills.'

'She made a fortune,' Godfrey remarked. 'Retired in 1893 and married money both times. I wonder what she has left?'

'She was before my time, of course,' said Mabel Pettigrew.

'Nonsense,' said Godfrey.

'I beg your pardon, Mr Colston, she was before my time. If she retired in 1893 I was only a child in 1893.'

'I remember her,' said Charmian. 'She sang most expressively – in the convention of those times you know.'

'At the Gaiety?' said Mrs Pettigrew. 'Surely –'

'No, I heard her at a private party.'

'Ah, you would be quite a grown girl, then. Take your pills, dear.' She pushed the two white tablets towards Charmian.

Charmian pushed them back and said, 'I have already taken my pills this morning. I recall quite clearly. I usually do take them with my early tea.'

'Not always,' said Mrs Pettigrew. 'Sometimes you forget and leave them on your tray, as you did this morning, actually.'

'She was the youngest of fourteen children,' Godfrey read out from the paper, 'of a strict Baptist family. It was not till her father's death that, at the age of eighteen, she made her début in a small part at the Lyceum. Trained by Ellen Terry and Sir Henry Irving, she left them however for the Gaiety where she became the principal dancer. The then Prince of Wales –'

'She was introduced to us at Cannes,' said Charmian, gaining confidence in her good memory that morning, 'wasn't she?'

'That's right,' said Godfrey, 'it would be about 1910.'

'And she stood up on a chair and looked round her and said, "Gad! The place is stinking with royalty." Remember we were terribly embarrassed, and –'

'No, Charmian, no. You've got it wrong there. It was one of the Lilley Sisters who stood on a chair. And that was much later. There was nothing like that about Lydia May, she was a different class of girl.'

Mrs Pettigrew placed the two pills a little nearer to Charmian, but said no more about them. Charmian said, 'I mustn't exceed my dose,' and shakily replaced them in the bottle.

'Charmian, take your pills, my dear,' said Godfrey and took a noisy sip from his coffee.

'I have taken two pills already. I remember quite clearly doing so. Four might be dangerous.'

Mrs Pettigrew cast her eyes to the ceiling and sighed.

'What is the use,' said Godfrey, 'of me paying big doctor's bills if you won't take his stuff?'

'Godfrey, I do not wish to be poisoned by an overdose. Moreover, my own money pays for the bills.'

'Poisoned,' said Mrs Pettigrew, laying down her napkin as if tried beyond endurance. 'I ask you.'

'Or merely upset,' said Charmian. 'I do not wish to take the pills, Godfrey.'

'Oh well,' he said 'if that's how you feel, I must say it makes life damned difficult for all of us, and we simply can't take responsibility if you have an attack through neglecting the doctor's instructions.'

Charmian began to cry. 'I know you want to put me away in a home.'

Mrs Anthony had just come in to clear the table.

'There,' she said. 'Who wants to put you in a home?'

'We are a little upset, what with one thing and another,' said Mrs Pettigrew.

Charmian stopped crying. She said to Mrs Anthony, 'Taylor, did you see my early tea-tray when it came down?'

Mrs Anthony seemed not to grasp the question, for though she had heard it, for some reason she felt it was more complicated than it really was.

Charmian repeated, 'Did you see –'

'Now, Charmian,' said Godfrey, foreseeing some possible contradiction between Mrs Anthony's reply and Mrs Pettigrew's previous assertion. In this, he was concerned overwhelmingly to prevent a conflict between the two women. His comfort, the whole routine of his life, depended on retaining Mrs Anthony. Otherwise he might have to give up the house and go to some hotel. And Mrs Pettigrew having been acquired, she must be retained; otherwise Charmian would have to go to a home. 'Now, Charmian, we don't want any more fuss about your pills,' he said.

'What did you say about the tea-tray, Mrs Colston?'

'Was there anything on it when it came down from my room?'

Mrs Pettigrew said, 'Of course there was nothing on the tray. I replaced the pills you had left on it in the bottle.'

'There was a cup and saucer on the tray. Mrs Pettigrew brought it down,' said Mrs Anthony, contributing what accuracy she could to questions which still confused her.

Mrs Pettigrew started noisily loading the breakfast dishes on to Mrs Anthony's tray. She said to Mrs Anthony, 'Come, my dear, we've work to do.'

Mrs Anthony felt she had somehow failed Charmian, and so, as she followed Mrs Pettigrew out of the door, she pulled a face at her.

When they were gone Godfrey said, 'See the fuss you've caused. Mrs Pettigrew was quite put out. If we lose her –'

'Ah,' said Charmian, 'you are taking your revenge, Eric.'

'I am not Eric,' he said.

'But you are taking your revenge.' Fifteen years ago, in her seventy-first year, when her memory had started slightly to fail, she had realized that Godfrey was turning upon her as one who had been awaiting his revenge. She did not think he was himself aware of this. It was an instinctive reaction to the years of being a talented, celebrated woman's husband, knowing himself to be reaping continually in her a harvest which he had not sown.

Throughout her seventies Charmian had not reproached him with his bullying manner. She had accepted his new domination without comment until her weakness had become so marked that she physically depended on him more and more. It was then, in her eighties, that she started frequently to say what, in the past, she would have considered unwise: 'You are taking your revenge.'

And on this occasion, as always, he replied, 'What revenge for *what*?' He really did not know. He saw only that she was beginning to look for persecution: poison, revenge; what next? 'You are getting into a state of imagining that all those around you are conspiring against you,' he said.

'Whose fault is it,' she said with a jolting sharpness, 'if I am getting into such a state?'

This question exasperated him, partly because he sensed a deeper sanity in it than in all her other accusations, and partly because he could not answer it. He felt himself to be a heavily burdened man.

Later in the morning, when the doctor called, Godfrey stopped him in the hall.

'She is damn difficult today, Doctor.'

'Ah well,' said the doctor, 'it's a sign of life.'

'Have to see about a home if she goes on like this.'

'It might be a good idea, if only she can be brought round to liking it,' said the doctor. 'The scope for regular attention is so much better in a nursing-home, and I have known cases far more advanced than your wife's which have improved tremendously once they have been moved to a really comfortable home. How are you feeling yourself?'

'Me? Well, what can you expect with all the domestic worries on my shoulders?' said Godfrey. He pointed to the door of the garden-room where Charmian was waiting. 'You'd better go on in,' he said, being disappointed of the sympathy and support he had hoped for, and vaguely put out by the doctor's talk of Charmian's possible improvement in health, should she be sent to a home.

The doctor's hand was on the door knob. 'I shouldn't worry too much about domestic matters,' he said. 'Go out as much as possible. Your wife, as I say, may buck up tremendously if we have to move her. It sometimes proves a stimulus. Of course, at her age ... her resistance ... but there's a chance that she may still get about again. It is largely neurasthenia. She has extraordinary powers of recovery, almost as if she had some secret source ...'

Godfrey thought: This is his smarm. Charmian has a secret source, and I pay the bills. He said explosively, 'Well, sometimes I feel she deserves to be sent away. Take this morning, for instance –'

'Oh *deserves*,' said the doctor, 'we don't recommend nursing-homes as a punishment, you know.'

'Bloody man,' said Godfrey in the doctor's hearing and before he had properly got into the room where Charmian waited.

Immediately the doctor had entered through the door so did Mrs Pettigrew through the french windows. 'Pleasant for the time of year,' she said.

'Yes,' said the doctor. 'Good morning, Mrs Colston. How do you feel today?'

'We wouldn't,' said Mrs Pettigrew, 'take our pills this morning, Doctor, I'm afraid.'

'Oh, that doesn't matter,' he said.

'I did take them,' said Charmian. 'I took them with my early tea, and they tried to force me to take more at breakfast. I know I took them with my early tea, and just suppose I had taken a second dose –'

'It wouldn't really have mattered,' he said.

'But surely,' said Mrs Pettigrew, 'it is always dangerous to exceed a stated dose.'

'Just try to keep a careful check – a set routine for medicines in future,' he said to Mrs Pettigrew. 'Then neither of you will make a mistake.'

'There was no mistake on my part,' said Mrs Pettigrew. 'There is nothing wrong with my memory.'

'In that case,' said Charmian, 'we must question your *intentions* in trying to give me a second dose. Taylor knows I took my pills as I always do. I did not leave them on the tray.'

The doctor said as he took her pulse, 'Mrs Pettigrew, if you would excuse us for a moment . . .'

She went out with a deep loud weary sigh, and, in the kitchen, stood and berated Mrs Anthony for 'taking that mad-woman's part this morning'.

'She isn't,' said Mrs Anthony, 'a mad-woman. She's always been good to me.'

'No, she isn't mad,' said Mrs Pettigrew, 'you are right. She's cunning and sly. She isn't as feeble as she makes out, let me tell you. I've watched her when she didn't know I was watching. She can move about quite easily when she likes.'

'Not when she likes,' said Mrs Anthony, 'but when she feels up to it. After all, I've been here nine years, haven't I? Mrs Colston is a person who needs a lot of understanding, she has her off days and her on days. No one understands her like I do.'

'It's preposterous,' said Mrs Pettigrew, 'a woman of my position being accused of attempts to poison. Why, if I was going to do that I should go about it a very different way, I assure you, to giving her overdoses in front of everybody.'

'I bet you would,' said Mrs Anthony. 'Mind out my way,' she said, for she was sweeping the floor unnecessarily.

'Mind how you talk to me, Mrs Anthony.'

'Look,' said Mrs Anthony, 'my husband goes on at me about this job now he's at home all day, he doesn't like me being out. I only do it for that bit of independence and it's what I've always done my married life. But we can do on the pension now I'm seventy and the old man sixty-eight, and any trouble from you, let me tell you I'm leaving here. I managed *her* myself these nine years and we got on without you interfering and making trouble.'

'I shall speak to Mr Colston,' said Mrs Pettigrew, 'and inform him of what you say.'

'Him,' said Mrs Anthony. 'Go on and speak to him. I don't reckon much of him. She's the one that I care for, not *him*.' Mrs Anthony followed this with an insolent look.

'What do you mean by that exactly?' said Mrs Pettigrew. 'What exactly do you mean?'

'You work it out for yourself,' said Mrs Anthony. 'I'm busy with their luncheon.'

Mrs Pettigrew went in search of Godfrey who was, however, out. She went by way of the front door round to the french windows, and through them. She saw that the doctor had left and Charmian was reading a book. She was filled with a furious envy at the thought that, if she herself were to take the vapours, there would not be any expensive doctor to come and give her a kind talk and an injection no doubt, and calm her down so that she could sit and read a book after turning the household upside down.

Mrs Pettigrew went upstairs to look round the bedrooms, to see if they were all right and tidy, and in reality to simmer down and look round. She was annoyed with herself for letting go at Mrs Anthony. She should have kept aloof. But it had always been the same – even when she had been with Lisa Brooke – when she had to deal with lower domestics she became too much one of them. It was kindness of heart, but it was weak. She reflected that she had really started off on the wrong foot with Mrs Anthony; that, when she had first arrived, she should have kept her distance with the woman and refrained from confidences. And now she had lowered herself to an argument with Mrs Anthony. These thoughts overwhelmed Mrs Pettigrew with that sense of having done a foolish thing against one's interests, which in some people stands for guilt. And in this frame of heart she repented, and decided, as she stood by Charmian's neatly-made bed, to establish her position more solidly in the household, and from now on to treat Mrs Anthony with remoteness.

A smell of burning food rose up the well of the stairs and into Charmian's bedroom. Mrs Pettigrew leaned over the banister and sniffed. Then she listened. No sound came from the kitchen, no sound of hurried removal of pots from the gas jets. Mrs Pettigrew came half-way down the stairs and listened. From the small garden-

room where Charmian had been sitting came voices. Mrs Anthony
was in there, recounting her wrongs to Charmian while the food was
burning in the oven and the potatoes burning dry and the kettle
burning on the stove. Mrs Pettigrew turned back up the stairs, and up
one more flight to her own room. There she got from a drawer a box of
keys. She selected four and putting them in the black suède handbag
which, perhaps by virtue of her office, she always carried about the
house, descended to Charmian's bedroom. Here, she tried the keys
one by one in the lid of Charmian's bureau. The third fitted. She did
not glance within the desk, but locked the lid again. With the same key
she tried the drawers. It did not fit them. She placed the key carefully
in a separate compartment of her handbag and tried the other keys.
None fitted the drawers. She went to the landing, where the smell of
burning had become alarming, and listened. Mrs Anthony had not
yet left Charmian, and it was clear to Mrs Pettigrew that when she
did, there would be enough to keep her busy for ten minutes more.
She took from her bag a package of chewing gum, and unwrapped it.
There were five strips of gum. She put the paper with three of the
pieces back in her bag and two pieces of gum in her mouth. She sat on
a chair near the open door and chewed for a few seconds. Then she
wet the tips of her fingers with her tongue, took the soft gum from her
mouth and flattened it. She next wet the surface of the gum with her
tongue and applied it to the keyhole of one of the drawers. She
withdrew it quickly and put it on Charmian's bedside table to set. She
took two more pieces of gum, and having chewed them as before,
moistened the lump and applied it to the keyhole of another drawer.
She slung back her bag up to her wrist and holding the two pieces of
gum, with their keyhole impressions, between the finger and thumb
of each hand, walked up the flight of stairs to her bedroom. She placed
the hardened gum carefully in a drawer, locked the drawer, and set off
downstairs, through the houseful of smoke and smell.

Mrs Anthony came rushing out of the garden-room just as Mrs
Pettigrew appeared on the first flight of stairs.

'Do I,' said Mrs Pettigrew, 'smell burning?'

By the time she reached the foot of the stairs Mrs Anthony was
already in the kitchen holding the smoking raging saucepan under the
tap. A steady blue cloud was pouring through the cracks of the oven
door. Mrs Pettigrew opened the door of the oven, and was driven back

by a rush of smoke. Mrs Anthony dropped her potato saucepan and ran to the oven.

'Turn off the gas,' she said to Mrs Pettigrew. 'Oh, the pie!'

Mrs Pettigrew, spluttering, approached the oven and turned off the gas taps, then she ran coughing from the kitchen and went in to Charmian.

'Do I smell burning?' said Charmian.

'The pie and potatoes are burned to cinders.'

'Oh, I shouldn't have kept Taylor talking,' said Charmian. 'The smell is quite bad, isn't it? Shall we open the windows?'

Mrs Pettigrew opened the french windows and like a ghost a stream of blue smoke obligingly wafted out into the garden.

'Godfrey,' said Charmian, 'will be so cross. What is the time?'

'Twenty past,' said Mrs Pettigrew.

'Eleven?'

'No, twelve.'

'Oh, dear. Do go and see how Mrs Anthony is getting on. Godfrey will be in any moment.'

Mrs Pettigrew remained by the french windows. 'I expect,' she said, 'Mrs Anthony is losing her sense of smell. She is quite aged for seventy, isn't she? What I would call an *old* seventy. You would have thought she could have smelt the burning long before it got to this stage.' A sizzling sound came round the back of the house from the kitchen where Mrs Anthony was drenching everything with water.

'*I* smelt nothing,' said Charmian. 'I'm afraid I kept her talking. Poor soul, she is –'

'There's Mr Colston,' said Mrs Pettigrew, 'just come in.' She went out to the hall to meet him.

'What the hell is burning?' he said. 'Have you had a fire?'

Mrs Anthony came out of the kitchen and gave him an account of what had happened, together with accusations, complaints, and a fortnight's notice.

'I shall go and make an omelette,' said Mrs Pettigrew, and casting her eyes to heaven behind Mrs Anthony's back for Godfrey to see, disappeared into the kitchen to cope with the disorder.

But Godfrey would eat nothing. He told Charmian, 'This is all your fault. The household is upside down just because you argued about your pills this morning.'

'An overdose may have harmed me, Godfrey. I was not to know the pills were harmless.'

'There was no question of overdose. I should like to know why the pills were harmless. I mean to say, if the fellow prescribes two and you may just as well take four, what sort of a prescription is that, what good are the pills to you? I'm going to pay the bill and tell him not to come back. We'll get another doctor.'

'I shall refuse to see another doctor.'

'Mrs Anthony has given notice, do you realize what that means?'

'I shall persuade her to stay,' said Charmian. 'She has been under great strain this morning.'

He said, 'Well, I'm going out again. This place is stinking.'

He went to get his coat and returned to say, 'Be sure to get Mrs Anthony to change her mind.' From past experience, he knew that only Charmian could do it. 'It's the least you can do after all the trouble . . .'

Mrs Pettigrew and Mrs Anthony sat eating their omelette with their coats on, since it was necessary to have all windows open. In the course of the meal Mrs Pettigrew quarrelled with Mrs Anthony again, and was annoyed with herself afterwards for it. If only, she thought guiltily, I could keep a distance, that would be playing my cards.

Mrs Anthony sat with Charmian all afternoon, while Mrs Pettigrew, with the sense of performing an act of reparation, took her two pieces of chewing gum, each marked with a clear keyhole impression, to a person she knew at Camberwell Green.

SEVEN

There was a chill in the air, but Godfrey walked on the sunny side of the street. He had parked his car in a turning off King's Road outside a bombed building, so that anyone who recognized it would not be able to guess particularly why it was there. Godfrey had, for over three years now, been laboriously telling any of his acquaintance who lived near Chelsea that his oculist was in Chelsea, his lawyer was in Chelsea, and that he frequently visited a chiropodist in Chelsea. The more alert of his acquaintance had sometimes wondered why he stated these facts emphatically and so often – almost every time they met him. But he was, after all, over eighty and, one supposed, inclined to waffle about the merest coincidences.

Godfrey himself was of the feeling that one can never be too careful. Having established an oculist, a lawyer and a chiropodist in the neighbourhood to account for his frequent appearances in Chelsea, he still felt it necessary to park his car anonymously, and walk the rest of the way, by routes expressly devious, to Tite Street where, in a basement flat, Olive Mannering, granddaughter of Percy Mannering, the poet, resided.

He looked to right and left at the top of the area steps. The coast was clear. He looked to right again, and descended. He pushed, the door open and called, 'Hello, there.'

'Mind the steps,' Olive called from the front room on the left. There were three more steps to descend within the doorway. Godfrey walked down carefully, and found his way along the passage into a room of many lights. Olive's furnishings were boxy and modern, coloured with a predominance of yellow. She herself was fairly drab in comparison. She was twenty-four. Her skin was pale with a touch of green. She had a Spanish look, with slightly protruding large eyes. Her legs, full at the calves, were bare. She sat on a stool and warmed these legs by a large electric fire while reading the *Manchester Guardian*.

'Goodness, it's you,' she said, as Godfrey entered. 'Your voice is exactly like Eric's. I thought it was Eric.'

'Is he in London, then?' said Godfrey, looking round the room suspiciously, for there had been an afternoon when he had called on Olive and met his son Eric there. Godfrey, however, had immediately said to Olive,

'I wonder if you have your grandfather's address? I wish to get in touch with him.'

Olive had started to giggle. Eric had said 'Ha – hum' very meaningly and, as Olive told him later, disrespectfully.

'I wish to get in touch with him in connexion with,' said Godfrey, glaring at his son, 'some poetry.'

Olive was a fair-minded girl in so far as she handed over to Eric most of the monthly allowances she obtained from Godfrey. She felt this was only Eric's due, since his father had allowed him nothing for nearly ten years past, Eric being now fifty-six.

'Is Eric in London?' said Godfrey again.

'He is,' said Olive.

'I'd better not stop,' said Godfrey.

'He won't be coming here today,' she said. 'I'll just go and put my stockings on,' she said. 'Would you like some tea?'

'Yes, all right,' said Godfrey. He folded his coat double and laid it on the divan-bed. On top of it he placed his hat. He looked to see if the curtains were properly drawn across the basement window. He sat down with a thump in one of the yellow chairs which were too low-built for his liking, and picked up the *Manchester Guardian*. Sometimes, while he waited, he looked at the clock.

Olive returned, wearing stockings and carrying a tea tray.

'Goodness, are you in a hurry?' she said as she saw Godfrey looking at the clock. He was not in a hurry, exactly. He was not yet sure of the cause of his impatience that afternoon.

Olive placed the tray on a low table and sat on her low stool. She lifted the hem of her skirt to the point where her suspenders met the top of her stockings, and with legs set together almost primly sideways, she poured out the tea.

Godfrey did not know what had come over him. He stared at the suspender-tips, but somehow did not experience his usual satisfaction at the sight. He looked at the clock.

Olive, passing him his tea, noticed that his attention was less fixed on her suspender-tips than was customary.

'Anything the matter, Godfrey?' she said.

'No,' he said, and took his tea. He sipped it, and stared again at the tops of her stockings, evidently trying hard to be mesmerized.

Olive lit a cigarette and watched him. His eyes did not possess their gleam.

'What's the matter?' she said.

He was wondering himself what was the matter. He sipped his tea.

'Running a car,' he remarked, 'is a great expense.'

She burst into a single laugh and said, 'Oh, go on.'

'Cost of living,' he muttered.

She covered up her suspender-tops with her skirt and sat hugging her knees, as one whose efforts are wasted. He did not seem to notice.

'Did you see in the paper,' she said, 'about the preacher giving a sermon on his hundredth birthday?'

'Which paper, where?' he said, reaching out for the *Manchester Guardian*.

'It was the *Mirror*,' she said. 'I wonder what I've done with it? He said anyone can live to a hundred if they keep God's laws and remain young in spirit. Goodness.'

'The government robbers,' he said, 'won't let you keep young in spirit. Sheer robbery.'

Olive was not listening, or she would not have chosen that moment to say, 'Eric's in a bad way, you know.'

'He's always in a bad way. What's the matter now?'

'The usual,' she said.

'What usual?'

'Money,' she said.

'I can't do more for Eric. I've done more than enough for Eric. Eric has ruined me.'

Then, as in a revelation, he realized what had put him off Olive's suspenders that afternoon. It was this money question, this standing arrangement with Olive. It had been going on for three years. Pleasant times, of course ... One had possibly gained ... but now, Mabel Pettigrew – what a find! Quite pleased with a mere tip, a pound, and a handsome woman, too. All this business of coming over to Chelsea. No wonder one was feeling put out, especially as one could not easily extricate oneself from an arrangement such as that with Olive. Moreover ...

'I'm not so strong these days,' he commented. 'My doctor thinks I'm going about too much.'

'Oh?' said Olive.

'Yes. Must keep indoors more.'

'Goodness,' said Olive. 'You are wonderful for your age. A man like you could never stay indoors all day.'

'Well,' he admitted, 'there is that to it.' He was moved to look longingly at her legs at the point where, beneath her dress, the tip of her suspenders would meet the top of her stockings, but she made no move to reveal them.

'You tell your doctor,' she said, 'to go to hell. What did you see the doctor about, anyway?'

'Just aches and pains, my dear, nothing serious of course.'

'Many a younger man,' she said, 'is riddled with aches and pains. Take Eric, for instance –'

'Feeling his age, is he?'

'I'll say he is. Goodness.'

Godfrey said, 'Only himself to blame. No, I'm wrong, I blame his mother. From the moment that boy was born, she –'

He leaned back in his chair with his hands crossed above his stomach. Olive closed her eyes and relaxed while his voice proceeded into the late afternoon.

Godfrey reached his car outside the bomb site. He had felt cramped when he rose from that frightful modern chair of Olive's. One had talked on, and remained longer than one had intended. He climbed stiffly into the car and slammed the door, suddenly reproached by the more dignified personality he now had to resume.

'Why does one behave like this, why?' he asked himself as he drove into the King's Road and along it. 'Why does one do these things?' he thought, never defining, however, exactly what things. 'How did it start, at what point in one's life does one find oneself doing things like this?' And he felt resentful against Charmian who had been, all her life with him, regarded by everyone as the angelic partner endowed with sensibility and refined tastes. As for oneself, of Colston's Breweries, one had been the crude fellow, tolerated for her sake, and thus driven into carnality, as it were. He felt resentful against Charmian, and raced home to see if she had made everything all right after upsetting Mrs Anthony and Mrs Pettigrew. He took out his watch. It was seven and a half minutes to six. Home, home, for a drink. Funny how Olive never seemed to have any drinks in her flat. Couldn't afford it, she said. Funny she couldn't afford it; what did she do with her money, one wondered.

At half past six Alec Warner arrived at Olive's. She poured him a gin and tonic which he placed on a table beside his chair. He took a hard-covered note-book from his briefcase. 'How are things?' he said, leaning his large white head against the yellow chair-back.

'Guy Leet,' she said, 'has been diagnosed again for his neck. It's a rare type of rheumatism, it sounds like *tortoise.*'

'Torticollis?' said Alec Warner.

'That's it.'

Alec Warner made a note in his book. 'Trust him,' he said, 'to have a rare rheumatism. How are things otherwise?'

'Dame Lettie Colston has changed her will again.'

'Lovely,' he said, and made a note. 'What way has she changed it?'

'Eric is out again, for one. Martin is put in again. That's the other nephew in Africa.'

'She thinks Eric is responsible for the telephone calls, does she?'

'She suspects everyone. Goodness. This is her way of testing Eric. That ex-detective is out.'

'Chief Inspector Mortimer?'

'Yes. She thinks it might be him. Funny, it is. She has no sooner got him working privately on the case, than she thinks it might be him.'

'How old is Mortimer?' he asked.

'Nearly seventy.'

'I know. But when exactly will he be seventy? Did you inquire?'

'I'll find out exactly,' said Olive.

'Always find out exactly,' he said.

'I think,' said Olive, defending her lapse as best she could, 'he'll be seventy quite soon – early next year, I think.'

'Find out exactly, dear,' said Warner. 'Meantime he is not one of us. We'll come to *him* next year.'

'She thinks you may be the culprit,' said Olive. 'Are you?'

'I doubt it,' he said wearily. He had received a letter from Dame Lettie asking the same question.

'How you talk,' she said. 'Well, I wouldn't have put it past you.'

'Mrs Anthony,' she said, 'had a row with Mrs Pettigrew this morning and is threatening to leave. Charmian accused Mrs Pettigrew of trying to poison her.'

'That's very hot news,' he said. 'Godfrey has been here today, I gather?'

'Oh yes. He was rather odd today. Something's put him off his stroke.'

'Not interested in suspenders today?'

'No, but he was trying hard. He said his doctor doesn't want him to go out and about so much. I didn't know whether to take that as a hint, or –'

'Mrs Pettigrew – have you thought of *her*?'

'Oh goodness,' said Olive, 'I haven't.' She smiled widely and placed a hand over her mouth.

'Try to find out,' he said.

'Oh dear,' said Olive, 'no more fivers for poor old Eric. I can see it coming. Do you think Mrs Pettigrew has it in her?'

'I do,' said Alec, writing his notes.

'There's a bit in the paper in the kitchen,' said Olive, 'about a preacher preaching on his hundredth birthday.'

'What paper?'

'The *Mirror*.'

'My press-cutting agency covers the *Mirror*. It's only the out-of-the-way papers they sometimes overlook. But thanks all the same. Always tell me of anything like that, just in case. Keep on the look-out.'

'O.K.,' said Olive, and sipped her drink, watching the old veined hand moving its pen steadily, in tiny writing, over the page.

He looked up. 'How frequently would you say,' he said, 'he passes water?'

'Oh goodness, it didn't say anything about that in the *Mirror*.'

'You know I mean Godfrey Colston.'

'Well, he was here about two hours and he went twice. Of course he had two cups of tea.'

'Is twice the average when he comes here?'

'I can't remember. I think –'

'You must try to remember everything exactly, my dear,' said Alec. 'You must watch, my dear, and pray. It is the only way to be a scholar, to watch and to pray.'

'Me a scholar, goodness. He had patches of red on the cheekbones today, more so than usual.'

'Thank you,' said Alec, and made a note. 'Notice everything, Olive,' he looked up and said, 'for only you can observe him in relation to yourself. When I meet him, you understand, he is a different personality.'

'I'll bet,' she said, and laughed.

He did not laugh. 'Be sure to find out all you can on his next visit in case he deserts you for Mrs Pettigrew. When do you expect to see him again?'

'Friday, I suppose.'

'There is someone,' he said 'tapping at the window behind me.'

'Is there? It must be Granpa, he always does that.' She rose to go to the door.

Alec said quickly, 'Tell me, does he tap on the window of his own accord or have you asked him to announce himself in that way?'

'He does it of his own accord. He always has tapped at the window.'

'Why? Do you know?'

'No – no idea.'

Alec bent once more with his pen over his book, and recorded the facts which he would later analyse down to their last, stubborn elements.

Olive fetched in Percy Mannering who, on entering the room, addressed Alec Warner without preliminaries, waving in front of him a monthly magazine of a literary nature, on the cover of which was stamped in bold lettering 'Kensington Public Libraries'.

'Guy Leet,' roared Percy, 'that moron has published part of his memoirs in which he refers to Ernest Dowson as "that weak-kneed wailer of Gallic weariness afflicted with an all too-agonized afflatus". He is fantastically wrong about Dowson. Ernest Dowson was the spiritual and aesthetic child of Swinburne, Tennyson, and Verlaine.

You can hear all their voices and Dowson was something of a French scholar and quite obviously under the spell of Verlaine as well as Tennyson and Swinburne, and very much in Arthur Symons' circle. He is fantastically wrong about Ernest Dowson.'

'How are you keeping?' said Alec, having risen from his chair.

'Guy Leet was never a good theatre critic, and he was a worse novel critic. He knows nothing about poetry, he has no right to touch the subject. Can't someone stop him?'

'What else,' said Alec, 'does he say in his memoir?'

'A lot of superficiality about how he attacked a novel of Henry James's and then met James outside the Athenaeum one day and James was talking about his conscience as an artist and Guy's conscience as a critic, and that whatever was actually committed to print –'

'Let the fire see the people, Granpa,' said Olive, for Percy was standing back-to-fire straddling and monopolizing it. Alec Warner had closed and put away his notebook.

The poet did not move.

'That's because Henry James is fashionable today, that's why he writes about Henry James. Whereas he jeers at poor Ernest – If you're pouring that brandy for me, Olive, it's too much. Half of that – Ernest Dowson, a supreme lyricist.' He took the glass, which he held with a shaky claw-like hand, and while taking his first sip seemed of a sudden to forget Ernest Dowson.

He said to Alec, 'I didn't see you at Lisa's funeral.'

'Sit down, Granpa,' said Olive. She worked him into a chair.

'I missed it,' said Alec, watching Percy's lean profile with concentration. 'I was in Folkestone at the time.'

'It was a fearful and thrilling experience,' said Percy.

'In what way?' said Alec.

The old poet smiled. He cackled from the depth of his throat, and the memory of Lisa's cremation seemed to be refracted from his mind's eye to the avid eyes in his head. As he talked, the eyes of Alec feasted on him, in turn.

Percy stayed on with his granddaughter after Alec Warner had left. She prepared a supper of mushrooms and bacon which they ate off

trays perched on their knees. She watched him while he ate. He
gnawed with his few teeth at the toasted bread, but got through all of
it, even the difficult crusts.

He looked up as he managed the last small rim of crust and saw her
watching him. When he had finished all, he remarked, 'Final
perseverance.'

'What you say, Granpa?'

'Final perseverance is the doctrine that wins the external victory in
small things as in great.'

'I say, Granpa, did you ever read any books by Charmian Piper?'

'Oh rather, we all knew her books. She was a fine-looking woman.
You should have heard her read poetry from a platform in the days of
Poetry. Harold Munro always said –'

'Her son, Eric, has told me there's talk of her novels being
reprinted. There's a revival of interest in her novels. There's been an
article written, Eric says. But he says the novels all consist of people
saying "touché" to each other, and it's all an affectation, the revival of
interest, just because his mother is so old and still alive and was
famous once.'

'She's still famous. Always has been. Your trouble is, you know
nothing, Olive. Everyone knows Charmian Piper.'

'Oh no they don't. No one's heard of her except a few old people,
but there's going to be a revival. I say there's been an article –'

'You know nothing about literature.'

'Touché,' she snapped, for Percy himself was always pretending
that nobody had forgotten his poetry, really. Then she gave him three
pounds to make up for her cruelty, which in fact he had not noticed;
he simply did not acknowledge the idea of revival in either case, since
he did not recognize the interim death. However, he took the three
pounds from Olive, of whose side-line activities he was unaware, for,
besides having small private means from her mother's side, she also
had occasional jobs as an actress on the B.B.C.

He carried the money by bus and underground to Leicester Square
where the post office was open all night, and wrote out, on several
telegraph forms, in large slow capitals, a wire to Guy Leet, The Old
Stable, Stedrost, Surrey: 'You are fantastically wrong in your reference to Ernest Dowson that exceedingly poignant poet who only just
steered clear of sentimentality and self-pity stop Ernest Dowson was

the spiritual and aesthetic child of Swinburne Tennyson and especially Verlaine by whose verse he was veritably haunted Dowsons verse requires to be read aloud which is more than most verse by later hands can stand up to stop I cried for madder music and for stronger wine new line but when the feast is finished and the lamps expire new line then falls thy shadow Cynara the night is thine new line and I am desolate and sick of an old passion etcetera stop read it aloud man your cheap alliterative jibe carries no weight you are fantastically wrong – Percy Mannering.'

He handed in the sheaf of forms at the counter. The clerk looked closely at Percy, whereupon Percy made visible the three pound notes.

'Are you sure,' said the clerk then, 'you want to send all this?'

'I am,' bawled Percy Mannering. He handed over two of the notes, took his change and went out into the bright-lit night.

EIGHT

Dame Lettie Colston had been happier without a resident maid, but the telephone incidents had now forced on her the necessity of having someone in the house to answer the dreadful calls. The mystery of it was, that the man never gave that terrible message to the girl. On the other hand, in the two weeks since her arrival, there had been a series of calls which proved to be someone getting the wrong number. When they had occurred three times in one day Dame Lettie began to bewilder the girl with questions.

'Who was it, Gwen, was it a man?'

'It was a wrong number.'

'Was it a man?'

'Yes, but it was a wrong number.'

'What did he say exactly? Do answer my question, please.'

'He said, "Sorry, it's a wrong number,"' shouted Gwen, 'that's what he said.'

'What kind of voice was it?'

'Oh mad-um. I said it was a man, didn't I? The lines must be crossed. I know phones like the back of my hand.'

'Yes, but was the voice young or old? Was it the same one as got the last wrong number?'

'Well, they're all the same to me, if they're wrong numbers. You better answer the phone yourself and then –'

'I was only asking,' said Dame Lettie, 'because we seem to be having such a lot of wrong numbers since you've been here. And it always seems to be a man.'

'What you mean? What exactly you mean by that, Mad*um*?'

Dame Lettie had not meant whatever the girl thought she meant. It was Gwen's evening out, and Lettie was glad Godfrey was coming to dine with her.

At about eight o'clock, when they were at dinner, the telephone rang.

'Godfrey, you answer it, please.'

He marched out into the hall. She heard him lift the receiver and give the number. 'Yes, that's right,' he said next. 'Who's that, who is it?' Lettie heard him say. Then he replaced the receiver.

'Godfrey,' she said, 'that was the man?'

'Yes,' he shouted. '"Tell Dame Lettie to remember she must die."' Then he rang off. Damned peculiar.' He sat down and continued eating his soup.

'There is no need to shout, Godfrey. Keep calm.' Her own large body was trembling.

'Well, it's damned odd. I say you must have an enemy. Sounds a common little fellow, with his lisp.'

'Oh no, Godfrey, he is quite cultured. But sinister.'

'I say he's a common chap. This isn't the first time I've heard him.'

'There must be something wrong with your hearing, Godfrey. A middle-aged, cultivated man who should know better –'

'A barrow boy, I should say.'

'Nonsense. Go and ring the police. They said always to report –'

'What's the use?' he said. And seeing she would argue, he added, 'After dinner. I'll ring after dinner.'

'That is the first time he has left that message since I took on Gwen a fortnight ago. When Gwen answers the telephone the man says, "Sorry, wrong number." He does it two or three times a day.'

'It may *be* some fellow getting a wrong number. Your lines must be crossed with someone else's. Have you reported this nuisance to the Exchange?'

'I have,' she said. 'They tell me the lines are perfectly in order.'

'They must be crossed –'

'Oh,' she said, 'you are as bad as Gwen, going on about crossed lines. I have a good idea who it is. I think it is Chief Inspector Mortimer.'

'Nothing like Mortimer's voice.'

'Or his accomplice,' she said.

'Rubbish. A man in his position.'

'That is why the police don't find the culprit. They know, but they won't reveal his identity. He is their former Chief.'

'I say you have an enemy.'

'I say it is Mortimer.'

'Why then,' said Godfrey, 'do you continue to consult him about the case?'

'So that he shall not know I suspect him. He may then fall into a trap. Meantime, as I have told you, he is out of my will. He doesn't know *that*.'

'Oh, you are always changing your will. No wonder you have enemies.' Godfrey felt guilty at having gossiped to Olive about Lettie's changes in her will. 'No wonder,' he said, 'you don't know the culprit.'

'I haven't heard from Eric lately,' Dame Lettie remarked, so that he felt more guilty, thinking of all he had told Olive.

Godfrey said, 'He has been in London the past six weeks. He returned to Cornwall last night.'

'But he hasn't been to see me. Why didn't you let me know before, Godfrey?'

'I myself did not know he was in London,' said Godfrey, 'until I learned of it from a mutual friend yesterday.'

'What mutual friend? What has Eric been up to? What friend?'

'I cannot recollect at the moment,' said Godfrey. 'I have long given up interest in Eric's affairs.'

'You should keep your memory in training,' she said. 'Try going over in your mind each night before retiring everything you have done during the day. I must say I am astonished that Eric did not call upon me.'

'He didn't come near us,' said Godfrey, 'so why should he come to see you?'

'At least,' she said, 'I should have thought he knew what side his bread's buttered.'

'Ha, you don't know Eric. Fifty-six years of age and an utter failure. You ought to know, Lettie, that men of that age and type can't bear the sight of old people. It reminds them that they are getting on. Ha, and he's feeling his age, I hear. You, Lettie, may yet see him under. We may both see him under.'

Lying in bed later that night, it seemed clear to Dame Lettie that Eric must really after all be the man behind the telephone calls. He would not ring himself lest she should recognize his voice. He must have an accomplice. She rose and switched on the light.

*

Dame Lettie sat in her dressing-gown at dead of night and re-filled her fountain-pen. While she did so she glanced at the page she had just written. She thought, How shaky my writing looks! Immediately, as if slamming a door on it, she put the thought out of sight. She wiped the nib of her pen, turned over the sheet and continued, on the back, her letter to Eric:

> ... and so, having heard of your having been in London these past six weeks, & your not having informed me, far less called, does, I admit, strike me as being, to say the least, discourteous. I had wished to consult you on certain matters relating to your Mother. There is every indication that we shall have to arrange for her to be sent to the nursing home in Surrey of which I told you when last I saw you.

She laid down her pen, withdrew one of the fine hair-pins from her thin hair, and replaced it. Perhaps, she thought, I should take an even more subtle line with Eric. Her face puckered in folds under the desk-lamp. Two thoughts intruded simultaneously. One was: I am really very tired; and the other: I am not a bit tired, I am charging ahead with great energy. She lifted the pen again and continued to put the wavering marks across the page.

> I have recently been making some slight adjustments in my own affairs, about which I could have wished to consult you had you seen fit to inform me of your recent visit to London.

Was that subtle enough? No, it was too subtle, perhaps, for Eric.

> These *minor* adjustments, of course, have some bearing upon my Will. It has always seemed to me a pity that your cousin Martin, though doing so well in South Africa, should not be remembered in some small way. I would wish for no recriminations among the family after my passing. Your position is of course substantially unchanged, but I could wish you had made yourself available for consultation. You will recall the adjustments I made to existing arrangements after your cousin Alan fell on the field of battle ...

That is good, she thought, that is subtle. Eric had got out of the war somehow. She continued,

> I could have wished for discussions with you, but I am an old woman and quite realize that you, who are nearing the end of your prime, must be full of affairs. Mr Merrilees is now drawing up the amended Will and I would not wish to further interfere with existing arrangements. Nevertheless, I could have wished to discuss them with you had you seen fit to present yourself during the six weeks of your recent stay in London, of which I did not hear until after your return.

That ought to do it, she thought. He will come wheezing down from Cornwall as fast as the first train will carry him. If he is the guilty man he will know that I know. No one, she thought, is going to kill me through fear. And she fell to wondering again who her enemy could be. She fell to doubting whether Eric had it in him . . . whether he had the financial means to employ an accomplice. Easier, she thought, for Mortimer. Anyway, she thought, it must be someone who is in my Will. And so she sealed and stamped her letter to Eric, placed it on the tray in the hall, took a tot of whisky and went to bed. Her head moved slowly from side to side on the pillow, for she could not sleep. She had caught a chill down there in the study. A cramp seized her leg. She had a longing for a strong friend, some major Strength from which to draw. Who can help me? she thought. Godfrey is selfish, Charmian feeble, Jean Taylor is bedridden. I can talk to Taylor, but she has not got the strength I need. Alec Warner . . . shall I go to see Alec Warner? I never got strength from him. Neither did Taylor. He has not got the strength one needs.

Suddenly she sprang up. Something had lightly touched her cheek. She switched on the light. A spider on her pillow, large as a penny, quite still, with its brown legs outspread! She looked at it feverishly then pulled herself together to try to pick it off the pillow. As she put forth her hand another, paler, spider-legged and fluffy creature on the pillow where the bed-lamp cast a shade caught her sight. 'Gwen!' she screams. 'Gwen!'

But Gwen is sleeping soundly. In a panic Dame Lettie plucks at the large spider. It proves to be a feather. So does the other object.

She dropped her head on her pillow once more. She thought: My old pillows, I shall get some new pillows.

She put out the light and the troubled movements of the head began again. Whom, she thought, can I draw Strength from? She considered her acquaintances one by one – who among them was tougher, stronger than she?

Tempest, she thought at last. I shall get Tempest Sidebottome to help me. Tempest, her opponent in forty years' committee-sitting, had frequently been a painful idea to Dame Lettie. Particularly had she resented Tempest's bossy activeness and physical agility at Lisa's funeral. Strangely, now, she drew strength from the thought of the woman. Tempest Sidebottome would settle the matter if anyone could. Tempest would hunt down the persecutor. Dame Lettie's head settled still on the pillow. She would go over to Richmond tomorrow and talk to Tempest. After all, Tempest was only seventy-odd. She hoped her idiotic husband Ronald would be out. But in any case, he was deaf. Dame Lettie turned at last to her sleep, deriving a half-dreamt success from the strength of Tempest Sidebottome as from some tremendous mother.

'Good morning, Eric,' said Charmian as she worked her way round the breakfast table to her place.

'*Not* Eric,' said Mrs Pettigrew. 'We are a bit confused again this morning.'

'Are you, my dear? What has happened to confuse you?' said Charmian.

Godfrey sensed the start of bickering, so he looked up from his paper and said to his wife, 'Lettie was telling me last night that it is a great aid to memory to go through in one's mind each night the things which have happened in the course of the day.'

'Why,' said Charmian, 'that is a Catholic practice. We are always recommended to consider each night our actions of the past day. It is an admirable –'

'Not the same thing,' said Godfrey, 'at all. You are speaking exclusively of one's moral actions. What I'm talking about are things which have happened. It is a great aid to memory, as Lettie was saying last night, to memorize everything which has occurred in one's experience during the day. Your practice, which you call Catholic, is, moreover, common to most religions. To my mind, that type of examination of conscience is designed to enslave the individual and inhibit his freedom of action. Take yourself for example. You only have to appeal to psychology –'

'To whom?' said Charmian cattily, as she took the cup which Mrs Pettigrew passed to her.

Godfrey turned back to his paper. Whereupon Charmian continued the argument with Mrs Pettigrew.

'I don't see that one can examine one's moral conduct without memorizing everything that's happened during the day. It is the same thing. What Lettie advises is a form of –'

Godfrey put down his paper. 'I say it is not the same thing.' He dipped an oblong of toast in his tea and put it in his mouth.

Mrs Pettigrew rose to the opportunity of playing the peacemaker. 'Now hush,' she said to Charmian. 'Eat your nice scrambled egg which Taylor has prepared for you.'

'Taylor is not here,' stated Charmian.

'Taylor – what do you mean?' said Godfrey.

Mrs Pettigrew winked at him.

Godfrey opened his mouth to retort, then shut it again.

'Taylor is in hospital,' said Charmian, pleased with her clarity.

Godfrey read from the newspaper, '"Motling" – are you listening, Charmian? – "On 10th December at Zomba, Nyasaland; Major Cosmos Petwick Motling, G.C.V.O., husband of the late Eugenie, beloved father of Patricia and Eugen, in his 91st year." Are you listening, Charmian?'

'Was he killed at the front, dear?'

'Ah, me!' said Mrs Pettigrew.

Godfrey opened his mouth to say something to Mrs Pettigrew, then stopped. He held up the paper again and from behind it mumbled, 'No, Zomba. Motling's the name. He went out there to retire. You won't remember him.'

'*I* recall him well,' said Mrs Pettigrew; 'when his wife was alive, Lisa used to –'

'Was he killed at the front?' said Charmian.

'The front,' said Mrs Pettigrew.

'"Sidebottome,"' said Godfrey, '– are you listening, Charmian? –

"On 18th December at the Mandeville Nursing Home, Richmond; Tempest Ethel, beloved wife of Ronald Charles Sidebottome. Funeral private." Doesn't give her age.'

'Tempest Sidebottome!' said Mrs Pettigrew, reaching to take the paper from his hand. 'Let me see.'

Godfrey withdrew the paper and opened his mouth as if to protest, then closed it again. However, he said, 'I am not finished with the paper.'

'Well, fancy Tempest Sidebottome,' said Mrs Pettigrew. 'Of course, cancer is cancer.'

'She always *was* a bitch,' said Godfrey, as if her death were the ultimate proof of it.

'I wonder,' said Mrs Pettigrew, 'who will look after poor old Ronald now. He's so deaf.'

Godfrey looked at her to see more closely what she meant, but her short broad nose was hidden by her cup and her eyes stared appraisingly at the marmalade.

She was, in fact, quite shocked by Tempest's death. She had only a month ago agreed to join forces with the Sidebottomes in contesting Lisa Brooke's will. Tempest, when she had learnt of Guy Leet's hitherto secret marriage to Lisa, had been driven to approach Mrs Pettigrew and attempt to make up their recent differences. Mrs Pettigrew had rather worked alone, but the heavy costs deterred her. She had agreed to go in with Tempest against Guy Lee on the grounds that his marriage with Lisa Brooke had not been consummated. They had been warned that their case was a slender one, but Tempest had the money and the drive to go ahead, and Mrs Pettigrew had in her possession the relevant correspondence. Ronald Sidebottome had been timid about the affair – didn't like raking up the scandal, but Tempest had seemed to have the drive. Tempest's death was a shock to Mrs Pettigrew. She would have to work hard on Ronald. One got no rest. She stared at the marmalade pot as if to fathom its possibilities.

Godfrey had returned to his paper. 'Funeral private. That saves us a wreath.'

'You had better write to poor Ronald,' said Charmian, 'and I will say a rosary for Tempest. Oh, I do remember her as a girl. She was newly out from Australia and her uncle was a rector in Dorset – as was also my uncle, Mrs Pettigrew –'

'Your uncle was not in Dorset. He was up in Yorkshire,' said Godfrey.

'But he was a country rector, like Tempest's uncle. Leave me alone, Godfrey. I am just telling Mrs Pettigrew.'

'Oh, do call me Mabel,' said Mrs Pettigrew, winking at Godfrey.

'Her uncle, Mabel,' said Charmian, 'was a rector and so was mine. It was the thing we had in common. We had not a great deal in common, Mrs Pettigrew, and of course as a girl she was considerably younger than me.'

'She is still younger than you,' said Godfrey.

'No, Godfrey, not now. Well, Mrs Pettigrew, I do so remember our two uncles together and we were all staying down in Dorset. There was a bishop and a dean, and our two uncles. Oh, poor Tempest was bored. They were discussing the Scriptures and this manuscrlpt called "Q". How Tempest was in a rage when she heard that "Q" was only a manuscript, because she had imagined them to be talking of a bishop and she said out loud "*Who* is Bishop Kew?" And of course everyone laughed heartily, and then they were sorry for Tempest. And they tried to console her by telling her that "Q" was nothing really, not even a manuscript, which indeed it wasn't, and I must confess I never understood how they could sit up so late at night fitting their ideas into this "Q" which is nothing really. As I say poor Tempest was in a rage, she could never bear to be made game of.'

Mrs Pettigrew winked at Godfrey.

'Charmian,' said Godfrey, 'you are over-exciting yourself.' And true enough, she was tremulously crying.

NINE

Partly because of a reorganization of the Maud Long Ward and partly because of Tempest Sidebottome's death, Sister Burstead was transferred to another ward.

She had been a protégée of Tempest's, and this had mostly accounted for the management committee's resistance to any previous suggestion that the sister could not cope with the old people's ward. The committee, though largely composed of recently empowered professional men and women, had been in many ways afraid of Tempest. Or rather, afraid to lose her lest they should get someone worse.

It was necessary for them to tolerate at least one or two remnants of the old-type committee people until they should die out. And they chiefly feared, in fact, that if Tempest should take offence and resign, she would be replaced by some more formidable, more subtle private welfare-worker and busybody. And whereas Tempest had many dramatic things to say in committee, whereas she was imperious with the matron, an opponent on principle of all occasions of expenditure, scornful in the extreme of physiotherapists and psychiatrists (everything beginning 'psycho-' or 'physio-' Tempest lumped together, believed to be the same thing, and dismissed) – although she was in reaction against the committee's ideals, she was so to the point of parody, and it was for precisely this reason, because she so much demonstrated the errors of her system, that she was retained, was propitiated from time to time, and allowed to have her way in such minor matters as that of Sister Burstead. Not that the committee were not afraid of Tempest for other, less evident reasons; but these were matters of instinct and not openly admitted. Her voice in committee had been strangely terrifying to many an eminent though small-boned specialist, even the bossy young heavily-qualified women had sometimes failed to outstare the little pale pebble-eyes of the great unself-questioning matriarch, Mrs Sidebottome. 'Terrible woman,' everyone always agreed when she had left.

'After the fifties are over,' said the chairman, who was himself a man of seventy-three, 'everything will be easier. This transition period . . . the old brigade don't like change. They don't like loss of authority. By the middle-sixties everything will be easier. We will have things in working order.' Whereupon the committee surrendered themselves to putting up with Tempest, a rock of unchanging, until the middle-sixties of the century should arrive.

However, she had died, leaving behind her on the committee a Tempest-shaped vacuum which they immediately attempted, but had not yet been able to fill.

In the meantime, as if tempting Providence to send them another, avenging, Tempest, they transferred Sister Burstead, on the first of January, to another ward. That the old people's ward was being reorganized provided a reasonable excuse, and Sister Burstead made no further protest.

News of the transfer reached the grannies before the news of the reorganization.

'I'll believe it when I see it,' said Granny Barnacle.

She saw it before that week-end. A new ward sister, fat and forceful with a huge untroubled faceful of flesh and brisk legs, was installed. 'That's how I like them,' said Granny Barnacle. 'Sister Bastard was too skinny.'

The new sister, when she caught Granny Green absentmindedly scooping the scrambled egg off her plate into her locker, put her hands on her slab-like hips and said, 'What the hell do you think *you're* doing?'

'That's how I like them,' said Granny Barnacle. She closed her eyes on her pillow with contentment. She declared herself to feel safe for the first time for months. She declared herself ready to die now that she had seen the removal of Sister Bastard. She sprang up again from her pillow and with outstretched arm and pointing finger prophesied that the whole ward would now see the winter through.

Miss Valvona, who was always much affected by Miss Barnacle's feelings, consulted the stars: 'Granny Barnacle – Sagittarius. "*Noon period best for commencing long-distance travel. You can show your originality today.*"'

'Ho!' said Granny Barnacle. 'Originality today, I'll wear me britches back to front.'

The nurses came on their daily round of washing, changing, combing and prettifying the patients before the matron's inspection. They observed Granny Barnacle's excitement and decided to leave her to the last. She was usually excitable throughout this performance in any case. During Sister Burstead's term of office, especially, Granny Barnacle would screech when turned over for her back to be dusted with powder, or helped out of bed to sit on her chair.

'Nurse, I'll be covered with bruises,' she would shout.

'If you don't move, Gran, you'll be covered with bedsores.'

She would scream to God that the nurses were pulling her arms from their sockets, she would swear by the Almighty that she wasn't fit to be sat up. She moaned, whenever the physiotherapist made her move her fingers and toes, and declared that her joints would crack.

'Kill me off,' she would command, 'and be done with it.'

'Come on, Gran, you've got to get exercise.'

'Crack! Can't you hear the bones crack? Kill me off and –'

'Let's rub your legs, Gran. My, you've got beautiful legs.'

'Help, she's killing me.'

But at the best of times Granny Barnacle really liked an excuse for a bit of noise, it livened her up. In a sense, she gave vent to the whole ward's will to shout, so that the others did not make nearly so much noise as they might otherwise have done. It was true some of the other grannies were loud in complaints, but this was mostly for a few seconds when their hair was being combed. Granny Green would never fail to tell the nurses after her hair was done.

'I had a lovely head of hair till you cut it off,' although in reality there had been very little to cut off.

'It's hygiene, Granny. It would hurt far more when we combed it if your hair was long.'

'I had a lovely head . . .'

'Me, too,' Granny Barnacle would declare, especially if Sister Burstead had been within hearing. 'You should have seen my head before they cut it off.'

'Oh, short hair is cooler when one is in bed,' Granny Taylor, whose hair had really been long and thick, and who actually preferred it short, would murmur to herself.

'Let's give you a nice wave today, Granny Barnacle.'

'Oh, you're killing me.'

On the day of the new sister's arrival, Granny Barnacle and her obvious excitement having been left to the last, it was found, when her turn came, that she was running a temperature.

'Get me out of bed, love,' she implored the nurse. 'Let's sit up today, seeing Bastard's gone.'

'No, you've got a temperature.'

'Nurse, I want to get up today. Get me a will-form, there's a bob in my locker, I want to make a new will and put in the new sister. What's her name?'

'Lucy.'

'Lucy Locket,' shrieked Granny Barnacle, 'lost her –'

'Lie still, Granny Barnacle, till we make you better.'

She submitted after a fuss. Next day, when they told her she must keep to her bed she protested louder, even struggled a little, but Miss Taylor in the opposite bed noticed that Granny Barnacle's voice was unusually thin and high.

'Nurse, I'm going to get up today. Get me a will-form. I want to make a new will and put in the new sister. What's her name?'

'Lucy,' said the nurse. 'Your blood pressure's high, Gran.'

'Her last name, girl.'

'Lucy. Sister Lucy.'

'Sister Lousy,' screamed Granny Barnacle. 'Well, she's going in my will. Give me a hand . . .'

When the doctor had gone she was given an injection and dozed off for a while.

At one o'clock, while everyone else was eating, she woke. Sister Lucy brought some milk custard to her bed and fed her with a spoon. The ward was quiet and the sound of grannies' spoons tinkling on their plates became more pronounced in the absence of voices.

About three o'clock Granny Barnacle woke again and started to rave in a piping voice, at first faintly, then growing higher and piercing. 'Noos, E'ning Noos,' fluted the old newsvendor. 'E'ning pap-*ar*, Noos, E'ning Stan-*ar*, E'ning Stah Noos *an* Stan-*ar*.'

She was given an injection and a sip of water. Her bed was wheeled to the end of the ward and a screen was put round it. In the course of the afternoon the doctor came, stayed behind the screen for a short while, and went.

The new ward sister came and looked behind the screen from time to time. Towards five o'clock, when the few visitors were going home, Sister Lucy went behind the screen once more. She spoke to Granny Barnacle, who replied in a weak voice.

'She's conscious,' said Miss Valvona.

'Yes, she spoke.'

'Is she bad?' said Miss Valvona as the sister passed her bed.

'She's not too well,' said the sister.

Some of the patients kept looking expectantly and fearfully at the entrance to the ward whenever anyone was heard approaching, as if watching for the Angel of Death. Towards six o'clock came the sound of a man's footsteps. The patients, propped up with their supper trays, stopped eating and turned to see who had arrived.

Sure enough, it was the priest, carrying a small box. Miss Valvona and Miss Taylor crossed themselves as he passed. He went behind the screen accompanied by a nurse. Though the ward was silent, none of the patients had sharp enough ears, even with their hearing-aids, to catch more than an occasional humming sound from his recitations.

Miss Valvona's tears dropped into her supper. She was thinking of her father's Last Sacrament, after which he had recovered to live a further six months. The priest behind the screen would be committing Granny Barnacle to the sweet Lord, he would be anointing Granny Barnacle's eyes, ears, nose, mouth, hands and feet, asking pardon for the sins she had committed by sight, by hearing, smell, taste and speech, by the touch of her hands, and by her very footsteps.

The priest left. A few of the patients finished their supper. Those who did not were coaxed with Ovaltine. At seven the sister took a last look behind the screen before going off to the dining-room.

'How is she now?' said a granny.

'Sleeping nicely.'

About twenty minutes later a nurse looked behind the screen, went inside for a moment, then came out again. The patients watched her leave the ward. There she gave her message to the runner who went to the dining-room and, opening the door, caught the attention of the ward sister. The runner lifted up one finger to signify that one of the sister's patients had died.

It was the third death in the ward since Miss Taylor's admittance. She knew the routine. 'We leave the patient for an hour in respect for the dead,' a nurse had once explained to her, 'but no longer than an hour, because the body begins to set. Then we perform the last offices – that's washing them and making them right for burial.'

At five past nine, by the dim night-lamps of the ward, Granny Barnacle was wheeled away.

'I shan't sleep a wink,' said Mrs Reewes-Duncan. Many said they would not sleep a wink, but in fact they slept more soundly and exhaustedly that night than on most nights. The ward lay till morning still and soundless, breathing like one body instead of eleven.

The reorganization of the Maud Long Ward began next day, and all patients declared it a mercy for Granny Barnacle that she had been spared it.

Hitherto, the twelve beds in the Maud Long Ward had occupied only half of the space in the room; they had been a surplus from another, larger, medical ward, comprised mainly of elderly women. The new arrangement was designed to fill up the remaining half of the Maud Long Ward with a further nine elderly patients. These were to be put at the far end. Already, while the preparations were still in progress, this end of the ward was referred to among the nurses as the 'geriatric corner'.

'What's that word mean they keep saying?' Granny Roberts demanded of Miss Taylor.

'It's to do with old age. There must be some very old patients coming in.'

'We supposed to be teenagers, then?'

Granny Valvona said, 'Our new friends will probably be centenarians.'

'I didn't catch – just a minute till I get the trumpet right,' said Granny Roberts, who always referred to her small hearing fixture as the trumpet.

'See,' said Granny Green, 'what they're bringing in to the ward.'

A line of cots was being wheeled up the ward and arranged in the new geriatric corner. These cots were much the same as the other hospital beds, but with the startling difference that they had high railed sides like children's cots.

Granny Valvona crossed herself.

Next, the patients were wheeled in. Perhaps this was not the best introduction of the newcomers to the old established set. Being in varying advanced states of senility, and also being specially upset by the move, the new arrivals were making more noise and dribbling more from the mouth than usual.

Sister Lucy came round the grannies' beds, explaining that they would have to be patient with these advanced cases. Knitting needles must not be left lying about near the geriatric corner, in case any of the newcomers should hurt themselves. The patients were not to be alarmed if anything *funny* should occur. At this point the sister had to call a nurse's attention to one of the new patients, a frail, wizened, but rather pretty little woman, who was trying to climb over the side of her cot. The nurse rushed to settle the old woman back in bed. The patient set up an infant-like wail, yet not entirely that of a child – it was more like that of an old woman copying the cry of an infant.

The sister continued addressing the grannies in confidential tones. 'You must try to remember,' she said, 'that these cases are very advanced, poor dears. And don't get upset, like good girls. Try and help the nurses by keeping quiet and tidy.'

'We'll soon be senile ourselves at this rate,' said Granny Green.

'Ssh-sh,' said the sister. 'We don't use that word. They are geriatric cases.'

When she had gone Granny Duncan said, 'To think that I spent my middle years looking forward to my old age and a rest!'

Another geriatric case was trying to climb over the cot. A nurse bustled to the rescue.

'A mercy,' said Granny Duncan, 'poor Granny Barnacle didn't live to see it. Poor souls – Don't you be rough with her, Nurse!'

The patient had, in fact, pulled the nurse's cap off and was now clamouring for a drink of water. The nurse replaced her cap, and while another nurse held a plastic beaker of water to the old woman's lips, assured the ward, 'They'll settle down. The moving's upset them.'

After a stormy night, the newcomers did seem quieter next morning, though one or two made a clamour in the ordinary course of conversation, and most, when they were helped out of bed to stand shakily upheld for a moment by the nurse, wet the floor. In the afternoon a specialist lady and an assistant came with draught-boards which she laid on the floor beside four of the new patients who were sitting up in chairs, but whose hands were crippled. They did not protest when their socks and slippers were removed and their feet manipulated and rubbed by the younger woman. Their socks and slippers were replaced and they seemed to know what to do when the draught-boards were set in front of their feet.

'Look, did you ever,' said Granny Valvona. 'They're playing draughts with their feet.'

'I ask you,' said Granny Roberts, 'is it a bloody circus we are here?'

'That's nothing to what you'll see in geriatrics,' said the nurse proudly.

'A blessing poor Granny Barnacle wasn't spared to see it.'

Miss Taylor absorbed as much of the new experience as she could, for the sake of Alec Warner. But the death of Granny Barnacle, her own arthritic pains, and the noisy intrusion of the senile cases had confused her. She was crying towards the end of the day, and worried lest the nurse should catch her at it, and perhaps report her too sick to be wheeled down next morning to the Mass which she and Miss Valvona had requested for the soul of Granny Barnacle who had no relatives to mourn her.

Miss Taylor dropped asleep, and waking in the middle of the night because of her painful limbs, still pretended to sleep on, and went without her injection. At eleven o'clock next morning Miss Valvona and Miss Taylor were wheeled into the hospital chapel. They were accompanied by three other grannies, not Catholics, from the Maud Long Ward who had been attached to Granny Barnacle in various ways, including those of love, scorn, resentment, and pity.

During the course of the Mass an irrational idea streaked through Miss Taylor's mind. She dismissed it and concentrated on her prayers. But this irrational idea, which related to the identity of Dame Lettie's tormentor, was to return to her later again and again.

TEN

'Is that Mr Godfrey Colston?' said the man on the telephone.

'Yes, speaking.'

'Remember you must die,' said the man.

'Dame Lettie is not here,' he said, being flustered. 'Who is that speaking?'

'The message is for you, Mr Colston.'

'Who is speaking?'

The man had hung up.

Though Godfrey was still tall, he had seemed to shrink during the winter to an extent that an actual tape-measure would perhaps not confirm. His bones were larger than ever; that is to say, they remained the same size as they had been throughout his adult life, but the ligaments between them had gradually shrunk, as they do with advancing age, so that the bones appeared huge-grown. This process had, in Godfrey, increased rapidly in the months between the autumn of Mrs Pettigrew's joining his household and the March morning when he received the telephone call.

He put down the receiver and walked with short steps into the library. Mrs Pettigrew followed him. She herself was looking healthier and not much older.

'Who was that on the phone, Godfrey?' she said.

'A man . . . I can't understand. It should have been for Lettie but he definitely said it was for me. I thought the message –'

'What did he say?'

'That thing he says to Lettie. But he said, "Mr Colston, it's for you, Mr Colston." I don't understand . . .'

'Look here,' said Mrs Pettigrew, 'let's pull ourselves together, shall we?'

'Have you got the key of the sideboard on you?'

'I have,' said Mabel Pettigrew. 'Want a drink?'

'I feel I need a little –'

'I'll bring one in to you. Sit down.'

'A stiff one.'

'Sit down. There's a boy.'

She came back, spritely in her black dress and the new white-streaked lock of hair among the very black, sweeping from her brow. Her hair had been cut shorter. She had painted her nails pink and wore two large rings which gave an appearance of opulent ancient majesty to the long wrinkled hand which held Godfrey's glass of brandy and soda.

'Thanks,' said Godfrey, taking the glass. 'Many thanks.' He sat back and drank his brandy, looking at her from time to time as if to see what she was going to do and say.

She sat opposite him. She said nothing till he had finished. Then she said, 'Now, look.'

She said, 'Now, look. This is all imagination.'

He muttered something about being in charge of his faculties.

'In that case,' she said – 'in *that* case, have you seen your lawyer yet?'

He muttered something about next week.

'You have an appointment with him,' she said, 'this afternoon.'

'This afternoon? Who – how . . .?'

'I've made an appointment for you to see him at three this afternoon.'

'Not this afternoon,' said Godfrey. 'Don't feel up to it. Draughty office. Next week.'

'You can take a taxi if you don't feel up to driving. It's no distance.'

'Next week,' he shouted, for the brandy had restored him. However, the effects wore off. At lunch Charmian said,

'Is there anything the matter, Godfrey?'

The telephone rang. Godfrey looked up, startled. He said to Mrs Pettigrew, 'Don't answer.'

Mrs Pettigrew merely said, 'I wonder if Mrs Anthony has heard it? I bet she hasn't.'

Mrs Anthony's hearing was beginning to fail, and she had obviously not heard the telephone.

Mrs Pettigrew strode out into the hall and lifted the receiver. She came back presently and addressed Charmian.

'For you,' she said. 'The photographer wants to come tomorrow at four.'

'Very well,' said Charmian.

'I shan't be here, you know, tomorrow afternoon.'

'That's all right,' said Charmian. 'He does not wish to photograph *you*. Say that four o'clock will be splendid.'

While Mrs Pettigrew went to give the message, Godfrey said, 'Another reporter?'

'No, a photographer.'

'I don't like the idea of all these strangers coming to the house. I had a nasty experience this morning. Put him off.' He rose from his seat and shouted through the door, 'I say, Mrs Pettigrew, we don't want him coming here. Put him off, will you?'

'Too late,' said Mrs Pettigrew, resuming her place.

Mrs Anthony looked around the door.

'Was you wanting something?'

'We did hope,' said Mrs Pettigrew very loudly, 'to have our meal without interruptions. However, I have answered the telephone.'

'Very good of you, I'm sure,' said Mrs Anthony, and disappeared.

Godfrey was still protesting about the photographer. 'We'll have to put him off. Too many strangers.'

Charmian said, 'I shall not be here long, Godfrey.'

'Come, come,' said Mrs Pettigrew. 'You may well last another ten years.'

'Quite,' said Charmian, 'and so I have decided to go away to the nursing home in Surrey, after all. I understand the arrangements there are almost perfect. One has every privacy. Oh, how one comes to appreciate privacy.'

Mrs Pettigrew lit a cigarette and slowly blew the smoke in Charmian's face.

'No one's interfering with your privacy,' Godfrey muttered.

'And freedom,' said Charmian. 'I shall have freedom at the nursing home to entertain whom I please. Photographers, strangers —'

'There is no need,' said Godfrey desperately, 'for you to go away to a home now that you are so much improved.'

Mrs Pettigrew blew more smoke in Charmian's direction.

'Besides,' he said, glancing at Mrs Pettigrew, 'we can't afford it.'

Charmian was silent, as one who need not reply. Indeed, her books were bringing in money, and her small capital at least was safe from Mrs Pettigrew. The revival of her novels during the past winter had sharpened her brain. Her memory had improved, and her physical health was better than it had been for years in spite of that attack of bronchitis in January, when a day and a night nurse had been in attendance for a week. However, she still had to move slowly and was prone to kidney trouble.

She looked at Godfrey who was wolfing his rice pudding without, she was sure, noticing what he was eating, and she wondered what was on his mind. She wondered what new torment Mrs Pettigrew was practising upon him. She wondered how much of his past life Mrs Pettigrew had discovered, and why he felt it necessary to hush it up at all such costs. She wondered where her own duty to Godfrey lay – where does one's duty as a wife reach its limits? She longed to be away in the nursing home in Surrey, and was surprised at this longing of hers, since all her life she had suffered from apprehensions of being in the power of strangers, and Godfrey had always seemed better than the devil she did not know.

'To move from your home at the age of eighty-seven,' Godfrey was saying in an almost pleading voice, 'might kill you. There is no need.'

Mrs Pettigrew, having pressed the bell in vain, said, 'Oh, Mrs Anthony is quite deaf. She must get an Aid,' and went to tell Mrs Anthony to fetch her tea and Charmian's milk.

When she had gone, Godfrey said,

'I had an unpleasant experience this morning.'

Charmian took refuge in a vague expression. She was terrified lest Godfrey was about to make some embarrassing confession concerning Mrs Pettigrew.

'Are you listening, Charmian?' said Godfrey.

'Yes, oh yes. Anything you like.'

'There was a telephone call from Lettie's man.'

'Poor Lettie. I wonder he isn't tired of tormenting her.'

'The call was for me. He said, "The message is for you, Mr Colston." I am not imagining anything, mind you. I heard it with my ears.'

'Really? What message?'

'You *know* what message,' he said.

'Well, I should treat it as it deserves to be treated.'

'What do you mean?'

'Neither more nor less,' said Charmian.

'I'd like to know who the fellow is. I'd like to know why the police haven't got him. It's preposterous, when we pay our rates and taxes, to be threatened like that by a stranger.'

'What did he threaten to do?' said Charmian. 'I thought he merely always said –'

'It's upsetting,' said Godfrey. 'One might easily take a stroke in consequence. If it occurs again I shall write to *The Times*.'

'Why not consult Mrs Pettigrew?' said Charmian. 'She is a tower of strength.'

Then she felt suddenly sorry for him, huddled among his bones. She left him and climbed the stairs slowly, clinging to the banister, to take her afternoon rest. She considered whether she could bring herself to leave Godfrey in his plight with Mrs Pettigrew. After all, she herself might have been in an awkward situation, if she had not taken care, long before her old age, to destroy all possibly embarrassing documents. She smiled as she looked at her little bureau with its secretive appearance, in which Mrs Pettigrew had found no secret, although Charmian knew she had penetrated behind those locks. But Godfrey, after all, was not a clever man.

In the end Godfrey submitted, and agreed to keep the appointment with his lawyer. Mrs Pettigrew would not absolutely have refused to let him put it off for another day, had she not been frightened by his report of the telephone call. Obviously, his mind was going funny. She had not looked for this. He had better see the lawyer before anyone could say he had been talked into anything.

He got out the car and drove off. About ten minutes later Mrs Pettigrew got a taxi at the end of the street and followed him. She wanted just to make sure he was at the lawyer's, and she merely intended to drive past the offices to satisfy herself that Godfrey's car was outside.

His car was not outside. She made the driver take her round Sloane Square. There was still no sign of Godfrey's car. She got out and went into a café opposite the offices and sat where she could see him arrive. But by quarter to four there was still no sign of his car. It occurred to her that his memory had escaped him while on his way to the lawyer. He had sometimes remarked that his oculist and his chiropodist were in Chelsea. Perhaps he had gone, by mistake, to have his eyes tested or his feet done. She had trusted his faculties; he had always seemed all right until this morning; but after his silly talk this morning about that phone call anything could happen. It was to be remembered he was nearly eighty-eight.

Or was he cunning? Could the phone call have come from the lawyer, perhaps to confirm the appointment, and Godfrey have cancelled it? After all, how could he have suddenly gone crazy like his sister without showing preliminary signs? Possibly he had decided to feign feebleness of mind merely to evade his obligations.

Mrs Pettigrew paid for her coffee, resumed her brown squirrel coat, and set off along the King's Road. She saw no sign of his car outside the chiropodist. Anyway, he had probably gone home. She glanced up a side turning and thought she saw Godfrey's car in the blue half-light parked outside a bombed building. Yes indeed, on investigation, it proved to be Godfrey's Vauxhall.

Mrs Pettigrew looked expertly around her. The houses opposite the bombed building were all occupied and afforded no concealment. The bombed building itself seemed to demand investigation. She walked up the dusty steps on which strangely there stood a collection of grimy milk bottles. The broken door was partly open. She creaked it further open and looked inside. She could see right through, over the decayed brick and plaster, to the windows at the back of the house. She heard a noise as of rustling paper – or could it be rats? She stepped back and stood once more outside the door considering whether and how long she could bear to stand in that desolate doorway and see, without being seen, from which direction Godfrey should return to his car.

Charmian woke at four and sensed the emptiness of the house. Mrs Anthony now went home at two in the afternoons. Both Godfrey and Mrs Pettigrew must be out. Charmian lay listening, to confirm her feeling of being alone in the house. She heard no sound. She rose slowly, tidied herself and, groping for one after another banister rail, descended the stairs. She had reached the first half-landing when the telephone rang. She did not hurry, but it was still ringing when she reached it.

'Is that Mrs Colston?'

'Yes, speaking.'

'Charmian Piper – that's right, isn't it?'

'Yes. Are you a reporter?'

'Remember,' he said, 'you must die.'

'Oh, as to that,' she said, 'for the past thirty years and more I have thought of it from time to time. My memory is failing in certain respects. I am gone eighty-six. But somehow I do not forget my death, whenever that will be.'

'Delighted to hear it,' he said. 'Good-bye for now.'

'Good-bye,' she said. 'What paper do you represent?'

But he had rung off.

Charmian made her way to the library and cautiously built up the fire which had burnt low. The effort of stooping tired her and she sat for a moment in the big chair. After a while it was tea-time. She thought, for a space, about tea. Then she made her way to the kitchen where the tray had been set by Mrs Anthony in readiness for Mrs Pettigrew to make the tea. But Mrs Pettigrew had gone out. Charmian felt overwhelmed suddenly with trepidation and pleasure. Could she make tea herself? Yes, she would try. The kettle was heavy as she held it under the tap. It was heavier still when it was half-filled with water. It rocked in her hand and her skinny, large-freckled wrist ached and wobbled with the strain. At last she had lifted the kettle safely on to the gas-ring. She had seen Mrs Anthony use the automatic lighter. She tried it but could not make it work. Matches. She looked everywhere for matches but could not find any. She went back to the library and took from a jar one of Godfrey's home-made tapers. She stooped dangerously and lit the taper at the fire. Then, cautiously, she bore the little quivering flame to the kitchen, holding it in one shaking hand, and holding that hand with her other hand to keep it as steady as possible. At last the gas was lit under the kettle. Charmian put the teapot on the stove to warm. She then sat down in Mrs Anthony's chair to wait for the kettle to boil. She felt strong and fearless.

When the kettle had boiled she spooned tea into the pot and knew that the difficult part had come. She lifted the kettle a little and tilted its spout over the teapot. She stood as far back as she could. In went the hot water, and though it splashed quite a bit on the stove, she did not get any over her dress or her feet. She bore the teapot to the tray. It wafted to and fro, but she managed to place it down gently after all.

She looked at the hot-water jug. Should she bother with hot water? She had done so well up to now, it would be a pity to make any mistake and have an accident. But she felt strong and fearless. A pot of tea without the hot-water jug beside it was nonsense. She filled the jug, this time splashing her foot a little, but not enough to burn.

When all was set on the tray she was tempted to have her tea in the kitchen there in Mrs Anthony's chair.

But she thought of her bright fire in the library. She looked at the tray. Plainly she could never carry it. She would take in the tea-things one by one, even if it took half-an-hour.

She did this, resting only once between her journeys. First the teapot, which she placed on the library hearth. Then the hot-water jug. These were the dangerous objects. Cup and saucer; another cup and saucer in case Godfrey or Mrs Pettigrew should return and want tea; the buttered scones; jam; two plates, two knives, and two spoons. Another journey for the plate of Garibaldi biscuits which Charmian loved to dip in her tea. She could well remember, as she looked at them, the fuss about Garibaldi in her childhood, and her father's eloquent letters to *The Times* which were read aloud after morning prayers. Three of the Garibaldi biscuits slid off the plate and broke on the floor in the hall. She proceeded with the plate, laid it on a table, and then returned to pick up the broken biscuits, even the crumbs. It would be a pity if anyone said she had been careless. Still, she felt fearless that afternoon. Last of all she went to fetch the tray itself, with its pretty cloth. She stopped to mop up the water she had spilt by the stove. When she had brought everything into the room she closed the door, placed the tray on a low table by her chair and arranged her tea-things neatly upon it. The performance had taken twenty minutes. She dozed with gratitude in her chair for five more minutes, then carefully poured out her tea, splashing very little into the saucer. Even that little she eventually poured back into the cup. All was as usual, save that she was blissfully alone, and the tea was not altogether hot. She started to enjoy her tea.

*

Mrs Pettigrew stood under the chipped stucco of the porch and looked at her watch. She could not see the dial in the gloom. She walked down the steps and consulted her watch under a lamp-post. It was twenty to five. She turned to resume her station in the bombed porch. She had mounted two steps when, from nowhere, a policeman appeared.

'Anything you wanted, Madam?'

'Oh, I'm waiting for a friend.'

He went up the steps and pushing open the creaking door flashed his torch all over the interior, as if expecting her friend to be there. He gave her a curious look and walked away.

Mrs Pettigrew thought, 'It's too bad, it really is, me being put in a predicament like this, standing in the cold, questioned by policemen; and I'm nearly seventy-four.' Something rustled on the ground behind the door. She looked; she could see nothing. But then she felt something, like the stroke of a hand over her instep. She shuffled backwards, and catching the last glimpse of a rat slithering through the railings down the area, screamed.

The policeman crossed over the street towards her, having apparently been watching her from some doorway on the other side.

'Anything wrong?' he said.

'A rat,' she said, 'ran across my feet.'

'I shouldn't stand here, Madam, please.'

'I'm waiting for my friend. Go away.'

'What's your name, Madam?'

She thought he said, 'What's your game?' and it occurred to her, too, that she probably looked years younger than she thought. 'You can have three guesses,' she replied pertly.

'I must ask you to move along, Madam. Where do you live?'

'Suppose you mind your own business?'

'Got anyone to look after you?' he said; and she realized he had not much under-estimated her years, but probably suspected she was dotty.

'I'm waiting for my friend,' she said.

The policeman stood uncertainly before her, considering her face, and possibly what to do about her. There was a slight stir behind the door. Mrs Pettigrew jumped nervously. 'Oh, is that a rat?'

Just then a car door slammed behind the policeman's bulk.

'That's my friend,' she said, trying to slip past him. 'Let me pass, please.'

The policeman turned to scrutinize the car. Godfrey was already driving off.

'Godfrey! Godfrey!' she called. But he was away.

'Your friend didn't stop long,' he observed.

'I've missed him through you talking to me.'

She started off down the steps.

'Think you'll get home all right?' The policeman seemed relieved to see her moving off.

She did not reply but got a taxi at King's Road, thinking how hard used she was.

Godfrey, on her arrival, was expostulating with Charmian. 'I say you *couldn't* have made the tea and brought it in here. How could you? Mrs Pettigrew brought in your tea. Now think. You've been dreaming.'

Charmian turned to Mrs Pettigrew. 'You have been out all after-noon, haven't you, Mrs Pettigrew?'

'Mabel,' said Mrs Pettigrew.

'Haven't you, Mabel? I made my tea myself and brought it in. Godfrey won't believe me, he's absurd.'

'I brought in your tea,' said Mrs Pettigrew, 'before I went out for an airing. I must say I feel the need of it these days since Mrs Anthony started leaving early.'

'You see what I mean?' said Godfrey to Charmian.

Charmian was silent.

'A whole long story,' said Godfrey, 'about getting up and making your own tea. I knew it was impossible.'

Charmian said, 'I am getting feeble in mind as well as body, Godfrey. I shall go to the nursing home in Surrey. I am quite decided.'

'Perhaps,' said Mrs Pettigrew, 'that would be the best.'

'There's no need, my dear, for you to go into a home,' said Godfrey. 'No one is suggesting it. All I was saying –'

'I'm going to bed, Godfrey.'

'Oh, dear, a supper tray,' said Mrs Pettigrew.

'I don't want supper, thank you,' said Charmian. 'I enjoyed my tea.'

Mrs Pettigrew moved towards Charmian as if to take her arm.

'I can manage quite well, thank you.'

'Come now, don't get into a tantrum. You must get your beauty sleep for the photographer tomorrow,' said Mrs Pettigrew.

Charmian made her slow way out of the room and upstairs.

'See the lawyer?' said Mrs Pettigrew.

'It's damn cold,' said Godfrey.

'You saw the solicitor?'

'No, in fact, he'd been called away on an urgent case. Have to see him some other time. I say I'll see him tomorrow, Mabel.'

'Urgent case,' she said. 'It was the lawyer you had an appointment with, not the doctor. You're worse than Charmian.'

'Yes, yes, Mabel, the lawyer. Don't let Mrs Anthony hear you.'

'Mrs Anthony has gone. And, anyway, she's deaf. Where have you been all afternoon?'

'Well, I called in,' he said, 'at the police.'

'What?'

'The police station. Kept me waiting a long time.'

'Look here, Godfrey, you have no evidence against me, you understand? You need proof. Just you try. What did you tell them? Come on, what did you say?'

'Can't remember exact words. Time they did something about it. I said, "My sister has been suffering from this man for over six months," I said. "Now he has started on me," I said, "and it's high time you did something about it," I said. I said –'

'Oh, your phone call. Is that all you have to think about? I ask you, Godfrey, is *that all* . . .?'

He huddled in his chair. 'Damn cold,' he said. 'Have we got any whisky there?'

'No,' she said, 'we haven't.'

He silently opened Charmian's door on his way to bed.

'Still awake?' he said in a whisper.

'Yes,' she said, waking up.

'Feeling all right? Want anything?'

'Nothing, thank you, Godfrey.'

'Don't go to the nursing home,' he said in a whisper.

'Godfrey, I made my own tea this afternoon.'

'All right,' he said, 'you did. But don't go –'

'Godfrey,' she said. 'If you will take my advice you will write to Eric. You will make it up with Eric.'

'Why? What makes you say that?'

But she would not say what made her say this, and he was puzzled by it, for he himself had been thinking of writing to Eric; he was uncertain whether Charmian knew more about him and his plight than he thought, or whether her words represented merely a stray idea.

'You must promise,' said Olive Mannering, 'that this is to be treated as a strictly professional matter.'

'I promise,' said Alec Warner.

'Because,' said Olive, 'it's dangerous stuff, and I got it in strictest confidence. And I wouldn't tell a soul.'

'Nor I,' said Alec.

'It's only for purposes of research,' said Olive.

'Quite.'

'How do you make your notes?' Olive inquired. 'Because there mustn't be names mentioned anywhere.'

'All documents referring to real names are to be destroyed at my death. No one could possibly identify my case-histories.'

'O.K.,' said Olive. 'Well, goodness, he was in a terrible state this afternoon. I was really sorry for him. It's Mrs Pettigrew, you see.'

'Suspenders and all that lark?'

'No, oh no. He's finished with that.'

'Blackmail.'

'That's right. She has apparently discovered a lot about his past life.'

'The affair with Lisa Brooke.'

'That and a lot more. Then there was some money scandal at the Colston Breweries which was hushed up at the time. Mrs Pettigrew knows it all. She got at his private papers.'

'Has he been to the police?'

'No, he's afraid.'

'They would protect him. What is he afraid of? Did you ask?'

'His wife, mostly. He doesn't want his wife to know. It's his pride, I think. Of course, I haven't met her but it sounds to me that she's always been the religious one, and being famous as an author off and on, she gets all the sympathy for being more sensitive than him.'

Alec Warner wrote in his book.

'Charmian,' he remarked, 'would not be put out by anything she learnt about Godfrey. Now, you say he's *afraid* of her knowing?'

'Yes, he is, really.'

'Most people,' he said, 'would say she was afraid of him. He bullies her.'

'Well, I've only heard his side. He looks pretty bad just now.'

'Did you notice the complexion?'

'High-coloured. Goodness, he's lost weight.'

'Stooping more?'

'Oh, much more. The stuffing's knocked out of him. Mrs Pettigrew keeps the whisky locked up.'

Alec made a note. 'Do him good in the long run,' he commented. 'He drank too much for his age. What is he going to do about Mrs Pettigrew?'

'Well, he pays up. But she keeps demanding more. He hates paying up. And the latest thing, she wants him to make a new will in her favour. He was supposed to be at the lawyer's today, but he called in on me instead. He thought I might persuade Eric to come and frighten her. He says Eric wouldn't lose by it. But as you know, Eric feels very bitter about his family, and he's jealous of his mother, especially since her novels were in print again, and the fact is, Eric is entitled to a certain amount, it's only a question of time ...'

'Eric,' said Alec, 'is not one of us. Go on about Godfrey.'

'He says he'd like to make it up with Eric. I promised to write to Eric for him, and so I shall, but as I say –'

'Has Mrs Pettigrew any money of her own?'

'Oh, I don't know. You never know with a woman like that, do you? I don't think she has much, because of something I heard yesterday.'

'What was that?'

'Well,' said Olive, 'I got the story from Ronald Sidebottome, he called yesterday. I didn't get it from Godfrey.'

'What was the story?' said Alec. 'You know, Olive, I always pay extra if it entails an extra interview on your part.'

'O.K.,' said Olive, 'keep your hair on. I just wanted you to know this makes another item.'

Alec smiled at her like an uncle.

'Ronald Sidebottome,' she said, 'has finally decided not to contest Lisa Brooke's will now that Tempest is dead. The case was really Tempest's idea. He said the whole thing would have been very distasteful. All about Lisa's marriage with Guy Leet not being consummated. Mrs Pettigrew is awfully angry about the case being withdrawn, because she was working in with the Sidebottomes when Tempest died. And she hasn't managed to get her hold on Ronald, though she's been trying hard all winter. Ronald is a very independent type at heart. You don't know old Ronald. He's deaf, I admit, but –'

'I have known Ronald over forty years. How interesting he should strike you as an independent type.'

'He has a nice way with him on the quiet,' she said. She had met Ronald Sidebottome while strolling round a picture gallery with her grandfather shortly after Tempest's death, and had brought the two old men back to supper. 'But if you've known Ronald for forty years, then you don't want to hear any more from me.'

'My dear, I have known Ronald over forty years but I can't know him as you do.'

'He hates Mrs Pettigrew,' Olive observed with an inward musing smile. 'She won't get much of Lisa's bequest. All she has so far is Lisa's squirrel coat, that's all.'

'Does she think of contesting the will on her own account?'

'No, she's been advised her case is too weak. Mrs Brooke paid her adequately all the time; there's no case. Anyway, I don't think she has the capital to finance it. She was depending on the Sidebottomes. Of course, under the will, the money goes to her when Guy Leet dies. But he's telling everyone how fit he feels. So you can be sure Mrs P. is going to get all she can out of poor old Godfrey.'

Alec Warner finished his notes and closed the book. Olive passed him a drink.

'Poor old Godfrey,' said Olive. 'And he was upset by something else, too. He had an anonymous phone call from that man who worries his sister – or at least he thinks he had. It amounts to the same thing, doesn't it?'

Alec Warner opened his notebook again and got his pen from the pocket of his waistcoat. 'What did the man say?'

'The same thing. "You are going to die" or something.'

'Always be exact. Dame Lettie's man says, "Remember you must die" – was that what Godfrey heard?'

'I think so,' she said. 'This sort of work is very tiring.'

'I know, my dear. It must be. What time of day did he receive this call?'

'The morning. That I do know. He told me it was just after the doctor had left Charmian.'

Alec completed his notes and closed his book once more. He said to Olive, 'Has Guy Leet been informed of the withdrawal of the law-suit?'

'I don't know. The decision was only made yesterday afternoon.'

'Perhaps he does not know yet,' said Alec. 'Lisa's money will make a great difference to a man of Guy's tastes. He has been feeling the pinch lately.'

'He can't have long to live,' said Olive.

'Lisa's money will make his short time pleasanter. I take it this information is not particularly confidential?'

'No,' said Olive, 'only what I told you of Mrs Pettigrew's hold on Godfrey – that's confidential.'

Alec Warner went home and wrote a letter to Guy Leet:

Dear Guy – I do not know if I am the first to inform you that neither Ronald Sidebottome nor Mrs Pettigrew are now proceeding with their suit in contest of Lisa's will.

I offer you my congratulations, and trust you will long enjoy your good fortune.

Forgive me for thus attempting to anticipate an official notification. If I have been successful in being the first to convey this news to you, will you kindly oblige me by taking your pulse and your temperature immediately upon reading this letter, and again one hour afterwards, and again the following morning, and inform me of the same, together with your normal pulse-rate and temperature if you know it?

This will be invaluable for my records. I shall be so much obliged.

Yours, Alec Warner.

P.S. Any additional observations as to your reaction to the good news will of course be much appreciated.

Alec Warner went to post the letter and returned to write up his records. Twice, the telephone rang. The first call was from Godfrey Colston, whose record-card, as it happened, Alec held in his hand.

'Oh,' said Godfrey, 'you're in.'

'Yes. Have you been trying to get me?'

'No,' said Godfrey. 'Look here, I want to speak to you. Do you know anyone in the police?'

'Not well,' said Alec, 'since Mortimer retired.'

'Mortimer's no good,' said Godfrey. 'It's about these anonymous calls. Mortimer has been looking into them for months. Now the chap has started on me.'

'I have an hour to spare between nine and ten. Can you come round to the club?'

Alec returned to his notes. The second telephone call came a quarter of an hour later. It was from a man who said, 'Remember you must die.'

'Would you mind repeating that?' said Alec.

The speaker repeated it.

'Thank you,' said Alec, and replaced the receiver a fraction before the other had done so.

He got out his own card and made an entry. Then he made a cross-reference to another card which he duly annotated. Finally he wrote a passage in his diary, ending it with the words, 'Query: mass-hysteria.'

ELEVEN

In the fine new sunshine of April which fell upon her through the window, Emmeline Mortimer adjusted her glasses and smoothed her blouse. She was grateful to be free of her winter jumpers and to wear a blouse and cardigan again.

She decided to sow parsley that morning and perhaps set out the young carnations and the sweet peas. Perhaps Henry would prune the roses. Henry was over the worst, but she must not let him hoe or weed or in any way strain or stoop. She must keep an eye on him without appearing to do so. This evening, when the people had gone he could spray the gooseberries with lime-sulphur in case of mildew and the pears with Bordeaux mixture in case of scab. And the black-currants in case of big bud again. There was so much to be done, and Henry must not overdo it. No, he must not spray the pears for he might over-reach and strain himself. The people would certainly exhaust him.

Her hearing was sharp that morning. Henry was moving about briskly upstairs. He was humming. The scent of her hyacinths on the window ledge came in brief irregular waves which she received with a sharp and pleasant pang. She sipped her warm and splendid tea and adjusted the cosy round the pot, keeping it hot for Henry. She touched her glasses into focus and turned to the morning paper.

Henry Mortimer came down in a few moments. His wife turned her head very slightly when he came in and returned to her paper.

He opened the french windows and stood there for a while satisfying his body with the new sun and air and his eyes with his garden. Then he closed the windows and took his place at the table. 'A bit of hoeing today,' he said.

She made no immediate objection, for she must bide her time. Not that Henry was touchy or difficult about his angina. It was more a matter of principle and habit; she had always waited her time before opposing any statement of Henry's.

He gestured with the back of his hand towards the sunny weather. 'What d'you think of it?' he said.

She looked up, smiled, and nodded once. Her face was a network of fine wrinkles except where the skin was stretched across her small sharp bones. Her back was straight, her figure neat, and her movements easy. One half of her mind was busy calculating the number of places she would have to set for the people this afternoon. She was four years older than Henry, who had turned seventy at the beginning of February. His first heart attack had followed soon after, and Henry, half-inclined to envisage his doctor as a personification of his illness, had declared himself much improved since the doctor had ceased to pay regular daily visits. He had been allowed up for afternoons, then for whole days. The doctor had bade him not to worry, always to carry his box of tablets, to stick to his diet, and to avoid any exertion. The doctor had told Emmeline to ring him any time if necessary. And then, to Henry's relief, the doctor had disappeared from the house.

Henry Mortimer, the former Chief Inspector, was long, lean, bald and spritely. At the sides and back of his head his hair grew thick and grey. His eyebrows were thick and black. It would be accurate to say that his nose and lips were thick, his eyes small and his chin receding into his neck. And yet it would be inaccurate to say he was not a handsome man, such being the power of unity when it exists in a face.

He scraped butter sparingly on his toast in deference to the departed doctor, and remarked to his wife, 'I've got these people coming this afternoon.'

She said, 'There's another bit about them in the paper today.' And she held her peace for the meantime about his having to take care not to wear himself out with them; for what was the point of his being retired from the Force if he continued to lay himself out on criminal cases?

He stretched out his hand and she put the paper into it. 'Hoax-Caller Strikes Again,' he read aloud. Then he read on to himself:

Police are still mystified by continued complaints from a number of elderly people who have been receiving anonymous telephone calls from a male hoax-caller since August last year.

There may be more than one man behind the hoax. Reports on

the type of voice vary from 'very young', 'middle-aged' to 'elderly', etc.

The voice invariably warns the victim, 'You will die tonight.'

The aged victims' telephones are being tapped by the authorities, and police have requested them to keep the caller in conversation if possible. But this and all other methods of detecting hoax-callers have so far failed, the police admitted yesterday.

It was thought at first that the gang's activities were confined to the Central London area. But a recent report from former critic Mr Guy Leet, 75, of Stedrost, Surrey, indicates that the net is spreading wider.

Among numerous others previously reported to be recipients of 'the Call' are Dame Lettie Colston, O.B.E., 79, pioneer penal reformer, and her sister-in-law Charmian Piper (Mrs Godfrey Colston) the novelist, 85, author of *The Seventh Child*, etc.

Dame Lettie told reporters yesterday, 'I am not satisfied that the C.I.D. have taken these incidents seriously enough. I am employing a private agency. I consider it a great pity that flogging has been abolished. This vile creature ought to be taught a lesson.'

Charmian Piper, whose husband Mr Godfrey Colston, 86, former Chairman of Colston Breweries, is also among the victims of the hoax, said yesterday, 'We are not in the least perturbed by the caller. He is a very civil young man.'

A C.I.D. spokesman said everything possible is being done to discover the offender.

Henry Mortimer put down the paper and took the cup his wife was passing him.

'An extraordinary sort of case,' she said.

'Embarrassing for the police,' he said, 'poor fellows.'

'Oh, they'll get the culprit, won't they?'

'I don't see,' he said, 'how they ever can, all evidence considered.'

'Well, you know the evidence, of course.'

'And considering the evidence,' he said, 'in my opinion the offender is Death himself.'

She was not really surprised to hear him say this. She had followed his mind all through its conforming life and late independence, so that nothing he said could surprise her very much. He had lived to see his children cease to take him seriously – his word carried more force in the outside world. Even his older grandchildren, though they loved him, would never now understand his value to others. He knew this; he did not care. Emmeline could never, however, regard Henry as a dear old thing who had taken to developing a philosophy, as other men, on their retirement, might cultivate a hobby. She did not entirely let her children see how she felt, for she liked to please them and seem solid and practical in their eyes. But she trusted Henry, and she could not help doing so.

She let him busy himself in the garden before she sent him indoors to rest. A few more weeks and he would be watching the post for that particular letter from his old friend in the country inviting him to come for a fortnight's fishing. It seemed miraculous that another spring had begun and that soon Henry would announce, 'I've heard from Harry. The may-fly's on the river. I'd better be off day after tomorrow.' Then she would be alone for a while, or perhaps one of the girls would come to stay after Easter and the younger children would roll over and over on the lawn if it was dry enough.

She sowed her parsley, and wondered excitedly what the deputation who were calling to see Henry this afternoon would look like.

The Mortimers' house at Kingston-on-Thames was not difficult to reach, if one followed Henry's directions. However, the deputation had found it a difficult place to find. They arrived shaken in nerve and body, half an hour late, in Godfrey's car and two taxis. In Godfrey's car, besides Godfrey himself, were Charmian, Dame Lettie and Mrs Pettigrew. The first taxi bore Alec Warner and Dame Lettie's maid, Gwen. In the second taxi came Janet Sidebottome, that missionary sister of Lisa Brooke; accompanying her were an elderly couple and an aged spinster who were strangers to the rest.

Mrs Pettigrew, spruce and tailor-made, stepped out first. Henry Mortimer came beaming down the path and shook her hand. Godfrey emerged next, and meantime there was a general exit from the two taxis, and a fussy finding and counting of money for the fares.

Charmian, from the back of Godfrey's car, said, 'Oh, I have so enjoyed the drive. My first this year. The river is splendid today.'

'Wait a minute, wait a minute, Godfrey,' said Dame Lettie who was being helped out. 'Don't pull me.' She had grown stouter and yet more fragile during the past winter. Her sight was failing, and it was obviously difficult for her to find the kerb with her foot. 'Wait, Godfrey.'

'We're late,' said Godfrey. 'Charmian, sit still, don't move till we've got Lettie out.'

Mrs Pettigrew took Dame Lettie's other arm while Henry Mortimer stood holding the door. Lettie yanked her arm away from Mrs Pettigrew, so that her handbag dropped to the pavement and the contents spilled out. The occupants of the taxis rushed to rescue Lettie's belongings, while Lettie herself drew back into the car and sank with a plump sound into her seat.

Young Gwen, who Dame Lettie had brought as a witness, stood in the gateway and laughed aloud.

Mrs Mortimer came briskly down the path and addressed Gwen. 'Look lively, young person,' she said, 'and help your elders instead of standing there laughing.'

Gwen looked surprised and did not move.

'Go and pick up your aunt's belongings,' said Mrs Mortimer.

Dame Lettie, fearful of losing her maid, called out from the car,

'I'm not her aunt, Mrs Mortimer. It's all right, Gwen.'

Mrs Mortimer, who was not normally an irate woman, took Gwen by the shoulders and propelled her over to the little group who were stiffly bending to retrieve the contents of the bag. 'Let the girl pick them up,' she said.

Most of the things were, however, by now collected, and while Alec Warner, directed by Henry Mortimer, stooped to fish with his umbrella under the car for Dame Lettie's spectacle-case, Gwen so far overcame her surprise as to say to Mrs Mortimer, 'I got nothing to do with *you*.'

'All right, Gwen. It's all right,' said Dame Lettie from the car.

Mrs Mortimer now kept her peace although it was clear she would have liked to say more to Gwen. She had been troubled, in the first place, by the sight of these infirm and agitated people arriving with such difficulty at her door. Where are their children? she had thought, or their nieces and nephews? Why are they left to their own resources like this?

She edged Gwen aside and reached into the car for Dame Lettie's

arm. At the opposite door Henry Mortimer was reaching for Charmian's. Mrs Mortimer as she assisted Dame Lettie, hoped he would
not strain himself, and said to Dame Lettie, 'I see you have brought
the spring weather.' As Lettie finally came to rest on the pavement
Mrs Mortimer looked up to see Alec Warner's eyes upon her. She
thought: That man is studying me for some reason.

Charmian tottered gaily up the path on Henry Mortimer's arm. He
was telling her he had just read, once more, her novel *The Gates of
Grandella* in its fine new edition.

'It is over fifty years,' said Charmian, 'since I read it.'

'It captures the period,' said Mortimer. 'Oh, it brings everything
back. I do recommend you to read it again.'

Charmian slid her eyes flirtatiously towards him – that gesture
which the young reporters who came to see her found so enchanting –
and said, 'You are too young, Henry, to remember when the book
first came out.'

'No indeed,' he said, 'I was already a police constable. And a
constable never forgets.'

'What a charming house,' said Charmian, and she caught sight of
Godfrey waiting inside the hall, and felt she was, as always when
people made a fuss of her, making him sick.

The conference did not start for some time. Emmeline Mortimer
consulted in low tones with the ladies of the deputation in the hall,
whether they would first like to go 'upstairs', or, if the stairs were too
much for them, there was a place downstairs, straight through the
kitchen, turn right. 'Charmian,' said Mrs Pettigrew out loud, 'come
and make yourself comfortable. I'll take you. Come along.'

Henry Mortimer piled the men's coats and hats neatly on a chest,
and, having shown the way upstairs to the male candidates, ushered
the rest of the men into the dining-room where, at the long table, bare
except for a vase of shining daffodils and, at the top, a thick file of
papers, Gwen was already seated, fuming sulkily to herself.

When Godfrey came in he glanced round at the furnishings with an
inquiring air.

'Is this the right room?' he said.

Alec Warner thought: He is probably looking for signs of a tea-tray.
He probably thinks we are not going to get any tea.

'Yes, I think this is most suitable,' said Henry, as one taking him into consultation. 'Don't you? We can sit round the table and talk things over before tea.'

'Oh!' said Godfrey. Alec Warner congratulated himself.

At last they were settled round the table, the three strangers having been introduced as a Miss Lottinville and a Mr and Mrs Jack Rose. Mrs Mortimer withdrew and the door clicked behind her like a signal for the start of business. The sunlight fell mildly upon the table and the people round it, showing up motes of dust in the air, specks of dust on the clothes of those who wore black, the wrinkled cheeks and hands of the aged, and the thick make-up of Gwen.

Charmian, who was enthroned in the most comfortable chair, spoke first, 'What a charming room.'

'It gets the afternoon sun,' Henry said. 'Is it too much for anyone? Charmian – another cushion.'

The three strangers looked uneasily at each other, simply because they were strangers and not, like the others, known to each other for forty, fifty years it might be.

Godfrey moved his arm to shoot back his sleeve, and said, 'This telephone man, Mortimer, I must say, it's a bit thick –'

'I have a copy of your statement here, Colston,' said Henry Mortimer, opening his file. 'I propose to read each one aloud by turn, and you may add any further comments after I have read it. Does that course meet with approval?'

No one seriously disagreed with that course.

Gwen looked out of the window. Janet Sidebottome fiddled with the electric battery of her elaborate hearing-aid. Mrs Pettigrew laid her arm on the table and her chin on her hand and looked intense. Charmian sat with her heart-shaped face composed beneath her new blue hat. Alec Warner looked carefully at the strangers, first at Mrs Rose, then at Mr Rose and then at Miss Lottinville. Mrs Rose had her eyebrows perpetually raised in resignation, furrowing deep lines into her forehead. Mr Rose held his head sideways; he had enormous shoulders; his large mouth drooped downwards at the same degree of curvature as his chin, cheeks and nose. The Roses must be nearly eighty, perhaps more. Miss Lottinville looked small and slight and angry. The left side of her mouth and her right eye kept twitching simultaneously.

Henry Mortimer's voice was not too official, but it was firm:

'. . . just after eleven in the morning . . . on three separate occasions . . . It sounded like that of a common man. The tone was menacing. The words on each occasion were . . .'

'. . . at various times throughout the day . . . the first occasion was on 12th March. The words were . . . The tone was strictly factual . . . He sounded young, like a Teddy-boy . . .'

'. . . first thing in the morning . . . every week since the end of August last. It was the voice of a cultured, middle-aged man . . . the tone is sinister in the extreme . . .'

'It was the voice of a very civil young man . . .' This was Charmian's account. Godfrey broke in. 'How could he be a civil young man saying a thing like that? Use your head, Charmian.'

'He was,' said Charmian, 'most civil on all three occasions.'

'Perhaps,' said Henry, 'if I could continue . . .? Then Charmian can add her comments.'

He finished Charmian's statement. 'That is correct,' said Charmian.

'How could he be *civil*?' said Godfrey.

'Mr Guy Leet,' Henry announced, taking up the next paper. 'Oh, Guy isn't here, of course –'

'Guy asked me to say,' said Alec, 'we could discuss his case as much as we like so long as we don't discuss his private life up to 1940.'

'Has to get about on two sticks,' commented Godfrey.

'Guy's account,' said Henry, 'is substantially the same as the others, with the most interesting exception that he gets Toll calls from London at between six and seven in the evening when the cheap rate is on. In his opinion the offender is a schoolboy.'

'Nonsense,' said Dame Lettie. 'A middle-aged man.'

'It is simple,' said Henry, 'to trace a Toll call from London to the country. And yet the police have not yet traced any caller to Guy Leet at Stedrost.'

'Quite,' said Dame Lettie. 'The police –'

'However, we will discuss these factors later,' said Henry. 'Next Mr Ronald Sidebottome – Oh, Ronald's not here either. What's happened to Ronald, Janet?'

'He was a youth – a Teddy-boy, as I've said,' Janet Sidebottome replied.

'Ronald,' roared Godfrey into her ear. 'Why hasn't Ronald turned up? He said he was coming.'

'Oh, Ronald. Well, he was to call for me. I suppose he forgot. It was most annoying. I waited and then I rang him up but he wasn't at home. I really can't answer for Ronald these days. He is never at home.'

Alec Warner took out a small diary and scribbled something in pencil.

'Ronald's statement,' said Mortimer, 'describes the caller as a man well advanced in years with a cracked and rather shaky voice and a suppliant tone.'

'There must be something wrong with his phone,' said Dame Lettie. 'The man's voice is strong and sinister. A man of middle years. You must remember, Henry, that I have had far more experience of the creature than anyone else.'

'Yes, Lettie, my dear, I admit you have been greatly tried. Now Miss Lottinville, your statement . . . "At three o'clock in the morning . . . A foreigner . . ."'

Mrs Mortimer put her head round the door. 'Tea is ready, Henry, when you are. I have laid it in the breakfast room so that –'

'In five minutes, Emmeline.'

She disappeared and Godfrey looked yearningly after her.

'Finally Mr Rose,' said Henry: '"I received the call at my business premises at twelve noon on two days running . . . the man sounded like an official person . . . late middle age . . ."'

'That sounds accurate,' said Dame Lettie. 'Only I would describe the voice as *sinister*.'

'Did he have a lisp?' said Godfrey.

'Mr Rose has not mentioned a lisp in his statement – Had he a lisp, Mr Rose?' said Henry.

'No, no. Like an official. My wife says an army man, but I would say a government chap.'

Everyone spoke at once.

'Oh no,' said Janet Sidebottome, 'he was –'

'A gang,' said Dame Lettie, 'there must be a gang.'

Miss Lottinville said: 'I assure you, Chief Inspector, he is a man of the Orient, I should say.'

Henry waited for a while till the noise subsided. He said to Mr Rose, 'Are you satisfied with your account as I have read it?'

'A hundred per cent,' said Mr Rose.

'Then let's continue the discussion after tea,' said Henry.

Miss Lottinville said: 'You have not read the statement of this lady on my left.' The lady on her left was Mrs Pettigrew. '*I* haven't had any of your phone calls,' she said. 'I've made no statement.'

Alec Warner wondered, from the vehemence of her tone, if she were lying.

Mrs Mortimer sat with her silver teapot poised at a well-spread table.

'Come and sit by me,' she said kindly to Gwen, 'and you can help to pass the cups.'

Gwen lit a cigarette and sat down sideways at the place indicated.

'Have you been afflicted with these phone calls?' Emmeline Mortimer asked her.

'Me? No, I get wrong numbers.'

Mrs Pettigrew said confidentially to Mrs Mortimer: 'I've had no trouble myself from any phone calls. Between ourselves, I think it's all made up. I don't believe a word of what they say. They're trying to draw attention to themselves. Like kids.'

'What a delightful garden,' said Charmian.

They were assembled once more in the dining-room where a fire sparkled weakly in the sunlight.

Henry Mortimer said: 'If I had my life over again I should form the habit of nightly composing myself to thoughts of death. I would practise, as it were, the remembrance of death. There is no other practice which so intensifies life. Death, when it approaches, ought not to take one by surprise. It should be part of the full expectancy of life. Without an ever-present sense of death life is insipid. You might as well live on the whites of eggs.'

Dame Lettie said suddenly and sharply, 'Who is the man, Henry?'

'My dear Lettie, I can't help you there.'

She looked so closely at him, he felt almost that she suspected himself.

'Lettie thinks you are the man,' said Alec wickedly.

'I hardly think,' said Henry, 'Lettie would attribute to me such energy and application as the culprit evidently possesses.'

'All we want,' said Godfrey, 'is to stop him. And to do that we've got to find the man.'

'I consider,' said Janet Sidebottome, 'that what Mr Mortimer was saying just now about resigning ourselves to death is most uplifting and consoling. The religious point of view is too easily forgotten these days, and I thank you, Mr Mortimer.'

'Why, thank you, Janet. Perhaps "resigning ourselves to death" doesn't quite convey what I mean. But of course, I don't attempt to express a specifically religious point of view. My observations were merely confined –'

'You sound most religious to me,' said Janet.

'Thank you, Janet.'

'Poor young man,' mused Charmian. 'He may be lonely, and simply wanting to talk to people and so he rings them up.'

'The police, of course, are hopeless. Really, Henry, it is time there was a question in the House,' said Lettie warningly.

'Considering the fairly wide discrepancies in your various reports,' said Henry, 'the police at one stage in their investigations assumed that not one man but a gang was at work. The police have, however, employed every method of detection known to criminology and science, so far without success. Now, one factor is constant in all your reports. The words, "Remember you must die." It is, you know, an excellent thing to remember this, for it is nothing more than the truth. To remember one's death is, in short, a way of life.'

'To come to the point –' said Godfrey.

'Godfrey,' said Charmian, 'I am sure everyone is fascinated by what Henry is saying.'

'Most consoling,' said Janet Sidebottome. 'Do continue, Mr Mortimer, with your words.'

'Ah yes,' said Miss Lottinville who was also enjoying Henry's philosophizing.

And Mrs Rose, with her longanimous eyes and resignation, nodded her head in sad, wise and ancient assent.

'Have you considered,' said Alec Warner, 'the possibility of mass hysteria?'

'Making telephones ring?' said Mr Rose, spreading wide his palms.

'Absurd!' said Dame Lettie. 'We can eliminate mass hysteria.'

'Oh no,' said Mortimer. 'In a case like this we can't eliminate any possibility. That is just our difficulty.'

'Tell me,' Alec asked the Chief Inspector with his piercing look, 'would you describe yourself as a mystic?'

'Never having previously been called upon to describe myself, I really couldn't say.'

'The question is,' said Mr Rose, 'who's the fellow that's trying to put the fear of God in us?'

'And what's the motive?' said Godfrey. 'That's what I ask.'

'The question of motive may prove to be different in each case, to judge by the evidence before us,' said Mortimer. 'I think we must all realize that the offender is, in each case, whoever we think he is ourselves.'

'Did you tell them,' said Emmeline Mortimer when they had gone, 'what your theory is?'

'No – oh no, my dear. I treated them to brief philosophical sermons instead. It helped to pass the time.'

'Did they like your little sermons?'

'Some of the women did. The young girl seemed less bored than at other times. Lettie objected.'

'Oh, Lettie.'

'She said the whole afternoon had been pointless.'

'How rude. After my lovely tea.'

'It was a lovely tea. It was my part that was pointless. I'm afraid it had to be.'

'How I wish,' said Emmeline, 'you could have told them outright, "Death is the culprit." And I should like to have seen their faces.'

'It's a personal opinion. One can't make up one's mind for others.'

'Can they make up their own minds, then?'

'No. I think I'll go and spray the pears.'

'Now, darling,' said Mrs Mortimer. 'You know you've done enough for one day. I'm sure it's been quite enough for me.'

'The trouble with these people,' he said, 'they think that the C.I.D. are God, understanding all mysteries and all knowledge. Whereas we are only policemen.'

He went to read by the fire in the dining-room. Before he sat down he straightened the chairs round the table and put back some of them in their places round the wall. He emptied the ash-trays into the fire. He looked out of the window at the half-light and hoped for a fine summer. He had not mentioned it to Emmeline yet, but this summer he hoped to sail that yacht of his for which, in his retirement, he had sacrificed a car. Already he could feel the bright wet wind about his ears.

The telephone rang. He went out to the hall, answered it. Within a few seconds he put down the receiver. How strange, he thought, that mine is always a woman. Everyone else gets a man on the line to them, but mine is always this woman, gentle-spoken and respectful.

TWELVE

'I told him straight what I feel,' said Mrs Pettigrew to Mrs Anthony. 'I said, "It's all a lot of rot, Inspector. It started with Dame Lettie Colston, then Godfrey feels he's got to be in the picture and one sets off the other. To my dying day I'll swear it's all make up." But he didn't side with me. Why? I'll tell you why. He'd be put out of Dame Lettie's will if he agreed it was all her imagination.'

Mrs Pettigrew, though she had in fact, one quiet afternoon, received the anonymous telephone call, had chosen to forget it. She possessed a strong faculty for simply refusing to admit an unpleasant situation, and going quite blank where it was concerned. If, for instance, you had asked her whether, eighteen years before, she had undergone a face-lifting operation, she would have denied it, and believed the denial, and moreover would have supplied gratuitously, as a special joke, a list of people who had 'really' had their faces lifted or undergone other rejuvenating operations.

And so Mrs Pettigrew continued to persuade herself she had not heard the anonymous voice on the telephone; it was not a plain ignoring of the incident; she omitted even to keep a mental record of it, but put down the receiver and blacked it out from her life.

'A lot of imagination all round,' said Mrs Pettigrew.

'Ah well,' said Mrs Anthony, 'we all got to go some day. But I shouldn't like to have that chap on the phone to me. I'd give him something to get along with.'

'There isn't any chap,' said Mrs Pettigrew. 'You hear what I say?'

'I got my deaf-aid in, and I hear what you say. No need to raise your voice.'

Mrs Pettigrew was overcome by that guilt she felt whenever she had lowered herself to the intimacy of shouting at Mrs Anthony, forgetting to play her cards. By way of recompense she left the kitchen aloofly, and went to find Godfrey.

He was sitting by the fire, maddeningly, opposite Charmian.

'Please, Godfrey, let us not have all this over again. Ah, it's you, Mrs Pettigrew,' said Charmian.

'She is not Taylor,' said Godfrey, with automatic irritability.

'I know it,' said Charmian.

He looked unhappily at Mrs Pettigrew. There was really no consolation left in the house for a man. He was all the more disturbed by Charmian's increasing composure. It was not that he wished his wife any harm, but his spirits always seemed to wither in proportion as hers bloomed. He thought, looking at his wife, It is only for a time, this can't last, she will have a relapse. He felt he was an old man in difficulties. Mrs Pettigrew had made another appointment for his lawyer that afternoon. He did not feel up to keeping it. He supposed he would have to see the lawyer some time, but that long fruitless going to and from Kingston yesterday had left him exhausted. And that madman Mortimer, making a fuss of Charmian – everyone making a fuss of Charmian, as if she were still somebody and not a helpless old invalid – roused within him all those resentments of the long past; so that, having made the mistake of regarding Charmian's every success as his failure, now, by force of habit, he could never feel really well unless she were ill.

Charmian was saying to him, 'We did talk over the whole matter quite a lot last night. Let us leave the subject alone. I for one like Henry Mortimer, and I thoroughly enjoyed the drive.'

Mrs Pettigrew, too, was alarmed by this mental recovery of Charmian's, induced apparently by the revival of those old books. In reality it was also, in part, due to an effortful will to resist Mrs Pettigrew's bullying. Mrs Pettigrew felt that there might now even be some chance of Charmian's outliving Godfrey. Charmian should be in a home; and would be, if Godfrey were not weak-minded about it, trying to play on his wife's sympathy and keep her with him.

Godfrey looked across the fireplace at his ally and enemy, Charmian, and at Mabel Pettigrew, whom he so tremendously feared, sitting between them, and decided to give Mrs Pettigrew the slip again this afternoon and go to see Olive.

Mabel Pettigrew thought: I can read him like a book. She had not read a book for over forty years, could never concentrate on reading, but this nevertheless was her thought; and she decided to accompany him to the solicitor.

After Charmian had gone to lie down after lunch Mrs Pettigrew came in to her.

Charmian opened her eyes. 'I didn't hear you knock, Mabel,' she said.

'No,' said Mrs Pettigrew. 'You didn't.'

'Always knock,' said Charmian.

'Mrs Anthony,' said Mrs Pettigrew, 'is getting too forgetful to manage the cooking. She has left out the salt three days running, as you know. There was a caterpillar cooked in yesterday's greens. She put all that garlic in the sweetbread casserole – said she thought it was celery, well, I mean to say. She boiled Godfrey's egg hard this morning, he couldn't touch it.'

'Keep an eye on her, Mabel. You have little else to do.'

Mrs Pettigrew's feelings – those which prompted every action – rose to her throat at this independent attitude which Charmian had been gradually accumulating all winter. Mrs Pettigrew's breath, as she stood over Charmian's bed, became short and agitated.

'Sit down, Mabel. You are out of breath,' said Charmian.

Mrs Pettigrew sat down. Charmian watched her, trying to sort out in her mind this new complaint about Mrs Anthony, and what it could signify, apart from its plain meaning. Her thoughts drifted once more, for reassurance, to the nursing home in Surrey, in the same way that, as she knew, Jean Taylor's thoughts would, in the past, rest on her savings in the bank when from time to time her life with the Colstons had become too oppressive.

Mrs Pettigrew's breathing was worse. She had been suddenly caught in a gust of resentment which had been stirring within her since Charmian's partial recovery. She felt a sense of great injustice at the evident power Charmian exerted over Godfrey – so strong that she did not seem conscious of it. It was a spell of her personality so mighty that, for fear of his miserable infidelities in Spain and Belgium with Lisa Brooke coming to Charmian's knowledge, he had been, so far, docile before all the threats and deprivations of the past winter. Mabel Pettigrew had only needed to indicate that she was in possession of the full correspondence between Lisa Brooke and Godfrey, dated 1902, 1903, and 1904, and his one immediate idea had been:

Charmian must not know. Tell Eric, tell everyone. But keep it from Charmian.

Mrs Pettigrew was aware that in this he was not displaying any special consideration for Charmian's feelings. That might have been endurable. The real reason was beyond her grasp, yet undeniably present. It was real enough to render Godfrey limp in her hands. What he seemed to fear was some superiority in Charmian and the loss of his pride before her. And, though Mabel Pettigrew indeed was doing better out of Godfrey than she had hoped, she sat in Charmian's bedroom and overwhelmingly resented the inexplicableness of Charmian's power.

'You seem to have a mild touch of asthma,' Charmian remarked. 'Better keep as still and quiet as possible and presently I will get Godfrey to ring the doctor.'

Mrs Pettigrew was thinking of that business scandal at Colston Breweries which had been hushed up at the time, the documents of which she now had in her keeping. Now, if Godfrey had been really frightened about her possible disclosure of these documents she would have understood him. But all he worried about was those letters between himself and Lisa Brooke. Charmian must not know. His pride before Charmian, Charmian, an old wreck like Charmian.

Charmian stretched her hand towards the bell-push by her bed. 'Godfrey will ring for the doctor,' she said.

'No, no, I'm better now,' said Mrs Pettigrew, gradually controlling her breath, for she had the self-discipline of a nun where business was concerned. 'It was just a little turn. Mrs Anthony is such a worry.'

Charmian leaned back on her pillow and moved her hand wearily over her heart-shaped face. 'Have you had asthma before, Mabel?'

'It is not asthma. It's just a little chest trouble.' Mrs Pettigrew's face was less alarmingly red. She breathed slowly and deeply after her ordeal, and lit a cigarette.

'You have great courage, Mabel,' Charmian observed, 'if only you would employ it to the proper ends. I envy your courage. I sometimes feel helpless without my friends around me. Very few of my friends come to see me now. It isn't their fault. Godfrey did not seem to want them after my stroke. When my friends were around me every day, what courage I had!'

'You would be better off in the home,' said Mabel Pettigrew. 'You know you would. Lots of company, your friends might even come and visit you sometimes.'

'It's true I would prefer to be in the nursing home. However,' said Charmian, 'Godfrey needs me here.'

'That's where you're wrong,' said Mrs Pettigrew.

Charmian wondered, once more, which of Godfrey's secrets the woman could have got hold of. The Colston Brewery affair? Or merely one or more of his numerous infidelities? Of course, one was always obliged to appear to know nothing where a man like Godfrey was concerned. His pride. It had been the only way to live reasonably with him. For a moment, she was tempted to go to Godfrey and say, 'There is nothing you can tell me about your past life which would move me in the slightest. I know most of your supposed secrets, and what I do not know would still not surprise me.'

But she did not possess the courage to do this. He might – he would certainly – turn on her. He would never forgive her for having played this game, for over fifty years, of knowing nothing while at the same time knowing everything, as one might be 'not at home' while actually in the house. What new tyranny might he not exert to punish her knowledge?

And the simple idea of *facing* each other with such a statement between them was terrible. This should have been done years ago. And yet, it should not have been done. There was altogether too much candour in married life; it was an indelicate modern idea, and frequently led to upsets in a household, if not divorce ...

And she, too, had her pride to consider. Her mind munched over the humiliations she had received from Godfrey. Never had she won a little praise or recognition but she had paid for it by some bitter, petty, disruptive action of Godfrey's.

But I could sacrifice my pride, she thought, in order to release him. It is a matter of courage. The most I can do is to stay on here at home with him. She envied Mrs Pettigrew her courage.

Mrs Pettigrew rose and came to stand by her bed.

'You're more of a hindrance to Godfrey here than you would be in a nursing home. It's ridiculous to say he needs you.'

'I shall not go,' said Charmian. 'Now I think I must have my nap. What is the time?'

'I came,' said Mrs Pettigrew, 'to tell you about Mrs Anthony. She can't do the cooking any more, we shall all have stomach trouble. I will have to take over the meals. And besides, this cold supper she leaves for us at night is not satisfactory. It doesn't agree with me, going to bed on a cold supper. I will have to take over the cooking.'

'That is very good of you,' murmured Charmian, calculating meanwhile what was behind all this, since, with Mrs Pettigrew, something always seemed to be behind her statements.

'Otherwise,' said Mrs Pettigrew, 'one of us might be poisoned.'

'Well, really!' said Charmian.

'*Poisoned*,' said Mrs Pettigrew. 'Poison is so easy. Think it over.' She left the room.

Charmian was frightened, and at the same time a long-latent faculty stirred in her mind to assess the cheap melodrama of Mrs Pettigrew's words. But Charmian's fear predominated in the end, and, as she lay fearfully in her bed, she knew she would not put it past Mrs Pettigrew to poison her once she took control of the food. A poisoning was not easy to accomplish, but still Mrs Pettigrew might know of undetectable methods. Charmian thought on and on, and frightened herself more and more. Another woman, she thought, would be able to go to her husband and say 'Our housekeeper is threatening to poison me' – or to insist on an investigation by her friends, her son, the doctor. But Godfrey was craven, Eric was hostile, the doctor would attempt to soothe her down, assuming she had started to entertain those wild suspicions of the aged.

Then it is settled, Charmian thought. This is the point where my long, long duty to Godfrey comes to an end. I shall go to the nursing home.

The decision gave her a sense of latitude and relief. In the nursing home she could be a real person again, as she had been yesterday with Henry Mortimer, instead of a frightened invalid. She needed respect and attention. Perhaps she would have visitors. There, she could invite those whom she was prevented from seeing here at home through Godfrey's rudeness. The nursing home was not far from Stedrost. Perhaps Guy Leet would be driven over to see her. Guy Leet was amusing.

She heard the front door slam and then the slam of the car door. Mrs Pettigrew's footsteps followed immediately, clicking towards the front door. Charmian heard her open the door and call, 'Godfrey,

I'm coming with you. Wait.' But the car had already started and
Godfrey was gone. Mrs Pettigrew slammed the door shut once more
and went to her room. A few minutes later she had descended the
stairs and left the house.

Mrs Pettigrew had informed Godfrey of her intention to accompany
him to his solicitor. When she found he had once more given her the
slip she felt pretty sure he had no intention of keeping his appointment with the lawyer. Within a few moments she had put on her hat
and coat and marched up the road to find a taxi.

First of all she went to the bombed building off the King's Road.
There, sure enough, was Godfrey's car. There was, however, no sign
of Godfrey. She ordered the taxi to drive round the block in a hope
that she would catch Godfrey before he reached his destination,
wherever that might be.

Godfrey, meanwhile, was on his way to Olive's flat, about seven
minutes' walk for him at his fastest pace. He turned into Tite Street,
stooping his head still more than his natural stoop, against a sudden
shower of rain. He hoped Olive would have tea ready. He hoped Olive
would not have any other visitors today, obliging him to inquire, in
that foolish way, for the address of her grandfather. Olive would be in
a listening mood, she was a good consoling listener. She would
probably have heard from Eric. Godfrey wondered what she had
heard from Eric. Olive had promised to write and tell Eric, in strictest
confidence, about his difficulties with Mrs Pettigrew. She had
promised to appeal to Eric. Eric would no doubt be only too glad to be
on good terms with his parents again. Eric had been a disappointment, but now was his chance to prove himself. Eric would put
everything right, and no doubt Olive had heard from Eric.

He reached the area gate and pushed it open. There was an unusual
amount of litter down in the area. The dust-bin was crammed full; old
shoes, handbags, and belts were sticking out beneath the lid. On the
area pavement were scattered newspapers, tins, rusty kitchen uten-
sils, empty bottles of numerous shapes, and a battered lampshade.
Godfrey thought: Olive must be having a spring-clean, turning out all
her things. Very wasteful and untidy. Always complaining of being
hard up; no wonder.

No one answered his ring. He walked over to the barred window of Olive's front room and it was then he noticed the curtains had gone. He peered in. The room was quite bare. Must he not have come to the wrong house? He walked up the steps and looked carefully at the number. He walked down the steps again and peered once more into the empty room. Olive had definitely departed. And on realizing this his first thought was to leave the vicinity of the house as quickly as possible. There was something mysterious about this. Godfrey could not stand anything mysterious. Olive might be involved in some scandal. She had said nothing, when he had seen her last week, about moving from her flat. As he walked away down Tite Street he feared more and more some swift, sudden scandal, and his one desire was to forget all knowledge of Olive.

He cut along the King's Road, bought an afternoon paper, and turned up the side street where his car was waiting. Before he reached it a taxi drew up beside him. Mrs Pettigrew got out.

'Oh, there you are,' she said.

He stood with the newspaper hanging from his hand while she paid the taxi, bewildered by guilt. This guilt was the main sensation Mrs Pettigrew touched off in him. No thought, word or deed of his life had roused in him any feeling resembling the guilt he experienced as he stood waiting for Mrs Pettigrew to pay the taxi and turn to ask him, 'Where have you been?'

'Buying the paper,' said Godfrey.

'Did you have to park your car here in order to walk down the road to buy the paper?'

'Wanted a walk,' said Godfrey. 'Bit stiff.'

'You'll be late for your appointment. Hurry up. I told you to wait for me. Why did you go off without me?'

'I forgot,' said Godfrey as he climbed into the car, 'that you wanted to come. I was in a hurry to get to the lawyer's.' She went round to the other side of the car and got in.

'You might have opened the door for me,' she said.

Godfrey did not at first understand what she meant, for he had long since started to use his advanced years as an excuse to omit the mannerly conformities of his younger days, and he was now automatically rude in his gestures as if by long-earned right. He sensed some

new frightful upheaval of his habits behind her words, as he drove off
fitfully towards Sloane Square.

She lifted the paper and glanced at the front page.

'Ronald,' she said. 'Here's Ronald Sidebottome in the paper. His
photo; he's got married. No, don't look. Watch where you're going,
we'll have an accident. Mind out – there's the red light.'

They were jerked forward roughly as Godfrey braked for the red
light.

'Oh, do be careful,' she said, 'and a little more considerate.'

He looked down at her lap where the paper was lying. Ronald's
flabby face beamed up at him. He stood with Olive simpering on his
arm, under the headline, 'Widower, 79, weds girl, 24'.

'Olive Mannering!' Godfrey let out.

'Oh, you know her?'

'Granddaugher of my friend the poet,' Godfrey said.

'The lights, Godfrey,' said Mrs Pettigrew in a tired tone.

He shot the car forward.

'"Wealthy ex-stockbroker ..."' Mrs Pettigrew read out. 'She
knows what she's doing, all right. "Miss Mannering ... film extra and
B.B.C. actress ... now given up her flat in Tite Street, Chelsea ..."'
The jig-saw began to piece itself together in Mrs Pettigrew's mind.
As heart is said to speak unto heart, Mrs Pettigrew looked at Olive's
photograph and understood where Godfrey had been wont to go on
those afternoons when he had parked his car outside the bombed
building.

'Of course, Godfrey, this will be a blow to you,' she said.

He thought: God, she knows everything. He went up to his
solicitor's offices like a lamb, while Mrs Pettigrew waited in the car
below. He did not even attempt to circumvent her wishes, as he had
half-hoped to do when finally forced to the alteration of his will. He
did not now even think of the idea he had previously dabbled with, of
confiding the facts to his lawyer. Mabel Pettigrew knew everything.
She could tell Charmian everything. He instructed a new will to be
drawn up leaving the minimum required by law to his son, and the
bulk to Mrs Pettigrew, and even most of Charmian's share, should
she outlive him, in trust for Mrs Pettigrew.

'Now,' said the solicitor. 'This might take some time to prepare, of
course.'

'It must be done right away,' said Godfrey.

'Would you not like some time, Mr Colston, to think it over? Mrs Pettigrew is your housekeeper?'

'It must be done right away,' said Godfrey. 'No delay, if you please.'

'Disgusting,' said Godfrey later that evening to Charmian. 'A man going on eighty marrying a girl of twenty-four. Absolutely disgusting. And he's deaf as a post.'

'Godfrey,' she said, 'I am going to the nursing home on Sunday morning. I have made arrangements with the doctor and the bank. Universal Aunts are coming tomorrow to pack my things. Janet Sidebottome will accompany me. I do not wish to put you out, Godfrey. It might distress you to take me yourself. I am afraid I simply can't stand these anonymous telephone calls any longer. They will bring me speedily to my grave. I must be protected from the sight of the telephone. I have spoken to Lettie, and she approves my decision. Mrs Pettigrew thinks, too, it will be the best course – don't you, Mabel? Everyone is agreed. I must say, I feel most sad. However, it had to be eventually. You yourself have often said –'

'But you don't mind the telephone calls!' he shouted. 'You don't care about them at all.'

'Oh yes, I do, I do. I can't put up with them any longer.'

'She does mind them,' said Mrs Pettigrew.

'But you don't need to answer the phone,' he shouted.

'Oh but every time the telephone rings I feel it must be *him*.' Charmian gave a little shudder.

'She feels so bad about the telephone,' said Mrs Pettigrew.

He knew he could not refute their words.

THIRTEEN

'What surprised me, I must confess,' Alec Warner said to Miss Taylor, 'was that, for a moment or two, I felt positively jealous. Olive, of course, was a friendly type of girl, and most conscientious in giving me all the information she could gather. I shall miss her. But the curious thing was this pang, this envy of Ronald, my first reaction to the news. Not that Olive, at any time, would have been my type.'

'Did you make a note of your reaction?'

'Oh, I made a note.'

'I bet he did,' thought Miss Taylor.

'Oh, I made a note. I always record these surprise deviations from my High Churchmanship.'

His 'High Churchmanship' was a figure of speech he had adopted from Jean Taylor when, at some buoyant time past, she had applied it to him, merely on account of the two occasions when he had darkened the doors of a church, to observe, with awe and curiosity, a vicar of his acquaintance conducting the service of evensong all by himself in the empty building – Alec's awe and curiosity being directed exclusively towards the human specimen with his prayer book and splendid persistence in vital habits.

'Granny Green has gone,' said Miss Taylor.

'Ah yes, I noticed a stranger occupying her bed. Now what was Granny Green?'

'Arterio-sclerosis. It affected her heart in the end.'

'Yes, well, it is said we are all as old as our arteries. Did she make a good death?'

'I don't know.'

'You were asleep at the time,' he said.

'No, I was awake. There was a certain amount of fuss.'

'She didn't have a peaceful end?'

'No, not peaceful for us.'

'I always like to know,' he said, 'whether a death is a good one or bad one. Do keep a look-out.'

For a moment she utterly hated him. 'A good death,' she said, 'doesn't reside in the dignity of bearing but in the disposition of the soul.'

Suddenly he hated her. 'Prove it,' he said.

'Disprove it,' she said wearily.

'I'm afraid,' he said, 'I've forgotten to ask how you are keeping. How are you keeping, Jean?'

'A little stronger, but the cataract is a trouble.'

'Charmian is gone to the nursing home in Surrey at last. Would you not like to join her there?'

'Godfrey is left alone with Mrs Pettigrew, then.'

'You would like to be with Charmian, surely.'

'No,' she said.

He looked round the ward and up to the noisy end. There the senile cases were grouped round the television and so were less noisy than usual, but still emitting, from time to time, a variety of dental and guttural sounds and sometimes a whole, well-intentioned speech. Those who were mobile would occasionally leave their chairs and wander up the ward, waving or talking to the bedridden. One tall patient poured herself a beaker of water and began to raise it to her lips, but forgetting the purpose before the act was accomplished, poured the water into another jug; then she turned the beaker upside down on her head so that a little water, left in the beaker, splashed over her forehead. She seemed pleased with this feat. On the whole, the geriatrics were keen on putting objects on their heads.

'Interesting,' said Alec. 'The interesting thing is, senility is somewhat different from insanity. The actions of these people, for instance, differ in many particulars from those of the aged people whom I visit at St Aubrey's Home in Folkestone. There, some of the patients have been mad most of their lives. In some ways they are more coherent, much more methodical than those who merely turn strange in their old age. The really mad old people have had more practice in irrational behaviour, of course. But all this,' said Alec, 'cannot be of much interest to you. Unless one is interested in gerontology, I cannot see that their company, day and night, can be pleasant to you.'

'Perhaps I'm a gerontologist at heart. They are harmless. I don't mind them, now. Alec, I am thinking of poor Godfrey Colston. What can have possessed Charmian to go away just when her health was improving?'

'The anonymous telephone calls were worrying her, she said.'

'Oh no. Mrs Pettigrew must have forced her to go. And Mrs Pettigrew,' said Miss Taylor, 'will most certainly make Godfrey's remaining years a misery.'

He reached for his hat. 'Think over,' he said, 'the idea of joining Charmian in the nursing home. It would so please me if you would.'

'Now Alec, I can't leave my old friends. Miss Valvona, Miss Duncan –'

'And this?' He nodded towards the senile group.

'That is our memento mori. Like your telephone calls.'

'Good-bye then, Jean.'

'Oh Alec, I wish you wouldn't leave just yet. I have something important to say, if you will just sit still for a moment and let me get my thoughts in order.'

He sat still. She leaned back on her pillow, removed her glasses, and dabbed lightly with her handkerchief at one eye which was inflamed. She replaced her glasses.

'I shall have to think,' she said. 'It involves a question of dates. I have them in my memory but I shall have to think for a few minutes. While you are waiting you may care to speak to the new patient in Granny Green's bed. Her name is Mrs Bean. She is ninety-nine and will be a hundred in September.'

He went to speak to Mrs Bean, tiny among the pillows, her small toothless mouth open like an 'O', her skin stretched thin and white over her bones, her huge eye-sockets and eyes in a fixed infant-like stare, and her sparse white hair short and straggling over her brow. Her head nodded faintly and continuously. If she had not been in a female ward, Alec thought, one might not have been sure whether she was a very old man or a woman. She reminded him of one of his mental patients at Folkestone, an old man who, since 1918, had believed he was God. Alec spoke to Mrs Bean and received a civil and coherent answer which came, as it seemed, from a primitive reed instrument in her breast-bone, so thin and high did she breathe, in and out, when answering him.

He stepped over to Miss Valvona, paid his respects, and heard from her his horoscope for the day. He nodded to Mrs Reewes-Duncan, and waved to various other occupants of the ward familiar to him. One of the geriatric set came and shook hands with him and said she was going to the bank, and, having departed from the ward, was escorted back by a nurse who said to her, 'Now you've been to the bank.'

Alec carefully watched the patient's happy progress back to the geriatric end, reflected on the frequency with which the senile babble about the bank, and returned to Jean Taylor who said:

'You must inform Godfrey Colston that Charmian was unfaithful to him repeatedly from the year after her marriage. That is starting in the summer of 1902 when Charmian had a villa on Lake Geneva, and throughout that year, when Charmian used often to visit the man at his flat in Hyde Park Gate. And this went on throughout 1903 and 1904 and also, I recall, when Charmian was up in Perthshire in the autumn – Godfrey could not leave London at the time. There were also occasions at Biarritz and Torquay. Have you got that, Alec? Her lover was Guy Leet. She continued to see him at his flat in Hyde Park Gate through most of 1905 – up to September. Listen carefully, Alec, you are to give Godfrey Colston all the facts. Guy Leet. So she gave him up in the September of 1907, I well remember, I was with them in the Dolomites, and Charmian became ill then. You must remember Guy is ten years younger than Charmian. Then in 1926 the affair began again, and it went on for about eighteen months. That was about the time I met you, Alec. Guy wanted her to leave Godfrey, and I know she thought of doing so quite often. But then she knew Guy had so many other women – Lisa Brooke, of course, and so on. Charmian couldn't really trust Guy. Charmian missed him, he did so amuse her. After that she entered the Church. Now I want you to give these facts to Godfrey. He has never suspected Charmian, she managed everything so well. Have you got a pencil on you, Alec? Better write it down. First occasion, 1902 –'

'You know, Jean,' he said, 'this might be serious for poor Godfrey and Charmian. I mean, I can't think you really want to betray Charmian after all these years.'

'I don't want to,' she said, 'but I will, Alec.'

'Godfrey probably knows already,' he said.

'The only people who know about this are Charmian, Guy, and myself. Lisa Brooke knew, and in fact she blackmailed Charmian quite cruelly. That was when Charmian had her nervous breakdown. And in fact the main reason Guy married Lisa was to keep her quiet, and save Charmian from the threat of scandal. It was never a proper marriage, but, however, as I say, Guy did marry Lisa for Charmian's sake. I will say that for him. Of course, Guy Leet did have charm.'

'He still has charm,' said Alec.

'Has he? Well, I don't doubt it. Now, Alec, write this down, will you?'

'Jean, you would regret it.'

'Alec, if you won't give Godfrey this information I shall have to ask Dame Lettie to do so. She would make the matter far more unpleasant for Charmian. I see it is necessary that Godfrey Colston should stop being morally afraid of Charmian – at least it is worth trying. I think, if he knows of Charmian's infidelity, he won't fear any disclosures about his. Let him go and gloat over Charmian. Let him –'

'Charmian will be shocked. She trusts you.' He put the case for the opposition, but she knew he was stirred and excited by her suggestion. He had never, in the past, hesitated to make mischief if it served his curiosity: now he could serve her ends.

'There is a time for loyalty and a time when loyalty comes to an end. Charmian should know that by now,' she said.

He looked at her curiously as if to find in her face something that he had previously overlooked, some latent jealousy.

'The more religious people are, the more perplexing I find them. And I think Charmian would be hurt by your action.'

'Charmian herself is a religious woman.'

'No, only a woman with a religion.' He had always found it odd that Miss Taylor, having entered the Church only to please Charmian, should have become the more addicted of the two.

He made notes of the information Miss Taylor gave to him. 'Make it clear,' she said, 'that this is a message from me. If my hands were in use I would write to him myself. Tell him from me he has nothing to fear from Mrs Pettigrew. Poor old man.'

'Were you ever jealous of Charmian?' he said.

'Of course I was,' she said, 'from time to time.'

Alec was wondering as he wrote down the details of Charmian's love-affair, if Godfrey Colston would be agreeable to taking his pulse and temperature before and after the telling. On the whole, he thought not. Guy Leet had been obliging in this respect, but then Guy was a sport. Still, one might try.

'You know, Taylor,' said Dame Lettie, ' I do not feel I can continue to visit you. These creatures are too disturbing, and now that I am not getting my proper sleep my nerves are not up to these decrepit women here. One wonders, really, what is the purpose of keeping them alive at the country's expense.'

'For my part,' said Miss Taylor, 'I would be glad to be let die in peace. But the doctors would be horrified to hear me say it. They are so proud of their new drugs and new methods of treatment – there is always something new. I sometimes fear, at the present rate of discovery, I shall never die.'

Dame Lettie considered this statement, uncertain whether it was frivolous or not. She shifted bulkily in her chair and considered the statement with a frown and a downward droop of her facial folds.

Miss Taylor supplied obligingly: 'Of course the principle of keeping people alive is always a good one.'

Dame Lettie glanced along the ward at the geriatrics who were, at that moment, fairly docile. One old lady sat up in her cot singing a song or something; a few were being visited by relatives who spoke little but for the most part simply sat out the visiting time with their feeble forebears, occasionally breaking the silence with some piece of family news, spoken loudly into the half-comprehending faces, and accepting with blank calm the response, whether this were a cluck or a crow, or something more substantial. The rest of the geriatric patients were grouped at the television corner, watching and commenting. Really, there was nothing one could complain of in them.

But Lettie had been, in any case, jittery beyond the usual when she arrived. She had not answered Miss Taylor's greeting, but had scraped the bedside chair closer to Miss Taylor and started talking immediately.

'Taylor, we all went to see Mortimer. It was utterly futile –'

'Oh, yes, Mr Warner told me yesterday –'

'Quite useless. Mortimer is not to be trusted. The police are, of course, shielding him. He must have accomplices – one of them is apparently a young man, another a middle-aged man with a lisp, and then there is a foreigner, and also –'

'Chief Inspector Mortimer,' said Miss Taylor, 'always used to seem to me rather sane.'

'Sane, of course he's sane. I am not saying he isn't sane. I made the great mistake, Taylor, of letting him know I had remembered him in my will. He always appeared to be so helpful on the committees, so considerate. But I see now, he has been a schemer. He did not expect me to live so long, and he is using these methods to frighten me to death. Of course I have now taken him out of my will, and I took steps to make this fact known to him, hoping his persecution would then cease. But now, in his rage, he has intensified his efforts. The others who receive the anonymous calls are merely being used as a blind, a cover, you see, Taylor, a blind. And Eric, I believe, is working in with him. I have written to Eric, but have received no reply, which alone is suspicious. I am their main objective and victim. Now, a further development. A few weeks ago, you remember I arranged to have my telephone disconnected.'

'Oh yes,' said Miss Taylor, closing her eyes to rest them.

'Well, shortly after that, as I was going to bed, I could swear I heard a noise at my bedroom window. As you know, my window looks out on the . . .'

Dame Lettie had, in the past few weeks, got into the habit of searching the house every night before going to bed. One could not be too careful. She searched the house from top to bottom, behind sofas, in cupboards, under beds. And even then there were creaks and unaccountable noises springing up all over the place. This nightly search of the house and the garden took three-quarters of an hour, by the end of which Dame Lettie was in no condition to deal with her maid's hysterics. After a week of this routine Gwen had declared the house to be haunted and Dame Lettie to be a maniac, and had left.

Thus, Dame Lettie was not in the mood for the geriatrics when she visited Miss Taylor in the Maud Long Ward.

'I suppose,' ventured Miss Taylor, 'you have informed the police of your suspicions. If someone is trying to get into the house, surely the police –'

'The police,' Dame Lettie explained with long-tried emphasis, 'are shielding Mortimer and his accomplices. The police always stick together. Eric is in with them. They are all in it together.'

'Perhaps a little rest in a country nursing home would do you good. All this must be very exhausting.'

'Not me,' said Dame Lettie. 'Oh no, Taylor, no nursing home for me while I have my faculties and am able to get about on my feet. I am looking for another maid. An older woman. They are so difficult to come by, they all want their television.' She looked over to the senile patients gathered round their television receiver. 'Such an expense to the country. An abominable invention.'

'Really, in cases like theirs, it is an entirely suitable invention. It does hold their attention.'

'Taylor, I cannot come here again. It is too distressing.'

'Go away for a holiday, Dame Lettie. Forget about the house and the phone calls.'

'Even the private detective whom I employed is in league with Mortimer. Mortimer is behind it all. Eric is. . .'

Miss Taylor dabbed her sore eye under her glasses. She wanted to close her eyes, and longed for the bell to ring which marked the end of the visiting hour.

'Mortimer . . . Mortimer . . . Eric,' Dame Lettie was going on. Miss Taylor felt reckless.

'In my belief,' she said, 'the author of the anonymous telephone calls is Death himself, as you might say. I don't see, Dame Lettie, what you can do about it. If you don't remember Death, Death reminds you to do so. And if you can't cope with the facts the next best thing is to go away for a holiday.'

'You have taken leave of your senses, Taylor,' said Dame Lettie, 'and I can do no more for you.' She stopped at the outer office and, demanding to speak to the ward sister, registered her opinion that Miss Taylor was off her head and should be watched.

When Gwen had left Dame Lettie's employment she quite understandably told her boy friend all about the nightly goings-on, how the mad Dame would go round the house, poking into all the cupboards and corners, and the garden, poking into the shrubberies with an electric torch, no wonder her eyesight was failing.

'And she wouldn't let me tell the police,' said Gwen. 'She doesn't trust the police. No wonder, they'd have laughed at her. Oh, but it gave me the creeps because when you're looking for noises, you keep hearing them all over the house and you think you see shapes in the darkness, and half the time it was herself I bumped into in the garden. Oh, but that house is just about haunted. I couldn't stand it a minute longer.'

Gwen's boy friend thought it a good story and recounted it at his work which was in a builder's yard.

'My girl was in with an old girl, some dame or countess or other up Hampstead way . . . went round the place every night . . . kept hearing burglars . . . wouldn't get the police . . . My girl walked out on her a week past, too much of it . . .'

'There's some cranky ones going about,' commented one of his friends, 'I'll tell you. I remember during the war when I was batman to a colonel, he . . .'

So it was that a labourer, new to the yard, picked up Gwen's story – a youth who would not have considered himself a criminal type, but who knew a window cleaner who would give two or perhaps three pounds an item for likely information. But you had to have an address.

'Where'd you say this countess was living?' he said to Gwen's boy. 'I know all up Hampstead and round the Heath.'

Gwen's boy said, 'Oh, this is a posh part, Hackleton Rise. My girl says the old woman'll be carted off looney in the end. She's one of them, did you see in the papers? – about the phone-call hoax. She's cut off her phone now . . .'

The young labourer took his information to the window cleaner, who did not pay him immediately. 'I got to check the address with my contact.'

The window cleaner himself never actually touched a job like this, but there was money in information. In a few days' time his contact expressed himself satisfied, and paid over ten pounds, remarking that the old girl in question wasn't a countess after all. The window cleaner duly paid a small share to the young labourer remarking that the information was a bit faulty, and that he'd better not be leaky with his mouth the next few days.

So it came about that Dame Lettie's house and nocturnal search-
ings fell under scrutiny.

On the day of her last visit to Miss Taylor she returned to
Hampstead by taxi shortly after five. She called in at the employment
agency to see if they had found her a woman yet, a middle-aged
woman, clean with good references, to live in. No, they had found no
one yet, Dame Lettie, but they were keeping their eyes open. She
walked the rest of the way home.

Gloomily she made a pot of tea and drank a cup standing in the
kitchen. She then puffed her way into her study and started writing a
letter to Eric. Her fountain-pen ran out of ink. She refilled it and
continued,

> ... I am thinking only of your poor mother put away in a home, &
> your poor old father who has done so much for you, and who is
> rapidly failing in health, when I demand that at least you should
> write and explain your silence. There has been bitterness between
> your parents and yourself, I know. But the time is come, surely, in
> their declining years, for you to make what amends you can. Your
> father was telling me only the other day, that, for his part, he is
> willing to let bygones be bygones. In fact, he asked me to write to
> you in this vein.

She stopped and looked out of the window. An unfamiliar car had
pulled up at the house opposite. Someone visiting the Dillingers,
apparently, not knowing the Dillingers were away. She began to feel
chilly and got up to draw the curtain. A man was sitting waiting in the
car. As she drew the curtains, he drove off. She returned to her desk
and continued,

> Do not suppose I am not aware of your activities in London and
> your attempts to frighten me. Do not suppose I am in the least
> alarmed.

She scored these last sentences through with her pen. That was not
what she had meant to write. She had, at first, thought of writing in
this manner, but her second thoughts, she now recalled, had decided
her to write something more in the nature of an appeal. One had to

employ cunning with a man like Eric. She took a fresh sheet and began again, stopping once to look over her shoulder at a potential noise.

I am thinking only of your poor mother put away in a home, & your poor old father, enfeebled and rapidly failing in health, when I . . .

She finished the letter, addressed and sealed it, and called Gwen to catch the six o'clock post. Then she remembered Gwen had left.

Dame Lettie laid the letter helplessly on the hall table and pulled herself together so far as to think of supper and to switch on the news.

She prepared her supper of steamed fish, ate it and washed up. She listened to the wireless till half-past nine. Then she turned it off and went into the hall where she stood for about five minutes, listening. Eventually, various sounds took place, coming successively from the kitchen quarters, the dining-room on her right, and upstairs.

She spent the next forty-five minutes in a thorough search of the house and the garden, front and back. Then she locked and bolted the front door and the back door. She locked every room and took away the keys. Finally she climbed slowly up to bed, stopping every few steps to regain her breath and to listen. Certainly, there was somebody on the roof.

She locked her bedroom door behind her and tilted a chair under the door-knob. Certainly, there was someone down there in the garden. She must get in touch with the Member tomorrow. He had not replied to her previous letter which she had posted on Monday, or was it Tuesday? Well, there had been time for a reply. Corruption in the police force was a serious matter. There would have to be a question in the House. One was entitled to one's protection. She put her hand out to feel the heavy walking-stick securely propped by her bed. She fell asleep at last. She woke suddenly with the noise in her ears, and after all, was amazed by the reality of this.

She switched on the light. It was five past two. A man was standing over by her dressing-table, the drawers of which were open and disarranged. He had turned round to face her. Her bedroom door was open. There was a light in the passage and she heard someone else padding along it. She screamed, grabbed her stick, and was attempting to rise from her bed when a man's voice from the passage outside said, 'That's enough, let's go.' The man by the dressing-table hesitated nervily for a moment, then swiftly he was by Lettie's side. She opened wide her mouth and her yellow and brown eyes. He wrenched the stick from the old woman's hand and, with the blunt end of it, battered her to death. It was her eighty-first year.

FOURTEEN

Four days passed before the milkman reported an accumulation of four pints of milk on Dame Lettie's doorstep, and the police entered her house to find the body, half in, half out of her bed.

Meanwhile Godfrey did not wonder, even vaguely, why he had not heard from Lettie. Now that her telephone was disconnected he seldom heard from her. In any case, he had other things to think about that morning. Alec Warner had been to see him with that extra-ordinary, disturbing, impudent, yet life-giving message from Taylor. He had, of course, ordered Warner out of the house. Alec had seemed to expect this and had departed with easy promptitude to Godfrey's 'Get out', like an actor who had rehearsed the part. He had, however, left a slip of paper behind him, bearing a series of dates and place-names. Godfrey examined the document and felt unaccountably healthier than he had been for some months. He went out and bought himself a whisky and soda while he decided what to do. And, over his drink, he despised Guy Leet yet liked the thought of him, since he was associated with his new sense of well-being. He had another whisky, and chuckled to himself to think of Guy bent double over his two sticks. An ugly fellow; always had been, the little rotter.

Guy Leet sat in his room at the Old Stable, Stedrost, Surrey, laboriously writing his memoirs which were being published by instalments in a magazine. The laboriousness of the task resided in the physical, not the mental effort. His fingers worked slowly, clutched round the large barrel of his fountain-pen. His fingers were good for perhaps another year – if you could call these twisted, knobble-knuckled members good. He glanced reproachfully at them from time to time – perhaps good for another year, depending on the severity of the intervening winter. How primitive, Guy thought, life becomes in old age, when one may be surrounded by familiar comforts and yet more vulnerable to the action of nature than any young explorer at the Pole. And how simply the physical laws assert themselves, frustrating all one's purposes. Guy suffered from an internal disorder of the knee-joints which caused one leg to collapse across the other whenever he put his weight on it. But although he frequently remarked, 'The law of gravity, the beast,' he was actually quite cheerful most of the time. He also suffered from a muscular rheumatism of the neck which caused his head to be perpetually thrust forward and askew. However, he adapted his eyesight and body as best he could to these defects, looking at everything sideways and getting about with the aid of his servant and his car, or on two sticks. He had in his service a pious, soft-spoken, tip-toeing unmarried middle-aged Irishman for whom Guy felt much affection, and whom he called Tony to his face and Creeping Jesus behind his back.

Tony came in with his morning coffee and the mail, which always arrived late. Tony placed two letters beside the paperknife. He placed the coffee before Guy. He stroked the fronts of his trousers, wriggled and beamed. He was doing a Perpetual Novena for Guy's conversion, even though Guy had told him, 'The more you pray for me, Tony, the more I'm a hardened sinner. Or would be, if I had half a chance.'

He opened the larger envelope. Proofs of the latest instalment of his memoirs. 'Here, Tony,' he said, 'check these proofs.'

'Ah, ye know I can't read without me glasses.'

'That's a euphemism, Tony.' For Tony's reading capacity was not too good, though he managed when necessary by following each word with his finger.

'Indeed, sir, 'tis a pity.' Tony disappeared.

Guy opened the other letter and gave a smile which might have appeared sinister to one who did not realize that this was only another consequence of his neck being twisted. The letter was from Alec Warner.

Dear Guy,

I'm afraid I sent Percy Mannering the last instalment of your *memoirs*. He would have seen it in any case. I'm afraid he is a trifle upset about your further reference to Dowson.

Mannering in replying to thank me for sending him the article, tells me he is coming down to see you, no doubt to talk things over. I hope he will not prove too difficult and that you will make all allowances.

Now, dear fellow, you will, I know, assist me by taking the old fellow's pulse and temperature as soon as it can conveniently be done after he has discussed the article with you. Preferably, of course, during the discussion, but this may prove difficult. Any further observations as to his colour, speech (clarity of, etc.) and general bearing during the little discussion will be most welcome, as you know.

Mannering will be with you tomorrow, i.e. the day on which you will, I expect, receive this letter – at about 3.40 p.m. I have supplied him with train times and all necessary directions.

My dear Fellow,
I am, most gratefully,
Alec Warner

Guy put the letter back into its envelope. He telephoned to the nursing home where Charmian was now resident and asked if he might call and see her that afternoon, and was informed, after the nurse had been to make inquiries, that he might. He then told Tony to have the car ready at three-fifteen.

He had intended to see Charmian, in any case. And today was warm and bright, though clouds came over at intervals. He held no resentment against Alec Warner. The chap was a born mischief-maker; but he didn't know it, that was the saving grace. He was sorry poor Percy would have to undergo the journey for nothing that afternoon.

When he left at a quarter past three he left a message on the door of his Old Stable, 'Away for a few days'. Quite improbable, it sounded, but Percy would have to take it or leave it.

''Tis a lie,' commented Tony, sliding into the car to drive his master off.

Charmian liked her new room. It was large and furnished with bright old-fashioned chintzes. It reminded her of her headmistress's room at school in those times when the days were always, somehow, sunny, and everyone seemed to love each other. She had been quite eighteen years of age before she had realized that everyone did not love each other; this was a fact which she had always found it difficult to convey to others. 'But surely, Charmian, you must have come across spitefulness and hatred before you were eighteen?'

'Only in retrospect,' she would reply, 'did I discern discord in people's actions. At the time, all seemed harmony. Everyone loved each other.'

Some said she was colouring the past with the rosy glow of nostalgia. But she plainly remembered her shock when, at the age of eighteen, she became conscious of evil – a trifling occasion; her sister had said something detrimental about her – but it was only then that Charmian discovered the reality of words like 'sin' and 'calumny' which she had known, as words, for as long as she could remember.

The window of her room looked out on a lawn in the centre of which stood a great elm. She could sit at her window and watch the other patients walking in the grounds, and they might have been the girls at her old school sauntering at their recreation period, and she with her headmistress taking tea by the window.

'Everything,' she said to Guy some time after he had made his difficult way across the room, 'has an innocent air in this place. I feel almost free from Original Sin.'

'How dull for you, dear,' said Guy.

'It's an illusion, of course.'

A young nurse brought in tea and placed it between them. Guy winked at her. The nurse winked back, and left them.

'Behave yourself, Guy.'

'And how,' he said, 'did you leave Godfrey?'

'Oh, he was most depressed. These anonymous telephone calls worry him.' She gestured towards her white telephone receiver. The civil young man had vaguely assumed in her mind the shape of a telephone receiver. At home he had been black; here he was white. 'Does he worry you, Guy?'

'Me? No. I don't mind a bit of fun.'

'They worry Godfrey. It is surprising how variously people react to the same thing.'

'Personally,' said Guy, 'I tell the young fellow to go to hell.'

'Well, he vexes Godfrey. And then we have an unsuitable housekeeper. She also worries him. Godfrey has a lot of worries.

You would see a change in him, Guy. He is failing.'

'Doesn't like this revival of your books?'

'Guy, I don't like talking against Godfrey, you know. But, between ourselves, he is rather jealous. At his age, one would have thought he had no more room for these feelings, somehow. But there it is. He was so rude, Guy, to a young critic who came to see me.'

'Fellow has never understood you,' said Guy. 'But still I perceive you have a slight sense of guilt concerning him.'

'Guilt? Oh no, Guy. As I was saying, I feel unusually innocent in this place.'

'Sometimes,' he said, 'a sense of guilt takes a self-righteous turn. I see no cause for you to feel either in the right or in the wrong where Godfrey's concerned.'

'I have regular visits from a priest,' she said, 'and if I want moral advice, Guy, I shall consult him.'

'Oh quite, quite.' Guy placed his gnarled hand on her lap; he was afraid he was forgetting how to handle women.

'And then,' said Charmian, 'you know he has estranged Eric. It is really Godfrey's fault, Guy. I do not like to say these things, and of course Eric was a disappointment, but I can't help feeling Godfrey's attitude –'

'Eric,' said Guy, 'is a man of fifty-five.'

'Fifty-seven,' said Charmian, 'next month.'

'Fifty-seven,' said Guy. 'And he has had time to acquire a sense of responsibility.'

'That,' sighed Charmian, 'Eric has never possessed. But I did think at one time he might have been a painter. I never had much hope of his writing, but his paintings – he did seem to have talent. At least, to me. But Godfrey was so mean about money, and Godfrey –'

'If I remember,' said Guy, 'it was not until Eric was past forty-five that Godfrey refused to give him any more money.'

'And then Lettie,' said Charmian, 'has been so cruel about her wills. Always promising Eric the earth, and then retracting her promises. I don't know why she doesn't do something for Eric while she is still alive.'

'Do you think,' said Guy, 'that money would make Eric any less spiteful?'

'Well, no,' said Charmian, 'I don't. I have been sending Eric sums of money for some years, secretly, through Mrs Anthony who is our daily woman. But he is still spiteful. Of course he disapproves of my books.'

'They are beautiful books,' said Guy.

'Eric doesn't approve the style. I'm afraid Godfrey has never handled Eric tactfully, that is the trouble.'

'Beautiful,' said Guy. 'I have just been re-reading *The Seventh Child*. I love particularly that scene at the end with Edna in her mackintosh standing at the cliff's edge on that Hebridean coast being drenched by the spray, and her hair blown about her face. And then turning to find Karl by her side. One thing about your lovers, Charmian, they never required any preliminary discussions. They simply looked at each other and *knew*.'

'That,' said Charmian, 'is one of the things Eric cannot stand.'

'Eric is a realist. He has no period-sense, no charity.'

'Oh my dear Guy, do you think these new young men read my books from charity?'

'Not from indulgence and kindness. But charity elevates the mind and governs the inward eye. If a valuable work of art is rediscovered after it has gone out of fashion, that is due to some charity in the discoverer, I believe. But I say, without a period-sense as well, no one can appreciate your books.'

'Eric has no charity,' she said.

'Well, perhaps it is just that he is middle-aged. The really young are so much pleasanter,' said Guy.

She was not listening. 'He is like Godfrey in so many ways,' she said. 'I can't help remembering how much I had to shut my eyes to in Godfrey. Lipstick on his handkerchiefs —'

'Stop feeling guilty about Godfrey,' Guy said. He had expected a livelier meeting with Charmian. He had never known Charmian to complain so much. He wished he had not inquired after Godfrey in the first place. Her words depressed him. They were like spilt sugar; however much you swept it up some grains would keep grinding under your feet.

'About your novels,' he said. 'The plots are so well-laid. For instance in *The Seventh Child*, although of course one feels that Edna will never marry Gridsworthy, you have this tension between Anthony Garland and Colonel Yeoville, and until of course their

relationships to Gabrielle are revealed, there is every likelihood that
Edna will marry one or the other. And yet, of course, all along one is
aware of a kind of *secret life* within Edna, especially at that moment
when she is alone in the garden at Neuflette, and then comes
unexpectedly upon Karl and Gabrielle. And then one feels sure she
will marry Gridsworthy after all, merely for his kindness. And really,
right up to the last page one does not know Karl's true feelings. Or
rather, one knows them – but does *he* know them? I must admit,
although l remembered the story well, I felt the same enormous sense
of relief, when I read it again the other day, that Edna did not throw
herself over the cliff. The suspense, the plot alone, quite apart from
the prose, are superb.'

'And yet,' said Charmian, smiling up at the sky through the
window, 'when I was half-way through writing a novel I always got
into a muddle and didn't know where it was leading me.'

Guy thought: She is going to say – dear Charmian – she is going to
say 'The characters seemed to take on a life of their own.'

'The characters,' said Charmian, 'seemed to take control of my pen
after a while. But at first I always got into a tangle. I used to say to
myself,

> Oh what a tangled web we weave
> When first we practise to deceive!

Because,' she said, 'the art of fiction is very like the practice of
deception.'

'And in life,' he said, 'is the practice of deception in life an art too?'

'In life,' she said, 'everything is different. Everything is in the
Providence of God. When I think of my own life ... Godfrey ...'

Guy wished he had not introduced the question of life, but had
continued discussing her novels. Charmian was upset about Godfrey,
that was plain.

'Godfrey has not been to visit me yet. He is to come next week. If
he is able. But he is failing. You see, Guy, he is his own worst enemy.
He ...'

How banal and boring, Guy thought, do the most interesting
people become when they are touched by a little bit of guilt.

He left at five. Charmian watched him from the window being

helped into his car. She was vexed with herself for going on so much about Godfrey. Guy had never been interested in her domestic affairs. He was such an amusing companion. The room, with its chintzes, felt empty.   .

Guy waved out of his car window, a stiff, difficult wave. It was only then that Charmian noticed the other car which had drawn up while Guy had been helped into his seat. Charmian peered down; it looked like Godfrey's car. It was, and Godfrey was climbing out, in his jerky way. She supposed he had come on an impulse to escape Mrs Pettigrew. If only he could go to live in a quiet private hotel. But as he walked across the path, she noticed he looked astonishingly bright and healthy. She felt rather tired.

Guy Leet considered, as he was driven home, whether in fact he was enjoying that sense of calm and freedom that is supposed to accompany old age or whether he was not. Yesterday he had been an old, serene man. Today he felt younger and less peaceful. How could one know at any particular moment what one's old age finally amounted to? On the whole, he thought, he must be undergoing the experience of calm and freedom, although it was not like anything he would have anticipated. He was, perhaps, comparatively untroubled and detached, mainly because he became so easily exhausted. He was amazed at Charmian's apparent energy – and she ten years his senior. He supposed he must be a dear old thing. He was fortunate in possessing all his material needs, and now that Lisa's will was being proved, he might possibly spend the winter in a really warm climate. And he had earned Lisa's money. And he bore no grudge against Charmian for her ingratitude. Not many men would have married Lisa simply to keep her quiet for Charmian's sake. Not many would have endured the secrecy of such a marriage, a mere legal bond necessary to Lisa's full sensual enjoyment of her many perversions. 'I've got to be married,' she would say in that hoarse voice, 'my dear, I don't want the man near me, but I've got to know that I'm married or I can't enjoy myself.'

Foolishly, they had exchanged letters on the subject, which might have upset his claim on Lisa's money. He did not think Tempest's suit would have succeeded, but it would have been unpleasant. But that eventuality had come to nothing. He would get Lisa's money; he had earned it. He had given satisfaction to Lisa and safety to Charmian.

He doubted if Charmian ever thought with gratitude of his action. Still, he adored Charmian. She had been wonderful, even when he had met her a year ago at a time when her mind was failing. Now that she was so greatly improved, what a pity she had this Godfrey trouble on her mind. However, he adored Charmian for what she had been and what she still really was. And he had earned Lisa's money. Trinidad might be delightful next winter. Or Barbados. He must write for some information.

When they drew up at the Old Stable Percy Mannering appeared out of the back garden and approached the car waving a magazine in the direction of the front door where Guy's message was pinned up.

'Away for a few days,' shouted Percy.

'I have just returned,' said Guy. 'Tony will give me a hand, and then we will go indoors for a drink. Meanwhile let us not alarm the lilies of the field.'

'Away for a few days,' shouted Percy, 'my foot.'

Tony trotted round the car and took Guy by the arms.

'I've been waiting,' shouted Percy, 'for you.'

Guy, as he was helped to his feet, was trying to recall what exactly he had written about Ernest Dowson in the latest published instalment of his memoirs which so enraged Percy. Guy was not a moment inside the door before he found out, for Percy then started to inform him.

'You quote from the poem about Cynara,

'"I have been faithful to thee, Cynara! in my fashion."

'You then comment, "Yes, that was always Dowson's way, even to the point of dying in the arms of another man's wife – his best friend!" – That's what you wrote, is it not?'

'It must be,' said Guy, sinking into his chair, 'if you say so.'

'And yet you know as well as I do,' shouted Percy, 'that Sherard rescued Dowson from a pub and took him home to be nursed and fed. And Dowson did indeed die in Mrs Sherard's arms, you utter snake; she was sustaining and comforting him in a sudden last spasm of his consumption. You know that as well as I do. And yet you write as if Dowson and she –'

'I am but a hardened old critic,' said Guy.

Percy banged his fist on the table. 'Critic – You're an unutterable rat.'

'A hardened old journalist,' said Guy.

'A steaming scorpion. Where is your charity?'

'I know nothing of charity,' said Guy. 'I have never heard of the steaming properties of the scorpion. I never cared for Dowson's verse.'

'You're a blackguard – you've slandered his person. This has nothing to do with verse.'

'What I wrote is the sort of thing, in my opinion, that *might* have happened,' said Guy. 'It is as near enough my meaning.'

'A cheap jibe,' yelled Percy. 'Anything for a cheap joke, you'd say anything –'

'It was quite cheap, I admit,' said Guy. 'I am underpaid for these essays of mine.'

Percy grabbed one of Guy's sticks which were propped beside his chair. Guy grabbed the other stick and, calling out for Tony, looked up with his schoolboy face obliquely at Percy.

'You will write a retraction,' said Percy Mannering with his wolf-like look, 'or I'll knock your mean little brains out.'

Guy aimed weakly with his stick at Percy's stick, and almost succeeded in knocking it out of the old man's quivering hand. Percy adjusted his stick, got it in both hands and with it knocked Guy's stick to the floor, just as Tony came in with a tray and a rattle of glasses.

'Jesus, Mary,' said Tony and put down the tray.

'Tony, will you kindly recover my walking stick from Mr Mannering.'

Percy Mannering stood fiercely displaying his two greenish teeth and gripping the stick ready to strike, it seemed, anyone.

Tony slithered cautiously round the room until Guy's desk was between him and Percy. He lowered his head, rolled up his eyes, and glared at them from beneath his sandy eyebrows like a bull about to charge, except that he did not really look like a bull. 'Take care what ye do,' he said to them both.

Percy removed one of his hands from the shaking stick and took up the offensive journal. He fluttered this at Tony.

'Your master,' he declared, 'has uttered a damnable lie about a dead friend of mine.'

''Tis within the realm of possibility,' said Tony, clutching the edge of the desk.

'If you will lay a piece of writing paper on the desk, Tony,' said Guy, 'Mr Mannering wishes to write a letter of protest to the editor of the magazine which he holds in his hand.'

The poet grinned wildly. The telephone, which was on a side table beside Guy's chair, mercifully rang out.

'Come and answer the phone,' said Guy to Tony.

But Tony was looking at Percy Mannering who still clung to the stick.

The telephone rang on.

'If ye will lift the instrument I'll lay out the paper as requested,' said Tony, 'for a man can do but one thing at a time.' He opened a drawer and extracted a sheet of paper.

'Oh, it's you,' Guy was saying. 'Well, now, sonny, I'm busy at the moment. I have a poet friend here with me and we are just about to have a drink.'

Guy heard the clear boyish voice continue: 'Is it Mr Percy Mannering who's with you?'

'That's right,' said Guy.

'I'd like to talk to him.'

'For you,' said Guy, offering the receiver to Percy.

'Me. Who wants me, what?'

'For you,' said Guy, 'a youngster of school age I should think.'

Percy bawled suspiciously into the telephone, 'Hallo, who's there?'

'Remember you must die,' said a man's voice, not at all that of a young person.

'This is Mannering here. Percy Mannering.'

'That's correct,' said the voice, and rang off.

Percy looked round the room with a bewildered air. 'That's the chap they're talking about,' he said.

'Drinks, Tony,' said Guy.

'That's the man,' roared Percy, his eyes gleaming as with some inner greed.

'Nice youngster, really. I suppose he's been over-working at his exams. The cops will get him, of course.'

'That wasn't a youngster,' said Percy, lifting his drink and draining it off, 'it was a strong mature voice, very noble, like W. B. Yeats.'

'Fill Mr Mannering's glass, Tony,' said Guy. 'Mr Mannering will be staying for dinner.'

Percy took his drink, laid down the stick, and sank into a chair.

'What an experience!' he said.

'Intimations of immortality,' commented Guy.

Percy looked at Guy and pointed to the telephone. 'Are you behind this?'

'No,' Guy said.

'No.' The old man drained his glass, looked at the clock and rose from his chair. 'I'll miss my train,' he said.

'Stop the night,' said Guy. 'Do stay.'

Percy walked uncertainly about the room. He picked up the magazine, and said,

'Look here –'

'There is a sheet of paper laid out for you to write your protest to the editor,' Guy said.

'Yes,' said the old man. 'I'll do that tomorrow.'

'There is a passage in *Childe Harold*,' said Guy, 'I would like to discuss with you. It –'

'No one,' stated Percy, 'in the past fifty years has understood *Childe Harold*. You have to *begin* with the last two cantos, man. That is the SECRET of the poem. The episodes –'

Tony put his head round the door. 'Did ye call me?'

'No, but while you're here, Mr Mannering will be stopping the night.'

Percy stayed the night and wrote his letter of protest to the editor next morning. He stayed for three weeks during which time he wrote a Shakespearean sonnet entitled 'Memento Mori', the final couplet of the first version being,

> Out of the deep resounds the hollow cry,
> *Remember – oh, remember you must die!*

The second version being,

> But slowly the reverberating sigh
> Sounds in my ear: *Remember you must die!*

The third being,

> And from afar the Voices mingle and cry
> O mortal Man, *remember you must die!*

and there were many other revisions and versions.

Eric Colston and Mrs Pettigrew were waiting for Godfrey's return.

'There's something funny going on in the old man's mind today,' Mrs Pettigrew said. 'I should judge it was something to do with a visit from old Warner this morning. He couldn't have stayed long. I had just gone across the road for cigarettes and when I got back there was Warner on the doorstep. I asked him if he wanted to see Godfrey. He said, "I've seen Godfrey, thanks." But I'll find out what it's all about – you just wait, I'll find out. Then, when I got indoors Godfrey gave me a really wild grin and then *he* went out. I was too late to catch him. He didn't come back to lunch, there's his fish fingers lying on the table. Oh, I'll find out.'

'Has he signed the will yet?' said Eric.

'No, the lawyers are taking their time.'

Eric thought: I'll bet they are taking their time. He had taken the first train to London on receiving that letter from Olive. His first action had been to call on the solicitor. His next was to get in touch with Mrs Pettigrew.

Mrs Pettigrew filled Eric's glass. She noticed, as she had done earlier in the day, his little hands, and she felt quite frightened.

Eric was a stocky man, rather resembling his mother in appearance except that the feminine features and build looked odd in him. His hips were broad, his head was large. He had Charmian's wide-spaced eyes, pointed chin and small neat nose. His mouth was large like that of Dame Lettie whose battered body was later that evening to be discovered.

But Mrs Pettigrew told herself, she was experienced with men like Eric. Not that she had ever encountered quite the same details of behaviour in any other man. But she was familiar with the general pattern; she knew he was not normal, for though he greatly desired money he yet seemed willing to sacrifice quantities of it to gain some more intense and sinuous satisfaction. She had in her life before met men prepared to sacrifice the prospect of money in order to gain, for instance, a social ambition.

To that extent she felt she knew her man. She felt it was not surprising that such a man would sacrifice anything for revenge. And yet, could she trust him?

'I am doing this,' he had told her, 'for moral reasons. I believe – I firmly believe, it will do the old man good. Teach him a lesson.'

Oh, but Eric was a mess! She looked at his little hands and the feminine setting of the eyes like Charmian's and felt perhaps she was foolish to trust him.

Eric was a mess. Olive's letter had told him his father was being blackmailed by 'a certain Mrs Pettigrew' into bequeathing a large portion of his fortune to her. Eric had acted promptly and without a moment's thought. Even in the train up from Cornwall he had not taken thought but had flirted all the way with delicious ideas – the discomfiture of Godfrey; the undermining of Charmian; the possible sympathetic-bosomed qualities of this Mrs Pettigrew under her possibly tough exterior; the thrill of being able to expose everyone to everyone if it proved expedient to do so; and the thrill of obtaining sufficient immediate cash to enable him to go and tell his Aunt Lettie what he really thought of her.

Not that he knew what he thought of her. He retained in his mind an axiom from his youth: the family had let him down badly. Everyone, even the family, had agreed upon that in the years when Eric was between twenty-two and twenty-eight, and the century was between twenty-three and twenty-nine years old. He had rejected every idea his family had ever held except this one idea, 'Somehow or other we have let Eric down. How did it happen? Poor Eric, Charmian has mothered him too much. Charmian has not been a mother enough to him. Godfrey has been too occupied, has never taken any notice of the boy. Godfrey has been too lenient, too strict, too mean, has given him too much money.' The elders had grown out of these sayings when the fashion changed, but by then Eric had taken them for his creed. Lettie bore him off on consoling holidays. He robbed her, and the hotel staff got the blame. She tried to get him interested in prison-visiting. He started smuggling letters and tobacco into Wormwood Scrubs. 'Poor Eric, he hasn't had a chance. He should never have been sent to that crank school. How could he ever be expected to pass an exam? I blame Charmian ... I blame Lettie ... Godfrey has never cared ...' He went to an art school and was caught stealing six tubes of paint. They sent him to a Freudian analyst whom he did not like. They sent him to an Adlerian, and subsequently to an individualist. Meanwhile, there was an incident with a junior porter of a club, in the light of which he was sent to another psychiatrist of sympathetic persuasion. He was so far cured that he got one of the maids into trouble. Charmian was received into the Church.

'Eric will grow out of this phase,' said Charmian. 'My grandfather was wild as a youth.'

But Eric was amazed when his elders eventually stopped blaming themselves for his condition. He thought them hypocritical and callous to go back on their words. He longed for them to start discussing him again in the old vein; but by the time he was thirty-seven they had said quite bitter things to him. He had bought a cottage in Cornwall, where he drank their money. He was in a home for inebriates when the war broke out. He emerged to be called up by the military, but was turned down on account of his psychological history. He loathed Charmian, Godfrey, and Lettie. He loathed his cousin Alan who was doing so well as an engineer and who, as a child, had always been considered dull in comparison with Eric. He married a negress and got divorced six months later, a settlement being made on her by Godfrey. From time to time he wrote to Charmian, Godfrey, and Lettie, to tell them that he loathed them. When, in 1947, Godfrey refused him any more money, he made it up with Lettie and obtained small revenues and larger promises from her. But Lettie, when she saw so little return for her cash by way of his company, reduced her bounty to mere talk about her will. Eric wrote a novel, and got it published on the strength of Charmian's name. It bore a similarity to Charmian's writing. 'Poor Eric,' said Charmian, 'has not much originality. But I do think, Godfrey, now that he is really doing some work, we ought to assist him.' She sent him, over a period of two years, all she possessed. Eric thought her mean, he thought her envious of his novel, and said so. Godfrey refused to write to him. Charmian had confided to Guy Leet, 'I suspect that Godfrey has a secret horror of another novelist in the family.' And she added, what was not strictly true, but was a neat conclusion, 'Of course, Godfrey always wanted Eric to join that dreary firm.'

By the time he was fifty Eric began to display what looked like a mind of his own. That is, instead of sending wild vituperative accusations to his family, he now sent cold reasoned denunciations. He proved, point by point, that they had let him down badly from the time of his first opening his eyes.

'In his middle-age Eric is becoming so like Godfrey,' said Charmian, 'though of course Godfrey does not see it.'

Eric no longer called Charmian's novels lousy muck. He analysed them piece by piece, he ridiculed the spare parts, he demolished the lot. He had some friends who applauded his efforts.

'But he takes my work so seriously,' said Charmian. 'Nobody ever wrote of it like that.'

Charmian's health had failed by the mid-fifties. The revival of her novels astonished Eric, for he had by some fractional oversight misjudged an element in the temper of his age. He canvassed his friends and was angered and bewildered to find so many had fallen for the Charmian Piper period-cult.

Charmian's remittances, smuggled through Mrs Anthony, were received with silence. His second book had secretly appealed to Dame Lettie. It had been described as 'realistic and brutally frank', but the energy which he might have put into developing his realistic and brutally frank talents was now dispersed in resentment against Charmian. The revival of her novels finished him off and he found he could no longer write.

Even the reports in the papers that Godfrey, Charmian, and Lettie had been recipients of threatening telephone calls failed to stimulate him.

Throughout the war, and since, he had been mainly living on women of means, the chief of whom had been Lisa Brooke. He had found it hard, after Lisa's death, to replace her. Everyone was hard up, and Eric put on weight with the worry of it all, which did not help. His difficulties were approaching a climax at the moment he had received Olive's letter. 'Your father is being cruelly blackmailed by a certain Mrs Pettigrew, the housekeeper. I think he would be willing to make up the past differences, if there was anything you could do without letting your mother know ...'

He took the first train up to London, in a state of excitement, and spent the journey visualizing the possibilities before him.

When he arrived at Paddington at a quarter to six he had no idea what he was going to do. He went into the bar and had a drink. At seven he emerged and saw a telephone box. He telephoned to the home of his father's solicitor, and on the strength of his communication, obtained an interview that evening. He got from the solicitor an assurance that preparations for the new will would be delayed as long as possible. He received some additional advice to which he did not listen.

He went to call on Olive, but found her flat deserted. He stayed the night with some reluctant acquaintances in Notting Hill Gate. At eleven next morning he telephoned to Mrs Pettigrew and met her for lunch in a café in Kensington.

'I wish you to know, Mrs Pettigrew,' he said, 'that I'm with you. The old man deserves a lesson. I take the moral point of view, and I'm quite willing to forgo the money.'

'I'm sure,' said Mrs Pettigrew at first, 'I don't know what you mean, Mr Eric.' She wiped the corners of her mouth with her handkerchief, pulling her lower lip askew in the process.

'He would die,' said Eric, 'rather than my poor mother got to know about his gross infidelities. And so would I. In fact, Mrs Pettigrew,' he said with his smile which had long ceased to be winning, 'you have us both in your hands, my father and I.'

Mrs Pettigrew said, 'I've done a lot for your parents. Your poor mother, before she was taken away, I had to do *everything* for her. There aren't many that would have put up with so much. Your mother was inclined to be – well, you know what old people are. I suppose I'm old myself, but –'

'Not a bit,' said Eric. 'You don't look a day older than sixty.'

'Well, I felt my years while I had your mother to attend to.'

'I'm sure you did. She's impossibly conceited,' said Eric; 'impossible.'

'Quite impossible. And, now, your father –'

'He's impossible,' said Eric, 'an old brute.'

'What exactly,' said Mrs Pettigrew, 'had you in mind, Mr Eric?'

'Well, I felt it my duty to stand behind you. And here I am. Money,' he said, 'means hardly anything to me.'

'Ah, you can't go far without money, Mr Eric –'

'Do call me Eric,' he said.

'Eric,' she said, 'your best friend's your pocket.'

'Well, of course, a little cash at the right time is always useful. At the right time. It's surprising, really, my father has lived so long after the life he's led.'

'Eric, I would never let you go short. I mean, until the time comes . . .'

'You can always get ready cash out of him?'

'Oh yes.'

Eric thought: I bet you can.

'I think we should see him together,' said Eric.

She looked at his little hands. Can I trust him? she wondered. The will was not yet signed and sealed.

'Trust me,' said Eric. 'Two heads are better than one.'

'I would like to think it over,' she said.

'You would prefer to work alone?'

'Oh, don't say that. I mean, this plan of yours is rather sudden, and I feel, after all I've done for Godfrey and Charmian, I'm entitled to –'

'Perhaps, after all,' said Eric, 'it is my duty to go down to Surrey to see Mother and inform her of her husband's little indiscretions. Distasteful as that course might be, in fact, it might save a lot of trouble. It would take a load off my father's mind, and there would then be no need for you to take any further interest in him. It must be a strain on you.'

She came back on him sharply: 'You don't know the details of your father's affairs. I do. You have no evidence. I have. Written proof.'

'Oh yes,' he said, 'I have evidence.'

Is it bluff? she wondered.

'When do you want to come and see him?' she said.

'Now,' he said.

But when they got back, Godfrey was still out. Mrs Anthony had left. Mrs Pettigrew felt quite frightened. And when Eric started roaming about the house, picking up the china ornaments and turning them upside down to look at them, she felt quite vexed. But she held her peace. She felt she knew her man. At least she ought to, with all her experience.

When he sat down, eventually, in Charmian's old chair, she ruffled his hair, and said, 'Poor Eric. You've had a raw deal from them, haven't you?' He leaned his large head against her bosom and felt quite nice.

After tea Mrs Pettigrew had a slight attack of asthma and withdrew to the garden, where she got it under control. On her return she thought she saw Godfrey in the chair where she had left Eric. But it was Eric all right. He was asleep, his head lolling sideways; although in features he most resembled Charmian, he looked remarkably like Godfrey in this pose.

Charmian's impression of Godfrey's brightness and health, when she saw him from her window, became more pronounced when he was shown into her room.

'Cheerful place,' he said, looking round.

'Come and sit down, Godfrey. Guy Leet has just gone. I'm afraid I'm rather tired.'

'Yes, I saw him leaving.'

'Yes, poor soul. It was kind of him to visit me. He has such difficulty getting about.'

'So different,' said Godfrey, leaning back in his chair like a satisfied man, and stretching his legs apart, 'from the way he got about in the summer of 1902 in the villa on Lake Geneva, up to 1907 at his flat in Hyde Park Gate, in Scotland and Biarritz and Torquay and then in the Dolomites when you were taken ill. Then nineteen years later when he was living in Ebury Street, up to the time of –'

'I should like a cigarette,' said Charmian.

'What?' said Godfrey.

'Give me a cigarette, Godfrey, or I shall ring and ask the nurse to fetch one.'

'Look here, Charmian, you'd better stay off cigarettes. I mean –'

'I would like to smoke a cigarette before I die. As to Guy Leet – you yourself, Godfrey, have hardly any room to talk. You yourself. Lisa Brooke. Wendy Loos. Eleanor –'

'The little rotter,' said Godfrey. 'Well, just look what he's come to and only seventy-five. Bent double over two sticks.'

'Jean Taylor must have talked,' she said. She stretched out her hand and said, 'A cigarette, Godfrey.' He gave her one and lit it.

'I'm getting rid of Mrs Pettigrew,' he said. 'A most domineering bitch. Always upsetting Mrs Anthony.'

Charmian inhaled her cigarette. 'Any other news?' she said.

'Alec Warner,' he said, 'is losing control of his faculties. He came to see me this morning and wanted me to take my pulse and temperature. I ordered him out of the house.'

Charmian began to laugh, and could not stop, and eventually had to be put to bed, while Godfrey was taken away and given a soft-boiled egg with thin bread and butter, and sent off home.

At eight o'clock they had finished supper. Mrs Pettigrew said, 'If he isn't home by nine I'd better ring the police. He might have had an accident. That car, it isn't safe. He's a menace on the road.'

'I shouldn't worry,' said Eric, reflecting that, after all, the new will was not signed.

'Oh, I always worry about him,' she said. 'That's what I mean when I say that I'm entitled to . . .'

Godfrey drove more carefully than usual. Having satisfied himself that Warner's information was accurate he felt that life was worth taking care of. Not that one had doubted Warner's information. Poor Charmian. At any rate, she had no call, now, to be uppish and righteous. Not that she really had been priggish; but she had always assumed that air of purity which made one feel such a swine. Poor Charmian; it was very catty of Taylor to gossip about her after all these years. Still, Taylor had done a good turn without knowing it . . .

Here he was at home. A long drive for an old man.

Godfrey came in with his glasses in his hand, rubbing his eyes.

'Where on earth have you been?' said Mrs Pettigrew. 'Eric is here to see you.'

'Oh, good evening, Eric,' said Godfrey. 'Have a drink.'

'I've got one,' said Eric.

'I'm keeping quite well, thank you,' said Godfrey, raising his voice.

'Oh, really?' said Eric.

'Eric wishes to speak to you, Godfrey.'

'Mrs Pettigrew and I are in this together, Father.'

'In what?'

'The question of the new will. And in the meantime, I expect to be remunerated according to the situation.'

'You're growing a paunch,' said Godfrey. 'I haven't got a paunch.'

'Otherwise we shall really have to present Mother with the facts.'

'Be reasonable, Godfrey,' said Mrs Pettigrew.

'Get to hell out of my house, Eric,' said Godfrey. 'I give you ten minutes or I call the police.'

'I think we're a little tired,' said Mrs Pettigrew, 'aren't we?'

'And you leave tomorrow morning,' he said to her.

The door bell rang.

'Who can that be?' said Mrs Pettigrew. 'Did you forget to leave the car lights on, Godfrey?'

Godfrey ignored the bell. 'You can't tell Charmian anything,' he said, 'that she doesn't know already.'

'What did you say?' said Mrs Pettigrew.

The door bell rang again.

Godfrey left them and went to open it. Two men stood on the doorstep.

'Mr Colston?'

'That's right.'

'Could we have word with you? It's the C.I.D.'

'The car lights are on,' said Godfrey.

'It's about your sister,' said the senior-looking of the men, 'Dame Lettie Colston, I'm afraid.'

Next day was Sunday. 'Hoax Caller Strikes at Last', declared the headlines. 'Aged Welfare Worker killed in bed. Jewellery and valuables missing.'

FIFTEEN

'If you look for one thing,' said Henry Mortimer to his wife, 'you frequently find another.'

Mrs Mortimer was opening and closing her mouth like a bird. This was because she was attempting to feed a two-year-old boy with a spoon, and as he opened his mouth to take each spoonful of soft egg, she involuntarily opened hers. This child was her grandson whom she was minding while her daughter was confined with a second child.

Mrs Mortimer wiped the infant's mouth and pushed a jug of milk out of his reach.

'Look for one thing and you find another,' said Henry Mortimer. 'They found twenty-two different wills amongst Lettie Colston's papers, dated over the past forty years.'

'Silly woman,' said Emmeline Mortimer, 'to change her mind so often.' She tickled the cheek of her grandson and clucked into his face, and while his mouth was open in laughter she popped in the last spoonful of egg, most of which he spluttered out. 'I was sorry for poor old Godfrey breaking down at the inquest. He must have been fond of his sister,' she said.

She gave the child his mug of milk which he clutched in both hands and drank noisily, his eyes bright above the rim, darting here and there.

When the child was settled in a play-pen in the garden Mrs Mortimer said to her husband,

'What's that you were saying about poor Lettie Colston's wills?'

'The chaps were checking up on her papers in the course of routine, in case they should provide any clue to the murder, and of course they checked up on all her beneficiaries. Quite a list out of twenty-two consecutive wills.'

'The murderer wasn't known to her, was he?'

'No – oh no, this was before they got him. They were checking up, and . . .'

Dame Lettie's murderer had been caught within three weeks of her death and was now awaiting trial. In those three weeks, however, her papers had been thoroughly examined, and those of the beneficiaries of her twenty-two wills who were still alive had been quietly traced, checked, and dismissed from suspicion. Only one name had proved a very slight puzzle; Lisa O'Brien of Nottingham, whose name appeared in a bequest dated 1918. The records, however, showed that Lisa Brooke, née Sidebottome, aged 33, had married a man named Matthew O'Brien aged 40 at Nottingham in that year. The C.I.D. did not look much further. Lisa O'Brien in the will must be a woman of advanced years by now, and in fact, it emerged that she was dead; O'Brien himself, if still alive, would be beyond the age of the suspect. The police were no longer interested, and ticked the name O'Brien off their list.

Henry Mortimer, however, as one acquainted with the murdered woman and her circle, had been approached, and had undertaken to investigate any possible connexion between the murder and the anonymous telephone calls. Not that the police believed these calls had taken place; every possible means of detection had failed, and they had concluded with the support of their psychologists that the old people were suffering from hallucinations.

The public, however, had to be satisfied. Henry Mortimer was placed in charge of this side of the case. The police were able to announce:

> The possibility of a connexion between the murder and the anonymous telephone calls which the murdered woman was reported to receive from time to time before her death is being investigated.

Mortimer fulfilled his duties carefully. Like his colleagues, he suspected the murderer to be a chance criminal. Like his colleagues, he knew the anonymous voice would never be traced in flesh and blood. Nevertheless, he examined the police documents, and finally sent in a report which enabled the police to issue a further statement:

The authorities are satisfied that there is no connexion between the murder of Dame Lettie Colston and the anonymous telephone calls of which she had been complaining some months before her death.

Meantime, however, Henry had noticed the details of Lisa O'-Brien, and was interested.

'You look for one thing and you find another,' he had said to himself. For he had never before heard of this marriage of Lisa's. Her first marriage with rich old Brooke had been dissolved in 1912. Her secret marriage with Guy Leet had recently come to light, when Guy had claimed her fortune. But Matthew O'Brien – Henry did not recall any Matthew O'Brien. He must be quite old now, probably dead.

He had requested the C.I.D. to check further on Matthew O'Brien. And they had found him quite quickly, in a mental home in Folkestone where he had been resident for more than forty years.

'And so,' said Mortimer to his wife, 'you look for one thing and you find another.'

'Do Janet and Ronald Sidebottome know anything of this husband?' said Mrs Mortimer.

'Yes, they remember him quite well. Lisa went touring Canada with him. They didn't hear from her for a year. When she turned up again she told them he had been killed in an accident.'

'How long has he been in this mental home?'

'Since 1919 – a few months after their marriage. Janet is going down to identify him tomorrow.'

'That will be difficult after all these years.'

'It is only a formality. The man is undoubtedly Matthew O'Brien whom Lisa Brooke married in 1918.'

'And she said he was dead?'

'Yes, she did.'

'Well, what about Guy Leet? Didn't she marry him? That makes them bigamists, doesn't it?'

'I shouldn't think for a moment Guy knew the man was still alive. Everyone, apparently, believed he was dead.'

'The police won't trouble poor Guy about it?'

'Oh, the police won't bother him now. Especially at his age.'

'What a woman,' said Mrs Mortimer, 'that Lisa Brooke was. Well,

I expect her money – Oh, what will happen to her money, now? Guy Leet is surely –'

'That's a question, indeed. Lisa's fortune belongs to Matthew O'Brien by rights, sane or insane.'

Henry went out into the garden and said to his squealing grandson,

'What's all this racket going on?' He rolled him over and over on the warm stubbly grass. He picked up the child and threw him into the blue sky and caught him again.

'He'll throw up his breakfast,' remarked Emmeline, who stood with her head on one side, and smiled proudly at the child.

'Up-up-ee,' demanded the child.

Henry rolled him over and over, left him yelling for more, and went indoors to catch Alec Warner on the telephone before he should go out.

'You're interested in the St Aubrey's Home at Folkestone?' Henry said.

'Yes. But only in the older patients. I've been visiting them on private research for ten years.'

'Do you know a man there called Matthew O'Brien?'

'Matt O'Brien, oh yes, a private patient. A dear old chap, nearly eighty. He's bedridden now. Quite batty, of course, but he always knows me.'

'Were you thinking,' said Henry, 'of going down there any time this week?'

'Well, I only go once a month, as a rule, and I went last week. Is there anything special?'

'Only,' said Henry, 'that Janet Sidebottome has agreed to go down to Folkestone tomorrow to identify Matthew O'Brien. I won't go into details, but if you would care to accompany her, since you are acquainted with the Home, it would be a kindness to Janet who will probably be distressed. Ronald can't go with her, he's in bed with a chill.'

'What has Janet Sidebottome to do with Matt O'Brien?'

'Can you go?' said Henry.

'Yes,' said Alec.

'Then Janet will explain everything. Do you know her number?'

'Yes,' said Alec.

'And one of our men will be there to meet you.'

'A copper?' said Alec.

'A detective,' said Mortimer. 'The affair might be of some inciden-
tal interest to you.'

'That's just what I was thinking,' said Alec.

Janet said, 'It is all most distressing. Ronald should have been here to
assist me. He met Matthew several times. I can't think why Ronald
should have a chill in this fine weather.'

Alec shouted above the rattle of the taxi.

'No need to be distressed. I shall do my best to replace Ronald.'

'Oh, no, don't distress Ronald,' she said. 'I only meant –'

He gave her a smile. She sadly adjusted her hearing equipment, and
said, 'My hearing is rather poor.'

'You may not be able to recognize Matt O'Brien,' he articulated.
'He's an old man, and the years of insanity may have changed him
beyond recognition. They get drugs, you know, and then the drugs
have an effect on the appearance. But don't worry if his features are
not familiar to you. I think the authorities already have evidence that
he's Lisa's husband. They have Lisa's signature, for instance, from
the time of his admission.'

'I will do my best,' said Janet. 'But it is a distressing experience.'

'He is gentle,' shouted Alec. 'He thinks he is God. He has never
been violent.'

'I am distressed about my late sister,' Janet said. 'I don't like to
admit it, but I must; Lisa was never straight in her dealings. It is a
blessing she was never found out in this business.'

'It would have been bigamy,' said Alec.

'It was bigamy,' she said. 'There was no excuse for Lisa, she had
every opportunity in life. But it was the same when she was a girl. She
caused our dear father a great deal of sorrow. And when Simon
Brooke divorced her, there was all that scandal. Scandal was serious
in those days.'

'What did you think of Matt O'Brien at the time?'

'Well, he was an Irishman, a lawyer. He talked a great deal, but then
he was an Irishman, and he was quite charming. And do you know,
when Lisa told me he was dead, I could hardly believe it. He had
seemed to me so lively. Of course, we did not suspect the truth. It is
very distressing.'

'It will soon be over,' said Alec. 'We shall not be with him for long.'

The interview with Matt O'Brien was soon over. The detective met them in the hall and a nurse took them up to Matt's room where he lay on his pillow among his loose white hair.

'Hallo, Matt,' said Alec, 'I've brought two friends of mine to see you.'

The detective nodded to the old man and stood back discreetly and formally beside the nurse.

Janet approached his bedside and lifted his limp hand in greeting. He raised his other hand in benediction.

The old man moved his pale eyes towards Alec.

'It's you, Alec,' he said in a blurred voice, as if his tongue were in the way.

'I was wondering,' said Alec, 'if you remember a lady called Lisa at all? Lisa Brooke. Lisa Sidebottome.'

'Lisa,' said the old man.

'You don't remember Lisa – a red-haired lady?' said Alec.

'Lisa,' said the old man, looking at Janet.

'No, this isn't Lisa. This is her sister, Janet. She's come to see you.'

The old man was still looking at Janet.

'Don't you remember Lisa? – Well, never mind,' said Alec.

The old man shook his head. 'I recollect all creatures,' he said.

'Lisa died last year,' Alec said. 'I just thought you might know of her.'

'Lisa,' said the old man and looked out at the sky through the window. It was a bright afternoon, but he must have seen a night sky full of stars. 'My stars are shining in the sky,' he said. 'Have I taken her to Myself?'

Janet was served with tea downstairs and invited to put her feet up for a while.

She put away her handkerchief. 'I did not,' she said, 'at first find any resemblance. I thought there must be a mistake. But as he turned his head aside to the window, I saw the profile, I recognized his features quite plainly. Yes, I am sure he is the same Matthew O'Brien. And his manner, too, when he spoke of the stars . . .'

Alec declined tea. He took a notebook from his pocket and tore a page from it.

'Will you excuse me if I scribble a note to a friend? – I have to catch the post.' He was already scribbling away when Miss Sidebottome gave him leave to do so.

Dear Guy – I believe I shall be the first to give you the following information.

A man named Matthew O'Brien has been discovered, who was already married to Lisa when you married her.

Mortimer will give you the details, which have now been fully established.

As it happened, I have been visiting this man, in the course of research, at St Aubrey's Home for mental cases, for the past ten years, without suspecting any such association.

I imagine there will be no blame imputed to you. But of course, as your marriage with Lisa was invalid, you will not now benefit from her estate. Lisa's money, or at least the great bulk of it, will, of course, go to her legal husband – I fancy it will be kept in trust for him as he is mentally incapacitated.

Be a good fellow, and, immediately on reading this letter, take your pulse and temperature, and let me know...

Alec begged an envelope from the receptionist. He slipped in his note, and addressed and stamped it. He slid the letter into the post-box in the hall, and returned to comfort Janet.

Alec felt, when he left Janet Sidebottome's hotel after escorting her painfully home, that he had had a fruitful though exhausting day.

Reflecting on Matt O'Brien's frail and sexless flesh and hair on his pillow, and how the old man had looked back and forth between Janet and himself, he was reminded of that near-centenarian, Mrs Bean, who had replaced Granny Green in the Maud Long Ward. So different from each other in features, they yet shared this quality, that one would not know what was their sex from first impressions. He resolved to make a note of this in Matt O'Brien's case-history.

He felt suddenly tired and stopped a taxi. As it drove him home he ruminated on the question why scientific observation differed from humane observation, and how the same people, observed in these respective senses, actually seemed to be different people. He had to admit that Mrs Bean, for instance, to whom he had not paid close attention, had none the less rewarded him with one of those small points of observation that frequently escaped him when he was deliberately watching his object. However, the method he had evolved was, on the whole, satisfactory.

A fire-engine clanged past. Alec leaned in his corner and closed his eyes. The taxi turned a corner. Alec shifted his position and looked out into the evening. The taxi was purring along the Mall towards St James's Street.

The driver leaned back and opened the communicating window.

'A fire somewhere round here,' he said.

Alec found himself on the pavement outside his block of chambers, in a crowd. There were policemen everywhere, smoke, people, firemen, water, then suddenly a cry from the crowd and everyone looking up as a burst of flame shot from the top of the building.

Alec pushed through to the inner edge of the crowd. A policeman barred his way with a strong casual arm. 'I live here,' Alec explained. 'Let me pass, please.'

'Can't go in there,' said the policeman. 'Stand back, please.'

'Get back,' shouted the crowd.

Alec said, 'But I live there. My things. Where's the porter?'

'The building is on fire, sir,' said the policeman.

Alec made a rush advance and got past the policeman into the smoke and water at the entrance to the building. Someone hit him on the face. The crowd fell back as a wave of smoke and flame issued from a lower window. Alec stood and looked into the interior while another policeman from the opposite side of the crowd walked over to him.

'Come back,' said the policeman, 'you're obstructing the firemen.'

'My papers are up there,' Alec said.

The policeman took him by the arm and pulled him away. 'There is a cat,' Alec said desperately, 'in my rooms. I can't let pussy burn. Let me dash up and let her out. I'll take the risk.'

The policeman did not reply, but continued to propel Alec away from the fire.

'There's a dog up there. A beautiful husky from a polar expedition,' Alec haggled. 'Top floor, first door.'

'Sorry, too late, guvnor,' said one of the firemen. 'Your dog must have had it by now. The top storey's burnt out.'

One of the residents among the crowd said, 'There are no pets in those flats. Pets are not allowed.'

Alec walked away; he went to his club and booked a room for the night.

SIXTEEN

The summer had passed and it was Granny Bean's birthday for which the ward had been preparing for some days.

There was a huge cake with a hundred candles. Some men from the newspapers came in with their cameras. Others talked a while to Granny Bean, who was propped up in a new blue bed-jacket.

'Yes,' Granny Bean answered them in her far-away flute, 'I've lived a long time.'

'Yes,' said Granny Bean, 'I'm very happy.'

'That's right,' she agreed, 'I seen Queen Victoria once as a girl.'

'What does it feel like to be a hundred, Mrs Bean?'

'All right,' she said weakly, nodding her head.

'You mustn't tire her,' Sister Lucy, who had put on her service medal for the occasion, told the news men.

The men took down notes from the sister. 'Seven children, only one now alive, in Canada. Started life as a seamstress hand at the age of eleven ...'

The matron came in at three o'clock and read out the telegram from the Queen. Everyone applauded. Granny Valvona commented, '"... on your hundredth birthday", doesn't sound quite right. Queen Mary always used to say, "on the occasion of your centenary".' But everyone said it came to the same thing.

The matron stood proxy for Granny Bean in blowing out the candles. She was out of breath by the twenty-third. The nurses took turns to blow out the rest.

They were cutting the cake. One of the news men called, 'Three cheers for Granny Bean.'

The hilarity was dying down and the men had gone by the time the normal visitors started to arrive. Some of the geriatrics were still eating or doing various things with their slice of cake.

Miss Valvona adjusted her glasses and reached for the newspaper.

She read out for the third time that day: '"September 21st – today's birthday. Your year ahead: *You can expect an eventful year. Controversial matters may predominate from December to March. People associated with music, transport, and the fashion industry will find the coming year will bring a marked progress.*" Now, were you not connected with the fashion industry, Granny Bean? It says here in black and white . . .'

But Mrs Bean had dropped asleep on her pillow after the nurse had given her a warm drink. Her mouth was formed once more into a small 'O' through which her breath whistled faintly.

'Festivities going on?' said Alec Warner, looking around at the party decorations.

'Yes, Mrs Bean is a hundred today.'

The deep lines on Alec's face and brow showed deeper. It was four months since he had lost his entire notes and records in the fire.

Jean Taylor had said, 'Try to start all over again, Alec. You will find a lot of it will come back to your mind while you work.'

'I could never trust my memory,' he had said, 'as I trusted those notes.'

'Well, you must start all over again.'

'I haven't got it in me,' he said, 'to do that at my age. It was an accumulation of years of labour. It was invaluable.'

He had seldom, since then, referred to his loss. He felt, sometimes, he said once, that he was really dead, since his records had ceased to exist.

'That's rather a metaphysical idea for you, Alec,' she said. 'For in fact you are not dead, but still alive.'

He told her, it was true he frequently went over his vast notebooks in his mind, as through a card index. 'But never,' he said, 'shall I make another note. I read instead. It is in some ways a better thing.'

She caught him looking with an almost cannibal desire at Granny Bean on her hundredth birthday. He sighed and looked away.

'We all appear to ourselves frustrated in our old age, Alec, because we cling to everything so much. But in reality we are still fulfilling our lives.'

'A friend of mine fulfilled his yesterday.'

'Oh, who was that?'

'Matt O'Brien in Folkestone. He thought he was God. He died in his sleep. He has left a fortune, but never knew about it. Lisa's money of course. No relatives.'

'Will Guy Leet – ?'

'No, Guy has no claim. I think Lisa's estate will now go according to her will to Mrs Pettigrew.'

'In that case,' said Miss Taylor, 'she will, after all, have her reward.'

Mrs Pettigrew had her reward. Lisa's will was proved in her favour and she inherited all her fortune. After her first stroke Mrs Pettigrew went to live in a hotel at South Kensington. She is still to be seen at eleven in the morning at Harrod's Bank where she regularly meets some of the other elderly residents to discuss the shortcomings of the hotel management, and to plan various campaigns against the staff. She can still be seen in the evening jostling for a place by the door of the hotel lounge before the dinner gong sounds.

Charmian died one morning in the following spring, at the age of eighty-seven.

Godfrey died the same year as the result of a motor accident, his car having collided with another at a bend in Kensington Church Street. He was not killed outright, but died a few days later of pneumonia which had set in from the shock. It was the couple in the other car who were killed outright.

Guy Leet died at the age of seventy-eight.

Percy Mannering is in an old men's home, where he is known as 'The Professor' and is treated with special respect, having his bed put in an alcove at the far corner of the dormitory – a position reserved for patients who have known better days. His granddaughter, Olive, sometimes visits him. She takes away his poems and letters addressed to editors; she types them out, and dispatches them according to Percy's directions.

Ronald Sidebottome is allowed up in the afternoons but is not expected to last another winter.

Janet Sidebottome died of a stroke following an increase in blood pressure, at the age of seventy-seven.

Mrs Anthony, now widowed, had a legacy from Charmian, and has gone to live at a seaside town, near her married son. Sometimes, when she hears of old people receiving anonymous telephone calls, she declares it is a good thing, judging by what she has seen, that she herself is hard of hearing.

Chief Inspector Mortimer died suddenly of heart-failure at the age of seventy-three, while boarding his yacht *The Dragonfly*. Mrs Mortimer spends most of her time looking after her numerous grandchildren.

Eric is getting through the Colston money which came to him on the death of his father.

Alec Warner had a paralytic stroke following a cerebral haemorrhage. For a time he was paralysed on one side and his speech was incoherent. In time he regained the use of his limbs; his speech improved. He went to live permanently in a nursing home and frequently searched through his mind, as through a card-index, for the case-histories of his friends, both dead and dying.

What were they sick, what did they die of?

Lettie Colston, he recited to himself, comminuted fractures of the skull; Godfrey Colston, hypostatic pneumonia; Charmian Colston, uraemia; Jean Taylor, myocardial degeneration; Tempest Sidebottome, carcinoma of the cervix; Ronald Sidebottome, carcinoma of the bronchus; Guy Leet, arteriosclerosis; Henry Mortimer, coronary thrombosis . . .

Miss Valvona went to her rest. Many of the grannies followed her. Jean Taylor lingered for a time, employing her pain to magnify the Lord, and meditating sometimes confidingly upon Death, the first of the four last things to be ever remembered.